INSHALLAH

Inshallah

ORIANA FALLACI

Translation by Oriana Fallaci
from a translation by James Marcus

NAN A. TALESE

DOUBLEDAY

New York   London   Toronto   Sydney   Auckland

Published by Nan A. Talese
an imprint of Doubleday
a division of Bantam Doubleday Dell Publishing Group, Inc.
666 Fifth Avenue, New York, New York 10103

DOUBLEDAY and the portrayal of an anchor
with a dolphin are trademarks of Doubleday,
a division of Bantam Doubleday Dell Publishing Group, Inc.

Library of Congress Cataloging-in-Publication Data

Fallaci, Oriana.
[Insciallah. English]
Inshallah/Oriana Fallaci
translation by Oriana Fallaci, from a translation
by James Marcus.—1st ed.
p.   cm.
Translation of: Insciallah.
1. Beirut (Lebanon)—History—Fiction. I. Title.
PQ4866.A4I5713   1992
853'.914—dc20   92-16701
CIP

ISBN 0-385-41987-2
Copyright © 1990 RCS Rizzol: Libri S.P.A., Milan
Translation copyright © 1992 by Doubleday, a division of
Bantam Doubleday Dell Publishing Group, Inc.
All Rights Reserved
Printed in the United States of America
November 1992
First Edition

1   3   5   7   9   10   8   6   4   2

The characters in this novel are imaginary. Their stories are imaginary, the plot is imaginary. The events from which the plot departs are real. The landscape is real, the war in which the story unfolds is real.

The author dedicates this work to the four hundred American and French soldiers slaughtered in the Beirut massacre by the Sons of God sect. She dedicates it to the men, the women, the old, the children slaughtered in the other massacres of that city and in all the massacres of the eternal massacre called war.

This novel is meant to be an act of love for them and for Life.

FIRST ACT

CHAPTER ONE

1

AT NIGHT the stray dogs invaded the city. Hundreds and hundreds of dogs who taking advantage of the people's fear poured through the deserted streets, the empty squares, the abandoned alleys, and where they came from nobody knew because during the day they never appeared. Perhaps during the day they hid in the rubble, inside the cellars of the shattered houses, in the sewers among the rats, or perhaps they did not exist because they weren't dogs but ghosts of dogs who materialized with the darkness to imitate the men who had killed them. Like men they divided into bands consumed by hate, like men they wanted only to tear each other to pieces, and the monotonous rite always took place under the same pretext: the conquest of a sidewalk made precious by food scraps and scum. They advanced slowly, in patrols led by a squad leader who was the strongest and fiercest of all, and at first you didn't notice them because they stalked without a sound: the strategy of soldiers who creep in wary silence to surprise the enemy and butcher them. But suddenly the squad leader let loose with a howl, almost the blare of a fanfare announcing the attack, the howl was followed by another howl then by another then by the collective barking of the group which deployed itself in a circle to close in the rival one and squeeze it in a siege that would prevent any escape, and hell burst forth. Rolling around in the scum assailants and assaulted snapped at each other's throats and spines, they bit each other's eyes and ears, they tore each other's bellies, and the rabid cries were more deafening than bombs. No matter what battle or clash among men lacerated the night, the uproar of the dogs slaughtering each other for the possession of a sidewalk surpassed the bursts of the rockets, the thuds of the mortars, the rumble of the artillery. And never an instant of rest, of truce. Only when the sky faded into the glimmering violet of dawn and the bands disappeared leaving behind small lakes of blood and carcasses of vanquished comrades would you once more hear the sounds of the war

waged with rockets and mortars and artillery. But at that point a new
tumult began, no less chilling: that of the roosters who crazed by fear
had lost all notion of time and who instead of heralding the rising of
the sun wore out their throats by commenting on those sounds with a
crow. A cannon shot and a crow. A machine gun burst and a crow. A
rifle shot and a crow. Desperate, terrorized, human. A double sob in
which you could almost hear the word help. "Help! Help!" Thousands
of roosters. It was as if every house, every courtyard, every terrace
sheltered a henhouse in delirium, as if every rooster lived for the single
purpose of shrieking out its own madness. Or the madness of the city,
the torments of the absurd place that the military maps indicated as
36S-YC-316492-Q15? Zone 36, tier S, grid YC, coordinates 316492,
altitude 15. That is, the headquarters of the Italian contingent in Beirut.

*   *   *

Stretched out on the cot he'd set up in the dugout of the basement,
and unable to sleep, Angelo listened and at each sob his pensive face
contracted in a scowl of exasperation. He detested them so much,
those roosters, that when he saw one he turned his head away. For the
dogs, instead, he felt a kind of dismal curiosity because they let nobody
approach them, from a distance you could perceive only a vague silhouette, almost the shadow of a shadow on the verge of dissolving, and he
had never seen them. He rose, careful not to wake Charlie, his captain,
who slept in the next room. He turned on a flashlight and began to
pace back and forth, but the space was so minuscule and his long legs
covered so quickly the distance from wall to wall that he gave up at
once: he went back to the cot and there he remained, immobile, to
steep himself in questions. What if his insomnia was not caused by the
piercing concerto but by the mess in which he'd entangled himself with
Ninette? A gorgeous woman, yes. Long and sleek chestnut hair which
waved in glitters of gold, disquieting violet eyes that inflamed all the
world's desires, harsh and fiery features of a barbarian queen, and a
body that took your breath away. The trouble is that beauty isn't
enough to justify a romantic attachment. When it has nothing to offer
but the monotonous invitation let-us-make-love, let-us-make-love, its
appeal to the senses becomes a nuisance and even a threat: an ambush
to your liberty. Damn that August day. They had met one August day
in a bookshop of the Eastern Zone where he was buying newspapers
for Charlie. A careless gesture, an accidental shove at someone behind

you, an approach that on the spot you consider innocuous: "Excusez-moi, Madame." "Don't worry, Sergeant." An impossible dialogue conducted by means of je-ne-comprends-pas, I-don't-understand, mish-fahèm. They had barely been able to exchange their names: "Je m'appelle Angelo." "My name is Ninette." Yet the next day she'd come looking for him. From base to base, post to post, she'd arrived at the headquarters. Defiant, intrepid, provocative. In a district where feminine immodesty was regarded as the worst insult to Allah, so that woe to the woman who didn't cover her head and conceal her body in an awkward pajama or a chador, she had come with her hair in the wind and a dress so tight that at first glance she looked naked. In her hands, a little bag of sweets. "For you." He had refused it, sent her away, but the next Sunday here she was again: dressed in the same way and with another little bag of sweets.

He sighed with irritation. He'd accepted, this time, and what a mistake! Since then, not a Sunday passed without her showing up at the headquarters. She came even if the 155mm guns were firing from the mountains, even if combat was raging along the Green Line, and each time she quivered with the joy of a cat who has found its mate. "Angelo, my angel!" Then she would festively run toward him, she would inebriate him with smiles and caresses and English words: incomprehensible phrases from which he could only gather that she was Christian, that she lived in the Eastern Zone, that she intended to take him to bed. That is, to rob him of himself. Let-us-make-love, let-us-make-love. How to resist her in spite of the desire she aroused in his body? How to tell her that he didn't want a sentimental adventure, that even a sentimental adventure is a form of love, an amorous commitment, a temporary bond that deprives one of freedom? How to explain that he didn't need any form of love or an amorous commitment because only through freedom could he understand who he was, what he was searching for, and what Life means? Lacking a language in common (he didn't speak Arabic and expressed himself in French, she didn't speak Italian and expressed herself in English), he could defend himself only by saying je-ne-comprends-pas, I-don't-understand, mish-fahèm, non-capisco: the tactic he used during those two months. Yesterday, however, along with the little bag of sweets she had brought a tiny package wrapped in brown paper. Inside it, a condom. And when a woman offers you a condom, can you go on repeating I-don't-understand? At the most, and at the cost of feeling ridiculous, you can refuse it. He had. But while doing so his eyes had met the disquieting violet eyes that inflamed all the world's desires, and he had fallen into them.

"Okay, Ninette. Demain, domani, tomorrow." Tomorrow was today and... Of course it was she who made him so nervous, who gave him insomnia! Or maybe not? No, it wasn't she... It was the crisis that consumed him since he had come to the city of the stray dogs and the crazed roosters: the absurd place the military maps indicated as 36S-YC-316492-Q15. It was the uneasiness that disoriented him since he had realized he did not know who he was, what he wanted, what Life means. It was the dissatisfaction that devoured him and surfaced at any pretext, including the one of rejecting his desire for the gorgeous woman who offered herself to him...

He started peevishly. Before Beirut, this didn't happen. He accepted his existence without discussing it, with the aplomb of an animal who eats and drinks and sleeps and couples at will. He enjoyed his youth. He didn't ask many questions. Now, instead, he didn't enjoy anything. His nerves were always on edge, his soul sank deeper and deeper into the mists of a rebellion without particular goals, into the fog of a meta-physical anguish, and he did nothing but torment his brain with one *why* after another. Why had he ended up here, why had he chosen a trade that didn't suit his character and his mental structure, the sol-dier's trade, why had he betrayed mathematics... Oh, how much he missed mathematics! How strongly he regretted having left it! It massages your meninges as a coach massages an athlete's muscles, mathematics. It sprays them with pure thought, it purges them of the emotions that corrode intelligence, it transports them to greenhouses where the most astonishing flowers grow. The flowers of an abstraction composed of concreteness, a fantasy composed of reality... "You are on a train traveling at 15 kilometers per hour and it rains. You are seated alongside the left-hand window, you look in the direction in which the train goes, and you watch a drop of rain fall onto the glass. From the right to the left, that is obliquely, and forming an angle of 30 degrees with respect to the vertical. Then the train accelerates, it speeds up to 20 kilometers per hour, and the angle formed by the raindrop changes: it becomes 45 degrees with respect to the vertical. In the first and in the second case, at what speed does the raindrop fall?" No, it's not true that mathematics is a rigid science, a severe doctrine. It's a seductive, capricious art, a sorceress who can perform a thousand enchantments. A thousand wonders. It can make order out of disorder, it can give sense to senseless things, it can answer every question. It can even provide what you basically search for: the formula of Life. He had to return to it, he had to start all over again with the humility of a school-boy who during the summer has forgotten the Pythagorean tables: two times two equals four, four times four equals sixteen, sixteen times sixteen equals two hundred fifty-six, and the derivative of a constant is equal to zero, the derivative of a variable is equal to one, the derivative of a power of a variable... Didn't he remember? Of course he did! The derivative of a power of a variable is equal to the exponent of the power multiplied by the variable with the same exponent minus one. And the derivative of a division? It's equal to the derivative of the dividend multiplied by the divisor minus the derivative of the divisor multiplied by the dividend, all of it, the whole thing, divided by the dividend multiplied by itself. Simple! Well, of course finding the formula of Life wouldn't be so simple. To find a formula means solving a problem, to solve a problem we must enunciate it, to enunciate it we must start with a premise and... Oh! Why had he betrayed the sorceress? What had made him betray her?

He tossed on the cot. Maybe the bus that carried him from Brianza to Milan and from Milan to Brianza when he attended the university. Every morning two hours of travel with a sleep that fogs your mind, every afternoon, two more with a weariness that numbs your body, so that you return home with a kind of rancor for the sorceress who demands such a sacrifice. Maybe the yoke of the family nagging you with the usual reproaches and complaints: we-work-to-send-you-to-school, to-give-you-an-education, and-you-don't-even-say-thanks. Maybe the boredom of the provinces where nothing happens and the only relief is to flirt with the girl next door, the only pastime is to accompany her to the movies and to see a film that you don't see because you brood over the indefinite integral and the dread of having gotten her pregnant. Or maybe your nature perpetually torn by uncertainties and doubts, because those who think very much end up seeing both the pros and the cons, thereby losing themselves in uncertainties and doubts. What will I do with a degree in mathematics? Will I discover new worlds, new stars? Will I invent a theory that will change the course of civilization? You believed it, at the beginning. For this you used to keep in your room the poster with Einstein's witty face and his divine equation $E = mc^2$. But the hours in the bus and the family's reproaches and the boredom of the provinces have worn down your self-confidence, at a certain point you have put yourself on trial and decided that you are just one among many. You won't discover anything, you won't invent anything. You'll use that degree for a job which exploits your knowledge of the indefinite integral, you'll marry the girl next door, you'll have children whom you'll nag with the same we-work-to-send-you-to-school etcetera, you'll soon become an adult with wrinkles in your soul. You'll lose your youth before it is time. Much better to delay those wrinkles by taking a vacation, by responding to the draft you avoided for the past three years, then. Yes, he had betrayed mathematics not to lose his youth before it was time. People think that the army makes you old. On the contrary. The army returns you to childhood, it crystallizes your childhood. It blocks it the way floriculturists block the growth of plants which, compressed at the roots and pruned of their foilage, become dwarf trees. Bonsai. Your intellect in place of the compressed roots, your maturity in place of the pruned foliage. Instruments of witchcraft, the toys with which the uniform entices and the salary with which it rewards you for a job that isn't a job but a game. Skip the hypocrisies: it's fun to march, to shoot like a marksman at the firing range, to handle explosives, to climb impervious mountains, to descend into the abysses of the sea, to leap into the sky with a parachute. To play at making war. If some accident doesn't occur or if they don't send you to a real war, you truly return to being a child. A thoughtless child in a thoughtless school called barracks. Not to mention the pleasure you feel in showing your vigor, exhibiting your body that mathematics had weakened and the army has strengthened, transformed into a perfect machine for playing and seducing: lofty stature, broad shoulders, narrow flanks, flat abdomen. So, to hell with the poster of Einstein's witty face and his divine equation $E = mc^2$.

He smiled sadly. Goodbye to the poster, goodbye to the dream of discovering new worlds, new stars, of inventing some theory that would change the course of civilization, he had become what the Italians call an incursore.* That is, a supersoldier: a modern samurai who shoots better than anybody else and better than anybody else handles explosives, scales impervious mountains, descends into the abysses of the sea, leaps into the sky with a parachute, and gets blown up in real wars. But he was twenty-six, dammit, and at twenty-six he was capable of doing nothing else: his mind had become so calcified that he couldn't even enunciate a problem to find the formula of Life, he scarcely remembered that the derivative of a power of a variable is equal to the exponent of the power multiplied by the variable with the same exponent minus one! He wanted to use his brain again, to bring it again into the greenhouses where he walked before the cynical floriculturist compressed the roots of his intellect and pruned the foliage of his maturity. He wanted to stop being a dwarf tree and to grow, to finally become an adult. At the cost of getting wrinkles in his soul. And then

* The Italian equivalent of the American Green Berets or Special Forces.

he wanted to die with those wrinkles, not to be blown up at twenty-six in a real war, because... One moment: what if his insomnia was not caused by Ninette and all the rest, but by the fear of being blown up at twenty-six in a real war? For weeks the Condor had been keeping them on alert: doubled defenses, triple guard duty, all leaves suspended. Yesterday the carabinieri* at the entrance had almost chased Ninette away: no-stopping-here, general's-orders. And the Condor was not the kind of general who gets alarmed over nothing. As for Charlie, all he did was to pester everybody with admonitions: look-out-here, look-out-there, I-want-you-to-have-eyes-even-in-your-ass, we're-waiting-for-something. Partly out of spite and partly out of incredulity, he had always refused to take it seriously. Now he did, though, and realized what he should have realized as he listened to the howls of the dogs and the crows of the crazed roosters. No, it was not the piercing concerto, it was not the amorous or pseudo-amorous mess in which he'd entangled himself, it was not the crisis ignited by his dissatisfaction that made him so restless: it was the waiting for the "something" that till yesterday did not exist and tonight existed. Something that moved, that advanced slowly in the darkness and while advancing spread a scent of death. Not the death that kills with gunshots, volleys, cannon shots: a different death. More frightening, more greedy. A death he couldn't imagine and yet he felt in every fiber of his body, with every nerve of his nervous system...

"Allah akbar, Allah akbar, Allah akbar! Wah Muhammad rassullillah! Inna shahada rassullillah... God is great, God is great, God is great! And Muhammad is his prophet! In truth I tell you that he is his prophet..."

The voice of the muezzin descended from the minaret of the mosque in rue de l'Aérodrome to mix with the howls of the stray dogs, the crows of the crazed roosters, the thud of the mortar shells. Modulating a plaintive singsong it swelled to psalmodize mysterious precepts, to divulge the prayer that precedes the dawn, and Angelo started. Five o'clock in the morning! He needed to get some sleep! Then he turned off the flashlight, he closed his eyes and fell asleep as if the muezzin had announced a whatever dawn of a whatever day. A Sunday just like any other.

---

* Special corps charged with the functions of the military police and the protection of the public order.

2

He was awakened by a tinkling of objects that banged against each other and the sensation of being at the center of an earthquake. The cot was swinging, the floor was shaking, the dugout seemed like a boat that pitches on a stormy sea. Then the earthquake stopped. A motionless silence fell, a stillness during which there was time to cast a look at the phosphorescent hands of his watch, to note that they pointed to six-twenty-four, and a monstrous rumbling ripped the air with an apocalyptic slap. He jumped to his feet. With convulsive movements he pulled on his camouflage outfit, slipped into his boots, jumped into the next room to call Charlie. But Charlie was already on his way out. His giant's frame shaken by a violent tremor, he was running toward the stairs that climbed up to the back of the courtyard and snarling: "God dammit! God dammit!" He followed him, and as he did he knew that the "something" had happened. An enormous catastrophe, a tragedy compared to which his own dramas became futilities. Yet he didn't expect to see what he saw in the uncertain light of the morning, and when he saw it he paled. It was a huge mushroom of red dust, the deep red of blood, that with striking slowness arose from a black cloud a mile and a half south, and as it arose it inhaled the earth like the trunk of an immeasurable cyclone. It sucked it, it absorbed it, it carried it up in the sky, and here it spat it out to suck it again, spit it out again, then unroll it like a carpet and form a flat crown that enlarged, spread, stretched into a blanket of obscurity: an unbounded darkness from which strange blotches rained. Strange shadows. Puppets with two arms and two legs.

"Chief! Down there!"

"Yes. The American headquarters," Charlie answered hoarsely. And almost at the same moment everything rocked again, shook again with the hiccoughs of an earthquake. The buildings seemed to wobble, the trees to flicker, and the flag at the top of the flagpole rippled in a dry blast of wind. Whoosh! Some windows broke, some chunks of plaster fell with a deafening thud, from the house next door a terrorized shriek resounded: "Yahallah!" Then the motionless silence fell once more, the stillness stagnated once more giving Angelo the time to cast another look at his watch, to note that it pointed to six-twenty-nine, and a second rumbling ripped the air with a second apocalyptic slap. A second mushroom of red dust arose from a second black cloud. This time a mile north. And this one also sucked up the earth, absorbed it, carried it up in the sky, spat it out, sucked it again, spat it out again, and again unrolled it to form the flat crown that enlarged, spread into a blanket of obscurity. The unbounded darkness from which the strange blotches rained. The strange shadows. The puppets with two arms and two legs.

"And down there, chief!"

"Yes. And down there is the French headquarters," Charlie answered hoarsely.

Not a word more, but Angelo heard what he was thinking: the-next-mushroom-is-for-us. And for a minute that seemed to both an eternity they remained still and mute, staring at each other as if the only thing to do were to wait for death standing still and mute, staring at each other. Or as if they wanted to exchange their souls and to engrave on their memories every detail of each other's features. High and smooth, Angelo's forehead, and half-covered by a rebellious tuft of fair hair. Lively and still full of illusions, his big eyes. Straight and imperious, his quivering nose. Taut and hollowed, his fresh cheeks. Stiff and yet softened by youth's hopes, his well-drawn mouth... Incised with ancient wrinkles, Charlie's forehead, and darkened by raven hair. Melancholic and deep, his dark eyes. Crooked and flattened by many wild fights, his nose. Withered and swollen by an endless discontent, his cheeks. And buried beneath bristly walrus mustaches, his mouth clenched in a grimace of infinite bitterness... Six-twenty-nine plus one. Plus two. Plus three. Plus four. Plus five, plus six, plus seven. Plus eight, plus nine, plus ten, plus eleven, plus twelve, plus thirteen, plus fourteen, plus fifteen... Six-thirty. As the minute elapsed, the mouth buried beneath the bristly walrus mustaches opened: "Let's get over to the Operations Room, son." Then they crossed the threshold of an entranceway half-hidden by sandbags and lunging into an uproar of officers with thick stubble and hastily donned uniforms, into a chaos of voices that anxiously asked what-happened, what-was-that, they crossed the ground-floor atrium. They reached a room full of radar screens, telephones, topographic maps, city plans, transceivers with radio operators nervously calling to order the state of alert.

"Eagle base, Eagle base, come in! This is Condor, Operations Room, Condor!"

"Sierra Mike base, Sierra Mike base, come in! This is Condor, Operations Room, Condor!"

"Ruby base, Ruby base!"

"Logistics base, Logistics base!"

"Attention all bases, all posts, attention! Maximum state of alert! Block all entrances, close them with tanks! Double surveillance, stop any vehicle, any vehicle! Search everybody, every package, every object, shoot if necessary: Condor's orders!"

In the middle of the room, a handsome man with general's rank who pointed at a large clock on the wall and screamed like a lunatic. The Condor.

"It is since six-twenty-six that I wait for the reports from Ost Ten and the Twenty-Seven Owl and the other observation posts! I want, I said I want, the exact coordinates and the precise distances! I want, I said I want, the ambulances and the rescue squads and the bulldozers to immediately go to the French, to the Americans! Tell the field hospital personnel to get ready, to prepare the operating rooms right away: understand? And I don't give a damn if there are not enough stretchers, understand? I demand the impossible! I repeat, the impossible!"

Beside him, his aide: an aloof colonel absorbed in the study of a map dotted with tiny Italian flags. The various bases and posts, the eventual targets of the next mushroom. Behind the aloof colonel, a frantic paratrooper captain who vented his anguish by shouting the most elaborate contumelies, then a bizarre character in a red-and-blue-striped robe who adjusting a monocle at his left eye and raising a nasal voice quarreled with him in Latin.

"Sufficit, non decet! Enough, this is unbecoming!"

"To hell with your sufficit, to hell with your non decet! I told you we couldn't trust those buttfuckers, those shitlickers, those dickpullers, rassullillah! I told you one day they'd give it to us up our ass!"

"Captain! Mind your language and your behavior, captain! It is no use to get hysterical and to shout vulgarities! Fortis animi est non perturbari in rebus asperis! Strong souls are not upset by misfortunes, Cicero teaches!"

With slow steps and with the air of someone who knows how to impose himself and his opinion, Charlie approached the Condor.

"Just what we were afraid of... Right, general?"

"Right, Charlie. I just spoke with the government: it was the French headquarters and the American headquarters. Two kamikaze trucks. A double slaughter."

"Two... And where's the third one? Where's ours?"

He pointed at the wall where the large clock read almost six-thirty-three.

"We'll know very soon, Charlie. There was an interval of five minutes between the first and the second attack. Now nine minutes have passed since the first one, four minutes since the second. If they keep the same interval..."

"In their place I wouldn't, general."

"Neither would I... If I were the third kamikaze, I'd give myself another ten or fifteen minutes. I'd move when those of the third target begin to relax."

"Yes, but..."

"Charlie, we've done what we could! And you know it. At this point, all we can do is wait."

They began to wait in silence. They were all silent by now. Even the furious captain who had been shouting elaborate contumelies, even the bizarre character with the monocle and the red-and-blue-striped robe who had quarreled with him in Latin, even the radio operators seated at the transceivers. And everybody's eyes were fixed on the large clock, everybody's ears were trained upon the only sound that could be heard in the room: the tick-tock of the clock spring which scanned the seconds. Each tick-tock a conquest and yet an exacerbation of the anguish, a hope and yet a multiplication of the tension, of the unendurable wait. A wait that did not involve only them because, though they were the easiest and most probable target, the next mushroom could arise from any of the bases that the aloof colonel's map indicated with tiny Italian flags and that the radio operators had been nervously calling before: Eagle base, Sierra Mike base, Ruby base, Logistics base. Tick-tock... six-thirty-three and one second. Tick-tock... six-thirty-three and two seconds. Tick-tock... six-thirty-three and three seconds. Tick-tock... six-thirty-three and four seconds. Tick-tock... six-thirty-three and five seconds. Tick-tock... six-thirty-three and six seconds... If-I-were-the-third-kamikaze-I'd-give-myself-another-ten-or-fifteen-minutes, the Condor had said, and everybody had heard him. Tick-tock, tick-tock... six-thirty-five. Tick-tock, tick-tock... six-thirty-six. Tick-tock, tick-tock... six-thirty-seven. Tick-tock, tick-tock... six-thirty-eight. Tick-tock, tick-tock... six-thirty-nine... At six-thirty-nine, the ten-minute mark, Charlie turned to Angelo who was biting his nails.

"Let's not despair, son."

"No, chief," Angelo murmured continuing to bite his nails.

"Maybe the third truck had some damage in its engine."

"Maybe..."

"Or maybe the kamikaze has changed his mind."

"Maybe..."

Tick-tock, tick-tock... six-forty. Tick-tock, tick-tock... six-forty-one. Tick-tock, tick-tock... six-forty-two. Tick-tock, tick-tock... six-forty-three. Tick-tock, tick-tock... six-forty-four. Tick-tock, tick-tock... six-forty-five... At six-forty-five Charlie stepped away from Angelo and reapproached the Condor.

"General, are you thinking what I'm thinking?"

"Yes, Charlie," the Condor nodded. "By now it's too late to re-establish the element of surprise. I think the third truck has spared us, for today."

"For today...!" was the bitter comment of a lieutenant with a large, eggplant nose.

"Dum fata sinunt vivite laeti! As long as destiny allows, let's live in joy, Seneca says! And Horace adds: Carpe diem! Seize the day!" shot back the bizarre character with the monocle and the robe.

"Fuck your carpe diem, fuck your today! I'll get them myself, those buttfuckers, those shitlickers, those dickpullers, rassullillah!" the frantic captain went back to shouting. But this time the Condor intervened.

"Shut up, Pistoia! And go to the Americans, go to the French! Find out what kind of trucks they were, what direction they came from, at what speed they got in, who drove them, which explosive they were loaded with, and how much." Then, turning to the lieutenant with the eggplant nose: "You too, Sugar. Quick!"

"Right away, general! I fly with my balls to the wind!" answered the first one raising a suddenly relaxed face.

"Yessir. At your orders, sir!" answered the lieutenant clicking his heels.

Then they ran off, followed by two jealous eyes. Angelo's eyes.

*   *   *

Now that the spasmodic tension was over, and with the tension the torture of the fifteen minutes spent staring at the clock and listening to its monotonous sound, he thought of nothing else but going there. But not to satisfy a curiosity or a sense of pity: to obey a call, a need that he confusedly felt linked up with his uncertain tomorrow and that almost in bad faith he disguised with sensible questions. How many soldiers like him were buried beneath the rubble of the American and the French headquarters? How many had been sucked up by the mushroom and carried into the sky to be spat out on the ground, puppets with two arms and two legs? How many Angelos who during the night had been listening to the howls of the stray dogs and to the crows of the crazed roosters or brooding over their Ninettes and their anxieties, who-am-I, what-am-I-searching-for, what-is-life? How many replicas of himself? Fifty, one hundred? He could not imagine himself dead fifty times, one hundred times. And he wanted to see. No, he didn't want to see. He wanted to understand. Aren't Life and Death the two faces of the identical problem? He turned to Charlie.

"Chief..."

"No," Charlie grunted, well knowing what he would ask. "What's it got to do with you? You work for me!"

"I could be of some use, chief. I could join the rescue squads..."

"The rescue squads don't need you."

"I could take pictures of them while they work... For our archive..."

"Leave me alone, son."

He did. Ignored by everybody, he went to wander into the atrium, now a feverish bustle of officers tracking the rescue operations. "Tell the Engineers to go with two Leopards and at least two cranes!" "Bring more shovels and more picks! The ones you sent are not enough!" "And don't forget your masks, your gloves and your masks! The dead stink, don't you know?" He stopped in dismay. He leaned against the door of an office where the nasal voice of the bizarre character now resounded.

"What a hateful attack, my illustrious friend! Really hateful! Nor could it come at a less convenient moment, for me. I mean, just today our colleagues of the English headquarters had invited me to lunch! You know, as I had the incomparable honor of serving in the Seventh Brigade during a Nato exchange, they have a special predilection for me. And Sir Montague, the commander, had even enriched the menu with a lovely pudding... I'll have to apologize in writing. It would be discourteous to do so by phone. A gentleman never indulges in discourtesies. Never! Not even in the midst of four hundred dead. Yes, we already have the number. Four hundred. Three hundred Americans and one hundred French. A big omelette. Sed quid novi? War is always an omelette, and one cannot have an omelette without breaking the eggs!"

He started in disbelief. Four hundred! Whether Charlie wanted him to or not, he had to go. He had to! And with his brain on fire he shot down the stairs to the basement. He burst into the Arab Bureau, snatched an M12, climbed back upstairs, ran back down again, seized the camera bag, climbed back upstairs, and was in the courtyard. As long as there was a jeep, he thought panting. A jeep was there, with the driver at the wheel. He jumped in.

"Go, Stefano, go!"

"Go where?" said Stefano raising his childish face still pale with fear.

"To the Americans. And to the French."

"But I'm waiting for Charlie! I must go with Charlie!"

"Forget Charlie! Move!"

Intimidated, Stefano started the engine and left the headquarters. He took rue de l'Aérodrome. It was daylight by now, the crazed roosters were no longer shrieking, the stray dogs had returned into the cellars of the shattered houses, into the sewers among the rats, and the two mushrooms of red dust had vanished. A clean, mocking sky shined over the city. A sky that seemed to say: go-and-see, go.

3

Themselves in a sturdy white building southeast of the airport, the thousand Marines of the American contingent: a four-story structure at the bottom of the avenue that skirted the control tower compound then the hangars. And, when you reached the terminal, you could already discern its outline standing with the red and the blue of the flag against the green of the trees. In front and around it, in fact, there were some mulberry trees and a row of palms. As they passed the hangars, however, Angelo realized that the unmistakable white structure wasn't there. Neither was the flag.

"Stefano! You took the wrong street."

"No, I didn't. After rue de l'Aérodrome I turned right, I took the avenue, I passed the terminal, then the control tower, then the hangars and... You're right! Where's the American headquarters?" Stefano mumbled, totally lost.

"Turn around. Quick!"

Stammering I-don't-understand, I-don't-understand, Stefano turned around. He drove back to rue de l'Aérodrome, made a U-turn, reached the airport for the second time, turned once more onto the avenue that skirted the terminal then the control tower then the hangars, and ended up in the same place.

"See? I didn't take the wrong street!"

"No, you didn't," Angelo admitted.

"Then the American headquarters should be there, at the bottom of the avenue..."

"It should. But it's not."

It was not. Yet several helicopters were flying in that direction, others were already landing beyond the row of palms, and also the ambulances which passed in a deafening racket of sirens were darting that way. So he told Stefano to follow them, and soon they reached a large fence enclosed by barbed wire along which dozens of journalists and photographers were disputing with the Marines of the sentry post.

"Let us in, let us in!"

"Get lost, dammit! Get lost!"

"Get back, dammit, get back!"

Inside the fence, chaos. Medics who frantically ran with the stretchers, frantically laid down the bodies, frantically loaded them on the helicopters or in the ambulances: "Make way, make way!" Rescue squads who desperately dug with bulldozers, shovels, hands, in search of someone to save: "Fast, fast!" Plastic bags piled up in pyramids or scattered around the ruins: the bags with the corpses already collected. Survivors who, covered with blood and soot, their eyes still full of terror and their uniforms torn, wandered calling for their mothers or Jesus. "Mommy... Jesus... Mommy..." And crumbled, disintegrated by the explosion that at six-twenty-four had surprised the thousand men in their sleep, the four-story building. In its place, an expanse of rubble no higher than a truck, and a stink of charred flesh that the wind spread around with the acrid smell of hexogen, the shouts, the curses, the laments.

"Help me! Get me out, help me!"

"My legs! Good Lord, my legs!"

"Ronnie! Where are you, Ronnie?!?"

"Junior! Answer me, Junior!"

"Oh, God! God, God!"

Stefano cowered in his seat.

"I'm not coming," he said in a small strangled voice.

"Right. Don't," Angelo answered. Then he put the M12 on his shoulder, the Nikon in his jacket, and plunged into the chaos. Every step, a stab of rage and horror. Here a finger, there a foot, or a hand, a forearm, an ear that improvised sextons picked up and threw in plastic bags like the garbage of a butcher shop: most of the bodies had been in fact dismembered into dozens of pieces. Some, instead, had remained beneath the iron scaffolding or the toppled walls to become heartrending bas-reliefs. Others were so charred that at the slightest touch they broke apart like embers. The wounded were few. But looking at their injuries you wished they would die as well, and often they did by means of the rescuers sent by the city. Devoid of technique or too accustomed to this kind of carnage, most of them worried only about moving the rubble swiftly. They used the scrapers or the shovels at random, and rather than extracting the victims with care they raked them like wreckage. They skewered them, they tore them apart. The Italian squads functioned better because they were directed by specialists from the Corps of Engineers and because they had the Leopards, with the cranes. But they worked almost always with the Marines and seldom spoke English. Still more rarely the Marines spoke Italian, and though they said the same thing they did not understand each other and the misunderstandings added disaster to disaster.

"No, puttana miseria, no-o-o! Prima bisogna segare la trave!"*

"What does he want? What is he saying? We've got to cut the girder!"

"La trave-e-e! Segare la trave! Perdio, come si dice in inglese segare, come si dice trave?"

"The girder! Cut the fucking girder! For God's sake, how do you say girder in Italian, how do you say to cut?!?"

"Cazzo! Siete contenti, cazzo?!? Era vivo, respirava, e ora è morto! Morto! Lo dicevo, io, che bisognava segare la trave!"

"Fuck you! Are you happy, fuck you?!? He was alive, he still breathed, and now he's dead! Dead! I told you we should cut the fucking girder!"

Then the desolate comments about the kamikaze. The bitter stories, the questions of the other rescuers.

"But who was he?!? Is there any way to know who he was?"

"A Son of God, of course. A Khomeinist. Didn't you hear the Marine who was at the sentry box? He saw him well. Right in the face!"

"No, I didn't. What did he say?"

"He said that around his head there was a black ribbon. The kind the Sons of God, the Khomeinists, wear. And then he said he was rather young, around thirty, that he had a beard, and that he smiled with happiness."

"With happiness?!?"

"Yessir! With happiness!"

"And how did he enter?"

"Easy. He passed right under the guard's nose with his truck full of hexogen. He knocked down the gate at the sentry post, got through the fence, burst into the lobby. Here he flipped the switch and blew himself up. The Pietro Micca way. Not even a hair left."

"That criminal!"

"That psychopath!"

The Pietro Micca way? A criminal, a psychopath? But Pietro Micca

---

* "First we must cut the girder."

was neither a criminal nor a psychopath, Angelo thought as he headed toward a third group working with picks. Pietro Micca was a hero. Italian children used to learn in primary school that he was a hero. "Pietro Micca, soldier in the Piedmontese Army, born at Vercelli in 1677, serving in the company of miners during the French siege of Turin. On August 29, 1706, in order to stop the French grenadiers who had broken into the tunnel leading to the citadel, he set off a mine and blew himself up with the enemy. His heroic act symbolizes the bravery of soldiers who defend the homeland from foreign invaders etcetera." Yes, they learned it at school, by heart, like the Pater Noster or the national hymn, and without a word of pity or respect for the French grenadiers whom Pietro Micca had dismembered, smashed, charred, reduced to heartrending bas-reliefs. And what if one day the Muslim children of Beirut would learn the same rigmarole about the Son of God who had massacred the three hundred Marines? The same sacrifice. The same circumstances. No, not the circumstances. Because the three hundred Marines weren't laying siege to the city: they were trying to bring it some peace, to placate the dogs that tore each other apart. They hadn't broken into a tunnel: they were sleeping in their cots! Right. But the kamikaze had been told that they were his enemies, that they had come for the same reasons the French grenadiers had gone to Turin in 1706, and... He-smiled-with-happiness, the Marine said. Is it possible to smile with happiness while you're about to die and to murder three hundred creatures? Maybe yes. Once he had been part of a simulated attack on a bridge, and the mission consisted not only of setting the explosive charges at the piers but of making them explode while the imaginary enemy was crossing it. Well, he had performed the hypothetical slaughter with diligence and dash, calculating to perfection the instant in which the piers would collapse with the troops, and when Sugar had exclaimed bravo-I'm-delighted-bravo he had smiled with happiness. Let's be honest: if there had really been some troops on the bridge, he would have set the same charges with the same diligence and the same dash. No refusals in the name of ethics. And afterwards he would have smiled the same smile: a truth which applied to the massacred Marines. They too knew how to make bridges collapse beneath enemy troops, they too had been taught to kill. "Kill, kill, kill!" was the scream they gave during training. Not to mention that a soldier has some chance to get away. A kamikaze does not. In every case he blows up with his victims and... And: enough with staying here to see horrors and to ponder bitter truths, he said to himself. Then he moved to leave but after a few steps he halted: struck by the sight of a marò* who kneeling on the ground, sobbed and clutched a helmet against his heart.

"John! John! John!"

He clutched it with the obstinacy of a child who refuses to give up an object very precious to him. Yet there was nothing childish in his aspect. He was a man of twenty-seven or twenty-eight, with a very masculine face, and Angelo grew impatient. Cut-it-out, aren't-you-ashamed-to-give-yourself-up-to-such-scenes, he wanted to yell. But when he reached him, his voice faded. Because it was not just a helmet that the marò was clutching against his heart. It was a decapitated head inside the helmet.

* * *

"Let go of it, marò!"

But the marò continued to sob and to clutch against his heart the decapitated head inside the helmet.

"John! Oh, John, John!"

"Leave it, marò."

"John! Oh, John, John!"

"Leave it, I said!"

"But it's John!" Then he went back to sobbing. "Oh, John, John!"

"Whoever he is, marò. Leave it and rejoin your squad. What's your squad?"

"What squad? Oh, John! John!"

"You came with a rescue squad, didn't you?"

"No... I came to look for John... Oh, John, John!"

"How did you get here?"

"I don't know, I don't remember... Oh, John, John!"

"What's your name?"

"Fabio... Oh, John, John!"

"Give it to me, Fabio, I'll put it in a bag."

"No! Not in a bag, no! Oh, John, John!"

There was no way to appease him, to make him leave that head. All at once, however, the sobs stopped. And though continuing to clutch it, to press it against his heart, he began to talk. A long talk, disconnected and interspersed with quiet-sergeant-quiet when Angelo tried to arrest that sudden loquacity. The story of a brief yet intense friendship. They had met on the firing range during a joint exercise, he and John,

* The Italian equivalent of the U.S. Marines.

and they had immediately understood each other because John spoke Italian. His family came from Umbria and at home his parents never used English. Quiet-sergeant-quiet. They resembled each other in so many ways, he and John. For example, though John too was a professional soldier, meaning one who'd suckered himself into it, he couldn't stand the war. "Fuck the war! fuck the war!" he said all the time, explaining that he hadn't joined the Marines to make war but to travel the world. Sign-up-and-see-the-world, the posters promised, and how could he imagine that he would get dicked? How could he guess that he would leave Parris Island, that place where they break you with drills and ill-treatments, only to come here to Beirut? Just like him who had joined the marò with the illusion of going to Japan and had left Brindisi only to find himself in this city of assassins. Quiet-sergeant-quiet. They used to meet often, he and John. To drink a beer, to make plans, to dream. Yesterday, for example, he had said: Fabio, as soon as this mess is over, I quit the Marines and you quit the marò. You come to my hometown which is Cleveland, Ohio, together we open an Italian restaurant, we get rich and travel the world on our own. Fuck the war, fuck the war. In fact this morning he'd woken up thinking of the Italian restaurant in Cleveland, Ohio, and of John: of his small blue eyes, his tiny pointed nose, his narrow lips, his funny red hair. The red of bricks. No, the red of boiled lobster. Yes, he was thinking of him when the explosion had gone off, the sky had darkened, the Hiroshima mushroom had arisen from that darkness, and somebody had shouted oddio, gli-americani-sono-saltati-in-aria. Oh, God, the Americans have blown up. Quiet-sergeant-quiet. Then the second explosion had gone off, the sky had darkened again, again the Hiroshima mushroom had arisen, and somebody had shouted oddio, the-French-have-blown-up-too, who-wants-to-be-included-in-the-rescue-squads. He'd asked to be included in those going to the Americans, there he'd yelled at once John-where-are-you-John, and at once he'd stumbled against a decapitated head inside a helmet. A head so black that anybody would have mistaken it for the head of a black Marine. Only by staring at it had he understood that its black wasn't the black of black skin, it was the opaque sooty black of burned skin. He had also realized that the eyes weren't the eyes of a black man, the nose wasn't the nose of a black man, the lips weren't the lips of a black man. Black men have black eyes, splayed noses, fleshy lips, and the eyes of the decapitated head in the helmet were light blue. The nose was pointed, the lips were narrow. Quiet-sergeant-quiet. He had felt like dying when he'd realized that the eyes were light blue, the nose was pointed, the lips were narrow, and in the hope that at least the hair would be black like a black man's hair he had shifted the helmet. But the hair was brick-red, the brick-red of boiled lobster. John's hair. John's nose. John's eyes. John's head... And here he interrupted to hand it to Angelo.

"Take it, sergeant."

He had always held it against his heart and showing the back of the helmet, during the disconnected talk, so Angelo had been unable to see more than its profile. Now, instead, he could see the whole face, and at seeing it he froze. The pupils wide open, the lips parted in an expression of astonishment, the head seemed to keep seeing, and seeing to keep thinking, and thinking to not believe that it had lost its body... Nonetheless he took it, and without looking at it anymore he went to throw it in a sack. Then he notified the Sierra Mike squad leader that a marò in state of shock needed to be hospitalized and rejoined the jeep.

"Hurry up, Stefano. Get me back to headquarters."

"And the French?" asked Stefano.

"No French," he answered. But in the same moment the radio crackled to bring him Charlie's infuriated voice.

"Where are you, rascal?!?"

"I'm coming back with Stefano, chief."

"Yes, I know you took him, I know! I'll fix you for this too, I will!"

"Coming right away, chief."

"Nossir, you don't! Now you go to the French, you go! General's orders! He wants photos of the rescue squads at work, I told him you'd already run off to the Americans, that I sent you there myself, and now he wants you to go to the French! Get there quick, rascal!"

"Yes, chief," he murmured hoping not to find another Fabio, another decapitated head inside a helmet. Then he went to the French where he found Ferruccio. And, with Ferruccio, something much worse.

4

Ferruccio grabbed the shovel, lowered his mask to wipe the sweat dripping down his cheeks, his adolescent face contorted in anger. Good Lord, how many fibs had they told him to snatch him away from Milan and dupe him all the way to Beirut! It will be a noble venture, they said, an experience to remember with pride, those poor people will welcome you with open arms as they need help and peace... Liars! Crooks! Swindlers! Why should a boy just out of school risk his skin for a country that for years has tormented the world with its bombs on the planes, its shootings and its killings in the airports, in the streets, in the supermarkets, its kidnappings, its blackmails, its arrogances? And to think that he had believed them at first, that almost gladly he had trained for the noble-venture, the experience-to-remember-with-pride! Interminable marches in the sun, exercises on the rifle range, man-to-man drills, simulated explosions to learn how to calculate the distance of a blast... Because of this bloody city he had even argued with Daniela who yelled if-you-go-I-leave-you. But on board the C-130 he had well understood, shit! That ice-cold, noisy crock where they had to stay lined up like birds on electrical wires, seated on those shabby benches and so squeezed one against the other that when you needed to take a leak you didn't have an inch to get up and walk. That toilet that wasn't a toilet but a fetid drum, those tiny urinals that filled up at once and sloshed the piss everywhere. Those frowning officers who hid their fear by pretending to read the newspaper and keeping it upside down. Those uneasy soldiers who didn't hide it at all yet tried to overcome it with their tasteless, macabre witticisms... "Did you make out your will?" "Did you buy a plot in the cemetery?" Not to mention the wringing that twisted his guts when the C-130 had landed with that deafening stroke: thump, thump! He'd almost fainted at hearing that double thump, and gripped his Fal. He'd made sure the cartridge was well inserted and thought: Good Lord, why didn't I say that I have a bifurcated rotula in my left knee? They pronounce you unfit for service if you have a bifurcated rotula in a knee, they send you back to Milan: why didn't I say it? Because I wanted to know the war I'd seen in the movies and on television, that's why. Because I'm a jerk, that's why. Mother was right when she ridiculed my wish to know the war, war-is-interesting, I'd-like-to-go. "Pirla, ciula! You jerk! You simpleton!" The proof had come at the base. Good Lord! He hadn't even put down his knapsack when two Rpg, the rocket-propelled grenades that punch through steel as if it were butter, had landed on the camp. Then a rain of mortar shells had followed, the colonel had ordered them to go down into the shelters, and here a guy nicknamed Onion was shitting in his pants, crying because he wasn't a faggot. "Ah, if I'd only been a faggot! In the army they don't want the faggots!" At a certain point he'd shouted Onion, it's-never-too-late-to-change, and left the shelter to go outside where a piece of shrapnel had missed him by a hair. By a hair! Filthy city. It gave him nothing but fears and discouragements and regrets, this filthy city. Including his regret over Daniela who had really left him. But this morning's carnage surpassed everything.

He lifted the mask back up, seized the shovel, and began to dig again. Good Lord, what a carnage! Who would have ever imagined that death could be such a carnage? In Italy death was the great-grand-mother who dies of old age and is laid out on the bed where she seems to sleep among the flowers and the candles and the relatives reciting the Requiem Aeternam. It was the motorcyclist who smacks into a car on the Florence-Bologna highway so that the traffic police cover him with a cloth, and passing by you see only the vague shape of a corpse and a smashed motorcycle. It was the Sicilian emigrated to Milan where another Sicilian has put a knife in his belly so that the authorities don't let you approach the scene of the murder and from a distance you perceive only a blood-spattered sheet and a woman who shrieks: "Turiddu, Turiddu!" It was a shiver that you soon forget, a funeral or a grave you think about rarely and with melancholy. But here! A while ago they had hoisted a slab beneath which a French paratrooper was still alive. So alive that despite his crushed arms he forced himself to smile and repeated: "Merci, merci!" But then the slab had dropped and now nothing of the paratrooper remained but a pancake of flesh and bones. And how death does stink! As much as the mouse which had drowned in the olive oil jug last summer. Mother hadn't noticed and kept complaining: "But what is this stink? Where does it come from?" It came from the olive oil jug, and for Christsake! Had he known, he wouldn't have even asked to be included in the rescue squads. No, he would have asked all the same. Because if he rescued a person today, just one person, he would feel less of a jerk, less of a simpleton. And think of how satisfying it would be to write Daniela: "Dear Daniela, you left me because of Beirut. But had I not come to Beirut, I would not have saved a person. Have you ever saved a person? Best regards, Ferruccio." So keep going, Ferruccio. Don't get tired. Don't get discouraged by the flesh and bones pancake, by the stink of the mouse which drowned in the olive oil jug. Give a meaning to your fears and discouragements and regrets: find somebody who's breath-ing, somebody to save. If you do...

He interrupted his monologue, he stopped his digging, to observe something that had emerged from the rubble. What was it? A water-closet...? Yes, a water-closet... But what was the stuff inside it? A shred of sky-blue fabric with little pink flowers...? Yes, but what was there inside the shred of sky-blue fabric with little pink flowers? He bent down to look better. Oh, Lord! Good Lord! There was... there was... Ferruccio dropped the shovel and it was at that moment that Angelo arrived at the French headquarters.

*   *   *

He felt as if nothing could upset him, by now. On the way, he had been worrying only about Charlie's rebukes at hearing that he hadn't snapped any photos of the rescue squads working at the American headquarters. He felt ready to face a thousand decapitated heads inside their helmets, to console a thousand sobbing Marines, and in a confident tone he told Stefano to wait in the jeep. With steady steps he crossed the wall of rejected journalists, plunged into the chaos of ambulances and bulldozers. With firm eyes he looked at what remained of the nine-story building the French had occupied: a chasm with a crooked pyramid on the edge. Here, in fact, the kamikaze had reached the underground garage and the truck had exploded underneath: at a side of the foundation. Rather than disintegrating, therefore, the building had slid down maintaining its structure: the nine stories had subsided one on top of the other and skewed like a layered pastry that collapses on a slant, forming steps. In place of the various layers, the ruins of each floor and the victims caught in their sleep. On the steps, the rescue squads dug only with the shovels and the picks because the bulldozers' weight would have altered the precarious equilibrium of the pyramid. Alongside the dark chasm, the corpses already extracted. Almost a hundred. Everywhere, the wounded that the rubble continued to yield in a turmoil of shouts, whispers, laments, agonizing invocations...

"Maman! Mother, maman!"

"Ne me touchez pas, je veux mourir! Don't touch me, I want to die!"

"Mes jambes! My legs! Où sont mes jambes? Where are my legs?"

"Aidez-moi, je vous en supplie! Help me, I beg you!"

Just a replica of what he had seen at the American headquarters, he thought. Then he took his Nikon, framed a group of Italians who were shifting an iron girder, and got ready to take the first picture. But he didn't. Because, right at that moment, his attention was drawn by a bersagliere* who motionlessly stared at an object on the ground. A very young bersaglieri. Even from a distance and in spite of the mask which half-covered his face, you could tell that he was extremely young. And his immobility expressed such a painful dismay that you felt the need to go see the object he stared at. He went, he looked.

* The bersaglieri are the oldest corps of the Italian army, now used in armored companies. Their characteristic uniform includes a hat and a helmet with feathers.

What he stared at was a water-closet which contained a shred of sky-blue fabric with little pink flowers... No, he did not stare at that. He stared at something which emerged from that. And the something was... was... Angelo looked again and a husky groan exhaled from his throat.

"No-o-o..."

It was a child, a girl, stuck head-down and with three-quarters of her body in the water-closet. Only the lower part of her stomach and one leg emerged from the shred of sky-blue fabric with little pink flowers: the rest sank into the water-closet, swallowed up by the drainpipe. It sank like the cork of a bottle sinks inside the neck of the bottle, and not even God could have told by which coincidence of dynamics this had happened because the drainpipe was very narrow and the girl's body was not very small. Yet it had happened, and what was worse for him was that he knew the girl for he used to meet her when he went to the French headquarters. Always wearing the same smock of sky-blue fabric with little pink flowers she sat in the corridor of the ground floor among the cartridge cases, her toys, and as soon as she saw him she ran to prattle: "Bonjour, Monsieur, est-ce que vous avez un bonbon pour moi? Good day, Sir, do you have a candy for me?"

"Sergeant..." stammered Ferruccio. "Sergeant, what was a girl, a child, doing here?"

"She was Fawzia, the doorkeeper's daughter," he answered.

"Oh, Lord!"

"She was three..."

"Oh, Lord!"

"She liked candy..."

"Oh, Lord!"

"Let's pull her out, bersagliere."

It took a long time to do so. It took almost an hour. Without anyone helping them: the rescuers cared for those they could save and didn't waste time with the dead. It took them so long because she had really sunk in there like the cork of a bottle inside the neck of the bottle, and because they didn't have anything but that little leg to extract the cork. They seized it in turn, with delicacy, as if they were afraid of hurting her, of adding desecration to desecration, then they yanked it with strength. But each time the pipe seemed to swallow her up even more, and when they gained an inch they lost it at once. When they regained it they lost it again. "I'm not capable," each of them panted. "She's not coming, I'm not capable..." Instead they were. They got her out all the way, in the end. A hard vermilion cylinder, a horrifying sausage from which a tail of bloody curls hung. She came out with the smacking sound of a cork drawn out by a corkscrew. Plop! Then Ferruccio placed her in a plastic bag, took off his mask, and vomited his soul with a curse.

"Murderer Christ, murdereeer!"

He did it as though along with his disgust for the horrifying sausage he wanted to vomit his delusion, his grief at discovering that Beirut hadn't even given him a chance to save a life. Then he recovered his shovel, went back digging, and: "I'm really angry, sergeant. Because I was eighteen, see, eighteen, and now I am not anymore. I lost my youth. I lost it, sergeant, as I don't believe in anything, in anybody anymore. Neither in Christ nor the Holy Virgin nor the Eternal Father nor the saints nor men. There's no Christ, Sergeant, there's no Virgin, there's no Eternal Father, there are no saints. There are only men, and it would be better if there weren't any. Men are so evil. Evil animals. No, not animals. Because animals kill each other, yes, they eat each other, yes, but they don't drive the trucks full of hexogen to blow up children. To hurl little girls into water-closets. What kind of being was that guy in the truck, sergeant? Who was he? Well, I tell you who he was: a man. Yes, a man with two arms and two legs and a heart and a brain. And I don't like being born among men, sergeant. Better to be born among hyenas or among cockroaches. Or not to be born at all. See, I used to say that men are superior to animals because they know how to build streets and bridges and houses and cupolas and boats and ships and airplanes. And because they know how to paint the Sistine Chapel and write *Hamlet* and compose *Nabucco* and transplant hearts and land on the moon, all things that animals don't know how to do. But I was wrong. What's the point of being so clever if we blow little girls into water-closets? No, I don't believe in men. And since I'm one of them, from now on I don't even believe in myself. Oh, sergeant, I shouldn't have come to Beirut. If I hadn't come here, I still would believe in myself. And I wouldn't have lost my eighteen years. My youth. Jerk! Simpleton, jerk: I wanted to see the war... That's why I didn't say I have a bifurcated rotula in my left knee. Well, I saw it. I see it. And I don't like it. I don't like the armies, I don't like the uniforms, I don't like the flags... Why did you choose this trade, sergeant? I didn't. I'm a draftee, I'm here by accident. By mistake. But you! War is your trade. You know very well how to do what the man in the truck has done. You learned to use bombs as a baker learns to make bread. Why? I don't understand why anybody should learn that stuff. I hate war too much. And if anyone tells me that war has always existed and will always exist, I'll break his bones. To revenge my eighteen years, my lost youth. Tell me I'm right, sergeant.''

"You're right," he said.

"Swear you'll never kill anybody, sergeant."

"I swear I'll never kill anybody," he said. Then he tossed his pack over his shoulder and went off without snapping a single photo.

"Stefano, let's get back to the headquarters."

And he returned to the headquarters where Ninette waited for him.

* * *

She waited pacing back and forth in front of the carabinieri sentry box, her splendid face twisted with anxiety, her beautiful body strained with impatience, and as soon as the jeep slowed down to enter she ran toward him with a joyous voice.

"Darling! You're alive, thank God!"

He looked at her as he would look at somebody he didn't know and wasn't interested to know. He turned to Stefano.

"What is she saying? What does she want?"

Stefano translated.

"But where have you been, darling? You look so pale, so tired, and there's blood on your shirt!"

He looked at her in the same way and turned back to Stefano.

"And now what is she saying? What does she want?"

Stefano translated.

"You should get some rest and forget, poor darling. Go to sleep, I'll pick you up at seven. We'll spend the night making love and you'll forget.''

Stefano translated.

"Life goes on, darling, and we must forget," the joyous voice insisted.

Stefano translated then asked if he wanted to tell her something. But the answer was a disdainful head shake.

"No. Move!"

Stefano moved, and the jeep entered the serpentine pathway that led to the courtyard.

It was by now noon, in the streets of West Beirut people celebrated the double slaughter, and at post number Twenty-Eight of Shatila Fabio prepared himself to betray John's memory.

5

He hadn't remained too long at the field hospital. The tents over-flowed with the wounded and the dying, in the operating rooms the surgeons worked at a fever pitch, the blood plasma grew scarce, the morphine ran short, and who had time to waste on a marò simply sick with sorrow? After a quick check to see if he had any physical lesion, a medical officer had dismissed him with a couple of aspirin and advice very similar to that of Ninette: "Report in sick, young man, and don't think about it anymore." So, after going back to his base and reporting in sick, he had really tried to stop thinking about John. I'm a slacker, he had told himself, a hysteric. I forget that I'm in a war: if every soldier who loses a friend in the war should go crazy, armies would turn into madhouses. But, like a chunk of wood that when tossed in the water bobs back to the surface, the image of the decapitated head inside the helmet had quickly reemerged with the nightmare of that black which wasn't the black of black skin but the opaque sooty black of burned skin and the nightmare had been soon overlaid by the image of John all whole and alive. John who exclaimed fuck-the-war, John who wanted to quit the Marines and have him quit the marò so they could open an Italian restaurant in Cleveland, Ohio and get rich and travel the world, John who helped him discover how precious it is to have in Beirut a friend who laughs and talks... Before John the only friend he had had in Beirut was Rambo, his squad leader, who never laughed or spoke or drank beer. And little by little he had started weeping again: "John! Oh, John, John!" So he'd asked Rambo to be put back on duty and now he stood with him at Camp Three, the Twenty-Eight's reinforce-ment at Shatila, up behind a low sandbag wall he watched the celebra-tion of the double slaughter. A real celebration. Waving black banners and green flags, the Palestinian banners and the Shiite flags, they poured out of the houses and huts then they ran to each other and embraced. They congratulated each other, they thanked Allah. Or else they yelled out their exaltation from the windows, the terraces, the rooftops, they circled the Italian posts, spreading the index and the middle fingers in the sign of victory and hurled sinister warnings.

"Al-amerikin matu, jah! The Americans dead, hurray! Al-talieni bukra, jah! The Italians tomorrow, hurray!"

"Al-faransin matu, jah! The French dead, hurray! Al-talieni bukra, jah! The Italians tomorrow, hurray!"

"Kaputt! Tomorrow Italians kaputt!"

Men and women. Young and old. Hundreds. And swarms of children who, egged on by the adults, participated in the uproar by chanting insults.

"Al-talieni akrùt! Thieves!"

"Haqkirin! Bastards!"

"Miniukin! Faggots!"

Among the children, an old mullah with a coffeepot in his right hand and a tiny cup in his left who hailed the massacre by offering coffee.

"Eshrabu! Wah Allah maacum, eshrabu! Drink! God be with you, drink!"

He didn't yell, no. Neither did he pronounce any sinister warning or insult. He offered coffee and that's all. At first sight, the most inoffensive creature in the world. Frail and rounded, his shoulders cloaked in a brown woolen tunic. Meek, his diaphanous face framed by a short white beard and surmounted by a gray turban. Benevolent, the tone in which he repeated drink-God-be-with-you-drink. But his invitation was gloomier than the hurrays and the cries Italians-tomorrow-kaputt, Italians-thieves-bastards-faggots, and along with amazement Fabio felt an indignation which restored his need to weep. Ugly jackal, he thought. Toasting on the dead, on John's death! And we let him do it, none of us moves a finger to chase him away. None. Not even Rambo. Look at him. They call him Rambo because he resembles the Rambo of the movies, same muscles, same clenched teeth, yet he takes it with the patience of Saint Francis. This is cowardice. It's an injustice, a betrayal of John's memory: I must do something. And, all at once, a scream ripped the air.

"Shit of a mullah! Get off, shit of a mullah, go away!"

As if he hadn't understood the affront, or rather behaving as if he had received a compliment, the mullah approached him. He smiled a smile of yellow teeth, refilled the cup, handed it to him.

"Eshrab," he said. "Drink!"

"Go away or I'll shoot, you shit!"

Placidly and still behaving as if he had received a compliment, the mullah placed the cup on the sandbag wall. Then he flashed two eyes full of hate and raised a cold voice.

"Eshrab! Qult eshrab! Drink, I said!"

"Go away. Or I'll shoot. Go away."

"Eshrab! Al-amerikin matu, the Americans dead. Al-faransin matu, the French dead. Eshrab, drink!"

"I'll shoot!"

"El naharda iom aazim. Great day, today. Eshrab, drink!"

"Ignore him," Rambo grunted. But at the same moment the mullah extended his hand toward him. He grasped one of his wrists, he stared him in the eyes.

"Enta kaman. You too."

In reality Rambo didn't deserve the nickname Rambo. He never indulged in belligerent or hasty acts, he never yielded to an impulse of rage, he never pronounced a bad word or called names. In spite of appearances he was a mild type, a good-natured guy, and if something disturbed him he calmed himself by touching a small medallion with the Virgin Mary's profile that he wore at his neck with his identification tag. But woe to those who hurt his pride. And that hand grasping his wrist hurt his pride more than the words enta-kaman, you-too.

"Shu hakita? What did you say?" he answered in perfect Arabic. Then, with contemptuous slowness, he freed his wrist. He put down his rifle, with leaden steps he went to place himself in front of the mullah, seized the cup, and tossed the coffee in his face. "Kuss inmak, ibn sharmuta. Go fuck yourself, you son of a bitch."

And the nightmare of the decapitated head inside the helmet, the image of John who wanted to quit the Marines and have him quit the marò to open the restaurant in Cleveland, Ohio, disappeared from Fabio's mind. Along with them, the indignation and the pride. His brain became a well of terror, and while the mullah rabidly thundered incomprehensible words in his language, while the black banners and the green flags waved menacingly, while a group of Shiite guerrillas advanced aiming their Kalashnikovs, while the crowd roared al-maut-al-talieni, death-to-the-Italians, he leaped out of the guard post. He ran toward the mullah, took the coffeepot from his hands, gulped down in one mouthful all the coffee it contained, then returned it empty.

"Jamil! Good, jamil!"

"Jamil, good?" the mullah exclaimed in surprise.

"Na'am, yes. Wa el naharda iom aazim. And great day, today."

"El naharda iom aazim, great day today?" the mullah repeated, incredulously.

"Na'am, wa inta sadiqi. Yes, and you my brother."

"Sadiqi, brother? Ba'a koblet el sadaka. Then let's have a kiss of brotherliness," the mullah smiled, now mockingly. And he kissed him on both cheeks.

The roar of al-maut-al-talieni, death-to-the-Italians, died out. The black banners and the green flags stopped waving. The guerrillas who had advanced aiming the Kalashnikovs yelled their exultation. Fabio returned the double kiss, and from the marò of the Twenty-Eight a chorus of taunts arose.

"Coward! Whore!"

"Chicken! Pussy!"

"Shitbird!"

Rambo, on the contrary, hardly moved his lips.

"You're even worse," he murmured. "You're a Judas. A traitor without dignity, a Judas."

Of course he was, Fabio thought lowering his head in shame. Of course his double kiss had been a Judas kiss. Of course he'd lost his dignity. He'd also betrayed his companions, the four hundred dead, and John's memory. But suddenly he didn't give a damn for his dignity. Nor for his companions, the four hundred dead, and John's memory. Because he didn't want to die. He wanted to live, dammit. To live. And by entirely different paths, the indirect paths of reason, Angelo was meanwhile reaching the same conclusion.

* * *

"You irresponsible fool! What do you mean I-didn't-take-a-single-photo?" Charlie had rebuked him. "But how?! You disobey my orders, you take my jeep and my driver, you sneak off to the Americans, the general looks for you, I protect you, I tell him I sent you to take pictures of the rescue squads, he answers then-send-him-to-the-French-too, I send you there, and you come back empty-handed?!? Beat it! Get out of here!" He'd gotten out of there. He'd stopped in the courtyard to sum up an anguish by now at the limits of delirium. Pietro Micca and the kamikaze who smiled with happiness. The other one that nobody had seen and who in any case was a man with two arms and two legs and a heart and a brain. Fabio and the decapitated head inside the helmet, that head with the wide-open pupils and the lips parted in astonishment as if it continued to see and to think, and thinking it couldn't believe it had lost its body. Ferruccio and the girl sunk into the water-closet like the cork of a bottle inside the neck of the bottle, that agonizing monologue with the finale swear-you'll-never-kill-anybody-sergeant and his answer I-swear-I'll-never-kill-anybody. And Ninette with her untouched beauty, her egoistic joyousness, her mania for making love. Life-goes-on-darling. Life? Was this life? No. This was a destructive, illogical, senseless chaos! One moment... And if Life were really a destructive, illogical, senseless chaos? More than a hundred years ago Ludwig Boltzmann, the Austrian physicist who introducing the methods of statistics into thermodynamics had put in mathematical terms the concept of entropy, meaning chaos, had upheld just that. Chaos, he had said, is the ineluctable and irreversible tendency of all things: from the atom to the molecule, from the planets to the galaxies, from the infinitely small to the infinitely large. Its goal is exclusively destructive, and woe to us if we attempt to oppose it, to make order out of disorder: to give sense to senseless things. Rather than diminishing or weakening, it increases. Because it absorbs the energy we employ in the effort: the energy of life. It devours it, it uses it to arrive more quickly at its final goal which is the destruction or rather the complete self-destruction of the Universe. And it always wins. Always... It was contained in an equation of five letters, the atrocious verdict: $S = K \ln W$. Entropy equal to the constant of Boltzmann multiplied by the natural logarithm of the probability of distribution. Before becoming a dwarf tree, a bonsai, he had studied it and... And if the formula of Life were this? No, impossible, no! This was the formula of Death! It upheld that Life is an instrument of Death, food for Death, and how to believe that Life is an instrument of Death, food for Death? It had to be the opposite! Oh, if one day he could discover the opposite and demonstrate that Death is an instrument of Life, food for Life, that dying is only a momentary standstill, a pause to rest, a short sleep that prepares us to be reborn, to live again, to die again yes but to be reborn again, to live again, to live and live and live forever!

He jumped to his feet, electrified by an irresistible hunger to live. To live and live and live forever, to infinity. And our story begins just here.

CHAPTER TWO

1

FOR A TIME that to many seemed immemorial and instead went back to a recent past, Beirut had been one of the most agreeable spots on this planet: an extremely comfortable place to live and to die of old age or illness. Whether you were rich and corrupt or poor and honest, there you found the best a city can offer: a mild climate in the summer and winter, blue sea and green hills, work, food, a thoughtlessness that put up for sale any kind of pleasure, and above all a great tolerance because despite the babel of races and languages and religions its inhabitants lived together in harmony. The Shiite or Sunni Muslims cohabited amiably with the Maronite or Greek Orthodox Christians or Catholics, the ones and others did the same with the Druzes and the Jews. The litanies of the muezzins mingled easily with the sound of church bells, the believers of the mosques weren't cursed in the churches, the believers of the churches weren't cursed in the mosques. Neither the first nor the second were despised in the synagogues, and the rites of the nineteen creeds permitted by the Constitution were celebrated without difficulty. A more or less democratic regime existed, civil liberties were respected, even too many little sins were permitted, thus committed, and people killed each other out of revenge or jealousy or robbery, not out of mandated hate or fanaticism or military exigency. War didn't exist. The massacres in which the two main tribes, the Christians and the Muslims, had slain each other for years were a vague memory. The raids undertaken over centuries by the Greeks, the Romans, the Crusaders, then Saladin, then again the Crusaders, then the Turks, then the Westerners always drawn to the city's geographic position and economic advantages, a forgotten story. In 1946 the French mandate had ended and along with independence had left a sense of well-being that amalgamated the various groups. It incorporated them through the faith in the only god that human beings worship without limit and without reservation: God Money.

It was called the Switzerland of the Middle East, at that time, and it was such a hospitable place that it welcomed whoever asked for refuge or success: adventurers, persecuted politicians, swindlers, spies, misfits, wretches in search of the Earthly Paradise. By the thousands they disembarked every day from the boats, the ships, the airplanes. To stay, fairly often, and get rich. It also was a beautiful city, though it didn't offer sublime monuments, and its beauty didn't lie entirely in the enchanting landscape. Splendid villas rose on the hills still embellished by the cedars of Lebanon, and immaculate gardens and verandas paved with superb Alexandrian mosaics. Stunning residences and exquisite art deco houses enlivened the park called the Pine Wood, so lush that its smell the odor of resin spread for miles. At the edge of it, a magnificent racetrack surrounded by stables which housed the most prized purebloods of the world. Next to the racetrack, a museum in which you could admire the anthropomorphic sarcophagi of the ancient forefathers, the Phoenicians, and the archaeological remains unearthed at Byblos. Sumptuous hotels de luxe lined the sunny seashore along with exclusive nightclubs, and restaurants famous for their wines and chefs. Among them the mythical Saint George. Poverty was not absent, of course: richness feeds itself on others' misery. But hunger didn't exist, and in every quarter you found some evidence of prosperity. In the Western Zone there was a grandiose Cité Sportive that contained a stadium for fifty thousand people, two Olympic-size swimming pools (one for swimming and one for diving), two tennis courts, two basketball courts, and lockers for the athletes, coffee shops, solariums. On the renowned street called Galerie Semaan stores overflowing with goods attracted customers from every part of the earth, and the banks paid dizzying profits: anyone who wanted to quickly double his money only had to deposit it in Beirut. Good schools to combat illiteracy existed as well, and good craft workshops in which to learn a trade, and an illustrious American university, a no-less-celebrated Catholic university which produced professors as distinguished in scientific as in humanistic doctrines. The hospitals worked efficiently. Theaters and concert halls and cinemas abounded. The traffic streamed rapidly along the wide two-lane avenues, the solid overpasses, the elegant ronds-points: the circular squares constructed by the French on the model of the Parisian ones. It streamed even better along the extraordinary Corniche that went from east to north, hugged the northern coast, reached the northwest promontory, then descended south through the beautiful and wind-kissed littoral. Construction flourished. The town planning scheme was comparable to those of the modern European capitals. An excellent road led to Damascus, an efficient railroad to Aleppo. The port, among the most well equipped in the Mediterranean, dispensed fabulous earnings. The airport, where hundreds of flights to and from Asia landed every day, contributed in equal measure to padding the city's pockets. And never mind if many of these fine things were polluted by a fist of multibillionaire mafiosi who controlled the economy. Never mind if the most conspicuous among these were a certain Pierre Gemayel, father of Bashir and Amin, and a certain Kamal Jumblatt, father of Walid. Never mind if the former was an admirer of Mussolini and the founder of a paramilitary corps known as the Phalange. The latter, a pioneer in the traffic of hashish and the powerful patriarch of the Druzes with the baggy pants pinched at the knee to shit out the Messiah. (According to their theological mysteries, to be delivered or rather defecated from a man.) Never mind. No earthly paradise is perfect, peace is well worth a few dirty tricks, and despite all this Beirut managed to be an almost happy place. (The "almost" indicates the caution to observe when using the equivocal adjective "happy.")

But one ugly day the Palestinians had arrived. With their anger, their pain, their money. An enormous amount of money. And thanks to that money, given the fact that in Beirut you could buy everything except immortality, they had bought the permission to establish themselves in three zones of the Muslim periphery: Sabra and Shatila, two quarters next to the Cité Sportive, and Bourji el Barajni. A quarter halfway along rue de l'Aérodrome. Here, using the same logic as the Israelis who had stolen their homeland, they had installed themselves in the place of the Shiites who at Sabra and Shatila and Bourji el Barajni had always lived. They had evicted them from their houses, taken their courtyards, effaced their streets to build new buildings. Then, not satisfied with such bullying, they'd sprawled beyond that territory to settle in some Christian neighborhoods as well. Deaf to the discontent their invasion provoked, they had established a state within the state: a nation with its own laws, its own banks, its own schools, its own clinics, its own army. A genuine army, outfitted with uniforms and barracks and armored tanks and long-range artillery. A military machine that lacked a navy and an air force yet received from abroad every kind of equipment including equipment necessary to excavate and build another city. Because, little by little, beneath the soil of the plundered city they'd excavated another city: invisible and impregnable. A labyrinth of catacombs sheltering tons of weapons and ammunition, passageways housing combatants and radio centers and secret entrances and well-ventilated tunnels that often extended for miles and led to the beach of the wind-kissed littoral. In short, an immense subterranean stronghold. A masterpiece of engineering. At the same time they'd reinforced their camps in southern Lebanon and, without caring for the ferocious reprisals with which the Israelis punished the country guilty of tolerating their enemy, they had intensified their attacks on the kibbutzim. Then Beirut had rebelled. Or, to be precise, the groups that could afford such a luxury like the Christians and the phalangists of Papa Gemayel. Clashes, at first, local skirmishes. But the clashes had soon degenerated into battles. The battles, into massacres like the massacre at Damour: the Maronite Christian town where the retaliating Palestinians had slaughtered dozens of old people, women, children. The massacres, into a real civil war. And the Switzerland of the Middle East had become a lugubrious stage setting of ransacked houses, gutted mansions, walls pierced by millions of bullets, mountains of corpses infecting the air that once smelled of resin. In the end, thanks to an armistice signed out of resignation and exhaustion, it had become a bisected Berlin. To the East, the Christian Zone or East Beirut. To the West, the Muslim Zone or West Beirut. In the middle, a border called the Green Line. An immaterial wall which sliced the inhabited area from north to south and gave the port to the Christians, the airport to the Muslims, but essentially favored the latter. West Beirut in fact got the larger portion of the area, most of the coast, the entire Pine Wood, the Old City with its prosperous quarters, the roads leading to southern Lebanon. Which, making the Palestinians the absolute masters, strengthened their aggressiveness and arrogance. It also solidified their control over the Israeli frontier and their attacks on the kibbutzim. So, another ugly day, the Israelis had come.

They had come with an army flanked by the navy and the air force, well known for the harshness with which it used to confront the enemy, and within a few days they had reached the Eastern Zone. Here, though, they had been blocked by the Palestinians. Their advance had converted into a siege, and for more than two months West Beirut had been crucified by an orgy of fire from the sky, from the earth, from the sea. Day after day, night after night, week after week, while the havoc extended to East Beirut because the besieged answered shooting from the Cité Sportive. In its stadium they had placed modified Sherman tanks and M48s, with 105mm cannons; on the tennis courts and basketball courts they had set up the mortars and the BM21s to launch Katyushas; on the solariums, the 12.7mm antiaircraft batteries: the same ones they had put on the roofs of the hospitals marked with the Red Cross symbol. They didn't bother with scruples. Thanks to the subterranean city, to its bowels which enclosed enough weapons and ammunition to resist for a year, they didn't surrender. In the end, however, they had. Cut off from water and food, tired of living in the passageways and tunnels, doubly hated by the Shiites who were dying like flies, they'd asked the Westerners to conduct negotiations with Jerusalem. And Jerusalem had answered with an irrevocable choice: either evacuate Beirut or resign themselves to a bloodbath. They had chosen to evacuate. Under the shield of a Multinational Force, after mining the subterranean city's passages and walling up its main entrances, almost ten thousand had left to scatter throughout Syria or Tunisia or Libya or South Yemen. Only the elderly, the mutilated, the children, the women, and those who defined themselves as noncombatants had remained: another ten thousand people now well contained inside the borders of Sabra, Shatila, and Bourji el Barajni. Then the Multinational Force had left Beirut as well. The Israelis had installed themselves as conquerors, with their consent the younger son of Papa Gemayel had become president, and a kind of peace had fallen over the inferno. But the beautiful city which had been one of the most agreeable spots on this planet, an extremely comfortable place to live and to die of old age or illness, no longer existed.

Now ruins, the splendid villas on the hills where the cedars of Lebanon would never grow back and the green would die stifled by the gray of the stones. Marble dust, the superb Alexandrian mosaics that paved the verandas. Crumbled or looted, the stunning residences and the exquisite art deco houses. Reduced to blackened trunks or ghostly stumps, the trees of the Pine Wood. And the magnificent racetrack had been demolished. The stables, knocked down. The prized purebloods, killed by the bullets. The museum with the archaeological remains of Byblos and the anthropomorphic sarcophagi of the ancient Phoenician forefathers, devastated. The sumptuous hotels de luxe, the exclusive nightclubs, the restaurants famous for their wines and their chefs, irretrievable. The grandiose Cité Sportive, literally crumbled. The rich stores of the Galerie Semaan, razed to the ground. The churches, the mosques, the synagogues, the banks that paid dizzying profits, reduced to ruins. The wide two-lane avenues, the solid overpasses, the elegant ronds-points, impracticable for the chasms the bombs had opened. The port, almost unusable. The airport, out of commission. And everywhere rubble, rubble, rubble. Corpses, corpses, corpses. Bourji el Barajni, the worst hit neighborhood, seemed a desert of stones. Even the traces of sidewalks or alleys were gone, and lucky those who found in that desert a few bricks to build a shanty. Sabra and Shatila, where many had survived in clandestine shelters dug beneath the houses, were less demolished. But two weeks later their inhabitants would bitterly regret not having died in the siege. Because two weeks later the young president and son of Papa Gemayel would be assassinated with sixty of his followers by a load of Tnt, and the phalangists would unleash their rage upon the Palestinians by now at the mercy of whoever wanted to punish them for their past arrogance and their responsibility in bringing the war to Beirut. A massacre that would horrify even those who don't understand why painting the Sistine Chapel and writing *Hamlet* and composing *Nabucco* and transplanting hearts and landing on the moon don't make us better than animals.

Well recalling the massacre they had suffered at Damour, Papa Gemayel's phalangists had pounced at nine o'clock on a Wednesday evening. A warm Wednesday evening of early September. And with the complicity of the Israelis, always happy to satisfy their inexhaustible thirst for revenge, they had surrounded both quarters blocking off any means of escape. A maneuver so swift, so perfect, that few had found the time to hide or to attempt a getaway. Then, inflamed with their faith in Jesus Christ and Saint Maron and the Virgin, protected by the sons of Abraham who lit the streets with flares, they had stormed into the houses to start the job by murdering those who were dining or watching television or sleeping. They had continued all night. And all the next day. And all the next night. Until Friday morning. Thirty-six straight hours. Without stopping. Without anybody saying enough. Anybody. Neither the Israelis, of course, nor the Shiites who lived in the neighboring buildings and from their windows could witness all. The men slain at once by machine gun fire and the elderly butchered in their beds had been lucky. Before being shot or stabbed, the women had been raped. Sodomized. Their bodies, churns for ten or twenty rapists at a time. Their newborns, bull's-eyes for target practice with cold steel or firearms: an eternal sport in which men who regard themselves superior to animals have always excelled and which for centuries has been called Herod's Slaughter. A wounded boy had managed to flee through the blocked routes and take refuge in the tiny hospital that three Swedish doctors ran in front of Shatila. But Herod's soldiers had chased him and found him on the operating table. A shove to the surgeon extracting the bullet, a bullet in the heart of the Palestinian nurse who tried to stop them, another one in the temple of the boy, and off. On Friday morning, tired of hunting and murdering, they had mined the houses where the survivors hid. At least half of those in Shatila. Then they had left singing defiant war songs and leaving behind a carnage worthy of a horror film. Children two or three years old who dangled from the beams of the exploded rooms like chickens hanging from a butcher's hooks. Newborns squashed or cut in two, mothers struck down in the useless gesture of protecting them. Seminude corpses of women with their wrists tied and their buttocks smeared with sperm and shit. Heaps of gunned-down men covered with mice who ate them up. Entire families killed at their dinner tables. And an unbearable stench. The stench of decomposition hastened by the September heat. Five hundred had been the initial word. But the five hundred had soon become six hundred. The six hundred, seven hundred. The seven hundred, eight hundred, nine hundred, one thousand. It had taken two bulldozers to dig the communal grave, almost a day to fling everyone into it. And in a fit of panic the government had recalled the Multinational Force. "Help, come bring us a little peace, help."

* * *

Four thousand Americans, Italians, French, and English (the latter numbering only one hundred) who upon disembarking believed they would settle things in a few weeks. Instead they were there for over a year and, far from having restored the peace, had to deal with a new war. In the Western Zone, in fact, now it was the Shiites who played the master. The pro-Khomeinist party which controlled them, the Amal party, represented another state within the state. Another tyranny within the tyranny. The new president, brother of the assassinated one, administered only the Eastern Zone and an army divided between those who wore the cross and those who didn't. Both of them, called the "governmentals." As if this weren't enough, the hallucinatory mosaic of groups and subgroups had given birth to the Khomeinist sect named Sons of God: the one that had revealed itself with the two kamikaze trucks. Two or three? This was the question that tormented the Condor while he waited to find out from Charlie if the third truck existed or not.

2

Charlie entered, sketched out a distracted salute, and without waiting for permission sat down in front of the desk. He looked very tired. Beneath the walrus mustaches his bitter grimace was more bitter than ever.

"It exists, general, it exists... My informers confirm that the trucks were three. One for us, one for the French, and one for the Americans. But at the last minute only two left."

The Condor started.

"How do they know it?"

"Simple. Last night the Amal were notified that at dawn three trucks would be passing through the streets they controlled. Three trucks which shouldn't be stopped or searched. But only two have been seen by their sentinels."

"What happened to the third one?"

"They don't tell me. But from certain indications I understand that there has been some conflict among the Sons of God: an argument between those who wanted to send it and those who didn't. Better-to-keep-the-Italians-on-tenterhooks-for-now,   better-to-make-them-nervous, etcetera. And the last ones have won. However, I'm sure of one thing: the third truck is in some courtyard and waits."

"We should find it. We should find out where they hide it, where they keep the explosives..."

"Impossible, general. Also because..." He held out a small poster with photos of two men behind a border of black tulips. The emblem of the Sons of God. The Condor grabbed it.

"Are they the kamikazes of this morning?"

"Yes."

"Shiites?"

"Yes."

"Did you know them?"

"No."

"Are you sure that neither of them is Mustafa Hash?"

"Yes."

"It would help to find him too..."

A couple of weeks earlier, in the bazaar in the Old City, Charlie had been approached by a strange individual. A Shiite with a wooden leg, a deadly pale face, feverish eyes overflowing with unhappiness who in perfect English had whispered to him: "Captain, the Sons of God are up to something big." A dialogue had followed, or rather an exchange of brief questions and brief answers. "An attack?" "Yes, a kamikaze attack." "Against whom?" "The foreigners." "Which foreigners?" "The Americans, the Italians, the French." "Who sent you?" "Nobody." "How do you know there will be an attack?" "I'm a Son of God." Then, in a muffled voice, the voice of a man with his conscience in tumult, he'd said that he'd joined the sect to enter as a martyr into the Garden of Allah but realized that he didn't like killing. "Killing is bad, captain. It is Mustafa Hash, one who has killed many times, who says this." Then staggering on his wooden leg and clearly relieved of his burden, he'd faded away into the uproar of the bazaar. And Charlie hadn't had the heart to run after him, to grab him and protest no-my-friend-that's-not-enough, now-spill-the-beans. Almost in a state of shock he had returned to the headquarters and related the episode to the Condor who'd immediately ordered the men to raise the ramparts, to dig the trenches, to erect the barricades. He'd also informed the Americans and the French. Pity that neither had taken him seriously. "Rumors, general. Should we believe all the crap we hear in this city... Si on croyait à toutes les bêtises qu'on raconte..." Yes, sure it would have helped to find Mustafa Hash, Charlie thought. He realized it so well that in those two weeks he'd returned every day to the bazaar, he'd searched and questioned each of the little spies he called my-informers. But all that remained of Mustafa Hash was the memory of two feverish eyes and a muffled, anguished voice. Finally, the news that he'd been killed.

"We'll never see him again, general."

"Why?"

"Because he has been killed, general."

"By whom?"

"By whoever found out that he tipped us off."

"Who told you?"

"Don't ask me, general..."

The Condor knit his brow.

"In that case the term third-truck becomes a figure of speech, a metaphor, Charlie. If they know that we know, there won't be a third truck. There will be a vehicle that ramparts and trenches and barricades and intelligence cannot stop..."

"I agree, general."

"A small airplane, for example. A twin-engine plane like a Bonanza piloted by a kamikaze who takes off from the Bekaa Valley and flies at low altitude eluding the radar. One who knows how to hit the target without getting scared off by machine guns on the rooftops. Or, even better..."

"A motorboat."

"Exactly. A motorboat directed against the ship that each week arrives and departs with the troops on leave or returning from their leave... If I were a Son of God who wanted to stage a spectacular slaughter, I wouldn't bother flinging myself at the bases or the headquarters with a truck or plane. I would take a motorboat and smash it into the ship."

"I agree, general..."

"An easy, unfailing, concentrated target. Four hundred corpses guaranteed. Not to mention that in the inlets next to the port there are many motorboats. How to tell what are the harmless and what the kamikazes?"

"I agree, general."

"Bad news. Because if the third truck isn't a truck, if it is an airplane or a motorboat, even with the navy surveillance there's no escape."

"There is, general."

"There is?"

"Yes, and it doesn't involve machine guns on the roof or surveillance of the navy."

"What does it involve, then?"

"Zandra Sadr, General. Zandra Sadr isn't only the Imam of the Lebanese Shiites, the highest religious authority they have in Beirut. He's also an astute politician. He aims at definitely splitting the city in two but realizes very well that to carry out his ambitious project he must face the governmentals who are allied with the Westerners. And as well he realizes that his followers aren't yet strong enough to crush an army which is allied with the Westerners. Consequently, he beats around the bush. With me he has always played the part of the benevolent host, of the pious man who wants peace. He has always expressed deep gratitude for the blood plasma we donate to the locals, always emphasized the hope that we continue to do so..."

"I know, Charlie, I know. Get to the point."

"The point is that nobody in West Beirut lifts a finger without Zandra Sadr's permission. Not even the Sons of God. The point is that in West Beirut orders are spread through the muezzins at the hours of prayer. Thus, if Zandra Sadr bids them to spread an appeal from the minarets, a sentence that asks his followers, therefore also the Sons of God, not to touch us... I mean the sentence I've prepared... Well, at least for a while we could be tranquil. Or slightly more tranquil. General, authorize me to ask him for a meeting, to open a dialogue."

"Charlie! The only dialogue to have with Mister Zandra Sadr is to tell him that if they touch the Italians I will shell him from the ships!"

"I could begin by saying exactly that, general."

"And with that you should end!"

"Here I don't agree, general. Because what we need is shrewdness:

force doesn't do any good. Did it do any good in the case of the Americans and the French?"

"Charlie! I won't accept the protection of the local Khomeini! I won't bow my head to somebody who directs my enemies!"

"We're not talking about accepting protection or bowing your head: we're talking about coming to terms, about adopting the system called you-give-something-to-me, I-give-something-to-you."

"Charlie! These are the words of the Neapolitan tarantella! I won't dance the tarantella! I'm a soldier!"

"A soldier in command of a thousand and six hundred soldiers who must not return home inside as many coffins, general."

There was a long silence. Then a long sigh.

"All right. Ask for the meeting. Open the dialogue."

"Immediately, general."

"As long as it doesn't injure my dignity!"

"Of course, general."

Charlie got up. He went to the door then turned around in the grip of a faint embarrassment.

"Now what is it, Charlie?!"

"A little problem regarding one of my aides, general: Charlie Two. Instead of taking the photos of our rescue squads he helped them and..."

"Who cares about the damn photographs, Charlie! Go ask for the damn meeting! Go at once or I'll change my mi-i-ind!"

Then he banged a fist on the desk and his eyes reddened. His eyelashes grew damp, and without any attempt on his part to restrain them, long tears began to roll down his cheeks.

3

It happened often. As soon as he felt a violent emotion, his eyes reddened. His eyelashes grew damp and, without any attempt on his part to restrain them, long tears rolled down his cheeks. The fact is that several creatures cohabit inside us, each of them in contrast with the others, and one of the creatures that cohabited inside him had a weakness for weeping. The others instead were characterized by boldness, haughtiness, and the ability to make his fellow men weep. An exorbitant pride drove them, an exaggerated need to stand out, to win, and the peculiarity of his character mostly came from these defects. Much less, from the gifts with which the gods had favored him: intelligence, courage, health, and a body that didn't age. At fifty-five he appeared

scarcely forty, amidst his harmonious features you couldn't see a wrin-
kle, and a few months before a soubrette sent to cheer up the troops
had yowled from the stage: "General, you are a stud, you are a cake!
Let's get together tonight!" He had inner qualities too. For example,
the passion he brought to everything he did, the inflexibility with
which he denied himself any privilege or laziness. He slept on a cot as
his men did, he worked till late in the night and at four in the morning
he was already up like a monk who awakens to pray, and took care of
the contingent as a dean should take care of his college: twice a day
inspecting all the posts, all the soldiers, all the guns, all the tanks, all the
armored cars, all the vehicles. So, never mind if noticing a crooked
helmet or a badly inserted cartridge or a loose bolt he shouted like a
savage; never mind if many hated him and accused him of authoritari-
anism, despotism, exhibitionism: in return, many loved him to the
point of veneration, and both groups agreed that he was a general
worthy of the title. Given the unlimited faith he had in himself, he
believed this as well. But today that faith was wavering: if the soubrette
sent to cheer up the troops had yowled again you-are-a-stud, you-are-
a-cake, he would have taken it as a mockery and his tears would have
redoubled.

   He dried one angrily, he picked up the telephone and called Crazy
Horse: his favorite victim and the head of his General Staff. He ordered
him to contact the various commanders, to make them place two antiaircraft machine guns at Logistics base, two at Eagle base, two at Ruby
base, four at Sierra Mike, and to call for a meeting with the ship's
captain tomorrow. Then he replaced the receiver and, overwhelmed by
the awareness of his impotence, took his head in his hands. Yes, Charlie
was right: force wouldn't do any good. The only way to block the third
truck was to accept the muezzins saying from the minarets that the
Italians were not to be touched. That is, to humiliate his profession, his
pride, to swallow the bitter pill. As long as it doesn't injure my dignity,
he'd told Charlie. But no matter which sentence Charlie had in mind,
the agreement with Zandra Sadr would injure his dignity. It would
humiliate his profession, his pride, it would be for him a defeat. He
dried another tear, this time with resignation. "You mustn't cry," his
parents used to say when he was a child. "You must be strong, you
must be harsh. If you're not strong, if you're not harsh, you can neither
lead nor win." And with those words, at age four, he had been entered
in a tricycle race. "And woe to you if you lose." He'd won. But it had
been worse than injecting a poison for which no antidote exists. A
poison called mania-to-win and inability-to-lose. At six he'd won the

swimming competition, at eight the Ping-Pong contest, at ten the cross-country race, at twelve the hurdle race, at thirteen the road race, at fourteen the juvenile boxing championship... The mechanisms of our temperament are so simple, after all, and old Sigmund was right: the clue to the problem is always to be found in the green season of existence. At a certain point, even Grandfather had contributed to the poison: "You must excel in everything, you must not get tired, not give up. You must be like a railwayman who drives the train on Christmas Eve. Remember that a railwayman drives the train even on Christmas Eve, that even on Christmas Eve the travelers entrust their very lives to him."

He attempted a smile that didn't come off. His grandfather was a railwayman and had a body covered with tattoos. Proud of being a railwayman, not of having the tattoos, he never removed his shirt. Once, however, he had, and what a marvel! On his chest there was a sailing ship so large that its keel touched the bottom of his stomach and the top of the mainmast reached the base of his throat. On his left forearm there was a heart that rippled with the slightest contraction of his hand, and beneath the heart the name "Maria." On his right forearm, a blue bass. On his back, a giant squid. On one bicep, a rose. On the other, a sombrero... One day he had asked him the reason, and the reason was that at twenty-two Grandfather had been a sailor on a sailing ship that made a trip around the world: the Liguria. At Ceylon the whole crew had decided to have the Liguria tattooed on their chests, in order to be forgiven by Grandmother who hated tattoos Grandfather had asked also for the heart with her name, Maria, and the double masterpiece had intoxicated him. At every port, a tattoo. The bass in Singapore, the squid in Hong Kong, the rose in Shanghai, the sombrero in Trinidad. But at his return Grandmother had started shrieking I-don't-want-a-husband-painted-like-a-convict, I-won't-go-to-bed-with-a-squid, and Grandfather had switched to the railroads. More than by the story, however, he had been impressed by the names Ceylon Singapore Hong Kong Shanghai Trinidad: symbols of a much-longed-for escape. The escape from the nightmare of the competitions, the contests, the races, the championships to win, of the railwayman who drives the train on Christmas Eve. That's why he had joined the Military Academy... He was sixteen, when he had, and he didn't even know how to handle a rifle. Still less did he know that the army was a tyranny much worse than the family, that it tormented with even worse nightmares of competitions, contests, races, championships to win, even worse threats of woe-to-you-if-you-lose, even worse refusals of defeat...

He attempted another smile which this time came off, and stopped crying. In the beginning he'd liked the army, of course. One thing is to go home late and find your mother with her forefinger pointed, your father with his icy look, where-have-you-been-and-with-whom, one thing is to go back late to the barracks and find an officer who punishes you in courteous language. "Ten minutes have passed since the bugle, cadet. Please return to your bunk, take your personal effects, leave behind your belt and your tie and your shoelaces, then make yourself comfortable in a cell and consider yourself under arrest." Only later had he understood that courtesy in the army is a luxury, that the military love to offend, that the further they rise in rank the more they offend. As if rank gave them a kind of immunity, or authorized them to scorn those who stay one step below. In fact he had learned to do the same, and this had revived the poison by which he had been intoxicated at four with the tricycle. Why? Because the military's trade is a constant climb toward higher and higher levels of authority, because if you're pushed by an intelligent ambition and by a solid vocation for leadership you can reach remarkable goals of supremacy and drive a train which at every goal gets longer and longer: increasingly crowded with people who entrust their lives to you also on Christmas Eve. Right: the image of that train had never left him. It had accompanied him more than the sailing ship and the heart tattooed in Ceylon, the bass tattooed in Singapore, the squid tattooed in Hong Kong, the rose tattooed in Shanghai, the sombrero tattooed in Trinidad: he had given up his freedom for that train... And now it risked being derailed in a tunnel that only led to his humiliation, to his defeat. There was nothing to win, in this city. As he hadn't been sent here to make war, there wasn't even an enemy to fight. Or maybe there was? Yes, there was! The third truck! The hypothetical airplane, the hypothetical motorboat: Death! A war had to be fought, then. A paradoxical, an unthinkable war, a war never fought by any soldier, in any era, in any country: the war against Death. What tricycle competition? What ping-pong contest? What cross-country race, hurdle race, road race, juvenile boxing championship? Here there was Death to vanquish! At the cost of coming to terms with it or whoever represented it. And never mind if the others did not understand: he hadn't to answer to anybody for the way he drove his train. Wasn't he the general?

"Come in, colonel."

Monocle in his left eye, mustache stiff with excitation, Crazy Horse came forward.

"Sir! I beg your pardon for bothering you, Sir, but necessity compels me to inform you of a mishap. At Eagle base they've placed the antiaircraft machine guns, at Logistics and at Ruby base also, but at Sierra Mike, no. The Sierra Mike commander shouts that he wants to know why and... and... General, Sir, I am a gentleman... And a gentleman cannot repeat certain terms: quod non vetat lex hoc vetat fieri pudor, what is not prohibited by law is prohibited by modesty, Seneca reminds us."

"Colonel! Drop Seneca and report what he says!"

"Well... He says that... that... whatever the fucking reason for the fucking order, the machine guns serve as much as... as..."

"As wha-a-at?"

"As a bloody dick of a dick superdick, General, Sir."

"Tell him that the bloody dick of a dick superdick is him! Tell him that if he doesn't set up those Brownings within five minutes I'll kick him in the ass then I'll get him in front of a court-martial!"

"Yessir, General. Still, please pardon my audacity... I think the officers should know the reason... Not even I have been informed, Sir, and..."

"Colonel! Don't bust my balls and carry out orders!"

"Hic et nunc, Sir. Immediately, Sir."

4

He sprang to attention, he returned to his office, he carried the orders out. Correct as usual, impeccable. Then he removed his monocle and abandoned himself to an examination of his torments. He was the Chief of Staff, by Jove! As such, he should be informed about everything! Instead that brute never did. He hadn't even told him about the kamikazes he expected. Because he expected them, by Jove, he expected them! That was the reason why in September he had summoned the battalion leaders, the explosives experts, the Corps of Engineers, and the troops had begun to dig, fill sandbags, erect ramparts, until each base had taken on the look of a Sevastopol under siege! How naive of him not to have understood it before! Yet a suspicion had grazed him. In fact he had risked a question: "General, Sir, are you expecting something, Sir?" The fact is that the brute had answered: "I expect you to shut your mouth." A brute, yes, a brute. The typical representative of an army ruined by democracy. Ever since the world had started prattling about equality, progress, democracy, you found nothing but coarse and vulgar officers: illiterates who didn't even know a motto of Seneca or a sentence of Cicero or a verse of Horace, bumpkins who couldn't even tell what took place the 14th of June 1800 at Marengo or the 8th of February 1807 at Preussisch-Eylau, barbarians who had no regard for gentlemen of the old stamp. Oh, what beautiful days, the days when being an officer meant being born of noble loins and having financial opportunities, so that if you didn't belong to the upper class you couldn't enter a military career!

He replaced his monocle which glimmered with flashes of contempt and panted bitterly. He knew, he knew that those illiterates and bumpkins and barbarians called him Crazy Horse like a redskin chief or a striptease parlor! And, if the second part of the appellative flattered him because of the association with the noblest animal that ever appeared on this earth, the first one filled him with disdain. Why crazy, why, good heavens?!? Because he was an erudite, meticulous, elegant person, and did things by the book? Because he admired the English and liked to resemble an Englishman? Well, he did! Pink freckled skin, long chin, narrow nose, carrot-colored mustache and hair, and the watery pupils of a Saxon raised in the fog. Even Sir Montague, who led the one hundred Dragoons sent to Beirut, used to tell him so. "Are you sure you're Italian, my friend? You look like one of us." And the lovely lady he'd met in London the unforgettable year he had served in the Seventh Brigade was kind enough to specify: "Not a common Englishman, though: a Royal Guard officer serving in India at the time of Queen Victoria!" But go explain certain things to the plebs. Once he had tried and the effort had doubled their lack of regard: prank phone calls, prank messages, malignities of every kind... Colonel, while-you-were-in-the-can-they-called-you-from-London. No, from-Ascot! No, from-Edinburgh! No, from-Buckingham-Palace! Or else they blunted the pencils he loved perfectly sharpened, they spattered with ink the immaculate reports he drafted for the Minister of Defense, they pilfered his fountain pen with its inscription God-Save-the-Queen and returned it to him with the inscription changed to God-Save-Lenin... In August they had stolen his Bulgarian leather riding crop with engraved initials, and now he had to use an uninitialed crop of artificial leather.

He panted with redoubled bitterness. What a milieu, good heavens, what a milieu! Here, if you wanted to be with somebody of your own rank, you had no choice but to associate with the head of the Operations Room: the distinguished major that those illiterates had baptized Old Grouse because of the tuft of hair which stood on his head like a crest. A worthy officer, that major: one of the very few aristocrats to-day's army could take pride in. To understand it one had to be a guest in his ancestral villa in Trieste, not so much a villa as a magnificent manor with four maids, three waiters, two scullery boys, a cook, a butler, a Swiss housekeeper, and a gamekeeper: luxuries you found nowhere, these days, but in the homes of boorish parvenus. Not for nothing had he chosen to share his quarters with him and the Professor, the Condor's aide. Well, in the absence of the distinguished colleague, you could also associate with the Professor. He didn't adorn himself with coats of arms, but he boasted two degrees, one in literature and one in philosophy. They called him the Professor because he'd come to Beirut with a trunk that on the dock had popped open spilling out a fountain of books very unusual in a military man's baggage: the *Dialogues* of Plato, *De Libero Arbitrio* by Erasmus of Rotterdam, Kant's *Critique of Pure Reason,* as well as other massive volumes whose dog-eared pages revealed the labors of a meticulous reader. He had a single defect, the Professor. He never opened his mouth. And multas amicitias silentium dirimit, silence cuts short many friendships, Aristotle reminds us in his *Topika.* As for the others, what dreariness! Eagle, the commander of the bersaglieri, was socially acceptable but had no class. You know, the kind of person who prefers pizza to pudding and Neapolitan coffee to tea. Falcon, the commander of the paratroopers, was a parvenu devoid of any style or character. Sandokan, the commander of the marò, a slob who deserved to hang from the mainmast for his filthy language and slovenliness. Charlie, a Barabbas who trafficked with the Arabs. Pistoia, a clod who would not be allowed in a gentlemen's club, even to wash the dishes... And how painful it was to eat with them at the mess, to listen to their trivialities, to watch their habit of piling pasta and dessert and salad on the same dish, for in-the-stomach-every-thing-mixes-up! How distressing to realize that for this he had left behind his beloved Speedy and entrusted him to that dolt of a stable-man! Every time he thought of it, he felt the need to leap into a bloody combat, to unsheathe his sword, to show what an aristocrat is capable of, then to die.

He leaned against the writing desk, a precious family relic he'd had brought from Italy and which he was very proud of because of an inlaid Tudor coat of arms: three helmets complete with gorgets and a row of twenty firs inside a cuneiform band. To die, yes. Lucky those who had died this morning! What sense does it make to live in a world that no longer respects refinement and good upbringing and people with class, a world full of boors who replace the inscription God-Save-the-Queen with an outrageous God-Save-Lenin, who don't put on a robe in the morning (not necessarily a cashmere robe with red and blue stripes, Her Britannic Majesty's colors, but any robe at all), who understand neither glory nor culture, who grow nervous because your prodigious memory retains every Latin text you studied in school, every war book you studied at the Academy, every name and surname and date? Better to die, yes. And since he couldn't die by the sword, that elegant weapon now as unfashionable as audacity, one of these nights he would go up to the terrace of the headquarters to challenge the snipers. "Shoot, you riffraff, hit me! Mors malorum finis est, death is the end of all woes, Quintilian says!" Because let's skip the talk, gentlemen: unhappiness has not only the face of hunger and cold. It also comes from the loneliness which saddens those who belong to a vanished or a misunderstood world, those who are forced to live in a milieu they don't belong to, among people who mock and ridicule and persecute with their vulgarity... Good heavens, the English! He hadn't written the note of apology nor called! What bad manners, what an unworthy gaffe! He sprang forward. He dialed the number of the former tobacco factory where the one hundred Dragoons of the English delegation were quartered. But today the telephone didn't work and, all disheartened, he left the office for his room. Here he changed his uniform, combed his mustache, splashed on his cheeks a few drops of 4711, thecologne-preferred-by-Napoleon: he prepared for supper in the manner that a gentleman of refinement and good upbringing should. Then he reached the mess where he sat beside a resigned Old Grouse to explain to him that war is always an omelette and one can't have an omelette without breaking the eggs. A subject that led him immediately to Marengo, then to Preussisch-Eylau, to Wagram. Thus, into the Condor's jaws.

*   *   *

"Distinguished colleague, at six-twenty-four I didn't even move an eyebrow. I kept on sleeping. Otia corpus alunt et animus quoque pascitur illis, sleep restores the body and the spirit, Ovid sustains. And God knows how my body and my spirit are exhausted since Speedy's tragedy. You never met my amazing Speedy, my dapple-gray hunter, did you? One meter seventy high. Slender, lean, lively. Unbeatable in jumping the obstacles. Everybody envied me, everybody. I used to feel like a king when I rode him to the fox hunt or to Piazza di Siena.* But when I left for Beirut I had to entrust him to a stableman, the negligence of that lout gave him emphysema so he had to be sent outside Rome to recover and last night I received the most heartbreaking call: 'Colonel, there's been an accident. Speedy has been gored by a bull and his intestines are hanging out. Colonel, we must shoot him at once.' All right, I'll buy the filly he was flirting with from his stall. Though a little low-slung and short-necked, she's graceful. She promises a lot. But no horse will ever replace my Speedy and... What I'm trying to say is that after such a trauma one doesn't get upset by four hundred dead, and has every right to assert it: by Jove! True?"

"Ah, yes," Old Grouse answered stoically.

"Just think of what happened the 14th of June 1800 at Marengo when Napoleon let the Austrian general Melas take him by surprise. Deprived of news about the adversaries he had fought on June 9 at Montebello, Napoleon believed that Melas was still in flight, as you well know. So, after sending Lapoype's column to the north, Desaix's or better Des Aix's to the south, he took up quarters at Marengo. Well realizing it, however, Melas had crossed the Bormida with the infantry led by Zach and suddenly jumped on the French with thirty-one thousand men. Thirty-one thousand concentrated on the same front against twenty-eight thousand scattered all over, do I make myself clear? Napoleon was almost crushed by it, and while Zach pursued his regiments he had to withdraw southeast then to order Lapoype and Des Aix to pull back. Lapoype couldn't make it, Des Aix did. The heroic Louis-Charles-Antoine Des Aix (please do separate well the Des from the Aix, otherwise it sounds like a common name not an aristocratic one), Chevalier of Veygoux, who immediately said: "Sire, this battle is lost. But it's two in the afternoon and we have time to win the next one." Then, flanked by Kellermann and by Marmont, Duke of Ragusa, he moved up to the contested area. He ordered Marmont to place his batteries facing the enemy and Kellermann to charge one flank with four hundred sabers, attacked Zach's infantry, and here the best comes. Because in such cases a cavalry charge used to end with a massacre of men and horses, as you well know..."

"Ah, yes..."

"Moreover, Zach's infantry was already in disarray because Zach had hurled himself in pursuit of the French he thought he had defeated, and Melas had repeated Napoleon's error: the one of not foreseeing

---

* Piazza di Siena is a renowned international equestrian competition which takes place in Rome.

the counterattack. Therefore it was easy for Des Aix to win. He fell, yes. He died with a bullet in his heart. But he triumphed. Because six thousand Austrians died that afternoon, my illustrious colleague, and eight thousand were taken prisoner. A considerable omelette, n'est-ce pas? And despite the seven thousand men lost by Napoleon, the next day Melas was forced to sign at Alexandria an armistice in which he promised to withdraw beyond the Ticino as well as to give up the fortresses he had conquered in Piedmont and Lombardy. A decisive day for the Second Italian Campaign, you'll agree!"

"Ah, yes..."

"But do you think the heroic Des Aix's death would teach something to Napoleon's stubbornness? By no means. Seven years later, the 8th of February 1807, in the battle of Preussisch-Eylau, during the campaign against Prussia, he did something almost worse. He sent Marshal Augereau's Seventh Army off into the fog. A mistake which caused the largest cavalry charge of all time, the one led by Gioacchino Murat with eighty squadrons and two thousand five hundred horses. Yes! Two thousand five hundred of which one thousand five hundred remained on the ground. And one thousand five hundred dead horses is a great many, my distinguished colleague! Well... It's not the four thousand five hundred lost at Wagram... Because, as you well know, in the battle of Wagram four thousand five hundred horses died, and by Jove! Just thinking of four thousand five hundred dead horses makes me sick, makes me cry... Still, one thousand five hundred horses is a great many too... Anyway, thanks to the fog, the Seventh Army was destroyed. And Augereau was so indignant that he addressed Napoleon with these very words: 'Sire, you have been wrong. You are wrong very often, Sire, and each time you are wrong you make a big, too big, mistake.' A fine character, that Augereau. Pierre-François-Charles Augereau, Duke of Castiglione, Marshal and Peer of France. Just realize what a great man is a man who, seven years after the battle of Marengo and eleven years after the battle of Castiglione, in fact the battle of Castiglione took place the 5th of August 1796, has the guts to address Napoleon the way he deserved!"

"Ah, yes..."

"Let's be honest: I prefer Collinet. Antoine-Charles-Louis Collinet, Count of Lasalle. One of my favorite models, my real master, is Collinet. A technician of the first order, a beau sabreur gifted with an irresistible charm. Moreover, the husband of a very beautiful and fabulously rich woman. Which doesn't hurt... But think of Collinet's career! At twenty, I said twenty, he was already Kellermann's aide-de-camp. At thirty, a brigadier general! Think of the campaigns he participated in! The campaign of Italy, of Poland, of Egypt, of Spain, of Austria where in 1806 he fought at Zhedenick and had the audacity to charge fourteen squadrons with only three of his own, of Prussia where on the 10th of June 1807, that is four months after Preussisch-Eylau, he saved Murat at Heilsberg... He died at thirty-four, Collinet. He died at Wagram with a bullet in his forehead. And I envy him. Because that bullet spared him the sorrow of seeing Napoleon's cavalry, that cavalry he had so perfectly molded, destroyed in Russia then at Lipsia then at Waterloo. I mean, he died long before his world collapsed... Because when our own world collapses, illustrious friend, when our own world vanishes and gives way to vulgarity, a bullet in the heart or in the forehead is a liberation."

"Ah, yes..."

"Even if one is young."

"Ah, yes..."

"Besides, I agree with Plautus who says: Quem dei diligunt adolescens moritur, those favored by the gods die young."

And it was at this point that he fell into the Condor's jaws.

"Colonel!"

"At your command, General, Sir!" he neighed, happy to have awakened his interest.

"If you don't shut up, I'll stuff that bullet into your ass."

The night was by now falling, nearly all the four hundred favored by the gods had been gathered up, Charlie had requested the audience with Zandra Sadr, and near the headquarters a melancholic woman's voice was singing the dirge of the hashashìn. The dope-growers.

> My hashish does no harm.
> It's good stuff, it comes from Bekaa,
> from the green valleys of Baalbèk.
> And it is cheap.
> Buy a kilo, soldier, and smoke it.
> Smoke it, smoke it!
> You have nothing else to forget
> this sad story
> and this sad city.

CHAPTER THREE

1

THE HEADQUARTERS was located at the beginning of rue de l'Aérodrome, the two-lane avenue which led to the airport, inside one of the few buildings spared from the shells of the Israeli siege: the villa that in the happy days an Emir of Qatar had built for his two wives, his two favorites, the twelve children born of those quadruple embraces, and that during the siege he had abandoned to the looters' barbarity. The carpets, the furniture, the chandeliers gone, the only two objects left were a large cherry-wood table that cluttered the former dining room and an oil painting in the atrium that provided an ominous portrait of the owner: hooked nose, inauspicious eyes, half-moon eyebrows, forked beard, cruel mouth, and a yellow turban from which a teardrop pearl dangled. On his shoulders, a blue cloak secured at the neck with a clasp of rubies and emeralds. (A detail for which Sugar saw in the painting a matchless work of art.) The other remnants consisted of the pompous boiseries and the equally pompous damasks that upholstered the rooms, the elaborate iron bars that protected the windows, plus a garden where the former flowerbeds and the rubble of a fountain evoked the memory of water lilies, rosebushes, blazing hibiscus. The location suited the purpose. On the opposite side of the avenue and two hundred yards south you had in fact the field hospital, the Logistics base, the Eagle base, and Bourji el Barajni. Five hundred yards north, Shatila. The access instead was uncomfortable because, after Mustafa Hash's tip, the Condor had erected a solid rampart that stealing a good part of the avenue's eastbound lane diverted the traffic and because a most elaborate system of defenses blocked the entrance with a series of obstacles. First of all, the carabinieri of the sentry box who stopped and inspected with metal detectors every vehicle. Then the serpentine pathway that crept through the rampart. Then the Leopard that blocked the passage at the end of the serpentine pathway and that only after a second inspection let you reach the courtyard.

That is, the piece of eastbound lane subtracted from the avenue. Then the final check to enter the garden when a solid wall with loopholes reinforced the entire perimeter, a guard tower with two men and a 12.7mm machine gun loomed at each of the four corners, and coils of barbed wire flanked electronic devices that at the slightest touch released a dense orange smoke. As for the building itself, it was completely wrapped in sandbags: from afar it seemed like a huge mummy swaddled in black and from the outside the headquarters projected an almost sinister look.

Inside, all the contrary. Except for the Emir's portrait, the inside offered scenery worthy of the tragicomedy played out by the protagonists. To the right of the atrium, a corridor with the Condor's office-lodging: tiny and dramatized by a desk full of radios and telephones as well as by a spartan blanket which concealed the cot. Next to the Condor's, the Professor's office: overflowing with papers and with the books which had earned him that nickname. Beyond the Professor's office, the private bathroom they shared with chilly politeness. By-all-means-go-ahead-colonel, by-all-means-go-ahead-general. To the left of the atrium, in the first room, Crazy Horse's office: always orderly and embellished by the writing desk with the Tudor coat of arms. In the second room, Pistoia's office: used by him only to torment Crazy Horse and to call Joséphine, Caroline, Geraldine, the three Lebanese to whom he was formally engaged though he had a wife. In the third, Old Grouse's office: impersonal and dignified. In the fourth, the Operations Room which spilled over into the glassed-in veranda. At the center, in the former dining room with the large cherry-wood table, the Briefing Room. To its right, in the former kitchen, the Post Office. On the second floor, in the former bedrooms of the Emir and his two wives, the administrative offices. On the third and fourth floors, in the rooms formerly occupied by the twelve children born of quadruple embraces, the lodgings of the officers on duty at the headquarters. On the top floor, in the two rooms formerly reserved for the favorites, the lodging of the carabinieri on sentry duty, and that of a bizarre group of draftees: the Condor's driver Gaspare, Pistoia's driver Ugo, Charlie's driver Stefano, the interpreter Martino, and the telephone operator Fifì. Next to them, the roof terrace where in the moments of despair Crazy Horse wanted to challenge the snipers and demonstrate that unhappiness has not only the face of hunger and cold.

Finally, the basement reachable through the stairway that Angelo and Charlie had rashly climbed after the first explosion. Located in the rear of the building, therefore hidden and out of intruders' reach, the basement consisted of a kind of crypt with two rooms mentioned as rarely as possible: one called Sugar Museum and one defined by an intimidating sign on the door. "Reserved area. Do not approach. Admission limited to the following personnel: Charlie-Charlie, Charlie Two, Charlie Three, Charlie Four, Charlie Five, Charlie Six, Charlie Seven, Charlie Eight." It was the office of Charlie and his aides, all of them named like him because whoever worked for Charlie became a Charlie, and here is what a hypothetical visitor would have found inside. On the floor near the entry, a jumble of hand grenades and sardine tins, helmets and cans of tuna in oil, M12 guns and sausages, cartridges and panettoni, nightscopes and chocolates, flak jackets and wine bottles, walkie-talkies, medicines. In short, the necessary provisions for the autonomy of a separate republic. Opposite the jumble, Angelo's dugout. A few steps farther, the real office: windowless, and beset by an even more entropic disorder. To the right, a cot leaning against the wall, Charlie's cot, and a kitchen sink that Charlie used as a lavatory. Plus, two radio receivers and two Charlies who listened with headphones. To the left, a series of filing cabinets with locked drawers and on every drawer the warning "Top Secret, Do Not Touch." After the filing cabinets, a gigantic poster of two delectable feminine legs on which somebody had scrawled in large letters: "If you don't have brains, have legs." In the middle, a long table with a pandemonium of newspapers and magazines and typewriters and intercoms and telephones that endlessly rang to ask for the captain or to leave him strange messages. "Albertine will come at five." "The electrician can see you tonight." "Grandma died this morning." The bizarre republic concealed in fact a rudimentary espionage service, and Charlie used it to hatch his plots of an improvised secret agent. That is, to stay in touch with his informers, to analyze and catalogue the news published in the papers, to intercept the Amal or the governmental radios, and to guard the documents he happened to get hold of. Which is the reason he'd named it after the office where Lawrence of Arabia worked in Cairo as special envoy of the Military Intelligence Service: Arab Bureau.

*　　*　　*

Not knowing Charlie and the nature of his real activity in Beirut, one might have asked why he identified himself with a Victorian aristocrat born in Wales and educated at Oxford, polished writer and impassioned archaeologist, incurable homosexual and highly sophisticated secret agent. Charlie was born in Bari, he had no degrees, he wrote badly, he couldn't tell an Etruscan vase from an Egyptian papyrus, and he liked women. But his taste for byzantine intrigue and his genius for double-dealing from the precisely temperament of an adventurer and the vocation of a spy. In other words, Lawrence of Arabia was for him what Antoine-Charles-Louis Collinet, Count of Lasalle, and Louis-Charles-Antoine Des Aix, Chevalier of Veygoux, were for Crazy Horse: a model, a master. He had met that master at eighteen, he said, in the darkness of a movie theater. That is, in the movie directed by David Lean and interpreted by Peter O'Toole. He had read his book *The Seven Pillars of Wisdom* to the point of dizziness, he added, but then had lost him: no love resists time. However, and thanks to a landscape that remained Lawrence's landscape, faces that remained the faces described by Lawrence, dramas that repeated the dramas lived by Lawrence, in Beirut his love had resurrected.

A lucid and mature love, now, accompanied by the discovery of a truth already accepted by Lawrence: when you're in somebody else's house, you must play by the host's rules. You must understand to what degree he wants you or doesn't want you, anticipate his hostilities, come to terms with them. And telling all this to the Condor, he had explained that, in order to survive the absurd mission they were charged with, they needed to create a network of information and contacts: to establish a miniature Intelligence Service. And the Condor had agreed. He'd given him the location in the basement, the telephones, the transceivers, the authority to choose his aides, and Charlie had chosen among those who had a good knowledge of French or English or Arabic. A certain Angelo who at that time worked for Sugar, a certain Martino, a certain Stefano, a certain Fifì, a certain Bernard le Français, plus a couple of radio operators. Except for Angelo, all draftees devoid of experience, simple guys who had never read *The Seven Pillars of Wisdom* or seen David Lean's film and who in most cases didn't even suspect the genuine nature of the work entrusted to them. But, as he wanted to be the only accountable member of that miniature Intelligence Service, Charlie didn't care for cunning aides: adults well trained in the art of espionage. Yet there was another reason why he had created the Arab Bureau, and this one lay inside the meanderings of his complicated personality: in the fact that he was a man inclined to hatred, capable of killing with the composure of an executioner, and at the same time a person who detested war more than the pacifists in civilian clothes. War accomplishes nothing, he used to say, it resolves nothing. As soon as it ends, you realize that the reasons for which it was fought have not disappeared or that new reasons have taken the place of the old: new pretexts for which another one will break out. One where the former enemies will be the new friends, the former friends the new enemies. War is the daughter of violence, violence is the daughter of physical force, and men cannot do without that stupid trinomial. He also maintained that he hadn't always spoken this way, that once he'd almost strangled a punk who had stolen his seat and giggled the-world-belongs-to-the-shrewd. With a single hand he had lifted him up and: "You're wrong, bloody idiot. The world belongs to the strong." But when he had understood that his powerful body concealed a potential violence that his temperament could make a bad use of, he'd felt as if he were the recipient of a curse. Since then he had never resorted to his lethal muscles and only if a danger threatened his life did he carry a weapon: a Browning High Power he hid at his left ankle. For the arsenal of bombs and rifles and ammunition jumbled on the floor of the Arab Bureau, he had in fact a kind of scorn. "I keep them as an exorcism." For intrigue, conspiracy, the occasional fraud, he had instead a blind admiration and he handled them with an aplomb bordering on cynicism. The same aplomb, the same cynicism, he'd used to launch the idea of giving away the blood plasma. Which brings us to the point.

It was difficult to get blood plasma in a city where even the doctors sold it on the black market, and one morning an elderly Muslim had gone to the field hospital to request some for his wounded wife. The field hospital personnel had answered sorry-we-can't, but Charlie had intervened: "Sure we can. Wait." Then he'd run to the Condor and: "General, the Arabs always honor their debts of gratitude. Let me manage this matter." Again the Condor had agreed, the plasma had been given, and the headquarters had become a bustle of people asking for the captain. Palestinians, Shiites, Sunnis, guerrillas, wretches who really needed plasma, hustlers who lied to make money with it. And, after accurate interrogations to determine if they were lying or not, the captain provided it. He even solicited transfusions from the soldiers. "It's a humanitarian initiative," he chanted. It was a coldhearted calculation, instead, a bargaining chip to use with his provisional allies, and a persuasive blackmail to wave in Zandra Sadr's face. "It seems that the Italians are under fire, Your Most Reverend Eminence. Are your followers forgetting that a great deal of Italian blood runs in their veins?" The sentence he wanted to be spread by the muezzins from the minarets emerged just from this blackmail.

2

The carabinieri in the sentry box called to report that a woman was asking for the captain, and Charlie puffed with annoyance: to speak with her, he should leave the office. Leaving the office, he would risk missing the telephone call from Zandra Sadr's secretary. A call that might come at any moment now: His Eminence had the habit of summoning at the last minute. He thus turned to Angelo.

"Go upstairs. See who she is and what she wants."

"Me?" Angelo protested. It made no sense to send him. He knew only six or seven words of Arabic. Na'am, yes. Là, no. Shukràn, thank you. Aamel maaruf, please. Lesh, why. Shubaddak, what do you want. Mish fahèm, I don't understand...

"Yessir, you!"

"But if she speaks Arabic..."

"If she speaks Arabic, you come back and get Martino."

"So why not send Martino?"

"Because I need him here. Move!"

He moved. He reached the sentry box, he approached the woman. She was very young, dressed in the Arab fashion with pink pants, pink blouse, pink head scarf. And she cried desperately. "Aamel maaruf, aamel maaruf!" Dismayed, he started the impossible dialogue.

"Parlez-vous français, faransìn?"

"Là, no! Aamel maaruf, là..."

"Parli italiano, talieni?"

"Là, no! Aamel maaruf, là..."

"Shubaddak? What do you want?"

"Capitàn! Aamel maaruf, capitàn!"

"Lesh? Why?"

"Dam! Aamel maaruf, dam!"

Dam? What did dam mean? It sounded familiar, but he didn't remember what it meant.

"Mish fahèm... I don't understand."

"Dam! Waladi biimut! Biimut, ambimut!"

And waladi, what did it mean? And biimut? And ambimut? He went to ask Martino. Charlie was finally on the phone with Zandra Sadr's secretary and didn't even notice him.

"Martino, what does dam mean?"

"Blood," Martino answered.

"And waladi biimut, ambimut?"

"My child dies, he's dying."

"Come, then! Come speak with her!"

Martino went. He questioned her, then translated.

"She says her child has been hit by a bullet. She says he has been brought to the Shiite clinic, but there they don't have the right plasma. She says he's bleeding to death and needs three units of B-negative. She says he is two years old."

"Two?!?"

He ran back to the office. He faced Charlie who had just finished the phone call and was ready to go. "Hurry up," Zandra Sadr's secretary had recommended.

"Chief, the woman is asking for three units of B-negative. If we don't give it to her, her child..."

"...will die of blood loss," Charlie retorted slipping the Browning High Power into the holster strapped to his left ankle. "Her son is six years old. No, five. No, four. No, three. No, two. He has been wounded by a bullet while he was playing in the street. No, while he was sleeping in the cradle. He has been brought to the Shiite clinic but there they don't have the plasma. Same old story to resell the stuff on the black market."

"But she cries! She is desperate!"

"They always cry, they're always desperate. In their place, I would do the same. Anyway, who is she?"

"A Muslim woman."

"What kind of Muslim? Shiite, Palestinian, Sunni? And who sent her? We need to know what kind of Muslim she is and who sent her. We need to make sure that her son truly exists, that he has truly been wounded, that truly there is no plasma at the Shiite clinic... Go over there and find the doctor who speaks Italian. I cannot. I have to go see Zandra Sadr! Don't you understand I have to go see Zandra Sadr?!?"

"Yes, but..."

"But what?!? Find the doctor, I said! Ask him if the child is there. Ask him if the woman has been sent by him. If yes, see whether it suits us to give her the plasma. If it suits us, go to the field hospital and take it."

"And what if it doesn't suit us?"

"If it doesn't, you get rid of her. Simple!"

Then he shot up the stairs with Martino, and Angelo had barely the time to ask a question.

"Martino! How do you say wait?"

"Intazer!" answered Martino in his shrill voice.

Intazer... Wait, intazer...

* * *

He jumped into the first jeep at hand. He argued with the tankman who was shifting the Leopard too slowly, threaded his way through the serpentine pathway, stopped in front of the sentry box where the woman continued to cry, and shouted: "Intazer! Wait, intazer!" Then he started the engine again, turned right into rue de l'Aérodrome, and reached a squalid building on the border between Gobeyre and Haret Hreik. The Shiite clinic. Here he asked for the doctor who spoke Italian. The doctor was performing surgery and couldn't be disturbed for a while, a nurse said to him in French. "Soyez patient et asseyez-vous, s'il vous plaît. Be patient and sit down, please." He sat on the entrance bench, he checked the time. Five in the afternoon, five, and he stayed here dawdling. But how?!? A mother cries because her child needs three units of B-negative, he needs it because he's dying, he's two years old and he's dying, and you waste your time finding out who sent her, if she's Shiite or Palestinian or Sunni, if it suits you to help her or not? And what if nobody sent her? What if instead of being Shiite or Palestinian or Sunni, she was Maronite Christian or Druze? What if helping her didn't suit the Arab Bureau games? You-get-rid-of-her. Simple. Right. You tell her my-dear, you're-no-use-to-us, so-I-don't-give-you-any-blood, your-child-can-drop-dead, good-night. His large blue eyes blazed with anger. He'd never liked that story of the blood donations. He'd always considered it a fraud, a vulgar trick to buy the favors of those who wanted them dead, a treachery. But the way Charlie managed the whole matter pleased him even less. Because when the suppliants were Shiites sent by Zandra Sadr, the plasma was delivered without a word; when they were Palestinians or Sunni, it was given with hesitancy or reluctance; and when they were Christians, eight times out of ten it was not given at all. Why-should-we, they-live-in-the-Eastern-Zone, they-are-no-use-to-us. Or: the-end-justifies-the-means. No, it is not true that the end justifies the means. If the means are questionable, even the noblest end becomes such. Anyway, he didn't like his Machiavellianisms and his Lawrence-of-Arabiaisms and his cynicism. Nor did he like his habit of playing mysterious, of always refusing an explanation. Listen-to-the-radio-and-keep-quiet. Read-the-newspapers-and-shut-up. Follow-me-and-don't-ask-questions. And woe to whoever approached his Top Secret drawers. What-are-you-looking-for, what-do-you-want, don't-snoop. Ah! There were days when he really regretted having left Sugar's squad. Besides, had he remained under Sugar's command, he wouldn't have met Ninette. Now he wouldn't be tormented on her account and... Five-thirty. He rose and called the nurse who spoke French.

"Est-ce qu'ils ont porté un enfant blessé aujourd'hui? Did they bring in a wounded baby today?"

The nurse shook his head with irritation.

"Monsieur, chaque jour ils nous portent des enfants blessés. Every day they bring us wounded babies. Asseyez-vous, s'il vous plaît. Sit down, please."

He sat down again, he returned to his brooding. How strange. In the last days he had never thought of Ninette, and suddenly it was as if she were seated beside him on the bench. He almost could sense her: unseizable yet tangible. Not the usual Ninette, though, voluptuous and shining with joy: a sad, apathetic Ninette, never seen and never suspected, a Ninette who wanted to die because she loved without being loved... He tried to reject the feeling with the idea of the child who was dying because the Shiite clinic didn't have three units of B-negative. Damn! If his blood group were B-negative, he would have given the three units himself... But his blood group was O-positive: entropy equal to Boltzmann's constant multiplied by the natural logarithm of the probabilities of distribution... In place of the probabilities of distribution, the blood groups: group A, group B, group AB, group O, factor Rh-positive, factor Rh-negative. And, as in love, it's very unlikely that A meets A or B meets B or AB meets AB etcetera: chaos always wins, and it's useless to deny it in the name of Life. Useless? He got to his feet. Ignoring the nurse who had reappeared and ran after him yelling Monsieur, le-docteur-peut-vous-parler-maintenant, the-doctor-can-speak-to-you-now, he dashed toward the door. He jumped again into the jeep, left with a screech of tires, reached the field hospital where he requested three units of B-negative. Captain's orders. After checking the refrigerator where the plasma was stored, the medical officer answered sorry: the B-negative group, also called the Mediterranean group, was common among Arabs not among Europeans. In fact they received very little of it, and in case of emergency they turned to the troops. They solicited a transfusion. The sergeant should do the same thing, and good luck: it wouldn't be easy to find one or two B-negative soldiers. "I'll find them," he snapped. Then he went back to the headquarters where the young woman in tears continued to wait, and called her.

"Dam na'am! Blood yes!'"

"Na'am, yes, na'am?" she sobbed in relief.

"Na'am, yes, na'am!" he repeated entering the serpentine pathway.

He knew exactly what to do. Once in the Arab Bureau, he would telephone Eagle and say: commander, we need a couple of volunteers who have B-negative. We need them immediately. General's orders.

3

Eagle made coffee in his Neapolitan pot, poured it into Aunt Concetta's Capodimonte cup which he'd brought from Italy with Uncle Ezechiele's menorah, then went to sip it beneath the Louis XVI gilded-wood canopy: perhaps the most valuable piece that furnished the sumptuous bedroom he had the luck to sleep in, and the one that most reminded him of his home in Naples. He liked to prepare the coffee that way, but most of all he liked to sip it beneath the Louis XVI gilded-wood canopy because from there he could comfortably admire the walls of faux blue marble, the high windows with crimson velvet drapes, the armoire inlaid with Chinese mother-of-pearl in the manner of the Piffetti brothers, precursors of Maggiolini, and particularly the chandelier. Nine bronze maidens who emerged naked from a bronze basket and brandishing nine pure-crystal torches revealed the expert hand of Viennese craftsmen as well as the good taste of the house's previous owner: a prince from Riyadh related to the family of Abd al Aziz ibn Saud, first sovereign of Saudi Arabia. Grand viveur and master of a harem that numbered four wives and six favorites, His Highness had really done things in style. With its numerous entrances, its semi-circular staircases, its arcades, its patios, the three-story mansion expressed by itself all the glories of a Sardanapalian Beirut: the garden parties in the enormous park green with century-old trees, the suppers of caviar and foie gras in the marble-paved halls, the orgies in the bedrooms with a double bidet in each bathroom... And never mind if upon his death which had occurred before the war because of an oysters-and-truffles indigestion, the estate had passed to Her Highness the First Widow who now in her nineties and immobilized within a mass of fat lived on the third floor with two of the minor widows, two of the favorites, two cooks, two nurses, two maids, a scullery girl, a eunuch. That is, thirteen people. According to some, a good-luck number. But according to Cabala, a source of bad luck and evil eye.

He finished sipping the coffee, got up to prepare another, then smiled gloomily. Well, it was a relief to be quartered in the mansion of a prince dead of oysters-and-truffles indigestion and only here could he bear his misfortunes. The misfortune of being in Beirut, of being bound to protect his people's worst enemies, of being nicknamed after a coarse brutal bird, a feathered creature accustomed to kidnapping newborns and robbing lambs... Eagle! Even physically, that appellative Eagle didn't suit him: his chest was so narrow that it floundered in any shirt; his neck was so slight that at the least gust of wind it risked snapping in two; his face was so meek that once, as a boy, he had been asked to pose for a painting of Saint Sebastian's martyrdom. In the hope of toughening it up, he had grown mustaches which stretched upward with curlicues, but next to his tender mouth and nose and bloodless cheeks they seemed like two question marks put there in fun. A prank. Finally, that appellative associated him with the rhetoric which characterizes military people: individuals who perniciously identify themselves with eagles, condors, falcons, hawks, never with courteous birds such as swallows or doves or sparrows. And he didn't like to be taken for a bully, a warrior: he detested warriors as much as weapons and uniforms. He felt ridiculous in uniform. Can you compare a gray double-breasted jacket, a white shirt, a striped tie, or a tailcoat with the uniform? As for the weapons, he even hated to display his pistol. He considered it an inconvenient, superfluous gadget. Superfluous, yes: what need is there to use weapons, to make noise, to get killed? If things take a turn for the worse, it's better to discuss: to look for a compromise. What's more, he couldn't stand the idea of commanding. It's a bad-taste thing, commanding, and very unpleasant. Because it puts you in contact with clods and dullards, it forces you to exercise the vulgarity of power, it limits the liberty of both the commander and the commanded, and it inebriates those who are conceited. He wasn't con-ceited. He perfectly knew that he didn't possess lofty qualitics or special talents. He perfectly realized that he offered the typical example of a weak and overeducated man, of an officer not to praise and not to blame: his life had always unfolded under the sign of mediocrity. Thus, he didn't feel any urgency to mount a throne, to shout orders. He could swear to it. Word of a Neapolitan!

He swore to it, he poured out a second coffee, and sighed in dismay. Eh! He also knew he practiced a trade he didn't belong to. If someone asked him why he had chosen the military as a career, he answered: "By a trick of fate, my friend. Fate is cruel." Then he said that, from a logical point of view, nothing justified such a mistake. He came from a well-to-do family of antiquarians and notaries, as an adolescent he had long hesitated between those two pacific professions, and everybody thought that he would choose the antiquarian trade. At eighteen, however, he had fallen in love with a girl from Modena. Soon after he'd received the draft notice, and you know how it works: almost always the draftees are yanked far away from the girl they love. If she lives in the North, be sure that they send you to the South; if she lives in the South, be sure that they send you to the North. So he had enrolled in the Military Academy at Modena where, disgrace of disgraces, he'd found himself elbow to elbow with Crazy Horse and... The second year, his love affair over, he wanted to return to Naples. But that nag, that donkey, had intervened. "What are you saying, my distinguished friend?!? What's gotten into you, my illustrious colleague? Quitting would be a sacrilege, an insult to our homeland, an act of cowardice unworthy of a gentleman! Perfer et obdura, dolor hic tibi proderit olim. Endure and resist, one day your effort will be repaid, Ovid teaches us." He'd endured, alas. He'd resisted. But at age forty-six, with a colonel's rank, he hadn't yet made his peace with it. And to have ended up again with that nag, that donkey, was the cruelest spite San Gennaro* could have inflicted upon him. Apart from being here to defend the Palestinians, of course. Because he was a Jew, Holy Moses! What's more, a Jew on the mother's side, and he never forgot that Judaism is inherited by way of the maternal line. Nor did Uncle Ezechiele and his mother. She'd almost fainted, poor thing, on hearing that he would be sent to defend the Palestinians. "There of all places, my son! To help our people's worst enemies!" And Uncle Ezechiele: "Think of our relatives in Jerusalem! Think of our cousins in Tel Aviv!" Nor had it been any use to yell: "Facite silenzio, m'avite scucciato! Shut up, leave me alone!" Every month his mother called to moan over the phone there-of-all-places, my-son, to-help-our-people's-worst-enemies, and for the last few weeks Uncle Ezechiele had found a new way to torment him: "Dear nephew, what will you do if an Israeli pilot bails out over Shatila?"

He finished his second coffee. A chilling question, and not at all silly, alas! Israeli reconnaissance planes were shot down quite often by the Druze artillery. Each time the pilots ejected with parachutes, and in September one had landed less than four hundred yards from Bourji el Barajni. By sheer good luck a Marine patrol had led him to safety. What would have happened if that pilot had fallen inside the quarter? I'll tell you: they would have eaten him alive. By the mouthful. Like dogs around a bone. Especially in Shatila, where the Israelis had helped the

* San Gennaro is the patron of Naples.

phalangists with flares etcetera. And what would he have done, in such a case? Would he have fired on the Palestinians he had come to defend, or would he have left the pilot to be eaten alive? He'd even asked Falcon, who at Bourji el Barajni had the same hypothetical problem, but as a Pontius Pilate who doesn't dare to take a position Falcon had replied: "Ask the Condor." He'd asked the Condor and gotten nothing but shouts. "Learn to make your own decisions, colonel! Have a little guts, don't be the usual marshmallow!" Because Mister General did not answer, no. He shouted, he pecked, he tore, he scratched. As a condor should. Besides, he loved to be called Condor. It's a bird who has a predilection for peaks, he said. Apparently nobody had told him that, peaks or no peaks, it is also an extremely disagreeable bird: winged, yes, but without feathers on the head and neck, made uglier by its fleshy comb and its habit of feeding exclusively upon rotting corpses. *Vultur gryphus* is its real name: greedy vulture. Oh, Jesus! Moses and Abraham and Isaac how did he dislike him! It was the only thing he had in common with the ruinous Crazy Horse, his dislike for that general! Uncouth, ill-mannered, always ready to criticize, to blame, to oppress. "Colonel, the M113 of the Twenty-One is ten inches from the sidewalk and you haven't noticed." "Colonel, the checkpoint at the Twenty-Two is insufficient and you don't take care of it." "Colonel, your bersaglieri smoke hashish and you don't stop them. You treat them like boys and soldiers aren't boys, they're men." And if you replied no, sir, at nineteen or twenty they're not men, they're boys, he doubled his Vultur Gryphus's pecks. Because he did not know what it means to be a soldier of nineteen or twenty in Beirut, to stand guard at Bourji el Barajni or Shatila twelve hours at a time, bitten by the mice during the night, pelted by the urchins' stones during the day, not seldom while you pick up their trash... Yes, their trash. Because those stinking Palestinians who would eat the Israeli pilot alive did not pick up their trash. They heaped it in front of their houses and hovels, or they threw it on the communal grave: on the tomb of their dead. So, in order to prevent epidemics, the bersaglieri had to collect it and burn it: to be their street sweeper.

He made his third coffee, he shot a glance at the nine bronze maidens who emerged from the Viennese chandelier, he sighed. Along with the urchins, the whores. Yessir, Mister General: the whores with their pimps. This morning a fat one had passed by the Twenty-Four with two guys. Her brothers, no doubt. She'd placed herself in front of the M113 gunner and while the two pimps were licking their lips, jamila-good-jamila, she had unbuttoned her dress to draw out a breast as big as a watermelon. "Khudu! Take it, khudu!" Then, as the gunner remained motionless and silent, the usual insults had started. "Miniuk! Faggot! Miniuk!" Which is why he told them: "Don't react, boys. Don't look at women. Don't defy fate. Resist. It doesn't matter if they call you miniuk, faggot, queers. Better queer than dead." Eh! It had become a kind of password, his better-queer-than-dead. In fact the bersaglieri never fell into the traps of love and sex. The marò, instead, all the contrary. They squabbled over Fatima, the harlot in blue jeans who'd left the brothel at Gobeyre and set up business on her own. They courted Farjane, the little fox in search of a fool who would marry her and bring her to Italy. They drooled over Sheila, the cute school-teacher who gave herself to the officers free of charge. They hooted at any mongrel who passed by. And if you protested to Sandokan, the boor sniggered: "He who has a cock hoists it high. My marò do have cocks." At Logistics, they even made use of the girls who accompanied by their fathers prostituted themselves for ten dollars a throw, plus some chocolates. As for Falcon's paratroopers, they were the Latin lovers of the contingent. They did not understand the risk, they did not see the lewd duplicity of those bedouins who in the name of decency covered their wives or sisters or daughters from head to foot and then sold them like goats. The other night a shriek had risen from a slum near the Twenty-Four: "Saedna, help, saedna!" He'd run over with Hawk, his sector leader, and found a little girl tied up to be raped by a guy who having paid her parents a good two thousand dollars claimed his right to use the merchandise. A question: what would have happened if she were a bersagliere's girl, a marò's girl, a paratrooper's girl? The answer: the third truck would have liquidated them all within a minute. And if the Condor weren't the Condor, he would tell him. The trouble is that the Condor was the Condor: just hearing his voice over the telephone scared him. Worse: each time the telephone rang, he trembled like a chick. And it didn't help to think, by Moses, I'm a battalion commander, a man of some intelligence, a guy who knows how to distinguish an inlay by the Piffetti brothers from an inlay by Maggiolini, it doesn't make sense to be frightened by some lousy bird's racket: the trembling continued. And rather than lift the receiver he would have shaken a Palestinian's hand.

*　*　*

The telephone rang. Eagle's body seemed to be jolted by an electric current, a trembling hand lifted the receiver.

"Yessir, general... At your command, sir, general..."

But it wasn't the general. It was Charlie Two, Charlie's aide, who in the general's name requested two or three volunteers for a transfusion of B-negative.

"And right away, sir!"

"Right away?"

"That's what the general said, sir."

"And who is this B-negative for?"

"For a child, sir."

"What child?"

"An Arab child, sir. Palestinian, Shiite, I don't know. Please, sir, it's urgent!"

A silence followed, heavy with irritation and perplexity. Irritation because the boy was Palestinian or Shiite, perplexity because the call came from Charlie's aide and not from the Condor himself. But then the relief at not having been called in person by the Vultur Gryphus prevailed.

"All right, Charlie Two. I'll take care of it myself," he replied. Then he quickly left the bedroom, went into the park, headed toward the southeast corner of the encampment.

It was an almost quiet evening, only the echo of some gunburst came from the Green Line, and in the tent at the southeast corner three bersaglieri named String, Nazarene, Onion were talking animatedly among themselves.

4

"Tonight I'm not going to Shatila. I swear I'm not," said an almost childish voice. "I'd rather tell them some fib like having diarrhea and stay in bed for a week!"

"If you invent the story of diarrhea and stay in bed for a week you're a fraud and a shit," protested an angry voice. "And I'll spit on that fat face of yours, all purple with booze, and I'll inform Hawk and won't talk to you anymore. Why you and not us? Do you think we enjoy freezing our butts off in the dark, waiting for a bomb or bullet? Then let's hear, let's hear, what would be the reasons for the fib of diarrhea?!?"

"You know it, String. We all do. He's afraid," a third voice put in, persuasively. "Don't scold him for that. He doesn't need to be scolded. He needs to be taught what we are never taught: that the point is not whether you have fear, it is to overcome fear with intelligence and dignity!"

"I'm not scolding anybody, Goddammit! I'm saying what I think! And I'm asking what right this enema, this clyster, has to make himself sick and not go to Shatila while we go! Come on, Onion, no, Clyster, answer me!"

"I answer, I answer! He's right, I'm afraid. Yes, afraid! And then I don't like to stand guard next to that grave which stinks!"

"It stinks?!?"

"Yeah, it stinks of the dead!"

"Of the dead?!?"

"Yeah, of dead! The dead who stay inside!"

"To hell with you, nitwit! It's not the stink of the dead! It's the stink of garbage! Are you blind, besides being stupid? Don't you see that those cavemen throw their garbage on it? How can the dead stink when they've been dead for more than one year?"

"They may have been dead for more than one year, but the stink is there, I tell you! And then there are the will-o'-the-wisps!"

"The will-o'-the-wisps?!?"

"Yeah! The will-o'-the-wisps, yeah!"

"Shut your trap, you mental deficient! You don't even know what will-o'-the-wisps are made of!"

"I do, I do! Because I saw them, once! In the Caserta cemetery! They're made like the little candles we stick in a cake! The only difference is that the candles we light them with matches and blow them out with the mouth, the will-o'-the-wisps light up and go out by themselves! And sometimes they walk. Or they fly! Because they're gas. Gas that comes from the dead!"

"Nazarene, tell this numbskull to shut up! He's getting on my nerves, he is."

"Eh, no, String. No! That's not fair. First you ask him why he wants to make up the fib of diarrhea, then you won't listen and insult him. It is not fair!"

"But why should I listen to him? There's nothing to listen to, nothing! He's a chicken, that's all. Do you believe there are will-o'-the-wisps at Shatila? Do you believe the dead stink after more than one year?!?"

"String, about will-o'-the-wisps I don't know. I've never seen them. But about odor I know. Because I have a good nose. When I was in India, I smelled the perfume of sage and jasmine even if I was in a stable! And I guarantee you that at Shatila the stink of garbage smells just like the stink of the dead. How can you miss it, since you're posted at the Twenty-One?"

"Bah! Nazarene, when it comes to good or bad odors, I only smell those of food. The smell of a roast, which I like, or the smell of fish, which I like much less, and so on. The only place I ever smelled the stink of the dead was over at the American headquarters."

Eagle pricked up his ears. He knew them well, those three. When he inspected the troops at Shatila, he often lingered to talk with them. The almost childish voice belonged to Onion, a youngster from the province of Caserta, who stood guard at the Twenty-Three: the post next to the communal grave. They called him Onion because his face was shaped like an onion, broad across the jaws and narrow at the temples, and because his round cheeks were purple like the purple of red onions. The angry voice belonged to String, a cook from Livorno who stood guard at the Twenty-One: the tower on the border between Sabra and Shatila. They called him String because, besides being very tall, he was as thin as a string and like a string he could squeeze nay strangle you each time he opened his mouth. The persuasive voice belonged to Nazarene, the Turinese student who stood guard at the Twenty-Seven Owl: the observation post at Shatila, located in the area under marò control. They called him Nazarene because he seemed like Jesus Christ: his face was intense and emaciated, his eyes both rebellious and serene, his hair so long that Hawk always grumbled: "Colonel, sir, if the general sees that hair, he'll shave it off and give us the third degree!" An agreeable young man, Nazarene. He'd been a leftist thug, a Red Brigader. Then he'd gone to India and converted to Jainism: a religion that prohibits one from harming any living being and preaches universal peace. Undoubtedly he would soon change the subject to stop that fight, but then the quarrel would flare up again and... There, he changed it.

"So you were at the American headquarters, String... Digging them out?"

"Sure. Didn't you know? Five days, for God's sake, five days of pulling out the dead! I thought I was there to dig out the survivors, instead all I did was dig out the dead... I found only one who was still alive, but on the stretcher he died as well. And I cried. Shit. I cried. Because I loved those poor dead, believe me. While I picked them up I kept thinking: what an idiot you were, String, when you cheered the Arabs and shouted yourself hoarse in anti-American marches! Butchers here, butchers there, imperialists here, imperialists there, buttfuckers-go-home... You didn't even understand that the Americans are sons of people like you. And I wanted to write a letter to the Central Committee of the Communist Party, to set this out in black and white, to tell them: fanatics, liars and fanatics, you must stop telling lies to young people!"

"I agree, String. I felt the same way while I was digging at the French headquarters. I still can't get it out of my mind, that sack that looked like a sack of potatoes but dripped blood. In fact, I cannot eat potatoes since then. And when I think of the way I hated everybody before going to India... Onion! What are you doing, Onion?!?"

"I scratch my balls, that's what I do! For good luck! Can't we talk about something else? I don't understand you, I don't! First you pump me up with your sermons about fear, then you scare me with blood potatoes... You'll give me a heart attack, that's what you'll do!"

"I'm sorry, Onion."

"But what are you sorry for, Nazarene? What do you apologize for?!? Don't you know that we can't talk about anything with him? Whatever we say, that enema and clyster ends up shitting his pants! For God's sake, even I was scared when I first got here! I told myself String, here you lose your skin. Or at the very least you lose an arm, a leg. String, your term of service should last four months. But you'll never get to the end: you'll be snuffed out much before! Then I got used to it. And now, if a bullet passes next to me I don't bat an eyelash. I look at it as if it were a fly."

"Liar!"

"Liar?!? Be careful who you're talking to, Onion! Don't even try calling me a liar! Otherwise I brown you, with that purple face I make onion soup!"

"You brown nothing! You make no soup! And I say liar, yes, liar! Because it's impossible to stay cool when a bullet passes by! Everybody gets scared! And the hotheads more scared than anyone else!"

"And who would these hotheads be? Let's hear!"

"People like you! Volunteers like you and the dolt who the other might kept beating his fists against the M113 and babbled why-am-I-here! In fact I got pissed off and I yelled nossir, you don't have the right to say that. You don't. Because you asked to come here! That right is mine, only mine! Because I did not ask. They sent me by force and they didn't give a damn that I was frozen by fear, freaked out for eight days! So freaked out that when the captain asked me where-do-you-think-you-are, I answered: at Spirinbergo, captain. I thought I still was in the Spirinbergo barracks and..."

"You just talk to hear your own ugly voice, Onion. You know very well that I'm not a volunteer, mongoloid."

"You're not a volunteer, but you always say that if they hadn't sent you, you would've made sure you got sent. You always say that being here is good, that here we're having our maturity tested etcetera! True or not?"

"True!"

"See? A hothead! That's what you are! You should've joined the paratroopers, the incursori!"

"And you should've stuck to your mommy's apron, chicken!"

Heedless of Charlie Two, of the dying child, of the B-negative blood, Eagle leaned against a tree and smiled. Now Nazarene would separate them a second time. But soon they'd find a way to come to blows again and... There, he separated them.

"Don't insult him, String. And you: don't exaggerate, Onion. I wanted to come too. I too was convinced that Beirut would do us some good. Because it's only by knowing war that we learn to reject it. You need to see it, in order to understand the poisonous attraction it has. And if we don't get slaughtered like the Americans and the French, I think that here I'll find what I'm searching for. Am I right, String?"

"Bah! I don't know anymore what I'm searching for. I don't know anymore what I want... Not even politically. I thought I was a communist, but now the communists make me sick and... What about you? What are you searching for?"

"Proof that we need to love life. Proof that we need to love love, and that life is love. Like Jainism says."

"Jane who?"

"Jainism. It's a religion I discovered in India. Want me to explain it to you?"

"No thanks, no. The only Indian stuff I like to know is tandoori chicken. But what are you politically?"

"Nothing. I don't believe in politics anymore, and the only ideology I respect is anarchism. What about you, Onion?"

"Me? About politics, I understand only this: that the rich are mean, the poor are nice, that you have to believe in God, and vote Christian Democrat. But what did you go to India for? Drugs?"

"No. To search for what I am searching for here. The proof that we need to love love."

"Here?!? Where is love, here?!?"

"There is. You don't see it but it's there. And when you see it, you understand it better than elsewhere. Even through the flowers, the plants. Look around, Onion. Flowers and plants hardly exist in Beirut. Almost all the trees in the Pine Wood have been burned down, almost every bush in the hills has been clear-cut. And the cedars of Lebanon... Have you ever seen a cedar of Lebanon, in this city? It is since the Bible, since the Song of Songs, that the world celebrates the cedars of Lebanon. And here you don't see a single one. All dead. Disappeared, vanished. But precisely because trees and plants and flowers are a luxury here, you love them more than anywhere else. And when you find a daisy among the rubble of Shatila, it seems more beautiful than any field of daisies at home. Know why? Because growing among that rubble a daisy proves that life is powerful, precious."

"Maybe, but I don't see any daisies in Shatila. And if there was one, I wouldn't bother looking at it. All I look at in Shatila is the shadows that can shoot at me. And I don't love anybody, there. I hate them all: the grown-up ones and the little ones. As a matter of fact, the little ones are those I hate the most. Always throwing stones at me, calling me son-of-a-bitch, sharmuta, talieni-kaputt, talieni-tomorrow-boom-boom. Why should I love those who throw stones at me?"

"Listen to this priest-kisser, this paternoster-mumbler who loves nothing but himself! Listen to this illiterate who doesn't even know how to conjugate verbs! Aren't you ashamed to say those things? Don't you think that those poor kids bother us because nobody's ever sent them to school and because they have nothing to eat? Don't you think that in the communal grave there are hundreds of them butchered like hogs?"

"No. I only think of my own skin. Nothing else."

"Then what do you have in place of a heart? A pancake?!? What did the priests teach you? What does a believer like you have to do with God? All you can say is that the rich are mean and the poor are nice! Hypocrite! Pharisee! That's what you are!"

"What I am is a guy who wants to stay alive to the end. A guy who has nothing in common with communists like you."

"I'll drink to that! I would get sick if I had something in common with you!"

"You do have it," the persuasive voice said at this point.

"In common with him?!?"

"Yes. In common with him."

"What?!?"

"Your blood group, B-negative. I saw it this morning in your clinical files."

B-negative?!? By the beard of Abraham and the bones of San Gennaro! He had said B-negative! Finally recalling Charlie Two and the reason he had come out to the encampment, Eagle burst into the tent.

"Who has the B-negative?"

"We two, colonel, sir," String replied with a glance of hate for Onion.

"You too, Onion?"

"Well... no... Actually..."

"Him too, him too! He doesn't want to because he's a selfish miser, a skinflint!" String shouted.

"No, it's that I..."

"Three units of B-negative are required for an Arab child who has been wounded," Eagle explained. "Naturally I don't want to force you, I can't force anybody. But the general has personally made the request, and if you feel that..."

"I'm at your service, colonel," String said. Then, turning to Onion: "And you should be too, you miser! Egoist! Skinflint!"

"But what does it have to do with me?" Onion tried to protest.

"Everything, stingy bastard!"

"I should remind you that blood donors are entitled to a day off," Eagle urged.

A day off?!? A whole day off without pretending to have diarrhea and without having to stay in bed?!? Onion raised his fat purple face and cleared his throat.

"If that's the way it is, sir..."

"Right. Go straight to the field hospital and report to the people who are taking care of this business. In the meantime I'll inform the general."

*　*　*

Angelo had waited for almost an hour when Eagle called back to say that two volunteers had been found, and he immediately ran over to the young woman in tears. He helped her into the jeep, brought her to the field hospital where he picked up Onion and String, then drove all three of them to the Shiite clinic. But too much time had passed. And the doctor mumbled sorry, the baby is dead.

CHAPTER FOUR

1

HE WAS DEAD and the fault was his. Charlie sat at the table in the Arab Bureau, held his head in his hands, and surrendered to the remorse that gnawed at him. Yes, according to the reconstruction of the facts, Eagle had lost too much time looking for the two volunteers. At least an hour. But Angelo had acted boldly, his initiative could have saved the baby. It hadn't because until six in the afternoon the captain's orders had been scrupulously followed and because the captain had refused to talk with the woman. Ah, if he hadn't rushed off in that hurry and that fear of losing his very important appointment with Zandra Sadr! Very important, too important. This was the point. Too important? More important than a two-year-old child who's dying, than a well of hopes, a lode of good possibilities that fade away? The night before the evacuation of the Palestinian guerrillas, he had met a boy. A handsome eight-year-old boy with dense black curls and immense eyes, named Salim. He'd met him in a bunker of Bourji el Barajni where he had gone to negotiate with a group who refused to leave the city. Salim was their interpreter, God knows why he spoke perfect English, and while translating he played with the weapons of the bunker. An arsenal of Kalashnikovs, M16s, rockets, pistols of every kind. He stripped them and reassembled them at an incredible speed, the way normal children fiddle with toys. They were his toys. They always had been. And by dawn, when the group had decided to leave, he had gravely said: "Captain, you have been kind to us. You deserve a gift." Then he'd held out a grenade, a Russian Rdg8. Answering no-thanks, Salim, don't-deprive-yourself, I-don't-want-it, he'd tried to decline. But Salim had insisted and tucked it in his pocket like a piece of candy. "Please, keep it, captain. And make good use of it." Well, he'd made good use of it: he'd thrown it away. Yet throwing it away he'd asked himself if Salim too would make good use of the weapons he stripped and reassembled with so much skill, if he too would throw them away, and had concluded that he wouldn't. Because he was already a man, poor Salim, an old man accustomed to killing. A damned soul. Because in Beirut a child of eight is no longer a child. He's a man, an old man accustomed to killing. A damned soul. A child of two, instead, is a well of hopes. A lode of good possibilities. When a two-year-old child dies, you don't think that a possible delinquent dies. A possible tyrant. You think that a possible savior, a possible redeemer dies. A hypothetical Jesus Christ, somebody who might make this filthy world a little less filthy.

He jumped to his feet, angry with himself. In this anger he grabbed the cot leaning against the wall, set it up next to the secret archive cabinets, then stretched out on it without turning off the light. It was already eleven, the meeting with Zandra Sadr had exhausted him, and he felt a tremendous need to sleep at once. But he also needed to know if His Eminence had actually ordered the muezzins to spread the sentence about the Italians, and this would keep him awake until their nocturnal prayer. That is, midnight. He grunted. Yes, somebody who might make this filthy world a little less filthy. A possible savior, a possible redeemer, a hypothetical Jesus Christ. That's why he loved children so much. The way he had loved the little girl whom twenty years ago he called my-daughter. Twenty years ago! He was twenty, twenty years ago... He studied Political Science at the University of Rome, he lived in the house of a harpy who rented out rooms, and here one October evening he'd been awakened by the mewling of a cat. He'd gone to chase it, but it wasn't a cat. It was a bundle of rags with two tiny hands poking out in an appeal for help. Whè! Whè! Whè! "She belongs to a couple who left without settling their bill," the harpy had said, "and I don't want her. You found her, you keep her." He'd kept her. He'd become her mother. Yessirs, her mother. A child belongs to those who accept it, who love it, not to those who conceive and abandon it. Besides, where is it written that a big mustached young man might not be a mother? Like a mother he changed her diapers, he fed her, he washed her, he rocked her to sleep. He calmed her each time she burst into screams. Like a mother he stayed up to watch her, he carried her to the park, he mingled with the nannies who in pity or amusement flooded him with advice. Keep an-eye-on-the-temperature-of-the-milk, pay-attention-to-the-consistency-of-the-poop, control-the-gums-when-the-first-tooth-sprouts. And-do-talk-to-her! He did, he did... To some people a newly born baby is a little body that grows and that's all. Wrong. Because in that little body he has a brain that expands, a consciousness. He never left her. He kept her even at the university, in the classroom. He hid with her in the last row, he fol-

lowed the lessons murmuring silence-baby-silence, and what an uproar
the afternoon she had burst into her whè-whè-whè. "Who's the lunatic
who comes with a newborn to class?!?" the professor had shouted.
Then, thinking that someone was mocking him, he'd sent him to the
dean. Thank God the dean was a credulous, courteous type. "Explain
yourself, young man. I'm listening." "She's my daughter, sir, and I
don't know where to leave her during lessons." "You can leave her
with your wife, can't you?" "I'm an unmarried father, sir. I have been
seduced and abandoned." "Well, in that case, I must grant permission
and congratulate you. You have a great deal of courage. You've taken
on quite a task, quite a burden." A burden?!? She wasn't a burden. She
was a joy. A challenge to bigoted rules, to doltish conformities, and a
joy. In fact he called her Gioia: Joy. And she called him Dada. "Gioia!"
"Dada!" The challenge, the joy, had lasted one autumn, one winter,
one spring, and one summer. Then on an ugly day the real parents,
meaning the bastards whom the law defines as parents, had returned to
take her back. They literally wrenched her from his arms. "Dada no,
Dada no-o-o-o!" she howled. What a torture to hear that Dada-no,
Dada-no.

He cleared his throat, looked at his watch. Eleven-thirty. He lit a
cigar and got ready to wait another half-hour. He'd never seen her
again. He'd never had news about her. And he'd never had a child.
Because among all the women he'd collected, so many that just thinking of them gave him nausea, there had never been one ready to get
pregnant for him. I-am-not-a-stallion-mare. If-you-want-a-child-
marry-me. Too bad men aren't snails, too bad human beings need an
ovum to reproduce. The maternal complex, however, had never left
him. And one could see it with his Charlies. Dammit, how he loved his
Charlies! Apart from the two radio operators Pistoia had fobbed off on
him, with them he felt like a mother hen raising chicks. And, for each
chick, waves of anxiety. Angelo, to begin with. So tough yet so vulnerable, so intelligent yet so stupid. He wanted to discover the formula of
Life, the daydreamer. He didn't have the faintest idea what it means to
live in this filthy world. Yesterday he had said: "In my opinion, dealing
with Zandra Sadr is unbecoming, disloyal." Unbecoming, disloyal? To
whom? To the Americans and the French who both had shaken their
heads mumbling bavardages-gossip-unfounded-rumors, when the
Condor had told them about Mustafa Hash? To that sleazy bungler
called Gemayel who gave his ass away to anyone and who was ready to
betray those who protected him? Open your eyes, son, he'd answered.
Here everybody plays his own game, there's nothing but lies and hy-

pocrisies, alliances disguised as enmities, enmities disguised as alliances: in such a dungheap you might as well sell your soul to the devil. And never mind if the devil stinks. When you wade into shit, you hold your nose and bear the stench. But it had been like talking to a brick wall. "I don't agree, chief." Moreover, the daydreamer was going through an existential crisis worthy of Hamlet. Sooner or later this would become clear also to his Ophelia, that gorgeous Ninette with whom he refused to grant himself a bit of happiness. They are dangerous, the Hamlets. They always end up making trouble for themselves and those around them... How many people die with Hamlet? Then, Martino. There was something strange about Martino: something concealing an uneasiness or a secret anguish. Maybe his excessive politeness, his excessive docility. Even if you scolded him, he didn't fly off the handle. Even if you abused him, he didn't rebel. As if he were seeking indulgence or pardon for a fault or sin. What fault, what sin? The sin of being a bad soldier, maybe? Or the sin of not being a male? Shit. He didn't want to think of that. The others would eat him up, if the so-called fault or sin were that one. As for Stefano, Fifì, and Bernard le Français, they moved him. Stefano, a bookbinder from Trieste, because at twenty he only knew about bindings, stitches, glues, and gutters. "Captain, is it difficult to find a girl?" Fifì, a rich Sicilian burdened by summers spent sunbathing on the beach and wasting money in the nightclubs, because he had nothing to give and would never know it. No wonder he stuffed himself with hashish. "For me it is a medicine." Bernard le Français, a former waiter and the son of emigrants from Brussels, because he was the most unlucky of them all. He possessed nothing, poor Bernard. Absolutely nothing. Not even a language. He spoke French but couldn't write it, he wrote Italian but couldn't speak it, and to overcome the embarrassment he always stayed by himself. "Mon capitaine, le problème c'est que je ne sais ni qui je suis ni quel est mon pays, ma patrie. Je me sens comme un poisson hors de l'eau. Captain, my problem is that I don't know who I am and which country is my country, my fatherland. I really feel like a fish out of water. Comprenez-vous, mon capitaine? Il faut que je prends racines quelque part, et le risque est que je prenne racine dans l'armée, que je devienne un militariste. Do you understand what I mean, captain? I need to put down roots somewhere. And the risk is that I put them down in the army, that I become a militarist."

"Allah akbar, Allah akbar, Allah akbar! Wah Muhammad rassullillah! Inna shahada rassullillah! God is great, God is great, God is great! And Muhammad is his prophet! In truth I tell you that he is his prophet!"

Midnight. Charlie sprang upright on the cot to listen to the singsong wafting from the minaret on rue de l'Aérodrome. Now the psalmodizing muezzin would invite his listeners to win salvation through prayer, then he would spread the Amal's messages and His Eminence's orders. Among these, the sentence about the Italians. Despite his scanty knowledge of Arabic, he wouldn't miss it: with Martino's help he had composed it word by word... He pricked up his ears. The messages followed the invitations, the orders followed the messages, but the sentence didn't, and this dismayed him. Could the old codger have swindled him? But then he decided that it would come with the dawn prayer, and went on brooding over Bernard le Français who didn't like the militarists. Comprenez-vous, mon-capitaine? Did he! It is a diabolical machine, the army. And militarism, a lethal gear. Have you noticed the recipe we use for fucking over the recruits when they arrive at the barracks, Bernard? First we assemble them in their civilian clothes to make it clear that they belong to a world devoid of equality: a society in which some dress well and some badly. Then we give them the uniform, so they think they've entered a fair brotherhood of equals: a society in which everybody wears the same clothes. Then we break them down with the drills, the marches, and while they march we make them sing. So-you-keep-in-step. (But keeping in step has nothing to do with it, Bernard. We make them sing because while they sing they don't think. And, not thinking, they don't realize they're being fucked.) Finally, we cancel their personality, their individuality. Because a soldier isn't supposed to be an individual, a person. He's supposed to be part of a perfect nucleus that acts in unison. And do you know what the main ingredient is for obtaining a perfect or near-perfect nucleus? Hate. Collective hate directed at one single target. And not even the target represented by the enemy a war provides or will provide: the target represented by a pariah with sergeant's stripes. The cloddish sergeant who subjects the soldiers to a tyranny which has been delegated to him by the lieutenant to whom it has been delegated by the captain to whom it has been delegated by the major to whom it has been delegated by the colonel to whom it has been delegated by the general to whom it has been delegated by the Machine. The unlearned sergeant who has been taught to shout the way a singer is taught to warble do-re-mi-fa-sol-la. To command, to mock, to humiliate. Like this: "So, you're a college graduate, huh? Good. Then go clean the toilets." Or, if the draftee is a farmer, a laborer: "You bumpkin, you lout, what sewer did you come from? Don't you even know how to count, you bumpkin, you lout?" Without knowing what he's doing, that is, without being aware of the role he's playing, he goes on until the college graduate and the farmer and the laborer hate him in equal measure, and at this point the near-perfect nucleus is obtained. Near-perfect because it lacks the finishing touch, the decisive ingredient. And guess what the decisive ingredient is: love. Love concentrated upon a single target which in this case is the lieutenant, or better the captain. The good, understanding, paternal captain who listens and consoles and addresses with jolly politeness. "So, you're a college graduate? Bravo. I'm glad to hear that. So, you're a farmer. Bravo, I'm delighted to know it. So, you are a laborer. Bravo. I'm happy to have you." Or: "Yes, the sergeant's reprimand was excessive: I'll have a word with him. Please turn to me, in case of need." Need? What need? By now their only need is to receive love, to give love. Thus, from the hate for the sergeant they pass to the love for the captain. My-captain. They will accept any sacrifice for their-captain. Any torment, any danger. For him and with him they will leap out of the trenches, they will fling themselves at the machine gun that mows them down, they will kill the enemy (meaning the wretch who's undergone the identical treatment on the other side), they will get slaughtered like oxen in the shambles. They will die without even suspecting they have been the victims of a lurid swindle, the cogs in a well-oiled and well-tested gear.

He relit his extinguished cigar, rubbed his eyelids which were growing heavy with sleep. Why, then, did he remain in the Machine? Why had he joined in the first place? Well... He had joined out of nausea, loneliness, pessimism. The nausea of living like a spineless bourgeois who pretends to redeem himself by means of mediocre adventures, now a docker who hates to unload, now a cook who hates to cook, now a student of Political Science who hates Political Science although it allows him to indulge his lawyer father and his dentist mother who are always whimpering please-get-a-degree. The loneliness he was drowning in despite his collection of women, the pessimism in which he withered thanks to his melancholy, the melancholy of the gloomy southerner who never hopes for the better and therefore is always resigned to the worst. What will I do with a degree in Political Science, he wondered, where will I go afterwards? Will I look for a job in some ministry, make a start in diplomacy, become a clerk in an embassy or a consul at Timbuktu? And one day, in an attack of masochism, he'd given himself to the Machine: presented himself at the Officers Training School. Sure, I understand what kind of trap you were falling into, Bernard: the army always offers roots to those who don't have any. It's the world's most hospitable club, the refugium peccatorum for anybody in search of a shelter in which to lodge his uncertainties or failures, and it rejects nobody. Least of all, the fish out of water. It provides him with a bed to sleep in, a mess to eat in, a friend to chat with. But above all, it decides for you: it manages your day, it organizes your tomorrow. Do-this, do-that; you-will-do-this, you-will-do-that. The future ceases to be a dilemma, in the army. And the barracks become your home, your fatherland. Yes, that's why he stayed. Why should he leave, anyway? He didn't have a wife, nor a steady mistress, a tie in the name of which to overthrow the overthrowable. All he had was an enormous rage that reignited wherever he found a new proof of how filthy this filthy world is. A rage that in Beirut was fed by the lies, the hypocrisies, the alliances disguised as enmities, the enmities disguised as alliances he'd mentioned to Angelo. For example, the enmity between President Amin Gemayel and the socialist-billionaire prince Walid Jumblatt: the two bastards who used to be inseparable buddies and together raced in their Ferrari and their Porsche along the Corniche Charles de Gaulle, together caroused in the swanky nightclubs of the coast, lounged around the swimming pools of the Saint George, piloted the speedboat with which one summer they had mowed down a poor boy. "Too bad for him. He should have known this stretch of sea is private." The two gangsters who after the expulsion of the Palestinian guerrillas had divvied up the warmaking loot inexplicably refused by the Israelis: a benison of Katyushas, Sherman tanks, Russian D30 long-range artillery...

He tossed away his cigar. He stretched out on the cot too short for his gigantic frame and groaned in disgust. Now the two former buddies were at war. Because when the rabble had elected Gemayel president, Jumblatt had gone crazy with jealousy. He'd brought his Katyushas and Shermans and D30s up into the Shouf Mountains, and started bombarding the residence of his former friend: the presidential palace at Baabda. Nevertheless they continued doing business together: weapons, ammunition, hashish, Coca-Cola, egg pasta, tomato sauce, medicines, banks. And, dulcis in fundo, the construction trade which turned a profit on every bombardment. Know why? Because on top of the rubble they could rebuild and thus raise the value of the land. To hell with their ideological and religious questions! The Gemayels and Jumblatts didn't give a shit about Jesus Christ, the Holy Virgin, Saint Maron, the Messiah who would be delivered or rather shat into a man's baggy pants. They shot and killed for economic interests, greedy rackets, and that's all. This country was the cradle of the most obscene privilege, the most degrading baseness, the most disgusting corruption.

It was a place where the laws existed only to benefit those who decreed them. A non-country. Right: the Muslims also ran their own rackets in arms and hashish, made money from the city's tragedy. And the Shiites were far from being saints: they cruelly avenged themselves against the Palestinians who had oppressed them, they collaborated with the Sons of God, they furnished them the trucks to massacre, they stowed those trucks in the courtyards of their quarters... But in the name of Jesus Christ, of the Virgin, Saint Maron, the Messiah to be delivered or rather shat into a man's baggy pants, they had been oppressed for centuries. The eternal serfs, the eternal ox-people who plow other people's land for a thread of hay. Among the litigants, then, he chose the eternal serfs: the eternal ox-people who plow other people's land for a thread of hay. He'd told it also to Zandra Sadr during the meeting. And the old codger had been so impressed that he had immediately accepted the sentence put together with Martino's help, then promised to spread it the way the captain desired: from the height of the minarets, five times a day, soon after the prayer... Dammit, how tired he was... He couldn't wait any longer...

He turned out the light and closed his eyes to sleep.

*   *   *

He reopened them in the glimmering that precedes the sunrise, woken by the voice of the muezzin who sang the first prayer. Allah-akbar, Allah-akbar, Allah-akbar... Again he sprang upright on the cot, again he cocked his ear, listened to the mysterious precepts: the invitations, the messages, the orders. And this time the sentence came. Eleven words that in the silence of the dawn resounded more heavily than eleven cannon shots.

"Ma'a tezi al-talieni! Al-talieni bayaatùna el dam! Al-talieni ekhuaatùna bil dam! Don't touch the Italians! The Italians give us blood! The Italians are our blood brothers!"

It was six o'clock, and soon the Condor would be calling him to ask: "Well, Charlie, did it work or not?" He was already up, the Condor. You could hear him shuffling around. You could also hear Crazy Horse's elegant trot mixing with the Professor's quiet comings and goings. In the basement Sugar was passing by, opening the door to his Museum, and on the contingent's stage the tragicomedy enriched itself with characters that until now have remained behind the scenes.

2

Sugar entered and his large eggplant nose twitched with an almost savage pleasure, his kindly face widened in a smile of happiness. He always did so when he entered the room they called his Museum: a meticulous collection of weapons from Russia, America, China, Czechoslovakia, Switzerland, Yugoslavia, Sweden, Israel, an infernal gallery of rifles and machine guns, pistols and bazookas, rockets and missiles, armor-piercing projectiles and illumination rounds, detonating cords and white phosphorus fuses, smoke bombs and time bombs, hand grenades, rifle grenades, mortar grenades, artillery shells, not to mention the antitank mines, the antipersonnel mines, the Tnt charges, the boxes of nitroglycerin, dynamite, penthrite, ballistite, the booby traps. In short, the instruments of death as it's given by war. He loved them. He collected them like Czars Alexander III and Nicholas II collected Carl Fabergé's eggs or Jean Duc de Berry collected illuminated manuscripts, and of course he knew about them as much as the two czars knew about enamels or Jean Duc de Berry about miniatures. He was in fact an explosives expert, and the infernal gallery represented the fruit of a year spent handling that stuff. "Put together a squad and secure the streets, the alleys, the overpasses of the Italian sector, clean down to the last cluster bomb," the Condor had ordered him after seeing the amount of deadly devices left by the Israeli siege and the Palestinian occupation. Sugar had put together the squad and for months had unearthed mines, gathered bombs, disarmed traps, seized weapons and ammunition. But can you ask a connoisseur to throw away the Fabergés given to Alexandra Feodorovna by Nicholas or to burn the pages of the calendar Paul de Limbourg painted for the *Très Riches Heures?* There were rare pieces among the deadly devices. And, instead of destroying them, Sugar had convinced the general to let him create that Museum which in his judgment surpassed the Kremlin's treasures or the Tower of London's crown jewels. With the Museum, a small workshop which in theory could blow up at any moment and destroy the headquarters. In reality, no. Because Sugar was a genius, in his field, and had the trust of all. Even that of Crazy Horse who esteemed him to the point of forgetting his simple rank of lieutenant without a coat of arms or financial prospects and compared him to Jean-Baptiste Bessières, Duke of Istria and commander of Napoleon's guard, dead of a bullet in the skull during the battle of Lützen. "Bessières wasn't a master of strategy and had no personal goods. But his bravery reached such heights that the Emperor commented on his death with these words: 'He lived like a Baiardo, he left us like a Turenne.' " Crazy Horse also extolled his mildness, his kindness of heart, and everybody echoed this judgment. Only those who were or had been under his command, like Angelo, knew that Sugar wasn't exactly a sugar.

They called him so because his gentle face emanated an almost sugary sweetness and because, rather than assuming arrogant or martial poses, he liked to appear poised: to offer the picture of a good citizen who would not harm a fly. The husband of a refined woman and the father of two refined children to whom he was extremely devoted, he always praised the joys of family as opposed to the worries of the barracks. A heartfelt Catholic, he went to Mass every Sunday and recited at least a Pater Noster before going to bed. In his youth, he explained, he had wanted to take up an ecclesiastical career and only because of family misfortunes he had later renounced his dream and accepted work in a firm in Busto Arsizio: the city where he was born. He blushed over the slightest trifle, he could hardly shout in the manner prescribed by the Regulations, yet these characteristics were tenuously related to his true nature, and Crazy Horse wasn't wrong in comparing him to Jean-Baptiste Bessières. Sugar was a born military man. He didn't abhor the Machine that exploits with the trick of love and hate, not at all, he didn't reject the system that erases the individual and fuses him into the perfect nucleus: on the contrary, he adored being a cog in the gear. "My trade is the finest in the world," he asserted. "I wouldn't change it even to become a king or a billionaire." And if you asked him who or what had led him to discover that vocation, he answered: "A click-clack." Then he said that in the Busto Arsizio firm he was very content: more than satisfied with his excellent job of technician, his fair salary, his kind of peaceful existence. But on arriving and leaving he had to punch a timecard which emitted an irritating sound, the typical sound of bourgeois boredom, click-clack, and one day he'd rebelled. He'd renounced the excellent job, the fair salary, the peaceful future, enlisted in the Incursori Battalion. Since then, not a single regret. Not a grain of nostalgia. And if you tried to understand how he could reconcile his trade with his shyness, his Sunday Masses, his Pater Nosters, you got lost in the labyrinths of the human soul. Those two aspects cohabited in him with disconcerting ease, they appeared in turn like the two faces of Doctor Jekyll who by night becomes the perfidious Mister Hyde and by day is again Doctor Jekyll.

He shut the door behind him, advanced on his treasures, began to inspect them one by one, and rather than a czar rapt in the contemplation of a Fabergé egg or a Duc de Berry absorbed in the enchantments of the *Très Riches Heures* he now seemed a floriculturist who examines every petal and pistil of his flowers to see if the greenhouse has been profaned by strangers. Excellent boys, the incursori in his squad, but a little undisciplined. They said be-sure-lieutenant-I-won't-touch, and instead they touched. That Palestinian matchbox, for example. Yesterday it was at the edge of the shelf, this morning half an inch farther in: someone had shifted it. He delicately picked it up, for the hundredth time he admired its ingenuity. You only needed to remove the matches, put a little Tnt in their place, slip a tiny fuse into it, then connect it to the flap, and when you pulled it to take a match: bang! The explosion caught you in the face. He placed the device back on the shelf. Ignoring the mechanical toys filled with penthrite that exploded when you wound the key, he halted in front of six plaster kittens and six doll's heads. He picked out a doll's head, he stroked its round face, its plump cheeks, its cute nose. Well, this one went beyond the effective crudity of the mechanical toys and the primitive ingenuity of the matchboxes. One picked it up saying what-a-pity, a-broken-doll, then tossed it away and blew up everything within a five-yard range. The same with the kittens. At Bourji el Barajni they were so proud of those doll's heads and kittens that, without explosive, they now manufactured them as souvenirs. Ten dollars apiece and the inscription "Palestinian Revolution." And what about the rain toy, the water pistol that instead of water emitted a jet of acid? What about cluster bombs, that is, the small antipersonnel mines the guerrillas had left on every sidewalk, in every alley, parking lot, abandoned house, and even in the schools?

He completed his inspection, he stepped next to a table where a four-hundred-pound bomb lay in a jumble of saws, drills, punches, screwdrivers, pliers, tongs, and hammers. It was an unexploded air bomb he had found in a courtyard and brought here to study its mechanism, but he didn't know its internal structure and though he'd deactivated the antidisassembly device he hadn't yet succeeded in defusing its ordnance... Can you imagine the funk one feels in dismantling a battery which may go off as soon as he skims it with a finger? Anyway, the real problem had cropped up when he'd tried to remove the cylinders containing the mechanical detonators: in the impact with the ground, the fuses had buckled so badly that their external grooving was almost gone. And the consequences were serious. The cylinders must be unscrewed with enormous caution, to unscrew them that way you must use a monkey wrench, but on the almost disappeared grooving the monkey wrench slipped away like a piece of wet soap and... Ergo, in a month he hadn't been able to move anything but the fuse in the tail: less crushed because the bomb had fallen properly. That is, head down. The fuse in the head, instead, hadn't shifted by a single millimeter. Yesterday he'd tried with the punch and the hammer. There was a tiny notch in the groove, so he hoped to turn it by resting the punch against the notch and tapping with the hammer. But with the punch and the hammer you strike blindly: you can't tell if the cylinder turns to the right or the left, and at the slightest error... "Sugaaar! You'll blow up the headquarters!" the Condor shouted. Well, maybe the best thing was to use his hands and nothing else. But in cases like this you need vigorous hands combined with a high-quality brain, and such an association could be found only in the league of two men: Angelo and Gino. Heh! With his bull's strength, Gino would move a greased mountain; with his intelligence, Angelo would immediately understand if the cylinder turned to the right or the left... But they were no longer under his command. Angelo had been stolen by Charlie and Gino had been taken by Falcon. All that remained from the old squad was a bunch of mediocrities like Rocco: a guy who boasted as many muscles as meninges. Meaning few. Furthermore, Rocco was in love. Always picking the daisy petals off and mumbling she-loves-me, she-loves-me-not. Who in the world would entrust an unexploded air bomb to a mediocrity in love?

"Condor Zed, Condor Zed!"

The walkie-talkie crackled with the Condor's authoritative voice, and Sugar almost snapped to attention.

"Condor Zed here, Condor One! At your orders, General, Sir!"

"Condor Zed! At Bourji el Barajni a suspicious truck is blocking the street between Camp Three and Camp Four!"

"A truck, sir...?"

"A truck, a truck! Head over immediately, I'll follow!"

"Yessir! Immediately, sir!"

And snatching up his tools, Sugar dashed out. Charlie, who was leaving the basement, had just the time to ask him were he was going and to wake Angelo. "Hurry up, son. Let's go and see what happens."

3

It was against every regulation to detach from the patrol, a squad leader should never stray far from his men, and in Bourji el Barajni it also was dangerous. Too many Shiites who came looking for a brawl, too many Khomeinists who joined the mullahs, tormenting the Italians on garrison. All of a sudden, however, Gino had halted between Camp Three and Camp Four, the two posts on the street where the Palestinians kept the monument to their Unknown Soldier. He had ordered his patrol to go and take a break at Camp Five, and remained alone. When a poem bursts inside you, and you stop to pin it down on paper, you can't have many people around: can you? Especially if you have a heavyweight's body and a ruddy face with an ogre's beard, plus two hands that seem designed to throw punches or employ a shovel, people don't understand that poems are for you a need like eating or drinking. They don't realize that through them you express your sadness, your dreams, your fears. That is, the anxieties of a disappointed twenty-five-year-old guy and the bad intuition the double slaughter has left you with... He made sure that the patrol had moved off. He sat at the foot of the monument, an ugly statue depicting a guerrilla armed with a Kalashnikov. Then, without putting down his M12, he opened the notebook Sister Françoise had given him, and wrote.

> The sun was bright that Sunday,
> a beautiful October sun,
> and I tasted it with my memory.
> Gulps of sweetness the remembrance
> of a childhood remote yet still present
> when the October sun rose
> ringing the bells of the first Mass
> and bringing the scent of the woods
> where I ran barefoot, pursued
> by my father's scolding voice.
> "Gino, come put your shoes on! We go to church!"
> The sun was bright and suddenly
> two blacks wings extinguished it.
> The wings of Death
> whose open beak pounced upon
> my unknown brothers
> my never met companions.
> It pounced, it seized them, it carried them up
> into the dark
> then flew away with no sound and yet
> promising to return.

Promising to return! Gino put Sister Françoise's notebook back in his pocket and curbed a shiver. How could he guess that Beirut had the black wings of Death? Until last year, for him, it was nothing but a tiny dot on the map. He didn't even know that the Palestinians lived here and not in Palestine, that there was bad blood between them and the Israelis, that besides those two there were the Sons of God and the Christians called Maronites after a Saint Maron who'd died fifteen centuries ago, that the Christians had it in for the Muslims, that the Muslims had it in for the Christians, that with the excuse of believing in different Gods they butchered each other like hogs... These details had emerged on the eve of his departure when he'd consulted a book then read the newspapers, and... He shook his head, dismayed. Don't think of it, he said to himself, don't get more sad than you are. Think of your Tuscany, of the Sundays when the sun rose to sound the bells for the first Mass and you ran barefoot in the woods. Think of your father who called out Gino-come-put-your-shoes-on, we-go-to-church. Think of the house where you were born... He smiled. For goodness sake, what a handsome house it was! So large that each room looked like a piazza. Sometimes he ran up to the attic, scrambled out onto the roof, and captured the sparrows that made their nests next to the gutters. To cook them. A cruelty. The fact is that children are cruel. Innocent and cruel, said the poet Rainer Maria Rilke. Mother, instead, used to say: "What doesn't poison, fills the stomach!" Which means, they didn't dine on steaks, at home. They dined on omelettes, potatoes, beans. Except for the days Father bought mortadella or went hunting. Once he'd gone with him, and with the first shot he'd bagged a wagtail. Poor wagtail. She was still warm when retrieved, a drop of blood gushed from her chest. But instead of arousing pity this had excited him, and driven him to fire at every creature that flew: finches, oxeyes, tree-creepers, thrushes. He was thirteen, in shooting he felt like a man, and nobody ever told him that the less you fire the more you are a man. But the poor wagtail had taken her revenge. And the finches, the oxeyes, the tree-creepers, the thrushes, also. Because on the way home he had been nabbed by the carabinieri and brought down to the station with Father. Questions and counterquestions, statements and counterstatements, admonishments, threats. "A boy cannot go hunting! Rifles are for adults!" Finally a loutish marshal had compiled a report full of syntactical blunders, not even a verb well spelled, and impounded the gun permit that Father had just renewed and paid for. What a sorrow. In fact he'd cried. "It's my fault, Father, my fault! Forgive me!" Then Father had done something he would never do again: he'd kissed him. On a cheek!

He closed his eyes, touched. Father was a peasant. One of those who like to be peasants and not follow the trend of settling down in the city to become greengrocers. He was called Bìghero, which means Hardy, and was small of stature but strong. He lifted the pig trough as if it were a soup bowl, tree trunks as if they were twigs, and he liked to say: "Gino resembles me!" He did. At seven he already drove the plow with the oxen, at ten he could hoe a field in a half-hour, at fourteen he lifted sacks weighing a hundredweight. Maybe because he ate so much. He started in the morning with half a loaf of bread, the one that mother made every Saturday, and at noon he could eat up an entire pot of sweet polenta. You know, the chestnut flour cooked with water and nothing else. Tasty! Not to mention the wine he drained instead of caffelatte. "One bottle of wine at the start of the day makes every problem go away," Father said. Beautiful times, beautiful places. In summer, when he didn't work the land, he went fishing for perch in the gully. He caught them with a sun-dried bamboo cane, a sewing thread for fishing line and a bent pin for the hook, then Mother fried them with the pumpkin blossoms. Tasty! After supper, the whole family played tombola with chickpeas, or stripped the corncobs and listened to Father's stories. Beautiful stories of witches and warlocks, because Father believed in enchantments and charms. The year the pigs had gotten sick, for instance, he had blamed it on a spell cast by the envious, and had asked the help of a warlock who dangling a coin with Pius IX's image had chanted: "Now go home, Bìghero. Your pigs are cured." Father had gone and found the pigs really cured. Sometimes, instead, he recounted the loves of the French kings and queens. Marie Antoinette, La Pompadour, etcetera. He knew them well because he wanted to compete in a television show called Lose-It-or-Double-It, and had chosen that subject because the TV people wouldn't let him choose Mussolini: a person he had loved a lot. "Sure, he made mistakes," he said. "But with him the trains ran on time." It was Father's only defect, this admiration for Mussolini. Otherwise, a saint. For example, he never slapped you in the face. Only a few kicks in the ass. Without hurting. Mother beat everywhere, instead. She hurt. And the reason was that at school he was very good in Italian and gymnastics. He wrote poems that the teacher praised and stood on the balance beam like an athlete, but he didn't do well in mathematics and smoked in class.

He closed his eyes, grumbled in amusement. His life had changed at eighteen, the summer they had sent him to visit Aunt Esmeralda who lived in Rome and had a suitor in uniform. A guy from Livorno who wore a red amaranth beret with a very strange badge: two wings springing from a kind of umbrella. "What beret is that?" he'd asked. "The paratroopers' beret, the beret of privilege," the suitor had answered. Struck by the word privilege, he'd gone to Livorno and enlisted and jumped. What a fear the first time! While plummeting downward at fifty yards per second, he only thought of Father's desperation: "It's a dangerous gadget, the parachute! If it doesn't open, you get smashed in a wheatfield!" So, with his heart in his throat he wondered: will it open? Well, it had opened. Suddenly he'd felt a tug, the enormous umbrella had swollen to pull him back upward for an instant, and what a shiver of happiness! He felt like a feather borne off by the wind, and fluttering in the midst of all that sky he shouted: "I'm flying! It's me, Gino, and I'm flying!" Thanks to the red amaranth beret, he had also discovered the sea. Another marvel. Because at home the water was only in the gully: the stream that tumbled among the moss-green rocks, and the pond where he fished for perch. A tiny pond that the shadow of the trees made very dark and melancholic. At Livorno, instead, it was everywhere: luminous, glorious, blue. By day the sea touched the horizon and by night it touched the stars. He'd learned to swim, to descend to the depths where he'd found fish of every kind and color, plants with tentacles, fairy-tale mountains, mysterious caverns. Stuff to write a hundred poems about. Then he'd been selected to serve in the incursori and never mind if among them there were many jerks who puffed out their chests, never mind if at a certain point he'd become a jerk too. One of those who go around with the roaring motorcycle as soon as they're off duty, and wear leather pants, boots with spurs, a jacket with the motto "Ride life and life will ride you." Or "Live to love and love to live." He had the mottoes sewn on by Aunt Esmeralda who in pursuit of her suitor now lived at Livorno and sewed them with a sigh: "Ma che lingua è, che vogliono dire queste parole, Gino? But what language is this? What do these words mean, Gino?" "È inglese, zia. It's English, Aunt," he answered. "Cuci, zia, cuci. Keep sewing, Aunt, keep sewing." He also wore T-shirts with phosphorescent skulls, spiked armbands, battery-powered earrings that lit up in the dark. He played the Californian macho and didn't care when Sugar protested Gino-you're-screwing-up-the-battalion's-dignity. Off duty one has the right to dress as he likes, right? The earrings hadn't lasted long. The battery ran out in a snap, without the light they weren't worth a damn, so he had given them up and bought a chain he kept in view on the handlebars of his roaring motorcycle. He felt so happy when people got scared and said: "Mind that guy. He's a hood." It was Angelo who made him understand that he was acting like a jerk. "Believe me, Gino: when you arrive at the pizzeria all dressed in black, with the skulls on your stomach, the spurs on your boots, I feel sorry for you." A real friend, Angelo. Apart from Sister Françoise, the only friend he had found in those years. Because, like Sister Françoise, Angelo judged him by what he was inside, not by how he seemed on the outside...

"Dakikatain, dakikatain!"

He opened his eyes, shaken by the sudden rumbling of a truck, then by a voice yelling deki-katein. Deki katein? What the devil did deki katein mean? And where had that truck come from, where was it going? Completely obstructing the street it now halted, the driver jumped to the ground, raised his right hand, spread his index and middle fingers in the V-shaped victory sign, then vanished into an alley and the doors of the houses slammed shut. Gino jumped to his feet. He dashed toward the abandoned vehicle, inspected it. How peculiar... Everything seemed normal and yet the driver had fled spreading his fingers in the V-shaped victory sign. Why? By Judas priest, the third truck! Without a kamikaze, this time! Armed with a time bomb! He grabbed the walkie-talkie. He called the Bourji el Barajni sector head: "Attention, attention! A suspicious truck has halted between Camp Three and Camp Four! The driver has fled, and I think it's about to explode! Take shelter, take shelter!" Then he crouched at the foot of the statue of the Unknown Soldier and waited for the explosion. But the explosion didn't come, and little by little he understood: what sense would it make to waste the third truck in order to kill him and a few inhabitants of the street? It was a harmless truck, then! The driver had jumped out because he needed to urinate! Spreading his fingers in a V-shape he didn't mean victory, he meant I'm-going-to-urinate, I'll-be-back-in-two-minutes! Dakikatain: two minutes. Now he remembered! He grabbed the walkie-talkie again. He called back to explain the mistake, to give the all-clear. But the sector head was already arriving with six paratroopers followed by Sugar, by his squad, by the Condor, by his escort, by Pistoia, and finally by Charlie with Angelo. And, with the exception of the last two, they all pounced on the truck without listening to explanations. Least of all, the Condor, who ecstatically led the assault.

* * *

"You'll tell us later, incursore!"

"But general..."

"Silence, I said, silence! And you, Sugar, search the cargo bed!"

"I searched it, general, and there's nothing! Now I'll search the cab!"

"The cab, right, the cab! Underneath the seats! In the engine compartment! Between the windows! Tear it all up, tear it all up!"

"I am, general, I am!"

"And the storage spaces: quick! The tool compartment!"

"The storage spaces are locked! We need a screwdriver!"

"Forget the screwdriver, God blasted! Break it with a pickax, Pistoia!"

"I am, general, I am!"

"And the spare tires, the spare tires! Deflate them, God dammit!"

"We have, general, we have. But they're empty! Now we deflate the others!"

"To hell with deflating! Rip them apart with a pickax! The explosive could be there!"

"The pickax won't rip them, general!"

"Rip them with a bayonet!"

"No, not the bayonet, general! My Sardinian pattada is better!" Pistoia yelled brandishing a sharp dagger, his Sardinian pattada, and hurling himself at the tires.

"The pattada, good, the pattada!"

They looked like grasshoppers in a wheatfield. Ripping the tires, uprooting the seats, unhinging the engine, breaking the tool compartment, whatever came under their pickax or bayonet or dagger, they dismantled the truck with the speed of grasshoppers who devour a wheatfield. And except for Angelo and Charlie everybody participated in the vandalism. So, when the driver returned, nothing remained of his truck but a picked carcass. And an agonizing wail in the street.

"Yahallah! Oh God, yahallah! Dakikatain, two minutes, I said! Dakikatain farsar, two minutes to piss!"

Along with the agonizing wail, Gino's disheartened grumbling.

"I knew it, but you didn't let me open my mouth!"

Along with Gino's disheartened grumbling, the Condor's pleased warning.

"The alarm must be given also for a mosquito, incursore!"

Along with the Condor's pleased warning, Pistoia's cheerful giggle.

"We've barked up the wrong tree, but we've had a good time!"

Along with Pistoia's cheerful giggle, Sugar's bitter comment.

"This isn't the way to do things. This wasn't a professional job."

Along with Sugar's bitter comment, Charlie's voice consoling the tearful driver.

"Sanafta lakom! We'll reimburse you!"

Angelo approached Gino and affectionately squeezed his shoulders.

"Don't blame yourself, Gino."

"But I do," Gino replied. "Look how they destroyed that truck! It looks like my father's tractor when it rolled into the bottom of the ravine!"

"Yes. S = K ln W."

"What?"

"It's an equation, Gino, a formula."

Gino smiled sadly.

"And what does it mean, what is it for?"

"It means chaos, Gino. And it is for finding another formula..."

"Which one?"

"Yes. The formula of Life."

"Is there one?"

"There must be. There is."

"Uhm... Know what? Whether there is or not, all I would like is to shave my beard and my head, then to go with the Tibetan monks. Yeah... the ones who dress in orange and keep a little bell on their toes to warn the ants move-along-otherwise-I-crush-you. I'm so tired of this work, Angelo... I thought the red amaranth beret would bring me into a garden full of fountains, and instead it brought me into a place without a drop of water. I feel so thirsty, here. I said it also to Sister Françoise..."

"Sister Francoise?"

"Yeah. The little nun from the convent who works at the Rizk... Ciao, Angelo."

"Ciao, Gino."

They separated, and Angelo went off with Charlie. Gino, with his patrol. Very soon, however, Gino stopped again. Once again he took Sister Françoise's notebook, and wrote a poem that was bursting inside him. A poem about himself.

> So I live inside myself
> day after day
> each day secretly expecting another day
> discouraged, disheartened, always alone
> over the chasm burst open by a garden
> that I loved and when I used to walk

to drink from a fountain now sealed up
I wished I fell inside it with my thirst.
But when I think of what I do not have
that I could have and that I need so much
I dare the chasm, I start again to walk
to write my fable
without a future, perhaps, and yet
brimful with dreams and rich in fountains as though
I faced a beautiful tomorrow.

In the headquarters courtyard, meanwhile, Angelo paced up and down like a glum Hamlet fidgeting on the misty glacis of Elsinore. And his thirst was about to be relieved by his Ophelia.

4

It had distressed him, that thousandth victory of Boltzmannian entropy: at each blow of dagger or pickax or bayonet, at each bite of the grasshoppers destroying the truck, a sense of nausea and defeat. It had saddened him, Gino's disheartenment: his need to take off the red amaranth beret and go with the Tibetan monks. Gino was the only friend he had, the only one who could penetrate the wall of his incommunicability. But, above all, he'd been disturbed by the remarks Charlie had made before going to the Condor. "I knew it would be a false alarm. Didn't you hear the muezzin this morning?" "No, chief. I was sleeping." "Well, if you didn't this morning, you will at noon. And at sunset, and every time the prayer comes from the minaret. Keep your ear cocked, son. And stop prattling about unbecomingness, disloyalty." Unbecomingness, disloyalty? He'd immediately rushed downstairs to ask what the muezzin had said. But nobody knew. "Bah! He probably said that Allah is great, Muhammad is his prophet, and woe to those who drink wine or eat pork," had answered Fifì. "Moi je ne parle même pas l'italien, penses-tu si je peux comprendre le muezzin qui parle arabe. I don't even speak Italian, how can I understand a muezzin who speaks Arabic," had answered Bernard le Français. And Stefano: "Why don't you ask Martino?" Martino was outside the headquarters. So he'd gone upstairs to wait for him, and he now paced up and down the courtyard like a glum Hamlet who fidgets on the misty glacis of Elsinore. He sighed. Ignoring two voices that argued nearby, the voice of Sugar and of a war correspondent called the-Saigon-journalist because she'd spent many years in Vietnam, he leaned against the outside wall of the veranda. Maybe the muezzin had said nothing that they should be ashamed of. Maybe his words somehow erased the cynicism of giving away plasma, and this was the reason why Charlie had jabbed at him stop-prattling-etcetera. Maybe he was forgetting the interminable minute during which they awaited death together, staring into one another's eyes as if they wanted to enter one into the brain of the other, into the heart of the other, to exchange their souls... Maybe he should have tried to understand him a little more, a little better... He sighed again. He started to listen to the two voices that argued nearby.

"But I wasn't raised in a monastery!" Sugar said. "They didn't teach me to turn the other cheek and forgive! They taught me to shoot, to cut throats, to kill in the most effective manner and with the fewest possible casualties! I tell you: the enemy must be eliminated when he's on his knees! It is then that we must stick the knife in his belly! Whether you're shocked by it or not."

"I'm not shocked, lieutenant," the Saigon journalist replied "I've seen it with my eyes, the wickedness you've studied on paper and in drills. About war I know more than you do, and human ferocity no longer shocks me. It doesn't even surprise me, anymore. Inconsistency does, instead. Because first you tell me you believe in a merciful God, a God who teaches how to turn the other cheek and forgive, then you tell me that the enemy must be killed when he's on his knees. So, do you believe in that God or not?"

"Sure I do, sure! But I'm a soldier, and the trade of a soldier is the trade of killing. It's other things too, in fact you don't choose it out of a taste for killing, but the final end is killing. And believing in God doesn't keep me from being a soldier who does his work well. That is, who knows how to kill well: by the most efficient means and without any arguments. Because a soldier must not argue. He must obey and that's all."

"No matter what the order is. Right?"

"Of course! No matter what the order is!"

"Then, if your general orders you to cut my throat, you cut it. Against your will, maybe, but you do."

"Of course I do! And, forgive me for saying so, without liking it or disliking it. When he kills, a soldier neither likes his task nor dislikes it. He does his job and that's all."

He moved away with a gesture of annoyance, went back to pacing the courtyard up and down. Well... He certainly wasn't the type who joins the Tibetan monks, Sugar. In order to obey and be obeyed, he would cut his own throat then place his own corpse under arrest. Once at Livorno, he'd sent him and Gino to practice nighttime orientation. Twelve miles on foot, no moonlight, no compass. I-want-to-make-sure-you-find-your-way-without-a-compass-and-keeping-the-North-Star-as-your-only-reference. They had immediately gotten lost in the wood. A wood so dense that the sky seemed to be made of leaves and you couldn't figure out which way was north and which way was south. So, they'd called him by radio: "Lieutenant, we're lost in a wood. We cannot tell which way is north and which way is south." Answer: "Look at the North Star!" "But there isn't any North Star, here, lieutenant." "What do you mean, there isn't?!? The North Star is halfway between the Great Chariot and Cassiopeia's Belt, five lengths from the lower rod of the Great Chariot, meaning the two stars on the other side of the cart: did you forget it?!?" "No, lieutenant. But we can't see the sky, we cannot see the stars. All we can see are leaves." "If you don't see the stars, look for them!" "In the wood?!?" "In the wood, yes, in the wood!" They'd started to look for the stars as if the stars were mushrooms, and at dawn Gino had really found the mushrooms. An entire meadow of boletus, agaric, pores, chanterelles. He'd filled his knapsack, brought them to Sugar, and: "Lieutenant, we didn't find the North Star but we did find these. They're good. Cook them." The result: six days of arrest for both. The sentence: "Guilty of diverting their attention and looking for mushrooms during an exercise in nighttime orientation." Just the opposite of Charlie who had never punished him. Never! Not even for the insubordination committed the Sunday of the double slaughter when he'd run off with his jeep and his driver. Not even for the trick committed yesterday when he'd hood-winked Eagle with the words General's-orders. A hell of a man, Charlie. The kind you could trust, he told himself. And at that very moment Martino arrived.

"Were you looking for me, Angelo?"

"Yes. What did the muezzin say this morning?"

Martino looked at him, surprised.

"The sentence, of course!"

"What sentence?"

"The sentence Charlie gave to Zandra Sadr!"

"To Zandra Sadr?"

"Yes. Charlie gave it to Zandra Sadr, and Zandra Sadr gave it to the muezzins."

"What does this sentence say?"

"It says: Ma'a tezi al-talieni! Al-talieni bayaatùna el dam! Al-talieni ekhuaatùna bil dam!"

"Translate it."

"Don't touch the Italians! The Italians give us blood! The Italians are our blood brothers!"

"What...?!?"

"Beautiful, huh? It sounds good in Arabic too. It has the cadence of a folk song, and when Zandra Sadr heard it..."

But Angelo was no longer listening. Overwhelmed by the impotent grief that smothers us each time we are betrayed by a person we loved and trusted, he had turned his back on Martino and approached the Leopard. He asked the tankman to shift the vehicle, let him pass, he passed, he turned in rue de l'Aérodrome. And if someone had asked him where he was going, he wouldn't have known how to answer. He didn't even see the people and the cars that darted along the avenue. So he didn't see the taxi that braked to an abrupt halt to drop off a gorgeous woman with long and sleek hair that waved in glitters of gold. He didn't see the gorgeous woman who ran toward him and called him with an exultant trill.

"Angel! My angel!"

He noticed her only when she was in front of him with her inviting smile and her disquieting violet eyes, her contagious gaiety. And as usual he understood almost nothing of what she said in English. A complaint about too many days spent without seeing him? An avowal of her burning impatience to see him again? Nevertheless he understood very well the monotonous invitation, the usual refrain let's-make-love. And suddenly he desired her as he had never desired anything, anybody. And, more than a desire, a need. The need of joining his body to her body, not to get from it a moment of ecstacy but to forget what he considered Charlie's betrayal. And he heard his voice saying what he had always refused to say.

"Tonight, Ninette."

The exultant trill became a shriek of joy.

"Tonight?!? Really tonight?"

"Really tonight, Ninette."

"Promise?"

"I promise, Ninette."

"Oh, darling, I'm so happy! I'll come back at seven, okay?"

"Okay, Ninette."

"We'll go to a hotel and stay there until morning, okay?"

"Okay, Ninette."

Then he went back to the headquarters, and it took him a while to realize that something very important and very dangerous had hap-

pened. Something that gave him an acute discomfort, almost the presentiment of a tragedy, of a catastrophe that because of his tonight-
Ninette would one day befall the two of them and the others. And
unexpected questions, unforeseen considerations, began to haunt him.
What if Ninette were an emissary of the Khomeinists, a lure dangled by
the Sons of God? In this treacherous city, this den of ambushes, every
suspicion became a hypothesis on the margins of reality. And since she
kept concealing her last name, her address, that hypothesis was more
than legitimate. Moreover, he sensed an odd side in Ninette: a peculiarity which was at the same time enigmatic and abnormal. The maniacal
tenacity with which she had circumvented him for months, for example. Or the uncontrollable gaiety, the irrepressible euphoria which at
moments turned into pools of inertia: gloomy bouts of abulia that
seemed to hide a tormenting secret... But all at once he decided that far
from being enigmatic or abnormal, far from being an emissary of the
Khomeinists, a lure dangled by the Sons of God, she simply was a
woman who offered love. Too much love. Thus, far from announcing a
catastrophe which one day would befall the two of them and the others, his acute discomfort came from the risk of being suffocated by her
excess of love... Or by his fear of love, his scanty knowledge of love? In
order to fill that scantiness, once he'd looked in the dictionary for the
word "amore" and found the following definition: "Masculine noun
which derives from the Latin word *Amor*. It means strong attachment
to a person; sentient rapture that makes one desire the affection and
company of a person; intense emotional or sexual attraction; total dedication to a principle." He'd shown it to the battalion chaplain and the
chaplain had shaken his head: "Oh, no. Love is much more than that.
It's giving ourselves to a human being, living for that human being, it's
renouncing ourselves for him or her. It's unselfishness, generosity. The
utmost generosity." Well... He'd never given himself to anybody, never
lived for anybody, and the idea of renouncing himself horrified him as
much as the idea of being loved in that way. If you love or are loved in
that way, you depend on the person who loves you or whom you love
as much as a newborn depends on his mother, a fetus on the placenta
that surrounds it, and you're no longer an individual. You're an appendix of the human being to whom you've given yourself or who has
given himself or herself to you, for whom you live or who lives for you,
and love becomes the worst form of slavery. No thanks. If so, he preferred friendship. A friend doesn't require what a lover requires,
doesn't demand exclusive contracts or total surrender, doesn't bind
you with the wicked fetters of sacrifice. And he had to tell it to her:

"Ninette, I need you. I desire you. But I don't love you nor do I want to love or be loved in the way the battalion chaplain describes." The point was the language, the fact that they hadn't a language in common. In French she went on refusing to murmur even a bonjour and, as for him, his English was still so poor that he couldn't even manage the auxiliary verb *do*. To say that he didn't love her, for example, where should he place the *do*? Where the French place the *pas*, Ninette-moi-je-ne-t'aime-pas? Or somewhere else? Ninette-I-do-love-you-not... Ninette-I-not-love-you-do... Ninette, I-do-not-love-you... He finally concluded that the problem could be resolved by writing a letter then having it translated by Martino, and did so. But when the letter was ready and closed in the envelope, he felt it needed to be mitigated by the offer of a gift and went out to look for a jewelry store.

He found it at Gobeyre, the Shiite quarter opposite Shatila, in a street called rue Farrouk. It was an old man sitting on a baby chair and smoking marghile who pointed it out. A blind old man whose sensitiveness divined at once the identity of the person near him and the purpose of his presence. "Cherchez-vous la bijouterie, mon soldat? Are you looking for the jewelry store, soldier?" a quiet voice asked while two milky pupils rose to see what they couldn't see. "C'est derrière vous, mon soldat. It's behind you, soldier." He entered it with the inexplicable feeling which had gripped him on the bench of the Shiite clinic in sensing Ninette's unseizable yet tangible presence. He doubtfully examined the goods. "Pour une femme musulmane ou chrétienne? For a Muslim or Christian woman?" the salesman inquired. "Chrétienne, Christian." "In that case I have just what you're looking for." And the last object one would expect to find in the most Shiite area of the Western Zone sprang out of a locked drawer: a gold chain holding a cross in the shape of an anchor. Or an anchor that was actually a cross. The upright and the crossbar formed in fact a cross with a tiny Christ and a minuscule ruby gushing from his chest. Certainly a residue of the happy Beirut, of the good days when the city wasn't divided in two and the Western Zone was inhabited also by the Christians, Angelo said to himself. So he bought it, and only later did he realize that a cross-shaped anchor was the least suitable gift to accompany a letter which contested ties and rejected love. But it was almost seven, by now: too late to return and change it. Ninette always arrived so punctually.

*   *   *

She arrived punctually as usual, and she sparkled with happiness. He felt nervous, on the contrary, pierced by unexpected guilt complexes. "À quel hôtel, to which hotel?" was the clumsy question he greeted her with. "A Junieh hotel," she trilled. Junieh? It was another city, Junieh: twelve miles from the center of Beirut and forty-five minutes from the headquarters. "No," he protested in dismay. "Yes," she retorted in amusement. Then she pushed him into a taxi that quickly reached avenue Nasser and rue Argàn and the Pine Wood boulevard where his anxiety surfaced again to bring back the presentiment of a tragedy to come. This time he didn't listen, though. His rationalism refused to. And when the taxi stopped at the passage of Tayoune, the nearest one to cross the Green Line and enter the Eastern Zone, the feelings dissolved. "Où allez-vous?" the French paratroopers standing at the checkpoint asked him, surprised to see an armed sergeant traveling with a woman. "À l'hôpital Rizk," he smoothly answered. "Bon, passez." The hotel was an ugly, rickety building. Its concierge, a boor full of hostility. "Sijil, documents." With contemptuous unconstraint Ninette placed a fifty-dollar bill in his hand, and at once the hostility became slavish obsequiousness. The slavish obsequiousness, a key with a tag: "Chambre Royale." Royal Room. Royal?!? It only contained a large bed with a blanket full of unequivocal stains, a night table with a little lamp, two wobbly chairs, a filthy washbasin, an equally filthy bidet, and tiled walls. A detail which suggested that before being a hotel the squalid place had been a brothel. The window overlooked an internal courtyard from which rough voices and nauseating cooking odors mounted. He drew back, disappointed.

"Ninette!"

"It doesn't matter, darling," she giggled, and with a shrug she tossed aside the blanket full of unequivocal stains. Then she made sure that the sheets were clean, she undressed, lay down on the bed, and held out her arms.

"Please, darling."

Naked, she was beautiful with an entirely different beauty. Her body lost its boldness and surprisingly evoked the fragility of a Murano glass, of a precious goblet which asks to be held with caution and grace. Delicate, her round breasts and her graceful hips. Transparent, her skin at times etched by the shadow of tenuous veins: almost a reminder that she could easily break. "Please, darling, please," she repeated while the barbarian queen's features languished with an almost imploring pliability. But Angelo remained near the door, without even putting down the M12. He had fancied a different approach, a slow and harmonious contact initiated together after the letter and the gift, and this impudent hurry displeased him. It offended him.

"First my letter and my gift," said, in English, an assertive voice.

The outstretched arms lowered, a sorrowful stupor darkened the disquieting violet eyes.

"What letter, darling? What gift?"

In silence he held out the envelope with the letter and the little box with the gift. In silence she took them, laid the envelope on the pillow, opened the little box, looked at the cross-shaped anchor. She looked for several seconds, with a mysterious smile, slowly caressing the minuscule ruby that gushed from the chest of the tiny Christ. Then she put it back in the box and made the gesture of leaving the bed to thank him with a hug. But the assertive voice stopped her.

"The letter."

"Now, darling?"

"Now."

"Okay, darling."

She knelt in the middle of the bed, opened the envelope, began reading the letter. Overcoming the displeasure, meanwhile, he struggled with doubts. Suppose his warnings and clarifications hurt her pride, suppose she burst into tears... All at once she looked so defenseless, so vulnerable. Maybe because a naked body always looks defenseless, vulnerable, even an insect can harm it, or maybe because her precious goblet's fragility dispelled the contemptuous unconstraint of the woman who had subdued the concierge with the fifty-dollar bill, she now seemed so easy to hurt... Her brow tightened, her lips clenched, she read with apparent detachment. But now and then she winced as if poked by a needle. He suddenly freed himself of the rifle. He placed it on the floor and went to her.

"Ninette..."

She stopped reading, refolded the letter, gave it back to him. Then she raised a grave, intelligent face, the face of a person who knows, and smiled again her mysterious smile.

"You're a very innocent boy, my angel. Maybe because you live too little and think too much. Think less, and live more."

What had she said? He looked at her in confusion.

"I don't understand, Ninette."

"It's better that way, darling. Much better... Because, if you did, I should tell you what I don't want to. Then you would run away and he would die again."

"I don't understand, Ninette."

"He would die again, and this time I would die too. I want to live, instead."

"I don't understand, Ninette."

"I hate death too much, darling. Too much. I hate it even more than loneliness, pain, sorrow, grief. And the word goodbye."

"I don't understand! Parle français, please! Speak French!"

"Never, darling. Never. Now come to me, please."

And before he could answer, two expert hands removed his belt which fell onto the floor. They removed his jacket, his shirt, his pants, all the rest. Then two tender arms encircled his body to drag it down into a well of sweetness, and the squalid room of the ex-brothel really became a Royal Room. In the courtyard the rough voices faded away, the nauseating cooking odors vanished, and so did the image of the filthy washbasin, of the filthy bidet, of those last days' nightmares. The decapitated head inside the helmet, the little girl sunk into the water-closet, the child dead of blood loss, the shattered truck. And Gino who wanted to join the Tibetan monks, Sugar who absolved the trade of killing, the muezzin who chanted don't-touch-the-Italians, the-Italians-give-us-blood, the-Italians-are-our-blood-brothers, Charlie who had disappointed him, of the equation $S = K \ln W$. And even the presentiment of a tragedy to come, of a catastrophe that because of that night would one day befall the two of them and the others. And he abandoned himself to the joy of living. Not of thinking: of living. And loving. Perhaps.

Along the Street Without a Name, meanwhile, an olive-green Mercedes kept passing by the Twenty-Three. And in Gobeyre two characters named Rashid and Khalid-Passepartout were about to enter the scene.

CHAPTER FIVE

1

THE REAL SOLDIER lies to himself when he says that he hates war. He loves it in a profound way. And not because he's a particularly wicked or bloodthirsty man but because, as paradoxical as it may seem, he loves the vitality that war carries inside itself. With the vitality, the challenge and the gamble and the mystery. On the stage of the ambiguous comedy called "peace," this mystery does not exist. You already know that the show consists of several acts and that after the first act you'll see the second, after the second you'll see the third: the uncertainties concern only the development of the story and its epilogue. On the stage of the unambiguous tragedy called "war," instead, you never know what will happen. Whether you're a spectator or protagonist, you always wonder if you'll see the end of the first act. And the second act is a possibility. The third, a hope. The epilogue, a hypothesis. You can die at any moment, in war, at any moment you can be removed from the cast or the audience. Everything is an uncertainty, there, an interrogative which makes you hold your breath. But precisely for that, in war you vibrate with an exasperated vitality: your eyes are more alert, your senses more awake, your thoughts more lucid. So you notice any detail, you perceive any odor, any sound, any taste. And, if you have brains, through it you study existence as no philosopher ever will; you analyze men as no psychologist ever will, you understand them as you will never understand them in a time and in a place of peace. Finally, if you're a hunter or a gambler, in it you amuse yourself as you never had and never will in the forest or on the tundra or at the roulette table. Because the atrocious game of war is the hunt of hunts, the challenge of challenges, the gamble of gambles. The hunt for Man, the challenge to Death, and the gamble with Life. All excesses which the real soldier needs.

He needs them because in such excesses he sees the positive sides, the advantages he gains. Farewell to the quotidian problems, the worries that in a time and in a place of peace seemed so grave and maybe were so: the children to raise, the taxes to pay, the debts to settle, the exam to take, the job to keep. Farewell to the necessities that there and then appeared to be inescapable: the air conditioner to install, the car to buy, the overcoat to replace, the molar to crown, the vacations to organize. When death can snatch you at any moment, and survival is the only thing that counts, the rest becomes a laughable business. As a consequence, the real soldier cannot stay away from war, and as soon as he finds a pretext he rushes to it without considering the dangers he'll have to face: the discomforts he'll have to undergo, the pains he'll have to suffer, the infamies he'll have to perform. And if he doesn't die there, if he doesn't leave there a piece of his body, back at home he will feel for the war a nostalgia which will consume him till the next pretext: a regret will accompany him to his grave. He'll talk about nothing else. He'll bore his relatives and friends with his memories of war, his war stories, his war experiences. The eternal story of the day a bullet missed him by a hair, of the night he was nearly hit by a bomb, of the dawn his company got hemmed in by such shelling that each of them feared he would never see the sun again, but they did because they launched a counterattack that left three hundred twenty enemy corpses on the field etcetera. Yes, for him no enjoyment or adventure will ever be comparable to those he had in the war. And without it he'll fade, he'll get heavy, he'll age. The real soldier is a masochist. He is also an egoist who doesn't worry about what he does, about the consequences his acts will have for himself or his fellow men, and very rarely does he pose himself moral questions. While the train or the ship or the airplane carries him toward the dangers and the discomforts and the sufferings he will endure, the infamies he will bear or commit, he only thinks of his liberation. Hallelujah! The bonds of social brotherhood are cut, the annoyances of the family are set aside, the yawns of boredom are forgotten. And so are the rules that fix what is good, what is bad. Hallelujah, hallelujah! Soon he will again meet Death, meaning Life, and he'll be at peace with himself.

Whether they admitted it or not, this was the case of many Italians in Beirut. It was the case of the Condor, it was the case of Charlie, it was the case of Sugar, of Crazy Horse, of Sandokan. But above all it was the case of Pistoia, a great gambler and a real hunter, who stayed in Beirut for the sake of his personal amusement. The one just described. And this explains the incident that tonight would insert itself in the mosaic of causalities upon which destiny feeds.

*   *   *

Pistoia twisted his lean face into a wrathful frown, opened his large mouth wide, vomited out a couple of dreadful curses, then removed the blue jacket he had put on to visit his fiancées and slipped back into his uniform. By Christopher Columbus, what a swindle! Just today, when he had his triple rendezvous with Joséphine and Geraldine and Caroline! He was sorry especially for that pressure cooker called Joséphine, a wolfess who surely did not use her bed to preach the Gospels. Because experience counts: right? It prolongs the embrace, it doubles the fun... Geraldine, no. She lacked experience, Geraldine, training. Seventeen years versus his own forty-two, understand? In fact, to give her a bang you had to settle accounts with her mother. Where-are-you-going, captain, where-are-you-taking-her. Just-around-the-corner, madame, to-have-a-coffee. Don't-bother, captain, I'll-make-the-coffee. After which, she really made the damn coffee, and goodbye to the bang. However, if you managed to sneak away and get her into a hotel, what freshness! What candor! "T'è piaciuto, Pistoia? Sono stata brava? Did you like that, Pistoia? Was I good?" As for Caroline, what to say? Appetite comes from eating, one cherry leads to another, and when you have at your disposal a basketful of cherries, you don't bother counting! They lived in the same building, Joséphine and Geraldine and Caroline. The first on the third floor, the second on the second, the third on the first. Actually he had met Geraldine on the second floor while descending from Joséphine's third floor, and Caroline on the first floor while descending from Geraldine's second floor. And, since Caroline was a friend of Joséphine and Geraldine who told her all their secrets, she had stopped him. "Come, monsieur le capitaine, come, make yourself comfortable, let me offer you a drink." Then, between drinks: "Ah, how lucky those two are! My husband falls asleep as soon as his head hits the pillow... I'll die without knowing love." He had immediately offered his services: "Don't cry, Madame Caroline. I'll take care of it. That's how I stay in shape." Let's be honest: staying in shape on each floor was a chore. Afterwards, he felt like an octogenarian who's made the circuit of the Seven Churches on foot, and the Condor got angry. "Pistoia-a-a! You have the cock where the gray matter should be!" More or less, what his wife shouted on the telephone. A lovely woman, his wife, a beauty. But more jealous than Othello cuckolded by Desdemona. No use gulling her with the answer: "Silly goose! Having three little fiancées in Beirut doesn't mean I am unfaithful! It is you whom I love!" Nor was there any point in answering the Condor: "General, what else can I do if I'm a romantic and a generous person?" He didn't even understand that the triple chore was a challenge to fate. Because Joséphine and Geraldine and Caroline were Guelphs, meaning Christians, and being Guelphs they lived in the Guelphs' district. Meaning the Eastern Zone. So, in order to visit them, he had to cross the Green Line. That is, to deal with Ghibellines on guard at the checkpoints. Meaning the Amal etcetera. By Christopher Columbus! If on your way you run into a gang of Ghibellines with more buttfuckers and shitlickers and dickpullers than usual, at the very least you risk being kidnapped: right?

He snorted sardonically. Guelphs and Ghibellines, right. No matter how hard you turn it over, you end up realizing that in this fucking world nothing new ever happens. What else was Beirut if not an eternal battle of Montaperti with the Christians in place of the Guelphs and the Muslims in place of the Ghibellines? Just for that reason he had enjoyed so much destroying the Ghibelline's truck in Bourji el Barajni! Enjoyed, yes. Had it been possible, he would have plunged his Sardinian pattada even into the driver's heart. In fact this morning, when he'd woken to that al-talieni-ekhuaatùna-bil-dam, he'd rushed to the Condor and: "General, as your Austrian colleague General Radetzky used to say, fucking abroad helps one learn languages. So, I've learned a little bit of Arabic and I know that al-talieni means the-Italians, ekhuaatùna means are-brothers, bil-dam means of-blood. And I want to inform you that I don't have any brothers, here. All my brothers are in the town that gave me this name, Pistoia. So, what kind of game are we playing?" But the Condor hadn't batted an eyelash: "An intelligent game, Pistoia." Intelligent?!? Was it intelligent to respond to hexogen with gifts of blood plasma, to answer threats with salaams? Was it intelligent to bear the contempt of those goddam Saracens, to let them run around with their Kalashnikovs and Rpg, to hold fire when they burst into Shatila or Bourji el Barajni provoking the Italians and frightening the Palestinians? Not that he cared about the Palestinians, let's be clear. They were Ghibellines too, and until yesterday they'd broken Beirut balls more than their ancestors at the time when they used to ransack Livorno... The fact is that the Condor listened too much to Charlie, he hung upon his advice like Marie de' Medici hung upon Richelieu's suggestions, and Charlie trusted too much the ferocious Saladin. That is, Zandra Sadr. He wouldn't get it into his head that promises don't mean a thing to the Arabs, that in the same moment they whimper blood-brothers they send you trucks and kamikaze. And if you ex-

plained this to him, if you reminded him that the Koran doesn't prohibit lying, that it even praises and encourages those who tell lies for
the glory of Islam, he growled: "Shut up, you fascist." Or: "Close your
trap, you friend of Gassàn." Yessir, he was. Every time he went to
dance on the mattress with Joséphine and Geraldine and Caroline, he
stopped at the Bodaru barracks of the Eighth Brigade to exchange a
few words with him. Because he was a guy on the ball, that Gassàn. A
Superguelph with the trimmings, a real lansquenet. Moreover, he
spoke perfect Italian. He had learned it at the Military School of Civitavecchia during a course for foreign officers, and perfected it at the
Paratrooper School in Pisa where they had met. Plus he had guts.
Whether it was necessary or not, he eliminated the Ghibellines without
moving an eyebrow. And, finally, he knew what Charlie would never
understand: forget the communists and the capitalists! The next war
wouldn't take place between the rich and the poor: it would break out
between the Guelphs and the Ghibellines! That is, between those who
eat pig meat and those who don't, those who drink wine and those
who don't, those who mumble the Pater Noster and those who whimper Allah rassullillah! "Pistoia, we are returning to the Crusades," Gassàn always grumbled. And at times he added: "Or have we already
returned?"

He swung his gaunt slouching body, he rolled his playful and covetous eyes. If only! Hadn't he come to Beirut with that hope? These
Multinational Forces remind me of the Crusades, he'd said to himself,
they make me think of the great days when we fought the Moors. Fine,
fine! With the excuse of protecting the Palestinians, let's go to fire a few
shots from arquebus and springald. And while leaving Pisa he felt like
Tancredi of Altavilla: the Crusader who along with his uncle
Boemondo of Taranto followed Godfrey of Bouillon, delivered the
Holy Sepulcher, pilfered the treasure of the mosque of Umar, collected
scads of Clorindas and Florindas and Teodolindas living on the same
floor. That is, in the harem. By Christopher Columbus, what a godsend! Instead, and apart from the Clorindas and Florindas and Teodolindas, here he was: playing the good samaritan who hands out
plasma and busts his balls in Shatila. Yessirs, Shatila! This was the goddam place where he had to go in a while! Because, distrusting Falcon
and Eagle, every night the Condor inspected by himself the Bourji el
Barajni and Shatila posts. But tonight he had to scold Sandokan for the
bad job done in placing the antiaircraft machine guns at Sierra Mike,
and which scapegoat to send in his place? Which, if not poor Pistoia
who already dressed in blue was set to go dancing on the mattress with

Joséphine and Geraldine and Caroline? To say nothing of the responsibility. Because the problem was not Bourji el Barajni, it was Shatila!
The fucking casbah of Shatila, the bloody rectangle of five hundred by
a thousand yards in which the cravings of both the Shiites and the
governmentals concentrated. The Shiites', for the simple reason that
they needed it for ruling the Western Zone; the governmentals', for
keeping their control over the city.

Besides, to understand the fucking problem, you only had to look at
the fucking map. The north side intersected with Sabra over which the
French hardly presided anymore: merde-alors, je-me'en-fiche, and so
on. In fact the goddam Saracens wandered through Sabra as if in the
desert. They only lacked the camels... The south side skirted the Street
Without a Name: a most important artery because on the right it became the Damascus Road, on the left it flowed into the littoral of
Ramlet el Baida... The west side was bordered by avenue Chamoun, a
good road to reach the Old City and the northern coast... The east side
opened into avenue Nasser and consequently fronted Gobeyre, the epi-
center of the Amal militia and the spearhead of the Shiite advance... By
Christopher Columbus and Giovanni da Verrazzano and Amerigo Ves-
pucci put together! To overrun Shatila, the Ghibellines only had to pass
through Sabra or to cross avenue Nasser and slip into some alley or lane
or path: it seemed like a slab of cheese with holes, the fucking casbah.
Each hole, a bait to attract the mice that don't eat pig meat. And the
posts manned by the marò or the bersaglieri certainly were not enough
to repel them. Besides, what do you repel when instead of shooting you
waste time with the salaams, the ialla-iallas, the get-back, please, get-
back? Tonight, however, the mice would have it rough: at the slightest
attempt, rat-tat-tat! Pistoia would fan his arquebus and send them to
the Creator. A pleasure which would compensate him for the missed
rendezvous and avenge Joséphine Geraldine Caroline. Either fuck or
shoot, Tancredi of Altavilla used to say. Right? And on this profound
deduction Pistoia concluded his moaning, grabbed his M12, called out
to his driver.

"Get your ass in gear, Ugo!"

"At your command, captain, sir!" answered Ugo in his loud, coarse
voice. "Where are we going, sir?"

"Hunting, Ugo. Hunting."

"Hunting what, sir?"

"Mice, Ugo. Mice."

"Mice, sir?"

"Mice, mice! The Ghibelline mice that sneak in through the holes!

Move over, 'cause I want to drive myself!'' And seizing the wheel, he drove off to search for a good hunting site to await his prey.

*   *   *

They were eight, the possible hunting sites. That is, the posts with which the Italians garrisoned the troubled quarter. Seven of them, with an M113 and six wardens. One, with a guard tower also. One, with a guard tower only. Posts Twenty-One, Twenty-Two, Twenty-Three, Twenty-Four, and Twenty-Five, held by the bersaglieri; posts Twenty-Five Alpha, Twenty-Seven, and Twenty-Eight, held by the marò. (The Twenty-Seven Owl, held by a marò and a bersagliere, was an observatory.) And the Twenty-Four was the first one you found when you came from rue de l'Aérodrome. In fact it guarded the southeast corner of the rectangle, meaning the corner where the Street Without a Name met avenue Nasser, and overlooked the rond-point of Shatila. But it plugged the least exploited hole, a pathway that creeping inside the quarter ended next to the communal grave, and Pistoia didn't stop. He entered avenue Nasser, drove five hundred yards, then made a U-turn and stopped at the Twenty-Two: the post on the northeast corner.

"Tutto bene, all okay, guys?"

"Yessir, captain."

The Twenty-Two secured a little square cluttered by a gas station that gave the Amal a fair pretext to approach, and just in front it had the final stretch of Gobeyre as well as rue Argàn: a street always full of guerrillas. To the north, the houses of Sabra and the road leading to the French observatory named the Tower: a theater for many appetites. In return, both to the west and to the south it was bordered by shanties that formed a solid barrier. The only hole consisted of a lane that connected it with the Twenty-Five. A lousy hunting site, then. And driving back two hundred yards he moved to the Twenty-Five: placed right in front of the Gobeyre sidewalk.

" Come va, how's it going, babes?"

"Looks quiet, captain."

A good spot, the Twenty-Five. It occupied a vacant lot which was closed to the left by a bunch of ruins concealing an old bunker and, to the right, by the wreck of a cottage called Habbash's house because the Palestinian leader George Habbash had lived in it. Therefore it plugged the most accessible hole: the long narrow street which led from avenue Nasser to the heart of the quarter. But Pistoia ignored it and, avoiding a vast bomb crater that pierced the ground near the lane connecting with the Twenty-Two, he slipped into the long narrow street. Here he passed the Twenty-Five Alpha, the post which didn't have the M113 because it consisted only of a guard tower on the roof of a three-story house, continued for another three hundred yards, and reached the Twenty-One: the post located at the junction of the Main Street of Sabra and the Main Street of Shatila. Above a hut at a corner of the junction was the other guard tower. String's guard tower.

"Nulla di nuovo, nothing new, String?"

"No, sir."

An excellent spot, a real hunting site, the Twenty-One. Because, besides plugging the biggest hole, meaning the hole of the mice that came from Sabra, it offered an absolutely perfect view. This should be the place to stop after the inspection, Pistoia thought. Then he turned to the left and, looking suspiciously at a lane that vanished inside a labyrinth of hovels, he reached the Twenty-Three: the post on the south side of Shatila, located on the Street Without a Name, which was used by intruders with a car. In fact he flared his nostrils as if he had detected something that wasn't there yet was there or about to be there, and hesitated a little.

"Occhio alle ombre, eyes on the shadows, clear?"

"Yessir."

"And fingers on the trigger."

Then he exited onto the Street Without a Name. He turned right, drove five hundred yards, passed a sandbag wall behind which two marò watched over an alley and an abandoned shelter (the camp where the Sunday of the double slaughter Fabio had drunk the mullah's coffee and Rambo had called him Judas) and got to the Twenty-Eight: the post at the southwest corner. That is, the intersection of the Street Without a Name and avenue Chamoun. Turning once more to the right he entered avenue Chamoun, covered the five hundred yards of the west side, turned right again, got to an open space with the remains of a swimming pool, and reached the Twenty-Seven: the post at the northwest corner, sited among the ruins of the Cité Sportive. Here he should have stopped to leave the jeep and go up the stairway leading to the Twenty-Seven Owl's observatory. Intead he turned around and retracing the route went back to the Twenty-One, where he braked, shut off the headlights, stiffened like a bloodhound on the scent of a hare or a pheasant. Neck taut. Ears upright. Pupils dilated. Teeth bared.

"What is it, captain, sir?" Ugo asked in surprise.

"Mice. Ghibellines. Mice," a tense voice answered.

An instant later an olive-green Mercedes burst from the Street Without a Name. It passed by the M113 of the Twenty-Three, almost grazed Onion who had uselessly yelled halt and raised his rifle, continued for a hundred yards or so, then plunged into the lane that Pistoia had suspiciously looked at, and vanished inside the labyrinth of hovels. On the front seat there were two young men.

"You mean those, captain?" Ugo asked.

"Those," he growled ecstatically. Then he started the engine, steered into the long narrow street, reached the Twenty-Five, jumped to the ground, loaded his M12. And, legs apart, he placed himself near the M113. "Those, Ugo, those. And they'll come out from this post."

"This one, captain, sir?"

"This one, Ugo. This one."

"How do you know it, captain?"

"I know it."

It made no sense to say so. Nothing authorized him to suppose that the two wouldn't remain in the labyrinth of hovels or leave Shatila from another hole: the Twenty-Three or the Twenty-One or the pathway behind the Twenty-Four. But the hunter-hound, the soldier who profoundly loved the war, the gambler who amused himself in the war as he would never do in the forest or the tundra or at the roulette table, knew that they would leave from there and so he had to wait for them there. He didn't wait long. After three or four minutes, the olive-green Mercedes popped out of the darkness and broke into the vacant lot.

"Halt! Stop! Halt!" the bersaglieri on the ground shouted.

"Halt! Stop! Halt!" the bersaglieri on the M113 shouted.

"Halt! Stop! Halt!" the gunner at the Browning shouted.

Pistoia, instead, didn't shout anything. He just fired. A long, confident, precise burst of M12. A volley of bullets that rained upon the hood, the windshield, the wheel. So that the driver slumped on the seat and, by a hair missing the bomb crater, the car went to bang against Habbash's house. Then it rolled over and stopped in the lane where the ecstatic voice resounded.

"I got you, mice, I got you! Barrah, out!"

One came out, covered with blood and blind with terror.

"Aamel maaruf! Please, aamel maaruf..."

The other remained slumped against the seat, moaning.

"Saedna... help... saedna..."

"Captain, we'll be lucky if we get them to the hospital alive," the squad leader said.

But Pistoia silenced him.

"Calm down, tender heart, calm down! First these two mice have to tell me what they wanted."

2

They didn't want a thing, Eagle sighed turning away from the nine bronze maidens of the Viennese chandelier, and they weren't mice. They were two youngsters stoned on hashish, two potheads. But the Vultur Gryphus hadn't even thought of rebuking the clod who had shot the pointless volley: he'd taken it out on the bersaglieri and their commander. "If those marshmallows you call my-boys were more alert, these things wouldn't happen! The fault is yours, colonel! I'm fed up with your indulgence, your stupid paternalism, your weakness!" And meanwhile the poor kids of the Twenty-Five bore the insults, the provocations, the spittles of the Amal arrayed like crows on the Gobeyre sidewalk. Yes, even the spittles. Certain gobs that looked like eggs in a frying pan. And, as they gave them back, avenue Nasser seemed a tennis court with spittles and insults in place of the ball. "Khoda, ibn sharmuta! Take that, you son of a bitch!" "And you take this, shitty bedouin!" Which increased the risk of vengeance, of nocturnal raids and... Eagle touched the coral horn he kept in his pocket to exorcise bad luck, sent out a silent prayer to his saints and prophets, then left for his evening inspection at Shatila. First stop, the Twenty-Three where a little shadow was on guard near the grave.

"Ciao, Onion. Everything okay?"

"Yessir, colonel..." Onion mumbled in a shaky voice.

"Let's not make any mistakes, tonight, hmm?"

"Nossir, sir..."

"This is a lousy post, I know."

"Nossir, sir."

"It is, it is..." He stared at the sinister quadrangle full of garbage and weeds. By Moses, what kind of tomb was that? From sunrise to sunset, goats nibbling and scattering their dung. From sunset to sunrise, moles feasting on it... They hadn't even set up a gravestone, those barbarians, or an epitaph to record who was buried within! To mark the contents, there was only a cane with a gray rag: once a black banner, the banner of the Palestinians. He shook his head. "I'll tell Hawk to move you to another post, kid..."

"No, colonel, sir! Please don't move me! I do want to stay here!"

"You do? Since when?!?"

"Since this afternoon, colonel, sir."

"This afternoon? Why?"

Onion twisted his body, coughed.

"Because this afternoon the general came, sir. And he gave us a sermon for the Mercedes story. He told us that we behaved like marshmallows not like men, that men must be men and behave like men, etcetera. And the word 'men' bothered me a lot, sir. I felt like answering no, general, I'm not a man. I'm nineteen and not even ready to become a man. But then I thought it over, and I realized that instead I'm ready for that and for many other things. Not everything, yet many things. So I better start becoming a man by staying here with the dead. Do you see them, sir?"

"See whom?"

"The will-o'-the-wisps, sir."

"They are not will-o'-the-wisps, Onion!"

"They are, sir, they are!"

"They are fireflies, Onion."

"Fireflies in the winter, sir? Look down there in the middle!"

Eagle looked down and started. But not because he had seen a will-o'-the-wisp or a firefly. Because at the foot of the cane with the gray banner there was something he hadn't seen before: a flower. A yellow gladiolus.

"I see nothing but a yellow gladiolus, Onion."

"Yessir, I put it there, sir."

"You?!?"

"Yessir. It broke my heart to see only that garbage and trash... Those dead people were people, right? Muslim people but people! So I stole the gladiolus from the Eagle base chapel and I brought it to them. Let's hope the Lord isn't angry for the theft, sir."

"The Lord won't be angry, Onion."

He got back into the jeep, drove along the Main Street, reached the Twenty-One where he stopped at the guard tower to hearten String. Here he was, bent over his rifle and with a double mess ration resting on a sandbag.

"Ciao, String. I see your appetite's not flagging."

"Nossir. Eating keeps me awake."

"Are you tired, String?"

"Nossir, I'm fine. If it wasn't for those rotten boys who live down there in the hut..."

"Why? What's wrong with them?"

"They have it in for me, sir. They always torment me with the Italians-tomorrow-kaputt, Italians-boom-boom, and..."

"Would you like a transfer, String?"

"Oh, no, sir! No! Don't bother, sir!"

"No bother, String. I'll tell Hawk."

"Please, colonel, don't!"

"I see. You too are anxious to become a man..."

"A man, sir?"

"Yes. Like Onion... I wanted to pull him off the guard post near the grave, and he refused. He said that staying with the dead helps him become a man."

"Sir, I don't think I'll become a man by hanging around the living and the dead in Beirut."

"Then why don't you want me to transfer you to a different post?"

"Because the air is healthier up here, sir."

"The air?!? String, is it a matter of women?"

"No, sir. Better-queer-than-dead, sir."

"Good. I see you've learned the lesson..."

"Yessir..." Then String watched Eagle go down and let out a sigh of relief. For Christsake, what would Jamila eat if the colonel pulled him off this guard tower? She already was so thin, poor Jamila... And so good. She didn't resemble at all her rotten brothers. She stole food and that was it. Because if you offered it, she wouldn't take it. She would put her hands behind her back, lower her eyes, and shake her head to say no. If instead you silently placed it somewhere, she took it to go and devour it in a corner. Like the day she had stolen his chicken. Look for the chicken, look for the chicken, where's-my-chicken, who-stole-my-chicken, and Jamila had stolen it. She was picking it clean in a corner. That's why he always came with a double ration: one for him, one for her. Only the other day he had eaten both of them, and in order to eat the poor baby had been forced to go rummage in the street garbage. Just the contrary of his little sister Monica, who was the same age, nine years, and wasted the food like a billionaire. She shredded it, she squashed it, she left it on the plate even if it was first-rate stuff. For example, the pancakes he personally cooked. In fact this morning he'd sent her a postcard that read: "Dear Monica, you waste even the pancakes I personally cook. Do you know that Jamila has to steal her food or rummage for it in the garbage?" He'd also written a letter to his parents: "Dear Dad and Mom, as you know I became a communist because of the bums sleeping in front of our house. That is, because of the poor and the hungry we have in Livorno. But those are poor and hungry in a manner of speaking: always with a pizza in their mouths or an ice cream in their hands, and fat. If you knew poor Jamila, you would understand what is real poverty and real hunger..."

"String!" Eagle shouted from the jeep.

"Yessir..."

"Don't eat too much, okay?"

"Don't worry, sir."

"I wish I could..." Eagle murmured. Then he ordered the driver to take him to the Twenty-Seven Owl. The anguishing worry that some trouble might burst had returned. So he wanted to take a look from the height of the Twenty-Seven Owl.

*   *   *

Filled with that worry he climbed the half-destroyed stairway and got to a rough platform: the rubble of a solarium that in the happy days had been part of the Cité Sportive. On the rough platform, a sentry box totally swaddled with sandbags and almost invisible because of the darkness. Inside the sentry box, Nazarene and a marò who spotted through the loopholes. All around, an arsenal of nightscopes and binoculars, radios, walkie-talkies, maps to consult with flashlights. Eagle entered and raised a voice that didn't belong to him. Annoyed, harsh.

"Nazarene, have you noticed anything unusual?"

"Nossir. As calm as a millpond, tonight," was the answer.

"Never trust a millpond in Beirut. Sooner or later it boils. Give me those nightscopes."

He lifted them to his eyes, impatient. From loophole to loophole he swept Shatila's perimeter. First, avenue Nasser. Then, the Twenty-Four's corner and the rond-point with the overpass. Then, the Street Without a Name. Then, its intersection with avenue Chamoun and the side bordering Sabra. Nothing, there was nothing that justified his anguishing worry. He thus shifted the scopes to rue de l'Aérodrome and the headquarters, the field hospital, the Logistics base, his base, Bourji el Barajni, the airport... Nothing. He moved them south, toward the barracks of the Sixth Brigade, then west: toward the littoral of Ramlet el Baida and Sierra Mike base... Nothing. He turned them again to avenue Nasser, to the little square of the Twenty-Two, to the vacant lot of the Twenty-Five, to the sidewalk of Gobeyre... Nothing. Not even the exchange of spittles, tonight. Around the M113 the bersaglieri looked quiet, on their sidewalk the Amal seemed to be conferring among themselves, and the militiaman who guarded Gobeyre's main alley sat on a stool lazily stretching his arms. He returned the scopes to Nazarene who was staring in the direction of Tayoune.

"What are you looking at?"

"A horse, sir. A mare."

"A mare?"

"Yessir. There's a mare at the Tayoune crossing. I saw her yesterday, when I passed with the ambulance that transferred the two wounded Shiites to the Rizk Hospital. A beautiful white mare with a golden mane and enormous, violet eyes. She stood in the middle of the rotary's grassy bed, eating the weeds, and... A hymn to life, sir. A hymn!"

"What hymn, what life, dammit? Do I keep you here to lose time with a horse?!?"

"Sorry, sir... It has been a moment of distraction, sir..." Nazarene stammered in dismay. "I always wanted a horse, as I couldn't have it once I bought a donkey, and..."

"What do I care about your donkey and your horse! Stop talking nonsense and keep your eyes open, instead!"

"Yessir, colonel, sir..."

"And give me the nightscopes again! Where did you hide my nightscopes?!?"

"Here they are, sir. You put them down yourself," the marò intervened, also in dismay. How strange. Eagle was always so kind...

He took the scopes back, pointed them again on the Twenty-Two, on the Twenty-Five, on the Twenty-Four, then once more on the Twenty-Five where he stopped to scan the bersagliere who all alone and several yards from the M113's crew watched the rear of Habbash's house. That is, the lane connecting with the Twenty-Two.

It was Ferruccio, and Nazarene would have given a lot to be at his place. In fact his guard post, an enclosure formed by a low sandbag wall, was located near the rubble of an edifice destroyed during the Israeli siege. And, thanks to a seed brought by the wind, from that rubble a magnificent fig tree had bloomed.

3

Ferruccio too felt nervous. He did because in the morning Hawk had called him and... "Put on the cleanest uniform you have, the best-pressed scarf you have, and come with me." "Where to, captain?" "To the Condor." "Why?" "Because he'll take you to the French who want to give you a medal." "For what, captain?" "For the little girl in the water-closet." He had taken it badly. He had deemed it a mockery, an insult, both for him and the little girl. Nevertheless he had put on the clean uniform, the best-pressed scarf, and gone off to the Condor who'd welcomed him with a shout. Those-boots-are-dusty. Christ! Is it possible to keep your boots polished in a city like Beirut? A loathsome man, that Condor. Just the opposite of Eagle who addressed everybody with courtesy and cared for his men as if they were his sons. Are-you-hungry, are-you-sleepy, are-you-wearing-wool-socks. Yes, you could confide in Eagle. You could say to him colonel, sir, I don't want to be decorated. This medal is a mockery, an insult, for me and for the little girl. Yesterday, for instance, he'd said to him: "Colonel, sir, I can't handle anymore standing under the fig tree. Send me out on patrol for a few hours." Eagle had, and what an interesting sight! Women on their way to the market, boys playing in the streets, old people standing in the doorways to get the sun... He'd also met Farjane, the fetching Palestinian who wearing her Sunday best, golden sandals and an organdy dress, went from post to post and asked the soldiers: "Will you please marry me? Will you please get me to Italy?" Gee! Had he not been in love with Daniela, he would've answered: "I'm the one who'll marry you, Farjane." And then he had met Fatima, the marò's prostitute. Ugly. Real ugly. A butt that under her jeans looked like a mattress. What jerks, the marò, to bang her in the jeep at the bottom of the pool! During the Israeli siege an explosion had flung into the diving pool a jeep that had neatly landed on the bottom, so the marò used it as a garçonnière with Fatima and... Ferruccio gripped his rifle tighter. There had been a rustling, like the soft padding of a cat, and now a shadow was moving to blend with the shadow of the fig tree.

"Mahomet! Is that you, Mahomet?"

Nobody answered, yet he didn't get worried. It always happened with Mahomet: he crept to him in a squat, sometimes coming from the long narrow street, sometimes from the rubble near the fig tree, then he crouched at his feet and it was useless to protest Mahomet-you-have-to-stop-this. Mahomet promised and then forgot. Because he was afraid of nothing, that kid. Not even of rifle shots. He was so used to war that he considered them just another sound, a normal thing like the rain. Who's afraid of the rain?

"Mahomet! Answer me, Mahomet!"

Again nobody answered, and this time he worried. He even was tempted to shoot at the shadow which had reappeared. And if Hawk were right? Yesterday Hawk had made a scene. "Soldier, don't you understand that allowing strangers on the posts is prohibited?!?" "Yes, captain." "Can't you get it through your head that in this city the kids aren't harmless?" "Yes, captain." "Don't you know that they drill like military men, that at eleven or twelve they're already soldiers?" "Yes, captain." "Don't you realize that somebody could send him over to distract you, to attack you?" "Yes, captain." "If a shadow doesn't answer the who-goes-there, you must shoot!" "Yes, captain." He had answered yes, yes, yes, yes, yes, but he would never shoot at Mahomet. Christ, he didn't shoot at kids! He'd rather be blown away than shoot at a kid. He put down his rifle.

"Mahomet! Come out, Mahomet. I know it's you!"

"It's me, it's me!" a cheerful little voice answered. And the shadow materialized to become a cute eleven-year-old boy with clean shorts and clean shirt and clean hair who at his feet held out a bag of pumpkin seeds. "I brought you pumpkin seeds, Ferruccio!"

He refused them, pretending outrage.

"I don't want your seeds! I'm angry! I was about to shoot you, dammit! You have to stop doing this, understand?"

"Yes, Ferruccio. Afuàn, Ferruccio. Excuse me..."

"No, I don't! You always say afuàn, afuàn, and then you do it again! Go away! I don't want to see you anymore!"

"Ferruccio... Aamel maaruf, please, Ferruccio..." The cheerful little voice began to crack. "I'll be quiet, I'll stay still... Please don't chase me away, please."

"Go away, I said! Go!"

Keeping back his tears, Mahomet placed the bag of pumpkin seeds on the ground. He rose, went off, became once more a shadow blending with the shadow of the fig tree, and Ferruccio gave the sandbags a kick. Christ, to chase him away like that! He shouldn't have chased him away like that! Rather than all those yes-captains, he should have answered Hawk that Mahomet didn't come to help the Sons of God and kill the Italians: he came to bring him pumpkin seeds, to keep him awake with some company! It's hard, you know, to stay twelve hours all alone pricking up your ears and peering out into the darkness. At a certain point you get sleepy, you slump over. But if you have somebody chattering beside you, the hours fly. Not that he had cheerful things to recount, poor Mahomet. His father had been murdered in the massacre of Sabra and Shatila with his grandfather, his uncle, and his sister, only his mother had survived, and in uncertain Italian he spoke exclusively of this. "Io e mia mamma vivi perchè noi nascondere sotto morti. Me and my mother alive because hid under bodies. My sister no hide under bodies, she said bodies weigh too much, too heavy, and before killing they did very ugly things to her. Very ugly. Me saw it. With my eyes.

Because my sister, fourteen years old: understand? Now my sister and my father and my grandfather and my uncle be in communal grave near my house. But I never look. My mother not want. She says: if you look, you become like Kadijia." "Who's Kadijia?" "Kadijia essere pazza di Shatila. Kadijia be crazy woman of Shatila. You not know her? Very very crazy. Always laughing, singing, dancing. Kadijia crazy because always look in communal grave. Her husband and her five children there." To avoid listening to these horrors, at times he said stop-Mahomet-stop and did all the talking. He told about his parents who were very much alive, about his sister who was even more alive than his parents, about his fiancée Daniela and his city which was named Milan and had no rubble. Or he sent him to the Syrian who had a grocery near the Twenty-One and stayed open all night to sell hashish under the counter. "Go get me a little hashish and don't get cheated on the price, Mahomet." Superfluous advice since Mahomet wasn't easy to cheat. If the Syrian tried, he began to yell akrùt-thief-akrùt and demanded compensatory damages in pumpkin seeds and pistachio nuts. Or he pilfered them. Certainly he'd pilfered tonight's seeds from the Syrian. He was so intelligent, Mahomet. And so special. Had he not met Mahomet, he would never have overcome the trauma of the little girl extracted from the water-closet. And it goes without saying that all the kids of Beirut were intelligent kids. Special kids. They learned languages at an astonishing speed, they resolved any problem in a flash, and they never slept. They stayed up until two, three in the morning, and at dawn they were in the streets again. God, was he sleepy... An irresistible drowsiness was coming over him, and it was hardly midnight: there were still six hours to pass under the fig tree... What a pity this wasn't a fig tree with figs... He would have counted the figs and... It was a sterile tree, alas, a fig tree without figs... A real Beirut fig tree...

He lit a hashish joint. Careful to hide the weak glimmering, he smoked it in voluptuous mouthfuls that numbed him even more, and his fear of falling asleep grew. I must wake up, he then told himself. I must stand guard over the lane at the Twenty-Two: to keep an eye on Habbash's house. It offers too many holes, that half-destroyed house: breached walls, gaping windows. The opening facing the alley doesn't even have a door. If an Amal wanted to take advantage of the darkness and get inside, the M113 crew wouldn't even see him. And, once inside the house, he could easily pop into the lane: take me by surprise. Hawk keeps saying it again and again: "Don't close your eyes, don't fall asleep." So I must be ready, if they come. Ready to shoot, to use my Fal. My-Fal? What a shithead I am. I dragged it out so much with the sergeant who helped me extract the little girl from the water-closet, I-don't-like-armies, I-don't-like-uniforms, I-don't-like-weapons, and now I say my-Fal. Let's be honest: I love it. I clean it, I dismantle it, I reassemble it. I even bring it to bed with me. I sleep with it. Because I believe in it and... Good Lord, what a need to sleep. And what an idiot I have been to chase Mahomet away, to lose his company. I need company. I need somebody to talk with. I'll talk with my Fal, tapping it with my fingernails. Like this: tock-tock, you're a friend... Tock-tock: after Mahomet, the best friend I have in Beirut... Tock-tock, tock-tock: you defend me, you help me stay awake... Tock-tock, tock-tock: no, you're not helping me... It's too quiet, here, too dark. I'm too sleepy... So sleepy... And at this point his eyelids grew heavy as lead, he closed them, propped his head on the Fal. So he didn't see the eight Amal who, having snuck through the breached walls and the gaping windows into Habbash's house then into the lane, now burst into the Twenty-Five's vacant lot to be joined by another group that was crossing the avenue. Or, rather, he saw them when they had already surrounded the M113.

More or less when they were noticed by Eagle who continued to point the nightscopes on the fig tree and the lane and the vacant lot and avenue Nasser, to search for the cause of his anxiety.

*   *   *

"Nazarene, I think something's happening at the Twenty-Five. Take a look and tell me what you see. You too, marò."

Both Nazarene and the marò scanned the Twenty-Five and started.

"I see a big mess, colonel."

"A real jumble, sir."

By Moses and Abraham and Isaac and all the prophets in the Torah! By San Gennaro and San Gerardo and San Guglielmo and all the saints in the calendar! While his heart beat like a drum, Eagle snatched the walkie-talkie and called Hawk.

"Hawk, attention Hawk! Eagle here, answer!"

"Eagle, this is Hawk!" a fuming voice answered.

"Hawk, what's going on at the Twenty-Five?!?"

"What's going on is that a gang of bedouins has surrounded the M113, colonel! The squad leader just called me and I was about to inform you that I'm going down there with a reinforcement patrol! And if they don't quit right away, this time it's me who fires a volley!"

Well, it was only a gang of a few bedouins: innocuous riffraff. Eagle relaxed and his heart went back to beating normally.

"No volleys, Hawk. And wait for me at the bottom of the Main Street: understand? We'll go together." Then, darting at Nazarene a glance full of I-told-you-never-trust-a-millpond-in-Beirut, he left the Twenty-Seven Owl and ran over to the Main Street. It was ten after midnight, the embarrassing the-Italians-give-us-blood, the-Italians-are-our-blood-brothers wafted from the minarets, and at the Twenty-Five the bersaglieri were shouting themselves hoarse to chase away the intruders who answered in a way Charlie would have never suspected.

"Al-talieni ekhuaatùna bil khara! Italians shit brothers!"

"Ekhuaatùna bil khara! Shit brothers!"

"Khara, shit, khara!"

4

A lanky thug with a thick beard and a peculiar fourteen-year-old blond with three hand grenades at his belt were leading them, and they weren't at all innocuous riffraff. Despite the worn jeans and the half-uniforms stolen or purchased God knows where, they were people who knew their trade. Moreover, armed with new Kalashnikovs, good ammunition belts, and Rpg. Nor were they so few: twelve had crossed avenue Nasser to join the eight who'd passed through Habbash's house and taken Ferruccio by surprise. A team of twenty, then, the most massive commando to attack a Shatila post with a well-coordinated maneuver. Arriving from two directions, in fact, they had enclosed the five bersaglieri in such a solid circle that only an exchange of fire could have broken it. The most disconcerting thing, however, wasn't their numerical superiority or their professionalism: it was not to understand what they wanted. To kill those few Italians and so avenge the two potheads in the olive-green Mercedes? To push their way onto the street that led to the Twenty-One and settle a kind of landing zone in the center of Shatila? They didn't touch the weapons they wore on their shoulders or belts, they didn't budge toward the M113. They didn't make alarming movements. They roared Italians-shit, khara-shit, and that's all. Only the little blond didn't limit himself to insults. A cigarette butt glued to his lips, a disdainful scowl on his young yet disagreeable face, he constantly touched the hand grenades hanging from his belt, three Russian Rdg8. And, without dropping the butt, he promised death in three broken languages.

"Me kill you. Io ammazzare voi. Moi vous tuer."

With the tacit consent of the lanky thug who clearly granted him special privileges, he also tormented Ferruccio: the only one outside the circle and the only one who didn't shout himself hoarse to drive them away. After overcoming his shame at falling asleep and being taken by surprise, Ferruccio had in fact realized that it was better for him to stay silent and to take advantage of the fig tree which concealed his enclosure under its foliage. But the little blond had seen him, and all of a sudden he removed a grenade from his belt. Though without pulling off the safety tab, he made the gesture of launching it.

"Me kill you first. Io te ammazzare primo. Moi te tuer premier."

Hawk's jeep and Eagle's jeep and the jeep with the reinforcement patrol broke into the vacant lot right at that moment thus forming around the circle another circle which imprisoned the twenty Amal and nullified their advantage. Then Hawk jumped on the little blond and ripped the Rdg8 from his hand, tossed it away. But, as he seized his wrists to disarm him completely, Eagle intervened with a courteous smile.

"Calm down, Hawk, calm down. Things can be discussed quietly and be solved through reason and dialogue, by Moses! Let's ask these gentlemen what they wish, why they're here!" And turning to the little blond who peered around in search of his grenade: "Good evening, young man. What do you want?"

"Khara!" he answered continuing to peer in search of his grenade.

"I don't understand. What did you say?"

"He said shit, colonel," Hawk rumbled.

"How rude! Anyway, who is in charge among them?"

"I'd say the beanpole with the beard, colonel."

"Fine." And, always offering his courteous smile, Eagle moved toward the lanky thug. "Good evening, bon soir, buonasera. Do you speak English, parla italiano, parlez-vous français?"

"Khara. Talieni khara." He grinned confirming his escort's lack of cooperation.

"He said that the Italians are shit, colonel!" Hawk shouted, now panting.

"They've been saying it since they arrived," the squad leader echoed. What are we waiting for, why don't we pump them with a burst of bullets?!?"

"Because there is nothing that cannot be solved through reason and dialogue," Eagle repeated stubbornly. "Let's call the Operations Room."

The call was taken by Old Grouse who immediately went looking for the Condor. But the Condor had gone to the Ruby base, and his substitute, the Professor, entrusted Charlie with the task of fixing that mess.

"With an escort and an interpreter, captain."

*   *   *

To hell with the escort, to hell with the interpreter, Charlie grumbled tying the Browning High Power to his left ankle. In certain cases escorts and interpreters are a ball and chain: he would do it alone and with the little Arabic he knew. Then he took his jeep and left with his disappointment. Dammit! All Pistoia's fault. On the fragile bridge that Zandra Sadr had agreed to build, that M12 volley had produced more damage than a cannonade. Or not? Maybe not. Maybe that M12 volley was the pretext that Gobeyre extremists had chosen to answer the muezzins' appeal, to oppose the order given by His Most Reverend Eminence. Maybe it had been a mistake not to foresee that in the muddle of factions, internal struggles, a group or subgroup would refuse the sentence al-talieni-ekhuaatùna-bil-dam. But who could have sent those twenty Amal? A loose dog or somebody with a head on his shoulders? Hmm! Apparently somebody with a head on his shoulders. For instance, one like Bilal the Sweeper. And if the twenty had been sent by Bilal the Sweeper? According to the rumors, Bilal had become a very important man in Gobeyre, a leader respected by all the factions and groups and subgroups... He should find him, knot again the threads of their friendship interrupted by the double slaughter, exploit the fact that he spoke good Italian... And with these thoughts Charlie reached the Twenty-Five, stopped to watch the absurd scene of the besieged besiegers. Then he approached to see who the lanky thug in command was, and started. Rashid! It was Rashid, the most Khomeinist of all the Khomeinists, the most ferocious ally of the Sons of God. A wild animal. He knew him well. In September when he tried to track down Mustafa Hash, he'd met him several times and one morning he had surprised him beating a militiaman guilty of insubordination. Blows to the head, kneecaps to the teeth, kicks to the genitals, and promises to "keep on going." "Keep on going, Rashid?!?" "Yes, captain. When one of my men transgresses, death is the lightest punishment." He also knew the little blond who escorted him: a neurotic skunk, a cowardly and despicable faggot. Once he had pointed his Kalashnikov at Sugar who was defusing a rocket at Shyah and: "Quick, maccarone, quick. Or me shoot you in your stomach." And, when Sugar had disarmed him, he'd whimpered help-help. They called him Passepartout, but his real name was Khalid, and he was the wild animal's lover. His whore. As such he allowed himself any abuse, any infamy, and aroused the hate of everybody. Even Rashid's friends. Ignoring the other eighteen, simple followers and therefore unworthy of any consideration, Charlie cast a meaningful look at Eagle. Then he put on the expression of a man who has been disturbed for a most boring trifle and stopped in front of the thug.

"Shubaddak, Rashid? What do you want, Rashid?"

"Badi iba bibati. To stay in my home," a surly voice answered.

"Heida eno bitàk, Rashid. This isn't your home, Rashid."

"Heida bitàk, heida bitàk! It's my home, it's my home!"

"Bitàk bi Gobeyre, Rashid. Your home is in Gobeyre."

"Bitàk bi Gobeyre, bi Sabra, bi Shatila, was bi sha'obi mahal badi. My home is in Gobeyre, in Sabra, in Shatila, and anywhere I like."

"Enta rhaltan. You're wrong."

Rashid sneered.

"Min rhaltan. I am not."

"Enta rhaltan. You are. Taala, Rashid. Come on," Charlie said moving forward a step.

"Enruhe? To go where?"

"Enda Bilal. To Bilal."

The sneer vanished in a strangled exclamation.

"Enda Bilal?!"

"Enda Bilal."

"Tares minno Bilal? Do you know Bilal?"

"Ana minno. I do. Bilal i sadiqi. Bilal is my friend."

"Sadiqi kum?! Your friend?!"

"Na'am, yes. Come on, Rashid." Then, always with the expression of a man who has been disturbed for a most boring trifle and thus cannot waste his time, he placed himself at his side. With the left arm he clasped his shoulders, with the right hand he clutched his right hand: the hand which held the strap of the Kalashnikov. And, imprisoning him in a grip that seemed a fraternal embrace, using all the tremendous force of his gigantic body, he pushed him out of the double circle. He led him toward the edge of avenue Nasser. Here he stopped, with phony mildness he forced him to turn halfway around, and pointed to the eighteen Amal he had ignored.

"Ull lahkni, Rashid. Tell them to follow us, Rashid."

Uncertain whether to try freeing himself with the risk of failing and losing face or to remain within the grip and let everybody believe it a fraternal embrace, Rashid gave the command. Then Hawk ordered the bersaglieri to make the besieged besiegers pass. The circle opened and, preceded by a vexed Passepartout, the eighteen too reached the edge of the avenue. Following Rashid who remained locked to his captor they crossed the avenue, got to the sidewalk of the Amal, entered the alley guarded by the militiaman who sat on the stool, and vanished in it with Charlie who reassured Eagle.

"Don't worry, colonel. I'll be right back."

Though not even the reflection of a streetlight or a gas lamp interrupted the darkness, he felt suddenly calm. He had won and could permit himself that luxury. But soon the alley turned into a deserted lane, the deserted lane into a silent pathway, a silent pathway narrowed by a sewer which let only one person pass at a time: they had to proceed in single file. So the powerful grip ended, he found himself behind Rashid who led the group and ahead of Passepartout who mocked him khara-talieni-khari, and was gripped by fear. An incongruous and inexplicable fear which had nothing to do with the danger he now faced, that is, with the risk that Rashid would avenge his humiliation by conducting him to one of his dens where death was the lightest punishment. A mysterious fear which came from the future, from a threat projected into the future, into the tomorrow that the compromise with Zandra Sadr aimed to avoid. With the fear, an anxiety that grew when he looked at Rashid's shoulders and felt Passepartout's breath on his back. Especially that breath. There was a danger which exceeded any other danger, in the little skunk: a particularly insidious snare that multiplied the well-known perniciousness of his lover. And being squeezed between the two he sensed it as an electric spark, a lethal odor. He arrived in this manner at the end of the pathway narrowed by the sewer. And here Rashid plunged into another alley and reached a little square surrounded by hovels. Among the hovels, a shanty with the lights on.

"Bitàk Bilal. Bilal's house," he said pointing at it. Then, turning to Passepartout: "Affettasciak. Search him. And, all excited by the prospect of playing the role of policeman, Passepartout moved forward. He eyed the gigantic body which towered over him by twelve inches at least.

"Down! En bas! Giù!"

"Haqqan, walad. Sure, kid," Charlie answered, happy to delay the moment in which the little skunk would pat down his ankles and find the Browning High Power. Then he squatted on his heels, pretending to facilitate the search he offered the upper part of his body, and Passepartout's experienced fingers began to ransack it. Shoulders. Armpits. Thorax. Stomach. Jacket pockets. Here the fingers stopped in disappointment.

"Up! Lève-toi. Alzati."

He got back on his feet and the experienced fingers began to ransack again. Belt. Pants pockets. Hips. Pelvis... Soon they would descend to the legs, they would find the Browning High Power hidden at the ankle, and one thing is to carry a weapon in full view, one thing to hide it at the ankle. How to interrupt him? Maybe by calling Bilal. He called him.

"Bilal! Bilal!

"Bilal! Do you hear me, Bilal?

"Answer, Bilal!"

Thighs. Knees. Calves... The fingers were dropping to the calves when the door of the shanty opened and on the threshold loomed the silhouette of a very tall, very fat, very pregnant woman.

"Min waes Bilal? Who's looking for Bilal?"

Behind the very tall, very fat, very pregnant woman, an extremely tiny man who drowning inside a jacket full of multicolored patches raised a proud bony face. Bilal the Sweeper.

"Uskut, silence!" he ordered her. Then with cadenced, solemn steps, surprisingly long for a person of such small stature, he advanced toward the group. He shot a quick and surprised look at Charlie, gave a rough shove to Passepartout who had interrupted the search to excitedly run toward him, glanced at the eighteen guerrillas who snapped to attention, and went aside with Rashid. He grunted something, angrily. Finally he dismissed all of them, ialla-ialla, and turned to Charlie.

"Afuàn, capitàn. Please, captain," he said. And pointing to the shanty door he added in perfect Italian: "Entra nella mia casa. Come into my house."

CHAPTER SIX

1

IT'S A NOBLE TRADE, the street sweeper's trade. It consists of sweeping the filth we produce, of making our existence less ugly and less infected. Stupid and ungrateful are those who use the word sweeper in a disparaging way, who don't understand how extraordinary and precious the sweepers are. We would die of stench and shame and plague without the sweepers. A city without sweepers or with bad sweepers is a den of poison and death, a physical and a moral barbarity. And in Beirut nobody wanted to be a sweeper. The few who accepted that work did it to the delight of the rats, of the stray dogs, of the flies. They gathered the filth randomly, breaking the bags and sloppily emptying the dustbins, they listlessly threw it in trucks that lost it on the way. Instead of burning it they spilled it into shallow holes where it remained to taint the air already putrid with miasmas, and they never unclogged the sewers. They never swept the alleys, the lanes, the pathways, the sidewalks. In short, they were bad sweepers. The world's worst sweepers. Not Bilal. He always swept the alleys and the lanes and the pathways and the sidewalks, he always unclogged the sewers, he always emptied the dustbins down to the bottom. He never broke the bags, he never lost the filth on the way, he spilled it into deep holes and burned it. He was in sum a fine sweeper, a sweeper who practiced his trade with pride and meticulousness. Because in practicing it with pride, meticulousness, he felt like a doctor who cures diseases and because he considered his broom one of the two medicines that Beirut needed to heal its wounds. The other was his Kalashnikov.

He employed his Kalashnikov with the same skill he employed his broom, Bilal: without wasting ammunition and without missing a shot. He brandished it with the same pride, and never mind if in his hands those two objects became disproportionate tools. In fact he was little more than a dwarf: four feet seven inches high. He also was gaunt, so gaunt that looking at him you wondered whether he weighed more than sixty pounds, and awfully poor. So poor that the only clothing he owned was a pair of broken-soled shoes, a torn-up pair of pants, that jacket full of multicolored patches, and to soothe such poverty he only had Zeinab: his very tall, very fat, very pregnant wife. Yet he was rich in intelligence. He knew how to read and to write, he learned languages with ease, and from his four-foot-seven-inch size he saw much more than tall people do. Charlie had met him by chance, in an Old City street. Look how carefully that boy sweeps the sidewalk, he had thought, then he'd approached and realized it wasn't a boy: it was a man, the epitome of those he called the eternal serfs, the eternal ox-people who plow other people's land for a thread of hay. They had immediately started to talk, and Bilal had said: "Capitàn, at age forty the only things I am familiar with are my broom and my Kalashnikov. With the broom I support eight children, a wife who is expecting a ninth, and an infirm father. With the Kalashnikov I defend my quarter and Allah. Capitàn, I do not know how to express myself with fancy words. But I know how to tell you that in this part of the city I do not want any Christian. Nor do I want you strangers who came to Beirut to take not to give, as the mullah explained to me. So, if I have to kill you, I kill you." A threat that Charlie had managed this way: "The mullah told you a lie, Bilal. You must not take as holy writ the lies they tell from the minarets and in the mosques. This time we've come to give, Bilal, not to take: we're not your enemies. The Christians as such aren't your enemies either. You'll find plenty of Bilals among them: a poor Christian understands you better than a rich Muslim. Bilal, your enemies aren't the Christians: they are the rich and the priests. The rich who profit from your misery by exploiting you and the priests who profit from your ignorance by telling you lies. There are two kinds of malnutrition, Bilal: the one of the body, which comes from not eating, and the one of the soul, which comes from not knowing. And since both of them prevent us from growing, we need to know as well as eat. Have you ever read a book, Bilal?" "No, capitàn. Books are expensive. More expensive than meat," Bilal had answered. "But now I understand why I am hungry even when I eat! Mine is not a hunger for food: it is a hunger for knowing! Oh, I would like so much to know, capitàn! To discover why the world turns, why at times it turns to the right and at times to the left, why some people have five or six jackets and some have only one full of multicolored patches... Promise you will bring me a book, capitàn!" Charlie had promised. But then the double slaughter had taken place, and besides: what book do you bring a man who's never read a book?

* * *

He followed him, with a sigh of relief. He cast a glance at his watch to check the time and said to himself dammit, almost twenty minutes had passed since he and Rashid had crossed avenue Nasser. In the meantime the Condor had surely reached the Twenty-Five to crucify poor Eagle with accusations, and imagine the bawls: "What do you mean he-went-off-with-them? Who escorted him, God blasted, whom did you send with him?!?" "Nobody, general, sir..." "And you let him go without anybody?!?" "They seemed to be friends, general, sir. They were walking arm in arm." "Friends?!? Arm in arm?!? Don't you realize he's made himself a hostage to get us out of this mess?!?" "I'll go search for him right away, general, sir." "Where, how? You?!? You who can't even find your own nose?!? Don't you know how large Gobeyre is?" No, there was no time to lose. And thinking this he crossed the threshold, entered the shanty that Bilal called my-house: a large room badly lit by a pair of gas lamps divided in two by a curtain. On the external side of the curtain, a large portrait of Khomeini. Plus a table, a coal stove, several chairs, a very high seat which looked like a throne, a wooden chest, the broom, the Kalashnikov, and a sofa where you could dimly see a long bundle wrapped in rags. On the other side, a ripple of childish giggles and the catarrhal grumbling of an old man who chided them to be silent. Obviously the eight children and the infirm father.

"Bilal..."

In silence Bilal took a chair, placed it with the back to the sofa, invited Charlie to sit. Then he clambered up into the high seat which looked like a throne, settled himself with his feet dangling over the floor, and crossing his arms on his chest spat out a cold haughty voice.

"Perché sei qui, capitàn? Why are you here, capitàn?"

"Per parlare, to talk, Bilal," Charlie stammered. Given the courtesy with which he'd been received, he hadn't expected such a chilly welcome.

"To talk about what, capitàn?"

"About what occurred in Shatila, Bilal. And as we understand each other..."

"We did a thousand years ago, capitàn. Many things have changed since then."

"Yes, Bilal. Many. Four hundred Americans and French have died, Bilal."

"We die every day, capitàn. Tell me why you are here."

"Because I want to avoid episodes like the one that has taken place in Shatila, Bilal. Because I need your help. You don't know it, but this evening twenty Amal burst into the Twenty-Five and..."

"I know, capitàn."

"You know?!?"

"Yes, capitàn. I sent them."

"You?!?"

"Me."

Incredulous, Charlie observed the tiny man who sat on the throne with his feet dangling over the floor and his arms crossed on his chest. He saw him again while he told him how much he'd like to know things, to discover why at times the world turns to the right and at times to the left, why some people have five or six jackets and some only one full of multicolored patches, he heard again his voice promise-you'll-bring-me-a-book-capitàn, and wondered what had happened to him.

"What happened to you, Bilal? Don't you listen to the muezzin?"

"I do, capitàn."

"Don't you hear the sentence His Eminence ordered the muezzin to say at the hours of prayer?"

"I do, capitàn."

"Well, then..."

"Then I must not take as holy writ the lies they tell from the mina-rets and in the mosques, you said to me. The priests profit from your ignorance, you said. And I realized it is true. First they told us you were enemies who had come to take not to give. Now they tell us you are friends who have come to give not to take, our blood brothers. You are not blood brothers, capitàn. You are shit brothers. Shit that shoots at my people. You almost killed two of them, capitàn."

Charlie looked at him as before, and as before he wondered what had transformed him.

"They didn't stop when we ordered them to halt, Bilal. We couldn't know they were stoned on hashish and..."

"They were my people, capitàn."

"They burst into Shatila like persons who intended to harm, Bilal. They didn't stop at any checkpoint, they..."

"Shatila is our home, capitàn. It has been stolen from us but it is still our home. So is Sabra. And I sent my men to remind you and the muezzins that it is our home, that we enter when we want. As we want."

"You sent us crooks, Bilal. The lanky thug who led them is a butcher and a sadist. You know that. And his little friend is a skunk, a despicable faggot. I'm familiar with them, Bilal. I can even tell you their names: Rashid and Khalid alias Passepartout..."

"They are the kind of crooks I need, capitàn."

On the other side of the curtain a baby began to cry, and once again the old man protested with his catarrhal grumbling. Zeinab scolded them both, and her shouts smothered a faint moan which seemed to come from another area. Charlie cast a second glance at his watch and asked himself what to answer a man who has learned the lesson well enough to turn it back against the teacher. Does he answer him no, my friend, I was joking, the priests must be listened to, you're a poor sweeper and should obey them, you should thank us even if we gun you down? Or does he congratulate him, does he tell him bravo, you're a perfect student, next time double the dose and kill me as well? Of one thing he was certain: he had lost him, really lost. And he would have given a lot to win him back. He sought the words to win him back. He found them in the only possible question.

"Aren't we friends anymore, Bilal?"

Bilal swung his feet dangling over the floor, loosened his arms, leaned against the back of the throne which seemed to swallow him up.

"Capitàn... You are not a shit brother. But friendship is a luxury at war."

"Who says it, Bilal?"

"The book."

"The book? What book?"

"The book you never brought me, capitàn."

"I couldn't decide which book to choose, Bilal..."

"It does not matter. I got one all the same, capitàn. I found it."

"Where?"

"In the trash."

"You mean you read a book you found in the trash?"

"Yes. I read it and I grew up."

"Which book is this book? What's the title?"

"I do not know."

"You don't know?!?"

"No, because..."

With hieratic solemnity Bilal descended from the throne. He went over to the chest, took out a filthy packet of papers smeared with grease and mud, the remains of a book, and returned to Charlie.

"I do not know it because the cover was not there. Nor the first pages and the last ones. But what remained told me all I wanted to know: why the world turns, why at times it turns to the right and at times to the left, why some people have five or six jackets and some only one full of multicolored patches, and what must be done to make the world turn a little better."

"What must be done, Bilal?"

"Fighting. In fact the book says that when they steal your home you have to take it back and keep it with your teeth. Otherwise they will steal it again. Look." He opened the book to a page marked with a piece of twine. He cleared his throat and: "Beasnani saudàfeh haza al bitàk, beasnani! Beasnani saudàfeh haza al quariatna, beasnani! Beasnani oudamiro ainai wa lisan itha iktarabbom menni, beasnani... Well, I will translate it for you: With my teeth I will defend my home, with my teeth! With my teeth I will defend my quarter, with my teeth! With my teeth I will rip out your eyes and your tongue if you come close to me. With my teeth! Beautiful, heh?"

"Yes..." Charlie murmured. "Beautiful." Then he said to himself that his pupil had grown too much, that he couldn't win him back, and got up to go. But at that very moment the faint moan that didn't come from behind the curtain repeated. Very distinctly.

"Yahallah... Yahallah..."

Strange. Who was moaning? The old man? No, it wasn't the old man's voice. A baby, then? No, it wasn't a baby's voice. Zeinab? Not even. It wasn't a woman's voice. And it came, now he realized, from the long bundle on the sofa behind him. He turned around. He looked. He understood.

"Is it a wounded man, Bilal?"

"Yes..." Bilal admitted in a low voice. He had very much hoped that the captain wouldn't notice, and his discovery made him uncomfortable.

"Where is he wounded?"

"In the legs..."

With determination Charlie approached the sofa, removed the rags wrapping the bundle, looked at him: it was a man of about thirty, certainly a guerrilla, and his face was flushed with fever. He touched his brow. It was burning. He took his pulse. It was racing precipitously. He uncovered him down to the feet to examine the rest of the body. There was still a bullet in the right leg, and the left leg showed a black festering gash: the sign of an advanced infection that was developing gangrene. He delicately covered him up again.

"It's serious, Bilal."

"I know, capitàn."

"He risks dying. At the very least, losing his legs."

"I know, capitàn."

"Why haven't you brought him to the Shiite clinic?"

"Because the governmentals check there too. And they know who he is. They would arrest him."

"Who is he, Bilal?"

"I cannot tell you, capitàn."

"Don't, but let me bring him to the field hospital. He'll be admitted without a name."

Bilal's hard eyes grew milder. His bony face reddened. His haughty voice became tremulous.

"Would you really, capitàn?"

"Of course."

"When?"

"Right away. I'll send the ambulance."

They stared at each other in silence. Charlie with his head bowed because Bilal didn't even reach his stomach, and Bilal with his head bent almost backward because Charlie's face was as distant for him as the ceiling. Then Bilal stretched out his right hand.

"Capitàn, now we are friends forever. If one day you ask me to do something, I will do it even if the book tells me not to. I promise."

"Me too," Charlie said clasping the outstretched hand. Then he grabbed him by the armpits, lifted him up as he would lift up a child, kissed him on both cheeks, then placed him back on the ground and returned to Shatila where things were going the way he'd imagined.

*   *   *

Just that way, except for a detail that Charlie wouldn't have ever hypothesized. As soon as he was informed, in fact, the Condor had run to the Twenty-Five and crucified poor Eagle with rebukes. Along with the Condor, however, Pistoia had come. And for half an hour his despair over the vanishing of the man who called him fascist had unexpectedly resounded in the vacant lot. "General, I feel the Ghibellines grabbed him and I cannot bear it." "General, I'm afraid he's in trouble and I feel sick." "General, I shall not stand here scratching my nuts and asking myself is-he-alive-is-he-dead. General, now I must tell them turn-him-loose-right-away, shitty-Saracens, or-I'll-cut-out-the-balls-you-don't-have." Then, all at once, he had crossed avenue Nasser. Waving his M12 he had entered the alley guarded by the militiaman on the stool and shouting Charlie-where-are-you-Charlie, he too had vanished into the darkness.

"What are you doing here? What do you want?" Charlie exclaimed when he met him in the pathway where his inexplicable fear had arisen.

"What am I doing here?!? I came to look for you, sadsack! Do you think I'd leave you in the clutches of those buttfuckers? I'd rather become a monk, I'd rather cut my dick off! Ah, what a joy to find you healthy and safe and more unpleasant than ever!"

It was a generous answer, and it deserved a generous thank-you. But instead of saying it, Charlie grunted a chilly you-could've-saved-yourself-the-trouble. Then he returned to the Twenty-Five, reported to the Condor, convinced him to send the ambulance for Bilal's wounded man, and with a nonchalant gesture picked up the Rdg8 that Hawk had snatched from Passepartout's hands.

2

"Martino, what's this grenade doing here?" Angelo asked, pointing to the Rdg8 that rested on the Arab Bureau table.

"Charlie wants to give it to Sugar for his Museum," Martino answered.

"Where did he get it?"

"At the Twenty-Five. An Amal had it. The very young and blond one who wanted to toss it at the bersagliere under the fig tree."

"Ah!"

"What a scoundrel!"

"Yes..."

He picked it up, he examined it. A bizarre coincidence: the serial number stamped on the safety tab corresponded to the coordinates of the headquarters: 316492.

"And what guts Charlie had, to go off with them! Don't you think so?"

"Yes..."

He placed it back on the table. Who cared about Charlie's guts and the Amal who wanted to toss the Rdg8 to the bersagliere under the fig tree? Other things filled his mind, this morning. To begin with, the bitter taste Junieh had left in his mouth with the memory of the filthy washbasin, the filthy bidet, and so on. Because the illusions of the Royal Room had not lasted too long. When Ninette had fallen asleep, replete and exhausted, the usual throes had reemerged. Reemerging they had doubled his need to know who she was, and he'd rummaged through her purse. Warily, with the caution of a thief. He hoped to find a document that would draw her out of anonymity, some piece of paper with a name, a surname, a date of birth, a telephone number, an address. But the purse contained nothing but a wallet with dollars and Lebanese currency, a comb, a holy card with the Virgin's profile, and two wedding rings. One small, suited to the circumference of her ring finger, and one large. A man's. Then, overwhelmed by the anger that comes with powerlessness, he had awakened her: "Who are you?!?" But smiling with unforeseen sadness, she'd answered: "I am Ninette and I love you." Then she had gone back to sleep and, far from being flattered or touched he had felt a kind of distress.

"Thank God Charlie found Bilal! And thank God the wounded man was at Bilal's house!" Martino went on.

"Yes..."

The kind of distress that hampers us when we feel in debt or at fault because we are loved by somebody we don't love. In the letter accompanying the absurd gift of the cross-shaped anchor he had told her that the reason he refused sentimental involvements was a crisis he had to face and resolve all alone. And certainly he hadn't lied. But the truth included something else: the nature, the cause, of that crisis. A cause he had never explored, never analyzed. What if the howls of the stray dogs and the crows of the crazed roosters weren't the reflection of a discontent with the others but with himself? What if the nightmare of entropy and the anguished search for the formula of Life were the product of his fear of love or his inability to love? He shuddered. He asked himself if at twenty-six he had ever loved anybody, his parents for example, or the girl in Milan. And the answer was no. What he felt for his parents wasn't love. It was an obligation to love, a duty imposed by the bond called family. We-gave-you-life-so-you-have-the-obligation-and-the-duty-to-love-us. Nor had he loved the girl in Milan. Rather than love, the love the chaplain described, that one had been a state of euphoria: an enthusiasm due to the enchantment of overcoming together the hurdle of virginity, discovering together the mysterious pleasures of sensuality. After leaving her, in fact, he had transferred the mysterious pleasures to women with whom there wasn't any hurdle to overcome, any discovery to make, and he had forgotten her.

"Charlie caught the ball. He said to Bilal this-man-has-to-be-hospitalized, and this set up the whole business."

"Yes..."

Forgotten the way we forget a stranger encountered on the bus. Well, probably the only person whose love he'd answered with a little love was his grandmother. "Remember that nobody loves you more than Grandma. Remember that you can tell Grandma everything, ask her for everything. Even a bicycle," she used to say. And, each time she did, he felt a fire inside. With that fire he cried: "Don't ever die, Grandma!" He hadn't spoken or eaten for days, after her death, and hated his parents who continued to speak and to eat. But little by little he had forgotten her too, and now it was as if she had always been dead. When he thought of her, he didn't even feel nostalgia... Maybe in order to overcome the crisis, the nightmare of the stray dogs and the crazed roosters, he simply needed to relinquish himself to another human being: to give up his own self, to accept the slavery of Ninette's love. Maybe... But the cure sounded so difficult, so contrary to his temperament and to what he was searching for, that only a miracle or a cataclysm could have dragged him to it.

"As for Bilal, he paid the debt right away. Know how?"

"No..."

"He had a militiaman tell Charlie that eleven Khomeinists have arrived here from Bekaa with a huge quantity of explosives to slaughter the Italians, and that they are hiding in the Harek Hreik quarter."

He started.

"And how do you know it?"

"I know it because I was with Charlie when the militiaman blurted it out, of course! The result is that Charlie asked for another meeting with Zandra Sadr, got one for tonight, and..."

"Martino, shut up and get ready," Charlie ordered, bursting into the office. "You too, Hamlet. You too, Stefano."

They left the headquarters. With the headlights off they drove to Haret Hreik, stopped in front of an elegant building protected by a machine gun and a dozen guards.

"Should I come too, chief?" Angelo asked.

"No. You stay here with Stefano and wait," Charlie grunted.

He was brusque because the night before he'd seen him sneak off with his Ophelia and now he felt hurt. Not for a matter of discipline, of course, but because he'd missed the occasion to mutter go-ahead-son-go-ahead: it doesn't take a miracle or a cataclysm to learn how to love and be loved.

But Angelo didn't blink.

"Good," he answered.

*　*　*

And he meant it, he thought. He wasn't eager to witness the show that in a while would be staged at the third floor of the elegant building. He knew it so well, by now, that staying in the jeep he could recount it down to the smallest detail. Preceded by three muzzles armed with Kalashnikovs and trailed by an ultrapolite Martino, Charlie entered a room furnished with nothing but an enormous Bukara rug, a tiny inlaid table, and many cushions. On the best cushions, His Most Reverend Eminence with a black cloak, a black turban, his long white prophet's beard: more motionless than a vulture crouched on a tree to await his daily portion of corpses to devour. At his sides, and in the same posture, his two sons. One lean and swarthy, bearded, who resembled him as a rapacious bird resembles another; one athletic and blond, clean-shaven, who looked like a sluggard in blue jeans. The first, just graduated in theology at the Khomeini university in Qom and impatient to inherit the paternal scepter. The second, still a student in economics at the American University in Beirut and anxious to emigrate to the not so hated United States. Then the three Kalashnikov-toting muzzles withdrew, Charlie and Martino moved forward. They greeted His Most Reverend Eminence who kept his head very low, so low that all you could see was a pair of white and shaggy eyebrows, and invited them to sit on the rug. Martino obeyed promptly. Charlie, rather slowly and taking care not to expose the Browning High Power strapped to his ankle. Soon after a woman in a chador entered with five glasses of hot syrupy tea. Humble, frightened, she placed it on the tiny inlaid table and His Most Reverend Eminence interrupted his crouched-vulture motionlessness. Raising his head and revealing a huge lumpy nose, he pointed to the glasses. Charlie took one, Martino too, and a heavy silence followed: a ridiculous hush during which you heard nothing but the gurgle of swallowing throats. And so the overture that precedes the curtain raising.

The curtain rose on the sweet cabaletta that Charlie performed without changing a note he'd written with the Condor. Harps and violas, lutes and harpsichords, fifes and such hypocrisies to make your skin crawl. Most Reverend Eminence, I hope that You are enjoying good health and I beg Your pardon for having requested this audience at such a late hour. Translate, Martino. Martino translated and the old bastard faintly answered: Captain, Our health is excellent and We are happy to receive you at any hour, but what is the reason for your visit this time? The reason is very serious, Most Reverend Eminence, but before exposing it I must thank You for giving the muezzins the sentence we worked out. Translate, Martino. Martino translated and the old bastard answered: Captain, We have kept Our promise and We hope that Allah the Merciful and Omniscient and Omnipercipient will continue to protect Our Italian brothers. Then Charlie assumed a less mellifluous tone and giving up the harps, the violas, the lutes, the harpsichords, the fifes, the hypocrisies, began sounding the trumpets. Number one, he said, Allah the merciful and omniscient and omnipercipient is protecting those brothers rather little and badly: not all the faithful respect their Imam's orders. They even mangle them with a noun that refers to a bodily function. In all due respect, Most Reverend Eminence, talieni-khara. Shit-Italians. With such a noun a gang of rascals has invaded the Twenty-Five etcetera. In short, he indirectly denounced his friend Bilal. He did it to demonstrate to the old bastard that his authority was crumbling, to make him uncomfortable and consequently to obtain major concessions. Number two, some dissidents had informed him that eleven terrorists from the Bekaa had come to Beirut with a huge quantity of explosives meant for slaughtering the Italians etcetera. The eleven were hiding in Haret Hriek, His Most Reverend Eminence's quarter. That is, a neighborhood where a leaf shouldn't fall without the Imam knowing about it. Translate, Martino. Martino translated, and the old bastard counterattacked with a trombone blast. Captain, what you have said distresses Us deeply. Indeed a very ugly thing is ignoring the orders of this Allah's messenger, and We are not consoled by reminding you that the fields of every church are sown with the weeds of the deaf. Nevertheless, captain, Our blood brothers haven't behaved too well either. A serious mistake was firing on the green automobile in Shatila. Then Charlie gave up the trumpets and switched to the drums nay the tam-tam, and intentionally skipping the adjective Most-Reverend he thundered: Eminence, the Italians have behaved so well that they've even admitted to their field hospital a guerrilla who would be otherwise dead or in the hands of the government police. Boom! They also have continued to dole out plasma and to patiently bear the spittles, the insults, of your followers. Boom, boom! But now they are fed up, and those who are fed up often end with changing their minds. What if Allah the merciful and omniscient and omnipercipient left them no choice but to defend themselves by more effective means than a gunburst? What if friends became enemies and brothers killed brothers? This is the message from my general: a man who doesn't like to turn the other cheek. Boom, boom, boom.

He sighed. Don't think it, he said to himself, clean your meninges instead. See if you still know how to pick the astonishing flowers of mathematics, of the abstraction composed of concreteness, of the fantasy composed of reality. Think about the problem of the raindrop or the indefinite integral of a constant. You do remember what that is: right? It is the product of the constant multiplied by the variable, the whole increased by an arbitrary constant etcetera. And the indefinite integral of a variable raised to a power? Well, that one needed a pen and paper and a light. He dug in his pockets, found the pen and the notebook he always carried with him, turned the flashlight on, and began to write murmuring, "Let's see... The integral of x raised to n multiplied by dx is equal to x raised to $n + 1$ divided by $n + 1$, the whole increased by c. Therefore the indefinite integral of a variable raised to a power is equal to a fraction with, at the numerator, the variable raised to the primary power plus one unit and, at the denominator, the exponent of the power plus one unit. The whole increased by an arbitrary constant... And the integral defined in an interval? Let's see. The integral defined in the interval between a and b of $f(x)$ multiplied by dx is equal to the difference between $f(b)$ and $f(a)$. So the integral defined in an interval equals the difference between the value of the indefinite integral calculated to the greatest extreme and the value of the indefinite integral calculated to the least extreme... Yes, he still knew how to pick the astonishing flowers of the abstraction composed of concreteness, of the fantasy composed of reality. He still knew how to swim in the clear waters of pure thought! He smiled, turned off the flashlight, turned to Stefano who kept silent and intimidated by the incomprehensible mumblings. He wondered if he should say something to keep him company. But he didn't have time because Charlie was returning with Martino and joyously jumped in the jeep.

"Home, boys, home! Get in back, Stefano: the chief is driving!"

Joyously? He licked his chops like the cat who has eaten a mouse.

"And where should I sit, chief?" Angelo asked.

Forgetful of the brusque tone, the cat snorted.

"Up front with me, Hamlet! Come on!" Then he flipped on the walkie-talkie and: "Condor One, Condor One! Charlie-Charlie here!"

"Charlie-Charlie, Condor One here," answered the general's vigorous voice. "Did it work?"

"Fully, Condor One, fully! We return with flying colors!"

Martino instead was wailing.

"Oh! Oh, oh!"

3

What a job, tonight! What responsibility, what emotion! When Charlie had cut off the words Most-Reverend to thunder what-if-Allah-the-merciful-and-omniscient-and-omnipercipient-left-us-no-choice-but-to-defend-ourselves-by-means-more-effective-than-a-gunburst, he had felt like dying. This time we won't get out of here alive, he had thought, this time they'll cut our throats. Zandra Sadr was so offended! His sons were so angry! All three were panting like people suffering from an attack of asthma. It had taken several minutes to see them calming down and to hear the old voice faintly say: "Captain, tell your general that friends should not become enemies and that brothers should not kill brothers. We'll find out where the eleven bearers of evil have hidden, we'll rip the harmful weeds from the garden." An answer that meant: agreed, my friend, I'll give the order to bump them off. So Charlie had resumed the harps and the violas, the lutes and the harpsichords, the fifes and the hypocrisies, not to mention the words Most-Reverend, and: "I'm sure of it, Most Reverend Eminence. Besides, whose eyes see better than the master of the house's eyes? Whose ears hear better than his ears?" The worst, however, wasn't this. It was being a soldier. My God, what a fool had he been not to pronounce the three words which prevent one from joining the army! What an idiot had he been to show up at the barracks!

"Oh! Oh! Oh!"

Martino wailed again and Stefano turned in surprise.

"Martino, why do you wail?" he whispered.

"Because I'm unhappy, dear."

"And why are you unhappy?"

"Because I'm a soldier, dear."

To begin with, as soon as he'd arrived at the barracks, they had cut his long hair and shaved his head à la Yul Brynner. "What's this mane? Come here, curly boy, and let's take care of it!" After shaving him à la Yul Brynner, they had given him the uniform: a most unbecoming garment which didn't fit his body and his taste for close-fitting, brightly colored suits. Moreover, in a greenish color that clashed with his complexion. With the uniform, two instruments of torture called boots. And with these they had forced him to walk, to click his heels, to march until each of his feet had become an immense painful sore. He who adored soft leather moccasins and to spare his feet always took a taxi... The third day, he'd burst into tears: enough, murder-me, I-believe-ineuthanasia. Then he'd sat on the ground to watch the others keep walking, clicking their heels, marching, one-two, one-two, and the corporal had punished him. Know how? By sending him to clean the latrines and the showers. The latrines were a terrible place because of the stink, of the urine that was squirted everywhere, of the excrement that floated in the paper-clogged toilets. The showers were almost worse because by using shoddy laundry soap instead of good lanolin bath soap those animals lost their body hair. The body hair mingled with lather, the lather got stuck in the drains, the drains needed to be cleansed by hand, and again he'd burst into tears. How could they impose such a thing on a university graduate, a cultivated person, a young man of courtesy and style? In tears he'd asked to speak with the lieutenant and: "Sir, instead of shooting, marching, clicking the heels, the army should tell the soldiers how to flush a toilet and toss away the hair-clogged lather. Please give me rubber gloves to clean the showers and a mask to clean the toilets." The lieutenant, a very nice and civilized guy, had wrapped him in a strange look of complicity. Then he'd given him gloves and a mask, and: "Do you speak English, French, and possibly Arabic?" "Yessir. I have a university degree in languages and I've done my thesis on popular Arabic literature. Summa cum laude." "Then why clean the toilets? Go to Beirut. They're desperate for interpreters, there." Ah, what a mistake had he made listening to his suggestion!

"Don't you like being a soldier, Martino?" Stefano whispered.

"No, dear, I don't."

"Why don't you, Martino?"

"Because soldiers are filthy, dear. They don't flush the toilets, they leave the hair-clogged lather behind them, and on top of that they make war."

War had never interested him. Not even in an intellectual sense. He had never read a book on war, never seen a war movie, and he knew so little about it that at his arrival in Beirut he thought he'd come to a city devastated by hurricanes. But what made him unhappy wasn't really the war. It was the silly, presumptuous, aberrant machismo that characterized everyone in the army. It was the glorification and the deification of the testicle as a symbol of masculinity, the exaltation and the apotheosis of the cock as a symbol of virility... The need to prove that you're more male than the other males, that you shoot straighter, you hit harder, you drink more wine and beer and never stagger. The urgency to talk all the time about women, about fucking, about screwing, to admire people like Pistoia, to praise his exploits, his notorious bravura in simul-

taneously seducing three women named Joséphine Caroline Geraldine.
Taking the Condor as a model, considering him a man's man, a super-
man, a supermale who shoots better than the others, hits better than
the others, drinks better than the others, screws better than the others
though nobody knows whom he screws, maybe he doesn't screw at all,
but nobody would ever believe it because he's so special. He even
opens the bottles of champagne in a special way: instead of uncorking
them, he decapitates them with a bayonet swipe across the neck. Slash!
And the neck shoots off, leaving the guillotined bottle splashing champagne as a guillotined body would splash blood. He'd seen him do this
numberless times, and each time he'd felt a sort of disgust because it
wasn't an innocent gesture: it was a macabre rite, a macho rite of
destruction, the gesture of an executioner who delights in brandishing
the ax and executing. But of course the idiots wanted to imitate him.
Know how? With the little wine bottles that have metal caps instead of
corks. And if you told them that the metal cap can be removed with the
fingers, employing a bayonet is more than superfluous, they got mor-
tally offended. The bayonet was an appendix of their genitals, see.
Their real phallus. To figure this out, you only had to take a look at the
Pink Room.

"Are you thinking about war, Martino?" Stefano whispered.

"No, dear."

"What are you thinking about?"

"About us, dear. About the Pink Room."

The Pink Room was located on the top floor, next to the billet of the
carabinieri on duty at headquarters, and they called it so because it was
upholstered in pink velvet. Including doors and wardrobes. The one of
the carabinieri, similarly upholstered in blue velvet, was called the Blue
Room. Both of them had belonged to the emir's favorites who liked to
make love surrounded by pink or blue. Well, the pink velvet no longer
existed. Slashing at it with their bayonets, Gaspare and Ugo and Fifì
had destroyed it completely. Again, the phallus as a symbol of destruction. And this principle extended to the bathroom: a place that must
have been astonishing at the time of the favorites. Black marble floor,
gilded swan-shaped faucets, bidet and shower with adjustable jets, circular bathtub. Well, his bunkmates had soiled the tub so thoroughly
that the shower could hardly be used. They'd also unhinged or up-
rooted the faucets, scratched the black marble floor, broken the bidet.
Not to mention the obscene images they hung above their cots. An
orgy of breasts, vaginas, buns, garter-bedecked thighs. A bacchanalia of
blondes and brunettes with their nightgowns half-opened over tanta-

lizing nipples or pubis... And the specter of Lady Godiva. Because the ultimate product of machismo in uniform was named Lady Godiva. Thumbing through a porno magazine Gaspare had come across the photo of an erotic doll and the following blurb: "Lady Godiva, the ideal companion for your solitary nights. Perfect human measurements: 99-69-99. Thermal-sound system. She laughs, cries, turns you on. Price, eighty thousand liras. Mail orders promptly filled. Maximum discretion." And he'd gone crazy with exultation. Ugo and Stefano and Fifì, as well. "A sixty-nine-centimeter waist! What a gas!" they shouted. "Ninety-nine in the tits, ninety-nine in the ass! What a pussy, boys, what a pussy!" Fifì even insisted that he had tried one out in New York. "It works, guaranteed, it works!" They were also excited by the name Godiva. They thought it came from the verb *godere*, to enjoy. So it had been useless to explain that the verb had nothing to do with the name, that Lady Godiva was the heroine of an English medieval legend: a lady who in order to protest the taxes imposed by her husband Leofric, Earl of Mercia and Lord of Coventry, had crossed the city on horseback and clothed in nothing but her long golden hair. This had increased their enthusiasm. "Nude? Completely nude?!" Then stuffing the eighty thousand liras in an envelope they'd placed the order, and since then he had lived in the nightmarish fear of the obscene toy's arrival. Ah, if only he could confide his anguish to a friend and ask him why he hadn't pronounced the three words! Charlie, for example. The trouble is that Charlie wasn't a friend. He was a mother. And how can you confide such a secret to a mother? You might as well stab her in the heart.

"Off to bed, boys!" roared the mother bursting with the jeep into the headquarters. And still licking his chops, still rejoicing like the cat who has eaten a mouse, he rushed up to the Condor who waited for the details of the showdown with Zandra Sadr.

Poor Charlie. He would have been less happy had he imagined the recondite threads that would eventually connect Lady Godiva to Bilal's destiny. But who can imagine the unimaginable? That night he didn't even suspect what the next day would bring.

*   *   *

The next day Radio Amal spread a communiqué full of praise for the Italians, and at Haret Hreik eleven bodies were found pierced by 7.62s: the Kalashnikov bullets. A settling of accounts between rival factions, the newspapers commented. Immediately after, six Gobeyre notables with a bouquet of roses showed up at the headquarters sentry box to see the Condor and give him a message of peace. Charlie went outside, searched them as well as the roses, then led them to the former dining room and improvised a ceremony in the presence of all the officers. Pistoia excepted. The six thanked the Condor for the wisdom displayed by their blood brothers during the deplorable attack on the Twenty-Five and for accepting in the field hospital a peaceful citizen who had been wounded in the legs while crossing the street. Afterwards they kissed him on the cheek, one by one, three times apiece, and the Condor was so pleased that the usual tears trembling on his lashes tumbled down like hailstones. Unaware that his weeping was due to an emotive allergy, the six considered it their duty to imitate him or rather to surpass him. So they burst into a chorus of heartrending sobbing and everybody ended up breaking down in earnest.

Everybody but the Professor. That is, the only one who knew how to look with detachment at this strange world where men make you laugh and cry at the same time.

4

The Professor closed the door of his office, sat at his desk, rolled a sheet of paper into the typewriter: an object as precious to him as the *Dialogues* of Plato, the *DeLibero Arbitrio* by Erasmus of Rotterdam, Kant's *Critique of Pure Reason,* or the other pithy volumes contained in the trunk that had burst open at his arrival raising amazement and incredulity. He loved transferring his thoughts to paper, for the well-written page he had an almost maniacal veneration, and a quotation hanging on the wall behind him said: "The spoken word is by its own nature slipshod and imprecise. It offers no time to reflect, to use language with elegance and reason, it leads to reckless judgments, and doesn't keep us company because it requires the presence of others. The written word, on the contrary, offers time to think and to choose terms. It eases the exercise of logic, compels us to give well-pondered judgments, and keeps us company because it is practiced in solitude. Especially when we write, solitude is a great companion." Which explains the ironic half-smile that creased his face neither young nor old, neither handsome nor ugly, and the care he took in sustaining his role as a nonprotagonist or as a witness who stays behind the scenes. What's more, it explains why he spoke so little and why he wanted to write a book on the tragicomedy unfolding before his eyes. The novel we are reading.

But, more than a character, the Professor was a charade: a game of mirrors, a mise-en-abîme. That's why we only have this means of knowing him: three letters addressed to a wife who didn't exist. The one that follows is the first one.

*   *   *

You asked me how things were going in Beirut. I replied that they were going as always, and surely you guessed that this was a trick to avoid subjects I didn't want to face on the phone. You know to what extent I abhor that barbaric nay primitive instrument, that most hideous gadget which doesn't permit us to see the face of the person we are speaking with, and you know that I am not a great talker. When I speak, I never manage to fully say what I want. When I write I do, instead, and here's the truth: things couldn't go worse. By now the tragedy has become a farce, and the farce cohabits with madness. We degrade ourselves with questionable compromises, we play at dice with cunning and fraud, we buy our safety with blackmail and plasma and lies... Not by chance we just exchanged tears and kisses with the ones who would like to slaughter us. Not by chance five times a day the muezzins sing out from the minarets "Don't touch the Italians, the Italians give us blood, the Italians are our blood brothers" and yet we live in the expectation of death: every deed of ours aims at the duel which sooner or later we'll fight with her. What kind of duel I don't know, though the third truck still is the face that death offers up, and none of us has overcome the trauma of that terrible Sunday. I, even less than the others. Ah, those handsome ripped-up boys! Those fine young men each of whom could have been our son! They arrived at the field hospital without legs, without arms, with their intestines hanging out... I saw only one who was intact: a twenty-year-old black Marine who had lost his mind instead of his limbs and who gulping distilled water repeated: "Wine, Italians, wine." But the point is another one. It is what I thought while I watched them. I thought: in the end, what distinguishes me from a kamikaze in civilian clothes? Soldiers in uniform can commit massacres identical to those of a kamikaze. And in a logical process (logical, thus alien to the appeal of rage or grief) I identified myself with the ferocity of the kamikaze in civilian clothes. I steered my boat toward the comfortable harbor of cynicism. Or of coherence? Let me anticipate your answer: "You are an intellectual, and an intellectual cannot allow himself the partisanships of faith or passion or morality. An intellectual must identify himself with everybody, he must understand everything and everyone." Granted. But those who understand everything and everyone end up absolving everything and everyone; those who absolve everything and everyone end up forgiving everything and everyone; those who forgive everything and everyone believe in nothing. And those who believe in nothing are cynics. That simple.

Coherence or not, and at the cost of giving in to the partisanships of faith or passion or morality, I intend to keep myself very distant from the comfortable harbor of cynicism. And if you argue that I didn't need to come here to discover that the uniform isn't a monk's robe, that in the barracks we don't learn to hunt pheasants, that the military commits slaughters identical to the one we suffered, I'll defend myself by insisting that one judges his or her profession by the way he or she performs it. I never performed it for the purpose of killing. For me, the uniform has never been a symbol of abuse and violence. It has always been a Franciscan concept, an act of humility. Indeed, a monk's robe. The barracks, not factories of homicides and suicides but human and social structures: abbeys where young individuals lodge and receive an education in order to become men. I hate the martyrdom as I hate the fanfares, the banners in the wind, and the authority. I consider the last one a harmful principle, a trap that leads to violence by syllogism: authority equal weapons, weapons equal force, force equal oppression, oppression equal violence. And, you'll admit it, I don't teach my soldiers how to commit violence. I teach them how to grow, to make use of their lives with intelligence and dignity and possibly without fear: the draft is not and should not be an abuse to bear. It is and should be a privilege, a school that cuts the umbilical cords of the young people still glued to the tiny cosmos of the family: Mommy who spoils them with her cares, breakfast-is-ready-and-the-button-is-stitched, Daddy who weakens them with his worries, don't-speak-with-strangers, pay-attention-when-you-cross-the-street... If I'm wrong, tell me why the period of military service is never forgotten, why old people speak of it with ill-concealed nostalgia, with the unconfessed wistfulness one has for a good experience. All right, in some cases the memory nay the nightmare of bullying and cruelty remains: nobody can deny that the barracks often resort to over-coercive methods, that certain officers treat the soldiers like acephalous bodies or victims to rampage over. The army is a mixture that contains any kind of elements, it reflects the society it belongs to, and all societies are full of imbeciles. No surprise that so many of them end up joining the army. But it's wrong to judge us from that perspective or that perspective only, and those who do so lose track of an important detail: despite our many defects and our many imbeciles, we're indispensable.

Once we talked about this, you and I. And in spite of your sigh of reproof you had to admit that in the entire history of this planet not a single society has managed to exist without soldiers. The recognition cheered me as much as the sigh of reproof made me unhappy. My dear, no society has ever existed without soldiers for the simple reason that no society can exist without soldiers: the protoanthropoid who club in hand prevented the wild beasts from entering the cave where his tribe lived was a soldier. And since it's legitimate to suppose that also at those times soldiers were chosen from among the most robust, the most accustomed to toil, it's equally legitimate to deduce that other thankless tasks were entrusted to them. For example, removing the mass of stones that blocked the cave's entrance, or capturing the wild boar to roast or lighting a fire in the rain. Does it seem like so little to you? The Countess of Castiglione loved to assert that military men are babies. Had she said that to me, I would have answered: Madame la Comtesse, then how is it that, as soon as an emergency arises, you immediately turn to those babies? A dam breaks, a valley is flooded, and you call for us. An earthquake breaks out, a city gets destroyed, and you call for us. A rebellion bursts, looting rages, and you call for us. You send us to die at Caporetto, at Anzio, at Cephalonia, at Stalingrad, at Giarabub, at Iwo Jima, in Normandy, in Korea, in Vietnam, in Afghanistan, wherever you need butchery flesh. Yesterday, today, tomorrow. In any age, under any regime. Madame la Comtesse, I lose my temper when the dyed-in-the-wool antimilitarists stick us in the pillory with the accusations warmongers-dolts-ignoramuses... As if the warmongers and dolts and ignoramuses existed only among the citizens in uniform. As if the citizens in civilian clothes were by definition veritable saints and lofty intellects and fonts of wisdom... I lose my temper and answer: nossir, I'm not a baby. I'm not a warmonger. I'm not a dolt. I'm not an ignoramus. The uniform doesn't blindfold me. It doesn't shut down my humanity and my intellect. It doesn't keep me from loving culture, from reading Plato and Erasmus and Kant. It doesn't prevent me from taking sides with Man, from understanding that despite his treachery and foolishness he truly is the measure of all things. In any case, the only scale we have for weighing life. The only benchmark to explain it. So I believe in my trade, and...

And yet, since things have gone as they're going in Beirut, since I saw those handsome ripped-up boys and that black twenty-year-old Marine who had lost his mind instead of his limbs, this trade gives me a sort of dissatisfaction. It pinches me like a pair of narrow boots, like a love that doesn't gratify anymore and so throws us into the arms of another love... My dear, about this tragedy that sometimes degenerates into tragicomedy and sometimes into farce I want to write a book. A novel. You know that the novel has always attracted me because it's a vessel into which one can simultaneously pour reality and fantasy, dialectics and poetry, ideas and feelings. You know that it has always seduced me because its medley of reality and fantasy, dialectics and poetry, ideas and feelings, has the potential to provide a truth more true than real truth. A reinvented, universalized truth in which everybody can identify and recognize himself. It never ignores Man, the novel. Whatever story it recounts, and in whatever time or space a story unfolds, the novel tells about men. About human beings. And I want to tell about men, about human beings. For years I've wanted it, for years I've waited for the occasion to do it, and the occasion has finally arrived: a miniature Iliad is stirring around me. A modern Iliad where (with a little humor) I can locate almost all the heroes of the divine poem. Beginning with Helen and Paris and Menelaus, given the fact that Helen is Beirut itself. Paris and Menelaus, the two halves of the contested city. And of course there are the other kings and warriors, there are the women, the priests, the shrewish gods wrangling among themselves. There is Agamemnon, here a general with the ravenous energy of a lion who lacking a forest spouts his rage on us and yells, deafens, tyrannizes. There is Ulysses, here a mustached giant who prefers the sophistries of intrigue to the crudities of warmaking and whips up a new one every day. His Ithaca, his dream and goal, to imitate Lawrence of Arabia: an archetype he resembles as a wolf resembles a greyhound. There is Achilles, here an innocuous pirate we never see because he stays next to the seashore to uselessly yearn for combat. And then Philoctetus, here a mild colonel we see even less because he stays up on a hill to avoid confrontation. Then Ajax, here an amusing Don Juan whose tent swarms with Brissidas and Cressidas and whose mania for coming to blows has brought us woe. Then Nestor, here an aristocratic horseman of little wisdom but undoubted eloquence who oppresses his fellow men with Latin proverbs and Napoleonic anecdotes. Then Antenor, here a meek Neapolitan Jew who would sell Vesuvius and the Weeping Wall to avoid waging war. Then Diomedes, here a meticulous technocrat who lives for the Regulations and collects booby traps with the pedantry of a philatelist. Then Hector, here a magnificent dwarf armed with a Kalashnikov and dressed in a patched jacket, who sweeps the streets of the Old City...

Fictitious comparisons, pretentious quibbles? Perhaps. Actually, the character who most intrigues me has nothing to do with the models offered by the divine poem. He is the hamletic squire of Ulysses, a handsome pensive sergeant who deludes himself with the hope of resolving via mathematics two most unsolvable problems: the stubborn love that a Lebanese woman as mysterious as gorgeous throws upon him, and an existential crisis that Ludwig Boltzmann's theories have doubled. One evening I *asked him what he was searching for, and he gravely answered: "The formula of Life, sir." Then he sketched out an equation composed of five symbols, $S = K \ln W$, said that this was the formula of Death, that according to it Death always wins, and concluded: "Nevertheless there must be a way to demonstrate the contrary, to prove that it's Life who always wins. And I intend to find it." I'm intrigued, nay fascinated, also by his gorgeous and mysterious Lebanese, though. I sense such a heartbreaking tragedy, such a heroic unhappiness, behind her whirlwind of desires. And finally I'm captivated by the crowd that languishes inside the walls of Troy. For instance the archers who suffer in the encampments of the Achaeans, and whom Homer never speaks of. You know, studying the Iliad I often wondered who were the soldiers that Agamemnon and Ulysses and Ajax and Nestor and Achilles had brought to die in a war that didn't concern them. Now I no longer do. They were the boys I see on the guard towers, at the checkpoints, at the posts, in the offices or on patrol: the marò, the bersaglieri, the paratroopers, the incursori, the young men who risk getting killed and whom the army indicates with the anonymous word "troops." One was named Fabio and on a terrible Sunday he betrayed his slaughtered friend. One was named Ferruccio and to forget having lost his eighteen years, his youth, he spent the nights chatting with a little boy who had escaped the massacre of a thousand Trojans. One was named Onion and standing guard along the edge of a ditch full of dead he shook with terror. One was named String and used to give his food to a malnourished child, one was named Nazarene and preached peace, one was named Gino and wrote tender poems, one was named Martino and tore himself apart in an unsuspected drama... Fictitious comparisons or not, pretentious quibbles or not, the story doesn't change. The eternal story, the eternal novel of Man who at war manifests himself in all his truth. Because nothing, unfortunately, reveals us as much as war. Nothing exacerbates with the same strength our beauty and our ugliness, our intelligence and our stupidity, our bestiality and our humanity, our courage and our cowardice: our enigma. In fact the danger lies in narrating a story already narrated, in writing a novel already written. But I don't worry. The art of writing consists of repeating things already said and of repeating them in a way that people believe they read them for the first time, Remy de Gourmont used to maintain. And I know how to repeat the already said things in a way that they seem said for the first time: writing in my way. That is, without yielding to the temptation of sermons or to the fear of judgments. In both cases, merchandise exposed to the inclemencies of fashion or time. Therefore perishable. Look: to tell about men, these bizarre animals that make us laugh and cry at the same time,* *it takes two sentiments which in the end are two reasonings: pity and irony. In other words, all we need is a smile on the lips and a tear in the eyes.*

Just the point of view expressed by the phantasmagorical extra who now roves among us with a pencil in hand: the woman we call the-Saigon-journalist. Because guess what her definition of men is. The icy one we find in every encyclopedia. Yet enriched by a note as contemptuous as tender. "Two-handed mammals fitted for standing erect and capable of articulate language, characterized by a cranial volume and a cerebral mass which in respect to the facial portion of the skull are larger than those of the other mammals. Consequently, much funnier than the other mammals and more touching than any other animal."

(What if she is my alter ego, what if she intends to write my book?)

SECOND ACT

CHAPTER ONE

1

NOW THAT THE STORY spreads out to give us characters so far kept in the shadows, other actors of the tragicomedy the Professor is using to write his miniature Iliad, a smile on the lips serves us better than a tear in the eyes. Without that smile, in fact, we wouldn't be able to bear the scenery in which the events unfold: the orgy of foolishness that favors the sadistic intelligence of Chaos, the triumph of masochism that feeds the madness of the city. Everybody shoots at everybody, each member of each group or subgroup has a Kalashnikov or an M16 or an Rpg, and he drags it around the same way normal people drag an umbrella on rainy days. When you least expect it, rat-tat-tat! Bang! Just to exercise his fingers, at times, to overcome the tedium and kill who-ever happens by: an old woman crossing the street, a child playing in a courtyard, a newborn sleeping in its mother's arms. Why not? Muni-tions abound. They come from all over the world, in the harbor there's always a ship that unloads them on the pier, in the bays there's always a boat that unloads them on the beach. They cost very little and the prayer that Christians and Muslims recite in their hearts goes like this: "Our Father and Our Allah who are art in Heaven, supply us with the daily 7.62s and 5.56s and rockets and bombs, lead us not into the temptation of making peace, and free us from any goodness, amen." Don't try to understand. The process of understanding requires a mini-mum of logic, and here logic doesn't exist. The Palestinians, for exam-ple, have split into two sects: one loyal to a certain Abu Mussa and one loyal to a certain Arafat. In nearby Tripoli, the only place they haven't been kicked out of, they slaughter each other with artillery. In Bourji el Barajni, in Sabra, in Shatila, they do it with revolvers. To satisfy their desire to see them dead, their enemies no longer need to perform massacres: they only have to cast a glance at the alleys and garbage heaps. In nine cases out of ten, there's the corpse of an Abumussian eliminated by an Arafatian, or of an Arafatian eliminated by an

Abumussian. Essentially, the same thing that happens between the Amal and the Sons of God: until yesterday united by a secret alliance and accomplices in abominations. Aren't the Amal the ones who have carried out Zandra Sadr's order and liquidated the eleven Khomeinists from the Bekaa? (But don't worry: tomorrow they'll be friends again.) Squabbles take place between the phalangists and the Kataeb, both devoted to the Holy Virgin and to Gemayel, and on the Shouf Mountains the Druzes are crucifying the Maronites. They cut off their arms and their legs, then they leave them to bleed. And as if this weren't enough, serious disagreements are splitting the governmentals: the Eighth Brigade, made up of Christian soldiers and Christian officers, sneers at the Sixth Brigade, made up of Shiite soldiers but almost always led by Christian officers. Each time the Christian officers order a shelling of Haret Hreik with the mortars placed along the Galerie Semaan, the Shiite soldiers alter the trajectory and hit the hill shielding the quarter. A lovely hill in the Eastern Zone, already mauled by the artillery of the socialist-billionaire prince Jumblatt who tries to hit the Baabda presidential palace where Gemayel lives, and already tormented by the clashes shredding the hottest stretch of the Green Line. That is, the three hundred yards from the church of Saint-Michel to the Galerie Semaan. Attention, attention: the church of Saint-Michel is the last outpost of Gobeyre, the place where the Amal are concentrated to defend the Shiite quarters and to try encroaching on the Eastern Zone; the Galerie Semaan is the last outpost of Hazmiye, the place where the governmentals are concentrated to defend the Christian quarters and to try encroaching on the Western Zone. The lovely hill overlooks those three hundred yards, and guess what sits on its top: a convent. Guess who stays in the convent: the paratroopers, the carabinieri, and the incursori of the Ruby base. Consequently, every day the battalion under Falcon's command sucks up a good portion of the grenades and Katyushas and stray bullets that fly in the area.

Yet the dramas which characterize this base have nothing to do with that gunfire's torment: at the Ruby our heroes despair, sigh, suffer for very different reasons. Let's see what reasons, now that the story spreads out to give us characters so far kept in the shadows. And to confirm how funny and how touching is the two-handed mammal fitted for standing erect, capable of articulate language, characterized by a cranial volume etcetera. It's a late November day, one month has passed since the terrible Sunday, and we find ourselves at the Ruby where an angry Condor is pacing Falcon's office. Falcon himself has slunk off with the excuse of going to the latrines.

* * *

No, he didn't like the sloppiness with which Jumblatt's Druzes aimed at Gemayel's palace and peppered this base. He didn't like the cynicism with which the Shiite gunners altered their mortars' trajectory and shelled this hill instead of Haret Hreik. He didn't like the friction that was growing between the Sixth and the Eighth Brigades and inside the Sixth. If the crack widened into a break, the governmentals would be split and the Green Line would become impassable. But even less he liked what he had just discovered by accident. By accident! Thanks to a nitwit incursore who'd taken advantage of his visit to pose him a life-or-death-question! The blood went to his head as he thought over that absurd conversation. "Go ahead, let's hear your life-or-death-question. Is it the usual ailing mother or dying grandfather you all resort to for getting a leave and going to Italy?" "Nossir, general. I don't want to go back to Italy. I want to stay in Beirut and get married." "Get married?!? What does it mean get-married?!" "It means I'm in love, general, sir." "In love?!? You come to your general to say you're in love?!?" "Yessir. And to ask for a loan." "A loan?!?" "Yessir. Six thousand dollars." "Six thousand dollars?!?" "Yessir. That's all I need to put together eight thousand. Having been here six weeks, I've received two thousand dollars in salary and..." "Eight thousand dollars? Why the hell do you need eight thousand dollars?!?" "To pay the ransom, general, sir." "What ransom?!? Who's been kidnapped?!?" "Nobody, sir. I mean the ransom to redeem the future mother of my children. In accordance with local custom, she has been sold by her parents to another guy. To step aside this guy demands eight thousand dollars. If he doesn't get it, he marries her. And I kill myself." "Kill yourself?!?" "Yessir, general. The heart does as it will." He had eaten him alive. You-delinquent, I'll-ship-you-back-to-Italy. And the answer had been: "General, sir! If you ship me back, you have to ship back the whole battalion. At the Ruby base, almost everybody is in love with a Lebanese woman and wants to marry her, to pay the ransom." So he had chased the nitwit away, set up a rapid inquiry, and... It was true, God blasted. Sacrosanctly true. You sent them on patrol, and they fell in love. You posted them at a checkpoint, and they fell in love. You dumped them up on a guard tower, and they fell in love. You shut them inside an M113, and they fell in love. It was a bank of love, this fucking base. It consumed love like a bakery consumes flour, it scattered love like a perfume factory scatters the fragrance of lavender and bergamot. Or like a contagious disease scatters a virus. But not the jolly and inoffensive love that Pistoia assuaged with his Joséphines and Geraldines and Carolines, not the lewd carnal love the marò satisfied with their Sheilas and Fatimas and the various prostitutes of Shatila: the sugary, languorous, romantic love of Pierrots sighing in the moonlight! The love that longs for weddings and orange blossoms and Mendelssohn's march! The love that weakens, cretinizes, distracts, and leads you to say imbecilities like the-heart-does-as-it-will! His paratroopers... His incursori... The battalion that was considered the most virile, the most manly, ladykillers par excellence!

He stopped pacing up and down, sat at the desk, rested in dismay. The fucking hill! All he got from this fucking hill was preoccupations, disappointments, pains in the neck. And to think that when Gemayel's government had given the Italians that abandoned convent and its surrounding property, he'd felt like the winner of a lottery! He hadn't even considered the risky nearness of Baabda, already Jumblatt's target. He hadn't even worried about the mess left by the Syrians and the Palestinians who during the siege had employed it as their headquarters. Unhinged doors and windows, plundered rooms, bloodstained walls, corridors filled with booby traps. And, in the cellars used as torture chambers to interrogate prisoners, even some mummified fingers. This is an earthly paradise, he'd thought ticking off the advantages. To begin with, the advantage of being located in the Eastern Zone and atop a height that controls the most dangerous stretch of the Green Line. Then, the advantage of a being in a spot with all the requisites to house a battalion: fine olive fields and groves to shade the troops' tents, large clearings for parking, vacant spaces for the garages and offices, huts for storing munitions... As for the convent building, constructed next to solid cliffs and enriched by a wide esplanade that overlooked the three hundred yards from the church of Saint-Michel to the Galerie Semaan, it was all he could desire. Reinforced-concrete walls, cellars deep enough to be transformed into shelters, space to burn. On the ground floor, an immense hall and six smaller rooms plus the chapel. On the first floor, connected to the immense hall by a stairway, the chambers of a school and a kindergarten. On the second floor, a nice kitchen and several bedrooms with baths. The building also had two entrances. The main one, consisting of a big wooden door, in the rear. The secondary one, consisting of a little iron gate, in the side street that originated from the three-hundred-yard stretch. And, thirty yards away, the side street offered the utmost advantage: an unfinished skyscraper which seemed tailor-made to house Ost Ten: the international observation post that would be manned by a squad of Italians and a squad of Americans. Well, he'd grabbed the earthly paradise so quickly that he scarcely had found the time to ask whom the property belonged to. It belonged to twenty nuns of a French order who ran an elementary school with a kindergarten and who had fled during the Israeli siege, he'd later found out. However, the risk of seeing them again was nonexistent. Fifteen had gone back to France and five had died. Killed by a bombardment while they were fleeing. Disintegrated with their primers, their dictionaries, their church vessels including the cruets of holy water and wine, the Blessed Sacrament, the Missal. But, not even one month after the installation, Falcon had called him in a tizzy and: "General! They're back!" "Who?" "The dead owners! The disintegrated nuns!"

He slammed his fist on the desk, infuriated. He'd hurried over, and here they were: in excellent health and arrayed with their primers, dictionaries, church vessels including the cruets of holy water and wine, the Blessed Sacrament, the Missal. Four nuns in gray frocks, gray veils and wimples; a novice in black half-length garments, white veil, and no wimple. At their head, Sister Espérance: a tall and wiry Norman in her fifties who darting an icy blue glance and spouting more haughtiness than a king on his throne left you as frozen as an iceberg. "Ça c'est notre maison, messieurs. Déménager immediatement! This is our home, sirs. Out! Move immediately." Next to Sister Espérance, Sister George: a tiny Parisian in her forties, with a small spiteful nose and enormous eyes magnified by double-lens glasses. "Are you deaf, messieurs? Didn't you understand what the Mother Superior just said? Sortez, donc! Get out!" Next to Sister George, Sister Madeleine: a ruddy-faced Marseillaise in her sixties, with the bosom of a wet nurse ready to suckle and hips as massive as a tank. "Déménager, oui, bouger! Leave, yes, move!" Next to Sister Madeleine, Sister Françoise: a thirty-year-old nurse from Nice, very shy and not very attractive, who never opened her mouth but stared at him so reprovingly that he had felt guilty of every crime. Finally, Sister Milady, the novice: a Lebanese about twenty-five and a beauty. A real beauty. Her body, as slender and sinuous as the body of a model. Her features, as exquisite as the features of a Gothic madonna. And never mind if an inopportune down darkening the corners of her lips evoked the shadow of two faint mustaches. Among the others she emerged a black swan in a brood of gray ducks. What a witch, though! What a viper! She didn't even let you speak. "Taisez-vous, messieurs! Sonnez le retraite! Shut up, sirs! Sound the retreat!" He had tried to appease them. "Sisters, we are not here unlawfully. This residence has been assigned to us by your government." The black swan had yelled. "Our government has no right to assign what belongs to us!" At a certain point, however, and with the leniency of a sovereign who deigns to pardon an unruly subject, the Norman had proposed a compromise. "I want to be generous, sirs. Hand over immediately the first and the second floors, the main entrance, the cellars, and keep the ground floor, the esplanade, the rest. The chapel, in common." He'd accepted, and let's be honest: the cohabitation worked. Yes, it worked. But the supposed earthly paradise continued to be a source of headaches, and the lovesickness matter was the worst of them. For God's sake, where did the virus come from? Who scattered it, who kept it alive? The devil, the Eternal Father, the...

And suddenly the Condor jumped to his feet, pierced by an intuition which was rather a certainty. The nuns! It came from the five nuns! It was scattered by the five nuns, kept alive by the five nuns! Five. Only five, and two of them more than mature: but women. Covered by inviolable garments, strangled by wimples, withered by veils: but women. Inaccessible, incorruptible, asexual, chaste: but women. Women who lived under the same roof, who breathed the same air, who underwent the same risks with a remote yet constant presence... A rarefied yet disquieting intimacy, an illusory yet concrete attraction: their windows opened onto the esplanade, dammit, and the classrooms on the first floor were right above the immense hall where the mess was located. This meant hearing their footsteps, picking up their voices, conjecturing their gestures... It seems nothing, a footstep. Or a voice, a gesture. But if the footstep is a woman's footstep, if the voice is a woman's voice, if the gesture is a woman's gesture, if all this strikes the imagination of four hundred young and healthy men who are forced to live in abstinence from senses and emotions, the effect can be catastrophic. It can set off an amorous psychosis that in a little while goes out of control and transforms the most ladykilling ladykillers into languorous Pierrots at the mercy of any little fox ready to empty their pockets at eight thousand dollars a pop. Why hadn't he thought of this before?!?

2

The question was legitimate. The analysis, correct. But the truth was more complicated, because it included a phenomenon that characterizes the two-handed mammal even better than his (or her) upright posture, articulate language, cranial volume, cerebral mass etcetera.

That is, the masochism with which he (or she) strives to be accepted by those who don't want him and loved by those who don't love him; the stupidity that often leads him (or her) to give his heart to the very same people who reject it. Poor ladykillers, how much had they had to suffer before idyll would begin! How had they been brought to their knees by the five nuns! Excluding Sister Françoise, who was almost never at the convent because she daily worked at the Rizk Hospital and who in any case didn't oppose anybody, each one had chosen a victim to rampage over. Sister Espérance had chosen Falcon. Two or three times a week she summoned him to the chapel and: "Monsieur, I'm disgusted. Your boors do nothing but shout vulgarities and march around in their underwear. I demand that they quiet down and dress in a decent way." No use answering that the boors were twenty-year-olds whose vocal cords couldn't be cut, that the vulgarities were simply love songs, that the underwear was the shorts prescribed by military regulation, that soldiers need to relax. She turned into an ice statue, gripped the sapphire crucifix that enhanced her impeccable frock, and raised it like a sword. "Monsieur! My convent isn't a barrack! This lack of decency is an outrage to my person, to my sisters, to this pious place! God does not want it!" Sister George had chosen Falcon's deputy: Gigi the Candid. At the slightest pretext she swept down on him with her double-lens glasses, and: "Monsieur! What's this uproar on the esplanade? Don't you even know how to control your troops?!?" So both of them lived in the nightmarish fear of meeting their respective persecuters and languished in the dream of receiving a smile. "A smile! Just a smile! Instead she strikes me with that sapphire crucifix, she pins me to the wall with that icy blue glance, she kills me. That is not a nun, it's a warrior! A Genghis Khan!" "Ah, Sister George is worse! Besides, what kind of nun is a nun who uses a man's name? George means Giorgio, right? And Giorgio is a man's name. Damn! I'd give a finger to get a gesture of kindness out of her, and this morning too she shot an assez-basta-enough that hissed like a Katyusha. Let's face it: Sister Madeleine is better!" Sister Madeleine, instead, was no better. She had chosen the boors whose vocal cords couldn't be cut, and tortured them with a subtle treachery: opening the windows in the morning to trill out a laugh that would have awakened the desire of a saint. Visceral, joyous. A moment later, however, she raised a nasty voice and: "Un peu d'air, un peu de soleil, pour oublier que les brutes sont ici! A little air, a little sunlight, to forget that the brutes are here!"

As for Sister Milady, the beautiful novice the Condor had called a black-swan-in-a-brood-of-gray-ducks-yet-a-witch, a-viper, she was a special case. Because it was she, not Sister Espérance or Sister George or Sister Madeleine, who had assumed leadership of the hostilities. And, as a personal victim, she had chosen a robust and attractive forty-year-old guy with fiery eyes and hatchet-hollowed features who spoke excellent French. The marshal* of the carabinieri whom Gigi the Candid kept under his direct command and who, because of his ability to resolve any problem of the practical kind, was called Armando Golden Hands.

*   *   *

One rifle shot is sufficient to start a war, and within a few days Sister Milady had fired two. The first, with a placard she had lettered and hung in the mess: "Les hôtes réunis dans ce salon sont invités à limiter leur tapages bestiaux de façon à ne pas trop troubler le travail et la prières des religieuses qui ont le malheur de les loger. The guests assembled in this hall are asked to limit their bestial racket in order not to disturb the labors and prayers of the nuns who have the misfortune of lodging with them." The second, with a little stairway of sixteen steps that went from the mess hall to the first floor where it ended in a door that gave access to the school and the apartments. A door now locked from the inside with a sturdy bolt. Claiming that the bolt wasn't sufficient and that the door represented a hypothetical entry, she'd asked to have the stairway clogged with obstacles. And Armando Golden Hands had assumed the task. "Leave it to me. I understand the nuns, and the French nuns even more. I spent my childhood in a boarding school run by them. They're particular women: women soldiers. With them it's no good to wave an iron fist. You must use velvet gloves." Then, piling up seats, armchairs, mattresses, he'd blocked the final seven steps. "Ça vous plaît, is this okay, Sister?" The answer: "No. Neuf restent vides. There are still nine clear steps." He'd blocked another five steps. "Now is it okay?" "No. There are still four." He'd blocked those too. Finally he'd shown her the result of his toils and good-humoredly said: "This is a Maginot Line, that would discourage hordes of rapists, Sister Milady. If you're not satisfied, all I can add is a high-tension wire." Far from being amused, though, she'd reacted with a shriek: "Impudent, insolent, effronté!" No use stammering I-was-joking-Sister-Milady, no use begging for her forgiveness with a thousand favors, continuous amends in the chapel or in the cellars or on the convent grounds. From

* Rank corresponding to warrant officer in the carabinieri.

that day on, she'd even started to rebuke his courtesies, to treat them as faults. Complaints and accusations compared to which the diatribes of Sister Espérance and Sister George or the subtle treacheries of Sister Madeleine seemed compliments. "Monsieur! You cut off our electricity in the basement!" "On the contrary, Sister Milady. I hooked it back up!" "Monsieur! You clogged the opening of our drainpipe!" "On the contrary, Sister Milady. I unclogged it." "Monsieur, you tore up the bench in the chapel!" "What are you saying, Sister Milady? I glued it back together!" Amidst such torments the spring had elapsed, and the afternoon had come on which Sister Milady had surprised the poor guy while he was shutting off the flow of water from the mess to the first floor. An event, by the way, which had taken place before a knot of officers. Among them, Falcon.

"Voleur, thief! Bandit!"

"But Sister Milady...!"

"You're stealing our water! Voyou, thug!"

"No, Sister Milady, no! I shut the flow off to locate a leak that I think is connected to your bathroom..."

"Menteur! Liar! Hypocrite! In my bathroom there's no water because you're diverting it to your soldiers!"

"Don't insult me, Sister Milady. Don't mistreat me. As soon as I find the leak and patch the pipe, I'll open the valve and you can take the best shower you ever had."

"Misérable! You wretch! How dare you speak of a thing as private as my shower?!? I'm fed up to here with you! I won't take it anymore, compris, understand?!"

And this time Armando Golden Hands had lost his temper. Hurling the wrench to the ground, he had grabbed the black swan by one arm, shoved her against the wall, and: "Listen to me, you little harpy. Because I'm the one who's had enough. I'm the one who can't take it anymore. For Christsake, for months I have been doing my best to please you, to get a smile out of you, and in spite of that you always kick me in the mouth. You accuse me, you humiliate me in front of the battalion, you call me a thief, a bandit, a thug, a liar, a hypocrite, a wretch. Sister Milady, you've busted my balls. Do you understand the word balls? Have you ever seen a pair of balls? Well, you certainly couldn't see mine: they're in pieces. Thus, you have two alternatives: either you stop it, or you keep going. If you stop, I'll try to grant you an armistice. If you keep going, I swear I'll give you back all the torments you've imposed on me. I'll drive you crazy. I'll make you cry until you run out of tears. And to begin with, I'll really shut down the fucking water in your fucking bathroom. So you won't be able to wash that lovely little mug of yours." Then he'd given the pipe a mighty kick, had left abandoning his toolbox, and she'd left as well, quivering with disdain. But the next day, here she is again with an adorable smile and a voice that seemed to be on loan from the mildest angels of Paradise.

"Armandooò..."

Gosh, what emotion at hearing her pronounce his name! And how precious she made it by shifting the accent to the third vowel then stretching out the *o* and detaining it between her half-open lips! Armandooò... Uttered by her, it seemed like a caress, a kiss.

"Yes, Sister Milady."

"Armandò, voulons-nous signer l'armistice? Shall we sign the armistice?"

He'd signed it immediately. And five minutes later, Falcon had signed his with Sister Espérance. Gigi the Candid, his with Sister George. Both, with Sister Madeleine. Then, to put a seal on the deed and transform the armistice into a peace treaty, the five nuns had been invited to dine with the troops, and the next day had come down to the mess. Wittily holding small olive branches and spreading an indefinable yet bewitching perfume which was simply woman's perfume, they'd answered the troops' hurrays, then taken their seats at the officers' table where Armando Golden Hands had been admitted as an exception, and who would ever forget that unforgettable evening? Not Falcon who pale with emotion devoted himself to Sister Espérance and passed her the salt, poured her the wine, offered her the most succulent morsels... Not Sister Espérance who accepting those attentions recounted the vicissitudes of the flight from the convent and explained that the false news of their deaths had been purposely given by the looters, then whispered something in Falcon's ear that made Falcon exclaim three times: "Madame!" Not Gigi the Candid who flirted with Sister George and at a certain point even asked her if she was a man or a woman! Not Sister George who far from being shocked by the question placed on his nose her double-lens glasses and laughed: "Monsieur Gigì, vous en avez plus besoin que moi! You need these more than I do!" Then she scolded him for speaking bad French and invited him to study it with the children at the school which had just reopened. Not Armando Golden Hands who, paralyzed with ecstasy, couldn't tear his gaze away from Sister Milady. Not Sister Milady who, electrified by the same emotion, incessantly adjusted her veil or fingered her mustached down as if she wanted to pull it off. Not Sister Madeleine who, without a

speck of jealousy for lacking an admirer of her own, continuously warbled her visceral laughter and shook her wet nurse's bosom in tremors
that drew greedy glances and heavy wisecracks. "Old hens make the
best broth!" Not Sister Françoise who, staring silently at the corner
where Gino was seated, suddenly got up and went to hand him a
notebook then said in perfect Italian a phrase whose meaning nobody
understood: "Ecco, signor sergente. Le auguro molti starnuti di Dio.
Here, Mister Sergeant, I wish you many of God's sneezes." So a flurry
of whispers arose, what-did-she-give-him, what-are-God's-sneezes, and
Gino blushed up to his ears. The consequences of the evening were
fatal especially for Falcon, Gigi the Candid, and Armando Golden
Hands. Before retiring, in fact, Sister Espérance had asked them to
represent the battalion at a small and informal supper on the second
floor, the trio had replied yes-oh-yes, and the following Thursday had
gone up to their former enemies' kitchen. Tête-à-tête they'd eaten
couscous and drunk Kzara, a wine that tastes of resin and inebriates,
and since that night the suppers on the second floor had become a
custom repeated every Thursday. Only during the two months that
Falcon and Gigi the Candid and Armando Golden Hands had spent in
Italy, as we shall see, had the custom suffered an interruption. In short,
the truth really went beyond the correct yet incomplete analysis made
by the Condor. The five nuns' presence wasn't so remote, the intimacy
wasn't so rarefied, the attraction wasn't so illusory, and the virus which
characterized the Ruby base was indisputably due to them. What's
worse, it wasn't at all innocuous: it already contained the seeds of tragedy. But the Condor couldn't know this. Nobody could have known it
that late November morning, as a shout ripped through the office of
the virus's first victim.

"Get me Falcooon!"

3

With long steps or rather falcades, the only thing he had in common
with the nickname that a malicious chance had foisted on him, Falcon
was meanwhile crossing the esplanade to reach the officers' latrines.
And his sharp face, the face of a fifty-year-old man more than dissatisfied with himself, looked distorted by anguish: he detested those latrines built on the slope of the hill. Every time the need urged him to
go, he held it back till it reached the most unbearable limits: only at the
very last moment did he set out for the goddam stalls exposed like a
shooting range to the fire that came from the church of Saint-Michel or

the Galerie Semaan. The stray bullets and the fragments showered with such an intensity, in fact, that the sheet metal walls seemed like a colander, and through the holes you could see the landscape. Yesterday a major had caught a 7.62 in his buttock. A captain, two fragments in his hip. Last week a fragment had missed a lieutenant's genitals, and in each case the comment had been: "Why don't we use the troops' john, by God?!?" Once he had. But he'd told himself: never again. He was the base commander, alas, the colonel of the paratrooper carabinieri. He had to set a good example, to exhibit what the army calls disdain-for-danger. Disdain for danger? One thing is to die while going to the attack and one thing is to die while taking a dump, your pants down. Imagine the comments: "How did Falcon die?" "Bare-assed in the officers' latrine! What a lousy way to go, huh?" Lousy, yes, he sighed. Humiliating. It made him remember the death of a carabiniere who, having found his wife in bed with another, had shot himself inside the battalion lavatories. The others wondered why the fool hadn't killed his wife and her lover. He wondered why he'd shot himself in such a place, instead, and would have liked to execute his corpse then shout: "You bastard, cuckold! Aren't you ashamed of the discredit you have thrown on us by committing suicide in a latrine?" No, he couldn't bear the idea of dying in a latrine. And given the fact that death cannot be avoided, that this is the real injustice of life, he had the sacrosanct right to hope for a less embarrassing end. In combat, let's say, or in performing some noble act, or on the tennis court: with the racket in his fist. Yes: to be honest, what he really hoped was to die on a tennis court. He loved that civilized sport so much! He loved it more than he'd ever loved a woman. To believe it, one simply had to count the trophies he'd won in thirty years and to hear those who said he's-more-than-a-professional. He was. To better execute the topspin and the drop shot he'd even invented what he called the Achilles-heel: a movement that consisted of shifting the body's weight to the right heel. Yet he'd chosen a trade which threatened to make him die in a latrine. A trade which in his heart he abhorred.

He stopped for a moment, listened to the gunshots that the Sixth Brigade and the Amal kept exchanging along the three hundred yards, and a shiver shook the tall lean body that the uniform mortified but the tennis whites enhanced by stressing its inbred elegance. With that shiver he reached the latrines, chose a central stall that made him feel more protected, and promptly dropped his pants. He should evacuate in the shortest time possible, and unfortunately he belonged to the category of those who like to do it while reading the newspaper or puzzling out the problems of humanity. What's more, when he was nervous it took him twice as long. And the Condor's visit had unnerved him a great deal. He sat on the bucket. He tried to relax. Come on, he said to himself, try to calm down: take all the time you need. But then he shook his head. Time? It wasn't a matter of time: it was a matter of luck! Even if the hypothetical bullet did not kill him, he could get wounded. Have his right foot smashed, for example. And, in that case, goodbye to the Achilles-heel. Damn war! Pain and fear, fear and suffering: that's what war consists of. And the fear, well: he had so much of it that sometimes he wondered whether his veins ran with blood or fear, if his brain contained gray matter or fear. Besides, they were such old friends, he and fear. Loyal friends. Friends who can't bear to be separated. Also in Italy they met so often. When with his carabinieri he had to face the raging rallies, the demonstrators who attack with iron bars and heavy stones and Molotov cocktails, for instance. Or when he had to arrest a dangerous gang, a punk with an itchy trigger finger. Or when he had to jump with the parachute. In fact he could describe every sign of it, every symptom: the throat that closes up, the nape that grows numb, the belly that gets paralyzed, the sphincter that slackens, the pride that vanishes and leaves you with a great exhaustion... He had even coined its definition: "Fear is something that steals your pride and leaves a tremendous exhaustion in its place." Was he a coward? No, he wasn't. Because with the parachute he jumped, after all, the dangerous gangs and the punk with the itchy trigger finger he faced, and the raging rallies as well. Being afraid doesn't mean being a coward. Still, he would have given a lot to be more courageous. To resemble Gigi the Candid, for example, who marched into the damn latrines whistling and laughing. "Bravo, forza! Good! Béccalo, hit him!" He was afraid of nothing, Gigi the Candid. Truly nothing? The other night the Ruby base had been racked by a howl of terror, he had rushed to see who'd howled, and found his deputy out of his senses. "Gigi, what happened?" "A toad, commander." "A toad?!?" "Yes, a toad. When I was a little boy, I used to fall asleep next to a pond, and once I woke up with a toad on my stomach. It wasn't doing anything wrong, poor thing. Just looking at me. But I got so frightened that, since then, if I see a toad I faint." So, even those who fear nothing are afraid of something. And maybe the definition to give was another: fear is a toad that spares nobody. Beirut, the last place to flee from it.

He contracted his abdominal muscles, tried to set off a peristalsis, the attempt failed, and he sneered sarcastically. Why, then, had he returned here? Why, when asked if he would interrupt his leave and reassume command of the Ruby base, had he answered yes? Certainly, not to pursue professional ambitions: in the Carabinieri Corps one had more to gain from handcuffing a thief or a mafioso than from staying in Beirut. And, even less, to flee from some conjugal unhappiness: with his wife he wasn't unhappy at all. The good woman didn't even scold him for the Sundays he spent on the tennis court. Perhaps he'd returned for the opportunities that war offers to men who are dissatisfied with themselves and want to put themselves on trial... War is such a test! The most extraordinary test that a man can take to judge himself, to compete with fear and discover what he's capable of at the moment of truth. What did he know about himself before coming to Beirut? What risks had he faced besides the minor ones offered by the dangerous gangs or by the iron bars and the weighty stones and the Molotov cocktails? What else had he done besides practicing the policeman's trade, that is, playing the cop who arrests and intimidates and punishes? Agreed: those minor risks had introduced him to swarms of toads. But he'd never checked, really checked, himself. He'd never exposed himself to the examination that counts. He'd never faced the test that concludes with the verdict I-made-it or I-didn't-make-it. And no compromises in between, no half-measures, no appeals to the jury, since the only judge of the victory or the defeat is yourself. Ah! What a relief, being able to say I-made-it, I-defeated-fear, I-won! What consolation, what pride! Yes: it had to be this one, the reason why he'd returned. But then he made a mistake in detesting these latrines where he risked a lousy and inglorious death or the bullet that smashes the right foot preventing you from playing tennis! He did because sitting on this bucket and shivering at every gunshot, squeezing his bowels and trying to overcome fear, was already a way of preparing for the examination. It was an exercise, a rehearsal like stretching your fingers on the piano before playing a difficult piece. Before facing the Great Test and proving to yourself that you aren't a coward. And after this diagnosis (rather accurate and yet unrelated to the real reason he had returned to Beirut) Falcon obtained the long expected peristalsis. He widened his sphincter, achieved what he needed to achieve, and leaving the john of his sorrows headed back up the hill slope.

He was still far from the point where he would begin to feel safe: it took three minutes to reach the convent building. But the victory he'd won over his intestines filled him with pride, and almost in a state of euphoria he reached the esplanade where he stopped in a sudden perplexity. There were Sister Milady and Armando Golden Hands, right in

front of the mess hall: the spot where one year before the furious
argument had taken place. A delicate, delightfully black-cloaked silhouette with the rosary hanging from her waist, Sister Milady. A solid and
glamorously tanned figure, Armando Golden Hands. They were speaking animatedly, her eyes in his eyes, and, as in a film never erased from
memory, Falcon resaw Armando Golden Hands hurl the wrench to the
ground then grab Sister Milady and shout listen-to-me-you-little-
harpy-because-I'm-the-one-who's-had-enough-I'm-the-one-who-
can't-take-it-anymore. He resaw Sister Milady leaving with disdain and
coming back the next morning with the adorable smile, with the voice
that seemed to be on loan from the mildest angels of Paradise. He
resaw the supper that had transformed the armistice into a peace treaty,
the former enemies who arrived wittily holding the small olive
branches, Sister Espérance who advanced in her impeccable frock and
sapphire crucifix then sat beside him and melted the ice of her usual
haughtiness. He reheard her voice telling about the vicissitudes of the
flight from the convent then whispering the revelation which had
caused his clumsy Madame-Madame-Madame. "It seems that the two
of us have something in common, mon colonel." "What's that, Madame?" "A passion for smashes, lobs, drop shots and topspin, mon
colonel." "Madame!" "Yes, before becoming a nun I was a tennis
champion." "Madame!" "Do you know what I miss most on this hill?
A racket and a tennis court, mon colonel." "Madame!" He also
reheard what had brought his enchantment to paroxysm: the fact that
she belonged to an aristocratic family related to the house of Orléans,
that in Normandy she had a castle with drawbridge, that to impose on
her family the choice of taking the veil she had struggled like a soldier
in combat... But, above all, he relived the Thursday suppers: the happy
anxiety with which he went up to the second floor with Gigi the Candid and Armando Golden Hands, the indulgence with which he toler-
ated the flirtations of his deputy and his deputy's aide, the displeasure
with which he had accepted the rotation that sent the battalion's officers back to Italy, the unconfessed melancholy that had crushed him
in Livorno. And the perplexity blocking him on the esplanade became a
suspicion that made his legs wobble. My God! What if his reason for
returning to Beirut wasn't the need to judge himself and to compete
with fear and to discover what he was capable of at the moment of
truth? What if the real reason was Sister Espérance?

He leaned against the baluster. He wiped away a drop of sweat that
had flowered on his brow, took a deep breath, and looked around in
confusion. Poor Falcon. Despite his honesty and good intentions he

didn't know how to descend into the depths of the soul, how to penetrate the dark meanders of the psyche. Even when he arrested people in Italy he never managed to identify the reasons why a crime or an alleged crime had been committed. Faithful to his role of policeman or rather executioner, he worried only about establishing which article of the Penal Code had been violated: the suspicion that life could go beyond the narrow borders of Law had always remained buried in a cemetery called Rejection of Feelings. The question he had just raised, therefore, terrorized him more than the idea of dying in a latrine or losing his right foot. Sister Espérance?!? Impossible! No, possible... Yes, no, yes: it took him a long time to accept the yes. It took him at least a dozen deep breaths and many droplets of sweat. To have returned for her! For a nun his own age, an incorruptible Mother Superior, an unattainable woman who invited him to supper and nothing more! For an ice statue who would never lavish anything on him besides a hand squeeze and a measured sympathy! Love is truly blind, devoid of any good sense. Love?!? Was it really a matter of love? Yessir, love. Platonic, maybe, cerebral, and so repressed that it could be rather considered a wish for love. A slight fever. Yet that wish for love had been more than enough to bring him back here, that slight fever was more than sufficient to reveal the presence of the illness. He needed to cure himself. He needed to avoid meeting Sister Espérance, to skip the Thursday suppers. And above all, he needed to redeem himself, to transform the reason why he'd returned into the reason why he should have returned: preparing himself for the Great Test, proving that he wasn't a coward... Then, finally in control of his body, he tore himself from the baluster. He crossed the esplanade, passed in front of Sister Milady and Armando Golden Hands, broke into the corridor leading to his office, and almost knocked over a carabiniere who waited for him: an odd guy with a face that resembled a bas-relief inside a circle. At the bottom of the circle, a trembling little mouth. In the middle, an invisible nose. At the top, two tiny trapped-rat eyes. He questioned him rudely: "Who are you? What do you want?" "Lance Corporal Salvatore Bellezza son of the late Onofrio* reporting, sir!" a kind of peeping answered. "Ah, you!" he grunted recalling that he had summoned him for the stupidities he'd committed out of love for a little slut. "We'll settle our accounts later, you and I!" Then he knocked, entered, and the Condor's bawl exploded piercing everybody's eardrums within a range of a mile.

"Falcooon! What the fuck is going on at the Ruby?!?"

* Bellezza means beauty in Italian. Following the last name with the name of the father is an old police custom still practiced in some parts of Italy, particularly by the carabinieri.

The scene lasted thirty minutes, enriched by the frightening words are-you-in-love-too-dammit, and reawakened Falcon to his role of the executioner who considers life a code to be pitilessly administered. In fact it persuaded him that a sacrificial lamb, a victim to string up as an example, was required. Meanwhile, Salvatore Bellezza son of the late Onofrio waited. He waited, waited, and his small loved-crazed mind drifted like an oarless boat. Waves of foolish fantasies and baffling truths, the thoughts that tossed his boat in the fog of his naiveté and against the rocks of his desperation.

4

They would execute him. They'd put him up against a wall, wrap a rag around his head, and shoot him like the painter Mario Cavaradossi in the opera *Tosca*. The one where Caravadossi sings sweet-kisses-and-languid-caresses, the-hour-has-fled-and-I-die-in-despair. Or like the soldiers who in certain war movies end in front of a firing squad because they deserted the trenches and went home. No doubt about it: the general was shouting too much. "This shame has to stop!" he shouted. And the colonel added: "It will stop, sir. It will stop." Well, he didn't care. As a matter of fact, it almost pleased him. Because when reading the news in the papers, Sanaan would go blind with grief and commit suicide like Tosca who kills herself by jumping from the ramparts of Castel Sant'Angelo. And she would repent of the cruel things she had said. Go-to-hell, she had said in spite of the sweet kisses and the languid caresses they'd exchanged that fatal day at Plage Hollywood. And the expensive gifts he used to give Alì... And the heart-shaped stone on which he'd carved the initials SS with a pocketknife... Oh, it had been such a job to carve them with the pocketknife! Not to mention the nasty comments of those who watched him. "Moron! Don't you know who the SS were?" Sure he knew. He'd seen them in the movies. They were Germans soldiers dressed in black, with the swastika on their left sleeve and collars. Along with the swastika, the letters SS that meant Schutz Staffeln: Department of Protection. Military police, in short, Hitler's carabinieri. Well, according to the movies, they were less lovable than the carabinieri... They used to beat people, kill them, and married nobody but blondes. But what could he do if the names Salvatore and Sanaan began with the letter S and if engraving them in full was too difficult? On the golden medallion, the one he'd bought for her after the first kiss, the jeweler had engraved names in full and even the motto "Joined Forever." Forever! Cruel, ungrateful woman. Or maybe she didn't really know English... Maybe she hadn't understood the concept of "joined." It's a complicated verb, the verb "to join." Sometimes it means to enlist, like join-the-army, and other times to attach, to glue. Perhaps it would have been better to engrave the word "united." America is called the United States, not the Joined States. The point is that with Sanaan he didn't feel merely united like the United States: he felt attached, glued. He should see her again. He should tell her the concept of "joined." But how could he, if they shot him? Well, maybe they wouldn't shoot him: in Italy the death penalty no longer existed. No, it did. For espionage, sabotage, desertion. And, all things considered, his was a crime of desertion. That's why the general and the colonel were shouting that way.

"Colonel! I demand an exemplary punishment!"

"It will be, general, sir. It will be!"

Salvatore Bellezza son of the late Onofrio held back a moan. All Glass Eye's fault. Meaning His Excellency the Italian Ambassador. If Glass Eye had kept quiet, nobody but a few close friends would have been aware of it. Instead: "Why don't you intervene, sergeant, why do you permit such things to happen? I sacrifice myself for our country, and at night I cannot sleep because your lance corporal is making a racket on the roof!" In cases like these, the sergeant must report the complaint. The complaint goes to the colonel then to the general, and together they condemn you to death. Well, before ending in front of the firing squad he would avenge himself. He would tell the whole world that Glass Eye had a glass eye because he used to imitate James Dean with another Italian ambassador. One who had been appointed to Cuba, famous for his idiocy and for his unbearable wife: a vulgar billionairess, known in the diplomatic circles as the Laundress, who kept him with her money but was enamored of Fidel Castro. They were great friends, Glass Eye and the Laundress's husband. Together they played like children. They raced their cars one against the other, and only at the last moment did they brake. A game which had been inspired by James Dean's movie *Rebel Without a Cause* and required good reflexes. The two ambassadors had very bad reflexes, instead, and one day: bang! They'd collided with such violence that the Laundress's husband had cracked his skull becoming even more stupid, and Glass Eye had shattered his face losing the eye now replaced with the glass one. Yes, he would tell. And then he would tell how Glass Eye was afraid of being kidnapped then crucified by the Druzes. Which was the reason why the undersigned Salvatore Bellezza son of the late Onofrio had ended up standing guard on the embassy roof: a post where you broke your spine bending over a machine gun twelve hours on end. Yet, if Glass Eye had deigned to greet him at least once, to say at least once I-thank-you-Salvatore-Bellezza-son-of-the-late-Onofrio-for-breaking-your-back-for-me, he would have answered: thank you, Your Excellency! Thank you because without you I wouldn't have met the girl who lives across the street. Have you ever seen her, Your Excellency? A reedlike body, a fairy's face, skin as gold as amber, and black waist-length hair. The black of ebony. She lives on the sixth floor, Your Excellency, and her bedroom opens onto a wrought-iron terrace. Well, when she leans over the terrace, she looks like Juliet waiting for Romeo. And with my nose in the air I look like Romeo waiting for Juliet.

He held back a second moan. That's how it was. The embassy had three floors and in order to admire Sanaan on the sixth-floor terrace, he had to look up like Romeo... He hadn't noticed her, at first. He only thought of the Druzes and of how to stop them from kidnapping Glass Eye and crucifying him, at first. But one morning he'd raised his eyes and there she was. That afternoon, also. The following morning and the following afternoon, the same. In fact he'd actually wondered: could she be sitting out there for me? Then they'd fucked him over with the night shift, and he'd told himself: I'll never see her again. Instead, there she was. Night after night, always reading a book. So the fourth night he had spoken to her. In English, a language he'd studied to become a parking attendant and get lavish tips from American tourists. "Hello!" he'd shouted. "Hallò!" she'd answered. "I'm Salvatore Bellezza son of the late Onofrio. Do you speak English?" "Yes." "What is your name?" "Sanaan." "What are you reading?" "I'm studying." "What do you study?" "Architecture." "Architecture?!? Gee! Would you like all the same to go out with me?" And this time she'd answered with a question that had taken his breath away: "Are you married, are you engaged?" Married! Engaged! To whom?!? He had nobody, dammit. He'd never had anybody. With all the handsome young men in circulation, all the rich and city-born guys, what girl would look at a nickel-and-dimer born among the sheep of the Abruzzi? Furthermore, somebody who knows about physical love even less than the Virgin Mary? Because people think that nowadays everybody knows everything about everything. But they're mistaken. When it comes to physical love, certain guys only know what they see on TV when the lovers strip and roll around on the bed: at twenty, he'd received just one kiss. The one from Nidal, the ugly one who'd dropped him at once for the American with the jeep. Anyway, what do we do after the kiss? When do we get to strip and roll around on the bed? And what does the operation really consist of? Judging from the remarks of the guys in the barracks, it consisted of a kind of piston up and down that ended with a shiver: a sneeze that shook all over and left you very satisfied. True or false? To figure it out, he'd spent a leave at Cyprus, an island near Beirut rich in brothels. Here he had visited a nightclub full of indecent women, bought six whiskeys for the Greek harlot who touched his pants and said let's-go-upstairs. But at the last moment he hadn't had the guts and...

The moan burst and a gush of tears erupted from the tiny trapped-rat eyes. Oh! How impetuously had he answered no, Sanaan, I'm-not-married-or-engaged! So she'd gone back to her room, closed the window, turned out the light, and the following night she'd tossed a note in English: "Dear Salvatore, I would be happy to go out with you. The problem is that I'm very virtuous and I can't come unless somebody accompanies me. Your Sanaan." *Your* Sanaan! He'd felt drunk while reading that "your." She loves me, she loves me, he stammered. She loves *me,* Salvatore Bellezza son of Onofrio, a nickel-and-dimer born among the sheep of the Abruzzi, somebody who knows about physical love even less than the Virgin Mary! Then he'd picked up a piece of coal fallen from the chimney, wiped clean the wall of the building next to the embassy, and written in block letters: "Sanaan, I live at the Ruby base. If you do not come today, I kill myself." Well, it had worked. At one in the afternoon, while he was napping on his cot, a cry had reached him. "Wake up, Bellezza, wake up! Your girl is looking for you." *Your* girl! He'd run to the checkpoint, and there she was: a dream dressed in a long gown and a long-sleeved white blouse, her hair gathered in schoolgirlish braids, and not a hint of makeup. "I came because I don't want you to kill yourself," she'd said tugging him into a car where a handsome and mustached guy with sunglasses was at the wheel. "My cousin Alì." They'd taken off for a drive, the two of them in the back seat but separated by a big cushion set up by that bastard who spied on them in the rearview mirror and sounded the horn each time he saw it removed... beep, beep, beep! Sanaan was so enraged she smoked like a smokestack. However, at the end of the drive, she had promised to return the next day.

He dried his tears, blew his nose. She'd returned every day, since that day. Always with Alì as her escort, always at dinnertime, always so famished that you always had to take them to a restaurant. And always with the cushion and the rearview mirror and the horn. Beep, beep, beep! He couldn't even give her a kiss or caress her neck. At the most he could graze her hands or whisper I-adore-you. So, though his love

was a very spiritual and chaste love, though in Sanaan he saw Saint Rita
of Cascia, the saint who grants impossible graces and asks nothing in
return but a Salve Regina, though she hadn't a single vice, a single
fault... Well, a couple of vices she had: the one of smoking one cigarette
after another and the one of never answering a question. For example,
the question about how she studied architecture. Don't you have to
attend the university, to become an architect? Or is it enough to read a
book on the terrace? If you asked, she zigzagged. But maybe Saint Rita
of Cascia too had the vice of smoking and zigzagging when questioned, and he felt happy all the same. So happy that he no longer
wanted to die at twenty. Because before Sanaan he had wanted to die at
twenty. He used to think what is there for me in this world? Nobody
loves me, my father died throwing himself in the ravine on account of
his debts, my mother speaks with me only to yell, you-cannot-be-my-
child, you're-too-stupid, you-weren't-even-able-to-become-a-parking-
attendant... Better to die at twenty. Now, instead, he was happy to live.
Even with Alì under his feet. Besides, how could he object to Alì's
presence? A virtuous girl can't go out all alone with her fiancé. He
understood this so perfectly that he did nothing but cover that lousy
scum with gifts. Today a tie, tomorrow a shirt, the day after a quartz
watch. Not to mention the daily restaurant and the money he lent him.
A business which had started the afternoon he'd said: "Today you're
my guest, Salvatore. I want to pay for lunch." But at the moment to
pay: "Sorry, I forgot my wallet. Lend me fifty dollars." Then, instead
of settling the debt: "Lend me another fifty. So I'll give you back one
hundred." Well... Not only had the hypocrite never given back the one
hundred, but he had never stopped playing that music. Lend-me-fifty-
dollars, I-forgot-my-wallet, lend-me-another-fifty, I'll-pay-you-all-to-
gether. There were times when he wanted to take off his sunglasses and
see what there was underneath. A money box, a branch of a bank?! Oh,
how sad to die without recovering his dollars, his ties, his shirts, and
the quartz watch plus the restaurant bills! Salvatore Bellezza son of the
late Onofrio repressed another gush of tears, and right at that moment
the door opened. A humiliated Falcon appeared with the Condor who
was leaving for the headquarters.

"I'll take care of it, general. Trust me."

"An exemplary punishment, I said!"

"Yessir, general. Be sure."

"At once!"

"Yessir, general. At once."

"And be energetic, God blasted!"

"Yessir, general. Energetic."

Then Falcon cleared his throat, resumed the voice of the policeman who arrests and intimidates and punishes, of the executioner who considers life a code to be applied without pity, and casting a vacant look at the possible victim of exemplary punishment he cracked the first lash.

"Come in, criminal, come in. Let's play Torquemada."

5

He went in with the wobbly step of a convict who delivers himself to the hangman. The method was so familiar to him that he could anticipate every phase of the torture. First lash, second lash, and a sweetish warning. Third lash, fourth lash, and a caramelized threat. Fifth lash, sixth lash, and death. His sergeant in Livorno called it Scottish-shower. "The Scottish shower eases the flow of blood to the brain and helps morons like you." Falcon called it Torquemada-technique after a certain priest who burned heretics during the Inquisition, and before starting he said: Let's play Torquemada." He nervously coughed. Still wobbling he reached the desk, tried to stand at attention.

"At your command, colonel, sir."

A second lash was the answer.

"Head high, God dammit! Shoulders back, belly in, arms at your sides! Is this how a carabiniere presents himself to his commander?!?"

"Nossir, sir."

And raising his head, thrusting back his shoulders, sucking his belly in, holding his arms at his sides, Salvatore Bellezza son of the late Onofrio awaited the sweetish warning which came inexorably after the pause.

"Good, Bellezza, good. Now that you're standing at attention the way you're supposed to, I can talk man to man. Because you are a man: aren't you, Bellezza?"

"Yessir, sir."

"Wrong, Bellezza. Wrong. You are not. A man doesn't behave the way you do. And in my battalion I want men. Men with balls. Carabinieri with balls. Is that clear?!?"

"Yessir, sir."

"What's clear? What did I say?"

"Balls, sir. You said balls."

"Whose balls?"

"The carabinieri's balls, sir."

"I didn't say carabinieri's balls, Bellezza. I said carabinieri *with* balls! You're not listening, Bellezza."

"Yessir. I'm listening, sir."

Sure he was listening, sure. But the Torquemada technique was overlaid by the memory of the unforgettable day when Sanaan had come without the hypocrite, simply escorted by her sister and wearing a pair of tight jeans... Over the jeans, a skimpy jersey in which she seemed to burst. Over the jersey, her waist-length hair falling loosely. My God, what a tingling! No restaurant, that day. No cushion, no rearview mirror, no beep-beep-beep. They'd taken a taxi to a Christian beach called Plage Hollywood where the sister had immediately fallen asleep. Not to spoil their spiritual chaste love they'd gone searching for shells, found the heart-shaped stone, and... While they were admiring it, a big wave had run over Sanaan drenching her jersey. Gesù! Mamma mia, Gesù! Beneath the jersey she wore nothing. Nothing. Not even a bra! You could deduce it from her nipples stiffened by the cold water, see... And at the sight of those nipples his tingling had doubled, a bayonet had grown between his legs. No, really a bayonet. Such a bayonet that he didn't know what to do, where to look, and he thought: let's hope that Sanaan will not notice! But Sanaan had noticed, and guess what she'd done: she'd stretched out on the beach, drawn him down to her, and kissed him inside his mouth. Inside! Gesù, nobody had ever told him about kissing inside the mouth. Nobody! Not the Greek harlot of Cyprus, not Nidal the ugly one who'd dropped him for the American with the jeep, not the guys in the barracks. He had always thought that in order to kiss one should give a smack on closed lips. Nothing more. Sanaan, instead, opened your lips. With her tongue. Then, always with her tongue, she parted your teeth and searched for your own tongue and bit it, rubbed it, worked it. Meanwhile she took care of the bayonet until you lost your breath. With your breath, your mind. Because all at once she'd stopped. Laughing let's-cut-it-out she'd run off to wake her sister, she'd brought him back to the base, and the next day here she'd come with Alì. Again wearing the white dress and the schoolgirlish braids. A guy can lose his head. Can't he? Even more so if he's subjected again to the torment of the cushion, of the rearview mirror, of the beep-beep-beep. She had never given him that kiss again. Never, though he'd asked for it a thousand times. Never, though he'd incised the SS on the heart-shaped stone. Never, though he'd spent all that money for the golden medallion with the engraving Salvatore-Sanaan-Joined-Forever. Never, though he'd increased the loans and the gifts to the lousy scum. "Forget about it, Salvatore." Forget?!? When you re-

ceive such a kiss, you don't forget. You cannot forget! Because the
spiritual chaste love is no longer enough, and...

"Then uncork those ears of yours, Bellezza. Or rather Bruttezza."*

"Yessir, sir."

"The fact is that you have no balls, Bruttezza. No balls and no cock.
Between your legs there isn't even a pinhead. One can tell by looking at
your face. The face of a castrated sheep, of a eunuch without pride or
dignity. And this report confirms it. See this report, Bruttezza?"

"Yessir, sir."

"It's a list of your crimes, Bruttezza. And I won't lose time in men-
tioning those you committed in the past. The walls smeared with amorous messages, the insubordinations. I'll limit myself to what you did
last night."

"Yessir, sir."

"Number one, you abandoned your guard post and your machine
gun. Your guard post! Your machine gun!"

"Yessir, sir."

"You're a lunatic, Bruttezza. Besides being a castrated sheep, a eunuch without pride or dignity, you're a lunatic. A delirious paranoid, a
schizophrenic."

"Yessir, sir."

Could he deny it? He'd become that way from never receiving that
kiss again, and from seeing what took place in Sanaan's bedroom. Because in October Sanaan's family had moved from the sixth floor to the
fourth floor, and the fourth floor was almost at the same level as the
embassy roof. Sanaan's bedroom, almost in front of his guard post. So
he could see everything. Everything, including Sanaan when she
stripped down to the buff. What a tingling, my God, what a tingling!
And how many bayonets, my God, how many! If the Druzes had come
then, he wouldn't have moved a finger. At the most, he would have
said: "Go on, Druzes, go on. Kidnap that Glass Eye as you like. Crucify
him. Do what you want." But the worst thing wasn't seeing her nude.
It was seeing Ali who at a certain hour of the night went to her: who
entered on tiptoe, stealthy, turned out the lights, and amen. Not that
there was any reason to doubt his Saint Rita of Cascia, let's be clear: he
would have stuck his hand in the fire for Sanaan. But what right did a
cousin have, a simple cousin, to stealthily enter her room in the night?
And why did this cousin turn the light off? To save electricity, to talk in
the dark? And to talk about what, about whom? Each time this hap-

* Bruttezza means ugliness in Italian.

pened, he ate his heart out. For hours he went on asking himself what-do-they-talk-about, whom-do-they-talk-about, and wept. So, last night... Well, last night Alì hadn't shown up. But something worse had happened. God knows why, all of a sudden Sanaan had a nervous breakdown and began smashing chairs, knickknacks, mirrors. Then she collapsed on the floor and a moment later her mother, her father, grandfather, grandmother, sister, brother-in-law rushed in and threw themselves on her. To slap her, to punch her, to howl: "Miha, bad, miha! Sharmuta, whore, sharmuta!" Well, he hadn't been able to stop himself. He'd abandoned his guard post, his machine gun, the roof, the embassy, and sweeping past the sentry who cried bloody-idiot-where-are-you-going he'd slipped into the building across the street. He had reached the fourth floor, broken down the door with his shoulder, and burst into Sanaan's room. "Sanaan, my love, what are they doing to you?" She was keeping her eyes closed, see. She seemed dead. At the sound of his voice, however, she'd raised one eyelid. She'd stared at him with an icy pupil and: "Mind your own business, you fucking meddler. Go to hell." Then her mother, her father, grandfather, grandmother, sister, brother-in-law had shoved him down the stairs with kicks and prods and smacks in the head. He'd found himself back on the roof with the desire to kill himself with the machine gun. The trouble is that to kill yourself with the machine gun you need very long arms. And his arms were as short as those of Mark Antony who in the film *Cleopatra* has a real hard time shoving the sword into his belly.

"And for who? For a little tramp, a cheap hooker, a whore who leads you by the nose!"

"Nossir, sir!"

"Nossir?!? You dare to argue with me, Bruttezza?!?"

"Yessir, sir! My fiancée isn't a little tramp, a cheap hooker, a whore! She's a virtuous young girl, a saint! My Saint Rita of Cascia! She doesn't lead me by the nose!"

"And you're a dolt, Bruttezza. Along with everything else I said, a dolt. The most doltish dolt I ever had in the battalion. Such a dolt that you should be granted a plea of extenuating circumstances. An acquittal due to your incapacity for judgment or will. But I shall grant you nothing. And you know it."

"Yessir, sir."

"Number two. Upon your return to the roof you started screaming nonsense and woke up the ambassador, the neighbors, the entire quarter. You made a laughingstock of your country, of the contingent, and of the Carabinieri Corps. A corps that covered itself with glory both in the First and in the Second World War, in Northern Italy, in Greece, in Albania, in North Africa, in the antifascist Resistance!"

"Yessir, sir."

"Number three, you raised your fist against your squad leader. You broke his two upper premolars and his two lower premolars, for a total of four teeth that will have to be replaced. Yes or no?"

"Yessir, sir."

He couldn't deny this either. Sanaan-forgive-me, Sanaan-come-to-the-window, he'd shouted for at least twenty minutes. Sanaan hadn't. But others had. On every balcony, somebody protesting shut-your-mouth-you-moron-let-us-sleep-you-shithead. Which is why His Excellency the Ambassador Glass Eye had sent the squad leader to scold him. "Are you drunk, Bellezza?" "Nossir, I'm desperate. Sanaan told me go-to-hell." "If she did, she is a smart trollop and I want to know her, to shake her hand." A trollop?!? True: the colonel had just called her a tramp and a hooker and a whore. But a colonel is a colonel. A sergeant is only a sergeant. He'd leaped on him, yes. Such blows that the swine had spat out the four teeth like cherry pits. "That'll teach you to call my Sanaan, my Saint Rita of Cascia, a trollop!" Hey, wait a minute... Her mother, her father, grandfather, grandmother, sister, and brother-in-law had also called her a trollop. Sharmuta means prostitute. That is, trollop. Could they have known about the kiss? Maybe her sister hadn't been sleeping that fatal day at Plage Hollywood. Maybe she'd seen the kiss. Or had he made a mistake by confiding in her brother-in-law, Bashir? Yet Sanaan had warned him: "If you meet a snake with a little beard like a goat's, and he speaks Italian, that's my brother-in-law, Bashir. Be careful." The fact is when things must happen, they happen. When he had been moved to the embassy entrance, the other day, the snake had approached. "Me speak Italian. My name Bashir." "Mine, Salvatore Bellezza son of the late Onofrio." "You like Beirut, Salvatore Bellezza son of the late Onofrio?" "Yes, because in Beirut I have a fiancée." "A fiancée? And who is your fiancée?" "Somebody you know. Your sister-in-law Sanaan." Surprise. Amazement. Then a third-degree interrogation. What kind of relationship is there between you and Sanaan, what does your father own, what's your salary, how do you intend to guarantee your wife a comfortable existence, how much can you pay for the matrimonial contract, and so on. Well, he'd answered truthfully... That their relationship was serious because at Plage Hollywood she had kissed him inside the mouth and also taken care of the bayonet till he'd lost his breath etcetera. That his father owned nothing because he was dead and when alive he'd owned even less, which is why he'd hurled himself into the ravine. That his salary was a carabiniere's salary plus the monthly indemnity of two thousand dollars that each Italian soldier received in Beirut, but recently he'd frittered away his dollars on loans and presents and meals for Alì. However, for Sanaan he felt ready to rob a bank, and for the matrimonial contract he could put together three thousand. So Bashir had objected that Sanaan was worth at least ten thousand, that plenty of people would plunk down even twenty thousand, that in any case the banks shouldn't be robbed and... Yes, it had been Bashir!

"Of course you'll pay for the false teeth."

"Yessir, sir."

"He who breaks, pays. And the law is the law, Bruttezza. It doesn't give discounts."

"Yessir, sir."

"And now let's sentence you."

"Yessir, sir."

"A sentence that will hang you out to dry, Bruttezza, and will serve as an example to those who discredit the battalion and the Carabinieri Corps."

"Oh, colonel, sir!"

Overwhelmed by impotence, Salvatore Bellezza son of the late Onofrio began to sob. And, knowing he'd exaggerated, performed a cruelty that bordered on sadism, Falcon had the temptation to say come-on, don't-cry, I'm-not-going-to-kill-you! But then he saw again Sister Espérance's face, he heard again the Condor's frightening words, are-you-in-love-too-dammit, and uttered the three final lashes.

"Weep, criminal, weep."

"Yessir... sir..."

"Drown in your tears, drown. Because you'll not enjoy your little whore again. I'm sending you back to Italy, Bruttezza."

"To... Italy... sir...?!?"

"To Italy. You leave with tomorrow's ship, Bruttezza. Under arrest. And, once there, not even God can save you from thirty years in prison. About-face, march!"

*   *   *

He about-faced, he marched. Moving like a robot he left Falcon's office, reached his tent, threw himself on his cot, and now more than ever his small mind drifted like an oarless boat. To Italy! On tomorrow's ship! Thirty years in prison! Then he wouldn't be shot like

Cavaradossi when he sings sweet-kisses-and-languid-caresses! Sanaan wouldn't kill herself like Tosca, that is, jumping from the ramparts of Castel Sant'Angelo! What a disgrace! If only he could see her one last time and ask for her pardon! If he could speak to her, explain the situation! Like this, for instance: "Sanaan, because of you I've been condemned to a worse punishment than being shot: thirty years of prison in Italy. But I know you love me, and what are thirty years when we love and are loved? Thirty days, thirty minutes. Wait for me, Sanaan, and in thirty years we'll get married."

"Bellezza! Somebody's looking for you, Bellezza!" a sergeant shouted.

He didn't move. Who could be looking for him at this point?

"Bellezza! Come to the checkpoint, Bellezza!"

He unwillingly left the tent.

"Me?"

"Yes, you, stockfish!"

"Really?"

"Really, diphead!"

"And who's asking for me?"

"Your girl, I think! And the guy with the mustache and sunglasses."

He paled. Sanaan! His Saint Rita of Cascia, his Sanaan, had forgiven him! She'd returned to say Salvatore-I-love-you, I-never-stopped-loving-you, my-precious!

"Really-really?"

"Really-really, stupid fuck. Move!"

He sprang forward. In a few moments he reached the esplanade, the iron gate, the street that led to Ost Ten, the checkpoint. And here he stopped in confusion because his Saint Rita of Cascia wasn't there. In her place there was a very blonde blonde with a lot of makeup. And so transformed she sat in the car, embracing Alì like an ivy vine.

"Sanaan...!"

Sanaan didn't even relax her entangling embrace.

"I came to tell you that if you ever dare set foot in my house again, if you ever dare break down my door again, if you dare shout out nonsense again and write my name on the walls, Alì will snap your spine. I came to tell you that you don't amuse us anymore. Alì is my fiancé, I'm pregnant by him, and we're going to get married."

Then Alì burst into a tremendous laugh, drove away in the ivy's embrace. And, whimpering incomprehensible sounds, Salvatore Bellezza son of the late Onofrio fainted before the checkpoint where he was picked up by a couple of paratroopers who happened to pass by. Rather than a living being, a corpse to be handled by the armpits and ankles. A fragile larva of this poor world which really is a vale of tears and swindles.

CHAPTER TWO

1

THIS POOR WORLD really is a vale of tears and swindles, and to forget such a truth Gino wanted to get blind drunk. Having made this decision he headed toward the Ruby's canteen-bar and grumbled over the new reasons for his discontent. By Judas priest, was it fair asking him to obey Sugar who since the destruction of the truck kept breaking his knickknacks with every kind of scolding, orders-are-orders, Reg-ulations-are-Regulations, after-Pistoia's-mistake-we-must-be-diplo-matic?!? Was it proper expecting him to endure the threats and mocker-ies of a provoker like Passepartout, a prostitute on sale for a hand grenade or three bullets, and what's worse the lover of that Khomeinist butcher named Rashid?!? By Judas priest! He was patrolling those shitty alleys of Bourji el Barajni, this morning, when bang! Here comes Passepartout with his damn yellow hair and his damn cigarette butt and his damn Kalashnikov over his damn shoulder. The remark: "Come on, Passepartout! Stop parading that gun around! Leave it at home!" The response: "Why, maccarone? You no like my Kalashnikov? You afraid me kill you, fatty?" He'd lost his temper, and was about to shoot a warning volley when bang! Here comes Sugar who happens to pass by and growls: "Gino! Don't you dare, Gino!" Then off he goes with the usual twaddle about orders, regulations, diplomacy which has become a major commodity, an intransgressible necessity etcetera. In front of Passepartout who rejoiced and giggled and laughed scornfully! As a result, around noon the bitch had reappeared with his damn yellow hair and his damn cigarette butt and his damn Kalashnikov plus a mess of Russian Rdg8 on his belt. He had pointed to them and: "You can no touch me, maccarone. Your boss no want, fatty. With these bombs me go where I like, with these bombs me kill you when I want. Under-stand?"

"Three beers," Gino grunted entering the canteen-bar and sitting at a table that overlooked the esplanade.

"Three?" the bartender exclaimed.

"Three. No, four."

"Four?!?"

"Four. And as many cognacs."

"But sergeant..."

"Do as I say."

He lined them up in a row like sheaves of grain. He began to drink in a scientific manner. A mouthful of beer, a sip of cognac, pause. Another mouthful of beer, another sip of cognac, pause. The technique of the drinker who knows the art of getting drunk slowly. And today even more slowly because he isn't on duty, he has all the time he needs, he knows that the longer it takes the harder he thinks, the harder he thinks the better he understands that he doesn't suffer because of Passepartout and Sugar: he suffers because humanity is an unpleasant breed, an assembly of fools who don't even give a young man some sentimental education. They teach him that two plus two equals four, that Paris is in France, that Cleopatra lived in Egypt, and nothing whatsoever about love. At the most they tell him about sex. As if a relationship could be measured with sex or expressed only through sex. By Judas priest, he'd been forced to figure it out by himself that with a woman you must also talk, that meeting your twin soul means finding somebody who goes along your way, that having a cute little bum isn't enough. The girl from Val d'Aosta had a cute little bum. A doll from head to foot. But she was a brainless butterfly with whom you could neither talk nor read a poem: she wanted to be kissed and that's all, beanbagged and that's all, and she doped herself more than Jumblatt. Heroin, cocaine, whatever was on hand. No, she didn't go along his way. Even when he kissed her and beanbagged her, he felt so alone. Always thinking that love should be companionship, that it should keep you company even when the person you care for is far away. Which is why he had taken up with the one from Livorno who didn't have a cute little bum and wasn't a doll. She was as lean as a nail, older than he, she kept her hair short and at first glance she looked like a concentration camp inmate. But she knew about every problem and subject, she could explain why Picasso used to paint three noses or three eyes and why Marx maintained the theory of surplus value. She played Brahms's Third on the phonograph, she was intelligent and didn't smoke a single joint... They had met in the pizzeria, back in the days when he dressed like a punk with phosphorescent skulls, and her first words had been: "What are you? A man or a cartoon?" Something which had offended him deeply, and made him blush. Nevertheless he had risen, sketched out a bow, and answered: "A man who would like to buy you an aperitif, ma'am. Please, sit down." She'd sat down, and what a motormouth! In ten minutes she'd informed him that her name was Barbara but her parents had baptized her Agnese, that she hated the military, detested the paratroopers, didn't believe in God, wanted to smash capitalism even though she was a capitalist's daughter... He'd offered a pizza. And after the pizza, dessert. After dessert, coffee. Then he'd taken her home on his roaring motorcycle, he'd recited a couple of his poems.

He emptied his powerful lungs in a spurt of nostalgia. At the beginning they spent their evenings talking so: about Picasso, Brahms, Marx. And as soon as he wrote a poem he said to her: "Read it. Tell me if you like it." Love is this too. It is the joy of showing your poems to somebody who reads them, it is the pleasure of producing things for which you'll be praised not by the crowds but by the person you care for and who cares for you. And for her he cared so much that when Angelo had told him Gino, if you want to keep Barbara you better stop dressing like a punk, he'd immediately thrown away the boots with the spurs and the spiked armbands and the T-shirts with the phosphorescent skulls and all the rest including the jacket with the Ride-life-and-life-will-ride-you. He'd kept only the one with the Live-to-love-and-love-to-live. The trouble is that one night they'd ended up in bed, and goodbye Picasso. Goodbye Brahms, goodbye Marx. Like the girl from Val d'Aosta, all she wanted was to be kissed and beanbagged. And every pretext was good for a fight. For example, the fact that she posed as a half communist–half anarchic revolutionary and scorned women who wear furs but she wanted the fur for herself: a mink coat with sable collar. Or the fact that she wanted him to quit the army and open a judo or karate school. Or the one that she no longer read his poetry. "Yuck!" Yes, after the kissing and beanbagging, his poems no longer counted for her. Nor his mind, his soul. All she saw was his dick and his muscles, his muscles and his dick. This bothered him very much and he often said it to her. He said: Barbara, you feminists always scream that a woman isn't a sexual object. And I agree. But by Judas priest, a man isn't either! A man too suffers seeing that he arouses only physical desire! If you keep treating me as a sexual object, I may as well return to the girl in Val d'Aosta who has a cute little bum and needs somebody to help her detoxicate! He'd returned to the girl in Val d'Aosta. He'd helped her to detoxicate. But while he kissed her and beanbagged her, he thought of nothing else but Picasso's noses and ears, Marx's theory of surplus value, Brahms's Third, and didn't understand anymore if he loved the one or the other. So, one day he'd told her:

Listen, I must clarify my ideas, I must go to Beirut. And her answer had been to go back to drugs. Wired on drugs she'd shown up at the port where she'd been picked up by the carabinieri who were there to record everything: who came to see you and who didn't, who wished you a bon voyage and who didn't. They even took photos, those ruffians, and seeing the poor wretch spouting dope the way a fountain spouts water.... They arrested her right under his nose, by Judas priest!

He gulped down the fourth beer and the fourth cognac. They'd approached her and: "What's in your bag, sweetheart?" There was a snort, unfortunately. So it had been no use howling at them damn-gestaps, damn-flatfeet, you're-no-soldiers, you're-damn-fucking-stooges, and-you-behave-as-such-even-on-an-occasion-like-this: they'd dragged her off. And he had left with that weight on his conscience: the weight of having caused her arrest. By Judas priest! Did he hate the carabinieri! For the story of the gun license confiscated from his father the day of the wagtail, to begin with. Then for their arrogance, their contempt toward the other citizens and the law... If you see a car zip through a red light at one hundred miles per hour and run over a pedestrian crossing on the green, you can be sure that in the driver's seat there's a policeman dressed as a carabiniere. And if you shout at him: bastard, where-do-you-think-you-are, in-a-TV-movie-with-the-Los-Angeles-police, didn't-you-see-the-red-light-and-pedestrian-cross-ing-on-the-green, he reports you for insulting a public official. The same thing if you argue with one of them while he is in civilian clothes or in a bathing suit on the beach. By Judas priest, when a stooge is in civilian clothes or in a bathing suit, is his public official's qualification written on his forehead? Plus, they're alien to friendship. Never invite a carabiniere to supper. He's capable of snapping the cuffs on you while he gobbles up the pizza and the wine you pay for. One evening, at Livorno, he'd invited a carabiniere to the pizzeria. He was always alone, not even a scabby dog dated him, so: come-on, let's-have-a-pizza-and-drink-a-glass-of-wine-together. Well, the bastard had devoured two pizzas: one with anchovies and one with artichokes. He had drained not a glass but a whole bottle of wine, at the moment to pay the check he'd stared at the ceiling without even attempting a let's-split-it, and the next morning he'd slapped him with a fine because the roaring motorcycle was parked crookedly. Is it normal, is it human? Finally, he hated them for the way they resolved their sentimental problems. They always have tremendous crushes, the carabinieri. And if the object of their desires leaves them, they pull out their service revolver: I'll-kill-you-and-I'll-kill-myself. Then, with the excuse let's-see-each-other-one-last-time, they take her out in the car, and nine times out of ten you find the couple stone dead. The stooges slumped over the wheel, the object of their desires on the seat. Is it normal, is it human? The worst thing, anyway, was to have them at this base: continually pierced by Cupid's arrows. Officers included. Those nun-chasers. One lost his head over the head nun, another over the vice head nun, another over the nun, another over the quasi nun... No matter what those stooges thought about him and Sister Françoise, the here present Gino was the only one whose heart remained intact. Because when it came to the veil and the wimple, Gino had the same idea as his father: "One nun brings sighs, two nuns give you bad luck, and three bring you disaster. So, when you meet a nun in the street, you'd better knock wood." By Judas priest! He'd finished all the cognacs and the beers, yet he wasn't drunk.

"Bartender! Four more beers!"

"Four more, sergeant?!?"

"Right. And another four cognacs."

He lined up the cans and the bottles of the second round, he started again to drink in the scientific manner. Yet Sister Françoise was his friend. Apart from Angelo, the best friend he'd ever had. It's very difficult, you know, the friendship between a man and a woman. It is because you have a dick, she doesn't. And if you forget it or try to forget it, the moment always comes when a glance or a fortuitous contact of skin reminds you that you have a dick and she doesn't. Yet this didn't happen with Sister Françoise. And not because she was ugly like those stupids said. She wasn't ugly. She was not! She had marvelous black eyes, marvelous ivory hands, a hypnotic velvety voice, and everything considered she was more attractive than Barbara. Had he met her dressed as a woman rather than as a nun, he would have probably ended up in bed with her. Moreover, she had an intelligence that Barbara didn't even dream of, and who says that being beautiful means having beautiful features? Sometimes it means having brains, grace, dignity. Hmm... Maybe with Sister Françoise he could forget that men have a dick and women don't because they had met in Beirut. That is, at a point of his life when having a dick no longer meant much to him... And love, even less. The kind of love that takes place in bed, let's say, the one that looks for its twin soul in bed... He had understood it the day they had met. It was raining, that day, and he'd stopped at the checkpoint to write down a verse which asked to be nailed to a piece of paper. While writing it he had felt two eyes burrow into his back, he had turned around, and there was Sister Françoise:

motionless beneath the drizzle and patiently waiting to pass. Mumbling in French please-excuse-me, I-was-nailing-a-verse-I-don't-want-to-forget he'd jumped out of the way, and in perfect Italian she'd answered: "Non deve giustificarsi, signor sergente. La poesia è uno starnuto di Dio. You shouldn't apologize, sergeant. A poem is God's way of sneezing. If that sneeze isn't grasped immediately and nailed to a piece of paper, it fades into the air." Then she had looked at the sheet of paper with the scribbled verse and: "Signor sergente, le serve un quaderno. Sergeant, you need a notebook. I'll give it to you." Then she had, and by Judas priest! Nobody had ever told him that a poem is God's way of sneezing, that if you don't immediately grasp that sneeze and nail it to a piece of paper it fades into the air! Nobody had ever given him a notebook to preserve God's sneezes, and what else did he want to realize that Sister Françoise was his twin soul? Besides, in spite of her shyness or apparent shyness, she knew life much more than those who don't wear the veil. "Sister Françoise," he'd said once, "I wonder why I've never written a poem about happiness for two." "Because happiness for two doesn't exist, sergeant," she'd replied. "Happiness is solitary. So solitary that I found it only in the solitude of monastic life, in the peace that comes from giving up love expressed through the senses." So he'd told her about his dream of joining the orange-clad monks in Tibet and... By Judas priest, God was about to sneeze! Full of excitement Gino shoved the beers and the cognacs aside, then wrote down the poem.

> Happiness for two doesn't exist.
> Happiness is solitary.
> It's a dream that goes
> along the paths of a world
> faraway and unknown,
> there where the peaks of the Himalayas rise.
> It's a monk who walks all alone
> delighting in his silence
> and in the silence that surrounds him.
> It's the stick upon which he leans,
> an innocuous stick not a cudgel.
> It's the little bell tied to his toe
> to warn the ants and tell them:
> pay attention, I don't want to crush you.
> Yellow trees that gush with mangoes
> blazing bushes that burst with hibiscus

line the silent road.
When he's hungry for food he picks
a ripe mango,
when he's hungry for beauty he caresses
a hibiscus in bloom,
then he retraces his way and arrives
at the monastery that stands
on a peak of the Himalayas.
Happiness is a monastery
that stands on a peak of the Himalayas.
White glaciers and taciturn monks
slender horns which at sunset and sunrise
exhale a pure sound
always the same and equal to itself.
And he
without regretting the melodies
of a time now buried
with his memories, his desires
listens and smiles because
he knows
he is finally at peace.

He read it with satisfaction. He returned to his drinking, and all of a sudden the drunkenness exploded dissolving the mirage: telling him that his dream of becoming a Tibetan monk would never come true. He was not a man free to go where he pleased. He was a caged bird, a bird destined to be caught like the wagtail and the finches and the oxeyes and the tree-creepers and the thrushes he'd killed the first time he'd been given a gun, and the prisoner of a city that in its organic antipathy for peace would sooner or later fuck him. How, he didn't know. But he knew that never would he get to the monastery that stands on a peak of the Himalayas; never would he walk with the innocuous stick and the little bell tied to his toe along the silent road; never would he pick a mango from the yellow trees and caress a hibiscus on the blazing bushes and listen to the pure sound of the slender horns and find the peace that means happiness. He looked at his hands which were so big and heavy but with a pen and paper became so light, so delicate. He thought of Bourji el Barajni, of its alleys, its smell of roast mutton, its ambushes. And the certainty of a disaster, unidentifiable yet very precise, contorted his broad bearded face. Then he downed the final beer, the final cognac, he furiously lurched out of the bar. He broke onto the esplanade where Armando Golden Hands was working on the usual water pipe, overturned his toolbox, trampled on the holy card that blessed it, stumbled off.

"Watch where you put your feet, buffalo!" protested Armando Golden Hands.

"And you shut up, nun-chaser, stooge, gestap! 'Cause this isn't the moment to provoke! It is Gino who says so!" he answered. And letting out enormous belches, mumbling by-Judas-priest, by-Judas-priest, he got back into his tent.

2

Nun-chaser! Stooge! Gestap! Armando Golden Hands picked up the trampled holy card, a Saint Lucy offering a tray on which her eyes swam like fried eggs in a skillet, he carefully dusted it off, and shrugging his shoulders replaced it in the toolbox. It wasn't worthwhile arguing with a drunk, he grumbled. And besides, people always scowl at the carabinieri. They always call them gestaps, stooges. Except when they appeal to them for help. We've-been-robbed, call-the-carabinieri. I-have-been-threatened, tell-the-carabinieri. As for being a nun-chaser, that buffalo really had nerve! Wasn't he in love with Sister Françoise? As soon as he finished his shift at Bourji el Barajni he placed himself at the gate to await her return from the Rizk, and didn't move even if there was a storm of shells. So-if-she-arrives-I'll-run-to-shelter-her. Hmph! Maybe he'd been drinking out of disappointment at seeing her too rarely, poor guy. It certainly isn't pleasant to love somebody whom you never see, somebody with whom you can exchange nothing but a few words at the gate!

He shot a benevolent glance at the tent in which the buffalo had entered belching, he smiled, and his hatchet-hollowed face had a flash of self-irony. Well, he could afford some altruism, he thought. It was Thursday, and in a few hours he would dine with Milady. With her, with Sister Espérance, Sister George, Sister Madeleine, Gigi the Candid... Not Falcon, however. A little while ago Falcon had asked him to convey his regrets to the Mother Superior and there had been no way to make him change his mind. "Come at least for the toasts, colonel!" "Sorry, I can't." Yet Falcon never missed the Thursday night suppers, and knew very well that tonight they would celebrate Milady's birthday. He also knew that Sister Espérance planned to make his favorite dish, a soufflé aux épinards. Well... It would have been better if the one to drop out were Gigi the Candid, always so malicious toward him and

Milady. Always. Even when she came looking for him on the esplanade. "Armandò! Guess who's here, guess who wants you, Armandoòò!" Or: "Here he is, Sister! He's coming! He's running!" He did, yes, he did. He couldn't resist the sound of those drawling *r*'s and those stretched-out *o*'s, nor the enchantment of that perfect Gothic madonna face. So perfect that he didn't understand why everybody saw mustaches on it. Too-bad-about-the-mustaches, she-should-get-rid-of-the-mustaches. What mustaches? They weren't mustaches! They were just a shade, an invisible shade which did not alter at all her orchidlike beauty. Orchidlike... They are bewitching flowers, the orchids, and they'd had such a definitive role in his relationship with her... Because after the armistice supper he had done something crazy. He had called his wife and: "Please send me five orchids." "Five orchids? For whom?" "For the five nuns of the convent." "Then wouldn't lilies be more appropriate?" "Orchids travel better and last longer." Afterwards he had blamed himself. You're a scoundrel, a cynic, he'd said to himself. But the orchids had arrived all the same with the C-130 that delivered the mail on Wednesday mornings. Carefully wrapped in a cellophane bundle, well enclosed in a polystyrene box and... "Des fleurs pour vous. Flowers for you," he'd said handing the box to Milady, and not for an instant had he considered the ambiguity of the "you": the danger that the phrase could be interpreted in the singular as well as in the plural. Flowers-for-you, flowers-for-all-of-you. She'd interpreted it in the singular, alas. "Pour moi, for me?!? Des orchidées, mes fleurs préférées? Orchids, my favorite flower? Oh, Armandò, Armandò! I'll have to tell Sister Espérance that they're for all five of us or for the Infant Jesus on the altar!" Then she'd run off blushing with excitement.

He continued to work on the water pipe and smiled again. They'd really been nabbed by the terracotta Infant Jesus who slept on the chapel altar, but the misunderstanding had acted like gasoline poured on a fire. With the pretext of conveying the other Sisters' thanks, the following day she'd returned and: "Armandò, you're an exquisite man. I want to know everything about you." He'd tried to protect himself by saying that his everything amounted to nothing, that his life could be summarized in broad strokes: he lived in Livorno, he had a wife whom he loved and two children whom he adored; his native city was Anzio, the place where the Americans had landed during the Second World War; he had lost his parents to a Fifth Army artillery barrage and passed his childhood in an orphanage run by French nuns who spoke only French, which was why he knew French so well; during his adolescence he had lived with a gang of thieves who used him to pickpocket

tourists, and at twenty he had enlisted in the carabinieri to avoid becoming one of society's dregs. But, rather than getting horrified, she'd
been touched. "Oh, Armandò! What an exceptional story! A pickpocket who becomes a guardian of the law!" Then she'd told him
about herself, her rich family, her vocation born by reading Saint Teresa
of Avila, the day when she'd informed her family and her mother had
burst into a laugh. "You, a nun?!? I wouldn't believe it even if I saw
you in a cloister!" Her father had taken her seriously, instead, and
opposed the idea like the father of Saint Teresa of Avila. " I can't even
imagine you under a monastic veil... For you I want a comfortable and
prosperous existence, my dear: have you forgotten that at my death
you'll inherit a fortune? Get a law degree rather. It will help you manage your wealth." She'd gotten it. But twenty-four hours later she had
entered the convent, and since then the poor man lived in the hope
that she would change her mind. "My only solace is to know that the
novitiate is a test, and that you'll never withstand the test. You're too
impetuous, too inclined to passions, and soon you'll realize it," he
wrote her from Rhodes where he had moved. The worst, however, had
taken place the following Wednesday. Because his wife had told the
florist that the five orchids were for the Beirut nuns whose convent had
been invaded by the Italians, the good man had answered from-now-
on-I'll-send-them-myself, and the following Wednesday the C-130 had
unloaded another five. The wednesday after, the same. The next one,
also. As inexorable as destiny, each week the C-130 had kept unloading
five orchids that an enraptured Milady grabbed then passed to the
terracotta Infant Jesus who slept on the altar. And the idyll had grown.

He landed an angry hammer blow on the water pipe. The most
innocent idyll in the world, good heavens: nothing was going on between Milady and him. They talked and that's all. About his anticleri-
calism and the fact that it was reinforced by an inborn atheism never
erased or lessened by the French nuns who had sheltered him in Anzio,
for instance. Or about her inflexible faith and the fact that her father
was mistaken in hoping she would never make it through the novitiate... "Mistaken, Armandò, mistaken! I'm not interested in the pleasures of this earth. I believe in the Church much more than my father
believes in his wealth or you believe in your uniform." And each time
she flooded him with little crosses, blessed medals, holy cards depicting
Saint Teresa of Avila or Saint Agnes or Saint Agatha or the Saint Lucy
who offered a tray on which her eyes swam like fried eggs in a skillet.
But why, then, why, were there moments in which the novice garments
seemed so heavy for her and she loosened the veil, she panted what-a-

bother-this-stuff-is? Why did she forgive him for not believing in God and for hating the priests? Why did she always look for him, why did she appear sad when the conversation touched upon his wife and his children? Because she was in love: that's why. He certainly was. He'd been aware of it from the very beginning. So aware that for months he'd racked his brains with scruples, remorse, reproaches... I'm not a kid, he said to himself, I'm a forty-year-old man. I'm not a philanderer, I'm a happy husband, a happy father: how is it that I go around loaded with little crosses and blessed medals and stupid cards of Saint Teresa, of Saint Agnes, of Saint Agatha, of Saint Lucy, how can I be in love with a nun or quasi nun? And leaving Beirut to go back home on rotation with Falcon and Gigi the Candid he'd felt a sort of relief. He'd even been able to coldly answer her question will-you-return-Armandò. "I doubt it." He really doubted it, he was so certain that distance would heal his sickness. Out-of-sight-out-of-mind, the proverb says, and in the beginning it seemed to be true. Relaxing vacations with his seductively tanned wife, nights full of lust kindled by abstinence. One day, however, he had found himself in a movie theater watching an old film with Ingrid Bergman dressed as a nun; another day he had almost fainted at the sight of a nun who from afar resembled Milady; one evening he had almost beaten a friend who had jokingly said nuns-never-bathe and slapped his son who'd run off crying: "Do you miss Beirut, Dad?!?" So he'd understood that distance doesn't reduce a thing, proverbs are nonsense, and he had gone to buy five orchids. He had sent them with an ambiguous note: "Une pour chacune et toutes pour vous. One for each of you and all of them for you." Plus a post-script: "Beyrouth me manque. I miss Beirut." A month later Gigi the Candid had asked him if he would like to return, and the yes had been loud enough to wake an entire army of the dead.

He finished his work, began replacing the tools in the box with Saint Lucy. An ugly trip, the return trip. Always on the ship's bridge to stare at the sea and ruminate over his children who had taken his departure as a tragedy, his wife who had wept. "You said yes?!? You don't love me anymore, you don't love us anymore!" Always asking himself what had bewitched him beyond that perfect face, that enchanting figure, and why Milady was attracted to him: a forty-year-old without special quali-ties, a poor devil whose only talent was patching water pipes and hook-ing up electrical wires and changing locks, an anticleric, an atheist, and finally a married man. But above all he was consumed by impatience to see her again, to hear again her drawling r's and stretched-out o's, and by the fear of not finding her at the convent. Not finding her? She was waiting like a Madame Butterfly who's finally seen the thread of smoke arise from Pinkerton's ship. All trembling, happy, and full of apparently innocuous yet dangerous questions. "What did you miss the most Armandò?" "What did you mean by saying one-for-each-of-you-and-all-of-them-for-you?" While the idyll continued to grow... There was a yardstick to measure its growth: the progressive decrease of the barricade on the stairway that led from the mess hall to the upper floors. The day after his return, in fact, an incursore had broken his right knee by knocking into the first step's hurdles, and Falcon had blamed him. Your-fault, Armando, your-fault. Milady had leaped to his defense, then suggested removing the objects against which the incursore had knocked, and... Imagine a necklace which comes unstrung. Once the first step had been cleared, the second step had followed. And the third, the fourth, the fifth, the sixth: each time somebody needed a stool or a table or a bench, he took it from there. In less than two months, the Maginot-Line had become a symbolic screen that obstructed only the last five steps and that Milady pointed to with a meaningful remark: "Inversely proportional!" Milady?!? Was he saying Milady, not Sister Milady? For Christsake, he should pay attention, tonight... Armando Golden Hands closed the toolbox. He straightened his sturdy body, raised the handsome and masculine face which concealed the very simple reasons why Sister Milady had fallen in love with him, and was about to go when the enchanting figure pounced upon the esplanade like a swallow that announces the spring.

"Armandò, Armandò! Is it true that the colonel isn't coming tonight?"

"Yes, Mi... Sister Milady."

"But why?"

"I don't know, Mi... Sister Milady."

"What a pity, Armandò! Sister Espérance is so disappointed! Is there any chance he'll come for a few minutes only, I mean to toast my twenty-sixth birthday?"

"I'm afraid not, Milady."

It was really difficult to keep that "Sister" in place. Just as difficult as controlling the impulse to clutch her hands and confess I can't hold out anymore, Milady: to hell with your novice's veil, with my scruples, my remorse, my family, your Church and your God. Tell me that your father is right when he says you-won't-withstand-the-test. Tell me that you feel what I feel. And for an endless instant he was on the point of doing so. But, as if the Good Lord had listened and taken his precautions, Sister Espérance's regal face leaned out of a window.

"Sister Milady! What are you doing down there, Sister Milady?"

"I came to check if the colonel is coming tonight, Mother Superior!" the swallow twittered.

"Sister Milady! Nobody asked you to check anything!"

"Yes, Mother Superior, but as I know that you are very disappointed..."

"Sister Milady! Stop saying silly things and get inside immediately!"

"Yes, Mother... Right away, Mother..." And, turning to Armando Golden Hands: "Were you about to tell me something, Armandò?"

"No, Sister Milady."

Then the swallow flew off in a twirl of wings, and a white-haired colossus advanced raising a mocking voice.

"Don't worry, Sister, he'll come! He'll come right on the dot! I'll bring him there myself!"

It was Gigi the Candid who holding a book as huge as an encyclopedia headed for the side street and the Ost Ten skyscraper.

3

Full of regret for his harmless wisecrack, Gigi the Candid turned to apologize, and seeing that both had left the esplanade, he opened the little iron gate with a curse at himself: if a sensible man lodged on that hilltop, this was the bizarre colossus afraid of nothing except toads. Pity the others didn't understand it. But how could they? The child that with our lost innocence sleeps inside our heart very seldom awakens, and the one inside Gigi the Candid's heart never slept. An uncontaminated purity hid behind his prematurely white hair. An almost childish simplicity. He always was dressed in a slovenly way, with an unbuttoned shirt and his neck girded by a red scarf he regarded as an omen against misfortune and illness, rather than a gun he used a hunting knife, and had a rather disconcerting habit for a lieutenant colonel who is second in command of a battalion. When he needed something, he didn't bother to buy it or to get it by legitimate means. He stole it. All the construction work that Armando Golden Hands had lavished on the Ruby base, the hydraulic and electrical installations, the reinforcing walls, were due to the thefts committed by Gigi the Candid: rails extracted from Beirut's former railroad, pipes and pillars pinched from the dockyards in the Eastern Zone, bricks plundered from Bourji el Barajni where he could no longer venture without being followed by hordes of Palestinians shouting akrùt-thief-akrùt. And uselessly Falcon fretted, Crazy Horse despaired, the Condor bellowed that such a habit soiled his name as well as the contingent and the honor of the flag. Do children know what is right and what is wrong? The feature that most characterized Gigi the Candid's personality, though, was another: the idiosyncrasy he had about any intellectual tasks. Between him and learning, him and the printed page, there was such a pathological incompatibility that at the mere sight of a book he was struck by atrocious migraines. And yet (see how unpredictable the miracles of love are) he now held a volume as huge as an encyclopedia. The title: *Mot à mot, sept cents leçons de français.* Word by word, seven hundred lessons of French.

It had been given to him by Sister George the day after the fatal supper in the mess hall. Seduced by the gesture with which she'd removed her double-lens glasses and placed them on his nose then said Monsieur-Gigì-you-need-these-more-than-I-do, the eternal child had in fact lost all restraint and set up an impudent courtship. What-a-spirited-woman, what-an-intelligent-lady, tell-her-that-for-a-dame-like-her-I-would-dive-into-a-pond-full-of-toads-or-iguanas-with-sickle-shaped-lobes. Touched by the homage, Sister George had answered that rather than diving into a pond full of toads or iguanas with sickle-shaped lobes he should learn some French. Hence, the monstrous grammar entitled *Mot à mot, sept cents leçons de français.* "Voilà, Monsieur Gigì. At the rate of one lesson per day, seven hundred lessons would take almost two years. As I don't think they'll keep you in Beirut that long, I order you to study four lessons per day." "Four, Sister?!?" "Four. And don't kid yourself: I won't make any exception for your rank or your venerable white hair. Allez, hop! I expect you in my class tomorrow morning at nine." The next morning at nine he sat on a bench among the children. But the bench was too small for his tall sturdy body, the other children got distracted by his presence, so Sister Madeleine had suggested teaching him on the second floor and his classroom had moved to the kitchen. Regular and irregular verbs, acute and grave and circumflex accents, thirty words to learn by heart for each session. And scoldings. "Monsieur Gigì, you don't apply yourself! You're not studying!" "I'm studying, Sister George, I'm studying! But you must understand that the army doesn't keep me in Beirut to study French. I'm an officer, I take care of the troops!" "That's not my problem, Monsieur Gigì. Study at night." He did. He would have undergone any sacrifice to please her. She was so cute when she said Monsieur-Gigì and liquefied the *g* as if she wanted to savor it. Much cuter than Sister Milady when she drawled the *r*'s and stretched out the *o*'s in Armandò. When she praised, then... Well, she had a strange way of praising. She tapped you on a wrist and laughed: "Très bien, Monsieur Gigì. Today donkeys fly!" And, said by her, the word donkey wasn't offensive. Nor was her way of rewarding. To reward him, she gave him the candies he liked best: marzipan balls covered with grated chocolate and wrapped in yellow or green or violet tinfoil. Each time he answered a question correctly, she unwrapped one and popped it in his mouth: "Une petite carotte pour les ânes! A little carrot for the donkeys!"

He reached the Ost Ten skyscraper and snorted. As the unfinished building lacked an elevator and the observatory was at the fourteenth floor, now he had to climb step by step. And this was a pain in the neck. At the same time, however, it was a kind of pleasure. Because it resurrected the afternoon when Sister George had asked for one of the benches piled up in the anti-rape barrier and, seeing all those cleared stairs, she'd amusedly observed: "Well, I must say there's not much left to defend our virtue." Simpatica! When and where had he known a woman like that? Sister George's charm, anyway, went far beyond the allurement that Italians call simpatia. Maybe her brio. The careless ease with which she carried her infinitesimal figure and her double-lens glasses. Or the erudition he'd always rejected? By God, how many things she knew! All the history and philosophy of Muhammad, of Buddah, of the sage they pray to in China, Confucius... All the gospels of Saint Mark, Saint Matthew, Saint Luke, and Saint John... The life and death and miracles of two guys named Luther and Calvin... A dictionary, rather than a woman. A library. And yet she didn't boast or put on airs. "True wisdom comes from intuition and the heart," she said, "not from the information you find in books. I do well with the donkeys and the children because they understand more than cultivated people. Monsieur Gigì, I would never spoil your exquisite ignorance by teaching you anything but a little French." What's more, you could tell her anything without fear of being mocked. Hah! While eating the marzipan balls and with the pretext of practicing French, he had told her a lot: secrets he'd never revealed to anybody. That he liked plants and trees far more than weapons, for instance. That agriculture was his passion but he had never succeeded in studying it at the university because he had hopelessly failed all the exams for admission. Or that at his tender age, forty-eight, he had discovered the joys of painting and painted landscapes about which the experts used to say: "Not bad, not bad!" He had painted one for her, too. It reproduced the beautiful olive grove below the officers' latrines, and in spite of the latrines which he'd brainlessly included she had liked it very much.

"C'est plein de tendresse, it's full of tenderness, Monsieur Gigì. I'll hang it in my room, near the bed." He even had told her the story of the toad and of his premature white hair: during a trip to the Caribbean he'd found himself face to face with two sickle-shaped iguanas, bigger than toads and much more terrifying, and... She had burst into laughter and switched the Monsieur-Gigì to Gigì. Too bad his rotation to Italy had come a few days later.

He halted to catch his breath and to ask himself what he had felt when informed that he should go back to Italy. A sense of emptiness, he concluded, a dejection very similar to the dejection we feel after failing an exam at school. And with that sense of emptiness, that dejection, he had given her back *Mot à mot*. But she had refused. "Keep it, Gigì. So you'll remember your teacher." He had kept it, and at home he'd locked it in a wardrobe. He couldn't bear its sight. From the wardrobe he had retaken it only on the eve of his return to Beirut, and holding it in his arm he had entered the base...bloody idiot! Did he think that she would be waiting on the esplanade like Sister Milady? After four hours she'd come downstairs! Four! And she wasn't even moved: "Look who's here!" Yet the lessons in the kitchen had been resumed, and the taps on the wrist, and the carrots. Meaning the marzipan candies. "But you don't deserve them, Gigì. You're again a donkey that doesn't fly. You've forgotten everything!" He really had. He even screwed up the conjugation of the verb *aimer*, to love, which from a grammatical point of view is the simplest verb in the world. From another point of view instead... Once he'd lost his heart to a real bitch: a knockout who exploited him, swindled him, cuckolded him with everybody. And at the moment of buzzing her off, he hated her with every fiber of his body. In spite of that hate, however, he desired her with a longing that anybody would have defined as love, and continuously tormented himself with the question is-she-balling-another-man etcetera. As to his wife... Well, he hadn't desired his wife for a million years. She wasn't attractive, poor woman. She was so fat that each time she turned herself on the bed she broke the springs, and in a certain sense he didn't see her as a wife. He saw her as a wet nurse, a mother. Yet she was a part of him like his eyes, and he loved her so much that when he slept alone he felt like an orphan. Well: what he felt for Sister George had nothing to do with the sentiment he felt for his wife or the one he had felt for the bitch. Yet she gave him shivers almost identical to the shiver the bitch used to give him. And though she wasn't a part of him like his wife, the idea of losing her made him sick. Was this love? And if it wasn't, why did he go to Ost Ten with the damn *Mot à mot?* Eh! Because at the Ruby base he couldn't even open the bloody book. They called him, they interrupted him, they disturbed him all the time. At Ost Ten, instead, nobody did. Stretched out in the tub of the bathroom located on the southwest corner, he could study the verbs' conjugations and taste the joy of making her happy. "Bravo, Gigì, bravo! Today donkeys fly! Today they really deserve their little carrot!"

He started climbing the stairs again. No, to be honest, today he had another reason for going to Ost Ten: Rocco and the five Marines who since the double slaughter were trapped in the observatory that the Americans manned with five paratroopers of the Ruby. Crossing the Green Line, returning to their headquarters, meant the risk of falling into the hands of the Amal. So the Condor didn't let them leave the building. Well, dressed in an Italian uniform, Lieutenant Joe Balducci could have made it. He was the son of immigrants from Lucca, he had pale skin and blond hair, he seemed Italian. But the other four were blacker than pitch and had such splayed noses, such football players' physiques, that even under a chador or disguised as muezzins they would have been recognized. Poor guys! Not that he liked them: let's be clear about it. They never smiled, they never granted the shadow of a laugh, in all that time they hadn't even learned to mumble a buongiorno and a buonasera and an arrivederci and a grazie. And the only time they moved their lips was to grunt the typical curses of the Marines who God knows why can't open their mouths without invoking some obscenity associated with the lower half of the body. Fucking, fucked, fuck-you, fuck-off, fuck-out, fuck-over, fuck-up etcetera. To display more manners, to pay you a compliment, old-fart. As for Joe Balducci, who usually limited himself to a hail of shit-shit-shit, he was the most boring and gloomy guy one could find in Beirut: he used his mouth only to talk about Vietnam where he'd seen the whole nine yards. My Lai here, Pleiku there, Saigon on the right, Da Nang on the left. Well... In the hope of cheering them up a little, last week he'd come up with a pot of spaghetti with tomato sauce. Still hot, mind you, and enriched by fresh parmesan with fresh basil: stuff to make you lick your chops. But, instead of hailing that bounty, they all had complained: "Sir, how about a fucking hamburger with fucking fries and fucking ketchup?" Agreed: moldering on the top of a skyscraper forgotten by God and by men is no picnic. Nor is feeling a prisoner of yourself and of your dead comrades, thinking that if you leave the damn observatory you'll be eaten alive by people who rather than giving up the pleasure of killing an American would convert to Christianity. But a little courtesy never hurts, right? He reached the top floor. He entered a large room with the roof barely covered by a girderless loft, the walls lined with sandbags. On the floor, an arsenal of grenade launchers, machine guns, bazookas, hand grenades, machine gun belts, cartridges, rifles. At each loophole, an observer with binoculars and nightscopes. In the middle, the transceivers. Everywhere, tables littered with topographic maps and diagrams. And, bent over the map of Beirut, a young Marine officer who mumbled to himself.

"Shit! Shit! Shit!"

"Ciao, Joe," Gigi the Candid said with a poke at his shoulders.

"Hey, sir," Joe Balducci answered with a little smile. "Did you bring us any hamburgers with fries and ketchup?"

"Nope. And this will teach you to scorn my spaghetti," he shot back, still offended. Then he turned to the Italian who stood at the northeast loophole. A scrawny and desperately ugly youngster.

"Ciao, Rocco. Still in the doghouse?"

"Yessir, colonel," replied Rocco with a sigh.

Poor Rocco. He didn't belong to the Ost Ten squad. He was an incursore and usually stayed at Bourji el Barajni. They'd banished him up here to prevent him from leaving his guard post and going in search of the girl he'd lost while back home for an attack of measles. A girl who was looking for him in her turn. He really needed help, Gigi the Candid thought before reaching the bathroom and opening his *Mot à mot* to study the simplest yet most complicated verb in the world. Because, if a place existed where two creatures in love would never find each other, this was the top of a skyscraper forgotten by God and by men.

4

"Two hundred ninety-five degrees, altitude church of Saint-Michel, outgoing fire."

"Three hundred five degrees, altitude Galerie Semaan, incoming fire."

"Two hundred ninety-five degrees, altitude church of Saint-Michel, incoming fire."

"Three hundred five degrees, altitude Galerie Semaan, outgoing fire."

Pressing his eyes to the nightscopes, Rocco scrupulously noted the pingpong of shells that the Amal and the governmentals were lobbing along the three-hundred-yard strip below the hill. But his mind was far away and his soul was sweating out all the despair of his twenty-four unhappy years. What if Imaam were at this moment in the vicinity of Saint-Michel or Galerie Semaan? What if one of those shells killed or wounded her? He wouldn't even have known! Oh, God! Why hadn't he ever tried to get her address? Why hadn't he opposed her diktat, the first day? The first day... It was springtime, the first day, and he didn't work anymore in Sugar's squad. Off duty he used to stroll in rue Hamrà and practice the French he knew by ear, that day he'd done the same, and all of a sudden here are three girls coming down the sidewalk. Two of them, so-so. One, really beautiful. Not beautiful in the sense of the movie stars: beautiful to his taste. Brunette, very short, very plump. And a smile, a mouth! As full of stars as an August night. Bonsuar, good evening. Comansavà, how's it going? The two so-so's stupidly giggle without answering. She looks at him seriously, instead, and answers: "Italièn ou sirièn? Italian or Syrian?" Because of his dark complexion and his tiny eyes, she would later explain. He'd invited them for a cup of coffee, and the two so-so's hadn't accepted. She had, and the coffee had been followed by an orange juice. The orange juice, by pastries and conversation. "My name is Imaam. I was born next to Cannons Square and I'm twenty-two years old. I'm a Muslim and I live near the Cité Sportive." Then: "No, I won't give you my address. My father is very strict and you would come looking for me. If you want to see me again, you must promise you'll never ask for my address." He'd promised, yes... He had because he'd been swept away by the fact that a girl of such beauty could prefer him to the handsome guys of the Ruby base. God, there were such handsome guys at the Ruby base! Tall, strong, with actors' faces. His body was short and skinny, instead, the body of a malnourished peasant, and his face was so unattractive that just looking at it made him feel inferior. Narrow temples, low forehead. Nose like the butt of a snuffed-out candle, tiny eyes stuck one beside the other. And inset beneath shaggy eyebrows which joined to become a single black stripe. Which is why he was so suspicious, at first. For sure she hangs around me out of curiosity, he thought, or because she sees me as a chicken to pluck: everyone knows that in Beirut Italian soldiers earn a pile of money. And to avoid any misunderstanding, he'd blurted out the truth: that despite the Beirut salary he was poor, that he didn't come from Rome or Milan but from a southern town called Diamante in Calabria, that his parents worked as peasants. But instead of dropping him cold she'd gripped one of his wrists and murmured: "Tell me more, tell me more."

"Fifteen degrees, altitude Eighth Brigade barracks, outgoing fire."

"Three hundred ten degrees, altitude Shyah quarter, incoming fire."

"Three hundred twenty degrees, altitude Tayoune crossing, incoming fire."

He had. It is such a comfort to speak with somebody who murmurs tell-me-more, tell-me-more. He'd told her that the years of his childhood had been the best because they had been so free: like the children of Beirut, he was always out and around. Then he'd been sent to school, from the school to the olive groves to pick the olives, and he'd forgotten what it means to be free. Come-here, get-over-there, do-what-I-tell-you. The same at eighteen, when to escape the olive harvest he wanted to become a waiter. The waiter's trade isn't bad at all, see. You get tips and you eat the same food as the customers. But to get the job you need a hoteliers' diploma which he didn't have, thus he had ended up washing dishes in the kitchen of a seaside inn. The kitchen was in a basement lit by a tiny window at beach level, and this was torture. Through that tiny window he watched people's feet filing by, and would have given his soul to be a foot among those feet: as soon as the cook said boys-I-need-salt-water-to-clean-the-clams, he seized the bucket and ran. To bathe his arms and his legs, see, to feel the splash of the waves. The trouble is that to feel the splash of the waves etcetera he had to cross the beach where the people sunbathed, that is, to wear himself out with jealousy, and one day the bucket had flown right into the sea. He'd gone back to the olive groves. The draft notice had arrived during the olive harvest. A joy. Many people don't like to receive the draft notice. They're afraid of losing their job or a university year, and they have a grudge against the military. He had no job to lose, no university year, and he'd always liked the military because of the bersaglieri who wear a hat full of marvelous plumes and trot sounding a fanfare and singing a very exciting song: "When the glorious bersaglieri / pass and trot throughout the city / my heart jumps with admiration / for those daring, sturdy boys!" In fact he had begged the recruiting officer: please-put-me-in-the-bersaglieri. God knows why, the recruiting officer had immediately assigned him to the paratroopers. There he had become an incursore, and the military trade now was his trade. His father was against it. He said: "Prison and barracks are the same thing!" Not true. The kitchen is a prison, the olive grove is a prison: the barracks are freedom. Like childhood. Besides, soldiers travel. They go to Beirut, see. If it wasn't for the military, he never would have come to Beirut: a city where he was perfectly comfortable because of the Arabs. Yes, those Arabs his colleagues treated so haughtily and called bedouins, Saracens, bumpkins. He didn't. Because he too was a bumpkin. He too was a Saracen, a bedouin. And in Beirut he felt like a bumpkin among bumpkins, a Saracen among Saracens, a bedouin among bedouins.

"Three hundred five degrees, altitude Galerie Semaan, outgoing fire."

"Two hundred ninety-five degrees, altitude Saint-Michel, incoming fire."

"One hundred ten degrees, altitude presidential palace, Katyusha explosion..."

Imaam had been very happy to know that he got along with the Arabs, that among them he felt like a bumpkin among bumpkins, a Saracen among Saracens etcetera. And she'd asked to see him a second, a third, a fourth, a fifth time. Every afternoon, in short. They used to meet downtown and, to avoid making people think sharmuta-whore-sharmuta, they followed this system: she passed at a preestablished point, pretended not to know him, and he followed her to the bar of the Bristol, a rich hotel where nobody gets scandalized if a young man and a girl have an orange juice or a coffee together. Just at the bar of the Bristol, one unforgettable afternoon, she had whispered: "Your adorable Syrian eyes." Then she'd caressed his eyelids, very slowly, very softly, and added: "You're not ugly, my love. You're handsome. Because you're handsome inside." Oh! Nobody had ever told him that he was handsome inside or outside, nobody had ever stroked his eyelids! Who would have ever imagined that his tiny and close-set and hollowed-out eyes were Syrian eyes, that Syrian eyes were adorable? And, the day after, he had discovered the oasis. He was walking along a path that bordered the farm next to the convent property, and all of a sudden here is an enclosure rimmed by lime trees: an oasis where you enter by climbing over the fence. In the middle, a dozen trucks without motors or wheels: the parking lot for unusable vehicles. By a stroke of luck that very same day he had been shifted to night duty, a blessing that left him free until sunset, so every morning they met near the farm where she waited with a lunch basket. Laboring a little he boosted her over the fence, then they reached the oasis and clambered into the back of a truck. If it was raining, a covered truck. If it wasn't, an open one from which they could enjoy the lime trees that interlacing their branches formed a ceiling of leaves. Oh, it was so sweet to make love beneath the ceiling of leaves! They made love, yes. Not all the way because, if you're not married, the Koran forbids it. But he contented himself with what the Koran permits, then he slept in her arms and awoke to eat the lunch she kept in the basket. As they ate, they spoke like husband and wife. How-much-was-this-chicken, it-was-too-expensive, you-shouldn't-have-bought-it, etcetera. Besides, weren't they really husband and wife by now? They even had a house, an address. Their house, the broken-down truck. Their address, the oasis rimmed by the lime trees that formed the ceiling of leaves.

"One hundred ten degrees, altitude presidential palace, Katyusha explosion."

"One hundred forty degrees, Shouf Mountains, incoming shells."

"One hundred thirty degrees, Shouf Mountains, outgoing shells."

After lunch, Imaam taught him Arabic. Words like *habibi* which means my-treasure if it's addressed to him, *habibati* which means the same if it's addressed to her. Or *ana-behebbak* which means I-love-you when it is said by her, *ana-behebbeki* which means the same when it is said by him. He taught her Italian, instead, with a single question and a simple answer: "Mi vuoi sposare?" "Sì!" "Do you want to marry me?" "Yes!" They wanted to get regularly married, of course, and their only uncertainty had to do with the rite they would choose to celebrate the marriage: Muslim or Catholic? To resolve the dilemma, they'd planned to exchange a Bible and a Koran. "One of us will read the Koran, one of us will read the Bible. Then, if we decide that the Bible is better, we'll get married in the Catholic church. If we decide that the Koran is better, we'll get married in the mosque." The trouble is that he had caught the measles, damn the measles. Isn't the measles a kids' illness?!? Well, he'd caught it anyway. High fever, red dots all over, field hospital, and Imaam who came all the same to bring him the lunch and to say mon-amùr-tu-es-bò-mem-comsà. My-love, you're-handsome-even-so. It had taken two weeks to heal, and at that point they'd sent him to Italy for convalescence. To Italy! Informing him at the last minute, that is, the evening before his departure! Pack-your-bag, quick, your-ship-leaves-at-noon. At noon! When Imaam would arrive! And there was no way to let her know! He'd remained so dumbstruck that he hadn't even been able to plead no, I-beg-you, don't-send-me. Dumbstruck he'd packed the bag, and everybody thought he was speechless with joy. "You devil! You lucky thing! How did you manage to catch the measles?" they laughed. Or: "Rocco, could you spare me a few measles?" Oh, don't ever expect the others to understand the pain that comes from the soul. If you get a bullet they immediately shout quick-medic-plasma, if you break a leg they solicitously plaster it, if you have a throat inflammation they promptly offer you a medicament. But if your heart is shattered and you're so dumbstruck you cannot open your mouth, they don't even notice. And yet the soul's pain is a sickness much graver than a broken leg or a throat inflammation, its wounds are more dangerous than those inflicted by a bullet. They are wounds that don't heal, that bleed again at every pretext. The proof was that he'd never healed from the ones inflicted on him by the come-here, get-over-there, do-what-I-tell-you, or by the sight of the feet going to the beach while he washed dishes... Anyway, and to make a long story short: only at the checkpoint had he been able to open his mouth and to leave a message. "Boys, at noon a beautiful girl will show up. Brunette, very fleshy, delightfully plump. Her name is Imaam and she speaks French. Do me a favor, tell her to come to the port. If the ship is late, we can say goodbye to each other." He had said so because the ship was always late. That morning, it had left on the dot.

"One hundred fifty degrees..."

Rocco lowered the nightscopes. His eyes were swollen with tears and instead of the explosions they saw a watery curtain. Oh, also on the ship he'd wept. Also in Livorno. How to avoid it? He couldn't write her. The only address he had was the one of a sewing school she used to attend in April and that in summer was closed... What days, my God, what weeks! To bear the sorrow, he continuously bought her gifts. Today the Gucci scarf that costs a fortune, tomorrow the Chanel Number Five which costs as much as the scarf because it's Marilyn Monroe perfume, the day after tomorrow the amethyst bracelet that costs less than a diamond but still costs plenty, and the shoes. She liked Italian shoes. In the oasis she'd kept saying: "As your wedding gift I want Italian shoes!" So, while in Diamante where he had gone to tell his parents about the engagement, he'd bought them: chestnut-colored lizard skin with black velvet tassels, no heels or she looked too tall beside him, and very expensive. Two hundred thousand liras. A good thing the shoemaker had promised to change them if the size wasn't right, and at his return to Beirut... God, how many struggles to be sent back to Beirut! Forget-it, they answered, you-spent-too-much-time-up-there. But one day he'd turned to the captain. "I beg you, captain. If you love somebody, do help me: send me back to Beirut." The captain loved somebody, and... As soon as he'd arrived in Beirut, he'd run over to the sewing school which usually reopened in September and slipped a note under the door. "Imaam, I am back and I wait for you with the shoes. Your Rocco." But the school hadn't reopened, the note had remained underneath the door, and he'd started thinking that she was dead. Well, she wasn't dead. She wasn't even wounded, he'd soon discovered through an incursore. "Rocco, if you're not on duty Sunday, let's go to the beach at Ramlet el Baida. It's out of artillery

range, and many girls come there. Last Sunday one of them was looking for you." "For me?!?" "Yeah. A nice fatty named Imaam. She kept
asking: Do-you-know-Rocco? Did-Rocco-come-back? When-is-Rocco-
coming-back?" "And what did you answer?!?" "That we didn't know
you. Just in case you dumped her..." Dumped her?!? He'd howled
wretches, morons, villains, and spent the whole Sunday at the beach.
But Imaam hadn't come, and God knows why Falcon had reassigned
him to Sugar's command.

"Two hundred twenty degrees..."

He raised the nightscopes again. A nasty blow, being reassigned to
the command of an officer who peeks over your shoulder even when
you go to the bathroom and punishes you for nothing. As nasty as that
Sunday disappointment. However, he'd worked it out and told himself:
if Imaam is searching for me at Ramlet el Baida, it means she can't get
from the Cité Sportive to the Ruby base. On the other hand she can
still travel to Bourji el Barajni, and sooner or later she will. So, with the
pretext that I need to readjust, I should convince Sugar to place me in
the M113 of Post One which is on rue de l'Aérodrome and controls all
the people entering or leaving the quarter. He had. The trouble is he
never stayed in the M113. Every ten minutes he left it to go and
request help from his comrades on duty at the other posts. "I beg you,
if you see Imaam, tell her that I'm at Post One." When he didn't do
that, he went off to mobilize the children: to show them her photograph and to harangue them. "Look at it carefully, kids! She's a beautiful girl: brunette, very fleshy, delightfully plump. And her name is
Imaam. If you see her, tell her: Rocco is back! He's back with the
shoes! In the M113 at Post One!" And finally Sugar had caught him.
"Why isn't Rocco here?!?" "He went to take a leak, sir. He'll be right
back," his crew had replied. But in the very same moment here is Gino
passing by with his head in the clouds: "Don't worry, lieutenant. I saw
him around. Poor Rocco, he has lost his girlfriend and sometimes he
goes looking for her." Then he'd understood the blunder and tried to
correct it. But Sugar had shouted don't-change-your-story, my-hear-
ing-is-fine, and: "From now on you stay at Ost Ten, Rocco. And there
you eat, you sleep, you live without going downstairs. Like the five
Americans. Understand?!?"

"Oh my Go-o-d!"

From the northeast corner of the room the groan reached the bathroom at the southwest corner. And, leaping out of the bathtub inside
which he studied the simplest yet most complicated verb in the world,
Gigi the Candid ran over to Rocco to console him.

"Come on, kid, don't take it so hard. I'll ask Joe Balducci to spell you. Tell me the whole story and we'll try to fix it up." But instead of saying thanks, Rocco pushed him toward the loophole.

"Look, sir, look!"

*   *   *

In fact it wasn't Imaam who had made him groan. It was the volcano of flames, black smoke, sparks, that rose upward at three hundred ten degrees. That is, the munitions dump at Sierra Mike. Sandokan's base.

CHAPTER THREE

1

SANDOKAN'S BASE was located at the quietest and most pleasant spot of the west coast: the littoral called avenue Ramlet el Baida which to the south joined the Street Without a Name and to the north flowed into avenue de Gaulle then climbed to the northwest promontory. There the sea caressed picturesque outcroppings of periwinkle granite, pink-pebbled beaches like the one that had witnessed Imaam's useless search for Rocco and Rocco's useless wait for Imaam, tiny inlets which in the happy days were known as Anse Montecarlo or Crique Côte d'Azur, and despite the rubble left by the Israeli siege the signs of war were few. The houses appeared almost intact, the hotels rather frequented, the stores enough supplied, and just where avenue Ramlet el Baida flowed into avenue de Gaulle a Luna Park joyfully stood. A real Luna Park with merry-go-rounds, slides, shooting galleries, plus an enormous wheel similar to the one in the Prater: Vienna's amusement park. A paradoxical image in which the optimists saw the triumph of Life over Death, the pessimists the symbol of a city incapable of separating right from wrong, the aesthetes and the cynics a pictorial touch bordering on surrealism, the wheel rotated to the rhythm of *An der schönen blauen Donau,* the Blue Danube Waltz. And even when a nearby quarter was burning you saw people on it. In fact the littoral didn't offer any targets that drew rifle or artillery fire, the Green Line was two miles away, and the stray bullets didn't travel that far. If they did, they arrived more tired than birds which have flown too much and didn't hurt anybody. As for the battalion's residence, two six-story buildings that Sandokan had rented from a rich Sunni official, it enjoyed the additional benefit of being located almost on the seashore and therefore being protected by the ships crisscrossing the coast. Naturally the nightmare of the third truck existed here too. In order to understand it, you only had to look at the barriers, the checkpoints, the sandbag embankments, the antiaircraft guns the Condor had wanted on the roofs, and finally the fence which enclosed the base. But in comparison to the other bases it seemed an El Dorado of security, and the presence of the Sunni official who lived with his wife and daughter in a large cottage inside the fence was the first demonstration. The second was the helicopter field that stayed a couple of hundred yards away, and the munitions dump: one hundred fifty yards away. Dulcis in fundo: set inside a carefully concealed hole and well protected by a wall of cement plus by the outcroppings of periwinkle granite, the dump could be considered the most unreachable and unattackable of the whole contingent. So unreachable, so unattackable, that there was hardly any need to guard it. Yet somebody had hit it dead center, with a professional's precision. Why? And who had it been?

Everybody wondered. In the hope of finding an answer Charlie had mobilized his best informants, Pistoia had opened an investigation, Sugar had searched the site for hours. But he'd found only the fragments of three mortar shells. A kind of shell that both the Amal and the governmentals used. And the Condor foamed with rage. "I want to know who! Who, who!"

*   *   *

Sandokan leaned out over the ditch now empty and blackened, he voluptuously inhaled the scent of ashes and explosive that remained in the air, and a smile of beatitude lit up his pirate's scowl. Long drooping mustaches, goatish sideburns, disheveled eyebrows, shaggy and sun-bleached beard, windburned skin. Who...? Bloody dick of a dick superdick, he couldn't care less to know. Whoever it was, he thanked him with all his heart. Nobody had been killed, the sentries merely got their asses scorched, and shouldn't he be a protagonist too, once in a while? He'd had it up to the balls with staying on the margins of war, with commanding a base where nothing ever happened and you got so bored that to hear the sound of a bullet you had to go to Shatila! War was his job, bloody dick of a dick superdick! It belonged to him as a fire belongs to a fireman, and what kind of life is the life of a fireman who doesn't have a damn fire to extinguish? A military man without war is unemployed, God dammit, and when he acts like a dove with an olive branch in his mouth he's a fucking liar too: a hypocrite, a lackey of the squishheads who preach pacifism. If you hate war, why do you choose a trade which deals with arms? Why don't you change your job? Go be a missionary, go! Become a greengrocer or a bank clerk! It had become fashionable to speak badly about war, to insult it and defame it with the

let's-love-one-another, but Sandokan didn't buy it. He never forgot
that war is the sap of life, a sap that comes with life, that runs in man's
veins like his blood. He never forgot that every living being makes war.
Every element of nature. No, he wasn't ashamed to love war: to respect
it, to invoke it, to be jealous of those who had the luck to fight one.
Oh, how did he envy the Russians in Afghanistan! How had he envied
the Americans in Vietnam! Had it been possible, he would have run to
Saigon and begged them: take me, please! I'm a good officer, an officer
who knows the profession of leading an assault, of conducting a
roundup and a reprisal, of cutting throats: give me a chance, dammit!
Bloody dick of a dick superdick, for years he'd hoped to see Italy involved in some conflict, even a minor one, for instance a few weeks'
showdown with Yugoslavia or Albania or Malta! Or the Principality of
Monaco, the Republic of San Marino! Forget it. After wedding themselves to democracy, the Italians had become less warlike than the
Swiss. And thank God they had sent him here to protect those Palestinian louts...

He left the ditch and returned to his quarters: a former bedroom on
the second floor of the main building, characterized by a wall-to-wall
carpet that was a rainbow of filth. Coffee stains, grease spots, mud
streaks. He sat at a desk cluttered with cartridges, hand grenades, revolvers, other tools like the Camillus knife that Gigi the Candid had
stolen for him from Joe Balducci and that Balducci had used in Vietnam. He smiled contentedly, but then his glance fell upon the foot-
prints his boots had added to the rainbow of filth, and the contentment
faded. Bloody dick of a dick superdick, the Sunni official had begged
him so much! "Please commander: take good care of my property. And
above all, don't ruin this white carpet." The poor man had even provided a vacuum cleaner. "Use it as often as you can, commander." And
he used it. But when your shoes have picked up soot from a fire-
blackened ditch, you can't walk across a white carpet without leaving
tracks. He got up. He grabbed the vacuum cleaner and for a few minutes the pugnacious pirate became what he really was. That is, a gentle
thirty-nine-year-old guy whose bellicosity could be compared to the
restlessness of children who play with tin rifles, a good man who un-
awares resembled his father: lawyer, pacifist, blind admirer of Bertrand
Russell, as well as distinguished member of Amnesty International and
president of the Anti-Hunting Society at Vicenza. A beautiful city, Vicenza, he growled. Who could deny it? Beautiful churches, beautiful
palaces, and blessed by the Prealps. But what plugged-up horizons!
Each time you went with Papa to pick edelweiss or to fish for trout and

to listen to his discourses on peace among people, you wasted away with boredom and anxiety. "Aren't these mountains full of harmonious splendor? What a sense of peace, son!" "Yes, Papa." "Never turn your back on peace, son." "No, Papa." "Like Bertrand Russell says, we must vanquish with tolerance the old mechanism of hate which leads us to attack other tribes. Such mechanism derives from ancestral, savage instincts, is therefore unhealthy and harmful to our mental equilibrium. Are you following me, son?" "Yes, Papa." "Tolerance is intelligence. Never forget that, son." "No, Papa."

Yes-Papa, no-Papa, but what was there beyond those trout-laden lakes, those mountains blossoming with edelweiss, those noble teachings? One Sunday it rained. No trout, no edelweiss, no noble teachings. "Can I go to the movies, Papa?" "Sure, son." He'd chosen one at random and seen John Wayne in command of the battleship *West Virginia* which bombarded the Philippine beaches to prepare the ground for MacArthur. Bloody dick of a dick superdick, what a movie! A wild foamy ocean, bold Marines rushing to their battle stations in the blink of an eye, cannons ripping the blue with golden blazes of death, and finally the American flag fluttering in the sky to confirm the victory over the perfidious Japanese. He'd returned home in the grip of an unfamiliar excitement, and next Sunday: "Can I go to the movies, Papa?" "Sure, son." This time there was Henry Fonda aboard the submarine *Seahorse* chasing Admiral Yamamoto, and he'd liked him even more than John Wayne. Up periscope, down periscope, give the coordinates, prepare the torpedoes, fire, bang! After Henry Fonda, Robert Mitchum who landed in Normandy with an amphibious craft and upheld by very exalting music secured solid beachheads at Omaha Beach. Meaning Saint-Laurent-sur-Mer. After Robert Mitchum, any war movie that was shown in Vicenza. A fixation. And while the fixation covered the walls of his bedroom with photos of gunboats, destroyers, frigates, cruisers, corvettes, minelayers, submarines, the meek boy became more and more of a war-lover. His father smiled and said: This is a transitory illness, son, a moral tonsillitis. You're searching for yourself: that's why you oppose my principles. But one day you'll get a law degree, you'll join my firm as a leading light of the bar, you'll keep a golden watch in your fob, a Rotary card in your wallet, and you'll talk like me." At nineteen, however, the future leading light of the bar had said: Papa, I'm not getting a law degree, I don't want to join your firm, I'm not interested in keeping a golden watch in my fob and a Rotary card in my wallet. And Vicenza is too choking, the lakes are too little, the Prealp mountains hide the sky. I love the wild foamy oceans, the open spaces, the war." And the next day he'd been admitted to the Naval Academy where his moral-tonsillitis had crystallized giving birth to the bizarre character who loved to stay in Beirut and trembled at the idea of being scolded because of a soiled carpet.

No, the damn soot wouldn't come out. The more he tried to suck it up, the more it penetrated into the texture. He then put the vacuum cleaner away and went back to his desk. Bloody dick of a dick superdick, there was so much to do besides cleaning a spot! He had to fix the ditch and replace the munitions dump, to call the headquarters and get the new supplies before evening, to write a report for the Condor who wanted the precise list of the blown-up material... How many pounds of Tnt, how many mortar shells, how many bazookas, how many machine gun rounds, how many rifle rounds... "Everything, understand? And be serious, for once!" Be-serious! All that cobra did was criticize and provoke and insult him! "Sandokan is a fascist, a cartoon." "Sandokan looks like the boatswain in the ads for canned tuna fish." "Sandokan is a discredit to the contingent." Or: "What kind of officer names himself after a Malaysian corsair, after a caricature in a boys' adventure story?" Nor did that cobra like his habit of expressing himself in American with roger, right, over, go-ahead, Sierra-Mike-One. "We're not in Vietnam, God blasted! We're in Beirut! This is not the American army! This is the Italian one! In Italian we say *sì*, not *roger*! We say *d'accordo*, not *right*! We say *chiuso*, not *over*! We say *vai avanti*, not *go ahead*! We say *uno*, not *one*! Understand?!?" He had it in for the marò, too. Ever since poor Fabio had swallowed the mullah's coffee, he slandered them in any possible way. Clods, slobs, cowards. Cowards? You only had to take Rambo's example to see how brave the marò were. Slobs? You only had to cast a glance at Roberto, his extremely tidy driver, to see how clean and orderly the marò could be. Clods? Well, maybe they were a little cloddish. Sailors don't bother with etiquette, are not used to snapping to attention and clicking their heels for every crap. The ships roll: if you snap to attention or click your heels, you end up with your ass in the air. As for the hashish, everybody smoked it. Including paratroopers. But try saying the truth to the snakes. That cobra hated the marò so much that in Bourji el Barajni they hadn't a single garrison, and in Shatila they had only three posts. No, two and half, since they split the Twenty-Seven Owl with the bersaglieri. Superbloody dick of a dick superdick!

He grabbed a sheet of paper. He began to list the material blown up. "One hundred thousand cartridges of 5.56... Thirty thousand of Nato 7.62... One thousand two hundred 120mm mortar shells... One thou-

sand two hundred heavy machine gun belts..." But here he interrupted, finally aware that the Condor was right to ask who had done it:
maybe there was something big behind this attack, something that little
by little was ripening to wipe out his boredom... And while he said it,
he felt a strange nostalgia for Vicenza, for the trout-laden lakes, the
crags full of edelweiss, the noble paternal instructions. For a moment
which was infinitesimal and yet so intense that it deranged him, he felt a
strong desire to shave off his shaggy sunbleached beard, his long
drooping mustaches, his goatish sideburns and recover his face. The
face of a gentle thirty-nine-year-old guy whose bellicosity could be
compared to the restlessness of children who play with tin rifles. Then
he got up, furious. And as if he wanted to quash the intuition, defend
himself from it, he slipped a 9mm Beretta into his holster. He hung a
pair of hand grenades on his belt, slipped in its sheath the Camillus
knife, and called for his driver.

"Roberto!"

"Here I am, sir."

A nice young man with pubescent cheeks and a neat, crisply pressed
uniform entered the room.

"Take me to Shatila, Roberto."

"Yessir, at once."

Ten minutes later his jeep passed Camp Three of the Twenty-Eight
where, by unforeseeable paths, Fabio was about to discover what even
Sandokan now wanted to know.

2

Fabio had never overcome the trauma of John's decapitated head
and the shame of having betrayed his memory with that coffee. The
vitality that once electrified him was gone, the despair which had stirred
him was dissipated too, and he vegetated in a kind of apathy which had
become the talk of Sierra Mike. "Remember when he used to sing at
the top of his voice and you had to tell him shut-up?" "Remember
when he used to pester us with stories of his exploits and we had to yell
give-us-a-break?" He always pulled a long face, never opened his
mouth, and his apathetic eyes discouraged any attempt at conversation.
Yet his Camp Three post companion was no longer Rambo. That is,
someone who would cut him dead and didn't waste many words either.
Promoted to patrol leader, now Rambo roved the alleys of Shatila and
at his old guard post there was Matteo: a chatty guy who offered joints
and got people to open up. The most disconcerting thing, however,

was the indifference Fabio showed toward women. Fabio! The base's rooster, the Latin lover! He no longer looked at them, he no longer spoke about them, and listen to this. In front of Camp Three were some shacks that belonged to the thug of the quarter, a Shiite named Ahmed, and in one of them lived a blonde who took your breath away. A genuine blonde, okay? So genuine that instead of a Lebanese you would have called her a Swede. Not to mention her high thighs and her lady-from-the-Eastern-Zone gait. Well, every morning the beauty in question left the shack and marched down the south sidewalk of the Street Without a Name to go to the Kuwaiti embassy where she evidently worked. At sunset she returned, and believe it: each time the shouts of enthusiasm shattered the air. "Goddess! Princess! Super pussy!" Everybody desired her. Everybody. Fabio, instead, remained cold and silent. What's more, he didn't even look at Sheila, the cute schoolteacher who slept with the officers for nothing and who had a weakness for him. Vattene-Sheila, go-away, was the ingrate's answer to her trills Fabio-ciao-Fabio.

"Fabio, are you okay?" Matteo asked.

"Why?" Fabio grumbled.

"Because you're always silent. That's why!"

"Yeah."

"Want a joint?"

"Nope."

"A hit. Come on, take it."

"Nope."

"Fabio, war is war. If soldiers lose their mind over each buddy who gets killed, armies would turn into hospitals! Right?"

"Yeah."

"Let me give you a piece of advice, then. When Sheila comes, don't chase her away. In certain cases there's nothing better than a good fuck and... Are you listening to me, Fabio?"

"Yeah."

He was listening, sure, he was listening. But he didn't want his joint. He didn't want Sheila. He didn't want his advice. And what did Matteo know about certain sufferings?!? Had he ever picked up a friend's decapitated head? Had he ever betrayed that friend's memory, ever behaved like a Judas? Matteo wasn't even in Beirut, the Sunday of the double slaughter. He'd arrived afterwards, and by God! Does hashish cure a grief that strangles? Do women cure a shame that gnaws? He didn't like joints. He wasn't interested in women. And when he thought of himself on the beaches of Brindisi, wearing a tiny bathing suit to show his tanned body and keeping his shirt open to better seduce the mature bags who pay with a trip to Frankfurt or Stockholm, he felt guilty. Because that tanned body seemed to him another betrayal of John who had been cut in two. His head on one side and the rest on the other... No, he didn't care for Sheila. He didn't even care for Mirella, by now. Every time he read her soppy letters, I-miss-you-my-love, I-get-shivers-just-thinking-of-you, he was caught by nausea. Shivers? Only one thing gave him shivers, now: the terror of hearing again what Rambo had whispered before cutting him dead: "You're a Judas. A traitor without dignity. A Judas." Or what the others had howled spitting their contempt: "Coward, whore, chicken, pussy, shitbird." They didn't say it anymore: right. But those words thundered in his ears like drumbeats. Know why? For he was the one who now said them to himself.

"Là, là, là! No, no, no!"

A feminine voice rose out of the darkness, a moan of a wounded animal. And along with it, a series of thuds like the thuds of a mattress being beaten. Then, a hoarse masculine yell.

"Sharmuta, whore, sharmuta!"

It came from the south sidewalk of the Street Without a Name, and Matteo started.

"Fabio!"

"Yeah," Fabio answered without stirring.

"They're beating up a woman."

"Yeah."

"In one of Ahmed's shacks."

"Yeah."

"Who might it be?"

"Ahmed."

Yes, Ahmed. He knew him well. Because during the summer that pig used to spend hours on the sidewalk where with a bottle of whiskey in his right hand and a glass in his left he got drunk notwithstanding Allah. Other times, instead, he crossed the street and with his disgusting belly, his greasy face, his faggoty mustache came to tell stories of his dirty life... That he'd lived in Iran where he owned a Turkish bath and a brothel, that he'd learned the art of love in Esfahaan, that to make love skillfully one needed to be circumcised... One night the miserable lard wanted to circumcise him. Brandishing a sharp knife he shrieked: "Let me do it, let me do it! It lasts one minute and you don't feel a thing!" To drive him off he'd been forced to point his gun: "Don't you dare touch my equipment, you shitty bedouin, or I'll send you to the Creator." He also came to offer girls. He had five prostitutes, during the summer. He kept them in the shack next to his own, all together, and beat them often. Now the only one left was Miriam. Maybe he was beating her, tonight. Poor thing. She moaned more and more weakly. The là-no-là was hardly audible. But the thuds grew louder. Ah, if only he weren't a coward! Ah, if only he had the courage to cross the street, burst into the shack, and make him stop!

"He's slaughtering her..." Matteo said.

"Yeah."

"How come nobody stops him?!?"

"Don't know."

"But a lot of people live in those shacks! Are they deaf?"

"Nope. They're used to it."

"Then let's intervene ourselves!"

"We can't."

"Sure we can! All we need to do is go over there and point our guns!"

"Abandoning the post is prohibited."

"I know, Fabio, I know! But who's going to see us in this dark? I'm going!"

"It is not your business."

"It is! I cannot stand such a shame!"

"Try to stand it."

"But when a thing like this happened next to the Twenty-Four, Eagle intervened with the bersaglieri!"

"Eagle is a commander."

And Ahmed is a dangerous guy, he wanted to add. The kind who licks your boots and twenty-four hours later sends his Khomeinist pals, gets you killed. And I don't want to die. I'm a coward, a whore, a chicken, a pussy, a shitbird, a traitor without dignity, a Judas, so I don't want to get involved. All of a sudden he did, though. Because he had an impulse that he wouldn't have been able to explain, an impulse which went back to the mullah's coffee and yet originated in a more distant and complicated shame. Perhaps the shame of the days when on the beaches of Brindisi he strutted in his tiny bathing suit to show his tanned body to better seduce the mature bags who pay with a trip to Frankfurt or Stockholm. Perhaps his awareness of having never given a thing but a little friendship to the Marine with whom he wanted to open a restaurant in Cleveland, Ohio. And he moved away from the wall. He crossed the street, reached the shack from which the moans and the thuds were coming, kicked the door, burst into a dark room where Ahmed was cudgeling a bundle in the shape of a woman, and pointed his gun.

"Ahmed, you son of bitch, don't you get tired of beating people up? Stop it or I'll shoot you. Understand?"

The bundle whined weakly and hid its head beneath a rag. Ahmed dropped the stick and raised his arms in a gesture of surrender.

"Okay, Fabio, okay! Don't shoot! We two, brothers!"

"I'm not anybody's brother, you pig! And least of all yours. Understand, pimp?"

"Understand, Fabio, understand! You can take her! Hadeja, gift!"

"No hadeja, no gift! I don't want any gifts from you, tub of lard. And if you start again, I repeat it, I'll kill you."

Then he returned to Matteo who stared at him with incredulous amazement.

"Fabio..."

"Well, he stopped. Are you happy now?"

"Yes, but..."

"But what?"

"Who was the woman he was beating?"

"I don't know."

"Didn't you see her?!?"

"No. I didn't look," he said shrugging his shoulders.

*   *   *

He truly hadn't. He hadn't even felt the instinctive curiosity to scan the darkness and check if the long bundle with its head hidden beneath the rag was Miriam. What difference would it make, anyway? Toward dawn, however, the outline of a tall feminine figure wrapped in a black abaja appeared on the opposite sidewalk. And Matteo emitted a strangled exclamation.

"God dammit! It's her!"

"Who?"

"The goddess! The princess! The stunning blonde!"

Just so. Motionless on the sidewalk, she observed them as if she hadn't decided as yet to come forward or go back. With her right hand, meanwhile, she touched her left arm which hung in a sling. She touched it as if it were badly hurt and through her fingers she could soothe the pain.

"The one who works at the Kuwaiti embassy?" he murmured with indifference.

"Yes, Fabio, yes!"

You also had the impression that leaving that sidewalk would represent a tremendous labor for her, an arduous sacrifice, and for a while she continued to hesitate. But then she stepped down, resolutely, and with very slow steps she crossed the street. Always touching the arm in the sling she reached the low wall of Camp Three and halted offering to the dim light an extraordinarily gentle, disfigured face. Her right eye was in fact half-closed. The left, encircled by a purplish bruise. Her cheekbones were scratched and bloodstained. Her lips, swollen. She moved them to raise a feeble voice.

"Who is Fabio?" she murmured in English.

"Me," Fabio answered circumspectly.

"My name is Jasmine. I come to thank you."

"Never mind..."

"You are a very brave man, Fabio. What does Fabio mean?"

"I don't know..."

"I think it means courage."

"Oh, no!"

"Yes, it does. How do you say courage in Italian?"

"Coraggio," Matteo put it.

"Coraggio? Then I will call you Mister Coraggio."

She tried a smile that her swollen lips refused to grant, she sketched out a well-mannered curtsy.

"Now I must go. But I will be back. And maybe I will have important news to give you."

Fabio and Matteo looked at each other questioningly. Then Matteo said that at war important news is always bad news, to hell with the day he'd chosen to graduate with a thesis on Lebanon and the international problems of the Middle East, so to forget about it he would smoke a joint.

3

He lit it. He inhaled it greedily and his face, the face of a twenty-one-year-old not accustomed to suffering, twisted in resentment. No, the thesis on Lebanon and the Middle East's international problems had nothing to do with his insane idea of coming to Beirut. The true reason why he had committed such an insanity was that he could no longer bear Palermo and the existence of a little parasite who studies Political Science because Political Science is less difficult than Medicine or Engineering, yawns from September to June in university halls, and from

June to September in the typical idleness of the Sicilian bourgeois. Waking at noon to go to the beach with Rosaria who is beautiful and intelligent and elegant and returns your passion to the point of refusing a wealthy duke then a famous soccer player. I-prefer-you-Matteo, you're-so-sexy-Matteo. Staying at the beach until sunset, returning home to shower and wheedle money from Daddy who indignantly answers I-pay-for-your-education-not-your-high-jinks. Grasping the hundred thousand liras from Mommy who sighs don't-show-it-to-Daddy, stick-it-in-your-pocket. Using that money to take Rosaria to a cheap cafeteria or to some cheap nightclub, and secretly feeling ashamed of yourself. At a certain point he'd felt an overflow of nausea and wondered: what if I get myself sent to Beirut? I would rid myself of the headache of military service, have an unforgettable adventure, and at the same time gather material for the thesis on Lebanon and the Middle East's international problems. Then he had discussed it with Rosaria, and Rosaria encouraged him. "Sure, Matteo, sure. All you need is a notebook, a tape recorder, some tapes, a camera, and a supply of film. Go, Matteo, go." For Christsake! When the girl you love talks that way, you don't care if Mommy cries all her tears and Daddy screams idiot-you've-been-drinking-tonight. You buy the notebook, the tape recorder, the tapes, the camera, the film, and you volunteer. Worse: seeing that without recommendations a Sicilian can't even go to Beirut, you ask Rosaria to get in touch with the cousin of her sister in-law's aunt who knows the mafioso friend of the other mafioso on good terms with the colonel of the recruiting office. "I beg you, Rosaria." "My pleasure, Matteo."

He inhaled a second hit. How impatiently had he waited for the recommendation to work, how enthusiastically had he left Palermo and boarded the ship! At his arrival he wanted to kiss the soil like the Pope when he travels abroad. Everything seemed extraordinary, everything! The garbage heaps. The portraits of Khomeini. The ugly minarets. The young women in pink pajamas. The old women in chadors. The punks in blue jeans and Kalashnikovs. The barefoot children, the wrecked houses, the scorched trees, the terraces with hanging laundry, the mullahs with filthy turbans... And even the ruins, the rubble. Even the fires and the ambulances that passed in a racket of sirens... Between the port and Sierra Mike he'd snapped so many photos that he had almost run out of film, and in the first three days he had recorded so many interviews that he had almost run out of tapes. Questions about Gemayel, about Jumblatt, the Druzes, the Maronites, the Sunnis, the Shiites, the Amal, the Sons of God, the slaughter of the French and the Americans which had taken place two weeks before... He was especially interested in the two kamikazes. So he tried to build up an imaginary identikit of their personalities and enriched it with any kind of conjecture. Their age, their education, where they had spent their final evening, whether they had doped themselves before getting in the trucks... He was happy. What more can I hope for, he thought. I'm witnessing things I could never imagine, I'm gathering precious material, and in addition I'm paid a salary of two thousand dollars a month: cash that will permit me to offer Rosaria some chic restaurants and fancy nightclubs when I return. After a week, however, his eyes had opened. Because he'd realized that as a soldier he would never prepare his thesis on Lebanon and the Middle East's international problems. When you're on duty behind the wall of Camp Three or inside an M113 or above a guard tower, all you think of is protecting your skin. Nothing more. And when you finish your twelve-hour shift, all you want is to stretch out on a cot or suck on a joint. At the most, you can brood over the truths you've discovered.

What truths? Well, that Beirut is a Palermo multiplied a thousand times, a shitheap which makes Palermo look like Zurich or Lausanne. Forget the heroic Palestinian resistance, forget the heroic Shiite renaissance, forget the struggle to win independence or a homeland! Whichever group they belonged to, whichever faction or religion, they fought only for the interests of their own 'ndrangheta.* They murdered each other just like in Palermo where the Caruso family hates the Badalamenti family because the Badalamenti family controls the construction business, the Badalamenti family hates the Caruso family because the Caruso family controls the fish market, thus if you're born a Caruso you spend your days waiting for a Badalamenti to come and blow you away, if you're born a Badalamenti you pass your nights waiting for a Caruso to come and knock you off. No, this wasn't a war. It was a feud between mafiosi who rubbed each other out with mortars or cannons instead of shotgun pellets, and who did it for the same reasons as the Carusos and the Badalamenti. I-want-the-construction-business, I-want-the-fish-market, and-since-you-murdered-my-father-I'll-murder-your-son. Or your wife, your nephew, grandfather. They learned it as children, when they were six years old and instead of grammars they were given rifles or Rpg. In fact at ten they were already bullies. Like bullies they spoke, they walked, they shot, they provoked, they died... The only thing which distinguished them from their Sicilian comrades

* Criminal organization on the model of the Sicilian mafia, based in Calabria.

was their contempt for life. Because the Carusos and the Badalamenti of Palermo did respect life, after all, did weep over their dead. They brought them flowers, they gave them top-quality funerals, they buried them in a cemetery. The Carusos and Badalamenti of Beirut, instead, howled a few ululations and bye-bye: down into a communal grave, with garbage and goat shit. Yes. They liked to die. They liked it as much as they liked to kill. When you stumbled across a corpse, you could swear that eight out of ten times it was somebody who'd been as happy to die as he'd been to kill. But then the here present Matteo might as well have stayed in Palermo. And, rather than on Lebanon and the Middle East's international problems, he might as well have prepared his thesis on the home mafia. That is, without bothering the colonel friend of the mafioso who knows the other mafioso who knows the cousin of the aunt of the sister-in-law etcetera. And without giving up the comfortable existence of a little parasite, without learning to smoke hashish.

Yes, hashish. Before coming to Beirut, he didn't know hashish. If he was offered a marijuana cigarette, he got offended: beat-it-I-don't-touch-that-stuff. The only time he'd tried it, he'd felt lousy! Dizzy spells, stomachache, vomiting. In Beirut, instead, he lived on hashish. He bought it from the Syrian in the grocery next to the Twenty-One. Eighty dollars a brick, plus a free rolling paper which reproduced a five-dollar bill. On one side, Abraham Lincoln with his close-cropped beard; on the other, the Lincoln Memorial with the motto "In God We Trust." In fact, some called them dollars. Big dollar if the joint was long and fat, little dollar if it was short and thin. "Do you have a little dollar?" "Lend me a dollar." Cunning, that Syrian. The Palestinian who ran the gas station next to the Twenty-Two didn't give the free paper with Lincoln and the Lincoln Memorial. Nor did the Shiite who had the drugstore on avenue Nasser, just in front of the Twenty-Five. Yes, they too sold hashish. Everybody, here, sold hashish. The children, the old, the women, the guerrillas. The landowners produced so much of it! The Bekaa Valley was an immense hashish field. Pale hashish, red hashish, black hashish. According to the experts, better than the stuff you buy in Afghanistan or in Morocco or in Nepal. More fragrant, more tasty. He'd learned these things very soon. Because very soon he'd begun to smoke it. Out of need, not only out of curiosity. People think that a guy begins only out of curiosity. Nossir. He also begins out of need. Because he's afraid of going out on patrol, for example. Or because he can't stand a shelling. Or because he has understood that Beirut is a Palermo multiplied a thousand times, that wherever he goes to get away from Palermo he finds Palermo again, thus he cannot escape his destiny... At twenty-one it's hard to realize that you cannot escape your destiny. And to console yourself, you say: let's go to the Syrian, let's try some hashish. You go, you try it, and this time you don't feel any dizzy spell. Any stomachache. Any vomiting. In their place, an inebriation that alcohol doesn't give, a bliss that not even sleep grants. So you try a second time, a third, a fourth, and at a certain moment you're fucked. You can no longer live without it. You cannot, no. And you don't care about the officers who shout if-you-smoke-hashish-I'll-kick-your-ass, I'll-put-you-under-arrest, I'll-send-you-to-prison. Even less do you care about the field hospital doctors who every night come to collect your urine and analyze it. Worse: you fool them. Know how? By giving them the urine of somebody who doesn't smoke. Fabio's urine, for instance. Of course you must have one of the field hospital vials they use to analyze it. But getting one is easy, and keeping it filled with Fabio's urine even easier. So, when the doctor comes, you turn against the wall, pretend to urinate, then you draw the other vial out of your pocket, and: "Here it is, sir." Many did it, many. And just as many sold their urine. For a very high price, by the way. At the Twenty-Seven there was a marò from Genoa who asked fifty dollars a vial. The lousy shark, the usurer.

He took another greedy hit from the joint. Well, apart from Palermo and the fear of dying, these days he had an excellent reason for smoking hashish: the sentimental mess he'd gotten into with Dalilah, the daughter of the Sunni official who had rented the two buildings and lived inside the fence of Sierra Mike. A real mess. At his departure, in fact, Rosaria had said: "Matteo, I don't ask you to be faithful to me because I'm a beautiful girl and can marry whomever I want. That is, because I've turned down a wealthy duke and a famous soccer player. I ask it because loyalty is loyalty, consistency is consistency." Sacred words to which he had replied: "Rosaria, don't even say it. You're my Queen of Sheba." Moreover, and despite the resentment he felt for the part Rosaria had played in the materialization of the insane idea, he continued to be madly in love with her. She's unique, irreplaceable, he thought, where else could I find such a Queen of Sheba? Two weeks ago, however, he'd met Dalilah and... It had happened the day they'd placed him at the base entrance to check whoever entered, and she'd arrived with her parents in a Mercedes driven by a liveried chauffeur. Like a good neophyte he'd zealously rummaged through the trunk, the hood, the seats, and neither the Sunni official nor his wife had protested. We understand, marò, you-have-orders-to-obey. Dalilah, instead, had attacked him in a curious mishmash of English and French. "We're in our own home, jeune homme! Oubliez-vous, have you forgotten, that this property is ours?!?" A couple of hours later, however, she'd reappeared. "Pardonnez-moi, monsieur. Quelquefois, sometimes, I'm irrationnelle." Then she'd crouched down beside the gate and it had been no use saying signorina, you-cannot-stay-here, this-is-a-checkpoint. "Please, monsieur. Be gentil. I'm bored, and je veux chat a little." Charming. Yes, although she wasn't beautiful like Rosaria, she had a charm that Rosaria didn't have. The kind that comes from ease and arrogance, perhaps. The ease and arrogance of the very rich who look self-confident even when they apologize, uppish even when they are in an uncomfortable situation, and always manage to obtain what they want. "Let me look at you, jeune homme. You are a très beau garçon. Not tall, but athletic. I find quelque chose familière about you. The olive complexion, peut-être. Ou bien your round and black eyes. You look Lebanese. Dans quelle région d'Italie were you born? Avez-vous a sweetheart?" She had also told him about herself. Twenty-three, only daughter, engaged to a certain Jamaal now in France. And a student at the American University in Beirut. A student of what? "Political Science." "Political Science?!?" "Oui, and very close to getting my degree. I'm preparing a thesis on Lebanon and the Middle East's international problems." For Christsake! They'd become friends.

He sighed disconsolately. Friends? Some day somebody should really clear up the meaning of this word, should really explain where friendship ends and love begins, what betrayal consists of. Because if you have a woman and go to bed with another woman, they tell you that you're a betrayer; if you don't touch the other woman and keep her as a friend, they tell you that you're faithful. So it follows that in sentimental matters betrayal is a question of skin, of physical contact: not of thoughts and sentiments. But can't we betray also with thoughts, also with sentiments? And betrayal or not, is it possible to love two persons at the same time? He couldn't come up with an answer, yet he knew that since that first encounter he had been waiting for Dalilah with the same anxiety he used to wait for Rosaria. And, when they'd taken him off the base entrance to place him again at Camp Three, he'd almost burst into tears. "Dalilah, nothing must change! As soon as I finish my shift I'll come tap on your window!" Her window was on the ground floor of the cottage, and there wasn't any need of tapping: each time Dalilah waited for him on the balcony and: "Je viens, Matteo, I'm coming!" Then they hid in some corner to smoke and chat about whatever subject came up. The places they dreamed of going and where they had often been in their imaginations, for example. The pubs of London, the bistros of Paris, the churches of Rome, the museums of Florence, the canals of Venice, the skyscrapers of New York, the steppes of Russia, the world in color, as seen in the tourist brochures. Other times they spoke of the doubts and uncertainties that bother the young, of the irritation at not being understood or taken seriously by their elders. What-are-you-yakking-about, you-chatterbox, what-do-you-know-at-your-age. In other words, it was not the thesis on Lebanon and the Middle East's international problems that created their mutual understanding: it was also the similarities of their problems, tastes, dreams. Something that had always been lacking in his relationship with Rosaria. For Christsake! If you wanted to bang, Rosaria wanted to go dancing. If you wanted to go dancing, she wanted to bang. If you said I-like-to-travel, she said I-abhor-it. What's more, she adored Palermo. "It's my city!" Well, Dalilah couldn't care less that Beirut was her city. She always complained: "Tout est laid, everything's ugly here. Je deteste Beirut!" Yet there was a subject they never spoke about: Rosaria-Jamaal. They circled around it, they alluded to it and at the point of pronouncing the name Rosaria or Jamaal they drew back. "Have you written to...?" "Yes, a postcard." "Did you hear from...?" "Yes, a few days ago." Because, though they never exchanged a kiss or a caress, they were fully aware that their friendship wasn't a friendship but a love story. To believe it, one should have seen the vehemence with which they'd run toward each other after the shelling of the munitions dump. "Dalilah! Are you safe, Dalilah?" "Matteo! Es-tu blessé, wounded, Matteo?" Let's be honest: in Rosaria's place, Dalilah wouldn't have said to him go-Matteo-go. She wouldn't have looked for the recommendation of the colonel friend of the mafioso etcetera. And, in Jamaal's place, he would have already married Dalilah. Then why, as soon as he thought of his Queen of Sheba, did his cock rise up to the stars?

"Move it, marò, move it!"

Six in the morning. Time to change shifts. Matteo shot an inquisitive look at Fabio, and wondered whether Jasmine would return with the important news. How good if she really did and the news was connected to the shelling of the munitions dump! What a lesson for the officers who always said don't-worry, nobody-will-touch-the-Italians, nobody-has-it-in-for-us! Nobody? Did they believe that today's soldiers resembled their great-grandfathers, those fools who in the First World War died without opening their mouth or opening it only to say long-live-Italy? Nossirs. Even though some fools still exist, some simpletons ready to get slaughtered shouting long-live-Italy or long-live-France or long-live-England or long-live-America, today's soldiers don't resemble their great-grandfathers. They're children of progress and opulence, for Christsake! They go to college, they read books and newspapers, they have a mind of their own. And, even when they fuck themselves on hashish, they don't listen to fibs.

* * *

He was a little presumptuous, Matteo, and less wise than it seemed when he compared Beirut to a 'ndrangheta of mafiosi who murder each other with mortars or cannons instead of shotgun pellets. He didn't even understand (one day he would) that progress changes men very little, that opulence weakens them, that in the end his great-grandfathers were more intelligent than he. That is, than those who think they have a mind of their own because they go to college or read books and newspapers. But he wasn't wrong in hoping to uncover what he soon would uncover thanks to Jasmine. Her news was really important. It was the ultimate demonstration that chaos mounted, mounted, and while mounting advanced like a viper that crawls inside the dark.

4

A tough night on the Street Without a Name. Out of God knows what caprice, Jumblatt's Druzes had decided to shell the Sixth Brigade barracks and the whole area was paying the consequences. In the space of a few minutes, two 130mm grenades had missed the Twenty-Three by a hair and a third had passed over the Twenty-Eight to explode next to the Kuwaiti embassy. There were also shots of 106mm coming from the Green Line, Kalashnikov bullets coming from Gobeyre, and behind the low wall of Camp Three Matteo seemed a little bird that protects itself from the hail by closing its eyes. Fabio stood on his feet, instead, and didn't stop looking at the shack he'd burst into the day before with his gun pointed at Ahmed.

"Let's hope they don't send us inside the M113," he suddenly grumbled.

"Let's hope? Why?!?" Matteo protested, crouching.

"Because if she comes while we're in the M113 she won't find us."

"If she doesn't, she'll be back! Don't you think of my skin and your skin? Don't you worry about us?!?"

Sure he did. But he also thought of the tall woman in the black abaja who despite her aching arm and her disfigured face had crossed the street to tell him he was a brave man, a man to call Mister Coraggio, and wanted to see her again. Not to have the important news Matteo cared about, but to make sure that the pig hadn't beaten her up again. She had unfrozen his heart, that cudgeled creature. She had taught him a sentiment he had never believed in: compassion. He cast a look at his watch. Five after ten. Well, she might still come. Should she come now, there would be time to exchange a few words even if Hawk decided to send them inside the M113: the rigmarole preceding the order is so long! The sector leader must call the Operations Room, the Operations Room must call the commander, the commander must give his authorization...

"Take shelter in the M113, take she-e-elter!"

The order came. Matteo got up.

"Let's go, Fabio, quick!"

"But..."

"Run, for God's sake! They've opened the hatch!"

With a sigh of resignation Fabio put the rifle on his shoulder, started climbing the slope that led to the Twenty-Eight's M113, and was half-way there when the feeble voice rose from the sidewalk.

"Mister Coraggio!"

He stopped at once.

"Go ahead," he said to Matteo.

"Go-ahead?! Are you crazy?" Matteo yelled.

"Go ahead," he repeated. Then he descended the slope and reached Jasmine who smiled.

"I am back, Mister Coraggio."

She had dressed up, to come back. She'd chosen a sumptuous blue jalabiah with golden-silver embroidery, and taken her left arm out of the sling. But the eye that yesterday was half-closed now was totally closed, the other one had become black, the scratched and blood-stained cheekbones had turned green, and the swollen lips were more swollen.

"Did he beat you again?!?"

She shook her head.

"No, Mister Coraggio. I am much better tonight."

"Where is he?"

"Sleeping. Very, very drunk."

"Then go home, Jasmine. It's too dangerous here."

She shook it again.

"I don't want to go home, Mister Coraggio. I want to stay with you, I want to thank you."

A mortar shell passed overhead to fall nearby, a stray bullet whistled. From the top of the slope a chorus of protests rained down.

"Fabio-o-o! What in the hell are you doing there?!?"

"Come up, you idiot!"

"Run, imbecile! They're closing the hatch!"

He looked at her in confusion, without understanding what she meant.

"I must go, Jasmine."

With another smile she stretched out her good arm, took his left hand, and firmly tugged him toward the alley with the abandoned shelter.

"M113 no good, Mister Coraggio. Shelter much stronger. Follow me, Mister Coraggio."

The Druzes' artillery had been joined by the governmentals' rockets, on the rond-point of Shatila a house had been hit and was burning.

* * *

Many used the abandoned shelter as a latrine. He didn't. It stank too much of shit. Also, it was too dark. And he feared the dark more than the bombs or the crowds roaring death-to-the-Italians. As a child, when he entered a dark room, he felt as if a hundred mouths were panting over his neck to swallow him up or a hundred fingers were trying to grab him. And he cried. "Mommy, Mommy!" On the threshold, therefore, his cowardice resurrected. He was caught by an untamable fear, a terror that almost surpassed the terror of the moment when Rambo had thrown the coffee in the mullah's face. Maybe Ahmed has sent her to set a trap, to avenge yesterday's humiliation, he thought. Maybe he is not in his bed but here, and waits to slit my throat or kidnap me for the Sons of God. I don't even have the flashlight, I forgot to take it. Should he attack me, who would defend me? Who would hear my appeals for help? The M113 is too far, the noise of the bombs stifles any other sound... No, I won't go on. I won't. I'll run away, I will. And forgetting his youth, his sturdiness, his weapon, he squirmed. She had to use all the strength of her healthy arm to grab him again, all the gentleness of her voice to repeat follow-me-Mister-Coraggio and to convince him to cross the threshold. He crossed it trembling, hoping that she really dragged him to return his courtesy, to lead him to a safer refuge, and followed her because of another fear.

The fear that she would notice his fear. So together they plunged into the darkness, they sank into the stink of shit, and what an absurd sight if somebody could have seen them! Suffocated by the smell that grew more and more unbearable, weighed down by the rifle and the helmet and the flak jacket, he advanced with the uncertainty of a blind man who suspiciously probes the air in search of obstacles. Heedless of that smell and free of any hindrance, instead, she proceeded with the assurance of a bat that doesn't need eyes to fly in the dark. The leisure of a mole that in the dark can discern every hole in its sewer. Before working at the Kuwaiti embassy she used to bring several clients there, so she knew the place better than a bat knows the night and a mole the subsoil. She knew, for example, that after the entrance there was a corridor, that this corridor was twelve paces long, that after the twelve paces came a stairway of twenty steps, that after the twentieth step you got to a tunnel thirty feet long, that at the end of the tunnel there was a cubicle where you could find a packet of candles with matches. Thus she easily got to the cubicle, never loosening her grip on his hand. She found the candles, she lit one, she placed it on a rock ledge, then she leaned her back against the wall and did what she thought a woman should do to thank a man who has been good to her. She spread her legs and hoisted the blue jalabiah.

"Take, Mister Coraggio. Take."

Beneath the blue jalabiah she had nothing but the beautiful body scored with bruises and scratches and old scars left by the most disgusting vileness that exists: the one of cowards who beat children, elderly people, defenseless women. At the same time confused and horrified, Fabio drew back a step. By Jesus... Then she hadn't been sent by Ahmed! She hadn't come to lead him to a safer refuge either... She had come to pay off her debt by giving herself like a glass of beer or a sandwich... Oh, no! How to respond, now? What to do? He had never been in a situation like this. He had never known a woman who gives herself like a glass of beer or a sandwich. He couldn't accept her invitation take-Mister-Coraggio, take. Not even when he strutted on the beaches of Brindisi could he have! He was a good-for-nothing, yes. He was a jellyfish who shat in his pants just at hearing the outcry death-to-the-Italians, a mediocrity whose greatest aspiration was to open a restaurant in Cleveland, Ohio. But he wasn't an animal who fucks a cudgeled woman in a fetid latrine. And the more he looked at that beautiful body scored with bruises and scratches and old scars, the less he desired it. At a certain point however his stare fell upon her swollen lips, her greenish cheekbones, her closed eye, in the uncertain light of the flickering candle it met the pupil of her black-encircled eye. And everything changed. Because, through the clouds of his ignorance and of his meager sagacity, he intuited what a more cultivated and intelligent man would have probably been unable to sense: against that wall there wasn't merely a woman who spread her legs and hoisted her blue jalabiah, a slave who tried to thank him in the only way she knew. There was the image itself of grief, of solitude, of misfortune. The symbol itself of a wretched and unhappy humanity who, the more it is wretched and unhappy, the more it needs to give and receive love. In other words he understood that the cudgeled woman was giving herself to receive what she had never had: a little love made with love. Taking her and giving himself to her in a fetid latrine was therefore a duty he couldn't shirk: an opportunity to ransom his miseries, to redeem himself, to forgive that cupful of coffee. And the compassion he'd felt while waiting for her at Camp Three changed into tenderness, the tenderness into desire, the desire into a feeling which wasn't love yet resembled love and could become love. He shed his rifle, took off his helmet and his flak jacket, unzipped his pants, and carefully avoiding the bruises and the scratches he took her. He gave himself to her. Sweetly. At length. While the faint voice thanked him...

"Thank you, Mister Coraggio. Thank you."

Then they went up again. Hugging each other like two survivors that a shipwreck has flung onto the same piece of flotsam, they sat on the threshold to tell each other who they were. He told her about Brindisi, about Mirella, about John, the mullah, the accusations coward-whore-chicken-pussy-shitbird-traitor-Judas. She told him of her life never grazed by a speck of joy or dignity. She said that she came from a peasant family of hashish growers, that as a little girl she'd been sold by her parents to Ahmed, that Ahmed had made her the queen of his brothel because rich Arabs have a weakness for blondes. They pay them double and they rent them by the week. A thousand dollars a week, meals included. She said that being a prostitute didn't trouble her, then, because she didn't know that people could make love like tonight and because her clients lived in luxury hotels or magnificent villas up in the Shouf. The food is good in the luxury hotels and in the magnificent villas. The beds are clean, and bathrooms have hot water plus terrycloth towels and free soap. Only the night a Saudi emir had rented her for a party and forced her to service thirty businessmen had she realized how ugly her trade was. Thirty, yes. One after the other. In fact, she'd gotten sick and the frightened Saudi emir had called the doctor who wanted to bring her to a hospital... She said that she'd continued this way until the Israeli siege, and that the siege had been such a relief to her. She had rested, during the siege. Afterwards, though, she'd returned to service the local Arabs. And Ahmed had started beating her. "Beirut's boors don't care if you are bruised or not," he laughed. He was so cruel, Ahmed. Cruel to everybody. On the second day of the Sabra and Shatila massacre he had refused to let in a Palestinian who was fleeing with his son, and when the two had hidden in a nearby ditch he'd called the phalangists. Here-they-are, here. She also said that at the Kuwaiti embassy she worked as switchboard operator, a job she had found through a merciful client: a businessman from Bahrain who liked the poems of a certain Omar Khayyam. And finally she said that working at the embassy permitted her to make extra money with polite gentlemen out of Ahmed's sight. Western diplomats, government officials. One of the latter had confided to her that the munitions dump at Sierra Mike had been blown up by an officer of the Eighth Brigade, and this was the news she wanted to give him since yesterday. Really important, right? "Right," Fabio answered. But, as deranged as he was by the story of the thirty businessmen who had used her one after the other, and taken by the feeling which wasn't love yet resembled love and could become love, he answered without realizing what a hot potato had been put in his hands. It was Matteo who explained it to him when the shelling was over and they went back to Camp Three.

"What did she tell you, what?"

"That the Eighth Brigade took out the munitions dump."

"The Eighth Brigade?!? The governmentals with the cross at their necks, the Christians?!?"

"Yeah."

"Do you realize what it means?!?"

"No."

"No?!? Wake up, Fabio. In Palermo these things are called warnings, the mafia does them to scold the guys who slip up. We must inform Sandokan right away, and check if it's true."

*   *   *

It was true. It really had been a warning in the mafia style: an admonition launched by an officer of the Eighth Brigade, Captain Gassàn, to shout at the Italians what Gemayel's nongoverning government didn't even dare whisper: "Enough of your bargaining with Zandra Sadr. Enough of your giving plasma to our enemies and being called their blood brothers. Enough of your keeping us outside the Palestinians' quarters and particularly Shatila. Soon we'll have to go in, and woe to you if you try to stop us." In other words, the contingent was now between two fires.

And this happened while the threads of our characters were beginning to intertwine, to gradually construct the weft of episodes which would lead to the event Gassàn was getting ready for.

CHAPTER FOUR

1

WHEN SOMETHING BIG HAPPENS, something that changes the status quo or even provokes a tragedy, we don't wonder which weft of marginal and apparently trivial episodes has eased or determined its realization. We don't take account of the individuals and the tiny things that form the fabric of that weft: we look at it from afar, the same way we look at a forest on fire. That is, without seeing the single trees and without caring for the branch or the leaf upon which the first spark fell. A tree has little importance, we say. A branch or a leaf, none at all. And in saying so we forget that it was precisely that leaf, that branch, that tree, which lit the fire and spread it to the other leaves and branches and trees of the forest. Even less do we wonder if the weft of marginal and apparently trivial episodes belongs to a chain of events that self-proliferate through the inexplicable mechanics of A producing B, B producing C, C producing D and so forth. Leaf by leaf, branch by branch, tree by tree. Whether we like it or not, whether we want it or not: this is the point. Blinded by the presumptuous schemes of a culture that in the name of rationalism boasts and claims to explain all, diverted by the sacrosanct need to consider ourselves the masters of our lives, we don't in fact realize that we are at the mercy of a logic both alien and incomprehensible to the human mind. In other words, we deny the mystery that the ancients called Fate or Destiny, we maintain that it doesn't exist. And with good reason. It's a hateful word, the word Destiny: the symbol itself of an impotence that offends the concept of responsibility and the freedom to decide according to our judgment. The right to determine our own existence. God's-will-be-done, amen. Yet Destiny exists, unfortunately. It resides in what we call Chance, fortuitous coincidence. And, to exploit us at its will, it uses the most unexpected means: an insignificant phrase, a banal encounter, an innocuous toy, a joy, a sorrow. Or a friendship, a love, a bomb. Nevertheless the chain of events that self-proliferate through the inexplicable mechanics of A producing B and B producing C was already in motion when Matteo realized the meaning of Jasmine's report. The worsening of the situation, instead, became evident two weeks later: when Crazy Horse trapped Angelo in his office to chat a little and relieve his tragic loneliness.

"Come in, sergeant, come in!"

"Nossir... I prefer not to bother you, sir."

"No bother at all, sergeant. Why shouldn't a lower-ranking individual chat with a colonel? The question comes from an officer who respects formality as much as hierarchy, believe me. An officer who in front of a uniform hanging on a coat hanger comes to attention and in front of a general taking a shower doesn't move an eyebrow. Not even if that general is Napoleon! By Jove, a young man also learns through a colloquial relationship with his superiors, doesn't he? Provided that he deserves such honor, of course. If I'm not in error, though, you do. I sense a certain class in you, an elegance that has nothing to do with your lofty stature or your slender physique, and rather comes from a Teutonic composure I don't notice in the others. How strange that in this nest of plebs you haven't been nicknamed the Prussian. Does such comparison bother you, sergeant?"

"Nossir, but..."

Angelo fidgeted. At the come-in-sergeant-come-in he'd heard a turmoil from the Operations Room, an overlapping of alarmed shouts, and now a voice that sounded like Sugar's voice was yelling the word ambulances.

"The ambulances, dammit, the ambulances!"

"We sent them! They left at nine on the dot, so it's already ten minutes!"

"Sent where, dammit?!?"

"To Camp Six, of course!"

"No! Not to Camp Six, nooo! There the alley is blocked by another car! Only from Camp Seven the stretchers can pass: got it?!?"

"Got it! We'll tell them!"

"Never mind, they're already here! They're already moving the car!"

"But nicknames are unpleasant and I should know, you were about to answer. I agree, sergeant, I agree. Crazy Horse, they call me... The fact is that I don't fret about it: sometimes I would really like to be a horse. As for the adjective crazy, well... I remind you that Don Quixote was crazy, and mutatis mutandis I resemble him. I too mourn a heroic past and would like to revive the deeds of my models. I too live in a world which is monstrously changed and to which I don't belong... Anyway, I answer with scorn: Honi soit qui mal y pense! A famous motto that as you know was uttered by His Majesty Edward the Third, King of England. In 1347, to be precise. At a tournament during which his mistress, the Countess of Salisbury, lost the strap of a stocking... Edward the Third picked up the strap, said honi-soit-qui-mal-y-pense, cursed-are-those-who-think-ill, and founded the Order of the Garter. A dark blue velvet garter edged with gold and to be worn beneath the left knee, although Her Majesty Queen Elizabeth the Second wears it above the elbow... By Jove, what a sense of humor that sovereign has! Dear sergeant, life requires a great sense of humor. Not only because life is sad, but because humor is a quality connected to courtesy, and courtesy is a virtue connected to discipline. Discipline in courtesy, I used to preach, and courtesy in discipline. Do you know the definition of discipline, sergeant?"

"Yessir, but..."

The turmoil in the Operations Room continued, less dramatic but still intense.

"Have they taken them out?"

"Yes, they're at the field hospital now!"

"And how did they move those two cars?"

"With the M113s!"

"And who had placed them there?"

"Nobody knows, as yet. Maybe two Palestinians who happened to pass by and were caught by panic..."

"And Sugar?"

"He's there to pick up the fragments. He should be back soon and report to the Condor!"

Some remarks came also from the Condor's corridor, and Charlie was running in that direction. Crazy Horse, however, didn't seem to care.

"But what, sergeant?"

"In the Operations Room they're shouting, sir. They speak of ambulances, of an alley between Camp Six and Camp Seven, of two cars that blocked the passage... Sir, I'd like to know what's going on..."

"Trifles, my friend, trifles. An accident. Answer my question, rather. Do you know that definition or not?"

"I know it, sir, but... Did you say accident?"

"Yes. A mortar shell, it seems. Don't change the subject. If you really know that definition, give it to me. That's an order!"

"Yessir... Military discipline is a norm which sets a soldier's daily life and defines the limits of his personal freedom. It is based on the principle of obedience and subordination, it consists of the precise and conscientious fulfillment of duties through an innermost conviction of their intrinsic necessity, it is indispensable for training and for forming the environment in which the soldier lives. Its goals are to transform a citizen into a soldier, to facilitate the exercise of authority, and to strengthen respect for superiors as well as the dignity of the individual expressing that respect."

"Flawless! Impeccable! Perfect! By Jove, despite my remarkable memory I didn't remember the last sentence! You've surpassed me, sergeant, and this evokes in my mind a comparison with Courelie: an extraordinary character who appears in a book relating the life of General Antoine-Charles-Louis Collinet, Count of Lasalle. Yes, Lasalle: Kellermann's aide-de-camp who, please correct me if I'm wrong, distinguished himself in the Prussian Campaign and on the 10th of June 1807 saved Murat in the battle of Heilsberg. As you well know, Lasalle had a friend: the valorous Pierre-Édouard Colbert, Count of Colbert-Chabanis. Courelie, a quick-witted and audacious noncom, was under Colbert's command. Now guess what feat of bravery Courelie committed during the cavalry charge which almost a year before Heilsberg, the 28th of October 1806, led to the fall of Prenzlau where Prince Hohenloe surrendered to Gioacchino Murat with ten thousand men and sixty-four cannons! Guess what act of boldness he..."

"Colonel, sir, forgive the interruption: who has been wounded by the mortar shell?"

"Whoever was wounded, was wounded: war is war. When it's your turn, it's your turn, my dear sergeant. Anyway Courelie was bold enough to overtake his colonel, Pierre-Édouard Colbert, Count of Colbert-Chabanis, who was leading the cavalry charge. Militarily speaking, a tactlessness that a lower-ranking officer never does nor can do. Never! In fact Colbert was so offended that after the victory he put Courelie under arrest. He did it with the following words: 'I applaud you, young man. Nonetheless I put you under arrest. So you learn not to exceed your colonel.' Now, since that punishment didn't prevent Courelie from becoming a general at thirty, here is what I have to say. Dear sergeant, far from feeling offended like Pierre-Édouard Colbert, Count of Colbert-Chabanis, who incidentally was made a peer of France in 1832, far from placing you under arrest because you've exceeded me astride the horse of your memory, I announce that you'll become a general at thirty. And I snap to attention, I express my sincere esteem."

"Angelo!"

"It was Sugar's voice. But it didn't come through the radio, this time, and Angelo flew out of the room. He rushed to the atrium where in a bloodstained uniform Sugar stared at him. He stared back.

"Lieutenant..."

"I come from Bourji el Barajni," Sugar said blowing his big nose filled with the tears that the eyes held back. "They got an incursori patrol, you know..."

He stiffened.

"No, I don't."

"Between Camp Six and Camp Seven... Five. All seriously wounded."

"A mortar shell?"

"No. It was not a mortar shell. It was an ambush. A dirty ambush. I just picked up the fragments of two Rdg8. Still warm. And the patrol leader... He's still alive, though..."

His brow wrinkled.

"Who was the patrol leader?"

But Sugar didn't answer.

"The patrol leader is in bad shape. Real bad. His face is ruined, his neck is dislocated, one of his femurs is fractured, his legs and arms are torn apart. And his hands... Practically mangled, Angelo. In fact at the field hospital they could do nothing and he has been taken to the Rizk... Well, he should make it... He's so strong... He has always been so strong... Truly a bull. But he'll never be again what he was Angelo... Never again will he ride his motorcycle... Never again will he write his poems..."

"Lieutenant!"

Sugar let the tears run from his eyes too.

"Yes, Angelo... The patrol leader was Gino."

So the weft of marginal and apparently trivial episodes enriched itself with the thread it needed.

* * *

Nothing but the warm fragments Sugar had picked up authorized the use of the word ambush. Gino's testimony was in fact missing because when the ambulances had arrived he was in a state of unconsciousness and still unconscious he'd reached the field hospital, then the Rizk. The testimony of the other four wounded, the same, because two couldn't speak and two couldn't remember. The testimony of those who lived in the alley, still worse because all of them were entrenched behind a wall of fear and silence. "I didn't see anything, I didn't hear anything." And the two cars removed by the M113s could not be considered as evidence because almost certainly their owners had fled out of panic. Thus, the word ambush was avoided for many hours, and the version provided by Crazy Horse continued to circulate. A-mortar-shell, an-accident. In the afternoon, however, one of the two who couldn't speak began to speak, one of the two who couldn't remember began to remember, and the use of the word ambush became legitimate. They had been patrolling the deserted alley and getting near the intersection with the road of Camp Six, both said, when a car had halted and plugged that end of the passage. Soon after the driver had fled, at the opposite end of the alley another car had halted plugging that passage too, and a short guy with a Kalashnikov on his shoulder had leaped out. As swiftly as a lizard he had clambered up a stairway that led to a roof terrace, and Gino had pointed his gun then approached the stairway. The two grenades had been thrown from the roof terrace at that moment. Straight, precise, on target. Especially the one for Gino. A dirty ambush, yes. Sugar was right. And the Condor called up Charlie.

"This time it wasn't the Eighth Brigade, Charlie. This time it was the Amal."

"No doubt, general. The trouble is that we cannot admit it. It would be like saying that the muezzins' appeal doesn't do any good, and that getting us is easy."

"Neither can we deny what everybody knows, Charlie..."

"No, but we can support the story that the five have been wounded by a mortar shell. And we can spread it with a press release. Let me do it, general."

"Okay, do it."

So Charlie wrote a press release saying that a Bourji el Barajni patrol had been wounded by a mortar shell, he entrusted Angelo with the task of distributing it, this led to a discussion which concluded with an inopportune wisecrack, and... (It seems like a negligible episode, doesn't it? Yet, if Charlie hadn't entrusted Angelo with the task of distributing the press release, if this hadn't led to a discussion, if the discussion hadn't concluded with the inopportune wisecrack, Angelo wouldn't have gone to see Gino. If he hadn't gone to see Gino, he wouldn't have received a certain poem as a gift. If he hadn't received a certain poem as a gift, that night he wouldn't have behaved the way he did with Ninette. If he hadn't behaved the way he did with Ninette, the chain of events would have followed a different course and...)

"Take this press release, make several copies, and go distribute them with Stefano. Begin with the journalists quartered in the Old City and if they ask questions, don't add a thing. Understand?"

"No, chief."

"Why not?"

"Because this is a lie."

"What lie?!"

"A lie. It wasn't a mortar shell. It was an ambush."

"What ambush?"

"An ambush with two Rdg8."

"Then listen to me, son. If I say a-mortar-shell, you must say a-mortar-shell. If I say a-vase-of-geraniums, you must say a-vase-of-geraniums. And don't bust my balls. I know Gino's your friend. But let's not overstate it. He isn't dead. He's just wounded. Only wounded."

2

Just wounded, only wounded, he thought as he slipped into the driver's seat. At war people don't get impressed when they hear the word wounded. They react as if getting wounded were a fortune or a case of bronchitis. They don't think that it can mean losing a hand or both hands, a foot or both feet, an eye or both eyes: no longer being able to see, to walk, to grip objects. That is, having a mutilated body, being an incomplete person who wishes to die. Once, on TV, he'd seen a Vietnam veteran: a Marine wounded by a booby trap at Da Nang. Just wounded, only wounded. And since the camera pictured him from the head to the stomach, he looked like a complete person: a man with a whole body. Sturdy shoulders, powerful chest, full biceps, and a handsome hearty face. At a certain point, however, the camera had pictured him from the stomach down and... He was not a complete person, a man with a whole body: he was a man cut in two. From the stomach down, nothing existed. In fact he stayed on a table like a knickknack. Or a bust-length statue nailed to a pedestal. Inside the pedestal, a mechanism through which he performed his biological functions. His artificial intestines. Well, he didn't seem to worry: he quietly explained how he kept in shape by doing gymnastics, lifting weights, playing ping-pong, following a fat-free diet... But then the interviewer had asked him: "When you think that despite all this you're alive, don't you consider yourself lucky?" And bursting into a chilly laugh he'd answered: "Do you believe I'm alive? Eighteen times I've attempted suicide. Eighteen times I died." Gino wasn't dead, no. Neither was he transformed into a knickknack, a bust-length statue nailed to a pedestal. But, aside from his ruined face, his dislocated neck, his fractured femur, his torn-apart legs and arms, he'd lost his hands. And we cannot live without hands. We can without intestines, it seems. Without feet, without legs, without eyes. Without hands, instead... We can't even lift a glass of water, without hands. Nor wash our face, nor unzip our pants to urinate, nor caress a woman, nor write a poem: we're more mutilated than a man cut in two. Sugar cried. The impassive Sugar who didn't hesitate to abuse you in the name of Regulations, the implacable Sugar who sent you to look for the stars in the woods, the inexorable Sugar who gave you six days of arrest because you found the mushrooms instead of the stars, cried. Charlie, on the contrary: "Let's not overstate it. He isn't dead, right? He's just wounded. Only wounded." And repeating just-wounded, only-wounded, Angelo got to avenue Nasser. He followed it to boulevard Saeb Salaam, turned into rue Bechurà, arrived at the Old City, but here he suddenly swerved into a street leading to the Sodeco crossing, and Stefano started.

"Hey, weren't we supposed to begin with the journalists quartered in the Old City?"

"Yes."

"But this street leads to the Eastern Zone!"

"Yes."

"Where are we going, then?"

"To the Rizk Hospital."

"Why?"

Because he wasn't Courelie, that's why. That dull Courelie who exceeded that fatuous Colbert, Count of Colbert-Chabanis, and became a general at thirty. Because he didn't want to become a general at thirty. Nor at forty or fifty. Because he was fed up with discipline, obedience, subordination and the-fulfillment-of-duties-through-an-innermost-conviction-of-their-intrinsic-necessity. Because he wanted to go see Gino. Because he wanted to make him understand that if it were possible to transplant a hand the way they transplant a kidney, he would give him one of his own... And thinking this he pressed down on the accelerator, impatient to reach the Rizk. He reached it in a few minutes. He skidded to a halt, jumped out of the jeep, said to Stefano wait-here, hurried inside.

"Où est-il, where is he?"

He was in a room on the ground floor, and all you could see from the threshold was a mummy wrapped in gauze: a white human outline with the head immobilized by a neck brace and the arms stretched along the body. At the place of the hands, two shallow pans. And beside the pillow, a young nun who murmured: "No, Gino, no! You can't now, you can't! Don't mind if the sneeze fades in the air: the Good Lord will send you another one! He does nothing but send you sneezes, the Good Lord!" He called her. She came and urged him back into the corridor.

"You're Angelo, right?"

"Yes, Sister Françoise…"

"He told me so much about you that I could recognize you in a crowd…"

"How bad is it, Sister Françoise?"

She lowered her mild face framed by the wimple and the veil, then raised it again to lift her large eyes drenched with sorrow.

"Bad, Angelo, bad. I assisted in the surgery and… Maybe they'll save one leg, maybe his neck will set back in place, maybe he'll get used to his ruined face, but his hands! At the most, they can try to patch up the stumps of the ring fingers and the pinkies. The forefingers and the thumbs aren't there anymore, one middle finger is cut off nearly down to the root and… The doctors hope to put him on the hospital ship that leaves next week, anyway."

"Is he talking?"

"Is he! In spite of the sedatives, I'm not able to shush him up. Now he wants to dictate a poem."

"Let me go in, Sister Françoise."

"Yes, but don't weary him. And don't say a word about his hands. He still doesn't know, and I want to be the one who tells him." Then she escorted him to the bed, she left him there, and the mummy flashed two feverish pupils. Where the mouth was supposed to be, a slot parted the gauze.

"You came. By Judas priest, you came…"

"Sure I came… How do you feel, Gino, how?"

"Like an idiot, that's how. Because right at that moment I thought: Look at the usual fool who parks crosswise and blocks the alley. I did not understand. Then I saw that bastard clambering up the stairway, I understood, but instead of shooting… What an idiot I am, what an idiot!"

"I would've done the same thing, Gino."

"No, you wouldn't. I know you: you would've fired. You wouldn't have forgotten what he said to you, and you would've fired."

"Whom are you talking about, Gino?"

"Passepartout… Whom else?"

"Who is Passepartout?"

"An Amal from Gobeyre, a little faggot with blond hair and a cigarette butt always stuck on his lips whom they call Passepartout because he goes everywhere. Don't you know him?"

"No."

"He's only fourteen, but he's more evil than the adults he sells himself to. Didn't I ever tell you about him?"

"No, you didn't..."

"He has it in for me. He doesn't like my face, he doesn't like my beard, he doesn't like my belly... He always chants at me maccarone, fatty... Days ago we argued about his Kalashnikov. I said to him dammit, Passepartout, stop parading that gun around, and he answered: Why maccarone, you no like my Kalashnikov, you afraid me kill you fatty? So I pointed my M12. But Sugar stopped me with his prattle about orders, regulations, diplomacy, and a little later the bastard showed up again with a mess of Rdg8 at his belt and: with these bombs me go where I want, with these bombs me kill you when I want, he said. I might be wrong, but the short guy who leaped out of the second car and scrambled up to the roof terrace was him. I'm ready to bet on it. That's why I ran after him. That's why I feel ready to bet that the Rdg8 came from him... Oh! How it hurts! By Judas priest, how it hurts!"

"Where, Gino, where?"

"Everywhere. My hands, my feet, my head... I'm one big ache from head to toe..."

"Because you talk and get upset, Gino. Don't talk..."

"But I want you to know, Judas priest! Besides, it helps me. It reminds me that I still have my vocal cords! Because the rest... I can't even turn my head to see what is there and what is not. I can't even move my feet. Take a look at my feet. Tell me if they're still there."

"They're still there, Gino."

"Both?"

"Both."

"Good... If the feet are still there, the legs are there too. Ergo, they didn't cut a leg. Well, they may cut it later. Sometimes they wait and cut it later."

"They won't cut it, Gino..."

"Let's hope. Otherwise, goodbye Tibet. Goodbye Himalayas, goodbye orange monks. Can you imagine a monk going up to the Himalayas with just one leg?"

"Don't wear yourself out, Gino. Sister Françoise ordered me not to let you wear yourself out."

"She did, huh? She really cares for me, you know. And I care for her. A lot. Because she understands me. She understood me even when I said never-mind-if-I-end-up-lame, better-a-leg-than-a-hand. The hands are more important, right? The most important thing of all. Because of the fingers. Judas priest, what a pain! Even my fingers hurt. Why? I'd like to look."

"Don't move, Gino."

"I don't. This neck brace doesn't let me. But I would like to, because... Do you know what distinguishes men from the monkeys? The fingers. Especially the thumb and the forefinger. For the way they're placed. Because with the thumb where it is and the forefinger where it is, a man can do things a monkey can't. He can hold a pen, and write poetry and... Oh, how it hurts!"

"Gino..."

"I always thought of that, always. I thought: by Judas priest, among so many monkeys there must be one monkey who has a poem bursting inside its mind! A poem about bananas, or about the forest, or about friendship and love... But having the thumb where it is and the forefinger where it is, the poor creature can't hold a pen in his hand and all those poems get lost."

"Be quiet, Gino..."

"No, I won't. I cannot be quiet. Because with these hands bundled up I feel like a monkey who can't even write a verse about bananas. There is a God's sneeze, inside my head, see? A poem that bursts. And I cannot write it. Sister Françoise doesn't want me to. She says don't-mind-if-it-fades-in-the-air, the-Good-Lord-does-nothing-but-send-you-sneezes, and... Can I dictate it to you?"

"Sure, Gino. Sure..."

"Do you have a pen?"

"Yes."

"A piece of paper?"

"Yes."

He took out a copy of the press-release-lie.

"I'll pause to tell you where to break the lines. Okay?"

"Okay."

"Ready?"

"Ready."

" 'Speak to me and let me speak... my friend... Explain to me and let me explain... why... bled by a thousand razors... hung by a thousand ropes... suspended above the abyss... of a darkness that blinds... of a silence that deafens... I can still dream my fable... without a future and

yet... full of hopes as if... I had a tomorrow.' Period... 'Because one day
you gave me a notebook.' Period... 'With the notebook your friendship, your love.' Period... 'Love and friendship are the same thing, my
friend... two aspects of the same need... of the same insatiable hunger...
of the same unquenchable thirst.' Period... 'And if you tell me that...
they're two different things... then I answer you that... in friendship
there is... more love than in love.' Now read it back."

Angelo cleared his throat and, restraining a sob, read it back.

> Speak to me and let me speak
> my friend
> Explain to me and let me explain
> why
> bled by a thousand razors
> hung by a thousand ropes
> suspended above the abyss
> of a darkness that blinds
> of a silence that deafens
> I can still dream my fable
> without a future and yet
> full of hopes as if
> I had a tomorrow.
> Because one day you gave me a notebook.
> With the notebook your friendship, your love.
> Love and friendship are the same thing, my friend,
> two aspects of the same need
> of the same insatiable hunger
> of the same unquenchable thirst.
> And if you tell me that
> they're two different things
> then I answer you that
> in friendship there is
> more love than in love.

"Did I get it, Gino?"

The mummy remained silent for a moment. Then the slot parting
the gauze where the mouth should have been opened.

"Yes... You know? It burst inside my head because of her. So I
wanted to write it for her, to give it to her. But now I want to give it to
you. Take it. It's yours."

"To me? I never gave you any notebook, Gino..."

"You did, you did... A hundred times you did. And today, too. With that sob. I understood what it meant. It meant: if hands could be transplanted like kidneys, I would give you one of mine..."

"Gino! What are you saying, Gino?!"

"I lost them. Didn't I?"

"No, Gino, no!"

"I lost them. That's why you held back that sob."

"No, Gino, no..."

"I'm maimed... I'm less than a monkey with a monkey's thumb and a monkey's forefinger. I'm maimed."

"Gino..."

"He took off my hands, that criminal. He killed me."

"Gino..."

"Go away, Angelo. Come back, but now go away..."

"Gino..."

"Yeah. That criminal... He cut them off, he killed me. That criminal. Criminal... criminal... criminal..."

3

He trembled, when he left. And not so much because of the clumsy way he'd reacted to the words I'm-maimed, I-lost-them, I'm-maimed, but because of the words he-killed-me. He-cut-them-off, he-killed-me. Trembling he returned to the jeep, asked Stefano to drive, then he reread the poem and his grief turned into rage. A cold, lucid, rational rage. An Amal from Gobeyre. A little faggot with blond hair and a cigarette butt always stuck on his lips, whom they called Passepartout because he went everywhere. A fourteen-year-old who was more evil than the adults he sold himself to. And if you scolded him, he came back with the Rdg8. With-these-bombs-me-go-where-I-want, with-these-bombs-me-kill-you-when-I-want. Well, the grenade with the 316492 corresponding to the headquarters' coordinates that sat on the table of the Arab Bureau, wasn't it an Rdg8? And hadn't Charlie found it at the Twenty-Five where a young blond Amal wanted to toss it at the bersagliere on duty under the fig tree? He remembered very little of that story. While Martino told him about the drama which had taken place in Shatila, he thought of Ninette, of the entropy nightmare, of his fear to love, his inability to love, so he couldn't care less about Charlie's exploit and Martino's narration. Yet the words the-young-blond-guy remained in his memory like the number 316492, and the more he mulled it over the more he came to the conclusion that the young-blond-guy had to be Passepartout. He had to find out, then. He had to question the bersagliere on duty under the fig tree, ask him if his attacker was blond and had a cigarette butt stuck on his lips... But, before that, he had to sneak into Sugar's Museum and examine the fragments picked up in the alley. If the serial number engraved on the safety tab was directly or nearly consecutive with the 316492 of the Rdg8 Charlie had picked up at the Twenty-Five, his suspicion would become a certainty. And since Beirut was a small place, since the Gobeyre-Shatila-Bourji el Barajni triangle was even smaller, thus people could be located with ease, since love and friendship are the same thing, two aspects of the same need...

"Do you want me to go?" asked Stefano, braking in front of the Eastern Zone hotel where many journalists lodged.

"Yes."

"Won't they insist on some details?"

"You have no details."

The-same-thing. Two-aspects-of-the-same-need. But if friendship was love, if as a friend he loved to the point of fantasizing the death of Passepartout, then he had been wrong in saying to himself that the nightmare of entropy and the anguished search for the formula of Life were generated by his fear of love and his inability to love. They were generated by something very different: the lack of friendship which had always impoverished his loves and which now depreciated his liaison with Ninette. Yes, he and Ninette were lovers by now. They had discovered a little hotel next to the Museum, a clean and nice spot with the windows that opened on the Pine Wood, and at least twice a week they spent the night there: with the complicity of Charlie who grunted go-Hamlet-go-to-your-Ophelia, the one-night adventure had become a bond to which he surrendered like a hashish addict surrenders to hashish. Each time, lakes of oblivion. Rivers of ecstasy. As the oblivion dissolved, however, as the ecstasy faded, the uneasiness he had felt after Junieh reemerged. With the uneasiness, a dissatisfaction that until this moment he hadn't been able to identify and now he identified. She wasn't a friend, Ninette. She wasn't a companion who senses you ready to give one of your hands. Who understands the truth at hearing your restrained sob. She was only an enchanting statue of flesh. Thus, she didn't sate the insatiable hunger, she didn't soothe the unquenchable thirst. She made him drunk and that's all, she gave him indigestion and that's all. Let-us-make-love, let-us-make-love. Love or epidermic contact, sex that exhausts itself in sex. You couldn't talk with her, you couldn't exchange an idea. "I don't speak French." Was it possible that in a city where every illiterate spoke French, she didn't even pronounce

a *oui* or a *bonjour, bonsoir, merci*?!? "I can't." "Why?" "I don't want
to." Stupid! Besides, that French speaking gap was an alibi. As soon as
he tried to use it to stitch together some conversation, she shushed
him. Let-us-make-love, let-us-make-love. Dammit! Even if the person
in your arms is an enchanting statue of flesh that bewitches you, even if
she's a factory of pleasure and drugs you, the moment always comes
when you want to talk. To talk and confess that you feel like a dwarf
tree, a bonsai with its leaves pruned and its roots compressed. To talk
and confide that you dream of leaving the army, of returning to mathematics, to the poster with Einstein's witty face and his divine equation
$E = mc^2$. To talk and explain that when you hear the howls of the stray
dogs and the crows of the crazed roosters your dismay grows, your
crisis multiplies. To talk and reveal what the double slaughter has been
for you... The marò who wept John-oh-John, the little girl who'd sunk
into the water-closet, the bersagliere who howled Christ-murderer...

"Mission accomplished!" Stefano warbled, coming back to the jeep.

"Good. Now let's take care of the ones in the Old City."

One night he'd tried. Mixing English with French and Italian, he'd
told her about the terrible Sunday and Boltzmann. He'd explained to
her that according to Boltzmann chaos is the ineluctable tendency of all
things, from the atom to the molecule, from the planets to the galaxies;
that it always wins and if you try to oppose it, to make order out of
disorder, you increase it because it absorbs the energy you employ in
the effort: it uses that energy to arrive more quickly at its final goal
which is the destruction or rather the complete self-destruction of the
Universe. He'd said to her that for this reason he saw in the equation
$S = K \ln W$ the formula of Death, that because of this he searched for
the formula of Life... And this time the enchanting statue of flesh had
listened, even replied. Something about her father and the French. Or
the French language. Then something about a great love and a great
man. Then something about a car and a clinic. Maybe the story of a car
accident in which her father, a great man she'd loved very much, had
died in a French clinic. And he'd been touched. For a while he'd felt as
if in his arms there was a companion, a friend. Instead, no. Because all
of a sudden she'd exploded into a wild laugh, laughing that wild laugh
she'd started again to touch him and kiss him like a famished cat, and:
"We think too much! Thinking is bad!" Was she crazy? No, she was
simply stupid. So stupid that he no longer cared to know who she was,
where she lived, why she concealed her real name, her address. And
many things began to annoy him. Her short tight dresses, for instance.
Her excessive kindnesses, her excessive attentions, her excessive appear-

ances at the headquarters, or her never removing the chain with the damn cross-shaped anchor. Never! She wore it at her neck the same way married people wear their wedding ring on the finger. "It is my omen." What did omen mean? He'd asked Martino and Martino had replied: "A presage, an auspice, a sign of good or bad luck... Omen is an untranslatable word. An unpleasant word." He was also irritated by the peculiar mood swings she now indulged in. Her abrupt and unexpected swerves from cheerfulness to melancholy. She who used to be so joyous, so festive... Might she have perceived his uneasiness, his dissatisfaction, his decision to get free of her? Yes, to get free. As soon as possible. One of these evenings. Friday evening, for example. A final date and: "Ninette, our relationship is nothing more than an epidermic contact, a sexual exercise, a gymnastic. Which means, a dialogue between deaf-mutes. I don't love you and I'll never love you. Never. I've realized it in understanding that love and friendship are the same thing, that between us friendship does not exist, that for you I wouldn't bother checking whether the young blond Amal had a cigarette butt stuck on his lips or whether the fragments of the two Rdg8 had a serial number consecutive with 316492. Charlie always says go-Hamlet-go-to-your-Ophelia. But these goings don't help, Ninette. Nor would they help if you spoke French or Italian, if I spoke more English or Arabic. Because we have nothing, we'll never have anything, to say to each other. So goodbye, Ninette."

"Who does it?" asked Stefano, braking in front of the Old City hotel where the other journalists were lodged.

"You do," he murmured. Then his eyes turned to a little tree that glittered in the foyer with the inscriptions Merry Christmas, Bon Noël, Aid Milad Mubarik, Buon Natale, and his murmuring became an exclamation. "Stefano! When is Christmas?"

"Sunday," Stefano answered.

"Sunday?!?"

"Yes, in less than a week. Don't you know that five hundred sailed this morning on Christmas leave?"

No, he didn't. Nor had he realized that in less than a week it would be Christmas. Hadn't he because Beirut's winter wasn't winter and because in the Western Zone Christmas was meaningless? Nonsense. He hadn't because this year nobody was paying attention to it. Last year everybody did. Each base overflowed with pennants, ribbons, colored bulbs, next to the field hospital the Engineers had erected an enormous fir sent by boat from Italy, and on the esplanade there was already the Logistics marquee for the Cheer Girls who would entertain

the troops with a rock concert. This year, not a thing. Nobody cared.
With whom would he spend this Christmas that nobody cared for?
Certainly not with Charlie and his Charlies eating a slice of panettone
and drinking a glass of champagne in the Arab Bureau. And even less
with her in the nice hotel with the windows that opened onto the Pine
Wood... Well, he would spend it with Gino. At his bedside... Meaning,
he should pronounce that goodbye as soon as possible. This very day,
tonight... No, not tonight. Tonight he had to examine the fragments in
Sugar's Museum, to search for their safety tabs, to question the bersagliere under the fig tree, he concluded hoping that Ninette wouldn't be
waiting for him in front of the carabinieri's sentry box.

*　*　*

But she was. Gorgeous as always, yet different. Her long straight hair
drawn back and gathered on her nape in a manner which stressed the
fiery barbarian queen features, her body austerely covered by a black
cloak that hid her legs to the ankles, her face as pale and taut as the face
of a person who is about to be sentenced, she waited leaning against
the rampart and her unusual appearance radiated an almost nunlike
asexuality. Her composure, a melancholy and at the same time haughty
determination. In fact he felt an unforseen, instinctive respect. With the
respect, a kind of transport he'd never sensed. With the transport, an
astonishment inflated with doubts. And his first thought was: maybe
she's not an enchanting statue of flesh and that's all, a factory of pleasure and that's all. Maybe she's a woman who deserves to be loved. His
second thought was: maybe it's not true that love and friendship are
the same thing. Maybe love is a sentiment totally opposed to friendship, an incoherency that can include and at times includes hostility or
even hate. The third thought was: maybe one can love without knowing it, without wanting to. Maybe I love her. But the last thought
annoyed him so much that he refused to consider it, and asking Stefano
to stop he stared at her rudely.

"Shubaddak, what do you want, Ninette?"

The immense violet eyes flashed a lightning bolt of pained surprise.
The body austerely covered by the black cloak seemed to shudder.

"I came to ask if we're staying together on Christmas night and if I
should reserve our room at the hotel, darling."

"She says she's come to ask if you're staying together on Christmas
night and if she should reserve your room at the hotel," translated

Stefano well recalling his interpreter's role on the day of the double slaughter.

He coolly shushed him with a brusque stay-out, I'll-handle-this-myself. Then he collected the little English he had been studying for her, shook his head.

"No, Ninette. You should not."

"No...?"

"No. On Christmas night I stay with a friend."

"A friend?!?"

"Yes. My friend Gino."

The immense violet eyes flashed again. This time, with a lightning bolt of arrogance mixed with indulgence.

"Is this friend so important to you?"

"Yes. Very important."

"More important than me, than us?"

"Yes. More important than you, than us."

The immense violet eyes dimmed mysteriously. The pale and taut face blushed, then relaxed into a smile of tender irony.

"I understand, darling. Friendship is sacred. Love is not. And when will we stay together?"

"Friday night. We must talk, Ninette. Understand? Talk!"

Beneath the black cloak her body had another shudder. From her pale and taut face, any trace of irony dissolved.

"I do, darling. I do. We'll talk Friday night. Same place, same time. Eight o'clock."

And without saying another word, without even sketching a slight handshake, she left. Head high, dignified, she glided away with her composure, her almost nunlike asexuality.

It was six on the dot and from the end of rue de l'Aérodrome an infernal uproar was coming. A chorus of angry voices and a rumble of trucks that grew louder and louder.

4

A demonstration? Impossible. Beirut wasn't a city of verbal protests, and demonstrations are not held with trucks. The Condor pricked up his ears, perplexed, and called Crazy Horse.

"Colonel, what's going on out there?"

"A parade, General, Sir. A parade!" Crazy Horse answered, full of excitement. "Extremely vulgar and odd individuals are passing in front of the headquarters. They are on trucks and they shout as though they had a grudge against us. Quod Deus avertat! God forbid, Sir!"

"What are they shouting?"

"I don't know, General, Sir. I can't understand them! But de nihilo nihil, nothing comes from nothing, Sir. Et mala tempora currunt, and these are evil times, Virgil says!"

"Don't bust my balls with your goddam Latin, colonel! Where are they coming from, God blasted, where are they heading?!?"

"They're coming from the south, General, Sir, and moving north. Toward Sabra. The head of the parade has already reached the rond-point of Shatila, and its rear touches the airport. As a consequence, Sir, they're skirting both Bourji el Barajni and Shatila. And unfortunately it's almost six o'clock: at both Bourji el Barajni and Shatila the guard shift will take place in a few minutes!"

"I know. Tell all the posts not to shift. Tell all vehicles to avoid that route. Tell all the checkpoints to ignore any possible provocation, to fire only if fired upon." Then he went outside to see, and started.

There were at least a thousand. Men, women, children. The women in chador, a rare thing in Beirut, the men with the green armband of the Amal or the black headband of the Sons of God. Many of them, armed with Kalashnikovs or Rpg. Those who weren't raised posters with Khomeini's image or photos of the two kamikazes dead in the double slaughter or black banners. A forest of black banners that in the sunset light fluttered in waves of pitch. And, beneath the waves of pitch, a river of faces twisted by hate, eyes broadened by rage, mouths spitting incomprehensible phrases that scanned God knows what insults and threats. The most alarming thing, however, was the trucks. Dozens and dozens of open trucks inside which the thousand squeezed like bats in their nests. Where had they found them? What did they want to prove? That they had provided the two used by the kamikazes? That they owned plenty of them, that they could provide many others for many other slaughters? They proceeded with sullen slowness, the torpid but inexorable crawling of a snake that slides toward its prey to gulp it down, and near the headquarters the snake reared its scales even more. The black banners multiplied their waves of pitch, the incomprehensible phrases grew in volume and intensity, and the mouths spat a very familiar word: "Talieni, talieni, talieni." To restrain them, to hamper the assault, only one squad of carabinieri sent to reinforce their comrades in the sentry box. Plus, a little group of officers with revolvers. Among the officers, Pistoia and Sugar. Next to Sugar, Charlie who nevertheless kept his arms folded. Next to Charlie, Martino who registered the incomprehensible phrases in a notebook.

"Get another squad and post it along the rampart!" shouted the Condor. Then, in a much lower but scolding voice: "I don't hear hymns to brotherhood, Charlie. Am I wrong?"

"You're not, general," Charlie answered through his teeth.

"One might say they have a grudge against us..."

"Against us also, general."

"Also?"

"Yes, because the Americans beat us four to two, and the French three to two. But we beat the English two to one, so we're third on the list."

"Stop with your riddles, Charlie. Tell me what they say."

Still through his teeth, Charlie called Martino over.

"Martino, translate what they say."

"Yessir. They say: death-to-the-Americans, death-to-the-French, death-to-the-Italians, death-to-the-English. However, they repeat death-to-the-Americans four times, death-to-the-French three times, death-to-the-Italians twice, and death-to-the-English only once," Martino answered with his usual zeal. And almost at the same moment a boy with the green armband of the Amal leaped out of a truck. Slipping between the carabinieri he reached the sentry box, stuck on it a photo of the two kamikazes, and launched a delighted shriek.

"Tawaffi! Death to you, tawaffi!"

"Tear it down!" the Condor roared. Then, without waiting for the order to be executed, he hurled himself at the sentry box. He ripped down the photo. But other boys had meanwhile left other trucks, with the boys many women in chador, and each of them had the same photo. Each of them was attaching it somewhere: to the chevaux-de-frise, to the coils of barbed wire, the checkpoint barrels, to any object that offered a hook, a clasp. And each of them shouted the same threat, tawaffi-death-to-you-tawaffi, intermixed with a well-known invocation in English: "Go home! Talieni, go home!" It was no use to chase them. For every boy and every woman you drove back, a new one arrived. For every photo you tore down, another appeared. And the shouts of the officers who led the resistance only served to increase the grotesque pantomime. Particularly the shouts of Pistoia, blind with fury at not being authorized to shoot.

"Return to your filthy brothel, ugly sow!

"Drop dead, buttfucker!

"Tawaffi to you, shitty Saracen!"

It went on this way until the parade entered Sabra and here vanished leaving a pool of torn paper, Khomeini eyes and turbans, kamikaze noses and beards. Spiteful leftovers that Charlie stared at, still wounded by the Condor's reproach and overflowing with sadness. To hell with them and their phony promises, their hypocrisies, their lies, their frauds, he bitterly said to himself. I'd forgotten what Lawrence of Arabia wrote of them. Untrustworthy, more unstable than water, close-minded, empty-hearted, producers of religion and nothing else. I'd forgotten because I let myself be moved by the children who die from blood loss, by the Bilals who read the half-books they find in the garbage, by the ox-people who plow other people's land for a thread of hay, and because I thought I could play chess with the Zandra Sadrs. Stupid, deluded, naive! The game of chess has ironclad rules: the pawns can't go backwards, the knights must jump in an L-shape, the bishops must move along the diagonal, the castles vertically or horizontally, the king can move forward or fall back, and the queen goes where she likes. With the Zandra Sadrs, instead, the queen goes nowhere, the king dances a minuet, the castles move along the diagonal, the bishops jump vertically or horizontally, the pawns retreat. And when you think you've detected the trick, they change it under your nose with a sneer: the game is overturned, and His Most Reverend Eminence checkmates you. I-don't-hear-hymns-to-brotherhood-Charlie. Me either, general, sir. His Most Reverend Eminence has checkmated me: I lost the match so conclusively that I no longer understand what's going on. Poor Charlie. He was too frustrated to make use of his shrewdness and analyze the situation, see the meaning of that parade. But all at once he did. And, as if stung by a wasp, he leaped away from the pool of torn paper. He ran to the Condor's office.

"General!"

"What?" grumbled the Condor, looking at the telephone with the expression of somebody who's just received bad news.

"The parade headed for Sabra. It vanished into Sabra..."

"I know."

"And though the threats were aimed at the others as well, though we were third on the list, the route was tailored for us. Bourji el Barajni, the headquarters, Shatila."

"I know."

"So it wasn't a casual or gratuitous provocation. It was a warning like the one that the governmentals gave us with the mortar shells at the Sierra Mike munitions dump."

"I know."

"But if we disturb both sides, if both sides consider us a burden, an obstacle, talieni-go-home, it means that something big is brewing."

"Exactly so, Charlie," the Condor said pointing to the telephone. "The French just called to inform me that they're demobilizing their remaining posts in Sabra and after tomorrow they'll simply keep a symbolic presence. The observatory. The Tower."

"Only the Tower?!?"

"Only the Tower. And I wonder how long it can last. Fifteen days? Not even. One thing is sure: the day the French pull out, the damn building becomes the pretext the governmentals and the Amal have been looking for to start a battle and..."

"And the damn building is a few yards away from Shatila, general. On the road leading to the square of the Twenty-Two. And the square of the Twenty-Two is almost right across from Gobeyre. To reach the Tower, the Amal of Gobeyre simply have to cross avenue Nasser and pass our post."

"Exactly so, Charlie... You may add the rest."

"The rest is that a third of the contingent has already left for Christmas vacation. More than five hundred thirty are on their way to Italy and won't be back until the New Year. So, if the French don't keep the Tower even for fifteen days, if they abandon it earlier, if the fire breaks out before the New Year, you cannot even reinforce the Twenty-Two and the other posts on avenue Nasser or on the Sabra border."

"Exactly so, Charlie. If anything happens before the New Year, we're fucked."

"Then what do you intend to do, general?"

"I intend to show that we won't accept any tawaffi-go-home-tawaffi from anybody. We won't move an inch. We'll hang on to our posts, we'll defend them. And as the best defense is offense, now I'm calling a briefing and putting the ships on alert."

* * *

The briefing took place the next morning with the participation of the seventeen officers who had to be instructed in case the fire would break out before the New Year: the members of the General Staff, the Condor's most trusted men, and the commodore of the ships. Quickly crossing the atrium where the portrait of the emir with the yellow turban and the blue cloak peered at them more ominously than ever, they entered the former dining room. Anxious to know the reason why they had been summoned in such a hurry, they immediately sat down at the cherry-wood table where the seating arrangement obeyed a precise ceremonial according to the duties and responsibilities of each. At one end of the table, the Condor. At the other, the commodore of the ships, who had arrived at dawn by helicopter. On the Condor's right, the Professor. On his left, Crazy Horse. After the Professor, Eagle. Then Falcon, the sector leader from Bourji el Barajni, the sector leader from Shatila, meaning Hawk, the director of the field hospital, the head of Ordnance, the head of the Transmissions Office who was therefore to the left of the commodore. After Crazy Horse, Old Grouse. Then the head of the Logistics, Charlie, Pistoia, Sugar, the head of Information, and Sandokan who was therefore to the right of the commodore.

The Condor didn't waste any time in preambles and was very concise.

"You saw yesterday's parade," he said. "Or you have been told about it. You heard what the demonstrators were shouting. Or you have been told about it. You know that within two weeks we've undergone two attacks: one at Sierra Mike and one at Bourji el Barajni. You know that the French are demobilizing their remaining posts in Sabra except for the observatory called the Tower. What you don't know, what none of us knows, is when they'll leave the Tower. And, obviously, the abandonment of the Tower will unleash both the governmentals and the Amal of Gobeyre. For too long the Amal have nursed the dream of bursting out of Gobeyre, reaching the littoral at Ramlet el Baida, from there descending south and heading north to take control of the whole Western Zone. For too long the governmentals have wanted to reestablish the control they lost over the Western Zone. So let's face the truth: until today, we've been able to contain both of them because the dike we erected from Bourji el Barajni to Shatila extended all the way to Sabra. That is, because the French garrisoned Sabra. But without the French, the dike splits in two: the Tower becomes the apple of discord, and the two adversaries go to war. Should this happen, we'd be the first ones to pay. So we must be ready for the worst. And as the best defense is offense, the ships must be put on alert. Which means, they must be ready to shoot at whoever intentionally shoots at us. I've called you to state the procedure you should follow in such a case." Then he stated it. A plan that Old Grouse had drawn up with the information provided by Charlie and contained in a bundle of maps and diagrams which indicated all the Beirut firing positions: the

Druze and the governmental artillery posts, the Amal batteries, the Khomeinist nests, the various barracks. Every firing position, a target to strike for defense or reprisal. Every target, a spot marked with its coordinates and a number beginning with 100. Each of the contingent's bases was instead marked with the letter corresponding to the initial of its name: E for Eagle, H for headquarters, L for Logistics, F for field hospital, R for Ruby, S for Sierra Mike. The ships were marked with the names of aquatic birds: Pelican, Gull, Albatross, Tern. So the term R110 meant that the Ruby base had been hit by battery number 110, Albatross 110 meant that the cruiser Albatross was about to direct its fire on the battery which had hit the Ruby base, S120 meant that Sierra Mike had been hit by battery number 120...

And meanwhile Angelo was interrogating the bersagliere on duty under the fig tree of the Twenty-Five. A task made easy by the fact that the bersagliere was the one with whom he'd tugged the little girl out of the water-closet, at the same time made difficult by the fact that he also was the one to whom he'd sworn I'll-never-kill-anybody. Yes, Ferruccio responded, the Amal with the Rdg8 was a fourteen-year-old guy with blond hair and a cigarette butt stuck on his lips: a little prostitute who lived in Gobeyre and came to Shatila to stir things up. No, he didn't know he was named Passepartout: somebody had told him that the lanky thug with the thick beard called him Khalid. But why was the sergeant so keen on identifying him? Because, Angelo wanted to shout, last night I went to Sugar's Museum, I examined the fragments Sugar gathered in the alley where Gino was mutilated, among them I found a safety tab. On that safety tab, the number 316495 almost consecutive with the 316492 of the grenade he wanted to toss at you. This means that the three Rdg8 came from the same manufacturer's batch, the same crate, the same person. And this person has to settle accounts with me. I need to know where he goes, where he hangs around, where I can find him and kill him. Instead he quietly answered that it was simple curiosity. "Just wondering, Ferruccio. Thanks." Then he rejoined Stefano who moaned.

"Ah, if only she'd arrive! She could still arrive, couldn't she?"

*   *   *

He meant Lady Godiva: the ideal companion for your solitary nights, perfect human measurements, 99-69-99 in centimeters, thermal-sound system, she laughs and cries etcetera, price eighty thousand liras payable by money order. Poor Stefano: the doll had never arrived. And although Gaspare and Ugo and Fifì were resigned to the idea of having lost the eight ten-thousand-lira bills they'd stuffed in the envelope, he continued to wait for her. That is, to cherish the mirages of her unknown delights.

CHAPTER FIVE

1

SHE ARRIVED on Thursday, two days before the French demobilized the observatory called the Tower. More incongruous than a bagpipe played by the Sons of God she dropped onto the stage of the tragicomedy like an extra who escapes anonymity to wreak confusion among the actors, and aside from Stefano she surprised even the boisterous gang that had purchased her. In fact Gaspare, the Condor's driver, scarcely remembered the enthusiasm with which he'd pointed out the advertisement in the porno magazine. He was a moony and nervous youngster, made doubly nervous by the tension of a job that would have knocked out an adult with iron nerves, and his real dream wasn't a lovemaking toy but a less despotic boss. Ugo, Pistoia's driver, had by now resigned himself to the loss of the eighty thousand liras. Besides, he didn't really need such a toy. As coarse and bouncy as a colt, he tried to follow his captain's example, and in the past month he had lived for the promise of an authentic doll: Sheila, the cute Palestinian whom the officers could have for free, who had surprisingly said to him: "The moment I can, with pleasure." As for Fifì, he had given the money out of boredom. To the namesake of the Coventry lady, we know, he preferred hashish. So, that Thursday, they expected anything but the shout that in the evening thundered through the Pink Room.

"Guys! A package for you!"

"For us?!?" Palpitating with hope, Stefano looked at Ugo who looked at Gaspare who looked at Fifì. And suddenly any resignation or oblivion dissolved in a magma of frenzy.

"Yeah, for us! He said *us*!"

"Are you sure?!?"

"Positive!"

They shot down the stairs, they rushed into the Post Office. And there was the package. Twenty by twenty-four inches, badly wrapped with string but redeemed by a return address they were quite familiar with. In silence they grabbed it, carried it to the Pink Room, opened it, and bewilderingly stared at what it contained: a bundle of flesh-colored plastic, folded like a shirt in its cellophane wrapper and attached to a luxuriant wig of tow-yellow curls.

"But is it truly her?"

"Sure it is her!"

"I don't believe it. She's too flat."

"She's flat because she'd uninflated, silly!"

"Let's get her out!"

The responsibility was taken by Ugo, breathless and already forgetful of Sheila. With shaking hands he gripped the wig, and the bundle opened up just like a folded shirt when lifted by the collar. Opening up, it revealed two long appendages which could have been legs, two others which could have been arms, and a sort of frying pan which could have been the face.

"It looks like pajamas with hair!" he commented in frustration.

"A sweatsuit," Gaspare corrected with perplexity.

"What did you expect?" Fifì snapped sententiously.

Stefano said nothing. He was too moved. He couldn't speak.

"Let's inflate her!"

"Yes, yes! Where's the hole to blow the air in?"

The hole to blow the air in was at the navel. Ugo pressed his mouth against it, exhaled, and immediately the sweatsuit began to take shape: to become a rough outline of a woman. In a crescendo of promises it sketched the thighs, the shoulders, two breasts as big as pumpkins, two disproportionate buttocks, then also the arms and the legs materialized. After the legs, a ball that could be a face and soon was. Coquettish, mincing, with a tiny nose and a large purple mouth which led to a deep and obscene orifice. The eyes were merely drawn. The fingers and the toes, also. But the lower section of the abdomen was rich in refinements and, marvel of marvels, it contained two more orifices as deep and obscene as the one in the mouth.

"Mamma mia!" stammered Stefano, finding his voice.

"What are you surprised at, blockhead? If she didn't have them, she wouldn't do what she's supposed to do!" Ugo guffawed joyously.

They set her on her feet. She was very light but could stand up by herself. They observed her for a while, then they pronounced their verdicts.

"I'm not sure," Gaspare said. "The proportions are right, and the same for the height and the heft... I mean, she has what she must have. But why didn't they give her any eyes, why didn't they even put a pair of buttons? Dolls always have eyes. And even eyelids that open and shut."

"Dolls also have fingers and ears. And she hasn't fingers or ears, either. But who cares? What do we need the ears or the fingers for?" Ugo retorted.

"In my opinion she's beautiful," Stefano said. "Well made and beautiful. I like her very much."

"Because you've never seen a goddam thing and you're content with nothing!" Fifì said. "I've seen those they sell in New York, and they have eyes, ears, fingers, adjustable limbs... You can't even compare them to this abortion. Yes, abortion." Then he shrugged and left slamming the door.

But they weren't influenced at all.

"Where's the thermal-sound system?"

"Here! The syringe, the whistle!"

"And the directions?"

The directions were with the syringe and the whistle. The first one was to obtain human warmth by injecting hot water into the double layer of plastic located inside the breasts and vagina. The second one, to obtain ecstatic groans and happy giggles each time the orifices were penetrated. All you had to do was screw it into her nape. So Gaspare went to the bathroom, injected the hot water, screwed in the whistle, and announced that Lady Godiva was ready for use.

"Who's going to try her out?"

"You!" Stefano said with a mixture of prudence and generosity.

"Sure. You can use my garçonnière," Ugo added in the same tone. Then he pointed to his cot which, being placed in a corner, could hold on the outer sides a kind of curtain that gave the same privacy as an old canopy bed.

"If you insist..."

Without enthusiasm, however seduced by the honor, Gaspare took Lady Godiva and laid her on Ugo's cot. Then he closed the curtain, unbuckled his pants, and set about consummating that ius primae noctis. But after a few seconds, an uproar of excited voices burst outside the Pink Room's door.

"They got her, they got her!"

"You lucky guys! You solved the problem!"

"Let us in! We want to see!"

"Open up! Open up!"

And Gaspare emerged from the cot, defeated.

"Too much racket. I cannot do it. Besides, she is so passive, so inert. Go on and try, Ugo."

"No, no. It's up to Stefano," Ugo answered cautiously.

"Me?!?" Stefano mumbled blushing down to his throat.

"Yeah. You."

With uncertain steps, Stefano approached Lady Godiva. He stretched out a hand, withdrew it fearfully, pressed it to his racing heart. Mamma mia! One thing is to look at her standing up in the room like a tailor's mannequin, and one thing is to see her stretched out on the cot like a real woman. A real woman, yes. She looked so real that she reminded him of Lorena: the daughter of the greengrocer whose store was next to his house. The same little nose, the same purple-colored mouth, the same big eyes... She'd always intimidated him, Lorena. In fact, and though he did nothing but go to that store to buy fruits and vegetables, he'd never told her I-like-you. Only once had he spoken to her: the day he'd seen her crossing the street at a red light. "Attenta, signorina, attenta! Be careful, Miss, be careful!" But she'd rebuffed him with a disdainful mind-your-own-business-you-snotnose, and since that day it had been useless to go buy fruit and vegetables which in any case his mother refused. "Why did you buy all these pears, all these beans?!? I don't need them!" Worse: one month later, that cruel creature had got engaged to the shoemaker's brother.

"Well, what are you waiting for?" Ugo yelled.

"Do you think she bites?" Gaspare added.

He drew a little closer. Again he stretched out one hand, again he withdrew it. She didn't bite, no, but all the fears he'd felt with Lorena were reemerging, and he didn't know where to begin. Even if the woman is a plastic woman and you don't risk disdainful rebuffs, how do you behave? Do you unbuckle your pants at once, like Gaspare, or do you indulge in some preambles like a kiss or a caress? He hadn't the slightest idea.

"Well, are you going to try her or not?"

"I don't know..."

"Booby! What is there to know? Get on top of her and close the damn curtain, numbskull!"

"It's just that..."

"Step aside, then. Let me try."

Peevishly, Ugo regained possession of his garçonnière. In the blink of an eye he took off his pants, closed the curtain, inserted himself in Lady Godiva, and the cot had just begun to creak when the door was flung open. A nasal voice resounded.

"Gentlemen! What's going on in here, gentlemen?!?"

It was Crazy Horse. Hearing the uproar and catching the phrase you-lucky-guys-you-solved-the-problem, he had pulled aside one of the noisemakers and: "Facta non verba! Facts not words. What problem are you talking about?" "The problem of fucking, sir," had been the rash reply. Fucking?!? Good heavens, what kind of language was that? What kind of explanation? Second rash reply: "Colonel, sir, the guys up in the Pink Room have received a surrogate." "A surrogate?! What surrogate?!" "We don't know, sir. They wouldn't let us in, they wouldn't let us see." Nothing more. But the partial explanation had been enough to fill Crazy Horse with morbid curiosity and worry. Ah! He knew them, he knew them, those rascals of the Pink Room! Always making a din, smoking hashish, soiling the walls with photos and drawings of naked or scantily dressed females... Granted, not everyone is capable of enduring abstinence by reading Ovid's *Ars Amatoria* and the novels of Donatien-Alphonse-François, Marquis de Sade. But a head of the General Staff has to keep his eyes open! He must guard the moral conduct of the troops, prevent them from falling into illicit and licentious practices, into iniquities that damage the army's honor! Moreover, he must not forget that young people are like second-rate horses. If they commit a grave misbehavior, they have to be punished with the crop; if they commit a little prank, they have to be scolded with a tap on the nose. In both cases, woe to the rider who eases the reins and lets them off. They lose respect, when they're let off. They unsaddle him at the first opportunity. And brooding over these things he'd reached the top floor, flung open the Pink Room's door, entered with the whinnying gentlemen-what's-going-on-in-here-gentlemen.

"Nothing, colonel, sir..." Gaspare stammered.

"What about that racket, then? What about that coming and going on the stairs?"

"We don't know, colonel, sir."

"Don't you, gentlemen? Not even about a surrogate that might be in your hands?"

Caught up in his effort to penetrate Lady Godiva's warm depths, Ugo hadn't recognized Crazy Horse's nasal voice. But now he did, and his vigor declined like an unsuccessful soufflé. Damn Fifì and his big mouth! Damn those meddlers who'd come to make that fuss! Imagine the fuss if the ballbreaker realized that the surrogate lay on his cot and that he was inside it! He had to stay still, for Christsake, to not even breathe. And let's hope that Gaspare would go on handling the situation.

"A surrogate? What surrogate, colonel, sir?"

"An unbecoming gadget, gentlemen. A licentious device, I'm told. Et vox populi vox Dei. People's voice, God's voice, an old proverb says."

"Nossir. We have no device here. Not even a pair of scissors or a hammer."

"Not even, gentlemen?"

"Nossir. Word of honor, sir."

"Word of honor?"

"Yessir. Word of honor."

"In that case, the maxim of Diocletian applies: Vanae voces populi non sunt audiendae. The populace's rumors are not to be heeded. And so does Cicero's: Nihil est tam volucre quam maledictum, nihil facilius emittitur, nihil citius excipitur, latius dissipatur. Nothing is quicker than slander, nothing is spoken more easily, nothing is welcomed more readily, nothing is spread more widely."

"Just like that, sir."

"Good. And what is there behind that curtain?"

"Ugo's garçonnière, colonel!" Stefano put in.

"His garçonnière, huh?"

"Yessir. And you can't open the curtain because Ugo is sleeping!"

Nothing else was necessary to understand that the licentious device was there. And, if Crazy Horse had opened the curtain, if he had impounded Lady Godiva, many things would have developed in a different way. But making such a gesture seemed to him so unworthy of a gentleman of his stamp that he stylishly withdrew.

"I understand, gentlemen, I understand. Well, go to sleep. But while sleeping don't forget Phaedrus's aphorism: Solent mendaces luere poenas malefici. Liars always pay for their evil acts. Goodnight and see you tomorrow."

Night was falling, Martino was about to become the key character in this event, and in the Condor's office a very worrisome dialogue was taking place.

*　*　*

"General, the French have already decided to abandon the Tower."

"Impossible, Charlie."

"Possible, instead. They will do it within the next forty-eight hours. I got the information from a Sunni woman who lives in Sabra and is having an affair with a paratrooper on duty at the observatory."

"Charlie I repeat it's impossible. I just spoke with the French. They would have told me."

"Why should they have, general? The Multinational Force doesn't have a joint command, relationships between the contingents don't really exist, and a procedure like the evacuation of the Tower is delicate. It has to take place on the sly. In my opinion, the hope of being informed is utopian."

"Let's not exaggerate. They did tell me they were demobilizing the other posts, didn't they?"

"They told you at the very last moment, general. And I wouldn't be surprised if this time they don't."

"I can't believe it, Charlie."

"I'd be even less surprised if they informed the governmentals, instead, and if Sunday morning we wake up to see the Lebanese flag on the top of the Tower."

"Hmm... And how does that Sunni woman know?"

"Simple. The paratrooper had promised to spend Christmas Day with her, and last night he canceled the promise with these words: On Christmas Day I won't be here. Because on Christmas Eve we shall quit the Tower."

"The classic lie to dump a woman. The classic gossip."

"Maybe. But in Beirut we learn things through gossip. Also the information we got from the prostitute who works at the Kuwaiti embassy sounded like gossip. Yet it wasn't. General, whether we believe it or not, we should take measures."

"And how, Charlie, how?!? I cannot stop the French from leaving the Tower! I cannot stop the governmentals from settling down in their place! It's their right!"

"Yes, but the Amal don't think so, general. If the governmentals settle down in the Tower, the damn building becomes the apple of discord you spoke about on Monday. And the fire you mentioned breaks out."

"So?"

"So we must guarantee the neutrality of the Tower. Once the French leave, we must take it ourselves."

"Charliiie! I can't trespass outside my territory! I can't fill in for the French!"

"In chaos like this you can do anything, general."

"There are international agreements!"

"In Beirut all agreements last as long as a sneeze."

"Charliiie! It takes thirty men to hold the Tower! And when you add the second shift, the thirty men become sixty! With a group of re-inforcements, they become ninety! A whole company! Are you forget-ting that I cannot even reinforce the Twenty-Two, the Twenty-Five, the Twenty-One, and the posts closest to Sabra? Are you forgetting that I don't even have one company for the Tower?!?"

"I'm not forgetting, general. But I don't see any other way to douse the fire."

"In war the fires aren't doused, Charlie."

"They are, general. If we intervene at the right moment, they are. And if we prevent them, they don't break out."

"We'll see when the moment comes, Charlie. That is, when the French tell me they're leaving the Tower! Because they'll tell me, you'll see. They'll tell me!"

And let's move on to Martino.

2

"Oh, no!"

Martino had moaned a horrified gurgle when on reentering the Pink Room he'd seen Ugo emerge from the garçonnière with an odd pajama attached to a wig of tow-yellow curls. And now, from his cot, he stared at Lady Godiva with a dismay as deep as the grudge he bore his already sleeping roommates. My God, with what trepidation had that childish Stefano set her upright and yelped look-how-beautiful-she-is! With what exultation had that beastly Ugo displayed her obscene orifices, check-out-this-one, check-out-that-one, she-even-has-one-in-her-mouth! With what ease had that hysteric Gaspare said take-it, take-it, give-her-a-try! Then Fifì had showed up. Ugo and Gaspare had chal-lenged him to triumph where both of them had failed, and Fifì had answered if-I-feel-like-it. Thank goodness he didn't feel like it. Well, no. He did. Look, he was getting up. He grabbed her, he carried her into the bathroom, he placed her on the floor, closed the door, turned on the hot water tap to fill the layer inside the breasts and the vagina... My God, my God! How could they wish to make love with an inflated balloon?!? He didn't understand. Maybe because he'd never possessed a woman: it had always been the women who possessed him. Always. Beginning with Brunella, when he was in high school. With the excuse of studying Immanuel Kant she'd brought him home and, while he tried to explain the meaning of the Categorical Imperative: "Martino, I want you, Martino." Then she'd dragged him to the bed without even giving him the time to say: "Mind that..."

He let out a long sigh. The same thing with Lucia. Besides, who would have suspected that Lucia wanted to jump on him? They wanted to change the world, Lucia and he. Together they discoursed upon capitalism, communism, imperialism, together they attended the anti-American meetings and shouted Americans-go-home, together they attended the university and tried to make contact with the Red Brigaders... Yet one day he had found himself on the floor and: Martino-I-want-you-Martino. Again, without giving him the time to say mind-that. Adilé, the Turkish girl he'd met in Istanbul the year he was there on a scholarship, hadn't jumped on him: no. She'd given him all the time to say mind-that. Only after the mind-that, they'd started living together in the old house near the New Mosque: a marvelous place facing the Bosphorus, an attic where you never got tired of watching the blue sea, the star-studded sky, the ships anchored in the port, the yachts with their garlands of twinkling lamps, and overall her... Her black waist-length hair, her green eyes, her white squirrel's teeth. She was so pretty, Adilé... And so intelligent. She worked at the National Library as a restorer of ancient manuscripts and knew how to discern beauty: how to teach it, how to communicate it along with good taste... When she worked on a particularly precious parchment, she brought it home and: "Martino, I wanted to show it to you. Observe the delicacy of this engraving, the harmony of these colors, the glow of this gold..." Or a manuscript, an ancient embroidery, a book of poetry she read cradling him in her arms like a teddy bear. He loved her so! He loved her so much that each time he went to Italy for a holiday or an exam he couldn't wait to get back to Istanbul, as soon as he arrived he ran to kiss her through the windows at airport customs, and people smiled: "How sweet!" She loved him too. But one day she'd gotten pregnant and: "Martino, we've played enough. I don't want you anymore." Meaning, she'd thrown away him and the child.

He cocked his ear toward the bathroom where an unexpected silence had fallen, he wondered if Fifì had finished the procedure with the hot water, prepared himself to hear the ecstatic giggles and the victorious shout I-made-it, I-made-it, which would soon arise. Well, Giovanna had made it with him. Because after Adilé he had sworn that no woman would ever possess him again, but when he had told Giovanna she'd laughed: "I will." Then she'd pushed him toward her bed, and at the first mind-that: "I know, Martino, I know." She was tough, Giovanna, masculine. Each time you slept with her, you felt as if you were being raped. "Kiss me and shut up. Hug me and shut up." She wasn't bad, though, and she often indulged in attitudes of real feminine sweetness.

She ironed his shirts, bought him flowers, and never scolded him for his waddling in the streets. But she kept him as a toy, a gewgaw to betray with everybody and one day: "Cut it out, Martino! Do I steal them from you?" My God. He would rather have died. And in a way she had left him dead. Dead to women, to the hope of being able to love them, to overcome with them and through them a homosexuality always repressed but never extinguished. That's why he'd moaned that horrified gurgle when Ugo had emerged from the garçonnière with the odd pajama attached to the wig of tow-yellow curls. That's why he suffered so much at the idea of hearing the ecstatic giggles and the victorious shout I-made-it, I-made-it. The damn whistle. Not to mention that his homosexuality had burst precisely in a bathroom, and...

He licked a tear which was running down to his lips. He had been sent to the country with his grandparents and his cousin Beppe, that summer, and it was a sultry August afternoon. One of those afternoons that dissolve you into sweat while the cicadas chirp. Grandfather and Grandmother were sleeping, he and Beppe stayed on the veranda to look for a hint of breeze, but the breeze didn't come and Beppe had said let's-take-a-shower-Martino. So they had gone into the bathroom, taken a shower, and... He was a handsome boy, Beppe. He had a smooth sun-gilded body, round buttocks, mischievous eyes, and he looked at him the same way women do. Not even realizing what he was doing, he'd caressed one of his cheeks. After the cheek, a shoulder. After the shoulder, the belly. Nothing more, but during the night he'd slipped into his bed to caress the rest. The next night, too. For many nights. How could he know he was sinning? He was only thirteen and nobody had ever told him that the fleshy cylinder he urinated with could be used for that too. According to what the priest said, sin meant skipping church on Sunday or eating before Holy Communion. Then Grandmother had noticed that Beppe's bed remained intact, and asked: "You aren't sleeping together, you two, are you?!?" She had asked it with such indignation that they had answered no, and realized they were committing a sin much graver than skipping church on Sunday or eating before Holy Communion. Yet, and in spite of their fear, a very tantalizing fear, they'd continued to do that thing. Yes, they called it "that thing." And "that thing" had gone on for three years: till the day Brunella had ravished him with Immanuel Kant then delivered him to Lucia, to Adilé, to Giovanna. He'd returned to making love with men after Giovanna, the spring he'd won a scholarship to Cairo and met Albert: a young Frenchman who lived out a drama like his. Just roommates, at first. Friends who consoled one another for their misfortune.

Because both he and Albert were tremendously ashamed of being faggots. They felt as if they had an illness, being faggots, an infection to be cured with an antibiotic called Woman, and took much care not to fall into each other's arms. The trouble is that an embassy queer, one of those elegant diplomats who use too much perfume and never miss a party, had started to cruise them. Quando-vieni-da-me are-you-coming-over-to-my-place, Martino, quand-viens-tu-chez-moi-Albert. To mock him they had started wearing Pierrot shirts, prancing around him in shocking-pink outfits, flirting with each other, and the game had ended in bed. That is, with exacerbating the truth. Along with the truth, their refusal to accept it: to consider it an illness, an impure peculiarity, a fault to correct or to forgive.

He smiled bitterly. Here is why he had left Albert. "Goodbye, darling. I love you, thus I leave you." Here is why he had joined the army. And, until the eve of his departure for Beirut, this decision had worked very fine. He didn't like anybody in the barracks. The uniforms, the brutalities, the filthy showers, the repulsive toilets snuffed out any kind of desire. But on the eve of his departure he'd met Beppe again, and... He'd met him by chance, no, by bad luck, while he walked down a street near the barracks: a heavy man getting out of a car with a fat broad and two ugly children. "Beppe!" he'd stammered, and for an instant he'd thought: now I faint. Beppe, all the contrary. What-a-surprise, Martino, let-me-introduce-you-to-my-wife-and-my-kids. As if the afternoon of the cicadas had never existed. Nor the following nights nor the following years... Had he changed! And not only for the overweight body. His eyes were no longer mischievous, his expression had become dull, and he spoke like the idiots who play the role of respectable citizens. "Yes, thank God. I have a family, now, I've settled down. Are you married too, Martino?" "No, Beppe." "What?! Still single?!? Wrong, Martino, wrong. Marriage is good for the body and the spirit, and children are a blessing: don't you know?" "Yes, Beppe." "Well, I better say goodbye now. I parked in a no-stopping zone and I don't want to get a ticket. Ciao, Martino." "Ciao, Beppe. And congratulations on your lovely children." A squalid, sad encounter. Nevertheless that squalid and sad encounter had lighted a fire of nostalgia. With that nostalgia he'd embarked, and here... He felt attracted by everybody, here. Everybody! Despite the guillotined bottles and the shouts and the arrogance, even by the Condor: so stalwart, so appealing, so unreachable. Despite his motherly attitude, even by Charlie: so solid, so strong, so unbreakable. And by Angelo: so handsome, so grave, so mysterious. By Bernard le Français: so wild, so skittish, so alluring. By Stefano: so fresh, so immature, so pure. And above all by Fifì, who resembled so much the young Beppe he'd caressed under the shower. Well... He always talked about women, Fifì. The gigantic poster with the two beautiful female legs had been brought and hung by him. Yet he emanated the same perverse appeal that Beppe emanated and there were moments when he had to clench his fists to overcome the temptation of touching him. Think of the scandal if somebody noticed! Something to get you pilloried, transformed into the laughingstock of the contingent, treated worse than a criminal. Martino leaked another tear and jolted. Next to his cot there was Fifì, bending over.

"Martino! Are you awake, Martino?"

"Yes... What is it?"

"Gaspare's right. She really is so inert, so passive. I don't succeed either. You try."

"Me...?"

"Yes, you! Who cares if you didn't pay? You can have my share."

"No, thanks, Fifì, no..."

"Go ahead, Martino."

"But I..."

"Go ahead, I said, go!"

There was no choice but to pretend to accept and, resigned, Martino got up. He went into the bathroom where Lady Godiva sprawled supine on the floor, her legs spread apart and her arms wide open as if to beg for mercy. She also looked less solid, he noticed, almost shrunken. Could the air valve be faulty? He picked her up, he seated her against the wall, and immediately the tow-yellow head lolled with such a human movement that he remained still to observe her. Strange: in the shade of the night and in that posture, she didn't look like a doll. Even less like an inflated balloon. She looked like a real woman. A woman who's breathing. Why? Maybe because the Amal were shelling the Green Line and the explosions sent out flashes of light that flickered over her with the rhythm of a breathing body. Or maybe because a tuft of the wig had slipped down on her face and beneath it her sketched-in eyes seemed somehow real eyes, the tiny protuberance of her nose a real nose, the obscene orifice of her mouth a real mouth. He shook his head. No, she looked like a real woman because he needed to believe she was real. And with tender movements he crossed her legs, placed her arms in her lap. Then he sat down beside her, and began to talk in an inaudible whisper.

"See, not even Fifì has figured it out. Go-ahead, he said. Nobody has figured it out. Nobody. And sometimes I could shout it till my vocal cords break: I'm a faggot! Today I wanted to confess it to Charlie. We were in the jeep, and out of the blue he grunted: 'Martino, if you have a problem, tell me.' I wanted to, yes. With all his walrus mustaches and his rough air, Charlie really is a mother... Yet I hadn't the courage and mumbled no-chief, no-problem-at-all, thanks. Then I pretended to look at a girl passing by. I'm always pretending. Always. Pretending, pretending, pretending... And not only because I'm afraid to be pilloried, transformed into the laughingstock of the contingent, treated worse than a criminal, but because I cannot stand the faggots. I hate them. Yes, hate. Everything about them disturbs me, repels me. The way they speak, the way they move and walk, the way they flaunt what I consider a disgrace, an impure peculiarity, an illness... Faggots are arrogant, see. They're petulant, presumptuous. They don't hide what I call a disgrace, an impure peculiarity. They're not ashamed of what I call an illness: on the contrary. They display it in parades, they impose it through laws, they administer it with their mafias, they enoble it with their phony ideologies, they publicize it on the movies and TV, they exploit it in the brothels... And if you say it, if you don't like them, they flutter. They cackle, they pose as victims, they call you a bigot. They even seize on Michelangelo's name. As if the David had been carved by them, as if the Sistine Chapel had been painted by them, or as if homosexuality were a guarantee of genius. Normality, a guarantee of mediocrity. They have the cult of the phallus, Albert used to say, they think and act and live in the name of the phallus... Oh, Godiva, you can't imagine how hard it is to be a faggot who detests faggots! But there is something worse than being a faggot who detests faggots, and you know what it is? Being a faggot in uniform. Know why? Because when it comes to the phallus, the military have a cult even more profound than faggots. It is their real banner, that fleshy cylinder that at thirteen I thought was good for urinating and nothing else. It is their real god, the God Phallus. And they allude to it at any pretext, they invoke it at any opportunity. In every army, every language. Cock here, cock there, dick here, dick there, cocksucker, cockteaser, dick peddler, dick teaser. Or balls, ballocks, bollocks... The balls seen as a treasure, as a symbol of virility and courage. Virility-equal-courage, says their enthymeme. As if courage were an exclusively masculine virtue. The uniform, the instrument of such virtue. A-man-has-to-serve-as-a-soldier, to-become-a-man-you-need-to-become-a-soldier, etcetera. Bullshit. They say man but they don't mean man: they mean male. They promise to make a man out of you, but they don't give a damn about making you a man: what they care for is to make you a male, to see you become a male. Well, I cannot become a male. They cannot make a male out of me. I am not even interested in becoming a male. Because I don't want to be a male, Godiva: I want to be a man. Being a faggot doesn't mean not being a man: it means not being a male. And though I'm not a male, I *am* a man. A man who understands beauty, goodness, courage. A man who hates ugliness, wickedness, cowardice. A man who knows how to think, how to feel, how to rejoice, how to suffer. Therefore a man more man than the males who haven't been able to make love with you. I can, if I want. All I need is to see in you the Beppe I loved the afternoon of the cicadas, or the Albert I loved at Cairo, or the Adilé I loved when in the attic facing the Bosphorus she showed me the miniatures from the Istanbul National Library. And know what? Let's give a lesson to the dick-worshipers, the cock-idolizers, the balls-glorifiers, the followers of God Phallus. Let's wake them up with your whistle." And full of ardor Martino turned to Lady Godiva. He took her in his arms.

"Darling!"

But he found nothing, poor Martino. Because, while he spoke, the loosely closed valve in the navel had continued to leak. And instead of the inflated balloon in which he had seen or wanted to see a woman, a real woman who breathes, now there was a tow-yellow wig attached to a plastic pajama.

* * *

"No luck you too, huh?" sniggered Fifì who for forty minutes had been anxiously waiting to comment upon the fourth failure.

"None," Martino lied politely.

"Ah! Tomorrow it's Stefano's turn: what fun for us..."

And, accompanied by these little cruelties of existence, Friday arrived. That difficult Friday which would contribute so much to the lighting of the fire now ready to break out.

3

It rained for hours. A dense downpour that soaked the red soil turning it into a purple lake of mud and spread on every road a carpet of slippery slime. Alone in the taxi which carried him to the hotel near the Museum, Angelo thought: and if love were a sentiment totally opposed to friendship? Maybe it is. Maybe love includes hostility, even hate, and

I love her. Without knowing it, without wanting it, I love her... It must be so because I felt things I had never felt for anybody when I saw her in that black cloak, and I made such an effort to answer when she asked me if Gino was more important than her, than us. And when she glided away with her composure, her dignity, I had to restrain myself from running after her: begging her pardon, saying to her that yes, we would spend Christmas together. Maybe I always loved her. Maybe until today I've told myself a bunch of lies. Maybe I've done it to defend myself from a love that scared me, that threatened to rob me of myself. I couldn't otherwise explain why I haven't been able to leave her, and why even tonight I'm not ready to pronounce that goodbye. That's the truth. The truth? Which truth? Truth is a hypothesis, an opinion composed of many truths. Truth doesn't exist even in mathematics where two plus two isn't necessarily equal to four, four plus four isn't necessarily equal to eight, and five plus five equals ten only if we use the decimal system: if we count on ten fingers. A Martian who merely has the stumps of six fingers like Gino, three on one hand and three on the other, can count no further than six. Seven doesn't exist for him. Or it exists only as a multiple of six. Eight, nine, ten, the same. And the multiples of ten. Thus, for that Martian, two plus two still equals four, three plus three still equals six, but four plus four doesn't equal eight: it equals something equivalent to our fourteen. Six is for him what ten is for us, after six he needs to use a multiple equivalent to our eleven, let's call it onesix, and... And what in the hell do I say?!? Am I raving? I'm raving. No, I'm trying to divert my mind from her: to avoid thinking that I do not feel ready to leave her, to pronounce that goodbye. I'm taking time, I'm asking for help from a six-fingered Martian: from a mathematical problem. I should tell it to Gino, tomorrow. It would amuse him.

"So I've become some kind of Martian with a tail, huh? A nice way to console a maimed man!"

"No, Gino, not with a tail: with six fingers that for him are ten. The same as ten."

"The same?!? What kind of stupidity is this? Did you come here to jerk me around?"

"I'm not jerking you around, and it's not a stupidity, Gino. It's a mathematical problem. To understand it, you have to remember that our numerical system is based on ten. But the ten does not correspond to an absolute. It is a hypothesis, an opinion. So if the Martian has six fingers instead of ten, the calculations don't change. All you need to do is go from six to eleven. That is, to the equivalent of our eleven. And so forth and so on."

"But if there's no ten, there's no eleven either, by Judas priest! And no twelve, no thirteen, etcetera!"

"There is not and there is. I'm saying eleven, twelve, thirteen for convenience, see? Maybe the Martian says onesix, twosix, threesix, etcetera."

"Hmm... I'm beginning to like it... Foursix for fourteen, fivesix for fifteen, sixsix for sixteen... Then, for the Martian six plus six is sixsix! Meaning sixteen. Right?"

"Bravo, Gino. You understood, you understand!"

"Sure I do. I also understand that if you buy twelve eggs from me, with the story of the nondecimal system I give you eighteen eggs and I get the price of twelve. In other words, along with four fingers I lose six eggs and..."

He shook his head. Nonsense: tomorrow he would not be with Gino. Tomorrow he would be with Ninette. He would just because indeed love and friendship are not the same thing, because love really is a sentiment totally opposed to friendship: an incoherency that can include and at times includes hostility or even hate. Now he felt sure of it. And though he didn't need that incoherency, though he didn't accept it, didn't respect it, by now he could not give it up. He could no longer do without the masochistic muddle of repulsion and attraction, tenderness and acrimony, liking and disliking, that gradually had taken possession of him. He could no longer live without that stupid gorgeous woman who opened her mouth only to gurgle let-us-make-love, let-us-make-love, that silly mysterious creature who hid her identity and exploded in a wild laugh while talking about serious things. We-think-too-much, thinking-is-bad. Whatever the verb to love meant, he loved her: yes. He loved her with a love which in spite of the desire it came from went beyond the desire, which despite the absence of friendship had much in common with his friendship for Gino, and in any case reminded him of the love the battalion chaplain described... Instead of pronouncing that goodbye, then, tonight he would surrender to her, he concluded. And when he reached the hotel he didn't even ask if she'd arrived. He grabbed the key the concierge held out, rushed over to the elevator, and burst into the room like a gust of wind.

"Ninette!"

Silence answered. She hadn't arrived. He did not get alarmed, though, and overcoming his disappointment he started to wait; pretty sure that within five minutes she would show up with her joyous trill, he lay on the bed. But after five minutes she didn't appear, after fifteen then thirty the same, and at that point his anxiety erupted. Could she have had an accident, could she have been wounded? No... There hadn't been any shooting today, there wasn't even the echo of a gunburst around. Could she not come, then? Impossible. Before gliding away she had said Friday-night, same-place, same-time, eight-o'-clock... He cast a glance at his watch. Eight-forty-five, now. Almost nine. He jumped off the bed, began to pace the room up and down, he stopped, he lay on the bed again, got up again, went to the window, leaned out to check if she was arriving. No, she wasn't. All you could see in the dark was an Eighth Brigade column of tanks and armored cars coming from the northeast and heading toward Abdallah Aei: the avenue that bordered the Museum and the racetrack, that is, the north side of the Pine Wood. A nocturnal exercise? A movement of troops from one barracks to another? He pondered this for a second then stepped away from the balcony and began to pace the room again. Nine o'clock. Nine-ten. Nine-twenty. Nine-thirty. At nine-thirty his anxiety became unbearable. Not knowing what else to do, he went downstairs. He asked the concierge if by any chance there was a message for him, and the concierge leaped up.

"Oh, monsieur! Pardonnez-moi, monsieur! I forgot to call and tell you that Madame has come to leave a letter for you."

"She has come?!?"

"Oui, monsieur... Just a moment after you, in a very big hurry. Voilà la lettre, here's the letter, monsieur."

He grabbed it, deranged and incredulous. With shaking hands he tore open the envelope, extracted some sheets of ivory-colored paper. It was a very long letter, written in a firm elegant calligraphy, and it began with the words "Darling, somebody will translate this for you." He tried to read the rest. But he could only pick up some shreds of sentences, scattered phrases, so he desisted and assailed the poor man who now looked at him in distress.

"N'avez-vouz pas informé Madame que j'étais dans ma chambre?!? Didn't you tell the lady that I was in the room?!?"

"Oui, monsieur, bien sûr! Of course I did! But Madame replied ana 'araf, I know, ana 'araf..."

"You should have called me all the same! At once!"

"I wanted to, monsieur... But she ordered me to call you after she had gone..."

"What else did she say?!"

"Rien, nothing, Monsieur. She was crying."

"Crying?!?"

"Oui, monsieur. Crying."

He left the hotel like a drunk who can't manage to keep his balance. The rain had stopped and the governmentals' column had halted along avenue Abdallah Aei: a dozen M48s with the 105mm guns, another dozen jeeps with the 106mm recoilless cannons, and ten or so armored cars probably full of troops. They pointed toward avenue 22 Novembre, the extension of avenue Nasser, and not even a moving shadow or a rustle interrupted their silent stillness. Might this be connected with the Tower problem, rather than with a nocturnal exercise or a movement of troops from barracks to barracks? Might the Eighth Brigade be about to enter Sabra and occupy the observatory the French were to abandon next? Leaving the Condor's office, last night, Charlie was so nervous... "They won't tell him, they won't tell him," he kept grumbling. And when he'd asked what he was talking about, he'd burst out almost hysterically: "I'm talking about the French, God dammit! About the Tower, about the Condor! The Condor thinks they'll tell him before they go: bullshit! They will not, they will not! They'll tell the Eighth Brigade and nobody else! Nobody else!" He observed the guns which in spite of their hooded muzzles looked ready to fire, he instinctively concluded that the Eighth was preparing to invade Sabra, to take the Tower, and for an instant he felt the impulse to remain there and see what was going on. But then his impatience to have the letter translated, to know why Ninette had left it and ordered the concierge not to call him at once, prevailed. He stopped a cab, jumped in it.

"Italian headquarters, quick."

"Very dangerous night, tonight," the driver answered skidding away. And it wasn't clear whether he meant the carpets of slime that overlaid the streets or the M48s with the 105mm guns and the jeeps with the 106mm cannons.

* * *

"Angelo! What happened?!?" Martino exclaimed when he rushed into the Pink Room.

"I need you to translate a letter," he answered hoarsely.

"What letter?"

"A letter in English."

"I'm coming."

They went to the briefing room, the only place where at that hour nobody would disturb them. They sat at the cherry-wood table, and

Martino took the sheets of ivory-colored paper. He looked at the firm and elegant calligraphy, he read the first lines, he saw the signature, he blushed, and raised his eyes to say no: it's too personal, I can't. But the hoarse voice forewarned him.

"Word for word, Martino."

Then he obeyed and read what follows.

"Darling, somebody will translate this for you, and of course I don't like to think that you'll know its content through an interpreter. That is, a witness or rather a judge of our story. If I could, I would write it in French: a language I know more than perfectly. But I cannot. I must not. And it's not my fault if Mister Boltzmann's chaos includes the babel of languages, the disorder which better than any disorder expresses the accuracy of his $S = K \ln W$. Yes, I impressed it in my memory, as you can see. I listened carefully the night we talked, and my mind registered everything: from the anguish that the howls of the stray dogs and the crows of the crazed roosters inflict on you, to the nightmare of the decapitated head inside the helmet and of the little girl stuffed into the water-closet; from the crisis in which you wallow with the fear of having become a dwarf tree, to your dream of resuming your studies in mathematics and finding there the recipe to understand the incomprehensible, explain the inexplicable, find the formula of Life. All you said that night is part of me, by now, and I'll go further: jealous of the fascination Mister Boltzmann exerts on your brain, I decided to find out who he was. I went to the library, and among the biographical notes (born in Vienna in 1844, professor of physics and mathematics at the University of Graz then of Munich) I spotted a disconcerting detail. He didn't die of old age or illness. He died by suicide. Do you know where? In Italy. In the castle of Duino, near Trieste... Poor Boltzmann. Maybe he couldn't bear the dejection of having proved a fact that even newborns divine, the invincibility of Death, and out of consistency he surrendered to it before his time. Or maybe he concluded that, besides constituting the inevitable goal of every thing and every creature, Death is a relief: a repose. And out of impatience, or out of exhaustion, he ran up to it. Could I imitate him? Well, though I can't deny that sometimes Death offers repose or relief, though what we think and desire today doesn't usually correspond to what we'll think or desire tomorrow because every tomorrow is a trap of ugly surprises, my answer is no. I don't think I could run up to Death for impatience or exhaustion. Unless... No, no. I'll never yield, I'll never bend, to its invincibility. I'm too certain that Life is the measure of all, the mainspring of all, the goal of all. And I hate Death too much. I hate it as much as I hate solitude, suffering, pain, the word goodbye. Yes, dear, the word goodbye... There's something perfidious in that word. Something sinister, irreparable. Not by chance we say it to those who are going to die or who are dying... Which is why I don't want to hear the goodbye-Ninette you would pronounce if I joined you in our room with the windows that open onto the Pine Wood, why I'll leave this letter downstairs and give up the pleasure of spending a final night with the illusions and the misunderstandings that physical love carries in its womb.

"I like physical love. You'll have noticed it... But the reason for liking it doesn't lie in the shiver with which it inebriates us and consigns us to oblivion. It lies in the company it provides us before and after that shiver, in the solace we receive at possessing a body we're attracted by, in the assurance we sense at uniting our body with that body: at feeling it inside and around us. Some people maintain that physical love is merely a means to procreate, to continue the species, but they're badly mistaken. If it were nothing but this, human beings would mate only when they have an egg to fertilize. Like the animals. (Assuming that animals really mate for the exclusive purpose of fertilizing an egg.) Yes, physical love is much more than that. It's a way of talking, of communicating, of keeping each other company. It's a conversation conducted through the skin rather than through the voice. And, as long as it lasts, nothing wrenches us out of solitude as much as its materiality; nothing fills us up and enriches us like its tangibility. But it's also the most potent drug that exists, the biggest factory of illusions and misunderstandings that nature provides. The drug of oblivion, precisely. The illusion of enjoying oblivion forever. The misunderstanding of being loved with the soul by someone who only loves with the body, who out of egoism or fear, refuses the absolutenesses of love and prefers the false succedaneum of friendship... Your case. How do I know it? My dear, except for the night when you explained to me that the Universe will end with its complete self-destruction because entropy is equal to Boltzmann's constant multiplied by the natural logarithm of the probability of distribution, with the voice we've spoken so little: you and I. With our skin, our bodies, instead, we've spoken a lot. And I haven't missed a word of what you said. Ours is only an epidermic contact, you said. A sexual exercise, a pleasurable gymnastic, a dialogue between deaf-mutes. I need more, you said. I need friendship. Pity you never heard what I said. Friendship cannot replace love, I said. Friendship is an ephemeral remedy, an artificial substitute, and often a lie. Don't ever expect from friendship the miracles that love produces: friends cannot substitute for love. They cannot snatch you from solitude, fill your emptiness, offer real company. They have their own lives, friends. Their own loves. They're an independent entity, an alien presence, a transitory link without obligations. Haven't you ever noticed that our friends are often friends of our enemies, haven't you ever realized that they come and go at their whim or necessity? Oh! When they go, they promise us mountains. In good faith, even. Count-on-me, turn-to-me, call-me. But when you call them, you seldom find them. When you find them, they usually have some unavoidable engagement and don't show up. When they show up, in place of the promised mountains they bring you a handful of gravel. The scraps, the crumbs of themselves. And you do the same thing to them. No, thank you. As much as love isn't enough for you, friendship isn't enough for me. As much as you need friendship, I need love. Love to love and be loved with the obligations of love, the inconveniences of love, the absolutenesses and tyrannies of love. Body and soul. I need it the same way the others need to eat and to drink. I need it to survive. Yes, this I said. And then I said: darling, I'm not an enchanting statue of flesh and that's all. I'm not a stupid woman who opens her mouth only to gurgle let-us-make-love. I am...

"Who am I? At first you wanted to know. You wanted it so badly that at Junieh you rummaged through my purse. (I saw, darling, I saw.) And the night you told me about Boltzmann I satisfied you. I told you who my father was and why I cannot, I must not, I don't want to speak French. I told you who was the man I loved who loved me body and soul. I told you why I hide my identity and in the hotels I give lavish tips instead of producing my documents... But then an atrocious migraine burst out (speaking of these things gives me atrocious migraines) and I cut off my confession. I don't remember if I cut it off with a laugh or a sob, but I remember that I cut it off by seeking comfort in your arms and that this bothered you. It offended you. Well, if you still wanted to know, I now would repeat that confession. I would even provide you with the papers you were seeking in my purse. Papers with my real name and surname, my date of birth, my address, documents that in a certain sense reflect the story of this city. A happy past, a desperate present, a dubious future. I would also add that in the happy past I had everything a privileged woman may desire, that in the desperate present I have nothing but an absurd cross-shaped anchor and too many things I possess but despise. (A typical ingratitude of the rich, I admit it... In fact I know very well that weeping on a full stomach and in a beautiful house is much better than weeping on an empty stomach and in a hovel. Nevertheless, and at the cost of sounding banal, I remind you that to be rich doesn't mean to be lucky. Let alone happy.) But your curiosity about me has dried up, last Monday I had the ultimate proof of it, and this authorizes me to summarize my portrait in three words: I am Beirut. I am a defeated soldier who refuses to surrender, I am a moribund wretch who refuses to die, a crazed rooster who crows at the wrong time, a stray dog who howls in the night... Nor do I feel shame for it: there is so much unhappiness in the crows of those roosters, there is so much vitality in the howls of those dogs. And believe me: they don't howl only to devour each other and conquer a sidewalk made precious by food scraps and scum. Sometimes they howl to find a companion to love and be loved by, and if they are rejected they quietly return to their dens. At the most, they come back for an instant: to wag their tails in farewell. In fact they know very well that love must be soothed in pairs but its quantity and quality are never balanced by symmetry and synchronism: when she's available, he's not available; when he's available, she's not available. (Or maybe they're available at the same time but to soothe his need a mere sip is enough, to soothe her need a river isn't sufficient. And vice versa.) In other words, they know very well that the anathema God flung at Adam and Eve when he chased them from the Earthly Paradise was not you-will-give-birth-with-pain-and-you-will-work-by-the-sweat-of-your-brow. It was: when-he-will-want-you, you-will-not-want-him; when-she-will-want-you, you-will-not-want-her.

"Dulcis in fundo. You've probably wondered why I chose you, an unknown visitor, a stranger encountered due to an accidental shove, to soothe my need for love. And the answer will hurt your pride. No, darling, I didn't choose you because you have big blue eyes and a handsome thoughtful face and an attractive body: I chose you because those eyes and that face and that body resuscitated in me the eyes and the face and the body of a man who is dead and whom I loved very much. You may have also wondered why, in spite of your stubborn rejections, I ended with loving you rather than loving him through you. And the answer will heal your wounded pride. Because, notwithstanding your cerebral chilliness, you are so alive. Your crisis is alive. Your rebellions, your disobediences, your doubts are alive. Your lacerating efforts to understand the incomprehensible and explain the inexplicable. Your effort to deny the loathsome $S = K \ln W$. Besides, we cannot love a dead person forever. Life prevents it, prohibits it. But in the same way we cannot love a dead person forever, we cannot love forever a person who doesn't love us. In fact I don't love you anymore, I don't want you anymore. I wouldn't even if you loved me, if you came to our rendezvous to tell me that without knowing it and without wanting it you always did... Which I doubt, by the way, because I am firmly convinced that in order to be truly loved by you I should die like... Some years ago I read a book that infuriated me. A novel. The story of an unloved man who dies killed on a highway. He dies and, repenting of not having loved him, the entire city hastens to his funeral. Thousands and thousands of people who weep and cry: 'He's not dead! He lives! He lives, lives, lives!' Meaning: in order to be loved by those who don't love, we have to die. The fact is that I'm not ready to die for the sake of being loved: only if I yearned for the relief and the repose that on certain occasions Death may offer could I imitate Mister Boltzmann and run up to it. And in such a case I'd be crazy. Crazier than the crazy woman who sings and dances around the Shatila communal grave...

With this wise statement I leave you, my handsome Italian, my ex-companion of solitude, I wish you to find the formula you search for. The formula of Life. (It exists, darling, it exists. I know. I can even put you on its trail: it does not derive from a scientific calculus, it is not a mathematical term. It's a word. A simple word that here we pronounce at any pretext. It promises nothing, I warn you. Yet it explains everything and it helps.) Your, no longer your, Ninette."

A heavy silence followed. Then Martino handed the letter back to Angelo and headed for the door where he paused and raised a voice full of sad reproach.

"Oh, Angelo!" he said. "How lucky you were! And you didn't know it."

It was almost midnight, in the Pink Room Gaspare and Ugo and Fifì slept soundly to recover from the emotions of a difficult day, and on the roof terrace Stefano pined with love for Lady Godiva, the other thread in the weft of marginal and apparently trivial episodes that through the chain of events warp what the ancients called Fate or Destiny.

4

The farce had in fact generated the unavoidable: in his anxiety to uncover the nature of the surrogate the four rascals denied possessing, Crazy Horse had turned to the Condor. "I'm afraid it is an unbecoming licentious gadget, Sir, an illicit device that stains the honor of the contingent. Begging pardon for my audacity, I suggest you interrogate your driver who is one of the owners." Feeling pierced to the quick, the Condor had summoned Gaspare. Gaspare had blurted it out, and before supper a howl had stirred the headquarters: "Bring it to my office, you mental deficients!" They'd done it. But right at the same moment Eagle had called to report that at the Twenty-Two Hawk was arguing with the French, and the Condor's presence was needed. So the task of examining the illicit device had been taken on by Charlie and Pistoia, and farewell to the trial. "Children's trifle," Charlie had grunted hardly looking at the doll. "Bloody cheap." Pistoia had guffawed prodding her from head to toe and inspecting her various orifices with a finger. Then they'd come out with the verdict, she's-all-yours, and drunk with gratitude Gaspare and Ugo and Fifì had picked her up again. Thanks-chief-thanks, thanks-captain-thanks. Stefano, instead, had remained silent. In silence he'd climbed the stairs to the roof terrace, and here Martino found him when after his sad remark he returned to the Pink Room.

"Stefano! What are you doing out here?"

"Nothing..."

"It's dangerous, here. You could catch a bullet!"

"I don't care..."

"Come on! Get inside."

"No..."

"What's wrong, what happened?"

"Don't you know...?"

"Know what?"

"Gaspare blurted it out."

"To whom?"

"To the Condor! He told him about Lady Godiva, the Condor got furious, made us bring her downstairs, then he ordered Charlie and Pistoia to put us on trial and..."

"They confiscated her."

"No, they didn't. But Pistoia started poking her, sticking his finger all over, and... Oh, Martino! I felt so bad! I wanted to shout at him: you perverted bastard, you vicious libertine!"

"Come on, Stefano. She's just a doll."

"Not for me! Not for me!"

Martino granted himself a smile. The first one since he'd taken the ivory letter paper and looked at the elegant, firm calligraphy. He remembered himself observing Lady Godiva, thinking that under the flashes of light projected by the explosions she looked like a real woman, so although he knew that this happened because of his unhappiness, he had sat beside her and told her what he'd never told any-body...

"I believe you, Stefano. I believe you."

"Really?!?"

"Yes, dear, yes."

"She's not a doll to me, see? Even sharing her with the others makes me suffer... I feel like crying when Gaspare touches her or Ugo slams her around or Fifì says that she's ugly! D'you know why?"

"No, dear..."

"Because I've fallen in love with her. That's why!"

"Yes, dear."

"Is it possible?"

"Yes, dear."

Martino granted himself another smile. Of course it was possible: tonight he'd fallen in love with Ninette. He didn't know Ninette. He had never run into her: he'd always seen her from a distance, in front of the carabinieri's sentry box. Yet, in translating that letter, he'd fallen in love as if he had seen her nearby many times. And though he was aware that this transport was actually an envy, a regret for the love he'd never experienced with Brunella or Lucia or Giovanna or Adilé, tonight he loved her more than he had loved Beppe and Albert.

"All the more that real women only give us sorrows!"

"They give them and they get them, dear."

"Well, Lorena gave me sorrows and didn't get any from me. Lady Godiva, instead... Oh, Martino! I'd give three months' salary to show her my love!"

"Then you better show her, dear..."

"But I've never been with a woman, Martino! I don't know how these things are done!"

"It wouldn't help you to know, dear."

"True?!?"

"True."

"I have an idea, though, you know? Once I saw a film where the actor did it with an actress inside a tub full of water. He soaped her all over, then he entered with her in the water, and... Is it possible, Martino?"

"Yes, dear. It's possible."

"But I'm scared all the same! Since Gaspare failed, Ugo failed, Fifì failed, how can I succeed?"

"You will, dear. I'm sure you will."

"Why are you sure, Martino?"

"Because you love her, dear."

There was a brief silence, then an exultant cry.

"I'm going at once, Martino!"

And with his fear vanished, his pain vanquished, Stefano headed for the bathroom.

*   *   *

He felt like the luckiest man in the world as he locked himself in there, and resolutely he opened the box where Lady Godiva had been put back by Martino. Resolutely he blew into her until she risked exploding, resolutely undressed. Then, very pleased with his tiny but already turgid penis, he turned the light off. He filled the round tub with hot water, went inside it with her, soaped her, and at this point the troubles began. The soap made her so slippery that she squirted out of his hands like an eel. No way to embrace her as the actor had embraced the actress in the film. Worse: being stiffened and lightened by the excess of air, she refused to stay seated and assume the position the actress had taken in the film. After each attempt she came back to the surface and, her arms wide open, her legs spread apart, she remained afloat to pitch back and forth like a lifeboat. He thus gave up the cinematic method, placed her on her feet, got ready to perform the operation vertically, but at this point he noticed that her curls were all wet and stopped to examine the damage. Mamma mia! They weren't just wet: in place of the curly wig there was a hideous mop of slick tufts, and can you imagine the shouts if Gaspare and Ugo and Fifì were to see that disaster?!? "Blockhead, moron, clod!" He turned the light on, he hurriedly got dressed. Heedless of his faded turgidity, he tore off several pieces of toilet paper. He made some hair curlers, rolled the slick tufts, dried them with Martino's hair dryer, but when the damage was somehow repaired he saw that she looked at him with one eye only. Maybe in wiping her face with the towel or in fixing her fringe with the curlers, he had half-erased the left eye. Then he burst into silent, desperate sobs. And reviewing his endless misfortunes, the misfortune of finding himself in Beirut, the misfortune of having to justify himself to Gaspare and Ugo and Fifì who already mistreated him for every trifle, the misfortune of having no sexual experience because of Lorena who'd rebuffed him with an icy mind-your-own-business-you-snot-nose, the misfortune of loving a plastic woman who lost her curls when you bathed her and half an eye when you dried her off, he let himself drop on the floor with her. Overwhelmed by a dismay which (he would never know) was the solitude Ninette alluded to in her letter, the solitude from which any authentic or imaginary love is born, he leaned his head against her belly. "Oh, Godiva, Godiva. I'm so unlucky, Godiva! The unluckiest man in the world!" This gave him much relief, and he stretched out a hand to say thanks caressing her pumpkin breasts. The relief grew and, surprised, he caressed her belly. After the belly, her flanks, her legs, her buttocks, whatever he found. The relief doubled. Wrapping him in flames of boundless sweetness restored his faded turgidity, so like a somnambulist who obeys the impulse to get up and walk he undressed again. He jumped on top of her, kissed the obscene orifice that stood in for the mouth, and kiss by kiss he forgot his endless misfortunes. He forgot Beirut, he forgot the justifications he would have to give Gaspare and Ugo and Fifì, he forgot Lorena and her icy mind-your-own-business-you-snotnose, he forgot the ruined curls, the half-erased eye. And overwhelmed by the enthusiasm, the discovery that indeed he was the luckiest man in the world, he launched himself to the conquest of his first woman. That plastic woman who looked at him with one eye only and yet led him to places full of unknown enchantment. That air-filled woman whom nobody had ever possessed and who therefore belonged to nobody but him. That unreal woman who was more real than any woman of flesh and bones: that long-yearned-for dream. And awakening Gaspare, Ugo, Fifì, Martino, the whistle that had never squealed began to squeal. To squeal, squeal, squeal...

"Ah! Eh! Ih! Oh! Uh!"

It took an eternity, or what seemed to them an eternity, to hear the silence replace the lubricious sequence of groans and giggles and sighs. An equal amount of time to see the door open. But it finally opened. And weary, ecstatic, as red as a ripe tomato, Stefano went toward Martino.

"Martino..."

"Yes, dear," Martino whispered.

"You were right, Martino..."

"Yes, dear."

"And she loves me too. I feel it." Then, turning to Gaspare and Ugo and Fifì: "The whistle broke right in the middle, I'm sorry. But..."

"Right in the middle?!?" Fifì shouted, offended.

"Yes, but I'll reimburse you the sixty thousand liras for your shares and..."

"I don't take any reimbursement! I don't resell anything!" Ugo bawled.

"I'd rather kill her!" Gaspare howled.

"We'll kill her together!" Ugo added.

Stefano was snoring, Martino was dozing, and Fifì pretended to see nothing when two silent shadows glided into the bathroom where Lady Godiva was resting, thoughtfully covered by a bath towel and uselessly protected by a note that said: "Woe to those who wrong her."

CHAPTER SIX

1

CHRISTMAS. At midnight it would be Christmas. And Christmas is such a mockery, in war. Such a cruelty. To heighten the mockery, to aggravate the cruelty, today they would be joined by a three-star general and the Head Chaplain coming from Rome. Protected by a well-armed escort, impatient to leave, the first would prattle about honor and sacrifice, the second about love and mercy, and of course nobody would dare respond go-away-liars, leave-us-alone. The here present colonel included. On the contrary. He already saw himself obsequiously snapping to attention, respectfully barking out the present-arms to those poor boys who'd spent the last eight days on extended eighteen-hour shifts... Shaken by an unusual wrath, Eagle slammed a fist into the pillow of his canopy bed and looked at the clock. Almost five in the morning, Holy Moses, and he'd been awake since two. It had been that dream, by Jesus: unfortunately he believed in dreams, and they never came to help him hit the jackpot in the lottery. They always arrived to presage troubles, catastrophes, calamities. And the one that had awakened him tonight was the ugliest he'd ever had in Beirut. Listen, listen. He was at the Twenty-Two of Shatila with his bersaglieri and a squad of marò who God knows why had ended up there, when the comet of the Three Magi had appeared in the livid ill-omened sky. Leaving behind a tail of refulgent orange light and passing from east to west, it had fallen from the sky to disintegrate in a fan of silvery flames, gold particles, black smoke, and a moment later the Twenty-Two had been surrounded by redskins like a wagon of American pioneers in westerns. A terrible battle had burst. Mortars, machine guns, heavy artillery, rockets. And corpses piling up by the dozens. The worst thing, however, was not the deluge of fire: it was that there was no enemy to defend against. The redskins in fact, didn't attack the Twenty-Two: they attacked each other, in a paradoxical suicide. And to break up the siege, to escape from the circle he needed the authorization of the Condor who instead kept shouting by radio: "Hold the positions! Hold the positions!" He thus felt completely abandoned, paralyzed by his powerlessness, and looking at the marò he thought: "I cannot put them into the M113 because the M113 is already full. I cannot leave them out in the open because out in the open they would die at once. What should I do, San Gennaro, what should I do?!?" Then the marò had disappeared into a hovel. He'd gone to seek them and inside the hovel he'd found a crèche with an Infant Jesus who was a grown-up little girl, a cow that was a goat, a donkey that was a dog, and a manger that was a mattress. But Saint Joseph looked like Saint Joseph, he had a beard as well as a kaffiah, and the Virgin Mary looked like the Virgin Mary. Dressed in blue, she greeted him with a gentle smile and said: "Et faddàl, Colunèl, et faddàl. Come in, Colonel, come in. Huna el hami Allah, here Allah protects us, Colunèl." A good protection indeed, Allah's protection! After a while the crèche had collapsed on her, on Saint Joseph, on the Infant Jesus who was a little girl, on the cow that was a goat, on the donkey that was a dog, on the marò who had sought shelter inside, and he'd awakened in such agitation that he hadn't been able to sleep anymore.

Eagle left the canopy bed, more and more agitated began to pace the Louis XVI room. But had it been a dream or a nightmare caused by the awareness of a real threat? Dreams are nothing but the fruit of thoughts unearthed from our consciousness, fantasies that reflect specific fears or concrete worries, old Sigmund said, and what had happened last night at Shatila had been so alarming! Because last night, at Shatila, the French who garrisoned Sabra had trespassed onto the Twenty-Two. Led by an arrogant lieutenant, ten paratroopers had parked an armored car at the end of the road that led from the little square of the Twenty-Two to the center of Sabra, and when Hawk had asked them to return to their territory the arrogant lieutenant had answered no. "Moi je reste ici autant que je veux, merde. I'll stay here as long as I like, shit! I've got a maneuver to cover and I'm covering it, shit!" A quarrel had broken out, Hawk had finally chased the intruders then blocked off the lane with cans full of sand, but the incident had left a tormenting question. What maneuver? In Sabra there was only one maneuver to cover: the evacuation of the Tower. And if this was the reason why the ten paratroopers had parked the armored car outside their territory, the Head Chaplain could really spare himself the trouble of chattering about love and mercy: the holy Christmas would bring a clash between the governmentals and the Amal. Then the clash would degenerate into a battle, the battle would strike the whole quarter and especially the

Twenty-Two, the Twenty-Five, the Twenty-Four, the Twenty-One...
The Twenty-Two because it had the bad luck of being located a few
yards from the Tower, plus of offering a road to reach it, and would
draw the governmentals' fire like a magnet. The Twenty-Five because it
had the misfortune of being located in front of Gobeyre and would
draw the fire of both sides. The Twenty-Four because it had the mischance of being located at the corner where avenue Nasser crossed the
Street Without a Name, and would draw all the scraps. The Twenty-
One because it had the calamity of being located at the junction of the
Main Street of Sabra and the Main Street of Shatila and was an open
door to whoever wanted to invade Shatila from Sabra... All this with a
shortage of five hundred men. To hell with Christmas! And to hell with
his need for sleep! He'd better stay awake and ready to face the consequences of that bad luck, misfortune, mischance, calamity. To begin
with, making sure that the French flag still fluttered on the flagpole
which had been fixed to the former water tank at the top of the Tower.
It was such a small flag. So small that in the daytime haze you could
hardly see it, and at night you saw it only from the Twenty-Five Alpha:
the guard tower situated on the roof of a house in the middle of the
street that led from avenue Nasser to the Main Street of Shatila, between the Twenty-Five and the Twenty-One. As the crow flies, in fact,
the Twenty-Five Alpha was quite close to the Tower: practically across
from it. But instead of clearing the sky, last night's rain had left a mist
that thickened the darkness and the guard-tower was manned by two
freshly arrived marò: a very young draftee from Ravenna who hadn't
yet understood that he was in Beirut and a very young volunteer from
Venice who had understood even it too well. Let's be honest: can you
compare the mental capacity of a smart urchin born in the shadow of
Vesuvius to that of a polite family boy born in Venice or Ravenna? Keep
your eye on them, he'd told Hawk. Make sure they don't fall asleep,
they don't get distracted, they don't make a blunder. And if the French
flag gets hauled down, call me immediately. Hawk hadn't called but...
He turned on the walkie-talkie.

"Hawk! Eagle calling Hawk!"

"Eagle, Hawk here! I'm here, colonel!" a slightly worried voice answered.

"Anything new, Hawk?"

"No, colonel. Only some little problem with the two kids at the
Twenty-Five Alpha."

"What problem, Hawk?!"

"Nothing serious, colonel, don't worry! I've been there to check a couple of times, and now I'm sending Rambo."

"Rambo?"

"Yeah. The marò squad leader. I want him to take another peek at the damn Tower!"

"What do you mean another peek?"

"Nothing, colonel, nothing. It's just that in this haze we can't see a thing, and the two kids have no experience. They're too young, colonel, and kind of lost. But they watch it, poor kids. They watch it..."

"Hawk, we need to find out what time the sun rises!"

"I already asked, colonel: at six-thirty-seven. And by seven it's full daylight."

"Okay, Hawk. I'll come to take that peek myself. Over."

Then he recited a fervid Pater Noster that he addressed to San Gennaro and San Gerardo and San Guglielmo, saints specializing in miracles, to be impartial and remain on the safe side he also murmered a Shema Israel that he delegated to Abraham and Isaac and Jacob, and feeling consoled by all these influential relationships with the Eternal Father he prepared the usual Neapolitan coffee then poured it into Aunt Concetta's Capodimonte cup. But neither San Gennaro nor San Gerardo nor San Guglielmo nor Abraham nor Isaac nor Jacob were inclined to give him a break that night, and the precious cup slipped from his hands, to fall on the carpet where it splashed an appalling stain in the shape of an I. The first letter of Iella, Iettatura, Iattura: words that in Italian mean bad luck, misfortune, mischance, calamity, catastrophe.

And this slowed his going to Shatila where instead of watching the tower the two marò of the Twenty-Five Alpha were watching a Sabra's window.

2

Luca let out a big sigh, and his gentle face twisted into an exasperated frown. Was this the way to grow up? Was this the way to become a man? If becoming a man means turning into a tired and disappointed person, much better to remain a boy: a Peter Pan playing in Kensington Gardens and searching for Never-Never-Never Land. The Country That Doesn't Exist. All Hemingway's fault, goddam Hemingway, with his boasting about virility and courage. And all fault of his grandfather who had been Hemingway's friend and did nothing but force people to read his books. "Learn! Learn!" Learn what? To stay on the guard tower of the Twenty-Five Alpha and look at a flag that you want to see but you don't see, at a window that you see but don't want to see? They are not serious people, writers. They've nothing to teach. They talk for the sake of talking, for the pleasure of putting nice words together and take advantage of the printed page as they know that on the printed page every fib seems to be a sacrosanct truth! Becoming men, knowing war, facing fear and death: crap like that. Goddam Hemingway! If it wasn't for that damn writer, that shithead, that fool, he wouldn't be here on this roof! He would be in his beautiful house at Campo San Samuele, in his lovely Empire-style bed with the pillars and the Burano lace canopy. He would sleep the sleep of the just, of the nineteen-year-old who hasn't committed any sins besides reading Hemingway and failing to understand how blessed is a guy who's born rich in Venice. He would awake at nine with le petit déjeuner brought by Ines the head maid, he would take a hot shower in the bathroom wallpapered with ladies and cavaliers dancing the minuet, he would slip into his faded jeans and his Hermes sweater to go strolling with his friends in San Marco square then drinking an aperitif at the Café Florian... And to think that before coming here he didn't like the lovely Empire-style bed with the pillars and the Burano lace canopy! It makes me feel like a courtesan in a sarcophagus, he complained, please sell it to an antique dealer! Please buy me a normal bed! He didn't like awakening with the petit déjeuner brought in by Ines, either, and Venice bored him. I've had enough of its black gondolas, its stink of fish, its laces, its glasses, its tourists, its pigeons, he said. I want to go to Africa, to Cuba, Pamplona! I want to hunt lions, to catch swordfish, to defy the bulls, to be a war correspondent, to face fear and death, to become a man like Hemingway! And thank heaven that in spite of that he'd remained a good God-fearing boy, not somebody who snorts coke or plays the revolutionary leftist by murdering judges and syndicalists, thank heaven that... Enough. He was too tired, he couldn't go on... this scanning the dark in search of the damn flag fluttering on the damn flagpole at the top of the damn Tower... Luca laid the nightscopes on the sandbags, rubbed his eyelids.

"I can't take it anymore, Nicolin."

"You tell me!" Nicola answered.

"And when I think that tonight it's Christmas, I feel like crying."

"You tell me!" Nicola repeated.

"Goddam Hemingway, goddam Hemingway!"

Goddam Hemingway, yes. Because tonight, Christmas Eve, he wouldn't even be in Venice. He'd be in Cortina, skiing with Donatella who was a little bit of a snob but who cared for him. He'd convince her to organize something different from the usual chic dinner with the lobster Newburg and the Dom Pérignon, maybe a little supper of polenta and Tokai, they'd eat off paper plates and listen to Stevie Wonder's I-just-called-to-say-I-love-you, after dinner they would go to dance until dawn and return to the hotel as happy as Peter Pan in Kensington Gardens. Instead here he was, peering at a flag he wanted to see but didn't see and at a window he didn't want to see but saw, cursing the day he'd offered himself as a volunteer though Father didn't want him to answer the draft and said if-they-call-you-now, they-send-you-to-Beirut. If-they-call-you-now, I-better-phone-my-friend-the-socialist-minister-and-get-you-an-exemption. Volunteer, goddamn Hemingway, volunteer! And with another thirteen hours to go on this roof, with his legs aching, his arms aching, his temples aching... Everything was aching. But not from the strain of keeping his eye on the lousy flag which was so tiny that the white-red-and-blue got mixed up with the darkness and the fog: from the effort of forcing himself to ignore that window. Hawk had scolded them: "You mustn't get distracted, understand? You must look at the French flag and nothing else, understand? You must see if it is there or not, understand?" Understood. But when the window lit up, your glance shifted to it on its own. Worse than that: in waiting to see it light up again, your eyes fastened to it most of the time.

"I'd kill her," he whined.

"Me too," Nicola answered.

"It's a cruelty, a barbarity, a sadism! Can a person be more evil than her?"

"No. You're right. No..."

"If only I could close my eyes! But if I close them, I won't see if the flag is there!"

"In my opinion, this is just what she wants!"

"Yes, but who asked her to do it? The Amal, the governmentals, the Sons of God?!?"

"I don't know. I know nothing about politics. I don't even know why we're here. Luca... Why are we here?"

"Hawk says that we're here to watch the flag."

"No, no. Why are we in Beirut, I mean. Do you know why you are in Beirut?"

"If I do! I'm a volunteer, am I not?"

"Then tell me, tell me!"

"Because of Hemingway, Nicolin... It's Hemingway's fault I'm here!"

"Hemingway Ernesto, the guy of the bulls, the one who shot himself in the mouth?"

"Him."

"But what does Hemingway have to do with you?"

"Everything. Because Hemingway and my grandfather were friends, in Venice they were always together, and all my grandfather did was talk about him. His bulls, his lions, his wars, his books. Read them, he said to me, learn! I did and... Sure, it was Hemingway who sent me here!"

"But he's dead!"

"What difference does it make? He sent me with his writing and my grandfather's talks! I was reading *For Whom the Bell Tolls* when I volunteered, goddam him! And goddam me for not listening to my father! Because it's true that they would've drafted me anyway, but my father knows a socialist minister who would've got me the exemption and... I shouldn't have read that book. People shouldn't read any books. They are lies. Only lies, believe me."

"I do."

"Have you read any Hemingway?"

"No, I read the newspapers only. Didn't I tell you that I help my mother sell newspapers at my Aunt Liliana's newsstand near the mausoleum of Galla Placidia? The only thing I know about Hemingway is his movies. What does he say in *For Whom the Bell Tolls?*"

"The same stuff as always. He always says the same stuff. He says that in war a man becomes a man even if he's not such. Because in war one has to suffer, to face fear and death, to confront his own virility... So I told my father: if they call me, don't ask the minister for anything. Hemingway went to war when he wasn't even eighteen. I'm nineteen and I want to go. I want to suffer, to face fear and death, to confront my virility, to understand."

"I see. And what have you understood?"

"That I don't like suffering, that I don't like fear, I don't like death. That I was fine at Campo San Samuele. That I don't want to become a man and that there's nothing wrong with remaining a boy in Kensington Gardens."

"Where?"

"Kensington Gardens. In London. Where Peter Pan goes."

"Peter who?!?"

"Peter Pan: the boy who wants to remain a boy and searches for Never-Never-Never Land in Kensington Gardens."

"Searches for what?!?"

"Never-Never-Never Land. The land that doesn't exist."

"But if it doesn't exist, why does he search for it?"

"Because he's a boy."

"Your grandfather's friend says this?!? Hemingway Ernesto?"

"No, it is James Matthew Barrie who says it. A writer whom I read before I read Hemingway... Holy Virgin, she turned the light on again! Look! Oh! I'll shoot her, I'll shoot her!"

"Don't look, Luca, don't," Nicola murmured, turning his freckled face in the opposite direction.

Poor Nicola. He said don't-look-don't, but soon he would turn his face again and look at her just as much. Because it was impossible not to look at. Impossible! Who had ever seen such a thing, a naked woman at the window? Yes, naked. And guess what she did as she leaned against the panes of that Sabra window which wasn't even thirty yards away from the Twenty-Five Alpha: at precise intervals she turned on a lamp and keeping her face in the shadow she caressed herself all over. All over! And she was so ugly, by Galla Placidia! Her breasts were so long and flaccid, her thighs so immense and misshapen, her belly so fat and swollen that at looking you felt like vomiting. Yet she caressed herself as if she were beautiful. Could Luca be right? Could the governmentals or the Amal or the Sons of God have asked her to do it for the sake of distracting them? Well, in that case she fully succeeded. Because the Tower was less than a hundred yards behind the window, and when she turned the lamp on you got so blinded that you no longer saw the French flag. When she turned it off, the same. In fact you had to readjust to the darkness and it took a while to make out the white-red-and-blue at the top of the flagpole. What was worse, you unconsciously waited for the torment to begin again and instead of concentrating on the white-red-and-blue you peered out in search of the now invisible window.

"But it's impossible not to look, Nicolin!"

"I know, Luca, I know."

He knew, and each time he had the impression that she would do it to make fun of him. That is, of someone who hated the idea of becoming a man even more than Peter Pan of Kensington Gardens. Someone who did not need the war and Beirut to understand who he was... He was a nineteen-year-old boy who didn't live in a beautiful house at Campo San Samuele, by Galla Placidia who didn't sleep in an Empire-style bed, who didn't have a bathroom wallpapered with ladies and cavaliers dancing the minuet. Nor a maid who awakened him with le petit déjeuner, nor the money to drink aperitifs at the Café Florian and to spend Christmas at Cortina with Donatella, nor a grandfather who frequented famous writers, nor a father who could call the ministers willing to grant a draft exemption. He lived in a four-room apartment on the outskirts of Ravenna. He slept in an ordinary bed, he prepared his breakfast by himself, he drank an aperitif once a month at the corner bar, and on Christmas he didn't go anywhere. In summer, the same. As for his father, he worked in a factory, and couldn't call any minister. Socialist or not, ministers chat with the people who work in the factories only when they need their votes. So if he were stuck on this guard tower to be mocked by a hideous naked woman, it wasn't Hemingway's fault. It was the fault of the rotten luck which screws the sons of the factory workers while they sell newspapers at Aunt Liliana's newsstand! Because all of a sudden, that day, here was Aunt Liliana, all trembling and waving a blue postcard, the draft postcard. "Do you know what it means, Nicola?" "Sure, Aunt Liliana. It means the army." "No, my child, it means Beirut." He hadn't believed it. He'd consoled her. "Don't worry, Aunt Liliana! They only send volunteers to Beirut. It's written in the newspaper!" Well... Luca said that people shouldn't read books, that books only tell lies. And newspapers? People shouldn't read newspapers either. Because in the barracks there was a volunteer, a certain Marcello who said: "I got balls. So I'm going to Beirut and you're not." But instead of Marcello, who was a volunteer and got balls, they'd sent him who was no volunteer and got no balls.

"She stopped! Let's thank the Holy Virgin, let's say a Salve Regina. But is the flag there or not, Nicolin?"

"It's there, Luca. It's there."

They had sent him on the same ship as Luca, a month after the massacre of the French and the Americans, and halfway through the trip he had suffered a breakdown. Why me, he sobbed, why not Marcello who was a volunteer and got balls? The others had taunted him: "Mommy, Mommy, my bottle!" "Give the baby his bottle!" Luca, instead, had taken him by the arm and said: "Don't cry, Nicolin. You're not the only one who fell into this hitch. Look how many we are." Then he'd given a shove to a rogue who was sucking his thumb to mimic the feeding bottle and said: "Stop it or I'll throw you off the ship, down into the sea." A nice person, Luca. Usually the rich aren't nice. They're mean. And rude. They don't care about the others, they treat them with indifference or conceit, and so on. But if you find a nice one, he's really nice. If you find a courteous one, he's really courteous. He consoles you, he tells you about his family and his house and his bed and his maid who calls him Mister... On the guard tower, also about Hemingway and a certain James Matthew Barrie. In short, he helps you more than a poor wretch would. Even when the ship had entered the harbor, Luca had helped him. "Now be brave, Nicolin and say a Salve Regina with me." All right, he was a little zealot: he had this mania for reciting the Salve Regina. But while the ship entered the harbor, a Salve Regina was just what they needed. The guns on the mountains were pounding so hard! So hard that the ship's commander didn't want to open the ports, and everybody hoped that he never would. Then he had, though, and on the dock there was a captain named Pistoia who bustled around and yelled: "Kids, move your asses, hurry up! Do you think these farts are fireworks for Saint Anthony's Day? These are bombs! Bombs! We're in Beirut, kids, at the war!" At the war! The sound itself of those words had seemed unreal to him. Because despite the films on Vietnam, the newspapers, the months of drilling in the barracks, he had never been able to grasp the significance of the word "war." But tonight he did. Tonight he could say what the war is. It's a sickness that rots from within, a cancer that devours your heart, a leprosy that putrefies the soul and leads people to do things they would never do in a place and in a time of peace. War is a whore. A sow, a hideous naked woman at the window. By Galla Placidia, she'd turned on the lamp again! And now she turned it off, on and off, on and off, at intervals, like the flashing lights that advertise a product or a shop... Overrun by consternation, Nicola turned to Luca. But Luca had grabbed the nightscopes and pointing his rifle at the window he was shouting, shouting...

"Stop it, you whore! Go fuck your mother, you harlot, or I'll shoot you! I'll shoot you! I'll stuff a bullet up into your belly, I swear it!"

Then he bent over to aim at her, and at that very moment Rambo's huge silhouette appeared on the roof.

"Calm down, marò. You are here to watch the Tower, not to shoot at whores."

"Yes, sergeant, yes! But do you have any idea how long this has been going on?!? Two hours!"

"Hmm..."

Rambo glanced at the blinking light and shook his big head. If he had been one who liked to talk, he would've answered: what's this fuss about an old slut in heat? If you knew what I find on patrol! Yesterday I saw a child looking for food in the garbage dump behind Sierra Mike's infirmary. Don't, I said to him, don't: take these chocolates, instead. He took the chocolates, then he went back rummaging through the garbage, and among the infected gauze he found a piece of roast chicken. He cleaned it off and he ate it. Later I saw another one on whom a pan of boiling oil had spilled. He was covered with blisters from head to foot, and guess how his mother had doctored him: by spreading toothpaste and lemon juice. The medical officer immediately called was furious. "Who did this?!?" he shouted. And the mother: "Ana, me, ana! Toothpaste good, lemon good. Disinfect." When they wiped the slime off, a blister broke. And along with the spurt of pus came such a stench that I felt sick. Yes, my boy, yes... When we're on guard at a post, it seems that all the world's ugliness is concentrated in that point. But when we're on patrol we realize that it is everywhere. The only beautiful thing I come across on patrol is Leyda: the little girl who lives in the hovel near the Twenty-Two. She's five, she reminds me of my sister Mariuccia who died at that age, and as soon as she sees me she runs with a trill: "Rambo! Khidni maak, I want to come with you, Rambo!" Then she grabs my pants, she trots along behind me, and I love her so much that I have learnt Arabic just to talk with her... All the rest is ugly, my boy, and that old slut in heat is not any uglier.

"Two hours, Sergeant, two hours!"

"Do you think she's doing it to distract us, sergeant?" Nicola put in.

"No."

"But she does it anyway! That light blinds us and we can't make out the French flag, sergeant!"

"If it's there, you better make it out. Is it there or not?"

"It is, sergeant."

"Let me check."

Rambo took the nightscopes, pointed them at the Tower. Still thinking of Leyda he scanned the darkness to seek the white-red-and-blue blot, and turned to Nicola.

"Hmm..."

"It's there, sergeant: right?" Nicola asked.

"I'm not sure. Something is moving, I see a white reflection, but it could be a small cloud."

"I'm not sure either," Luca added, perplexedly. "It could be the flag and it could be the cloud. To be sure we should look when it lightens up. What time does it lighten up, sergeant?"

"Six-thirty-seven. But before then I'll be back because I cannot trust you, you two," Rambo said. Then he called Hawk to tell him that in his opinion the French flag was no longer there, all he saw above the Tower was a white reflection, probably a small cloud.

It was five-forty-five, the window with the old slut in heat continued to flicker like flashing lights that advertise a product or a shop, and in the Pink Room Stefano cried disconsolately.

"Martino! They murdered her, Martino!"

*   *   *

They hadn't murdered her, but almost. Completely deflated she lay lacerated by a bayonet thrust in the heart, and the gash extended from the left pectoral to the right intercostal area where they had maliciously speared the note that warned woe-to-those-who-wrong-her. "Don't be so discouraged, dear. With a rubber patch and a little putty she'll be just like new," Martino heartened him. Then he stuffed the one-eyed doll into his knapsack and, careful not to awaken the two perpetrators of the crime, led him out of the Pink Room.

"Where are you going?" asked the tankman in the Leopard when he saw them leaving the headquarters with a knapsack and without a rifle.

"To the hospital," Stefano whimpered.

"Where are you going?" asked the carabinieri at the sentry box, surprised for the same reason.

"To the hospital," Martino repeated.

The hospital was a Logistics workshop. The doctor, a mechanic who began his shift at six. It wouldn't be easy to convince him and have the plastic surgery performed right away, Martino pointed out listening to the muezzin who sent his appeals from the minaret of the mosque in rue de l'Aérodrome, but with a little luck they might be able to return before seven. And thank God Charlie was asleep.

3

He wasn't asleep. He was mulling over the Twenty-Two's quarrel, and drew the same conclusion as Eagle: no doubt the maneuver the French lieutenant had mentioned was the abandonment of the Tower or its prelude. Certain operations take place in the night, when the city sleeps! Yet the Condor continued to maintain the opposite: "I exclude it. The French would tell me. They will." And if you said to him general, then call them, ask them straight when they'll leave the damn Tower, he shouted: "I don't call anybody! I won't humiliate myself with such a question!" He behaved like wives who know they're being betrayed by their husbands and pretend not to know out of pride. Anyway, since the Italians could not guarantee the neutrality of the Tower, since they had not the ninety men that such a garrison would require, the problem was no longer knowing the day or the hour the French would pull out: it was preventing or at least delaying the clash between the Amal of Gobeyre and the governmentals who would replace the French. And this could be done exclusively through a catechizing of Bilal. Yes, Bilal. Just yesterday his informants had told him worrisome things about the dwarf who'd grown too much because of half a book found in the garbage. "Captain," they'd told him, "Bilal's lost his head. All he does is to preach, to explain why the world turns, why at times it turns to the right and at times to the left, why some people have so many jackets and some have only one full of multicolored patches... He also asserts that Sabra is his home, Shatila is his home, the whole Western Zone is his home, that when they steal your home you have to take it back, and he has made up a war hymn that says: 'With my teeth I will defend my home, with my teeth! With my teeth I will defend my quarter, with my teeth! With my teeth I will rip out your eyes and your tongue if you come close to me. With my teeth!' And people listen to him. They follow him, Captain." Charlie glanced at his watch. Six in the morning. And at seven Bilal left Gobeyre to go sweep the streets of the Old City: there was no time to lose. He got up. He called the Operations Room.

"Is the French flag still there?"

A cheerful voice answered.

"It's there, it's there! Hawk confirmed it ten minutes ago!"

He let out a sigh of relief and called Angelo.

"Move on, son."

A dull voice answered.

"Yes, Chief." And already dressed, pale from a night spent rereading Ninette's letter, Angelo came forward.

He stared at him, worried.

"Are you sick, son?"

"No, Chief."

"Then go wake Stefano and Martino. We're off to Gobeyre."

Angelo went up and returned at once.

"They're not in the Pink Room, Chief."

"They're not?!"

"No. And neither Gaspare nor Ugo nor Fifì know where they are."

"Go find them!"

Angelo left again, and returned after a while alarmed.

"They're at the hospital, Chief."

"At the hospital?!?"

"Yes. The tankman in the Leopard and the carabinieri in the sentry box saw them leave at quarter to six. They asked where they were going and both of them said to-the-hospital."

"The field hospital?!?"

"It seems."

"Stay here. I'll run to give a look."

At the field hospital nobody had seen them. For-sure-they-didn't-come-here, for-sure-they-fed-you-a-line. And hoping that they'd fed a line to go make an unauthorized call to Italy, Charlie rushed over to the telephone office. At the telephone office nobody had seen them either, then blinded by anxiety he started looking for them as a mother who has lost her children. Dada-no, Dada-no. He went to Logistics, to Eagle base, to the mess, to the battalion shop, to the warehouses... Everywhere except the garage where an amused mechanic was patching Lady Godiva's left pectoral and right intercostal area. Meanwhile the dawn arose, six-thirty, six-forty-five, almost seven, the daylight brightened and dispersed the haze. It was seven when the walkie-talkie sizzled to bring him the Condor's rage.

"Charlie! Come back immediately, God blasteeed!"

Charlie went back immediately and immediately realized what an error he had committed by wasting that precious time, by obeying his maternal instincts. Distracted by a window that blinked on and off to display a naked woman, the Condor said, the two marò of the Twenty-Five Alpha hadn't noticed that the French flag had been hauled down during the night. It had been been Rambo, around five forty five, who suspected that the blot at the top of the flagpole on the former water tank wasn't the white-red-and-blue of the French flag. So at sunrise he had gone back to the guard tower and found out what everybody could now see: the blot at the top of the flagpole was not the French flag. It wasn't even a small cloud, as he'd thought in the beginning. It was the flag with the cedars of Lebanon on a white field. The governmental flag. Move, Charlie, move: led by a lunatic who chanted God knows what and brandished a Kalashnikov bigger than himself, at five after seven the Amal had crossed avenue Nasser. They had burst into the little square of the Twenty-Two and started to build a barricade. Of course the six bersaglieri of the post were trying to drive them back: the little square was actually a mess of blows, kicks, shoves. But this didn't do any good, and uselessly Hawk shouted his ialla-get back-ialla. Uselessly Rambo said to them in Arabic you-can't-stay-here. "We can, we can," replied the lunatic.

"A tiny individual, Charlie."

"Yes, general..."

"A dwarf with a patched jacket who speaks almost perfect Italian."

"Yes, general..."

"Do you know him?"

"Yes, general. It's Bilal."

"The one who kept that wounded guerrilla?!?"

"Yes, general."

"Then, move! Go talk with him!"

"Yes, general. The fact is that he will not listen unless you guarantee the Tower's neutrality..."

"What neutrality, dammit! The governmentals have been in the Tower since last night and you speak of neutrality!"

"You must convince them to get out..."

"Get out?!? Even if I convince them, I don't have the ninety men to garrison the bloody place! How many times do I need to repeat it?!? How many?!?"

"General, please. Try all the same while I talk to Bilal."

And, this time oblivious of Stefano and Martino, he rushed to the Twenty-Two where things were much worse than the Condor thought.

* * *

Much, much worse. Like enraged dogs who rush out of their kennel, the Amal from Gobeyre continued to cross avenue Nasser and flood the Twenty-Two where the first group was building the barricade. Some brought chairs, tables, mattresses. Some attempted to demolish the post's embankments and take the sandbags then add them to the furniture. Some shot in the air to be heard by the governmentals in the Tower. Some ecstatically yelled neha-hunna, we're here, neha-hunna... In the middle of this, Eagle who stammered: "Holy Moses... San Gennaro, San Gerardo, San Guglielmo, Holy Moses! Jesus... Abraham, Isaac, Jacob, Jesus!" Poor Eagle. He looked like a shipwrecked man searching for a rubber ring to get hold of. The rubber ring was Charlie and while grabbing him he pointed at the dwarf who stood on the barricade and chanted beasnani-saudàfeh-haza-al-bitàk-beasnani, beasnani-saudàfeh-haza-al-quariatna-beasnani.

"What is he saying, Charlie?"

"He is saying that he'll defend his home and his quarter with his teeth, colonel," Charlie answered. Then he headed over to Bilal who promptly climbed down from the heap of chairs, tables, mattresses, went to him and raised his bony face.

"What do you want, Capitàn?"

"To talk, Bilal."

"I don't have time to talk, Capitàn. I have to lead my men."

Then he turned his back to climb once more onto the pile of chairs, tables, mattresses, but Charlie seized him by one arm.

"What is this barricade for, Bilal?"

"This isn't a barricade, Capitàn. It's a bridgehead."

"What is this bridgehead for, Bilal?"

"To attack again if they drive me back. To reinforce if I succeed."

"Succeed in what, Bilal?"

"In taking back what is mine, what has been stolen from me, Capitàn. Because the Tower is mine. It belongs to my people. Sabra is mine. It belongs to my people. And I want it back. Now let me go, Capitàn."

"No, Bilal. Because you must listen to me, Bilal."

And continuing to grip him by the arm, Charlie dragged him toward a spot less engulfed by the uproar. He crouched in front of him as we do when we talk with children and want to stare at them face to face, he looked into his eyes. They were very, very hard. Much harder than the night of the half book and the wounded guerrilla. Much tougher. They led to a well of determination.

"Bilal..."

"I said let go of me, Capitàn."

"And I said you must listen to me, Bilal. Do listen. Carefully. Nothing has been stolen from you: the Tower doesn't belong to you. And Sabra doesn't belong to you, either. It belongs to everybody, which means to the city. And the soldiers who now occupy it represent the government of the city. If you attack them, you give them the pretext they've been waiting for. The pretext to start a confrontation or rather a battle. Do you understand the word pretext?"

"I do. It sounds the same in almost every language. Pretext, pretesto, prétexte. But I do not like what you are saying, Capitàn."

"You'll like even less what I'm about to say, Bilal: you could never win a battle against them. Never. Because those are soldiers, Bilal. Real soldiers."

"So am I, Capitàn."

"Yes, but they're stronger. Well equipped. They have big guns, armored tanks, armored cars, radios to communicate. And a lot of ammunition."

"And I have my Kalashnikov, Capitàn. In the end I shall win. It's written in the book."

"No, Bilal, you will not win. You'll die. Your book is mistaken Bilal: when we are dead, we win nothing. So, go back to Gobeyre. Go, Bilal, go. If you don't go, they'll massacre all of you. All. And with you they'll massacre your people in Gobeyre, your eight children, your wife who's expecting a ninth, your old father. Not to mention the Italians who have nothing to do with your quarrels. Do you want me to die, Bilal?"

The hard eyes grew a little less hard. At the bottom of their well of determination, a gleam of tenderness flashed up.

"I don't want you to die, Capitàn, but you came too late. Too late... You should have come an hour ago, before I crossed the avenue. Where were you an hour ago, Capitàn?"

Charlie shifted his eyes to a jeep that was arriving, the Condor's jeep, and clasped Bilal's arm even tighter.

"It's never too late to fix things, Bilal. And if you have not forgotten what you said the night I brought that wounded guerrilla to the field hospital... Did you forget, Bilal?"

"No, Capitàn. I remember it well. I said: now we are friends forever, Capitàn. And if one day you'll ask me to do something, I will do it even if the book tells me not to do it: I promise."

"Exactly. And that day has arrived, Bilal. I'm asking you to dismantle the barricade. I'm asking you to leave the Twenty-Two. I'm asking you to go back to Gobeyre with your men."

The gleam of tenderness went out. The hard eyes became harder again and icily pierced Charlie's eyes.

"Do you ask it for the sake of me and my people, or do you ask it for the sake of you and your people, Capitàn?"

"For both, Bilal..."

"I don't believe you, Capitàn. But I will keep my promise. On one condition: that the governmentals leave the Tower and the Italians take their place."

"Agreed, Bilal."

And finally releasing his arm, Charlie got back to his feet. He joined the Condor who'd left the jeep and was ill-treating poor Eagle.

"A little energy, colonel! I guarantee you that your saints and your prophets don't give a damn for the Twenty-Two!"

He interrupted him.

"General, Bilal will go if the governmentals will go. And on the condition that the Italians take their place in the Tower."

The Condor stiffened.

"That's what the other side said. I just spoke with them. And since I don't have men to substitute for the governmentals, the subject is closed."

"If it's closed, let's reopen it, general... I mean... We could use Rambo's patrol..."

The inevitable scream burst forth.

"Charlie! Don't talk nonsense, Charlie! Not including Rambo, that's five men only! Five, God blasted!"

"Then we could double it, general... We could add the five marò of the other patrol..."

The scream repeated.

"Don't pile nonsense on top of nonsense! You know very well that in a case like this there's no difference between five and ten men! You know very well that in an empty building ten men are ten hostages proffered to the Sons of God!"

"They're also a way to gain time, general..."

"And to clear the square, that is, to avoid a confrontation," Eagle put in hopefully.

The Condor seemed to hesitate.

"That's true..."

Then he looked at the barricade which had by now reached the dimensions of a very long and very high truck. He looked at the Amal who continued to pile up tables and chairs and mattresses, at the six overwhelmed bersaglieri who had stopped dealing blows and kicks and shoves, at Rambo who out of resignation had stopped haranguing them in Arabic, at Hawk who out of discouragement had stopped shouting ialla-get-back-ialla, and seemed to change his mind.

"Do we have another five marò?"

"Yes, sir!" cheeped Eagle, more hopeful than ever.

"What time does the sun set?"

"At four fifty-six, meaning 16:56, sir. And by six-twenty-two it's dark."

"Good. Double Rambo's patrol and have it ready to garrison the Tower until sunset. That is, four-fifty-six. Or, say, five: 17:00."

"Sunset? Only until sunset?!?" Charlie exclaimed in alarm.

"Sunset, Charlie. 17:00. I do not proffer my men to the Sons of God. Tell it to your dwarf while I tell it to the governmentals."

"But if I tell him that you'll keep them only until sunset, he won't leave!"

"Then, don't tell him."

"But if I don't tell him, I'll cheat him! I'll betray him!"

"That's your problem, Charlie. Not mine. I want to clear the square, and that's that. Go!"

"Yes, General..."

And with his head bowed, Charlie reapproached Bilal.

"My general says yes, Bilal."

"You mean the governmentals will leave?" Bilal asked suspiciously.

"They will, Bilal. They've given the same condition, and in a little while we will occupy the Tower in their place."

"For how long, Capitàn?"

"I don't know... For as long as necessary, I guess..."

"Are you sure, Capitàn?"

"Yes. I promise, Bilal."

"Really?"

"Trust me, Bilal."

"I am trying, Capitàn."

He went to the barricade he called a bridgehead, ordered his men to dismantle it and go back to Gobeyre. Then he returned to Charlie. With a very sad gesture he stretched his right hand.

"It is hard to keep a difficult promise, Capitàn. But I kept mine. And you? Will you keep yours?"

Charlie blushed imperceptibly.

"Why are you asking, Bilal?"

"Because friendship is a luxury at war, Capitàn. And because there is a proverb that says: either you or me."

Charlie's blush deepened.

"Bilal..."

"Goodbye, Capitàn. And if we do not see each other again, remember that my book is not mistaken. I shall win. Dead or alive, I shall win."

* * *

It was cold that morning. Along with the mud, the rain had left a wintery chill in the air. But the shiver that shook Charlie was not from the cold, and crushed by a sentiment that resembled shame he thus returned to the headquarters where Stefano and Martino were happily smiling over a healed Lady Godiva. And where Crazy Horse was despairing over the acquittal which had concluded the four rascals' trial.

"Quod non vetat lex, hoc vetat fieri pudor! What the law does not prohibit is condemned by decency, Seneca warns us!"

The Three-Star general had arrived, and with him the Head Chaplain. The first with his chest full of gold and silver and bronze undeserved medals, the second with his collar sanctified by two minuscule yet sparkling crucifixes, they were really prattling about sacrifice, honor, peace and mercy. In his office, instead, the Professor was adding a bitter footnote to the letter that during the night he had written to the wife who didn't exist.

<h1 style="text-align:center">4</h1>

What an extraordinary, irreplaceable gift fantasy is. And how unlucky are those who don't have it! How poor, you can go where you want, with fantasy. You can be what you like. You can even invent what doesn't exist. And, as we know, the Professor's fantasy had invented a wife who didn't exist: a companion to whom he addressed the letters he wrote to relieve his solitude and to build up the novel we are reading. But, above all, with fantasy you can invent reality. You can prove that reality and fantasy are the same thing, the two aspects of the same dream. You can foresee the future which seems to us a hypothesis and is instead a certitude already established by the impenetrable logic of destiny.

Just what the Professor's second letter says.

*   *   *

I wonder why I have this irresistible need to write, dear. Maybe because tomorrow is Christmas and, though holidays connected to otherworldly mirages bore me deeply, I cannot escape the fascination of that day. It's the day which celebrates the birth of a man who blindly believed in the force of love and in the immortality of Life, so the idea of spending it amidst an orgy of hatred and death makes me feel more alone than ever. You can't imagine what I would give to spend it with you, in a bed warmed by you, holding you in my arms and listening to the bells that call for joy. (Is fantasizing no longer enough for me?) Or maybe Christmas has nothing to do with it and this need is a need to converse with myself, keep myself company, overcome the anxiety that suddenly disquiets me. So many mishaps have hit us in the last weeks and hours... The governmentals have shelled us and blown up one of our munitions dumps, the Shiites have torn apart one of our patrols with two Rdg8 and sponsored a parade pregnant with threats, and the French have abandoned Sabra. If the bomb primed by their withdrawal explodes, we won't be able to defend ourselves because last Monday Agamemnon sent on vacation-leave a third of the contingent. "It couldn't be avoided, it was already organized!" he answers when I say that he made a mistake. Already organized...! Once I heard a brilliant aphorism on the organizational skill of my compatriots: "Paradise is a place where the policemen are English, the cooks are French, the beer-brewers are Germans, the lovers are Italians (sic), and everything is organized by the Swiss. Hell is a place where the policemen are Germans, the cooks are English, the beer-brewers are French, the lovers are Swiss, and everything is organized by the Italians." But let's talk about more agreeable things: my miniature Iliad, my novel to be written with a smile on the lips and a tear in the eyes.

I began it! I'm working on it! Every night I shut myself in this office and work, work, work: I navigate through the treacherous waters of the longed-for novel and God knows what port it will lead me to. A novel doesn't yield its many secrets immediately. Not even to the writer does it reveal its real identity at once. Like a fetus still devoid of features it locks within itself a mine of hypotheses, a myriad of good and bad surprises, so everything is possible. Including the worst. Yet its body is already outlined, its heart beats, its lungs breathe, its nails and hair grow, on its dim face the eyes and the nose and the mouth are discernible, and I can introduce it to you. I can tell that the story unfolds over an arc of three months, (ninety days elapsing from a Sunday in late October to a Sunday in late January), that it opens with an allegory verging on a chronicle, (the dogs of Beirut), that it sets out with the double slaughter, that it follows the conducting thread of Boltzmann's mathematical equation $S = K \ln W$. And that I develop the plot through the hamletic squire of Ulysses: the one who searches for the formula of Life. (I've baptized him Angelo, a choice that suits his aseptic reasoning, and besides I haven't assigned anybody the divine poem's names: In order to prevent the usual imbecile in ambush from accusing me of presumption and mocking my effort, to the Achaean chiefs I have given names of pugnacious birds or cartoonish nicknames. To the others, whatever seemed suitable.) The characters are imaginary. They are so even when they're inspired by some model or alleged model. As soon as I can in fact I escape from my exile and, unobserved, I observe. I listen, I spy, I steal from reality. Then I correct it, I reinvent it, I re-create it to such a degree that often I no longer remember who the original was. And here is the despotic general who thinks he can defeat Death, here is his disenchanted and ingenious adviser, his erudite and bizarre head of staff, his officers now bellicose and now meek, as well as the faceted multitude of his troops. The soldiers I spoke of in my previous letter. The boys who in every civil or uncivil society are brought to suffer and to die beneath the walls of Troy... Yes, I do use the archetypes I mentioned. However they represent only a part of the human samples the novel will offer: the poor and ugly Calabrese, the proud and taciturn Sardinian, the lively and meddlesome Sicilian, the rich and disappointed Venetian, the loutish and witty Tuscan, the naive and scared Romagnan, the educated and optimistic Turinese... I'm also using the gorgeous and mysterious Lebanese I call Ninette, as a matter of tact I'm assigning her a decisive role, and the various symbols of the sad city. The eternal pariah whom the not always Merciful Lord fucks over with a half-book found in the garbage, the eternal master whom the always Almighty Lord entrusts with heavenly powers, the eternal instrument of Evil which in its omnipresence can assume the features of an obtuse and perfidious fourteen-year-old... And the children that war kills. The pimps that war favors. The bandits that war protects. The women that war sacrifices. Among them, a woman-surrogate named Lady Godiva and five adorable nuns whom I intend to involve in the tragedy. Between the protagonists and the extras, some sixty characters. But from day to day the cast grows, the stage gets more crowded, and other characters are about to arrive. Help me God. Can you imagine what a toil it is to apportion them, to insert them into the narrative structure, to shift them at the right moment and in the right manner, that is, to make them serve the plot? Certain nights I feel like a sloppy puppetmaster who doesn't have enough fingers to support the strings of his puppets. And I quiver.

The trouble is that I cannot limit them, reduce them. Reducing them would be like mutilating the novel, it seems to me, like portraying life the way silent and black-and-white movies did. I don't like black-and-white movies. And the silent ones, even less. I don't understand the phony aesthetes who go into ecstasies for the silence and the monochrome, who praise their "inimitable intensity" or "essentiality." That so-called intensity lacks the sounds of Life, that so-called essentiality lacks its colors. Life isn't a silent or black-and-white show. It is an inexhaustible rainbow of colors, an unending concert of noises, a phantasmagorical chaos of voices and faces and creatures whose actions intertwine to weave the chain of events that determine our individual destinies... Listen: one of the things I'd like to say in my miniature Iliad is precisely that our individual destinies are always determined by a chain of events that interwine because of actions we personally did not commit. For example the simple gesture of somebody whose individual destiny will be in its turn determined by the simple gesture of somebody else, to infinity, by means of a mechanism which is alien to our wishes or our free will... And to say this, or to try, I must use the greatest possible number of puppets. Something I enjoy, by the way, *because through them I can express myself. My many selves, all the selves who I didn't know I was and who I've discovered I am. Flaubert used to say Madame-Bovary-c'est-moi, Madame Bovary is me. Well... I am Angelo, I am Ninette, I am the Condor, I am Charlie, I am Crazy Horse, I am Old Grouse, I am Sugar, I am Pistoia, I am Eagle, I am Hawk, I am Sandokan, I am Falcon, I am Gigi the Candid, I am Armando Golden Hands, I am Gino, I am Martino, I am Fabio, I am Matteo, I am String, I am Onion, I am Nazarene, I am Rambo, I am Ferruccio, I am Stefano, I am Fifì, I am Ugo, I am Gaspare, I am Bernard le Français, I am Rocco, I am Luca, I am Nicola, I am Salvatore Bellezza, son of the late Onofrio, I am Jasmine, I am Imaam, I am Sanaan, I am Dalilah, I am Sister Espérance, Sister George, Sister Milady, Sister Françoise, Sister Madeleine, I am Bilal, I am his wife Zeinab, I am His Most Reverend Eminence Zandra Sadr, I am Passepartout, I am his lover Rashid, I am Alì the Swindler, I am Ahmed the Pimp, I am the little boy Mahomet, I am the little girl Leyda... And soon I'll be Captain Gassàn, Roberto the Laundryman, Calogero the Fisherman, Sergeant Natale, Rocky, Mahomet's mother, Leyda's mother: I'll be, nay, I am any creature born out of my imagination, all the creatures who exist thanks to my thoughts and feelings, sucking those thoughts and feelings like a vampire sucks his victims' blood. The symbiosis is so complete that I can no longer differentiate and separate myself from them. When they weep, I weep. When they laugh, I laugh. When they're afraid, I'm afraid. When they die, I die. No, I never part from them. Never! Agamemnon realized it last night. He was mulling over the problem of the Tower, the Sabra French observatory that may light the fuse, and since I was silent he asked me what I was thinking about. Ah! I was thinking about the way of using that tower in my story, of unleashing a battle to give a decisive turning to my novel and become its knot. Its crux. I could toss two-thirds of the characters into that crux, I thought, eliminate some of them and keep the others behind the scenes to use them in the final section. Then, once the battle is over, I could unroll the theme I care for: the inevitability of destiny. Finally I could exhume the third truck, reverse the equation $S = K \ln W$, provide the formula of Life. And I felt like Jove who ruling the Universe at his will and whim pulls up and down the strings of his puppets, chooses those to save and those to sacrifice, creates and destroys the colors of the inexhaustible rainbow, the noises of the unending concerto. So I answered the Condor with the disconcertment of a person who's been brutally awoken, and he got angry. "Colonel! Stop roaming in the stratosphere, God blasted!" What could I retort? It was true, it's true. I roam in the stratosphere. Always. I flutter in a* *kind of lucid madness. My dear, the fact is that to write one has to be lucid and crazy at the same time.*

Yet what a marvel, that monstrous union! What a privilege to flutter in it, what a sublime responsibility! I'll prove it to you with an argument that nowadays is the topic of scholarly essays and elaborate polemics, drawing room quarrels and bestsellers, but that almost everybody tackles by dodging the most pressing point. Here it is. We belong to an epoch in which cinema and TV have taken the place of the written word, of the written narrative. An epoch where the movie and TV directors, or rather the actors, have taken the place of the writers and nobody (including me) resists the narcotic lure of the screen: the perpetual amusement offered by a system of communication that transforms even the sacred intimacy of sex and the inviolable solemnity of death into public entertainment. Subdued, hypnotized by the modern Medusa, we spend hours looking at her images and listening to her sounds. Consequently we read much less, and many no longer read at all. They say that it's possible to live without reading. Without the written word, the written narrative, the writers. Wrong. And not only because cinema itself and TV itself cannot exist outside of or without the written word, the written story, the writers, but because the screen doesn't permit us to think the way we think when we're reading. Its images and noises distract, preclude concentration. Or they suggest reflections which are superficial, transient. Know why? Because the screen is too much concerned with the pledge of astounding us, entertaining us, and methods it uses to achieve this goal are too rudimentary. Too toyish. They don't require the use of meninges. (And needless to underline that reading requires a minimum of meninges, meaning intelligence and culture, needless to emphasize that any idiot or illiterate with two eyes and two ears can stare at the images and listen to the noises of the modern Medusa.) But to live, to survive, we must think! To think we must produce ideas! And who produces ideas better than the writer? Away with phony humility: the writer is a sponge who absorbs life to spit it out again in the form of ideas. He is an eternally pregnant cow who delivers calves in the form of ideas, a dowser who finds water in any desert and makes it gush in the form of ideas. He is a seer, a prophet: Merlin the Wizard. Because the writer sees things the others don't see, feels things the others don't feel, imagines and anticipates things the others can neither imagine nor anticipate, and not only sees them and feels them and imagines them: he anticipates them and transmits them. Whether alive or dead. Dammit! No society has ever evolved outside or without writers. No revolution (good or evil) has ever taken place outside or without writers. For better or worse, it has always been the writers who have moved the world and changed it. So, writing is the most useful work which exists. The most exalting, the most satisfying one in the world.

Do I exaggerate? Do I succumb to the rhetoric of enthusiasm, to the utopias of the neophyte? I'm anticipating your reply: "Calm down, sir, cool off. Don't forget what the mathematician and philosopher Jean-Baptiste d'Alembert said two centuries ago. On a wild and uninhabited island, he said, a poet (read writer) wouldn't be any use. A geometer, yes. Fire wasn't certainly first lit by a writer, the wheel wasn't certainly invented by a novelist. As for the most exalting, the most satisfying trade in the world, go ask the writers who write every hour of every day for years: the poor souls who sacrifice their existence to a book. They'll answer: Colonel, do you seriously think that writing for a few hours after supper in Beirut qualifies you to give such a judgment? Do you seriously think that having a few ideas or putting together a story is enough to write a book? Do you seriously think that writing is a joy?!? Let us tell you what the trade of writing is, colonel. It is the atrocious solitude of a room that gradually becomes a prison, a torture chamber. It is the fear of the blank page that stares at you mockingly. It is the torment of the word that you don't find and, if you find it, it rhymes with the adjacent word. It is the martyrdom of the sentence that limps, of the metrics that fall apart, of the structure that staggers, of the page that bores, of the chapter that you must dismantle and remake, remake, remake until the words seem to you food that recedes from the famished mouth of Tantalus. It is giving up the sun, the blue, the green, the pleasure of watching the sky, of walking in a wood, of moving, of using your whole body, not just your head and hands. It is a monkish discipline, a hero's sacrifice, and Colette was right when she said it is also a form of masochism. A crime against ourselves, a felony that should be punished by law like the other felonies. Sir, there are people who end up in psychiatric clinics or in the cemetery, because of writing. People who turn into alcoholics, drug addicts, lunatics, suicides. Writing destroys, sir. It kills more than bombs." I know. I also know that my miniature Iliad could be a chimera, the embryo of a book that will never be born, an illusion like the sham pregnancy of the women who desire a child to the point of subconsciously halting their menstrual cycle and swelling their bellies with air and deluding themselves that their womb contains a fetus. But happiness is always an illusion. And, sham or not, this neopregnancy gives me an interlude of happiness. Now I thank you for having helped me to converse with myself, keep myself company, overcome the anxiety, I wish you a Merry Christmas and...

P.S.: Merry Christmas? While I was writing my letter, the French were evacuating the Tower and the governmentals of the Eighth Brigade were installing themselves in their place. While I was ending it, Amal of Gobeyre were invading the little square of the Twenty-Two and led by the magnificent dwarf with the patched jacket they erected a barricade... I don't know through what oratorical or psychological shrewdnesses Ulysses persuaded them to undo it and return to their own quarter, I don't know for what tactical or strategic calculations the governmentals handed the cursed building over to us, but I know that ten of our marò are now inside it and cannot remain there any later than five in the afternoon. That is, sunset. This means that reality and fantasy are really the same thing, the two aspects of the same dream: the battle I wanted to unleash in my imagination will burst precisely at sunset, when the ten marò will leave the Tower. It will be a ferocious battle. And if we survive it, if I survive it, it really will give my novel a decisive turn. It really will become its knot, its crux. But overall it will permit me to unroll the theme I care for, the inevitability of destiny, thus reverse the equation $S = K \ln W$ and provide the formula of Life. (Assuming that such a formula exists. I never had so many reasons to doubt it.)

THIRD ACT

CHAPTER ONE

1

A TERRIFYING SILENCE stagnated over Sabra and Shatila, a stillness as heavy as a shroud of lead. From the courtyards and from the henhouses not a single cock-crow came, and in the deserted streets, in the empty alleys, not a single rat went in search of food. All of a sudden even the roosters who incessantly sang out their madness had fallen quiet, even the rats who feasted on the trash had disappeared, and along with the rats the goats who nibbled the grass on the grave of the thousand Palestinians massacred one year before. Along with the goats, the people. No need to ask why. At sunrise even the blind had seen the governmental flag fluttering at the top of the Tower then the Amal invading the Twenty-Two to erect the barricade then Bilal leading them back to Gobeyre, then the Italian flag climbing the flagpole on the former water tank. By sunset even the deaf had heard the cry at-five-in-the-afternoon-the-Italians-will-leave-the-Tower, and everybody had understood what would happen. Bolting the doors, closing the windows, lowering the rolling shutters, the inhabitants of the two quarters had shut themselves in their houses and only the bersaglieri with the marò had remained outside: immobile and voiceless behind the sandbags.

Look at them while immobile and voiceless behind the sandbags they count the minutes that separate them from five in the afternoon, from the deluge of gunbursts and artillery and rockets. Their Christmas bells. Some are unknown to us, we haven't met them as yet on our tragicomedy's stage. Others are familiar, instead: they are characters from the novel the Professor calls my-miniature-Iliad. On the top of the Tower there's Rambo who anxiously touches his medallion with the Virgin's profile and from afar stares at the yellow hovel of Leyda, the five-year-old girl who has stolen his heart because she resembles his dead sister Mariuccia. It's located in a dangerous spot, that yellow hovel: on the west side of the little square garrisoned by the Twenty-

Two. And should something happen to Leyda, should Mariuccia die again... At the Twenty-Three there's Onion who wants so much to become a man and for that purpose has conquered his fear of the dead nay realized that evil always comes from the living. At the Twenty-One there's String who would like to have his maturity tested but being hungrier than usual only thinks of the Christmas dinner he plans to stuff himself with when the shift ends. Will they have roasted the chicken more professionally, tonight, will they have peppered the potatoes enough? Ah, what a meal it would be if he could cook a lobster all'armoricaine or a duck à l'orange with his own hands! At the Twenty-Seven Owl there's Nazarene whose anarchic pacifism does not tolerate the stink of blood on the way. So he thinks of India where at sunset and dawn you can smell the perfume of sage and jasmine, and points his nightscopes on Tayoune to see the white mare who lives in the middle of the rotary's grassy bed. At the Twenty-Eight there are Fabio and Matteo, and Matteo thinks of Dalilah who yesterday gave him a kiss and a thousand guilt complexes about Rosaria. But he also thinks of the deluge that will burst and shivers: what will this battle be? The nightmare described by Great-Grandfather who lost a leg in combat, or an exciting experience to recount in Palermo's cafés? Fabio thinks only of Jasmine with whom he's fallen in love on the contrary, of the nickname Mister Coraggio that has made him overcome the shame of betraying John's memory, and smiles without realizing that soon he'll cry. At the Twenty-Five there's Ferruccio who realizes it very well and whose eyes restlessly search through the shadows cast by the fig tree. This morning Mahomet said he would bring him a pot of hummus and schawarma, creamed chickpeas and roast mutton, and should he really come... How to stop him, Christ, how to prevent him from poking his nose out of the shanty where he lives with his mother? At the Twenty-Five Alpha there are Luca and Nicola who have just caught an alarming phrase over the radio, the-two-guys-on-the-guard-tower-across-from-the-Tower-are-risking-the-worst, and blind with rage at himself Luca alternates insults to Hemingway with Salve Reginas: "Salve Regina, mother of mercy, our life, our sweetness, our hope... Goddam Hemingway! Go to hell, you and your bulls, your wars, your books!" Frozen in fright, Nicola limits himself to moaning: "You were right, Aunt Liliana, you were right!" At the Twenty-Two there's Hawk. He waits for Eagle who went to get Rambo and his ten marò, and peering at the Tower he nervously grumbles: "Now he's hauling the flag down the flagpole... Now he's folding it up... Now he's getting ready to take them down, now he's getting them down... Or did he already do it to avoid leaving at five, that is, at 17:00? Neapolitans are so superstitious, so afraid of the number seventeen! They say it seems like a gallows with a hanged man and fear it more than black cats or broken mirrors... Yes, they've already left. They already are on their way..." And everywhere there's a livid ill-omened sky that grows more and more livid, more and more ill-omened.

Look at it also, and then look at Eagle who really left before five to avoid the seventeen, and who's arriving followed by Rambo's jeep. He's very pale, poor Eagle. So pale that his curly mustaches stand out against his cheeks like black question marks, and he breathes with difficulty. "Hawk, move on to the Twenty-Five. I'm going to the Twenty-Two," he says with that difficult breath. Then he turns to Rambo who still stares at the yellow hovel and sighs: "Place your marò along the south wall of the square, Rambo. Unfortunately there's no room in the M113." Finally, he calls the Operations Room and gives a brief report: "The flag is hauled down. The Tower, evacuated. Hawk is going to the Twenty-Five, Rambo and his marò are staying with me at the Twenty-Two. Over." "Over and good luck," somebody answers coolly. It's five after five, the terrifying silence continues, and in his office the Condor explains to the Head Chaplain why midnight Mass cannot be celebrated. "I'm sorry, Excellency: my efforts to avoid the clash have failed. The battle will break out very soon, and we'll be dragged into it from Shatila to Bourji el Barajni. We'll find ourselves in the position of a referee trapped between two boxers who are slaughtering each other, sir, and many of their punches will fall on us. This means that I have to keep my troops under cover. No Mass." Fingering the minuscule yet shiny crucifixes that sanctify the collar of his uniform, the Head Chaplain listens with irritation and disbelief: "A battle on Christmas Eve?!?" Buffing his undeserved gold and silver and bronze medals, the three-star general listens instead with the air of believing it all too much, and sweats. He's never been in a war, his battlefield exploits have never gone farther than blank rounds at drills and orders fired from his armchair in Rome, but he knows the Condor is right. Besides, who doesn't? Everybody agrees with him, tonight: the Professor who explained it in the postscript of his letter and who now would give a great deal to write that reality and fantasy are not the same thing, Charlie who taken by the remorse of having cheated Bilal searches for justifications in the phrase friendship-is-a-luxury-at-war, Crazy Horse who anxious to imitate Des Aix and Collinet torments everybody with a new maxim: "Bellum nec provocandum nec timendum, Pliny says! War must be neither provoked nor feared!" And also Pistoia who by now deprived of his jollity mutters: "By Christopher Columbus and his mother's dirty underpants! We're going to dance, in a while, to dance!" Also Sugar who swaddling his undefused bomb with sandbags mumbles: "Let's hope for the best!" Also Sandokan who at Sierra Mike rejoices, happy to taste the-sap-of-life never tasted in a war against Yugoslavia or Albania or Malta or the Principality of Monaco or the Republic of San Marino, yet feels an inexplicable longing for the edelweiss and the trout of the Prealps. Also Falcon who a moment ago entered the convent's chapel to thank God for keeping him far from the fire, that is, letting him postpone his Great Test. His moment of truth. Also Lieutenant Joe Balducci who at Ost Ten is wondering how much the fucking battle will determine his fucking fate and that of his fucking Marines trapped in the fucking skyscraper. Also the medical officers who at the field hospital prepare the operating tables and check the supplies of morphine. (Will there be enough?) Also Bilal's militiamen who enraged over the barricade's dismantlement are impatiently waiting to recross avenue Nasser. But, more than everybody, Bilal and Gassàn. Because, back in Gobeyre, Bilal has ordered the lanky thug called Rashid to prepare the defenses. And Rashid has called up the young and the old, assembled every available weapon, placed two trucks at the border with Shyah, then equipped them for the launch of the most precious rockets they have: thirty 80mm Katyushas deployable at short range. As for Captain Gassàn, he's now leading the company of ninety men who are about to retake the Tower. Look at them, too.

Look at them while with their well-pressed uniforms, their camouflage helmets, their M16s, their machine guns, their mortars, and escorted by an M48 with the 105mm cannon and 12.7mm Browning they move through the deserted streets and the empty alleys of Sabra to approach the target. This morning Gemayel's army accepted the Condor's proposal because its strategists had started a badly coordinated operation and because the company chosen to replace the French on the Tower had been stupid enough to raise the flag with the cedars of Lebanon. That is, to warn Bilal. During the day, however, the same strategists have made up for the double mistake. They've mobilized two Eighth Brigade and two Sixth Brigade battalions, each battalion under the orders of a capable officer, each officer trained at the academy of West Point or Saint-Cyr, and prepared a serious operation: on the avenue leading from the Pine Wood to Sabra, the column of M48s and armored cars that Angelo had seen during and after his wait for Ninette; on the Ramlet el Baida littoral, near the Luna Park, a column of M113s and armored vehicles loaded with troops and jeeps equipped with 106mm recoilless cannons. (Two deployments, by the way, which will permit them to launch a pincer assault. In fact the first column will burst into Shatila from the north side of Sabra and the second from the Street Without a Name.) Finally, they have alerted the Sixth Brigade mortarmen who lodge in the barracks behind the Logistics and given Captain Gassàn the command of the company now moving with the M48 through the deserted streets and the empty alleys of Sabra. With a rapid and militarily perfect maneuver, the company will soon reach the road of the Tower. It will leave the M48 at its corner, that is, facing the one hundred fifty yards which lead to the Twenty-Two's little square, then it will break inside. Here, without raising any flag, Gassàn will set up his troops this way: twenty-five men on the ground floor with two 81mm mortars and two 12.7mm machine guns; ten men on the first floor which has three front windows to post at; fourteen men on the second and on the third and on the fourth floors which in addition to the three front windows have four windows overlooking the sides and the rear; eleven men on the roof where he will position four 6.75mm machine guns and three 60mm mortars plus ten cases of grenades and ten thousand rounds in belts. However, Bilal will be informed of this by his sentries, and crazed with fury he'll order Rashid to fire the first Katyusha. Then he'll gather his best militiamen and cross avenue Nasser again, again he'll invade the Twenty-Two's little square and hurl himself into the conquest of the damn building. It's five-thirteen. The terrifying silence continues, as does the stillness as heavy as a shroud of lead. After yielding to the Head Chaplain who's peevishly seeking a shelter to celebrate his midnight Mass, the Condor has brought the three-star general to the Operations Room where everybody stares at the large clock that haunts with its gloomy tick-tock. Standing beside the jeep he has parked between the M113 and the wall where Rambo is crouching with his marò, Eagle breathes with even more difficulty and waits for hell to explode. Five-thirteen... Five-fourteen... Five-fifteen... Five-sixteen... Five-seventeen which is twice bad luck because it means seventeen and seventeen... And to exorcise the double seventeen he stretches his fingers in the sign of the horns, he murmurs the appropriate incantation. But the Katyusha that Rashid has launched from one of the two trucks placed at the border with Shyah is already crossing the livid ill-omened sky.

* * *

It crossed it from east to west, like the comet in the dream. The comet of the Three Magi. It crossed it leaving behind a tail of refulgent orange light like the comet in the dream. The comet of the Three Magi. And all of them, except Eagle, opened their mouths in ecstasy. What a beautiful comet, thought Rambo forgetting Leyda and his little dead sister. What a beautiful comet, thought Onion forgetting his dream and his fear. What a beautiful comet, thought String forgetting his hunger and his roast chicken. What a beautiful comet, thought Nazarene forgetting the perfumes of India and the white mare of Tayoune. What a beautiful comet, thought Fabio forgetting his now beloved Jasmine. What a beautiful comet, thought Matteo forgetting both Rosaria and Dalilah. What a beautiful comet, thought Ferruccio forgetting Mahomet and the pot of hummus and schawarma. What a beautiful comet, thought Nicola and Luca forgetting Aunt Liliana and Hemingway. What a wonderful story to tell when we return to Italy. "Would you believe it? On Christmas Eve I saw the comet of the Three Magi." Then with shining eyes they followed the parabola that descended to land almost gently on the former water tank, and... On the former water tank?!?

A rumbling ripped through the silence. The former water tank disintegrated in a fan of silvery flames, gold particles, black smoke. A puppet clutching an M16 spurted upward where it vanished, swallowed by the darkness. Another five crumbled into a thousand pieces which rained down on the adjacent roofs. Eagle covered his eyes and hell exploded along with the cries of the inhabitants then the shout of Bilal who wearing his patched multicolored jacket and pointing his Kalashnikov hurled himself into the conquest of the Tower.

"Ila al Bourji! To the Tower! Ila al Bourji!"

2

"Yahallah! Oh God! Yahallah!"
"Ila al Bourji! To the Tower! Ila al Bourji!"
"Nedsa lokum! What a catastrophe! Nedsa lokum!"
"Ila al Bourji! To the Tower! Ila al Bourji!"
"Mama, ummi, mama! Mother, mommy, mother!"
"Ila al Bourji! To the Tower! Ila al Bourji!"
"Papa, pappi, papa! Father, daddy, father!"
"Ila al Bourji! To the Tower! Ila al Bourji!"
"Saedni, help, saedni!"
"Ila al Bourji! To the Tower! Ila al Bourji!"

They fired from the windows, the terraces, the sidewalks, the trenches: from every hole which existed on the opposite bank of the river. That is, avenue Nasser. Gobeyre seemed like a volcano suddenly awakened to erupt a magma of lava, laterites, lapilli. They fired with Kalashnikovs, with Rpg, with revolvers, with mortars, and meanwhile the two trucks on the border with Shyah spat out the other Katyushas. But the precision of the comet had been fortuitous, the other Katyushas passed over the Tower to fall on the Cité Sportive, so Gassàn could react at his will and most of the crossfire hit Shatila. It tore apart the houses, the shanties, the hovels on the strip parallel to avenue Nasser. Thus many bolted doors flew open, many lowered shutters rose, and like mice fleeing from a burning lair the inhabitants poured outside in search of a nonexistent safety. Entire families who fled dragging suitcases, kitchen utensils, television sets, cages in which roosters shrieked out their madness more loudly than ever: yahallah, yahallah. Old people who panting and wailing plodded along the alleys: nedsalokum, nedsa-lokum. Children who desperately called their lost parents: mama-ummi-mama, papa-pappi-papa... Women who holding their newborns roved at random: saedni-saedni. And on top of their laments, their groans, their invocations, the shout of Bilal who trailing hordes of Amal broke into the Twenty-Two's little square then slipped into the road that led to the Tower. Ila-al-Bourji, ila-al-Bourji. Nobody could have stopped him, tonight. Nobody. He was too possessed, and his men were too many. Elated by his shout, intoxicated by hate, they kept coming in disorderly waves and if one fell dead they stepped on his body as we step on a stone or a leaf. If one fell wounded and called for help they trampled on him as we trample on an obstacle we haven't time to pick up or remove. Gassàn's men confronted them well. Like true professionals. They let them get bottled up in the road, then wiped them out. Yet they weren't able to get Bilal who despite the weight of the cartridges he carried, five magazines in one pocket and five in the other, more than forty pounds of weight altogether, ran up and down like an elf. So the M48's Browning tried to get him by pounding the little square and several volleys fell near the jeep beside which Eagle watched as powerlessly as in the dream that had awakened him at two in the morning. Just as in the dream, in fact, he hadn't an enemy to fight because neither the Amal nor the governmentals were attacking the Italians. Just as in the dream he couldn't break the siege because this would have meant to shoot, to disobey the Condor who had ordered fire-only-if-fired-upon. Just as in the dream he couldn't tell Rambo to shelter his marò because the M113 was full. And just as in the dream he felt so abandoned, so paralyzed, that he couldn't move away from that jeep.

Of course he would have liked to go, to see what happened at the various posts or at least join Hawk at the Twenty-Five, and every now and then he said now-I-will. It was so close, the Twenty-Five... All he needed was to take the lane that from the Twenty-Two led to the Twenty-Five: a short distance, really. Only two hundred yards. But the more he wanted to go, the more he asked his body to move away from the jeep, the more he remained glued to it. The Twenty-Five seemed to him as inaccessible as a remote island, and wringing his fragile wrists he moaned: "San Gennaro, San Gerardo, San Guglielmo, what did I do to deserve this? Abraham, Isaac, Jacob, my mother's prophets and my own, I even recited a Shema Israel this morning. Why are you punishing me?!?" He also wondered what else from the dream would come true, which other dire portents. The crèche with the Infant Jesus who was a grown-up little girl, the cow that was a goat, the ass that was a dog, the manger that was a mattress, Saint Joseph who looked like Saint Joseph, the Virgin Mary who looked like the Virgin Mary, maybe? The gentle smile and the words et-faddàl-colunèl, huna-el-hami-Allah, come-inside-colonel, here-Allah-protects-us? The hovel that collapsed on the crèche and on the marò? Ah, how silly he had been to keep Rambo and his squad at the Twenty-Two! Why had he done it, why?

"Eagle, come in, Eagle! Hawk calling Eagle!"

An overexcited voice filtered through the turmoil, and he grabbed the microphone.

"Eagle here. Go ahead, Hawk."

"Colonel! I've got a couple of problems, colonel! One is that at the Twenty-Five they hit us hard so I ordered the squad to go inside the M113: correct?"

"Correct, Hawk, correct. But where are you?"

"On the southwest corner of the vacant lot, sir! The other problem is..."

"Do you mean outside?"

"Yessir, outside. The other problem is..."

"Hawk, I don't want you outside! You have a bunker there. Get in, by Moses, get in!"

"Impossible, sir. The opening's too narrow! To get in I should leave the jeep, and if I leave the jeep I leave the radio! Anyway, the other problem is..."

"Do without the radio! Use the walkie-talkie!"

"No way, sir, no way! If I use the walkie-talkie, I use the batteries. And I'm out of batteries, sir! Besides I need the radio for the other problem! I mean, to stay in contact with those kids!"

"What kids?"

"The two on the guard tower of the Twenty-Five Alpha, sir! The marò who were supposed to watch the French flag! As I said..."

"What's wrong with them now?"

"They're scared, sir, damn scared! They went nuts! I must drag them out and..."

"Order them to come down."

"I did, sir, I do! But they don't listen! One answers that his aunt was right and one curses that American writer or recites the Salve Regina! They went nuts, I tell you! I must go there and drag them out!"

"Don't even think of it, Hawk."

"But it's bad up there, sir! They might get killed! And they're no use anymore! I must go, I must!"

"I said don't even think of it, Hawk. I want you inside the bunker! Do you read me?"

"Yessir, I read you."

"Then leave the jeep and go. Over."

He switched off the radio feeling a sort of humiliation. By Moses, Hawk was ready to push as far as the Twenty-Five Alpha, and he didn't even have the strength to reach the Twenty-Five. Hawk knew how to solve the problem of the two nuts on the guard tower, and he didn't even know where to shelter those poor guys crouching against the wall. Yet a decision needed to be made: the Katyushas that passed over the Tower to fall on the Cité Sportive had been replaced by short-range rockets that burst near the little square and the M48 at the end of the road had intensified its Browning volleys. As if this weren't enough, two Amal had hoisted a Russian PK46 onto the roof of the gas station. They were shooting like crazy, those cretins. So they drew the fire of the riflemen Gassàn had posted on the various floors of the Tower, and should a bullet hit the fuel tank or the cylinders of compressed gas... He called Rambo.

"We have to put your marò somewhere else, Rambo!"

Rambo nodded.

"I agree, sir. But where?"

"In some house, some shanty! Don't you know a trusty Palestinian around here?"

Rambo started.

"Yessir, I know Leyda's mother and grandfather. You know them too, sir. They're always at the door with their dog or their goat and..."

The noise of an explosion choked his voice giving the details, and Eagle looked at Rambo in relief.

"Leyda? Who's Leyda?"

"The little girl who lives over there." Rambo pointed to the yellow hovel. "But it's a dangerous spot, sir. It's located on the trajectory of the shots directed against the Tower from the south side of Gobeyre and..."

"Better than out in the open, though!"

"Yes and no, sir..."

He wavered for a moment yet made the decision.

"Yes or no, get them there. Quick!"

"Now, sir?"

"Now."

"And you, sir?"

"Rambo, in Naples we say there are three kinds of men: men, dummies, and shits. Perhaps I'm a dummy, but I'm not a shit. Here I must stay and here I shall stay."

"Alone, sir?"

"Yes, alone. Hurry up, Rambo."

Then he informed the Operations Room and remained all alone to savor his deed. He felt almost good, now that he had made the decision: almost ready to cover the two hundred yards of the lane, reach the Twenty-Five, check if Hawk had gone into the bunker, and who knows? Maybe even to join the Twenty-Five Alpha and drag the two nuts down by himself. But something marred his victory. Something that reminded him of the dismay he'd suffered when the Capodimonte cup had fallen to the floor and splashed the appalling stain in the shape of an I. So at a certain moment he moved away from the jeep, went to the yellow hovel, entered, and Holy Moses! It was a stable, a real stable, lit by a gas lamp and warmed by a brazier. On one side of the door, along the wall facing the square, Rambo and his marò sitting on the ground like shepherds who had come to hail the newborn Redeemer. And on the other side, the crèche of his dream: a little girl who slept on a mattress and who in spite of a Khomeini badge hanging upon her chest really seemed an Infant Jesus in the manger, a dog, a goat, an old bearded man with a kaffiah, a young woman dressed in blue who addressed him with a long gentle smile.

"Et faddàl, colunèl. Come in, colonel. Huna el hami Allah. Here Allah protects us."

"She's Leyda's mother, sir," Rambo explained. "And the little girl is Leyda. The old man, her grandfather. Do you recognize them?"

Sure he did. All of a sudden he perfectly remembered the three always staying at the door with the dog and the goat. And this explained many things. But it didn't explain the et-faddàl, colunèl, huna-el-hami-Allah.

"Yes, Rambo..."

"They are more than happy to shelter us, sir. And you were right: better here than outside to catch bullets and fragments!"

"Yes, Rambo..."

"Something wrong, sir?"

"No, Rambo..."

"But you're shivering, sir, you look cold. Warm yourself at the brazier!"

His watch read five-forty, and a strange cloud of white smoke rose from the road of the Tower. Within the strange cloud of white smoke, a passionate voice that exhorted: "Ihkmil! Don't stop! Ihkmil!" Then another one, brimful with fury, that thundered: "B'suraa! Quick! B'suraa!"

* * *

It was Bilal's, the passionate one. And it was Gassàn's, the one brimful with fury. An icy fury, the fury that comes from frustration and impotence. Despite the Katyusha which had disintegrated the former water tank and killed six of his men as well as destroyed two machine guns and a mortar, Gassàn had in fact continued to rule out the possibility that the Amal would conquer the Tower. They're many but they're also hindered by insurmountable disadvantages, he'd been saying to himself. First disadvantage: their assault comes exclusively from the little square. Nor could it come from elsewhere because the other access to this road is located in the middle of Sabra. Second disadvantage: the road is almost an alley, a blind and rectilinear strip which doesn't offer any diversion or escape. Once trapped in it, you have no choice but to retreat or get slaughtered. Third disadvantage: without even using its 105mm cannon, totally superfluous with such a nearby target, the M48 can massacre them with the Browning. The final and definitive disadvantage: both in the rear and on the sides, the Tower is hemmed in by huts or hovels that prevent it from being surrounded. And, from a logical point of view, his reasoning was flawless. From a practical one, instead, it was mistaken because it didn't consider the one advantage that canceled all the disadvantages: Bilal who, weighed down by his Kalashnikov and his forty pounds of cartridges but buoyed by his ardor and irrationality, led the hordes ready to die for him. So, while the corpses of the Amal piled up forming trenches of flesh behind which the others sought cover, a good percentage of Bilal's fire hit the target: in less than half an hour Gassàn had lost twenty-five other men. Seven on the ground floor, fifteen at the windows, three more on the roof where the Katyusha had disintegrated the first six. Along with the twenty-five dead, thirty wounded. A number including three of the four men in the M48: the gunner who'd been hit by an Rdg8 fragment, the pilot who'd taken his place and caught a bullet in the chest, and the radio operator who'd caught another bullet while leaning out to pull the pilot inside. Not by chance, at five-thirty he had been forced to inform the Eighth Brigade's commander that the company needed reinforcement. But the commander had replied that a large-scale attack was about to be launched and that holding the Tower had become ineffectual: "Leave it with the survivors, captain, and shield yourselves with smoke bombs." Hence the strange cloud of white smoke, the passionate voice exhorting ihkmil-don't-stop-ihkmil, and the one thundering b'suraa-quick-b'suraa.

They're an ugly matter, smoke bombs. Anybody familiar with war can confirm it. They're an ugly matter because they neutralize your intelligence, your will, your courage, and make you feel completely defenseless: at the mercy of an incorporeal, intangible, invisible, therefore unbeatable enemy. You cannot see anything when that cloud swallows you up. Disoriented, blinded, you no longer know what is forward and what backward, where the shooting comes from and where you should return it. You no longer have any sense of space and an inch seems a mile. Your comrades, phantoms or shadows against which you bump as against solid yet insubstantial objects. If you extend an arm to grab someone who's near, you don't find him. If you call him, he doesn't answer or seems to answer from afar. Remote, muffled. Moreover, the gas you're breathing is phosphorus and phosphoric chloride. It closes your throat, it burns your lungs, your eyes. A torture. Of course the degree of the torture depends on length and intensity which in their turn depend on the wind direction: at times the direction changes and the wind blows back the cloud on those who inflicted it. But this evening the wind was blowing from north to south, meaning toward the attackers, and without any risk Gassàn had ordered his men to shoot twelve smoke bombs every minute for ten minutes. Both with mortars and rifles. Those shot by rifle lasted one minute and a half, those shot by mortar lasted three minutes and a half, thus the smoke never thinned away. On the contrary, it thickened. And the cloud obtained what the deluge of bullets had not: the Amal didn't advance anymore. They couldn't even shoot, at that point. Swallowed up by the white darkness, disoriented, blinded, suffocated, they could only grope and gesticulate to call each other. "Manzur! Where are you, Manzur?" "Naadir! I can't find you, Naadir!" "Kamaal! Give me your hand, Kamaal!" Bilal, instead, continued to proceed. Step by step, touching the walls of the houses so as not to lose his bearings and always exhorting them with the roar ihkmil-don't-stop-ihkmil, he got closer and closer to the Tower's entrance. Forty yards. Thirty-nine. Thirty-eight. Thirty-seven. Thirty-six. Thirty-five. Thirty-four. Thirty-three. Thirty-two. Thirty-one. Thirty... Protected by the white cloud, meanwhile, Gassàn had evacuated the wounded and begun the retreat. First, the survivors from the roof. Then, those from the fourth floor. Then, those from the other floors. Each time, a group of bloodstained uniforms that shot their last smoke bomb and ran down to the ground floor then out of the building to rush toward the corner and turn it and vanish leaving behind them the thunder b'suraa-quick-b'suraa. He frothed, Gassàn. His icy fury had increased so much that he didn't even check if all the remaining weapons and ammunition were carried away. The two machine guns and the two mortars which had survived the first Katyusha, for instance. The belts of 7.62 rounds and the boxes of 60mm mortar shells. Still less he worried about the M48 which had been abandoned soon after its wounded crew had been taken away. And, along with several 12.7mm belts, there were fifty-four 105mm shells inside it. All the shells the 105mm cannon had not fired. The fact is that he now cared about one thing only: to see the intruder who'd been shouting ihkmil-don't-stop-ihkmil, the enemy who had defeated and humiliated him in less than half an hour. He cared that much because he was determined to kill him.

"Kaofa aktòl, I'll kill him, kaofa aktòl!"

When the last survivor had turned the corner of the road, he thus placed himself near the M48. He loaded the M16 and with his forefinger on the trigger he started waiting for the cloud to dissolve. He didn't wait long, the cloud was already thinning, and suddenly the blurry shape of a boy with a Kalashnikov and a jacket full of multicolored patches loomed in the white wisps. A small boy who approached the Tower's entrance by touching the walls and who hurled a new roar at the shadows behind him: "Lahkni! Follow me, lahkni!" A small boy?!? The forefinger on the trigger grew numb, Gassàn's eyes narrowed to give him a better look and... No, it was not a small boy. It was a man. A dwarf. A minuscule, brittle, extremely ugly dwarf. A dwarf?!? Had it been a minuscule brittle extremely ugly dwarf who had led the assault and defeated him, humiliated him?!? The astonishment froze him because during that half-hour he had constantly thought of his foe as a tall, robust, handsome man: taller than he who was very tall, more robust than he who was very robust, more handsome than he who was very handsome. Frozen he remained there staring at the unexpected creature, and it took several seconds for him to raise the M16 and aim. But meantime Bilal had reached the entrance and he slipped inside it with a double triumphant yell.

"Al Bourji lanna! The Tower is ours!

"Nasru! Victory, nasru!"

It was six o'clock on the dot and the darkness was by now total, when an M48 crammed with Amal frantically waving their Kalashnikovs and Rpg broke from the Tower's road into the little square of the Twenty-Two. Squashing a couple of corpses it passed the M113 and the jeep of Eagle who had left the yellow hovel, burst onto avenue Nasser, headed for the rond-point of Shatila where it turned into a street parallel to rue Farrouk, and entered Gobeyre with its precious plunder: the 105mm cannon, the fifty-four shells. Thus Eagle realized that while he was recovering near the brazier with Rambo, the marò, the Infant Jesus who was a little girl, the cow that was a goat, the ass that was a dog, the Saint Joseph who looked like Saint Joseph, the Virgin Mary who looked like the Virgin Mary, the governmentals had fled. And with a long sigh he called the Operations Room, informed the Condor that Bilal the Sweeper had conquered the Tower.

3

As on the morning of the double slaughter, they all were in the Operations Room: the Condor, as tight as a bow that's about to fling its arrow; the Professor, unusually nervous and unmindful of his miniature Iliad; Crazy Horse, overcome by the frenzy of imitating Des Aix and Collinet; Pistoia, more and more impatient to hurl himself into the eye of the hurricane; Sugar, equally ready to go; Charlie, more crushed than ever by his remorse. Angelo, enclosed in his personal torment yet helping Martino who had been entrusted with intercepting the governmental frequencies and translating the Sixth or Eighth Brigade's radio contacts. Perched on a stool, there was also the three-star general who did nothing but wipe the cold sweat from his neck. And, next to him, the Head Chaplain who stubbornly repeated: "At the cost of popping off I'll say my midnight Mass, at the cost of popping off!" Eagle's call dropped into this atmosphere.

"Condor, attention, Condor! Bilal has taken the Tower!"

They all raised their heads, each of them aware of the dangers it meant. The first, that the victorious Amal of Gobeyre would goad the Amal of Haret Hreik into attacking the Sixth Brigade barracks which were so near the Italian sector. In such a case, the front would stretch along rue de l'Aérodrome and the battle would spread to Bourji el Barajni then to the Eagle base and the Logistics as well as the field hospital and the headquarters. The second, that the governmentals would unleash the offensive always dreamed of and now essential to smash the green snake's ambitions. In such a case, since Gobeyre was a triangle shielded by Haret Hreik on one side and by Shyah on another, yet unprotected on the third side facing avenue Nasser, the attack would come from Shatila. And in order to attack from Shatila the Sixth and the Eighth Brigades needed to dislodge the Italians or at least to neutralize them.

"They might ask us to leave the quarter," Charlie said.

"I know. But I won't leave," the Condor answered.

"Instead of the whole quarter they might ask us to hand over the Twenty-Two, the Twenty-Five, and the Twenty-Four," Pistoia added.

"I know. But I won't hand over a damn thing."

"Or they might position themselves alongside our posts without asking a thing. Which would mean an attack breaking through the Twenty-One and the Twenty-Three," the Professor concluded.

"I know. And this is what I'm most afraid of."

"Quod Deus avertat, may God forbid it!" Crazy Horse whinnied.

God, instead, had already permitted it. Two mortar companies had just left the Sixth Brigade barracks and were positioning themselves in the ditch which extended between the Twenty-Eight and the Twenty-Seven: the marò posts. Although without success, a patrol of their gunners was even trying to install itself inside the Twenty-Seven Owl. You could realize it from the wrathful voices that came by radio from the observation post. The voices of Nazarene and the marò standing beside him.

"I told you to chase them, dammit!"

"I did, I did! Don't you see that I did?!"

"No, you did not! Now they're on the stairway, and soon they'll be back!"

"If they come back we'll throw them out, head-down! And if you don't like violence, I'll do it myself! But who are they? What do they want?"

"Guys from the Sixth Brigade, that's who they are! Taking our post, that's what they want! Violence or not, if they come back I'll shoot!"

Then the voice of Sandokan, clearly just arrived.

"Shut up, bloody dick of a dick superdick! Shut up... Condor, attention, Condor! Sierra Mike One calling Condor One!"

"Go ahead, Sierra Mike One!" the Condor shouted jumping on the transmitter.

"Condor, I came to check my posts and, in the ditch along avenue Chamoun, the one between the Twenty-Seven and the Twenty-Eight, I found the shitheads of the Sixth Brigade! They are dug in with 120 mortars and refuse to leave! What's more, a patrol wants to position itself here in the observatory and if it doesn't scram we'll end up with a fight. Copy?"

"I copy, Sierra Mike One."

"That's not all! While coming here I ran into a column of the Sixth Brigade! Fifteen M113s with Brownings, twelve jeeps with 106mm recoilless guns, ten armored cars! They were moving down Ramlet el Baida and by now they should have reached the Street Without a Name! Copy?"

"I copy, Sierra Mike One."

Then the voice of the radio operator of the Twenty-Eight confirming the last information.

"Condor, attention, Condor! M113s, armored cars, and jeeps on the Street Without a Name! The M113s are halting in front of the Kuwaiti embassy, the armored cars are vomiting troops, the jeeps with the 106s are moving into firing position! It looks like they're pointing at Gobeyre and the Tower. Copy?"

"I copy, Twenty-Eight."

Then Sandokan's voice again.

"Condor, attention, Condor! The mortars in the ditch have just opened fire! They shoot at the Tower and Gobeyre! The Brownings and the recoilless guns also! Lots of shots, lots! It's a mess here, a mess! Do you still hear me?"

No, they no longer heard him. His words had faded away, smothered by the tun-tun-tun of the Brownings, the thunder of the mortars, the crashes of the cannons. But neither the Condor nor the others needed Sandokan's report to know that the large-scale attack announced to Gassàn by his commander, the offensive always dreamed of and now essential to smash the green snake, had begun. Even in the

Operations Room the windowpanes shattered one after the other, and to complete the picture Hawk was calling to give further bad news.

"Attention Condor, attention! Here the bedlam has doubled! It looks like it's coming from Sabra! The Twenty-One just informed me that a dozen M48s with 105 guns have dashed into the Main Street of Sabra and fire like crazy at Gobeyre!"

They were the Eighth Brigade's M48s that the night before Angelo had seen on the avenue Abdallah Aei, and they had dashed into the Main Street of Sabra while the Sixth Brigade's column seen by Sandokan along Ramlet el Baida was reaching the Street Without a Name to vomit troops in front of the Kuwaiti embassy. Bad news because the firepower of the M48's 105mm guns was highly superior to that of the 106mm recoilless guns mounted on the jeeps, and because many shells aimed at Gobeyre fell on the Twenty-Two or the Twenty-Five or the Twenty-Four. Having intercepted an argument over the governmental radio frequencies, Martino confirmed it.

"General, sir, d'you know what they said?!? The gunner said: 'Captain, we'll end up hitting the Italians!' And the captain answered: 'I don't give a damn. Keep going.'"

The same thing with the Amal. Still excited by the fortuitous success of the comet, Rashid was in fact returning fire with the captured tank: a shot against the Eighth Brigade, a shot against the Sixth. But, as devoid of brains as of artillery experience, he wasted the fifty-four shells in the way he had wasted the thirty Katyushas. And rather than falling on Sabra they fell on the Twenty-One, rather than on the column halted in front of the Kuwaiti embassy they fell on the Twenty-Eight or the Twenty-Seven or the Twenty-Seven Owl. As for Bilal, he contributed no less to the cavalry of the various posts. He did so with the mortars and the machine guns Gassàn had left on the roof of the Tower, all the while singing his mysterious hymn.

"Beasnani saudàfeh haza al bourji, beasnani! Beasnani saudàfeh haza al quariatna, beasnani! Beasnani oudamiro ainai wa lisan itha iktarab-bom menni. Beasnani!"

With everybody's help, in sum, the battle was crumbling into a thousand grains of unhappiness. The grains we are about to observe one by one. Starting with Roberto, Sandokan's driver.

4

Seduced by that heaven-sent gift of war which descended upon him like an unexpected Pentecost, at five-forty Sandokan had taken his paraphernalia of weapons (the big revolver, the hand grenades, the ordnance rifle, the Camillus knife stolen from Joe Balducci) and rushed as we know to Shatila. After the wrangle with the mortarmen of the Sixth Brigade he'd reached the open space between the Twenty-Eight and the Twenty-Seven, barking at Roberto Wait-beside-the-jeep-and-don't-move-for-any-reason he'd left him in the middle of it, then he'd gone up to the Twenty-Seven Owl where he'd remained to relish the single war adventure of his pacific existence. "Bloody dick of a dick superdick, here comes a good one! Bang! Here comes a better one! Re-bang! This one is for us, close your eyes, say a Requiem Aeternam! No, it fell on that shanty: bang! Bang! Bang! Bang!" In other words, he had forgotten his driver. And more alone than a dog ignored by God and by men, poor Roberto had really remained without moving beside the jeep.

He'd been there for an hour, by now. And much of that time on his feet because, though the open space was adjacent to the ditch where Rashid and Bilal directed most of their fire, he hadn't realized the danger. The ditch was hidden by a rampart which concealed the explosions, and both the incoming and outgoing shells passed too high over to scare him. Why should I be afraid, he thought, I'm not a governmental soldier or an Amal! I'm a marò who's in Beirut by accident, a nineteen-year-old boy who doesn't bother anybody! And so thinking he looked at the battle as he could have watched a ping-pong match between invisible players who bat big balls of fire rather than tiny plastic ones. Instead of the ping-pong net, the rampart. Only after two explosions on his side had he finally understood that bombs don't ask if you are a governmental soldier or an Amal or a marò who's in Beirut by accident, and full of disconcertment he'd started to pray for Sandokan's return then quit his upright position and squatted alongside the jeep. Taking care not to soil his uniform, though. That is, sitting on his heels. It was his good uniform, for God's sake, the one to wear on Christmas! He'd cleaned it himself with cold-water detergent and pressed it with a steam iron! Procedures that at Sierra Mike they didn't even know about. They were so unprofessional, the guys of the Sierra Mike laundry! They threw the uniforms in hot boilers, they pressed them with a hot iron even if they saw grease or mud stains... They didn't even know that the mud contains corrosive substances and must never be put in hot water or under a hot iron. Never! As for the grease, it must be skimmed off meticulously! Don't ever wash or press an unskimmed garment. Ever! You end up with discoloration! He knew it because he had been raised in the best laundry in San Remo, his parents specialized in dry cleaning, and because he couldn't bear stains. He hated them more than filthy nails, filthy hair, filthy shoes, people who stink of sweat, and... Oh, Jesus, what a torture it was sitting on his heels like this!

While his nice little face got distorted by pain, Roberto wondered if he should risk rising and stretching his numb legs. But for the last few minutes the ping-pong match had lost its symmetry, the outgoing shells continued to top the rampart but the incoming ones smashed into it showering fragments, and in his hurry Sandokan hadn't given him time to take his flak jacket and his helmet. Forget-the-jacket, for-get-the-helmet, I-never-take-them, they-are-no-use. No use? If they were no use, they wouldn't be manufactured and stuck in soldiers' kits, right? Especially the helmets. All soldiers use helmets. Even the Egyptians, the Persians, the ancient Greeks, the ancient Romans, the Vikings, the medieval squires used helmets. So why hadn't he let him take it, holy pin of a pin superpin? Because he was an oaf, that's why. If he weren't an oaf, he wouldn't have gone around with that arsenal of knives, revolvers, hand grenades, and other devices, he wouldn't have enjoyed seeing his munitions dump blown up, and every now and then he'd say the word thanks. Thanks, Roberto, for rushing over when I call you. Thanks for waiting at the wheel when I go for whores. Thanks for vacuuming my carpet. Yes, also for the vacuuming the carpet. Because it was he who took care of that disgusting rainbow of filth. The fact is that officers never say thanks. Instead of saying thanks, they humiliate you, they scold you, they take advantage of the fact that unions and strikes don't exist in the army. All of them. All. No, not all. An officer like Eagle would have given him time to change his uniform and grab his helmet. Nor would he have marooned him in the middle of an open space with shells raining down. He wouldn't have ordered him wait-beside-the-jeep-and-don't-move-for-any-reason. Because yes, this was what Sandokan had said: yes. Then he'd climbed the stairs of the observation post and forgotten him like an umbrella.

"I'm not an umbrella!" he shouted with a sob in his throat.

The shout got lost in the uproar like a spark smothered by a stone, and his disconcertment became an ocean of consternation. What to do? Whether right or wrong, he couldn't abandon the jeep, join the Twenty-Seven Owl, and ask Sandokan why he had left him all alone like an umbrella. He couldn't even go to the M113 of the Twenty-Seven. And he was so tired. His knees ached, his calves ached, his back ached, everything ached, and he dreamed of lying down as he'd never dreamed of anything in his life. On the ground, for instance. On the ground?!? He would get his uniform filthy with mud and grease, on the ground! One moment. There was a piece of cardboard fifteen yards away. Large, long, clean. If he reached it, dragged it here and arranged it next to the jeep, he could lie down without soiling his uniform! He rose. He wobbled for an instant, regained his balance, ran toward the cardboard, and after what seemed to him an infinity he reached it. He grabbed it, dragged it to the jeep, arranged it next to the right side, lay down on it. But in doing so he grazed his pants against a mud-spattered wheel. Full of worry he twisted to examine the damage, in the movement a sleeve caught on the door latch, it tore, and his consternation turned to desperation. Bursting into tears he leaped to his feet, and didn't see the grenade which was falling in the middle of the open space. A 60mm mortar grenade. A grenade of Bilal. Yet he heard the crash, he felt the hail of soil and fragments that rained all around, then a blow on his skull, then a needle that pierced his left eye, and panting in fright he let himself slip to the ground.

"Oh, Jesus, I'm dead. They've killed me. I'm dead."

He repeated these words many times, convinced he was dead and meanwhile surprised to discover that dead people speak as if they were alive. It took him several minutes to acknowledge that he was alive and also very lucky because if the grenade had fallen while he was grabbing the cardboard he now really would be dead. But at this point he touched his head, found a bump full of gelatinous stuff, realized that it was blood, real blood dripping down a temple to fill his unhurt eye, and the fright resurfaced. For Christsake, he wasn't dead but he might die of blood loss, if he didn't get immediate help... Once he'd read that the human body contains five or six quarts of blood: would those five or six quarts of dripping blood last long enough? Sandokan had to be informed! The field hospital had to bring plasma! Yet how could he call in this uproar that stifled his voice like a stone smothers a spark? How could he move with his legs that hadn't even the strength to carry him to the Twenty-Seven Owl stairway? Maybe by radio... Yes, by radio! There was a radio in the jeep, tuned to the Sierra Mike frequency. All he had to do was pluck up some courage and climb into the jeep, inform the base! He plucked up some courage, crawling on all fours reached the back of the jeep. Propping himself on his elbows and knees he climbed up, scrambled inside, slithered to the radio, located the microphone. Sighing with relief he stretched out an arm, clutched it. But, instead of twiddling the knob that turned it on, he twiddled a dial that changed the tuning. He lost the Sierra Mike frequency. Oh, Jesus! And now?!? There were dozens of frequencies, dozens! Finding Sierra

Mike's again would be like searching for a needle in a haystack! He tried all the same. He tried and tried, and finally a fidgety dialogue filtered through the nasty crackling.

"Eagle, attention, Eagle! Condor One here! I want to know what is happening with the two marò at the Twenty-Five Alpha!"

"They're still on the guard tower, general, sir!"

"Still there?!? But they're useless there, God blasted! They risk being snuffed out for nothing! Why aren't they inside an M113?!?"

"Because by radio Hawk hasn't been able to persuade them, to make them come down, sir!"

"If he couldn't by radio, tell him to go there and get them, dammit!"

"Impossible, sir! The Twenty-Five is under heavy fire!"

"Then go there yourself, dammit!"

"But here it's worse than at the Twenty-Five, sir!"

"That's your fucking business!"

"But general... sir..."

"I said it's your fucking business, over!"

Then, after a few seconds, a kinder voice.

"Eagle, attention, Eagle! Condor Zed here! The general has reconsidered the matter of the Twenty-Five Alpha and decided to send some of us!"

He choked down a sob. See? Everybody knew about those two on the guard tower! Even the general worried about them. But nobody knew about him, nobody worried about him. Not to mention that those two at the Twenty-Five Alpha didn't risk dying of blood loss or going blind, and he did. Those two were together, they could console each other, and he could not. He was alone, alone! And it is so ugly to be alone when everybody is with somebody! He cleared his throat, he started again twiddling the dial, and picked up the Ruby base frequency where God knows who was yelling at God knows whom.

"They're shooting at us, too, for Christsake!"

Then the Eagle base frequency where the operator was scolding a certain Natale.

"Don't you dare, Natale, don't you dare! D'you read me?!?"

Then the Logistics frequency where another operator was angry because the Head Chaplain had set himself up in the garage and insisted on celebrating his midnight Mass there.

"There's no way to get rid of him! He bawls that he'll say it at the cost of popping off!"

Then, among other nasty cracklings, the kinder voice calling Sierra Mike.

"Sierra Mike, Condor Zed here! The general wants to know what's going on at the Twenty-Seven and the Twenty-Eight!"

Twenty-Seven?!? Twenty-Eight?!? Sierra Mike?!? A miracle, Jesus, a miracle! He'd found Sierra Mike's frequency again. He could get in! He put his mouth on the microphone.

"Sierra Mike, do you read me? This is Roberto, Sandokan's driver! I'm wounded in the head! I'm blind in one eye! Sierra Mike, Sierra Mike, do you hear me?!?"

No, they didn't. They kept talking among themselves as though he didn't exist.

"Condor Zed, only the two marò of Camp Three are still outside: all the others are inside the M113s!"

All the others?!? He rebelled.

"No, Sierra Mike, not all! I'm outside! All alone! And wounded in the head, blind in one eye! Come get me, please! Come!"

But the only answer he got was the word "over" followed by the sound which closes the circuit: click! Then his despair became so boundless that it happened as it used to happen when as a child he woke up during the night to find himself alone in the dark: at finding himself alone in the dark he felt such an irresistible need to piddle that he couldn't hold it, he couldn't even call his mother or rush to the bathroom, and the pee flooded the bed. Yes, he was overcome by the urge to urinate. An urge so violent, so invincible, that he didn't have the time to open his pants and pissed all over himself. He, who was a model of good behavior, a champion of cleanliness, soaked himself like a sponge. And filthy as he had never been, stinking, he slid out of the jeep to wallow in the mud. Without giving a damn for the uniform he'd washed and pressed with such care. He didn't even care about being filthy and stinking and half-blind, about losing his five or six quarts of blood, at this point. Resigned to die, he only thought of his parents who crying Roberto-Roberto would receive the coffin with his body and bury it in the cemetery of San Remo. And yet, through that resignation, a kind of disbelief emerged. A kind of outraged astonishment. Did he, did his parents deserve this? Mother was only thirty-eight, holy pin of a pin superpin! Father, only thirty-nine. And outside of the laundry shop they had received so little from life. To avoid aborting him they'd married when she was nineteen and he twenty, they'd given birth to his sister twelve months later, thus squandered their youth for the sake of their children. Only recently had they started granting themselves a few dinners at the restaurant, a few vacations in the mountains, a stall at the San Remo Song Festival they used to watch on TV. Burying him in the cemetery of San Remo would age them before their time, and goodbye to dinners at the restaurant. Goodbye vacations in the mountains, goodbye stall and Song Festival, goodbye life. He then began to pray: "Jesus, if it's true that you're against abortion, remember that they didn't abort me. Be nice to them. Be nice to me, too. Don't let me die of blood loss and go blind. I don't deserve it. I'm a good guy, you know it. I'm the kind who doesn't drink or gamble and saves money instead of wasting it on foolish stuff: in fact the naughty ones call me stingy. Niggard, stingy! I'm a good citizen who knows how to stand in line at the bus stop and in the shops, a person who never says ugly words except for some Christsake or holy-pin-of-a-pin-superpin which is much less than what Sandokan says. I believe in you and in Mary Virgin. On Sunday I always go to Mass and, when I can, I take Holy Communion. I never go for whores. I never talk to Sheila, I never look at Fatima. In Italy I have a girlfriend, yes, but I don't touch her. Not even with a condom. And you know how hard that is. At school I've always studied to the best of my ability. In the laundry I always worked hard, getting up at five in the morning to turn on the machines. The only fault you can lay on me is having failed algebra. The only sin, having pierced my right ear to wear an earring à-la-James-Dean. I wasn't informed that faggots wear it in the right ear... However I took algebra over, and I stopped wearing the earring. Look: I don't have it anymore. The hole is closing up. True, in Beirut I smoke hashish. Everybody does, so once in a while I do too. And, to be honest, right now I would like a joint very much. But if it bothers you, I'll stop. Forever, I promise. As long as Sandokan remembers I'm here. As long as you realize that nobody suffers the way I do."

Those who suffer always believe they are the only ones who suffer, or that they suffer more than the others. So it wouldn't have done any good to explain to him that in different ways or for different reasons the other grains of unhappiness were suffering as much as he was, that not far away somebody was suffering twice as much. Somebody inside the M113 of the Twenty-Eight, therefore not far from Fabio and Matteo who would soon confront him.

*   *   *

The M113 of the Twenty-Eight stood at the end of the rampart which enclosed the ditch, on the edge of a little hillock overlooking the

Kuwaiti embassy's rond-point. In that stretch of Shatila, the spot most exposed to the fire coming from Gobeyre. Camp Three, on the contrary, stood at the street level. Which means, protected on the right and in the rear by the slope of the hillock. On the left, by Jasmine's shelter. So, rather than taking shelter in the M113, Fabio and Matteo had asked Hawk if they could remain at Camp Three. Hawk had answered yes, and squatting behind the low wall they now nursed their fear. They had plenty. They had so much that for the past hour they didn't even remember the existence of Jasmine, Mirella, Rosaria, Dalilah, and their only concern was to hide it. A most difficult task that Matteo tried to accomplish through his usual loquacity: Holy-cow, these-animals-don't-even-respect-Christmas-Eve, Palermo's-animals-do, have-you-ever-heard-of-a-Badalamenti-killing-a-Caruso-or-of-a-Caruso-killing-a-Badalamenti-on-Christmas-Eve, and so on. Fabio, instead, was singing as loud as he could his personal version of a popular song's refrain that started: Hello, Mister-Cairo, how-do-you-do. He'd substituted the words Mister-Coraggio for Mister-Cairo, then improvised a sequel of nonsense that rhymed with the sound of how-do-you-do, and now he shouted himself so hoarse that they could hear him at the Twenty-Seven Owl where they did not hear Roberto.

"Hello, Mister Coraggio, how do you do... Hallò, Mister Coraggio, you're in trouble too... Hello, Mister Coraggio, this is a real boo-boo... Hello, Mister Coraggio, you better stop to coo..."

But suddenly an inhuman howl, a supplication in a language which had nothing to do with Italian, came from the M113 of the Twenty-Eight.

"Aiutu, matri matruzza, aiutuuu! Iò nun à vuougghiu fari 'a motti ru surici! Iò nu vuougghiu mòrere cu vuautri inti! Help, mama, mommy, help! I don't want to die like a mouse! I don't want to die with you nasty people!"

And the silly refrain, as well as the nervous monologue, stopped.

"Who's that?" Fabio asked.

"The Sicilian who arrived twenty days ago," Matteo answered.

"The one who's out of his mind and they keep in the kitchens?"

"Yeah. Calogero the Fisherman."

5

They called him Calogero the Fisherman because he introduced himself by declaring I'm-Calogero-the-Fisherman, and they kept him in the kitchens because if they placed him in a guard post he escaped.

Iò-'cca-nun-ci-stajo, mi-scanto. Here-I-don't-want-to-stay, I'm-afraid. They said he was out of his mind because in the twenty days he'd escaped five times, each time running toward the sea in search of a boat to return home. He was eighteen and a half, he had a squat and clumsy body, a childish face burnt by the sun, and gentle black eyes perpetually opened in dismayed astonishment. He came from an islet in the Egadi Islands named Formìca, meaning Ant and as small as one. In fact its population didn't reach eighty people and this number included the priest, the schoolteacher, the druggist, and two carabinieri sent to enforce the law. There he'd come into the world, the only boy after four girls, and in his eighteen and a half years he'd done nothing but fish: the work that he loved and had learned from his father, a savage who'd dodged the draft by harpooning one of his feet and becoming crippled. He knew all, really all, about anchovies and sardines, mullet and bass, lobsters and octopus, shrimp and squid, crabs and clams. Nothing, absolutely nothing, about the creatures who don't live in the water. Aside from his parents, his four sisters, his grandmother, the wild rabbits and the hens behind the house, the only terrestrial animal he was familiar with was the dog inherited from his grandfather who had died during a tunny-fish slaughter, by mistake killing himself instead of the tuna. He wrote with enormous difficulty, making monstrous spelling mistakes, he spoke a mysterious language which was Sicilian and which Sicilians themselves decoded badly. At seven, in fact, he had stopped going to school where he felt unhappy, and before the draft notice he had never left Formìca. Not even to go to nearby Trapani which every Monday was reachable by the postal schooner. As a consequence, he'd never seen a city or a railroad or a highway or an airport: airplanes were for him gigantic birds that flew in a straight line and left behind strips of smoke. Trains and cars, bizarre vehicles about which he knew as little as about war: something he had scarcely seen on TV. Echoes of the world reached Formìca through the TV, yes, but he watched it seldom because that inexplicable box spoke Italian like the priest and the schoolteacher and he got tired trying to understand what it was talking about. Yet that islet had always been for him Paradise, and he'd never desired to leave it. What more do you want from God when you have a boat to fish with, a hold to pile the fish in, a house to shelter yourself from the rain and the cold, a church to hear Mass, a bar to buy an ice cream on Sundays, then a father and mother and four sisters and a grandmother and a dog who love you? But one terrible day in July the card his father always spoke about had arrived. A card informing him that he had to proceed immediately to Brindisi, show up at the marò barracks, and become a soldier.

Matri matruzza, what a sorrow! Night after night he'd wept over that sorrow. One morning he'd almost harpooned himself in the foot like his father. Only when his father had begun to cry don't-do-it, you'd-regret-it, I-did, better-to-be-a-soldier-than-a-cripple, had he decided to obey the summons. He'd filled his suitcase with bread and jars of tuna in oil, said goodbye to his boat, to his parents, his sisters, his grandmother, his dog, and taken the postal schooner to disembark at Trapani. That is, to see a city for the first time. Matri matruzza, what a city! Seventy thousand inhabitants, they said. And docks, smokestacks, palaces, cathedrals, stores, lights lit even during the day, streets... In the streets, a scary din of cars and bicycles and trucks and buses, a multitude of people who walked as if they were late, but nobody to show him where the train station was. Take avenue So-and-So, they answered, turn left and go straight for two traffic lights then turn right and go for another five lights. And if you don't know which is avenue So-and-So, if you don't understand the traffic lights? Now they're red, now green, now yellow: why? It had taken him a hundred years to find the station. Just as many to find that incredibly long train. A train? Many trains! One attached to the other and with the words First Class, Second Class, etcetera. He hadn't been able to enter the first class. Yours-is-a-second-class-ticket, you-cannot-stay-here. What a pity. Because there were less people in the first class. In the second there were so many. And they squeezed you, they stomped on you, they pushed you. They even stole the place you'd chosen. "Taken, taken!" Anyway, he had found a seat. In the smoking compartment, unfortunately: what a stink! And the train had left. From Trapani to Alcamo, from Alcamo to Palermo, from Palermo to Cefalù, from Cefalù to Messina, slamming everything and everybody. Pum-pum, pum-pum, pum-pum. With those people who smoked and talked and ate, ate. Oranges, bananas, tangerines, chocolates. Not him. All he ate was a little tuna with bread.

Ugly, the train. Real ugly. The only good thing about the train was the window: the countryside that flew away in gusts of coolness. And the fact that at Messina they had put it onto a ship. Yes, a ship! With the people! And the ship hadn't sunk! On the contrary, it had plowed across the strait and carried them to Reggio Calabria: on the continent. Extraordinary. So extraordinary that in his emotion he'd devoured an entire jar of tuna. At Reggio Calabria, however, they'd taken another train. One that skirted the sole of the boot then the heel of the boot, up and down. Because it's true that Italy is shaped like a boot: the train followed the contour of the boot as if instead of a train it was a pencil. After Reggio Calabria, Catanzaro. After Catanzaro, Crotone. After Crotone, Corigliano. After Corigliano, Taranto. After Taranto, Lecce... Thank God for the window. He always looked out the window because now it was the sea that flew away in gusts of coolness. And because the other travelers quarreled with each other. They quarreled so much and so loud that he could almost understand what they said in Italian. A gentleman with a Communist Party badge said that this railroad was a joke, an insult to southerners, that the government was a den of thieves, that those thieves had to be closed in a place called Siberia. Another one with a Christian Democrat badge said that all the communists should move to Russia where the citizens travel in cattle cars and police arrest them. A third one with a rather young face and shoes of very soft leather, rich people's shoes, mistreated them both using words never heard in Formìca and to the gentleman who wore the Christian Democrat badge he said: shut up, you lackey of the imperialist multinational state that serves the Americans. You'll end up as you deserve: with a bullet-riddled chest in the trunk of a car. To the gentleman who wore the Communist Party badge he said: don't open your mouth, you false comrade and traitor to the working classes. With your guilty silences you made yourself an accomplice of the system, and you'll end up the same way: the working classes forgive nobody. As a result, they almost came to blows and it took seven stops before they agreed on something. Meaning the fact that the train didn't go fast enough. In his opinion, instead, it did. Even too fast. He would have paid money for it to slow down and make him arrive at Brindisi the lastest possible.

He'd arrived at Brindisi on Wednesday afternoon: after two days, two nights, and six hours of travel, matri matruzza. Dying of exhaustion and with his stomach in turmoil because he'd eaten all the jars of tuna, he had crossed the city which was as big as Trapani and reached a seaside fortress. That is, the place the card indicated. He'd said goodevening, I'm-Calogero-the-Fisherman, and as an answer they had cut off his hair. He'd become bald. Then they had given him a uniform that pinched him everywhere, a pair of boots that crushed his feet, and for months he'd lived as in a bad dream. Shouts, reproofs, strange commands. "Forward, march! Right, march! Left, march! About-face, present arms!" Not to mention the exercises, the drills, the rifle that leaped out of your arms like a fish as soon as you touched the trigger and smacked you in the face breaking your teeth. And the cruel bunkmates. The cruel officers. Their insults. "Barbarian! Caveman!

Troglodyte! Where do you come from, the Jurassic Period?" Finally, the desperation when a Sicilian had said to another Sicilian: "They're sending us to Lebanon." Because instead of Lebanon he had understood Milano, which in Sicilian is pronounced like Lebanon, and lost his head. "No, I don't want to go to Milano! Milano has no sea!" For weeks and weeks he had continued to believe that Lebanon was in Milano. Only at the departure, seeing the ship, had a doubt arisen. And a very soothing conversation had taken place between him and the two other Sicilians. "Why are we going on a ship? Milano has no sea: people don't go to Milano by ship." "We're not going to Milan, Calogero." "No? Where are we going, then?" "To Beirut, Calogero." "Beirut?!? What is Beirut?" "The capital of Lebanon, Calogero." "Then Lebanon is not in Milano?" "No, Calogero, Lebanon is not in Milan." "Is Lebanon on the sea?" "Yes, Calogero, Lebanon is on the sea." "Then Beirut has the sea?" "Yes, Calogero. A lot of sea."

This had been a joy. Because for sure Beirut would not be Formìca. It wouldn't have its limpid pure waters, its beaches of clean white sand, its phosphorescent cliffs. Fish wouldn't dart alongside the beaches and reefs in flashes of red and yellow, cobalt and silver. Gardens of coral and sponge would not blossom in its sounding depths, nor seaweeds that waver as if caressed by the wind. His father, his mother, his four sisters, his grandmother, his dog would not be there. But there he would live in peace: as long as it doesn't have barracks and fortresses, a city on the sea is always a promise. And under this illusion he'd embarked, voyaged. Hours and hours in the forecastle, staring at the horizon and anxiously waiting for Beirut's contour. The final night he hadn't been able to sleep, and when the dawn had outlined the promised city, he had let out a cry of happiness. "Beirut! Beirut!" But then the ship had approached the coast, plowed through waters dirty with paper, syringes, dead rats, garbage of every kind, they'd disembarked onto a pier full of rubble, and matri matruzza! This wasn't a sea-city! It was a war-city! The war you see on television, with smashed houses and dead people! So, as soon as he'd arrived at the base, he'd run toward the beach to look for a boat to go back to Formìca. They'd caught him, and he'd escaped again. They'd stuck him in a guard post and he'd fled the guard post. They'd relegated him to a roof terrace and he'd fled the roof terrace. They'd closed him in the infirmary and he'd fled the infirmary. They'd shut him up in the kitchens to clean the fish, and there he'd remained. Fish! Yesterday, however, the marò who stood guard at the corner of avenue Chamoun and the Street Without a Name had been hospitalized for diarrhea and, given the personnel shortage, the

Twenty-Eight's squad leader had said: "Let's replace him with Calogero. He shouldn't give us problems, there. It's an easy post." And...

Matri matruzza, what a mishap! First of all, because of the rifle he had to hold in his hands and the helmet he had to keep on his head. Then, because of the mud that sucked him in to the ankles and prevented him from escaping. Then, because of the storm smell he'd scented in the morning and which increased minute by minute. They have an unpleasant smell, upcoming storms. A stench of rotten debris that returns to the surface. Scenting it, you feel as you do when you're fishing on the open sea and the southwest wind rises, the sea swells to warn you, so you haul in the nets and begin rowing toward the land, but the more you row the more the tide carries you back: out to the open sea. In fact he'd called the squad leader and said: "Sta arrivannu 'na tempestazza. There's an ugly storm on the way." Too bad the squad leader had not taken him seriously. "Shut up, caveman." The same at sunset, when a comet-shaped thunderbolt had furrowed the sky and he'd shouted: "U furmene! U furmene da tempestazza! Lightning! Storm lightning!" "Shut up, you troglodyte!" It was a real thunderbolt, instead. In fact it had struck the top of the Tower and immmediately after the ugly storm had started. Thunderbolts, thunderclaps, lightning, rumbling, and the order to get inside the M113. What fear, inside the M113. Each time a flash came from the sky, it rocked and rolled like a boat tossed by a seaquake. And at the bottom of the boat, him: squeezed and crushed like a sardine in a basket of sardines, asphyxiated by the farts of those who farted out of dread. Oh, how they farted! A stink to make you die. Yet, as soon as you said I-want-to-piss, they began cursing Garibaldi who had disembarked near the Egadi Islands to foster Italian unity. "To hell with that meddler who stuck us with you barbarians of the South!" they yelled. "Because of you and Garibaldi we became a country that doesn't count for anything anymore!" They also yelled that the South and Sicily in particular should have been sold to Libya in exchange for petroleum, that after having sold it to Libya the North should have built a wall like the Great Wall of China, that in order to visit Italy the caveman from Formìca should have to show a passport with a visa valid for a half-day only... Then they turned to him and: "Understand?!? Woe to you if you dare to piss a single drop." Anyway, the worst torment was not that. It was the fear of dying like a mouse inside the M113. Because we all end up dying, agreed: when you cast a net, every kind of fish gets caught in it. Old fish, young fish, newborn fish. Still, one thing is to die in your boat where you can piss as you like and where the wind carries away the farts, and one thing is to die like a sardine in a basket of sardines who stink and curse Garibaldi. Not to mention the wickedness of demanding a visa to enter Italy, or the cruelty of selling you to Libya in exchange for petroleum. No, he didn't want to die with them. He wanted to go back to Formìca, to its limpid pure waters, its beaches of clean white sand, its phosphorescent cliffs, its coral reefs, its sponges, and his parents, his sisters, his grandmother, his dog... So at a certain point he had flung himself at the hatch to escape, the others had blocked him, and because of this he now howled that inhuman howl.

"Aiutu, matri matruzza! Iò nun à vuougghiu fari 'a motti ru surici! Iò nu vuougghiu mòrere cu vuautri inti! Help, mama, mommy! I don't want to die like a mouse! I don't want to die with you nasty people!"

Then the hatch flew open. And a dumpy figure, a shadow without a helmet or rifle, leaped out of the M113. Uselessly pursued by the bawls of the squad leader who shouted where-are-you-going-you-troglodyte-you-caveman, Calogero reached the edge of the hillock and hurled himself down the slope that ended at Camp Three. He did it with the movement of a diver who jumps off the springboard: trunk rigid, legs straight, arms held out. And with the nimbleness of a diver he plunged headfirst into the mud-drenched ground, he sank into it. Then he resurfaced to tumble down at the feet of Fabio and Matteo: a mask of slimy muck within which two eyes glittered more than flames in the darkness.

"I'm Calogero the Fisherman and I want to pass."

"To go where, Calogero?" replied Matteo resting his rifle on the sandbags and grabbing his wrists.

"Home. I want to go home. Let me go."

"You cannot, Calogero. Get back to your squad."

"No. I don't want to die like a mouse and with people who don't let me piss, who fart, who ask for a visa, who want to sell me to Libya, and who curse Garibaldi. Let me go!"

"If they fart and they want to sell you to Libya and they curse Garibaldi, stay with us, Calogero. We're paesani, countrymen, see? We speak your language. We're Sicilians too. I'm from Palermo and he's from Brindisi. Didn't you know that?"

"I didn't know and I don't want to know. I don't like Brindisi, I don't like Palermo. I like Formìca and I want to go there. Let me pass."

"No, Calogero. Either you stay in the M113 with them or you stay here with us," repeated Matteo shooting a meaningful glance at Fabio who quickly placed himself behind Calogero and immobilized him.

"Good, Calogero, good. We love Garibaldi. And we love you."
Then, raising his voice to those in the M113: "Close the hatch, we got
him!"

Amid exclamations of relief and yells of bravo-thanks-bravo, the
hatch slammed shut. The matter seemed settled. But Calogero didn't
care to know that those two were Sicilians. He didn't believe in their
declarations of love. The bitter experiences he'd undergone in the last
months had taught him that people say I-love-you to swindle you better, and with the wriggle of a harpooned tuna he slithered out of his
jailers' hands. He struck Matteo with a tremendous punch on the jaw
that sent him straight to the ground, he knocked out Fabio with an
identical punch on the chin, then he stepped over their bodies: quietly.
He quietly pissed against the sandbag wall, quietly left the post, turned
on the Street Without a Name, entered into the pandemonium of the
Brownings and the 106s that fired at Gobeyre, went beyond it, continued in the direction of Ramlet el Baida. And, had you been on his way,
you would have seen something that even in war (that is, a place where
everything can be seen and nothing surprises) we seldom see: a little
soldier who disarmed and covered with slimy muck quietly walked away
from the battle, and quietly explained to himself the whys. "Thunderbolts, thunderclaps, lightning, rumbling, stink of farts. I don't understand. I really don't. 'Cause I'm only eighteen, I'm a kid, and I don't
want to die at eighteen in Beirut. I want to live, to fish, and to die old.
In Formìca. Fishing. You people think of yourselves, settle it amongst
yourselves. Stay there, stay with the wicked ones who want to sell me to
Libya. Wicked, yes, wicked. The northerners are wicked. The southerners, too. The southerners like those liars who say to me we-love-you,
we're-paesani, we-love-you, and then harpoon me like a tuna. What do
I have to do with them, with you? I told you, I don't like Milano. I
don't want to go to Milano. But you answered: it is not Milano, it is
Beirut, a city with the sea. And not a word about the thunderbolts, the
thunderclaps, the lightning, the rumbling, the farts. You made me
come and you closed me inside that basketful of sardines that fart, to
die like a mouse with the enemies of Garibaldi. No, I don't understand.
I don't. So I go to the shore and I steal a boat. A boat to return to
Formìca..."

And meantime the others called him.

"Calogero-o-o! Where are you, Calogero?!?"

"Calogero! Answer, you barbarian, you caveman, you troglodyte!
Calogero!"

"Calogero! Goddam you and Garibaldi who mixed the South with the North, Calogero!"

"Calogero, come back, Calogero!"

They called him for a long time. They also looked for him everywhere. Behind the rubble, in Jasmine's shelter, on the Street Without a Name, on Avenue Chamoun, among the vehicles of the Sixth Brigade, inside the Kuwaiti embassy. But at that point Calogero was far away. Muttering his soliloquy he had reached the littoral of Ramlet el Baida and already roved on the shore, in search of his boat.

This was happening as at the Twenty-Seven Sandokan groped in the difficult waters of another sea. The one named Crisis of Conscience.

*　*　*

They are like coughing fits, the crises of conscience: they come when you least expect them. (Assuming, of course, that you have a conscience.) And surely Sandokan didn't expect his when he had abandoned Roberto to go up to the Twenty-Seven Owl and relish the single war adventure of his pacific existence. Each of those explosions gave him such a longed-for shiver. John Wayne who in command of the battleship *West Virginia* bombards the Philippines and prepares the ground for MacArthur... Henry Fonda who aboard the submarine *Seahorse* chases Admiral Yamamoto and torpedoes him... Robert Mitchum who lands in Normandy and secures a solid beachhead at Omaha... Vietnam, Afghanistan, the dream of going to Saigon or to Kabul and beg please-take-me-please, I'm-a-professional, I-know-how-to-lead-an-assault, how-to-cut-a-throat... During the M48 shelling, however, something had hit the sandbags of the Twenty-Seven Owl with an unusual sound. Not the harsh sound of a fragment but the dull one of a soft object. Whump! Pushed by curiosity he had laid the nightscopes down, had run outside to see, and guess what it was: a small hand cut off at the wrist. A woman's hand with ringed fingers and red lacquered nails. Then the coughing fit had come, questions and answers and doubts he'd never believed he would face had awakened the good man hidden behind the scowl of the pirate happy to appear as such. Where did it come from, that woman's hand with ringed fingers and red lacquered nails? Whom did it belong to? Bloody dick of a dick superdick, he had never thought that war could be also this: a woman's hand with ringed fingers and red lacquered nails. Was his father right to hate weapons and uniforms, to say that pacifism is a moral imperative and a code of civilization? Was he wrong to love war, respect it, invoke it, tell himself that it is the-sap-of-life, that it runs in man's veins with his blood, that every living being makes it, every element of nature? No, bloody dick of a dick superdick, no: he was not! A dog who tears to pieces another dog commits an act of war, a bird who kills another bird commits an act of war, a fish who swallows another fish commits an act of war. The same with an insect who devours another insect, a tree that stifles another tree, a gas that expands or an acid that burns. Everything we do to live, to survive, to exist, is an act of war. Thus he was not mistaken... Or was he? Yes, he was. Because a man is not an acid or a gas. A man is not a tree, an insect, a fish, a bird, a dog! He's a person who reasons knowing that he reasons, who creates knowing that he creates, who destroys knowing that he destroys, who kills knowing that he kills. He's a mind capable of finding solutions different from those nature offers and... And whatever he was, this battle was beginning to turn his stomach.

Yes, with these thoughts (maybe a little different in their form but identical in their substance) Sandokan now looked at the unexpected Pentecost which had made him forget Roberto and ignore Calogero. Meanwhile the governmentals kept hammering the Tower and were about to subdue Bilal who resisted, singing.

CHAPTER TWO

1

BILAL RESISTED, singing. From the Main Street of Sabra the M48s' guns spat out ten shells a minute, from the ditch parallel to avenue Chamoun the 120mm mortars spat out twice that many, in front of the Kuwaiti embassy the M113s' Brownings machine-gunned with such intensity that their barrels were scorching. But Bilal resisted, singing. His militia in Gobeyre returned the fire more and more untidily, the obtuse Rashid had wasted all fifty-four grenades captured with the tank and didn't even worry about sending him reinforcements. But Bilal resisted, singing. On every side of the Tower now pierced like a strainer enormous gashes opened, from the ground floor to the fourth floor the stairways were half-crumbled, most of the Amal who had conquered the building lay dead or dying, on the half-destroyed roof only five exhausted men remained. But Bilal resisted, singing. A victorious concert of brass bands and bugles and drums, the tuneless voice that resounded amidst the explosions and the crashes. A chorus of glory, the strophes of the hymn in which he had replaced the word "home" with the word "tower" and which he had repeated since six o'clock. Stubbornly, obsessively, tirelessly.

"Beasnani saudàfeh haza al bourji, beasnani! Beasnani saudàfeh haza al quariatna, beasnani! With my teeth I will defend this tower, with my teeth. With my teeth I will defend this quarter, with my teeth! Beasnani oudamiro ainai wa lisan itha iktarabbom menni. Beasnani! With my teeth I will rip out your eyes and your tongue if you come close, with my teeth!"

Only once had he interrupted it: when his eyes had turned in the direction of the alley leading to the shanty where back in November he'd received Charlie. Yahallah, yahallah! There were his eight children in that shanty, there was his old father, there was Zeinab with her enormous belly that carried the ninth... A plague, his children. They did nothing but argue and whine. But they were his children and he loved them. A burden, his father. He did nothing but groan and cough. But he was his father and he loved him. As for Zeinab... She was a grumbler, Zeinab. All she did was scold him and yammer that politics was stuff for the rich, not the street sweepers, that human beings are ungrateful and spit in the face of those who give: "It's foolish to make sacrifices for the people, Bilal. It's foolish to give away things and even our own life for our so-called fellow men. People take, take, take, and the more they take the more they spit in your face!" But she was Zeinab, and he liked her so much that he never cudgeled her. He valued her so much that he never betrayed her. Not even with the prostitute in the Old City, the one who said Bilal-if-you-sweep-my-sidewalk-well-you-can-have-it-for-nothing. Ah, how he liked Zeinab! So fat, so juicy, so tall, twice his height, and always ready to welcome him into the well of her depths. Ah, how he enjoyed clambering up her immense body, diving into that well, drowning and discharging all the day's desires... Afterwards he felt more sated than a wolf who has devoured an entire ox. Moreover, she had such a good heart! Despite the scoldings, she covered him with so many kindnesses! If a patch on his jacket tore loose, she mended it with the same color thread. If rummaging through the trash he picked up a louse, she fished it out and crushed it with her fingernails. If somebody mocked him for his stature, she consoled him. "Men aren't measured by the yard, Bilal! What a man must have, you have. And big. You're like a pine tree that spits forth pinecones. And with the pinecones, seeds. Seeds and seeds and seeds." As if that were not enough, yesterday she had glued together the loose pages of the half-book he had found in the trash and stuck them in a green cover with the title "Kitàb." Book. Then she had gone to the butcher and stolen a ram's head she wanted to cook for him tonight. "Please, Bilal, don't be late tonight! I'm cooking the ram's head!" No, he was not ready to give up Zeinab. Nor was he ready to give up his father, his eight children, life. He wanted to live. And exasperated, discouraged by nostalgia, he had been on the point of raising the white flag: surrendering, retreating. But soon a 120mm shell had fallen on the roof. A shell from the Sixth Brigade's Shiite mortarmen who fired from the ditch parallel to avenue Chamoun. Its fragment had hit one of the five militiamen, who had died whispering they're-shooting-upon-themselves, Bilal, and this had snuffed out the temptation.

Upon themselves, yes. If you shoot at a brother you shoot upon yourself, he'd thought. And shooting that way they would have crushed him, in the end. They would have killed him along with the last comrades. Then they would have concentrated their fire on Gobeyre, added it to the fire of the Eighth Brigade, and... One moment! Didn't all the army's problems emerge from the Sixth Brigade, the brigade which was composed almost exclusively of Shiites? Weren't the Sixth Brigade's artillerymen those who used to quarrel with their Eighth Brigade colleagues at the Galerie Semaan? Weren't they the ones who, in order to spare Gobeyre and Shyah and Haret Hreik, disobeyed their Christian officers' orders and diverted the fire to the convent's hill or elsewhere? Tonight they didn't divert it, true: every grenade hit its target. Maybe, tonight, the Christian officers had warned them with a threat. Anyone-who-misses-the-target-ends-up-in-front-of-a-court-martial. Or maybe, they'd promised a reward. Any-one-who-hits-the-target-nabs-a-bonus-and-a-leave. Fear and money shout down the heart, we know that. But when they would have realized they had fired on their own houses and families and faith brothers, their hearts would speak again. Shame and wrath would spur them to rebel, Gemayel's army would split in two, the Sixth Brigade would chase the Eighth out of the Western Zone, and the dream of conveying three-quarters of the city to the Muslims would become a reality. Along with that dream, what he'd said to the captain: "I shall win. Dead or alive, I shall win." Oh, merciful Allah, the captain had really done him a favor by swindling him! He had really made him a present by hiding the fact that the Italians would occupy the Tower only until sunset, that later they would permit the governmentals to take it again! If the captain had not hidden it, he would not have gotten so angry to see that the Italians had left and the governmentals had moved back in. If he had not gotten so angry, he would not have led his men to this conquest: ila-al-Bourji, ila-al-Bourji. And if he had not done so, now his brothers of the Sixth Brigade would not be shooting upon themselves: Gemayel's army would not prepare itself to split in two... Yes, things were going in the best way possible. And after this thinking, this analysis worthy of a grand strategist, of a skilled politician, Bilal had started again to resist. Resisting, he had forgotten all the rest: his eight children, his father, Zeinab who welcomed him into her depths, who mended his patches with the same color thread, who fished out his lice and crushed them, who consoled him saying men-aren't-measured-by-the-yard-Bilal, who glued together the pages of the half-book and stuck them in a green cover with the title "Kitàb," who carried the ninth child and made him feel like a pine tree which spits forth pinecones and with the pinecones seeds. Forgetting all the rest he had returned to singing beasnani-saudàfeh-haza-al-bourji-beasnani, beasnani-saudàfeh-haza-el-quariatna-beasnani, and now his tuneless voice resounded with such vigor that it reached the Sabra rond-point where with a jeep-mounted 106mm cannon Gassàn was vainly launching his personal grenades at the Tower. Vainly because, owing to some mechanical defect he could not identify, they kept passing over the roof and falling on Shatila. Personal because they belonged to his private stock and each one was engraved with two strange words: *brahmet-bayi.*

And here is Gassàn.

* * *

He really was the opposite of Bilal, Captain Gassàn. He was very tall, as we know, very robust, very handsome, and he had all that Bilal did not have: a slim elegant wife, two gracious and polite children, a luxurious apartment in the residential zone of Ashrafieh, as well as many new jackets and many whole books with leather covers and real titles. But he no longer had his beloved family villa on the seaside at Ramlet el Baida. And, most important, he no longer had his beloved father: a Maronite Christian general, former commander of the Eighth Brigade, who had always distinguished himself by his moderation and wisdom, and who had reacted to the arrival of the Palestinians by saying: "Let them in. We have room." Before his death, by the way, this used to be said also by Gassàn: at that time a mild-mannered medical student who believed in forgiveness and mercy. "I want to heal people, not to murder them." Those who didn't believe him simply had to listen to his comment on the massacre at Damour: the Maronite Christian town where the Shiites and the Palestinians, then united by an ephemeral alliance, had offered a prescient version of Sabra and Shatila. "Woe to those who seek revenge. We must forgive, we must find a modus vivendi: a way to live together." The fact is that the Shiites and the Palestinians didn't want to find a modus vivendi: they wanted to reinforce the advantage they'd acquired with the Damour massacre and give a second show of force by liquidating a very important person. So, on Christmas Eve, some obsequious individuals had rung the bell of the seaside villa at Ramlet el Baida. They'd asked to be received by the general and wish him a happy holiday, the general had received them, and instead of holiday wishes he'd gotten several revolver shots in his head. Then, while he was being buried in the Christian cemetery of Saint Elias other less obsequious individuals had torched the villa. And Gassàn had concluded that forgiveness is a luxury of saints, mercy a weakness. Abandoning his medical studies he'd requested the honor of joining the Eighth Brigade then glued the image of the Virgin of Junieh to the butt of his rifle and become one of the most ferocious officers in the governmental army. An executioner with a captain's rank. "When they treacherously murder your father and burn your house during his funeral, vengeance is an irrefutable right nay a binding duty," he retorted to those who recalled his comment on Damour. And to exercise that irrefutable-right, that binding-duty, he used a private stock of projectiles bearing the words *brahmet-bayi* or the initials *bb*. If the projectiles were rifle or revolver or machine gun bullets, he limited himself to inscribing the initials with a felt-tip pen. If they were mortar or cannon shells, he engraved the whole phrase with a dagger or a bayonet. Brahmet-bayi, on-my-father's-grave.

Everybody knew. Nobody, however, knew how many had died of brahmet-bayi or bb. Not even Gassàn himself, since in every Shiite or Palestinian guerrilla he saw one of his father's assassins and the execution of his father's assassins was an undertaking he never tired of. He interrupted it only to eat and to sleep or to spend a few hours with his slim elegant wife and his two children. Or to go to church, to confess, to receive Communion. Giving his confession, he punctiliously listed negligible faults and insignificant flaws that he considered sins: not a single episode connected to his killing. "That's not a sin." Receiving Communion, he prayed to the Virgin of Junieh to help him kill more than he did. And on no occasion did he deny having taken part in the massacre of Sabra and Shatila. "We had a score to settle. We settled it. It was excellent work and a huge grind," he coldly declared. He seemed cold. Ignoring the sinister mania that possessed his soul, you would have defined him as a man without passions: a type who substituted reason and good manners for feeling. He never raised his voice, never cursed, never drank, and was courteous toward women even if they wore the chador, correct toward old men even if they wore the kaffiah. With animals, even tender. Once he'd come across a wounded cat and healed it as if it were a person. Another time he'd brought to his barracks a bird with a broken wing and reattached it with professionalism. He was also intelligent, cultivated, and capable of judging himself keenly. "In the epilogue to *La vie en fleur*," he used to say, "Anatole France observes that men rarely show themselves for what they are. Usually, they conceal the actions that would confer on them hate or contempt and exhibit those that confer on them esteem and respect. Not me. I conceal the actions that would make me esteemed and respected, I exhibit those that make me hated or despised. This doesn't mean I'm better or worse than the others. It means I'm not a hypocrite." And, when the Westerners blamed the Lebanese for their slaughters: "Corneille was right in saying that people look upon the ills of others with different eyes than they look upon their own. Have you forgotten the carnage of your own history?" Finally, he was courageous. Any clash or combat saw him on the front line and, well knowing himself to be the most loathed man in the Western Zone, each night he roved there like a panther in the dark. In fact it was easy to find him in avenue Nasser where heedless of the Amal he halted to chat with the bersaglieri and to display the perfect Italian he'd learned at the Military School of Civitavecchia then at the Paratrooper School in Pisa the year he'd met Pistoia. Perhaps, the only friend he had. But should we marvel? Men like Gassàn are always lonely men. Precisely because their ferocity comes from tragedy and not from an innate bestiality, precisely because two different and incompatible creatures coexist in their personality, nobody understands them. Nobody gives them the sympathy which is usually given to the Bilals. Yet they suffer no less than the Bilals, and forget the illusions: inside his or her heart each of us secretly holds a Captain Gassàn. An alter ego, a Lucifer that any sorrow can suddenly unleash to transform us into the opposite of what we are or seem to be or try to be.

"Holy Mother!"

Captain Gassàn's handsome face widened in an icy smile. By dint of seeking and seeking the mechanical defect, he'd finally understood why his brahmet-bayi passed over the roof and missed the damn dwarf who, not content with robbing the Tower and the M48, now mocked him by singing his vulgar hymn: the barrel of the gun and the barrel of the spotter that shoots the tracer shell weren't aligned. There was no other choice but to stop, then, and wait for that miscarriage of nature to give up his resistance: leave the Tower, cross avenue Nasser and reenter Gobeyre. Because he had to give up his resistance. He had to leave the Tower. He had to cross avenue Nasser. No doubt about it. And at that point the brahmet-bayi wouldn't miss him. It would hit its target as if hitting a pigeon in a cage. Without any spotter, without any tracer. At close range, and with the miscarriage of nature in the middle of the avenue, the spotter was useless. The tracer was superfluous. All he had to do was start the jeep, drive onto avenue Nasser, halt thirty yards before the Twenty-Two, then aim straight down the road, lower the gun to the level of a man nay a dwarf and remember that tonight was the anniversary of his father's assassination: that he owed his father this small tribute, this symbolic bouquet of flowers on his grave at Saint Elias's cemetery. Brahmet-bayi, brahmet-bayi. And murmuring the two words, Gassàn started waiting for Bilal to offer himself like a pigeon in a cage.

Meanwhile Bilal kept singing beasnani-saudàfeh-haza-al-bourji-beasnani, beasnani-saudàfeh-haza-al-quariatna-beasnani, with-my-teeth-I-will-defend-this-tower-with-my-teeth, with-my-teeth-I-will-defend-this-quarter-with-my-teeth, and his tuneless voice echoed from the rond-point of Sabra to the rond-point of Shatila. That is, to the Twenty-Four where Sergeant Natale was about to scuffle with Passepartout. And pay the consequences.

2

Sergeant Natale didn't know Passepartout. He had never seen him pass by with the cigarette butt stuck on his lips, the Rdg8 on his belt, the Kalashnikov over his shoulder. Those Arabs with the green armbands looked all alike to him, and if one of them was differentiated by some peculiarity he didn't notice. Sergeant Natale didn't even know that the night Rashid had burst into the Twenty-Five Passepartout had attacked Ferruccio. Nor had he ever heard the rumor that Passepartout was the one who tossed the two grenades at the five incursori patrolling Bourji el Barajni. And, for the good of the contingent, this represented luck. Sergeant Natale was in fact a Neapolitan from Pignasecca, a quarter where you grow up learning to give blows rather than take them, he handled a knife like d'Artagnan handled a sword, he doled out filthy language like Demosthenes doled out ideas, and had a Herculean physique. Biceps whose circumference surpassed that of his skull, a thorax whose potency resembled Rambo's, plus a crooked nose which seemed to be there for the purpose of demonstrating his boxing capabilities. Not by chance the Pignaseccans called him Natale the Hard and said: "If Natale the Hard gives you a backhand slap, he sends you to Paradise." In short, people preferred not to make him angry. Yet he was a nice guy who understood other people's miseries and got moved by them, a wise person who had joined the army to discipline his hot temper and avoid mixing with the criminal underworld. Finally, a soldier who truly loved his work. At the Eagle base, no bersagliere was as proud to wear the feathered helmet that characterized the battalion. "'O casc' ch'e penne. 'O casc' 'mmie. My helmet. My feathered helmet." No squad leader was as pleased with his M113: "Woe to those who touch it, who scratch it." Which is why at five o'clock he had moved it as far as possible from the corner of avenue Nasser, and until seven o'clock the Twenty-Four had been one of the posts least battered by the shelling. At seven, however, about thirty young Amal led by Passepartout had realized that taking shelter behind the Twenty-Four's M113 they could easily aim at the Sixth Brigade's troops jammed in front of the Kuwaiti embassy. So they had placed themselves along its left side to provoke the governmentals with Kalashnikov bursts, and now Sergeant Natale was uselessly shouting through the vehicle's loopholes to chase them away. He shouted in Neapolitan, a language not as mysterious as Calogero's Sicilian, maybe, but certainly as incomprehensible to those who have nothing to do with Naples.

"Jatevenne, beat it, figl'e troia! Caccaroni, babbilani! Beat it, sons of bitches! Shitheads, ragheads!"

"Shu? What?"

"Quoi? What?"

"Che cosa? What?"

"Mish fahèm, no understand, mish fahèm!"

"M'avite 'ntiso 'bbuono, fetenti! You understood me well, assholes! Don't act like you don't understand, you bastards! I said you cannot stay there. If you don't go, I'll kill you with my own two hands, filthy bedouins!"

"Shu?"

"Quoi?"

"Che cosa?"

"What?"

"Mish fahèm, mish fahèm!"

"Schiatta a vuje e a chi v'è muorto, stramuorto, a chi sta 'ncoppa 'e muorte vuoste, a chi ancora, v'ha da murì! Goddam you and your dead, and the dead buried over your dead, and your dead who are not yet dead! Get off my balls, dammit!"

"Shu?"

"Quoi?"

"Che cosa?"

"What?"

"Mish fahèm, mish fahèm!"

"What shu, what quoi, what che cosa, what what?!? Fuck your mish-fahèm and go! Hypocrites!"

Hypocrites, yes, he thought. And impostors, pharisees, liars: who doesn't understand Neapolitan?!? The whole world speaks Neapolitan! They took advantage of him because he couldn't leave the M113 and use his knife, those cuckolds! They mocked him to make him lose face in front of his squad, those sons of bitches. God knows how his men were judging him, now. Maybe they said: by San Gennaro's cock, is this the so-called Natale the Hard who sends people to Paradise with a backhand slap? Or: by Saint Lucy's nipples, what kind of sergeant is our sergeant? A pussy who doesn't even know how to swat away a gang of juveniles? A chicken who doesn't deserve his feathered helmet? Not to mention that sooner or later the governmentals in front of the Kuwaiti embassy would return the fire, they would get fed up with the Twenty-Four, and goodbye M113. Goodbye honor. Because a squad leader who doesn't know how to defend his vehicle is not a man of honor. He's a pussy, a chicken who doesn't deserve to wear the feathered helmet. And if his destiny were that of a pussy, of a chicken, he might as well have remained at Pignasecca where the mammasantissima (meaning the gangster) selling coke had offered him a steady job as parking attendant in Garibaldi Square. Three hundred thousand liras per day for a net of six million liras per month, and no taxes to pay: three times what you receive in the army where, wind or rain or snow, they nail you down with a million and a half a month. Mannaggia, goddam: the governmentals in front of the Kuwaiti embassy had started returning the fire! The thirty little bastards had stopped shooting, instead, and... And what in the hell were they doing, now?!? They banged on his M113, they cried, they implored...

"Eftah, eftah!"

"Eddina der el sadr!"

"Eddina der arrah!"

"Min fadlak, min fadlak!"

"Helmets, please!"

"Flak jackets!"

He turned to the rest of the crew, bewildered.

"What are they saying? What do they want?"

"They're asking us to open the hatch, sergeant. They want helmets, they want flak jackets," answered the radio operator who was already informing Hawk.

Flak jackets?!? Helmets?!? Now divided between astonishment and indignation, Sergeant Natale moved to the scopes. He peered at them one by one, and immediately the nice guy who understood other people's miseries took hold of him. By Saint Lucy's nipples! They were not sons of bitches, shitheads, ragheads, and cuckolds! They were kids, innocent kids like the urchins who played in the alleys of Naples with wooden guns! All of them, all. Including the kid with the cigarette butt and the Kalashnikov and the Rdg8 who led them! Oh, poor little thing! What pity he felt for him! Because without knowing him he knew him, that wretch: a look was more than enough to reconstruct the story of his ill-starred life. Born in some Pignasecca of Beirut, listed on the welfare rolls since birth and thank God if once in a while the municipality gave him a package with moldy cookies and a toy recycled by the Red Cross, rickety, tubercular, born of shabby parents... A father who was a professional loafer and maybe a thief, a mother who was broken down by multiple pregnancies and maybe a whore, a dozen brothers and sisters who slept in the same bed, and no school. In the Pignaseccas, the urchins don't go to school. They snatch purses or wallets from the tourists, they amuse them by diving from the cliffs and fishing for the coins they toss into the sea. Or they sell stolen goods, they get prostitutes, drugs. And they chain-smoke: they always have a cigarette butt stuck on their lips, a butt glued to their labial muscles with saliva. Finally, they handle weapons better than soldiers do. Yet they have a golden heart, inside their soul they're more innocent than Christ on the cross, and unable to hurt a fly. Poor little thing! Can you imagine how many weapons that gold-hearted urchin had handled, how many prostitutes and drugs he'd dealt with, how many purses and wallets he'd snatched, how many stolen goods he'd sold, how many dives he'd made from the cliffs of Beirut to amuse the tourists who tossed coins in the sea? No, he shouldn't mistreat him. He should talk to him patiently, explain that there was a real war going on. And, full of good intentions, Sergeant Natale put on his dear feathered helmet. Without tightening the loose chin strap he opened the hatch, stepped out, and approached Passepartout.

"Piccirì, kid, 'o capisce italiano de Napule? Do you understand the Italian of the Neapolitans?"

"Me understand all languages," Passepartout said quickly regaining his usual insolence.

"Si 'o capisce, if you understand it, listen to me good. You can't have any jackets, kid, you can't have any helmets. We're at war, here. We've got only what we wear."

"Not true. You many extra. I know."

"Extra or not, I give you nothing. So, go home. Run off with your friends. This isn't a place for children, okay?"

After reporting the matter to Hawk, though, the radio operator was shouting just the contrary.

"Sergeant! The captain says it's better to get rid of them by giving away a couple of spare helmets!"

"See? You have helmets. And your captain authorizes."

But Sergeant Natale shook his head indulgently.

"T'aggio ritto no, I said no, piccirì. No helmet. Not even if the colonel orders me to. Not even if the general does. Or God in person."

"Là? No?"

"Là. No, kid. E nun me scassà 'o cazz', and don't bust my balls, okay?"

At this point he turned his back and, with his back turned, he didn't see the kid leap on him to tear off his helmet with the chin strap still loose. But he felt a shove, along with the shove somebody who scalped him, he heard the triumphant cry ana-khutta, I-took-it. And what happened next is easy to guess. First, a long roar: "'O casc' ch'e penne, 'o casc' 'mmie! My helmet! My feathered helmet!" Then a huge body, his body, that sprang upon Passepartout, tore the helmet from his hands, slipped it back on his head, and let loose the renowned backhand slap of Natale the Hard. Then Passepartout who tumbled to the ground, remained there for a second, stunned, got up shrieking saedna-help-saedna, and fled to take cover beneath the arches of the overpass. Then the other poor-little-things who overcoming their amazement pointed their Kalashnikovs. But in the meantime Natale had grabbed his Fal, and holding it by the barrel, swinging it like a club, roaring all the dirtiest taunts in his repertoire, he knocked them down one by one. "This is for you and for your luetic slut of a sister. This is for you and for your open-assed squawk of a mother. This is for you and for your squirting jiz faggot of a father. And this, this, this, and this are for all your offspring, present and future." At each blow, at each insult, three or four poor-little-things ended up on the ground like Passepartout. Like Passepartout they remained there for a second, stunned, then got up shrieking saedna-help-saedna and fled to take cover beneath the arches of the overpass. At the end there was only Sergeant Natale, looking around in confusion and touching his head which felt scalped again. Mannaggia 'a miseria, goddam misery, his helmet! His feathered helmet! It wasn't there anymore! Had it fallen off in the turmoil? Had those sons of bitches, those shitheads, those ragheads, cuckolds, hypocrites, impostors, pharisees, liars grabbed it and given it back to that brother of a luetic slut, that son of an open-assed squawk, of a squirting jiz faggot?!? Yes. And this time he would wash away the stain with the knife. He took his bayonet, the only available knife, and, deaf to the pleas the five bersaglieri shouted at him from the hatch of the M113, started advancing toward the overpass.

"Don't go, sergeant, don't!"

"Leave it, sergeant, leave it!"

"We've got so many helmets here, please!"

He advanced grimly, with the slow sober steps of a mammasantissima who goes to recover his stolen honor, and as he advanced he narrowed his eyes in search of the feathered helmet. It didn't take him long to locate it. It was on the brother-of-and-son-of-etcetera's head. In the explosions' flashes the iridescent plumage sparkled like the beam of a lighthouse. But he didn't recover it. Because in the weft of marginal and apparently trivial episodes, in the mysterious fabric of fortuitous coincidences that make up our destiny, it was established that his helmet would remain on Passepartout's head. Only with his helmet remaining on Passepartout's head could the chain of events realize itself, could Boltzmann's equation materialize. And while Sergeant Natale advanced grimly with those slow sober steps, a 105mm grenade fell on the rond-point of Shatila. A hail of fragments stroked his face, his legs, his lower abdomen, stopped him in his tracks, and goodbye 'o casc' ch'e penne. 'O casc' 'mmie.

*　*　*

The first wounded-in-action is like the first killed-in-action: an event which was foreseen, expected, and yet a drama which deeply traumatizes the group the wounded one belongs to. It tears away self-imposed masks, it brings strength or weakness to the surface, it causes confusion, and almost all the members of the group react as they would to an unforeseen, unexpected event: growing enraged or desperate, or losing their heads. So, many lost their heads. But the one who lost it more than anybody else was Eagle. In fact, when he learned what meanwhile had happened to Hawk, he shifted the focus of his anguish onto him and committed the error which would cost the life of a little leaf in the forest. A boy named Mahomet.

3

"Hawk, attention, Hawk! Eagle calling Hawk!"
"Hawk, come in, Hawk!"
"Hawk, do you read me, Hawk?"
No, he didn't. His radio wasn't receiving. Eagle repeated the call on the walkie-talkie, a shout stifled by the crash of the explosions.
"Eagle, attention, Eagle! Hawk here!"
"Hawk, why didn't you answer, Hawk?!"
"Because the radio blew up with the jeep, sir!"
"Blew up?!?"

"Yessir, a mortar shell! Thank God I was in the bunker! Anyway, before it blew up I spoke with the Twenty-Four and don't worry: the ambulance for Sergeant Natale made it! It got there from the Twenty-Three then the path behind the grave and picked him up!"

"Good! Are you still in the bunker?"

"Yessir. But with the walkie-talkie I cannot contact the posts! I've got to go inside the M113! So I can use the radio."

The M113? Holy Moses! Holy prophets, holy saints! It was right in the middle of the vacant lot, the M113 of the Twenty-Five. And the vacant lot was just on the trajectory of the fire that the Sixth Brigade was aiming at Gobeyre. It had to be moved! But where to? Well, maybe in the crater near the lane that led to the Twenty-Two...

"All right, Hawk. As soon as you are there, move it!"

"Move it, sir? What?"

"What do you mean what?!? The M113!"

"Where to, sir...?"

"Into the crater!"

"What crater, sir...?"

"The bomb crater near the lane!"

"But colonel, sir! How can eight men..."

"Leave only the pilot and the gunner, inside!"

"But sir... And the others, sir...?"

"Get them into Habbash's house!"

"Habbash's house?!?"

"Yes, Habbash's house! And you stay there too!"

"Me too, sir?!?"

"Yes! You too!"

"But colonel, sir... In Habbash's house I would be without the radio again! I cannot contact the other posts with the walkie-talkie!"

"Take the portable!"

"The portable runs on batteries, colonel! Batteries die!"

"Do as I tell you, Hawk! That's an order!"

It was an order and it had to be carried out in spite of all the problems it presented. To begin with, the substantial quitting of the post. From the Operations Room the Condor kept shouting hold-your-posts, hold-your-posts, but Eagle practically abolished the Twenty-Five by moving it or rather dismembering it into a tumbledown house and a bomb crater. Then, the crater itself. The previous night's rain had transformed it into a funnel of slime: on the slime the tracks didn't grip, and during the maneuver the inexperienced pilot let the M113 slide into the crater where it remained in an almost upright position.

That is, with the rear hatch smashed against the bottom. Worse: since he engaged the reverse gear when the squad was still inside, the six bersaglieri assigned to Habbash's house had to exit from the forward hatch, almost two paces from the crater's edge. In attempting the leap, three of them fell over the slippery wall and lost several minutes in clambering up. It also took a long time to cross the eighteen yards that separated the crater from the house. Weighed down by the knapsacks, the rifles, the flak jackets, they proceeded like tortoises that awake from a long sleep and that not even a danger can stimulate. The one who took the longest was Ferruccio. He halted, looked around, hesitated.... Not even Hawk was able to spur him on.

"Dammit, Ferruccio! Are you coming or not?!?"

"I'm coming, captain, I'm coming..."

"What are you looking at? Who are you expecting?!?"

"Nobody, captain, nobody..."

As for Habbash's house, it offered shelter only in the ground-floor room with the gaping windows through which Rashid had crept with his guerrillas in November to assail the post. A very questionable shelter, by the way, because the wall next to the vacant lot of the Twenty-Five was crumbled and as a shield against the gunbursts there was just an embankment of sandbags less than two yards high. Grumbling with resentment, his coarse face distorted by worry, Hawk flicked on the flashlight. He examined the dark corners, then the middle area, and all at once his hands started to tremble convulsively. God knows when, perhaps during the chaos of the assault on the Tower, the Amal had placed there two cases of penthrite: an explosive that detonates at the simple impact of a bullet. The cases stood one beside the other, as sinister as coffins, and in the beam of the flashlight the inscription showed up more gloomily than the gloomiest warning: *Penthrite*.

"Captain!"

"Jesus Christ, captain!"

"Now what do we do, captain?!?"

"I don't know," he answered in a strangled voice.

Since the contingent had arrived in Beirut, nobody had ever seen Hawk tremble. Nobody had ever heard him answer in a strangled voice I-don't-know. And all had learned to admire what his good-natured temper was hiding: the courage of an iron man who never indulges in phony bravery and fancy boasts. In every circumstance he remained calm, to every threat he responded coolly, and during the past hours he'd well confirmed these qualities. For instance, when the mortar grenade had destroyed his radio and his jeep. Which is why Eagle had made him Shatila's sector leader and given him responsibilities he wouldn't have entrusted to himself. But fear is a mysterious phenomenon. Sometimes it spares those who get frightened by a trifle, sometimes it masters those who are never afraid of anything, and it can materialize out of any kernel. A rustle, a shadow, an image. Or two cases of penthrite standing like a pair of coffins in a room exposed to the fire of battle.

"You don't know, captain?"

"No, I don't," he replied. Then he turned off the flashlight, ordered them to squat behind the sandbag embankment, and avoiding their eyes which glittered in the dark like cat pupils, each eye a silent reproach, you-don't-know, you-don't-know, he squatted as well. Pretending unconcern he lit a cigarette. But the trembling hands couldn't even get it to his lips, and in vain, he said to himself: what's happening, Hawk? Are you cracking? If you crack, those six boys will crack too. Fear stinks, remember? It's contagious, it infects more than an illness. Calm down, Hawk. You're not a nineteen-year-old recruit. You're forty, you're a career soldier. An officer. It's your duty to set a good example. It has never been difficult for you to set a good example, and you've been through much worse in Beirut. You've suffered any sort of headache, you've swallowed any sort of troubles, and you've always had scandalous luck. Don't forget the fortune you got this evening with that mortar shell. If you'd been in the jeep or on the threshold of the bunker rather than inside it, now you would be hamburger meat. Why should a freakish bullet end up on those coffins? There's one chance in a million for it to happen. Get up. Stop pretending to smoke this cigarette you don't even bring to your lips. Flip on the walkie-talkie. Call that poor wretch Eagle who saved your life with that bunker, tell him that you've carried out his stupid orders. Switch on the portable radio, call the other posts. Call the Twenty-Seven Owl, ask Nazarene what he sees from his fucking loopholes. Call the two nuts of the Twenty-Five Alpha you didn't drag out, check if they're still alive. Recover your guts! But the more he said it, the more he trembled, the more he convinced himself that his destiny was to blow up with the two cases of penthrite. And soon this got him to the terrible Sunday: its atrocious details... The saw he had used to cut free the corpse of a Marine whose legs had lodged beneath a block of cement that the crane couldn't budge. The pick with which he had unwittingly pierced the remains of a French paratrooper covered by debris. The letters and the photographs blowing around the rubble with the words of love, the heartbreaking dedications. To-my-dear-son. To-my-darling-husband.

To-Jim-with-love. Pour-Michel-avec-amour... The fear doubled. For God's sake, he too had family photographs on him. And along with the photographs, a letter from his wife. It had arrived this morning with the helicopter of the Head Chaplain and the three-star general. "Darling, I miss you so! Our little girl, also. She keeps asking: when will Daddy come home? I bought her the tricycle she wanted. I'll tell her you sent it from Beirut. As for myself, I bought a shovel to sweep the snow from the front door. Would you believe it? It's snowing, here in Rome. All the seven hills are carpeted in white, and the dome of Saint Peter's looks like an immense canopy of whipped cream." The snow! He did not want to die without seeing the snow again: He had to see it again! The snow and his wife and his little daughter and Rome... He would flee. Yes, he would sneak off, desert. And to hell with duty. To hell with the good example, with those eyes that glittered in the dark like cat pupils, each eye a silent reproach, you-don't-know, you-don't-know. Right, boys. I don't know and I don't care. Because in a while I'll flee. I'll sneak off, I'll desert, I'll leave you with the two cases of penthrite, I'll go to see the snow again. The snow, the snow, the snow! And he jumped to his feet. To flee. But as he did so, a dark silhouette appeared in the doorway.

"Halt! Who's there?"

The dark silhouette moved forward, it became a bersagliere with a feathered helmet.

"It's me, captain, sir. Don't shoot!"

It was Vincenzo, the inexperienced pilot who had let the M113 slide backwards into the crater.

"What do you want, Vincenzo?!?"

"I came to take a crap, sir."

"A crap?!?"

"Yessir. I couldn't hold it anymore."

"You couldn't hold it anymore?! And why didn't you do it in the plastic container? Didn't I give the order to shit in the plastic containers from the rations?!?"

"Yessir. But I used them all, sir. That thudding gave me diarrhea, sir."

"Well, do it!"

"I'm already doing it, sir. Ah!"

He really was. Long before being authorized he had dropped his pants. And whimpering with gratitude he was discharging his terror right next to the cases of penthrite.

"No, not there, dammit! Do you want to be the first one to die if a bullet comes? Don't you see what it says?"

"Yessir. It says penthrite, sir."

"Right! Penthrite! And what happens if a bullet hits, you idiot?!?"

"Nothing, sir."

"What do you mean, nothing?!? It explodes, and you're the first one to die!"

"But it cannot explode, sir."

"What do you mean it-cannot-explode?!? Why wouldn't it explode?!?"

"Because you're here, captain, sir!"

He said it as if his captain were the bunker of bunkers, the guarantee of guarantees, the Eternal Father in person. He said it with such trust, such firm belief, blind persuasion, that Hawk's fear dissolved at once. With the fear, the atrocious details of the terrible Sunday, the saw he'd used to cut free the corpse of the Marine, the pick with which he'd unwittingly pierced the remains of the French paratrooper, the letters' words of love, the photographs' heartbreaking dedications, the temptation to sneak off, to desert, to return home and see again the snow, his wife, his little girl, Rome, the snow, the snow. And the shame of having yielded to fear overwhelmed him. For God's sake! Destiny had entrusted him with these six greenhorns who hadn't even the right to manage their own safety, so that when they were ordered to go into the M113 they went, when they were ordered to leave it they left, when they were ordered to stay with two cases of penthrite they stayed, and he dared to tremble? He dared to crack, to think of fleeing and abandoning them?!? He approached the cases of explosive. He sat on one of them.

"It's time," he said. "I'm here. And, as long as I'm here, nothing can happen to you. But if you shit near the wall, you spare us a little stink: right?"

"Yessir," replied Vincenzo without interrupting the operation and leaving a long stripe of dung while he moved to the wall. Then he contentedly buckled up his pants and came back to sit near Hawk who looked at him in surprise.

"Now what do you want, dammit?!"

"Nothing, sir. I'm staying near you, sir. So nothing happens to me."

"You cannot stay near me! You must stay in the M113!"

"Please, sir! Keep me one more minute, sir!"

"Not a minute, not a second! The gunner is waiting for you!"

"Oh, no, sir. It's him who sent me away."

"He sent you away?!?"

"Yessir. He said: go away, go away, I can't live with a hick who shits all over and leaves me out of breath! Take your gear and go shit on the others. See...I brought all my stuff, sir. The rifle, the canteen, the knapsack..."

"But the gunner cannot stay alone! He has to have somebody with him, dammit!"

"I can take his place, captain," Ferruccio put in.

"Shut up, Ferruccio! You're not a pilot!"

"I know, sir, but what driving is there to do now? All the gunner needs is somebody to help him keep contact with the Operations Room! By the way, sir: the Operations Room must be informed that the portable radio's batteries are dead."

"Dead?!?"

"Yessir. By mistake the squelch has been on all day and now the batteries are dead..."

"And you tell me now?!? Why didn't anybody tell me before?!?"

"We were afraid to get you angry, sir... But if you let me go, I'll take care of it. I'll call them, sir."

"Dammit!"

Hawk took his head in his hands. Dammit, yes, dammit. Also the batteries of his walkie-talkie had gone dead. If the Operations Room was not notified through the M113's main radio, he would end up totally isolated. And Vincenzo was too silly, he couldn't be entrusted with the responsibility of calling the headquarters. The gunner who had chased him, even less. Ferruccio was intelligent, instead, and so anxious to go...

"All right, go. But I'll accompany you," he finally said.

"Thank you, sir."

And Ferruccio left with him, followed by a wake of comments.

*　　*　　*

"I wonder why he cares so much!"

"Well, ever since we got here he's been fidgety..."

"He didn't want to leave the M113, remember? He dawdled, he was nervous..."

"No, no, he was nervous inside the M113 too! He didn't want to stay there either. Always staring out the loopholes and repeating I-would-like-to-go-back-under-the-fig-tree!"

"Repeating what?"

"I-would-like-to-go-back-under-the-fig-tree. Isn't he the one who stays at the guard post under the fig tree?"

"If you ask me, he is expecting somebody."

"And who would he expect with this hubbub?!?"

"A girl, of course. Love doesn't mind the bombs."

"Which girl? His girl lives in Milan! I'll tell you who he's expecting: his friend Mahomet!"

"Mahomet? Who's Mahomet?"

"The kid he sends to the Syrian's to buy hashish!"

"The little boy who speaks Italian?"

"Yeah. The one who escaped the massacre at Sabra and Shatila with his mother."

"Maybe you're right."

"I'd bet on it!"

The only one who didn't join the chorus of comments was Vincenzo. Having lost Hawk, he had repositioned himself behind the burliest guy in the group: a sulky Tyrolean named Franz who spoke almost nothing but German. And he didn't lose sight of his new protector.

"Where are you going, Franz?"

"Wohin es mir beliebt, Vinzenz! Falle mir nicht auf den Sack!"

"What did you say?"

"I zaid I go vhere I vant, Vinzenz! And zyou no bust my balls!"

"What are you doing where you want, Franz?"

"Ich pisse, Herrgott! Siehst du nicht dass ich eben pisse?!?"

"What did you say?"

"I zaid I'm pitsing, gozdammit! You no zee me pitsing?!? Verschwinde von hier, get out of here! Warum klebst du an mir als eine Schmeissfliege, vhy you buzz around me like blowfly?"

"Because I want to piss too, Franz..."

"Aber du hast ja vor fünf Minuten gepisst! You pitsed five minuten ago! Hast du nicht gepisst wärend du schissest? You no pits vhile you shitting?!?"

"Yes, but I want to piss again with you, Franz. So we stay together."

4

One, two, three, go! Lowering their heads, Hawk and Ferruccio dashed toward the M113 submerged in the crater, but the crossfire was so dense that after a few steps they had to squat on the ground and crawl. Something that snatched a couple of curses out of Hawk and cheered Ferruccio greatly. Going that way would take them a long time, and this increased his hope of seeing Mahomet arrive. That is, of sending him back. Eighteen yards, seventeen, sixteen, he thought measuring the distance with stabs of regret. Ah, if he arrived now or before they reached the crater! Because, as to whether he would come, there was no doubt. He cared too much for that pot of hummus and schawarma. He would rather die than fail to keep the promise of bringing his gift. Fourteen yards... thirteen... twelve... eleven... God knows how long he'd fretted over it. "Mama, afuàn, please! I must bring Ferruccio the hummus and the schawarma!" Probably, she had even given him a slap. "I said no! Don't you hear the bombing?!?" She slapped him often for his nighttime escapades. But there were no bombs, no slaps, that could dissuade Mahomet, and soon he would emerge from the long narrow street that ended in the vacant lot of the Twenty-Five. With his clean hair, his clean shirt, his clean shorts, he would approach the guard post under the fig tree, and: "Ferruccio! Me here! Me arrived to bring you pot of hummus and schawarma!" Then he would get inside the sandbag enclosure, he wouldn't find him, all surprised and disappointed he would search for the M113 and wouldn't find that either because from afar not even its muzzle was visible, so he would halt in the middle of the vacant lot to call again: "Ferruccio, you please come out, Ferruccio. Me here!" And this would expose him even more to the rain of grenades, fragments, gunbursts. Oh, Lord! Ten yards... nine... eight... seven... six... Ferruccio halted a second, scanned around the fig tree, looked for a shadow which wasn't yet there, and shuddered. Woe to him if Mahomet got wounded or worse. Woe to him because he hadn't forgotten at all the little girl in the water-closet: his rage at men who know how to paint the Sistine Chapel, how to write *Hamlet,* how to compose *Nabucco,* how to transplant hearts and land on the moon, but are more beasts than beasts and make you regret being born among men rather than hyenas or cockroaches. Five yards... four... three... two... one. Oh, Lord: one! They had reached the M113 and Hawk was already banging on the forward hatch to call the gunner.

"Corporal! Open up, corporal!"

The hatch opened just to let them inside, then shut again to imprison them in a reeking darkness. Hawk grabbed the radio microphone, called Eagle to report about the transfer and the penthrite cases and the dead batteries, the gunner went back to the scopes, and Ferruccio began pestering him to have his place.

"Want me to watch?"

"No thanks, Ferruccio."

"But you must be tired! Take a break..."

"Don't worry."

"That's what I came for!"

"All right! Have it! Watch!"

He sat down eagerly. He pressed his eyes to the rubber eyepiece, and what a bustle! Lord, what a bustle! Within a few seconds the fire had so increased that the vacant lot appeared as lighted as in daytime. How to think that Mahomet would really keep his promise? Not even the rashness of a kid born and raised in the war could have defied such an inferno! One moment... What was that profile which emerged from the long narrow street?!? Nothing, thank God, nothing... Just the shadow of a rag hanging from a shanty. A rag? No, it wasn't a rag! A rag doesn't walk. It was him! With his black curls, his short pants, his skinny legs... And the pot in his right hand. The pot, Christ, the pot!

"Mahome-e-et!"

The howl thundered through the M113 to fade within. The gunner jumped in astonishment, Hawk interrupted his communication with Eagle.

"Ferruccio! What in the hell..."

He continued to howl.

"Mahomet! I'm in here, Mahome-e-et!"

Meanwhile he raised his arms toward the hatch, threw it open, hoisted himself off the seat, and sliding out of the gunner's hands he threaded his way through the opening. He exited, clambered up the near-vertical muzzle of the M113, got ready to jump onto the rim of the crater.

"Look out, Mahomet, look out!

"Don't stay there, Mahomet, don't!

"Down, Mahomet, down!"

The leap which would carry him to the rim of the crater was the one that the three bersaglieri had missed at the moment of leaving the M113, and that he had made without difficulty. This time he did not, instead, and fell face-down against the sheer slippery wall. He wasn't discouraged, though, and smeared with mud, blinded with mud, he got back on his feet. He started to climb. While climbing he slid. He fell again. But again he got back on his feet, again he started to climb: step by step he remade his way to the rim. The fact is that he hadn't anything to grab, the more he approached the rim the more he slid and sank in the slush: every slide a sticky and nasty grip, every grip half a minute lost. And vainly he struggled, he panted, he cursed, deaf to the shouts of Hawk, to the crashes of the bombs, to the appeals of Mahomet who disconcerted and unable to hear him wandered around with his pot. Why wasn't Ferruccio at his guard post under the fig tree? Why was the M113 gone? Had the Italians left Beirut, had Ferruccio returned to Milan without telling him? And if so, how could he have done such a thing? Didn't he know that his friend Mahomet would bring him the pot of hummus and schawarma, that to do this he would risk making Mother angry and receive a slap? No, no, impossible. The Italians couldn't have left. Ferruccio couldn't have returned to Milan. For sure he was hiding somewhere with the others and the M113. He did not understand that tonight was a dangerous night and had hidden to play a joke on him: sooner or later he would hear and answer. So he called, poor Mahomet, he called... He called as much as Ferruccio.

"Ferruccio, me arrived with pot of hummus and schawarma!"

"Mahomet, don't stay there, Mahomet!"

"Ferruccio, you please answer!"

"Mahomet, to the ground, Mahomet!"

"Ferruccio, you no play, tonight many bombs!"

"Down, Mahomet, down!"

At a certain point, and despite the uproar, Mahomet made out Ferruccio's voice and turned in its direction. Always keeping the pot in his right hand he advanced toward a strange blob that jutted out of the bomb crater near the lane. He stopped, narrowed his eyes, and in the flash of an explosion he saw his friend who smeared with mud was surfacing from the rim of the crater to make frenzied gestures which could only mean help-Mahomet-help! He thought that somebody had hurt him, that he'd been wounded, and more than ever heedless of any precaution he ran toward him with a shriek.

"Ferruccio! Me here, me help you, Ferruccio!"

"No, Mahomet, no-o-o!"

"Me come, Ferruccio, me help..."

Nobody would ever know who had launched that fireball. Bilal? Gassàn? Rashid? The Sixth Brigade's mortarmen in the ditch? The Eighth Brigade's tankmen on the Main Street of Sabra? The Amal firing from Gobeyre, the devil who amuses himself by murdering children, the Eternal Father who enjoys receiving them in his merciful lap, let-the-children-come-to-me? What's certain is that it burst very near Mahomet and that in bursting it struck him like an apocalyptic wind, it sucked him like a whirl, a hurricane. And Mahomet flew into the sky like a bird: his arms spread like wings and the pot of hummus and schawarma at the tip of one wing. He flew up straight, weightless, and flying up he got very high. So high that at a certain point he disappeared as if he'd gone to Paradise. Soon after, though, he reappeared. Perhaps he'd really gone to Paradise but the Eternal Father had rejected him to spite Allah, or perhaps he'd refused to enter because before entering he wanted to bring Ferruccio the pot of hummus and schawarma, and folding his wings yet still holding his pot at the tip of one wing he returned to earth. He returned with the heaviness of a felled bird, and dropping down he fell with a thud on the fig tree where he snapped two branches and showered many leaves. This scared him, so he spread his wings again. Still holding his pot at the tip of one wing he ascended again, again he flew into the sky like a bird. Straight, weightless. Again he disappeared, reappeared, and forever folding his wings he forever returned to earth. This time to fall on the sandbags of the guard post enclosure and break. Crack! Here he remained, motionless, smeared with hummus and schawarma, and his right hand opened to release the empty pot which tumbled away while a hoarse voice stammered senseless words.

"Mahomet... What happened to you, Mahomet...

"You're all filthy, Mahomet...

"Look at what you've done, Mahomet..."

In the years to come, when he would sadly think over the sorrow which had been the first great sorrow of his life, Ferruccio would still ask himself what he was doing while Mahomet flew into the sky with his pot then descended to fall on the fig tree then ascended again then descended again to break on the sandbags. But he would never find any answer besides the senseless words Mahomet, what-happened-to-you-Mahomet, you're-all-filthy-Mahomet, look-at-what-you've-done, Mahomet. The shock would totally erase from his memory the moment when he had finally hurled his body out of the crater, the blow of air which had struck him also and glued him to the ground, the effort of getting up and running toward the fallen motionless bird. Equally vanished, his recollection of Hawk who pulled Mahomet away from his arms and cried they-should-be-skinned-alive, all-of-them, those-sons-of-bitches, those-assassins, and gently composed the small body inside the guard post enclosure, closed his eyelids, crossed his hands upon his heart, straightened his skinny legs. Equally dissolved, his memory of the gunner who violently shook him and shouted enough-for-Christ-sake-enough. By means of some mysterious defense of the soul which often reacts to pain by erasing the cruelest memories, he would only recall the radio that crackled and two voices that spoke very faintly.

"Hawk, what were you saying about Habbash's house?"

"I was saying that we jumped from the frying pan into the fire, sir!

There are two cases of penthrite down there, and I don't know what to do. What should I do?"

"Knock on wood, Hawk. But why did you interrupt the call?"

"Because I had to take care of a mess, sir."

"A mess? What mess?"

"Nothing, colonel, nothing... A kid got killed here at the Twenty-Five and..."

"A kid?"

"Yessir, the little boy who always came to visit the bersagliere under the fig tree. And I'm afraid he is taking it badly."

"I see... Anyway, since you're in the M113, call the Operations Room and tell them that my walkie-talkie's batteries are dead too. Then call the two marò of the Twenty-Five Alpha, check if they've left the guard tower. And, penthrite or no penthrite, get back to Habbash's house. Because things are getting worse."

* * *

They were getting worse, yes. Because it was nine in the evening, the hour Gemayel's strategists had chosen to launch the pincer maneuver, and the Eighth Brigade was preparing to invade Shatila with the M48s halted on the Main Street of Sabra. The Sixth Brigade, with the M113s halted in front of the Kuwaiti embassy. "Hold your posts, hold your posts! And fire only if fired upon!" the Condor repeated. But he was the first to realize that at least two posts could no longer be held, that to bring the Amal to their knees and break down Bilal's resistance the governmentals had to occupy Shatila, that to occupy Shatila they had to enter from the Twenty-One and the Twenty-Three.

At the Twenty-One, as we know, there was String. At the Twenty-Three, Onion.

5

Cuddling up inside the M113 of the Twenty-Three, his head tucked inside his shoulders, his eyes closed not to see the flashes that flickered through the loopholes, his teeth clenched with such vehemence that his reddish face had become purple, Onion was fighting his personal battle. The battle to become a man. He was fighting it with every fiber of his being, now that he'd understood the heart of the matter: to become a man, it is not enough to conquer the fear of the dead. It is not enough to steal a gladiolus from the chapel and place it on the communal grave while invisible fingers pop out of the turf to seize you by the feet and drag you underground. It is not enough to decide that the will-o'-the-wisps are fireflies as the colonel says and that in Beirut fireflies exist during the winter too. To become a man, alas, you have to overcome the fear of the living. The dead harm nobody, poor dead. They don't seize you by the feet, they don't drag you underground, and even less they kill you. It is the living who kill you. Thus, he had to start all over again with the living who wanted to enter Shatila. Yes, Shatila! The general in person was saying it by radio. "Attention, all posts, attention! Two governmental columns are heading for the Twenty-One and the Twenty-Three! Hold your posts, hold your posts and fire only if fired upon!" Something to cry about. Because if they came with two columns, how could you hold your post without firing?!? Not even a hero would have been able to do such a thing! Well, a hero would. A hero like the hero of the film he'd seen before coming to Beirut. The story of a soldier so afraid to die that there is no way to make him get a spark of courage. But when he finds it... mamma mia! Forty German tanks he destroys. Forty! All by himself! He'd liked it just because of that, and because of the actor who resembled him as one drop of water resembles another. The same round face, the same small stature, the same age. Nineteen winters. What if he repeated that enterprise and became a hero, a man, without firing a shot? For example, merely shouting ialla-ialla, back-back, Shatila-belongs-to-us, nobody-passes? Taken by surprise the invaders would retreat, run back to their barracks and the general would thank him with a medal of valor. "Here's a man with balls. I tip my hat to Onion who taught a lesson to the world and to each one of us," he would say, and imagine the welcome he'd get on returning home. Flags, paper streamers, confetti, people applauding from the windows... "Hurray for Onion! Bravo Onion!" Not to mention the band in full uniform and playing the triumphal march from *Aida*. "Tatata! Taratata-ta-ta taratatata ta-taaa!" On the platform, the mayor and the entire Town Council and his parents. Mother in her Sunday dress and Father in his double-breasted jacket. With his parents, Miss Caserta and the president of the Bank of Italy as well as the archbishop. The archbishop would convey the Pope's blessing: "Bersagliere Onion, His Holiness sends you a Dominus Vobiscum." The Bank of Italy's president would give him a check for one hundred million liras: "Distinguished Mister Onion, please accept this inadequate but respectful homage." As for Miss Caserta, two kisses on the mouth and her telephone number. "Call me whenever you like. I'm yours." But rather than receiving kisses and money and papal blessings and applause and promises of bed, he would be proud to be a hero. That is, a man. A man who can face the living and the dead, a man without fear. The damn fear that now grew to jeopardize his dream. The less he wanted to be afraid, in fact, the more he was. The more he was, the more he found reasons to be. The more he found reasons to be, the more he fed the suspicion that imitating the actor was pure baloney. And if instead of retreating, running back to their barracks, the governmentals rolled over him with their tanks? Better a hundred years as a sheep than one day as a lion, the old saying went. Or was it the other way around? Oh God, yes: it was the other way around...

Shut up in the M113 of the Twenty-One and half-sozzled, String was instead fighting a very concrete battle: the one to overcome the hunger which had been tormenting him since five o'clock. He wasn't alone in the ordeal, let's be clear: the missed shift change also had meant no dinner, and everybody in Shatila had an empty stomach. But his was emptier than all the others because it hadn't been filled with the twelve o'clock lunch. Goddam Lenin! It was a good lunch, today: fresh vegetable soup, meat with beans and sauce, cheese and fruit. No wonder he wanted to wolf it down from start to finish. The trouble is that Jamila had shown up with her undernourished voracity, and who would have had the heart to wolf it down without offering something? The drama had begun with the apple. A beautiful apple, ripe in the right way and no worms. Counting on the fact that Jamila liked to steal her food and rejected outright gifts, he had offered the apple. "Do you want it?" And goddam Lenin: she'd taken it with a resonant yes. Then, seeing that she didn't move but stared at the cheese: "You don't want the cheese too, do you?!?" Second resonant yes. Then, seeing that she continued to hang around and her eyes devoured the soup: "Dammit! Don't tell me that you want that too!" Third resonant yes. Then, seeing that she didn't move but gazed at the meat, the sauce, the beans: "To hell with communism, Jamila! Take the whole thing. I'll make it with the Christmas dinner." For Christsake, how could he suspect that they would end up fasting?!? Not even during the explosion of the comet had such a horrid idea occurred to him. Only at five-thirty, when Hawk gave the order to take shelter in the M113s, he'd thought: goddam-Lenin, here-we-miss-the-six-o'clock-change-and-skip-dinner! Then, terrified at the prospect, he'd rummaged the M113 in search of a spare ration but those bastards had swept away everything. In the plundered boxes he'd found nothing but two minibottles of coffee liqueur, two shots of grappa, two of cognac, and one of cordial. As a result, he'd drained them all and despite the small doses the alcohol had gone to his head rousing a desperate monologue that nobody could stop. He wasn't even concerned with the M48s that were about to enter from the Twenty-One where his M113 was positioned crosswise to block the passage. He wasn't even distracted by looking through the scopes, a task the squad leader had charged him with in the hope of shutting up his mouth...

"God, I'm so hungry. And this because of my generosity, my communism, Lenin, and his goddam preaching what's-mine-is-yours-and-what's-yours-is-mine. If I hadn't given my ration to Jamila I wouldn't be suffering so. I'm slender, see, I burn calories very fast, and I haven't eaten since last night. Doesn't anybody have a candy to suck or a piece of chewing gum to chew? Just chewing gum, just chewing gum! My whole salary for a piece of chewing gum!"

"Shut up, String!"

"No, I won't. I'm too hungry. My guts are writhing, my gastric juices are gone, now I'll faint. If only I had a sandwich! A sandwich with salame or mortadella! I'm wild about salame, I'm wild about mortadella. Should Lenin come back to life, I'd tell him: comrade, it was not enough to say bread-for-everybody. You should have said bread - and - salame - for - everybody. Bread - and - mortadella - for - every - body. Don't you have salame in Russia, don't you have mortadella? Is everyone stuck with caviar?!? Caviar's good too, of course. With butter and lemon, maybe some minced onion and boiled egg yolk, it makes a perfect hors d'oeuvre. But salame is better, mortadella is better..."

"String! Will you be silent, String?!?"

"No, I won't. 'Cause I cannot. This is too evil, too cruel. What does war have to do with dinner? War or peace, dinner is dinner. It's a cook who says that. A cook by trade, a cook who graduated from the International Culinary School. And being one, do you know what I would prepare tonight if I were at Livorno? A Pellegrino Artusi menu, a classic. Cappelletti Romagna style with raveggiolo cheese, veal, fresh parmesan and a touch of nutmeg. Then crostini Tuscany style, that is, small toasts spread with a paste of spleen and anchovies. Then a roast hare with a spinach timbale and a mixed salad. And for dessert, panforte of Siena followed by a mint ice cream which helps digestion. Not that I'm an enemy of nouvelle cuisine, mind you. Paul Bocuse is a genius. A real genius who knows the art of combining flavors with style. So, instead of Artusi, I might even choose Bocuse and begin with a soup of truffes Elysées. Then, a bass in pastry shell. Then, a poulet à la Joanne Nardon. As for vegetables, baby peas in butter along with chicory from Lyons. And for dessert, a meringue with marrons glacés drizzled with an old Armagnac or a fine Napoléon. However, Artusi is the father of us all, and..."

"String, dammit! Shut your trap and report what you see with the scopes!"

"What should I report if there's nothing to report? Those M48s are more still than my stomach!"

But suddenly he fell silent. And forgetting Lenin, Bocuse, Artusi, hunger itself, he peered more carefully at the governmental tanks. Standstill? No, they were not at a standstill. They were moving, advancing with the 105mm guns pointed at the Twenty-One! The Twenty-One?!? Didn't they see that his M113 was positioned crosswise on the border of the two Main Streets to block the passage? Sure they did. In fact the M48 that led the column now stopped, two officers of the Eighth Brigade came down and approached the M113 with a scornful expression... Scornful? He immediately stopped looking through the scopes. He flung open the forward hatch, leaned out, and directed the flashlight's beam at the faces of the intruders.

"What do you want, shubaddak?"

"We've got to pass. Move," one of the two answered in English, chewing.

Chewing?!? Chewing what?!? A candy, a chocolate, a piece of chewing gum? At the very least, chewing gum! And pierced by envy, jealousy, rage for the coveted chewing gum which could have been a candy or even a chocolate, String lost his head.

"It is you who must move, you fascist! Get your dirty ass out of here, you delinquent who dares to come chewing in my face! And thank your God that I have not eaten, that I feel so weak, otherwise I'd jump out and shove that chewing gum or candy or chocolate or whatever it is down your throat!"

Inside the M113, meanwhile, the squad leader was speaking convulsively with the Operations Room. And the Operations Room was answering in the same tone.

"Condor, attention, Condor! Here at the Twenty-One the governmentals want us to move the M113!"

"Twenty-One, hold your post, hold your post!"

"We're holding it, we're holding it, but they are many! Around fifteen tanks! Can we fire?"

"No fire, no fire! The order is to shoot only in case of direct threat! But don't let them pass, don't!"

And, along with the convulsive dialogue, the angry voices of the bersaglieri who yelled at the Operations Room or quarreled among themselves.

"But what do they believe, the headquarters blockheads, that we are Leonidas at Thermopylae?!?"

"Worse! Because Leonidas could shoot at the Persians!"

"You bet he could! His Browning was scorching!"

"Ignoramus, illiterate! The battle of Thermopylae took place in the year 480 before Christ! They didn't have guns then!"

"You witless dullard! It was a paradox, right? He meant that we should be permitted to fire, that the direct threat exists!"

"No, it doesn't!"

"It does! Ask String!"

"String doesn't count! He's drunk!"

"More than drunk, he's jealous of the guy who's chewing the gum under his nose!"

"True! In fact he's doing nothing to make him understand. Nothing! He insults him and that's all!"

The Eighth Brigade officer who chewed the chewing gum or whatever had understood perfectly, instead. He didn't have to be born in Livorno to guess that the madman leaning out of the hatch wanted to jam something down his throat and refused to let them pass. Followed by his colleague and determined to clear the passage, he had thus returned to his M48 and ordered the three following tanks to get close behind it: each one with the front end against the rear of the other. And now he egged them on to run over the M113.

"Ruha, hop! Forward!"

With the fourth pushing the third, the third pushing the second, the second pushing the first, and all of them together setting off a deafening racket, the M48s began to press against the left side of the M113.

"Ruha, hop! Forward!"

It was a scene at the same time absurd and ferocious. It was as if an extremely powerful train made up of locomotives instead of boxcars engaged the brakes and the tracks of the M113 in a monstrous arm wrestle, an impossible contest. At each shove the M113 screeched, seemed about to snap, to catapult String who still leaning out of the hatch went on bawling his useless insults, so you did not need much to realize that soon it would yield.

"Ruha, hop! Forward!"

At the seventh thrust, in fact, it yielded. And inch by inch, still in its crosswise position, therefore incising a large gash in the ground, it drew back until the Main Street of Sabra and the Main Street of Shatila

became the same uninterrupted street. It almost reached the labyrinth
of hovels near which the officer who chewed the chewing gum left it
raising a scornful look at String.

"Stay there and shut up."

A few seconds later the other M48s burst in too, and right at the
same moment the Sixth Brigade's M113s marshaled in front of the
Kuwaiti embassy moved to enter from the Twenty-Three along with
four trucks full of troops. The clock marked nine-fifteen, and Onion's
drama was about to conclude. Poor Onion. Thanks to the exact version
of the old saying, he had overcome the suspicion that imitating yet
surpassing the actor in the film would be pure baloney. And repeating
to himself better-one-day-as-a-lion-than-a-hundred-years-as-a-sheep he
now thought of nothing but leaping out of the M113, chasing the
invaders back to their barracks, becoming a hero. That is, a man capable of facing the living and the dead without fear. So, when the first
Sixth Brigade M113 loomed on the Twenty-Three to enter the south
side of Shatila, he didn't hesitate: he jumped toward the hatch, opened
it, got out, and at the risk of being squashed like a dog crossing the
street he placed himself in front of the column.

"Ialla ialla, back!" he shrieked. "Shatila belongs to us, and nobody
can pass!"

He was immediately grabbed by the squad leader who had run after
him shouting imbecile, what's - inside - that - pumpkinhead - of - yours,
you're-really-a-snotty-baby, you'll-never-become-a-man. And as the
Twenty-Three's M113 did not obstruct the thoroughfare, as its squad
had not another snotty baby eager to become a man nay convinced that
becoming a man means becoming a hero, as each of the others knew
very well that the two things don't necessarily coincide and that being a
man is already a tremendous chore, the Sixth Brigade's column could
file by undisturbed and meet the M48s entering from the Twenty-One.

It was at this point that Bilal stopped singing beasnani-saudàfeh-
haza-al-bourji-beasnani. And it was at this point that Captain Gassàn
moved forward with his jeep and his 106mm cannon to set himself on
the straightaway of avenue Nasser.

*   *   *

He did it with great calm: absolutely certain that the dwarf by whom
he'd been humiliated hadn't stopped singing his vulgar hymn because
he was dead but because he'd given up resisting and was ready to leave
the Tower. He did it with the gloomy logic and the grievous perfidi-

ousness he'd never relinquished since the Christmas his father had been killed, his Ramlet el Baida villa torched, and also in the blind confidence that the Virgin of Junieh would help him redeem his hurt pride. Along with his pride, the disconcertment that three hours earlier had prevented him from pulling the trigger. Suddenly, in fact, the sky filled with bengals, their transparent globes of bluish light illuminated avenue Nasser almost like daylight, and such luck could only be a sign of divine benevolence. To take aim with the bare eye, to hit the target without the spotter, he needed light. Lots of light. Ignoring the fire the M48s were already raining from Shatila, he thus started the engine. He moved away from the Sabra rond-point, advanced down the avenue, stopped about forty yards from the Twenty-Two. Here he left the wheel, jumped on the caisson of the jeep where the cannon was mounted, arranged the barrel to point it at the straightaway stretch that Bilal would have to cross to reenter Gobeyre. Then he got down, went behind the gun, opened the breech, and looking through the barrel made sure that it aimed in the right direction as well as at a dwarf's height. It aimed in the right direction but at a man's height. So he jumped again on the caisson, cranked the elevating arc, corrected the aim and again got down, again went behind the gun, looked through the barrel, and smiled his icy smile. Good! Now it aimed at a dwarf's height, a little more than three feet above the asphalt: he could finally insert the shell. He did it, careful to choose one whose ogive bore a clear inscription: b-r-a-h-m-e-t b-a-y-i. Then he closed the breech, returned to the side of the gun, and with his forefinger on the firing button he began to wait for his enemy to spring from the little square and cross the avenue and offer himself like a pigeon in a cage. Meanwhile, his lips clenched, he prayed to the Olympus goddess he believed in. He said: "Heavenly Mother, merciful Lady who loves and protects those who suffer, do hear me. There aren't enough bengals, on avenue Nasser, and most of them are burning out. If I shoot at that miscarriage of nature with little light or no light, I miss him. He goes back home safe and sound, and I don't redeem my hurt pride. I don't place my symbolic bouquet on the grave at Saint Elias's cemetery. Do help me, clement Virgin, blessed among all women and consoler of the afflicted, refuge of sinners and dwelling of the Holy Spirit. I'm not asking you to give me back my father, my torched villa, the M48 he stole, the men of my company he killed on that Tower. I only ask you to send me more light. The light I need when he crosses the avenue. So I plead with you, good Virgin: at the right moment, please send me another bengal. A big one. Amen." Precisely the opposite of what, with equal fervor, Bilal was about to ask of his Olympus god: Allah.

He no longer wanted to kill or be killed, Bilal. And, no longer wanting to kill or be killed, he no longer thought that Charlie had made him a present by swindling him: he no longer reasoned like a grand strategist or a skilled politician about the Shiite soldiers who would rebel and split Gemayel's army in two. The Sixth Brigade on one side, the Eighth on the other. Worse: he no longer cared that the Sixth would chase the Eighth out of the Western Zone, that the old dream of conveying three-quarters of the city to the Muslims would become a reality, that his defeat would become his victory. Also the two last machine guns were now destroyed, the four men who had survived the 120mm shell were dead as well, and the only person left on the roof of the tottering building was he: wounded in the right arm by a bullet that had torn his deltoid. The temptation stifled by the words they're-shooting-upon-themselves-Bilal had thus returned to deliver him to a total refusal of his vision. Why should he defend that Tower and that quarter with his teeth, why should he continue to kill and end up killed? For whom? For the beastly Rashids and their Passepartouts, for the indifferent, for the ingrates? Zeinab was right when she said that giving our life for our so-called fellow men is foolish, that people take, take, take and the more they take the more they spit in your face... He wanted to go. He wanted to abandon that roof full of corpses, of friends and enemies dead because of him, and hoist the white flag, surrender: resign himself to the unfair rules of a world that at times turns to the left, at times to the right, but in any case gives you the wrong side. To surrender, yes, and survive. To enjoy life which is beautiful even when it is ugly and exhausts you with its streets to sweep, even when it denies you a jacket without patches and a whole book and an adult's stature. To resign, yes, and reach the ground floor, the square, the other sidewalk of avenue Nasser. To return home and see again your old father, your eight children, Zeinab with her belly brimming with the ninth. To touch her belly, to wonder if it contains a boy or a girl and feel like a pine tree that spits forth pinecones and with the pinecones, seeds, seeds, seeds. To eat the ram's head stolen from the butcher, to burn the damn half-book which has caused you so many miseries. To sleep in your own bed and awaken with the sun. To see the sun again, tomorrow... But to do this he had to expose himself to the bengals which illuminated avenue Nasser almost like daylight, and in some confused way he sensed that inside those transparent globes there was a tremendous danger. The danger of not seeing the sun again. Not tomorrow, not ever. Therefore he hesitated, hesitated. And while he hesitated he prayed to his Olympus god. He said: "Heavenly Father, merciful Lord who loves and protects the poor wretches who always get the wrong side. Do hear me: there are too many bengals on avenue Nasser. If I cross the avenue with all that light, I'll get shot as easily as a pigeon in a cage, and I won't return home. I won't see the sun again. Not tomorrow, not ever. Do help me, God omnipotent and omnipresent and omniscient, consoler of the afflicted, and king of kings. I'm not asking you for a life without streets to sweep, for a jacket without patches or a whole book or an adult's stature. I only ask you for a little darkness to cross the avenue and return to Gobeyre and see the sun again tomorrow. So I plead with you, Allah: at the right moment, please blow out those lights. Amen."

The fact is that it took a long time for those lights to burn out: each one lasted one minute. So at a certain point he concluded that Allah didn't want to listen to him, didn't want to help him, he threw his Kalashnikov away, and staggering like a drunk he abandoned the roof. He started descending the stairs by now half-crumbled and without banisters. Step by step, nay step-scrap by step-scrap, each step-scrap a knife that pierced his arm and from the arm went to his brain fogging his mind, he moved down to the ground floor. He reached the road where he had fought against the white cloud of the smoke bombs, the road that led to the little square of the Twenty-Two. Leaping over corpses, the corpses of the other men who had died because of him, he got to the Italian post where the bersaglieri inside the M113 didn't recognize him and asked themselves who might be that tiny creature who staggered like a drunk: a child lost in the battle? Only Eagle understood that the tiny creature was the proud dwarf who had routed a whole company of the Eighth Brigade and who launching the howls ihkmil-don't-stop-ihkmil, lahkni-follow-me-lahkni had conquered the Tower. And moved to pity, he called him: "Bilal!" But Bilal didn't answer, and passing the gas station from which the two Amal continued to fire the PK46, he arrived at avenue Nasser. Here he saw that meanwhile the terrible light had been reabsorbed by the darkness, and full of shame for having thought that Allah didn't listen to his prayer he stepped off the sidewalk. Full of humility and anxious to be forgiven by the Celestial Father, the omnipotent and omnipresent and omniscient God, the merciful Lord who loves and protects the poor wretches who always get the wrong side, he started crossing the avenue diagonally. That is, heading toward the alley in front of the Twenty-Five. And he was standing in the middle of the street when, atop the Olympus of the litigious gods, the Virgin of Junieh tripped up Allah and granted Gassàn the miracle he needed to sight his target. An immense bengal, an enormous moon of light that slowly descended from the sky over his head. And while descending it radiated a glare so shining, so dazzling, so blinding, that from the rond-point of Sabra to the rond-point of Shatila it really seemed like day. He halted. Blinking his eyelids and feeling as dismayed and deluded as he had ever felt in his life, for a second he remained there wondering why the Celestial Father was neither celestial nor a father, why the merciful Lord was neither merciful nor a lord, why besides not loving and not protecting the poor wretches who always get the wrong side the omnipotent and omnipresent and omniscient God liked to mock them. Then he started walking again. But almost at once he felt two pupils, two icy stylets, stab his back. So he halted a second time. He turned around to look in the direction the stylets came from, and about forty yards away he saw the jeep with the 106mm cannon pointed against him. At a man's, no at a dwarf's, height. Next to the cannon, a very tall and very handsome officer in the uniform of the Eighth Brigade who motionlessly stared at him. He stared, he stared, and his motionlessness emanated such a threat that Bilal forgot his decision to give up killing: he groped for his Kalashnikov. He didn't find it, and in the same moment he understood that he would never reach the alley in front of the Twenty-Five. He would never embrace again his old father and his eight children and Zeinab. He would never know if the ninth child who grew inside her immense body was a boy or a girl. He would never enjoy life which is beautiful even when it is ugly and exhausts you with its streets to sweep, even when it denies you a jacket without patches and a whole book and an adult's stature. He would never eat the ram's head stolen from the butcher and cooked for him, he would never sleep again in his own bed, he would never see the sun again. So he refound himself, and mastering the pain of the thousand knives he lifted his right arm. The wounded arm. He clenched his fist, he thrust his eyes into the eyes of the officer, and for the last time he raised his haughty toneless voice.

"S'antasser!" he roared. "I shall win!"

"On my father's grave," Gassàn quietly replied. Then he pressed the button.

The 106mm brahmet-bayi, twenty inches long and four point five inches wide, left straight for its target and exploded with such thunder that the burst was heard even at the headquarters where Charlie had a shiver he didn't know how to explain and whispered who-the-hell-got-it. On avenue Nasser the walls trembled, in the little square of the Twenty-Two Leyda's hovel and the M113 and the gas station and

Eagle's jeep shook as during an earthquake. Eagle threw himself on the ground, and while doing so he felt the impulse to shout: "Watch out, Bilal!" Then he looked at the avenue, didn't see him, and thought: "He made it, thank God." Consequently nobody except Gassàn ever knew that the brahmet-bayi twenty inches long and four point five inches wide had disintegrated the pigeon in the cage and that of Bilal the Sweeper not even a patch of his patched jacket remained.

CHAPTER THREE

1

THERE IS NO PARADOX more absurd than the one of a soldier who can't use his weapons in battle, and the impotence with which the bersaglieri had been forced to stand the incursions of the Amal then the irruption of the Sixth and Eighth Brigades had exacerbated that paradox to the limits of the unbearable. At the headquarters, therefore, they all longed to return the fire. "Whacks are answered with whacks! By Christopher Columbus, even a doted dog bites you if you step on his tail!" growled Pistoia. "Contumeliam si dices audies, those who inflict abuse must expect to be abused, Plautus tells us. Moveatur, ergo! Let's move, then!" whinnied Crazy Horse. "The principle of self-defense is the very basis of the Regulations. Let's apply it!" pontificated Sugar. And the Condor was frothing with anger. Returning the fire meant giving the ships the order to use their cannons and their missiles against the targets marked on the map of Old Grouse. Giving that order was the same as becoming enemies of their allies, and on one hand he would have sold his career to give it. That's enough, he thought. I'm sick and tired of playing the good samaritan, of telling myself fables about the railwayman who drives the train or about the general who fights Death etcetera. It's my right to react. On the other hand, he would have paid gold not to do it, and repeating to himself the allegory of the referee trapped between two boxers he concluded no: I cannot, I must not. Besides, what would the ships' shells and missiles obtain when the real targets are the ants crawling around us, the Kalashnikovs and the Rpg that shoot from the roofs and the alleys near the posts, the machine guns and the mortars that fire from the ditches and the streets of our own sector? To react seriously, I would have to bombard myself. In the meantime, he studied Old Grouse's map and picked out the objectives: "This yes, this no..." But all at once Charlie moved away from the radio where he had remained with Angelo and Martino to intercept the governmental dispatches.

"I have a better idea, general."

"What idea?" he answered with irritation.

"Pressing for a truce."

"A truce?! And who can get a truce?!"

"We can, general."

"We? Don't speak bullshit, Charlie! We have not been able to stop the Amal at the Twenty-Two, the governmentals at the Twenty-One and the Twenty-Three, and you dare maintain that we can stop a battle?!?"

"Yes, general. Because all we have to do is blackmail the kingpins on both sides."

"With what argument?!"

"With your own, general. I mean, saying to both that if they don't cease fire, we'll bombard them from the ships. Even if this means bombarding ourselves. It's a good argument. An excellent argument."

"Hmm..."

Suddenly interested, the Condor looked at the Professor who nodded.

"I would give it a try, general. As a matter of fact, I can call the governmentals right away."

"And I can run over to Zandra Sadr's," Charlie insisted. "If it works, we have everything to gain."

They obviously had everything to gain. To make things worse, Rashid had assumed the command left vacant by Bilal and now directed the fire against the Sixth Brigade barracks which were next to the field hospital. But a truce requires laborious talks, unending negotiations, and the decision whether to deploy the ships became more and more urgent. It thus took a long minute for the Condor to answer.

"All right. As long as you act fast. Both of you. And try not to be noticed, Charlie. Take the interpreter and that's all."

"Of course, general."

So it was that Charlie took only Martino and left Angelo in front of the radio.

"And don't you move. Understand?"

"Yes," Angelo replied with indifference.

*   *   *

Twenty-four hours had passed since Martino had translated Ninette's letter for him. But time is not an objective reality, always equal to itself. It isn't always measured by the clock or the calendar or the changing of the seasons or the setting of the sun. Its dimension shifts like a rubber band that we stretch or slacken according to our soul's state and mood. Sometimes it elapses with a slowness that transforms minutes into centuries, sometimes it runs with a speed that exceeds the speed of light, and sometimes it stops: interrupted by something that has petrified its essence. An unbearable pain, a violent surprise, a heavy ordeal. Angelo's time had been stopped by the ivory-colored sheets of paper Martino had given him back saying "Oh, Angelo! How lucky you were! And you didn't know." Stopping, it had set him apart from what happened in the time which is measured by the clock or the calendar or the seasons or the sun, and had delivered him to an indifference which estranged his soul from the dramas of the battle. Yes, even the battle was followed by him without interest or participation. Even its dramas were overshadowed for him by the obsessive thought of that letter by now engraved in his memory with the force of a brand. He remembered every sentence of it, every word. The detail that she knew the French language perfectly but refused to speak it, for example. Or the fact that she had perfectly understood the meaning of the equation $S = K \ln W$ and found out a particular he wasn't unacquainted with: Boltzmann's suicide. The fact that in spite of her thirst for life, her wealth, her privileges, she brimmed with unhappiness and didn't believe in her future, the fact that she had chosen him for his eyes and his face and his body which revived the eyes and the face and the body of the man she had loved too much... Finally, the peculiar remark about the unloved dogs who come back to wag their tails in a dignified farewell. He couldn't get free of it. He couldn't because the awesome worry that she would come back tonight was haunting him.

He bent over the radio which kept bringing governmental dispatches. He pretended to take notes and tried to restrain his anguish. No, he said to himself, no: it would be suicidal to come back tonight, and doesn't she condemn suicide in her letter? "Only if I yearned for the relief and the repose that on certain occasions Death may offer, could I imitate Mister Boltzmann and run up to it. But in such a case I would be crazy. Crazier than the crazy woman who sings and dances around the Shatila communal grave." Right, right. The point is that crazy people are not aware of their craziness and... For the first time interested in what happened around him, he turned to hear Pistoia who was telling the circumstances in which Sergeant Natale had been wounded. "So the Amal started banging on the M113, Natale went out to chase them away, and guess who led those shitheads, guess who stole his helmet: the little blond with the cigarette butt always stuck on his lips. Yeah, the one who apparently tossed the two Rdg8 to our patrol in the alley of Bourji el Barajni." He frowned. The little blond with the cigarette butt always stuck on his lips?!? Then even tonight Passepartout was around with his Kalashnikov and his Rdg8 and his evil! Should Ninette come back, she would risk running into him... Nonsense. No logic justified such a fear. Well, it did not and yet the fear was taking shape. Taking shape it fed the awesome worry, and God knows why the awesome worry evoked the image of the cross-shaped anchor. Along with the image, the idea that the silly jewel might represent an indispensable tassel in the mosaic of events: an insuppressible link in the chain born of the double slaughter. Why? Because he couldn't forgive himself the blunder of having considered her a silly goose, he answered, because he couldn't resign himself to the tragedy of having lost her. Because he'd realized he loved her, obviously. Obviously? The obvious things are the most difficult to prove. Also the datum one-is-greater-than-zero seems obvious. But to prove it you must demonstrate that one exists, that zero exists, that one and zero are different. And even if you formulate the problem starting with the axiom that one exists, that zero exists, that one and zero are different, the demonstration gives you a headache. Maybe he should stop thinking of her and of that letter, maybe he should disobey Charlie and find an opportunity to return himself to himself, he concluded cocking his ear to a dialogue which was taking place between Sugar and the Condor.

"General, I just spoke with the Twenty-Two, the Twenty-Five, and the Twenty-Seven Owl," Sugar said. "Both Sandokan and Eagle, as well as Hawk, can't use the walkie-talkie because the batteries are dead. We've got to bring them some. Moreover, the two marò of the Twenty-Five Alpha are still on that damn guard tower. We've got to drag them down before a grenade blows them up. Can I go?"

"All right, Sugar," the Condor assented. "But take along an escort who knows his job. An incursore, I mean. Pull him out of Bourji el Barajni if you have to."

"Right away, sir."

An incursore?!? He got up, left the Operations Room, rushed down to the Arab Bureau, without answering Fifi and Bernard le Français who asked where-are-you-going, he slipped on a flak jacket. Then he took a helmet, an M12, a walkie-talkie, a flashlight, threw himself back up the stairs, reached the courtyard where Sugar was waiting for the Leopard to move over. Firmly deciding to grab the opportunity he planted himself in front of the jeep.

"Lieutenant..."

Sugar looked at him in astonishment.

"What are you doing here? What do you want?"

"To go to Shatila, lieutenant."

"Beat it. Charlie said don't-you-move. I heard him."

"I know. But I am no use at that radio, I don't speak Arabic. And the general ordered you to bring an incursore along."

"I'm going to look for one right now. Beat it."

"You don't need to, lieutenant. I'm here."

Sugar began to yield.

"Well, given the state of necessity and according to the Regulations... I see you have a gun."

"I have it."

"And a helmet..."

"I have it."

"And a flak jacket..."

"I have it."

"And a walkie-talkie, a flashlight?"

"I have them."

"Get in."

He got in with a leap.

"Thank you, sir."

"Hmm... Let's start from the Twenty-Seven Owl."

To get to the Twenty-Seven Owl they had to plow through the tangle of armored cars and jeeps that still clogged the area around the Kuwaiti embassy, then turn onto avenue Chamoun and enter Shatila through the lane of the Twenty-Seven. From here they reached the open space with the broken stairs that led to the observation post, halted near the empty jeep of Sandokan, and Sugar went up with the batteries. Still thinking of Ninette, Angelo remained to wait for him. It was almost ten, and the open space had ceased to be a dangerous spot because all the Amal's fire now concentrated on the Main Street of Shatila. However the Sixth Brigade mortars continued to shoot from the ditch and the hubbub of the outgoing shells drowned the faint voice of Roberto who was blaming Jesus for his miseries.

2

"Almost ten, Jesus, and he doesn't come. He doesn't return, he really has forgotten me like an umbrella. And you don't lift a finger to refresh his memory, to remind him that he left me alone. You don't give a damn about my bump on the head, my blind eye, my horrible stench, my filth. The fact is that you don't care for the people of my kind, for the good boys who don't drink, don't gamble, don't waste money, don't go to whores. You don't like the clean guys who love their mother and their father, who don't touch their fiancée not even with a condom, who give up hashish and the earring à-la-James-Dean, who know how to stand in line and don't say ugly words. You prefer the heartless people who say bloody-dick-of-a-dick-superdick. Well, now I'll say it too: bloody dick of a dick superdick. I'm so angry, Jesus. So angry. And more with you than with him. Because, to be honest, I never liked Sandokan. I never could stand his big revolver, his hand grenades, his knife from Vietnam, his boasts, I never was happy to vacuum his disgusting carpet. You, instead! I would have vacuumed the sky for you! Cloud by cloud. For you I went to Mass every Sunday. For you I forced myself to fast and take Communion. For you I didn't vote communist. Yeah, I thought you were a great man. A courageous, generous man, a saint. And I believed in your miracles. Even if I was not convinced and they seemed like conjurer's tricks to me, I believed all the stories about you walking on the water, multiplying the fishes, restoring sight to the blind, bringing Lazarus back to life. But now I am angry and I tell you: listen carefully, Jesus. Nobody walks on water, fish multiply by laying eggs, and the only way to restore sight to the blind is through a transplant. Something that in your days didn't exist. As for Lazarus, look: if he got up and left his grave, it means that he was not dead. Or that he was in a cataleptic state. So, I don't believe in you anymore. I don't pray to you anymore. Bloody dick of a dick superdick! For more than four hours I've been trying to get your attention by promising you this and that. And you won't even bother refreshing his memory. But if I get out of here alive, if I return to San Remo, I'll take my revenge: you'll see. No more Masses, no more fasting, no more Communion. I'll vote communist, I'll put my earring à-la-James-Dean back in, I'll start smoking hashish again, I'll refuse to stand in line, I'll waste money, I'll gamble at the casino, I'll get drunk, I'll go to whores, I'll change my life. I'll become an atheist, a bastard. The trouble is that I shall not get out of here alive. I shall not make it back to San Remo. My head and my eye hurt too much, and I'm too cold. The chill of death, I know. I'm about to die, I know. And it is your fault! Your fault, your fault!''

The faint voice swelled into a groan so sharp that Angelo peered into the dark brightened by the flashes of the explosions. When Sugar had gone up the broken stairs with the batteries, he'd had the impression of hearing a mournful and peevish buzz that came from Sandokan's jeep: almost the peeping of an abandoned chick. But then the turmoil of the mortars in the ditch had drowned it out, so he'd returned to his anguish. Now instead he was sure of having heard a voice that cried in Italian I'm-about-to-die, it-is-your-fault, and he promptly ran toward Sandokan's jeep. He searched it with the flashlight to see if somebody was under it, he called.

"Who's there?"

A shriek of relief filtered through the turmoil.

"Me! It's me! Roberto, Sandokan's driver! Who are you, who are you?"

"Don't get scared, I'm Angelo. The headquarters sergeant. You know me. Come out, quick."

"Angelo, the headquarters sergeant?!? Oh, Jesus, Jesus, forgive me for the bad things I told you! I didn't mean them, Jesus, they weren't true! I like you Jesus, I do! I believe that you walked on the water! I believe that you multiplied the fishes! I believe that you restored the sight to the blind and brought Lazarus back to life! And I will not take my revenge, no! I will not stop going to church! I will not go to whores and get drunk and waste money and vote communist etcetera! Thank you, Jesus, thank you!"

"Come out of there, I said."

He pulled him out. Holding his breath he cleaned off the dirt in his closed eye, he scrubbed off the clots of blood from his head, he accompanied him to the M113 of the Twenty-Seven. And when he returned to his jeep he no longer thought of Ninette, of the letter, of the cross-shaped anchor, of Passepartout who even tonight was around with his cigarette butt and his Kalashnikov and his Rdg8. Reinstated into the time we measure by the clock and the calendar and the seasons and the sun, restored to himself, now he only thought of the way to reach the Twenty-Five Alpha and the Twenty-Five with Sugar. The way to profit from the war games he had learned in Livorno, the assaults on the imaginary fortresses. But is it not always so in life? We sense a calamity hanging upon us or a person we love, we anguish over it through every fiber of our being, and when the calamity materializes we lose sight of it. We forget it. Something, for instance a frightened boy with a speck in his eye and a bump on his head, has distracted us just when we should have summed up and acted.

"I've mulled over what we can do, lieutenant," he said as soon as Sugar emerged from the dark.

"Fine..." grunted Sugar widening his immense nose's nostrils as if to sniff a smell which disturbed him.

"We could divide the chores: split up halfway."

"Fine..."

"While you go to the Twenty-Five and the Twenty-Two, I can stop at the Twenty-Five Alpha and drag the two marò down from the roof."

"Fine..."

"Then I can bring them to the Twenty-One and meet you there."

"Fine..."

They left the open space, they got to the Main Street now totally in the governmentals' hands. Behind the M48 and the M113 hammering Gobeyre with the 106mm cannons and the 12.7mm Brownings, you didn't even discern the Twenty-Three where poor Onion was crying over his failure. As for the M113 of the Twenty-One, it seemed like a wreck abandoned on the beach by a sea storm. And the communal grave swarmed with soldiers in the uniforms of the Sixth or Eighth Brigade. Shouting ialla-ialla they chased away anybody who approached, so they reached on foot the long narrow street that led to the Twenty-Five Alpha and the Twenty-Five. The only deserted stretch in the quarter. Nobody dared to go in, an officer of the Eighth explained, because from avenue Nasser the Amal were shooting like hell: just peeping out the corner you risked an enfilade.

"Well?" Angelo asked impatiently.

"We're going all the same," Sugar answered.

"Good."

"Straight on to the Twenty-Five Alpha. Then we split up."

"Good."

"And don't forget: from this corner to the Twenty-Five Alpha there are three hundred yards that run southeast. So the right side is more exposed to fire and we must stick to the left."

"Sure."

"Near the wall, head down. Remember?"

"Yes."

"Ready?"

"Yes."

"Go!"

They turned the corner with a bound. With their eyes peeled, their ears cocked, their nerves steady, and their minds concentrated on the only thought that mattered, the thought of arriving unhurt at the objective, they hurled themselves onto the left side and started to run inside an immediate crackling of fire: the machine guns and the

Kalashnikovs that Rashid had posted at every window of avenue Nasser. They seemed like two hares aimed at by hordes of hunters hiding inside the blinds and behind the branches, and like two hares they ran: now lightly leaping in search of a darker corner, now suddenly braking to take cover within a niche, then again launching themselves forward. But they weren't hares. They were professionals refined in the art of competing with the risk of risks, the risk of dying. About that art they knew every rule, every gimmick, and their courage resembled very little the reckless heroic courage of those who are urged on by an enthusiasm or a passion. It was the icy, lucid, well-calibrated courage of the acrobats or the stuntmen who know how to do without overdoing, and knowing it can pick the right instant to jump from a platform and grab a trapeze. Or to throw themselves from a speeding train and land on the spot where a soft mattress awaits them. Allez-oop! Without allowing themselves hesitations or uncertainties, without trusting too much in their boldness or infallibility, without indulging in any kind of optimism or pessimism. Perfect machines, they formed a perfect pair: an almost inhuman binomial. At a certain point, aided by his long legs and his youth, Angelo had managed to pass Sugar who was leading the trek; bolstered by his greater experience and the pride of the teacher who won't permit himself to be humiliated by a disciple, Sugar had immediately regained the lead. But a volley of bullets had missed him by a hair and Angelo had overtaken him again to shield him with his body. Between the first and the second had thus begun a contest to cover each other in turn, to alternate the roles with the dexterity of jugglers who swap places, allez-oop, allez-oop, and this had perfected their exploit even further. In this way they reached the three-story house on whose roof the Twenty-Five Alpha guard tower was located. And here they halted, panting, to exchange a look of mutual admiration. Bravo Sugar, bravo Angelo. Then they separated.

"Good luck, sergeant."

"Good luck, lieutenant."

"Be careful up there..."

"You too..."

And Sugar slipped around the bend, all alone.

*   *   *

Running straight as a plumb line to avenue Nasser, therefore fully exposed to the gunbursts coming from Gobeyre, the two hundred yards that extended between the Twenty-Five Alpha and the Twenty-

Five seemed like a rifle range reserved for whoever wanted to waste bullets. The shots fell there confusedly and incessantly with the sole purpose of discouraging the governmentals' advance, the barred doors denied any kind of shelter, and there wasn't a niche within which to take some cover, a recess in which to hide or at least flatten. The only advantage was that the bengals which had permitted Gassàn to disintegrate Bilal had completely gone out, and this favored Sugar who after the bend had started to run in a different manner. Forward for five or six steps along the left wall and then, with a sudden leap, forward diagonally toward the right wall; forward for eight or nine other steps along the right wall and then, with another sudden leap, forward in a diagonal toward the left wall. Zigzag, zigzag. But now that Angelo no longer engaged him, his professionalism had lost its verve and his features betrayed a secret discomfort. An unconfessed chafe.

They had betrayed it also before the race which had ended in front of the three-story house on whose roof the Twenty-Five Alpha was located. Thanks to the darkness, in fact, Angelo hadn't noticed that at the Twenty-Seven Owl Sugar was widening his immense nose's nostrils as if to sniff a smell which disturbed him. And, if he had, he would have probably thought that he sniffed the stink left by Roberto. Instead he was sniffing the acrid, pungent stink that impregnates the air during a battle: the stink of ashes and sulfur which an olfaction unaccustomed to war may mistake for an innocuous odor of medicine, of antiseptic sprayed to disinfect, and which on the contrary is the poisonous stink of gunpowder. The loathsome stink of battle. Sugar had always loved the stink of battle. It had never been loathsome for him, and not even a stink. "What a good perfume of balistite, of phosphorus, of trinitrotoluene!" he used to say. "What a fresh clean scent! I'd like to put it in a bottle and bring it home." At the Twenty-Seven Owl he hadn't loved it, however. With astonishment he'd found in it an effluvium of filth and rot that gave him a secret discomfort. An unconfessed chafe. And now, running all alone, he understood where it came from. It came from seeing the shattered houses, the corpses, the havoc his ethics had always accepted, from sensing a nostalgia he had never believed he would sense: the nostalgia for the days when he worked as a technician in the Busto Arsizio firm and punched the timecard which emitted the irritating sound, the click-clack of bourgeois boredom. It came from the regret at having given up that boredom for the trade he called the-finest-in-the-world, a-trade-I-wouldn't-change-even-to-become-a-king-or-a-billionaire, and that nonetheless he defined as the-job-of-killing. It came from the repentance at having dedicated twenty years to the cult of the deadly tools he collected like the czars and Jean Duc de Berry collected the Fabergé eggs and the illuminated manuscripts of Paul de Limbourg. It came from the sudden, unexpected, unsuspected discovery that he had wasted his life in respect for a work he no longer respected. It's atrocious to discover that we have wasted our life in respect for a work we no longer respect. Maybe it is worse than discovering that we have wasted it in the struggle for a wrong ideal or in the love for a despicable person... And with those thoughts in mind he concluded his zigzag race, he entered the vacant lot of the Twenty-Five, he called out.

"Hawk! It's me, Sugar!"

He was answered by a snapping of rifle shots that returned him at once to his professionalism. In fact, he quickly threw himself to the ground, rolled to the enclosure under the fig tree, took shelter in it. But here he touched something cold, he flicked on the flashlight to see what it was, and for Christsake! It was a small corpse without any wound or bloodstain, the body of a boy clearly killed by a displacement of air or a violent blow and arranged as on top of a catafalque. The eyelids, lowered. The skinny legs, straightened. The small hands, crossed over his heart... He flicked off the flashlight. With a strange itch in his throat, almost an urge to weep, he got out and started searching again for the M113 he didn't see.

"Hawk! Do you hear me, Hawk?"

He was answered by an unexpected noise, this time: the rattling of an empty pot he had bumped into and that rolled away among the stones. Perplexedly he continued crawling, bumped into it again, and the pot bounced toward the bomb crater where it fell on something that echoed with a metallic sound. Metallic? He moved to the edge of the crater, and here was the M113 slid backwards to remain in an almost upright position. At its hatch, a bersagliere who leaned out in search of the object that had fallen.

"Hawk!" he repeated.

"The captain is with the others in Habbash's house, lieutenant," Ferruccio murmured. And seeing the pot he seized it with a groan.

"In Habbash's house?!"

"Yessir. There's just two of us in here."

"Two?!"

"Yessir. Colonel's orders."

"And this M113 in the crater?"

"Colonel's orders."

Colonel's orders?!? Without informing the Operations Room, with-

out even asking the Condor's authorization? But this was abandonment of a post! A manifest crime, an unquestionable violation of the
Principles of Military Discipline, article 342! He would say it to Hawk,
he would say it to Eagle! And for an instant Sugar went back to being
the harsh Sugar of the Regulations, the inexorable Sugar who avowed
himself ready to kill the Saigon journalist if the general ordered him to,
the implacable Sugar who mistreated Gino and exiled Rocco, the inflexible Sugar who loved the loathsome stink of battle. But it only
lasted that instant.

"I understand, bersagliere. And that pot?"

"It belonged to a friend of mine, lieutenant... A kid who died to
bring me a gift of hummus and schawarma..."

"The kid in the guard post under the fig tree?"

"Yessir... Can I keep it, sir?"

"Of course, bersagliere."

And, afterwards, he didn't say anything to Hawk. He simply gave
him the batteries and the advice to cover the two cases of penthrite
with sandbags. Nor did he say anything to Eagle, by now completely
submerged in an ocean of impotence. Finding the body of that kid had
been so hard: it had canceled any residue of respect for the articles of
the Principles of Military Discipline. And at the Twenty-Two the stink
of battle was so poisonous, so nauseating. It didn't come solely from
the sulfur and the other components of the gunpowder: it came from
the corpses that lay in the square, along the road to the Tower, on
avenue Nasser...

"I brought you the batteries, colonel."

"Oh! God bless you, Sugar! Was it hard to get here?"

"No, sir."

"Did you stop at the Twenty-Five? Did you see Hawk?"

"Yessir."

"Wasn't that a good idea, to send them to Habbash's house, and
move the M113 into the crater?"

"Yessir."

At the Twenty-Five Alpha, meanwhile, Angelo was trying to convince Luca and Nicola to leave the roof and to follow him.

3

It hadn't been a picnic going up there. The ladder to the guard
tower was on the side that received the avenue Nasser fire, many of its
rungs had been broken by the gunbursts, and to shin up you had to put

your feet against a wall that didn't offer any grip. All this slowed the
climb multiplying its danger, and at least a couple of times Angelo had
believed he wouldn't make it. Yet he had. Using his arms he'd hoisted
himself onto the roof, he'd reached the sandbag sentry box, and:
"Boys, I've come to get you. Let's move." They hadn't, though. They
didn't. Like octopuses clinging to a rock with their suckers they
clutched at the sandbags, and even the most patient persuasion could
not drag them from there. Beginning with Luca.

"You're very kind, sergeant. Very generous indeed. But I'd rather
pray. Salve Regina..."

"Let's go, marò! Be brave!"

"No, no. They're shooting, sergeant. Don't you see?"

"I see. That's why I came to get you, marò."

"Thank you, sergeant. Much obliged, really. But I'm staying here. I
have the sandbags, here. Salve Regina..."

"The M113 is better than sandbags, marò. Let's go to the M113 of
the Twenty-One."

"No, no, no. The Twenty-One is too far, sergeant. And I want to
return to Venice, to my beautiful house at Campo San Samuele, to my
lovely bed with the pillars and the lace. To my parents, to Ines, to
Donatella. Salve Regina..."

"If you don't move, you won't return to Venice. So be brave. Show
some guts, be a man."

"No, no, no. I don't care to be brave, to show guts, to be a man.
That's Hemingway's stuff, to hell with him and his books and his wars
and his fibs about virility. To hell with all the writers. I'm not brave. I
have no guts. I'm no man. I don't go shooting lions in Africa and
teasing bulls in Pamplona and covering wars in the world. I'm a Peter
Pan, sergeant. I like to play in Kensington Gardens. And to pray to the
Virgin. Please let me pray. Salve Regina..."

"You'll pray later, dammit!"

"No, no, no. I pray now. Salve Regina, mother of mercy, our life,
our sweetness, our hope, salve! To you we cry, poor banished children
of Eve, to you we send up our sighs, mourning, and weeping in this
valley of tears. Turn then, most gracious advocate, your eyes of mercy
toward us! In this our exile show us the blessed fruit of your womb,
Jesus! Oh clement, oh loving, oh sweet Virgin Mary..."

As for Nicola, it was worse. Because his stubbornness and his loquacity benefited from excellent arguments, and you couldn't shut him up.

"Sergeant, you tell us to show guts, to be brave. But Luca is brave.
Now why? Because he is rich, he has a father who knows the ministers,

and if he wanted he could have avoided being sent to Beirut. He could have gotten an exemption. Instead he preferred to listen to that writer of the bulls who shot himself in the mouth, and he came here. As for me, I am not a coward. Once I raced in a motocross race and I won. People clapped their hands and shouted: 'Bravo, bravo! That's courage!' Because it takes courage to race in a motocross race, believe me. It's a dangerous sport. Another time, while I was driving Aunt Liliana's Fiat on the wet highway, a scoundrel passed me on the right. On the right! One of those things that make you swerve all of a sudden and lose control of the car and kill yourself! Yet I didn't swerve. I kept control, I was brave. But war isn't a wet highway, sergeant. Know what I mean?''

"I know, marò. Let's go."

"No, sergeant, no. I'm too afraid, too terrified. I'm so afraid that I could cry like I cried when we arrived and everybody made fun of me yelling give-the-baby-his-bottle. I'm so terrified that I don't even feel hunger, I don't even feel thirst, I don't even feel sleepiness or cold. All I feel is an enormous rage at the ministers who sent me to Beirut. If I could, I would personally shoot them. I, who last year at school wrote a theme where I sustained that the death penalty is barbaric. We must not kill anybody, I wrote, not even criminals, not even assassins, because life is sacred. Now I would shoot them, yes. One by one. And before shooting them, I would say: this will teach you to send nineteen-year-old boys to the war. This will teach you to stick them up on a guard tower to watch the French flag and the naked woman who turns the light on and off. Do I make myself clear, sergeant?''

"You do, marò. But let's move."

"No, sergeant, I cannot. Sergeant, I know you risked your skin to come up here and get us. And I thank you. From the bottom of my heart, I thank you. But I shall not leave this roof. Listen, it is since midnight of last night that I've stayed here. Almost twenty-four hours. In fact I can't take it anymore. But I shall not move. I said it also to Captain Hawk when he called by radio and ordered us to come down. I said: captain, sir, if I get out of this sandbag sentry box I'll catch a bullet and I won't make it back to Ravenna. I want to make it back to Ravenna, sergeant. To my parents and to my Aunt Liliana! Luca wants to return to Venice and I want to return to Ravenna. Right, Luca?''

"Right, goddam Hemingway, right. Salve Regina, mother of mercy, our life, our sweetness, our hope, salve..."

In a certain sense, they weren't wrong. The sandbags enveloping the guard tower formed a little bunker which protected them efficiently from fragments and bullets, inside it they risked much less than they would trying to reach the M113 of the Twenty-One, and all through his urgings Angelo kept wondering if the fears of the Operations Room weren't excessive: if it were wise to bring them down and expose them to the fire. All at once however he had a twitch, a start that had nothing to do with his growing impatience, and he brutally grabbed them both. He yanked them onto their feet, stuck their rifles on their shoulders, flung them out of the shelter, and shoved them toward the ladder.

"Out of here! Go down, quick!"

Caught by surprise, intimidated by the unexpected abuse, Luca and Nicola obeyed. They climbed down the broken ladder, they slid, they tumbled down on the ground where he yanked them to their feet again, dragged them away, run-dammit-run, and they had scarcely covered sixty or seventy yards when a piercing whistle tore the air. A grenade fell on the roof, slipped into the sandbags and exploded inside the sentry box of the guard tower. Then a second grenade arrived. A third, a fourth. All from Gobeyre and all directed at the three-story house or near it. A whistle and a crash, a whistle and a yellow blaze, a whistle and a wall that crumbled. While Nicola whined help-me-Aunt-Liliana-help-me, Luca wailed help-me-clement-loving-sweet-Virgin-Mary, Angelo shouted run-dammit-run and dragged them as if they were sledges. But they reached the Main Street. And here he left the two sledges to the squad leader of the Twenty-One then went back to his jeep and called Sugar.

"I got them, lieutenant. I'm back in the jeep."

"Good. I'll join you as soon as this mess quiets down," Sugar replied. "But where were you when the Twenty-Five Alpha blew up?"

"On the street, lieutenant. I had taken them out a couple of minutes before."

"Just a couple of minutes? Somebody must be praying for you, young man. A miracle."

"A lucky coincidence, lieutenant."

A lucky coincidence, yes. A billionth proof that in Boltzmann's entropy anything can happen. Even that two particles on the point of colliding with each other, let's say a bomb and the person or the three persons the bomb must hit, at the last moment miss their collision and favor Life instead of Death. Or had it really been a miracle and was somebody really praying for him? Thinking it over, he couldn't explain that impulse to grab Luca and Nicola, fling them out of their bunker, shove them toward the broken ladder. Yes, he could. With the word chance. Lucky or not, coincidences always occur by chance. And

Chance is always fortuitous, unforeseeable, therefore inexplicable. Guess how many fortuitous, unforeseeable, therefore inexplicable events Chance was preparing tonight... He looked around. On the Main Street the pandemonium continued, but at the Twenty-Three the M113s of the Sixth Brigade had cleared the thoroughfare to let their armored cars unload new troops and this too was a lucky coincidence: a random event which would permit the Condor to send reinforcements if he finally decided to do so. In the northeast direction, the shelling that until a while ago had been striking the Twenty-Five Alpha hammered rue Argàn: the street facing the little square of the Twenty-Two. And this was an unlucky coincidence. A random event that disfavored Eagle, the bersaglieri in the M113, and the marò sheltered with Rambo in the yellow hovel... He turned on the dashboard lights. Eager to cleanse his brain, he grabbed a piece of paper and began to work on the problem he had considered in the Operations Room while saying to himself that the obvious things are the most difficult to prove. The problem of proving that one-is-greater-than-zero. Start with the axiom that one exists, that zero exists, and that one and zero are different, he mumbled. Then proceed with a trichotomy and remember that, given the variables a and b, you have three hypotheses to consider: that a equals b, that a is greater than b, that a is less than b. Discard the hypothesis that a is equal to b, already invalidated by the axiom establishing that one is different from zero, and consider the other two: that a is greater than b (meaning that one is greater than zero) and that a is less than b (meaning that one is less than zero). Solve the theorem ab absurdo, that is, relying on the fact that if one hypothesis is correct, its contrary is mistaken. Prove that the hypothesis one-is-less-than-zero is wrong, and... And if somebody was really praying for him? And if that somebody was Ninette? And if Ninette was praying because she saw the shells falling over Shatila? And if she saw them because she had actually come into the Western Zone? For sure, she did not lack the courage it took to come here during a battle...

In this he was not mistaken.

* * *

It's the mainspring of life, courage. We lit the first fire because we had courage. We came out of the caves and planted the first seed because we had courage. We hurled ourselves into the water and then into the sky because we had courage. We invented words and numbers, we faced the toils of thought, because we had courage. The history of Man

is above all a history of courage: the demonstration that without courage we cannot do a thing, that if we lack courage even intelligence ends
up being useless. And courage has many faces. The face of generosity,
of vanity, of curiosity, of necessity, of pride, of innocence, of reckless-
ness, of hatred, of joy, of desperation, of rage, and also of fear (to
which it remains joined by an almost filial bond). But there exists one
kind of courage that has nothing in common with those: the blind,
deaf, boundless, suicidal courage that comes from love. It has no limits,
the courage that comes from love and through love realizes itself: it
does not see any danger, it does not hear any reasoning. In fact it thinks
it can move mountains, and often it moves them. Sometimes, it instead
gets crushed by them. Ninette's case.

But Ninette is still far away. Now we have to follow another love,
another tragedy the battle prepares: that of Rambo and Leyda who
inside the yellow hovel are living out the final minutes of their happiness.

4

"Rambo!"

Unfazed by the infernal racket she wasn't even aware of because she
didn't know or imagine the sounds of peace and normality, during
those hours Leyda had continued to sleep on the mattress with her
Khomeini badge hanging upon her chest. Next to the mattress, the dog
and the goat and her grandfather and her mother: the other characters
of the crèche placed at the bottom of the room. But when the shelling
had begun to hammer rue Argàn, she had woken up. She had seen
Rambo, she had run over to him, and sitting on his lap she now stared
with dismay at an object she'd never noticed: the little medallion with
the Virgin's profile that he kept on the chain with his identification
tags.

"Rambo! Lesh hamel hel mara ala sadrak, why do you wear this
woman around your neck?!?"

"Leyda!" her mother complained with embarrassment. But Rambo
smiled a smile full of tenderness, and pulled the string that held the
Khomeini badge.

"Ma enti, and you, why do you wear this man on your chest?"

"Because this man is Khomeini, Rambo!"

"And this woman is the Virgin Mary. Do you know who the Virgin
Mary is?"

"Yes, I know! A bad woman!"

"No, Leyda, no! The Virgin Mary is not bad! She is good!"

"Not true!"

"True, Leyda, true."

"No! The Virgin Mary kills children! I know it!"

"Leyda!"

"Yes, I do! Because many Virgins came to Shatila. And they killed many children."

"Enough! Come here!" her mother complained again, even more embarrassed. But Leyda shook her head resolutely.

"No. I want to stay with Rambo."

"You bother him!"

"Oh, she does not, madame, she does not!" Rambo protested.

Bother him! Could Mariuccia bother him?!? She really resembled Mariuccia so much! The same plump little face, the same fat little hands, the same black little braids fastened by a rubber band... Well, no: in the end nothing remained of Mariuccia but her eyes. To insert the drainage tube into her skull they'd shaved her head and she looked like the miniature of an old bald crone. The fact is that in his memory he never saw her as the miniature of the old bald crone with the drainage tube inserted into her skull. He saw her as she was before hydrocephaly destroyed her: with her plump little face and her fat little hands and her black little braids fastened with the rubber band... That's why the first time he had met Leyda he'd remained breathless and stammered, "Mariuccia..." That's why, to the astonishment of his marò, he always let her follow him on patrol. Under the illusion of walking with a revived, healthy Mariuccia, he even forgot that the resemblance was no more than physical. Because Mariuccia was not intelligent, poor Mariuccia. Especially at the end, she was so slow-witted. All she did was toy with that Virgin Mary medallion and whimper that monotonous rigmarole: "Witch, ugly witch, with the claws of a chick... The night comes to me... And I go to it... Witch, ugly witch..." Leyda, instead! She even pointed out the dangerous types of Shatila: "Talla alai, talla alai! Be careful of him, be careful!" And she never talked nonsense. Not even the phrase many-Virgins-came-to-Shatila-and-killed-many-children was nonsense. She was referring to the massacre she'd escaped with her mother and her grandfather, to the phalangists who had restaged Herod's Slaughter with the image of the Virgin Mary on their rifle butts.

"They weren't Virgin Marys, Leyda. They were soldiers."

"They were Virgin Marys, I tell you! Virgin Marys dressed as soldiers! I was there, I saw them!" Then, tugging at his medallion: "Please, Rambo! Take it off!"

"No, Leyda, no."

"Why?"

"Because it was a gift. Hadeja, gift!"

"And who gave you this gift?"

"Mariuccia."

"Your sister Mariuccia?"

"Yes."

"And where is she now, Mariuccia?"

"She is dead."

She had died like a sick bird in the snow. Little by little... The way hydrocephaly kills. She had died at home, in his arms. The drainage tube hadn't worked, the liquid in her brain kept expanding, so the hospital doctors had sent her home where he hadn't left her bedside for months. Always there, always there, without caring about his parents who grumbled that's-enough-now-get-some-sleep. He had lost his job, to stay with her. A good laborer's job in the Cagliari suburbs. And along with the job, his fiancée who'd given him back the ring. "Too much is too much! I'm sick and tired of being so neglected! Don't I count, don't I?" Sure she counted. He was fond of her, he wanted to marry her. But could he leave Mariuccia to those who grumbled that's-enough-now-get-some-sleep, to those who considered her a nuisance? Her head was full of water, she breathed with more and more pain, and she no longer ate. She no longer spoke. Even if you hummed her rigmarole witch-ugly-witch-with-the-claws-of-a-chick, she stared at you with indifference. Only a few minutes before dying she'd had a gleam of lucidity. She'd pointed to the Virgin Mary medallion, and: "Do you want it? If you want it, take it." He had taken it. The next day he had buried her, and the sighs of relief had begun. "It's better this way, poor Mariuccia! She's stopped suffering and making us suffer! She's flown to Paradise!" To Paradise?!? Why should a five-year-old creature fly to fucking Paradise with her head full of water from hydrocephaly?!? Why should she go there without knowing what it means to get old? People say: "It's bad to get old. It's humiliating to wither, to fade." Right. But if we don't get old, if we don't wither, we don't fade, it means that we die young. So getting old is also good. And dying of old age is a conquest. A consolation. He'd joined the marò to forget the ill-concealed sense of riddance with which his family had greeted her death, the cruel sighs of relief it's-better-this-way-poor-Mariuccia-etcetera. He had hoped that the distance and the uniform would help him recover some faith in his fellow men, the joy of the days when she had a plump little face and fat little hands and black little braids fastened by a rubber band. But the distance and the uniform hadn't helped him recover a damn thing. In three hitches he had not made a friend. He had not even replaced the fiancée who said too-much-is-too-much. He had become a good marò and nothing more. A touchy, muscular Rambo who always kept to himself and opened his mouth to grunt the essentials and that's all. Then they had sent him here, and how to explain his love for Mariuccia revived in Beirut? Once he had seen the photo of a Vietnamese family killed during a bombing of Saigon, and among the dismembered corpses of the adults was the body of a baby. Stretched out on a mat. Naked. Intact. Children killed by the war almost always remain intact, God knows why. Maybe because they're so light and the explosions lift them up like feathers. And at the idea that Leyda might end up like the baby in Saigon, naked and intact... At the idea that Mariuccia might die a second time...

"If Mariuccia is dead, you can take off her Virgin Mary. Right? She wouldn't know. Right?"

"No, baby, no..."

"But I beg you! Please, Rambo, please! Look, if you take off the Virgin Mary, I'll give you my Khomeini!"

"No, baby, no..."

"Khomeini good! Say it with me: Khomeini good, Virgin Mary bad."

"No, baby, no."

"Yes, Rambo, yes! Say it with me!"

"No, baby, no..."

"Please! For me!"

"Okay, Leyda, okay... Khomeini good, Virgin Mary bad."

"Very bad!"

"Very bad..."

A chorus of liberating giggles rose from the marò who sat on the floor with their backs against the wall facing the square. None of them had forgotten the afternoon of the terrible Sunday when Rambo had tossed the coffee at the mullah then whispered to Fabio you're-a-Judas. And hearing him say Khomeini-good-Virgin-Mary-bad was a hell of an event.

"Did you hear that, boys?"

"God dammit, yes! Here is a story to tell!"

"To Fabio!"

But Rambo didn't react. And casting an understanding glance at Leyda's mother, he pulled the black little braids.

"Are you happy now?"

"Not yet."

"Not yet?!?"

"No. I'll be real happy when you take off the Virgin Mary!"

"Leyda...!"

"Please!"

"I cannot do it, Leyda."

"Yes, you can! You can!"

"All right... And if I take off my Virgin Mary, you'll go to sleep?"

"Yes! And before going I'll give you my present!"

"Your present?"

"Yes! A present to replace Mariuccia's present! My Khomeini! And you will wear it forever."

"Forever?"

"Forever! Don't you love me?"

"Far too much, baby, far too much." Rambo murmured to himself. Then he took off the medallion of the Virgin Mary, slipped it into a pocket, placed around his neck the string that held the Khomeini badge, and went to put her back on the mattress of the crèche: next to the dog, the goat, her grandfather, her mother.

"Here we go. Now close your eyes."

"I close them, I close them!" she happily twittered while he crouched again with the others against the wall that faced the little square of the Twenty-Two. And right at that moment the rocket arrived.

It arrived from Gobeyre, and it pierced that wall with the ease of a knife sinking into a pat of butter. It pierced it through horizontally, a couple of yards above Rambo and his ten marò, then it dipped in a parabola that ended at the bottom of the room and here it crashed with a golden burst. A glare more dazzling than a thousand flashes in the dark. Bursting, it illuminated for a few seconds the five creatures of the crèche. It froze their image like a photograph, so Rambo was able to look at Leyda one last time and to think God: now she dies again. An instant later there was a dull, almost stifled detonation. With the detonation, a brief childish shriek. "Rambo!" Brief and yet so sharp, so intense, that all those who were in that part of Shatila could hear it. Including Sugar who, having left the Twenty-Two and reached the Twenty-Five, retraced his steps and returned to the little square where he got petrified. The yellow hovel did not exist anymore. In its place, a dense cloud of dust from which the ten marò were emerging covered with soot and soil but totally unhurt. With the explosion, in fact, the roof had flown away like a hat stolen by the wind, the wall facing the Twenty-Two had opened like a fan and collapsed onto the square, and the wave of fragments had winged over their heads. "What luck, boys!" they yelled hugging each other. "This time we really hit the jackpot!" Around them, the overjoyed bersaglieri who leaving the M113 shouted you're-alive-you're-alive, and Eagle who stammered: "San Gennaro... San Gerardo... San Guglielmo... Abraham... Isaac... Jacob..." Finally, Rambo who all torn and dirty with blood came out of the cloud squeezing against his heart a tiny body: a heartrending disarticulated puppet from which swung two black little braids fastened by a rubber band.

"Rambo!" exclaimed Sugar.

He squeezed her against his heart with the possessive and jealous gesture of a mother who protects her newly born child, and with the slow heavy gait of a robot he advanced staring at something nobody else saw. Maybe the scene his eyes had photographed when the glare more dazzling than a thousand flashes in the dark had illuminated the five creatures of the crèche and looking at Leyda he'd thought God: now she dies again. Maybe what he had seen when she'd shrieked his name: a minuscule shadow that squirted upward like a splash of water then returned and landed on the ground. Maybe what he'd seen soon after, when he had thrown himself toward the bottom of the erased room and frantically started to dig in the hot bricks: the unrecognizable corpses of her mother, her grandfather, the dog, the goat, and, farther away, a tiny naked body. Naked and disarticulated but intact. The replica of the baby killed by that bombing of Saigon. Or maybe Mariuccia who in a gleam of lucidity pointed to the Virgin Mary medallion. Do-you-want-it? If-you-want-it, take-it.

"Rambo!" repeated Sugar feeling again the itch in his throat, almost the urge to weep, that he'd felt under the fig tree at finding the body of the kid smeared with the strange gravy but without a scratch. "Where are you taking her, Rambo?"

Rambo didn't answer and kept walking.

"Rambo! Who's that child?"

Rambo didn't answer and kept walking.

"Why did you take her, Rambo?"

Rambo didn't answer and gently laid the tiny body in the back of the jeep. He wrapped it in his jacket, he tucked it in the way we tuck in a child we put to sleep, then he sat beside it and adjusted the string with the Khomeini badge that hung from his neck.

"Because she's Mariuccia," he answered. "And this is the second time that she dies."

On the third floor of the well-known house located in the Haret Hreik quarter, meantime, Charlie waited to ask Zandra Sadr about the truce the governmentals had already accepted. And while waiting he wore down, overwhelmed by the awareness that the end of the battle depended on this meeting. That is, on him.

5

He swallowed another sip of syrupy tea and thought of how much he would have liked to throw it in Zandra Sadr's face as Rambo had with the cup of coffee and the mullah. Dammit! It was for fifteen minutes that, attended by his odious sons, the old crow went on spitting his salaams without letting him broach the subject. Welcome-captain, we-are-always-glad-to-see-you, we-hope-that-the-battle-has-not-caused-you-excessive-discomforts, drink-your-tea-and-then-we'll-talk. Besides being more syrupy than usual, the bloody tea was scalding. He couldn't manage to get it down and, in the wait for it to cool, precious minutes passed. Interminable silences that increased his anguish. The old crow knew. But he didn't care, and with his mutism he seemed to say: "Half an hour or a minute, captain, what's the difference? Take your time, my friend, there is no hurry. The Merciful will decide for us. Inshallah." "Ah, no, Most Reverend Eminence. When we're under fire, one minute is a life. Half an hour, eternity. When we expect to die, time is measured by the beating of our heart, by the breathing of our lungs, and tomorrow doesn't count. It's the next heartbeat that counts, the next breath. Don't you know how many human lives each sip of your bloody tea is costing, how many mutilated people, how many houses razed to the ground? Why do you hold your fucking tongue and force me to hold mine? Do your shrewd calculations include this waste, the-more-who-die-the-better? Enough with your salaams, your hypocrisies, your cruelties: let's put the cards on the table!" And all at once Charlie placed the glass on the rug.

"Most Reverend Eminence, time is short and we must get to the point. I've come to propose to you what my general has proposed to the governmentals and what the governmentals are ready to accept. A truce."

Zandra Sadr's intelligent eyes flashed. And the most sticky-sweet singsong Charlie had ever heard filtered through his long white beard.

"You surprise Us, captain. On the basis of what logic do you ask Us to halt a battle that's not in Our control, and that doesn't involve you?"

"On the basis of the logic, Most Reverend Eminence, or rather the fact that the battle does involve the Italians. We're in the middle of it, we've already suffered the first wounded, and we don't want the first dead. Thus it is our right to ask for a truce. And your duty to get it."

"But We are simply a humble representative of Allah, captain. His humble representative, His negligible servant, a man of the Church. We can't interfere with the actions of the combatants. We can only assume that, if the others are ready to accept a truce, Our followers will consider the opportunity to do the same. Allah is great and His compassion is infinite."

"In that case, you should be reminded that patience has a limit, Most Reverend Eminence, and that ours has reached it. I'm informing you that our ships are in a state of alert. If the truce doesn't take place, my general will give them the order to shoot. And the targets he's chosen are governmental as well as yours."

Beneath his large black cloak, Zandra Sadr seemed to flinch. His tone became harsh.

"Captain, Our ears are weak and tired. They think they haven't well understood."

"Your ears are vigorous and keen, Most Reverend Eminence. They have understood perfectly. However I'll repeat what I said, and this time I'll give you more details. Two miles off the coast, our frigates and cruisers are waiting with their loaded guns and missiles. At the order of my general they will shoot at your sources of fire and at the governmental ones. Even though this will mean hitting our own bases and posts. Do I make myself clear, Most Reverend Eminence?"

"Yes, captain."

"What's your answer, then?"

"My answer is that you have told Us extremely serious things, captain, and that We must consider them by praying. By asking for Allah's counsel. Wait for Us here."

He rose slowly. Followed by his sons who during the squabble had remained as motionless as statues, the blond with a silly half-smile on his lips and the dark one with a grimace of hate, he left the room. And Charlie remained there to lacerate himself with speculations. Had the old crow left to cut short a conversation which offended him? Had he been wrong to attack him so harshly, to give up the mellifluous tone of the other meetings? Perhaps, and despite his pretentions of imitating Lawrence of Arabia, he had forgotten that a Westerner can't treat an Arab like a Westerner. To subdue an Arab, a Westerner must navigate the meanderings of his winding soul: adopt his ambiguous language, his lies which are often truths, his truths which are often lies... Zandra Sadr wasn't Bilal. He was a corrupt priest, a sophisticated hoodlum, a gifted politician: he understood perfectly well that, employing the navy at the cost of shelling their own bases and posts, the Italians would commit an act of war against an allied nation which had called out to them for help... Yes, he did. But he also knew that the Sixth and Eighth Brigades had entered Shatila for a frontal attack on Gobeyre, that the Amal in Gobeyre couldn't resist too long, that they needed to catch their breath and gather their wounded and bury their dead. So, rather than cutting short a conversation which offended him, he'd gone to telephone his followers: to convince them to accept the truce. Assuming that in Gobeyre the telephone still worked, though... Because, if it didn't, he had to send some emissaries and this would dash any hopes of arranging things quickly. Imagine the time it would take to reach Gobeyre through the shelling, contact the various groups and sub-groups, then come back... Moreover, Bilal might refuse. He would probably answer we'll-fight-down-to-the-last-drop-of-blood or some bullshit like that, and... Bilal? He knit his brow, stabbed by a new form of uneasiness. For the first time in those hours, he analyzed the shiver he'd been shaken by when the sound of the brahmet-bayi's explosion had reached the Operations Room and he'd whispered who-the-hell-got-it: he asked himself if Bilal were still alive, and the answer was no. A spasm in his stomach told him that Bilal was dead. Killed by his destiny, the destiny of the eternal ox-people who plow other people's land for a thread of hay, and with the aid of a real good trio: a doll called Lady Godiva, a couple of blameless recruits, and a Charlie who'd betrayed him. Swindled and betrayed because friendship-is-a-luxury-at-war, cap-itàn. And because there-is-a-proverb-that-says: either-you-or-me. But woe to him if he admitted it. He would lose faith in himself, in admitting it... And concluding so Charlie drank the tea, by now cold. He looked at the door through which Zandra Sadr had left, wondered when the old crow would return, grabbed his walkie-talkie.

"Condor One, Condor One. This is Charlie-Charlie."

"Go ahead, Charlie, Condor One here," the Condor quickly responded. "Did it work? Did he accept?"

"Not yet, general. I call to inform you that it looks like we're on the right track and..."

"Charlie! What does it mean it-looks-like?!? What does it mean we're-on-the-right-track?!?"

"It means that he's contacting the people he needs to contact! Give him time, general..."

"There isn't time and you know it!"

"We'll have to find it, general! Have some patience..."

"My patience is gone, God blasted! Have you forgotten that the other side has already said yes?!?"

"But the other side can communicate by telephone and radio, general! They have an army, they are organized! These are loose dogs, they don't have radios, and almost certainly Gobeyre's telephones are down!"

"Charlie, I give you twenty minutes. Not one more. Got it?"

"Got it, general."

He signed off, and a few moments later Zandra Sadr's elder son came to tell him that Merciful Allah had counseled His Most Reverend Eminence to welcome the captain's proposal. But in Gobeyre the telephone cables were severed, either cut or burned, and His Most Reverend Eminence had been forced to send emissaries. In all likelihood, there wouldn't be an answer before midnight.

And it was only ten-thirty.

* * *

Ten-thirty, and at the headquarters Angelo was reentering with Sugar who notwithstanding the Regulations had fully decided to hush up Eagle's mistakes. In the long and narrow street which had witnessed the splendid trek of the two professionals, Gassàn had positioned himself with three squads of riflemen and the firm intention of repelling whoever would try to pass through. With its usual irreverence, farce was about to ridicule tragedy and at the Twenty-Two Eagle shouted to obtain reinforcements. The reserve company called Rapid Intervention.

"Send me the Rapid Intervention, by Moses! Come give me a hand! Don't you know that we cannot count on fortune forever?!?"

CHAPTER FOUR

1

THE DICTIONARY defines "fortune" as the lot, now good and now bad, that befalls us every day or in the course of existence. It also explains that the term derives from the name of a Latin goddess, the goddess Fortuna, who according to the ancients dispensed good and evil without concern for the identity of her victims or beneficiaries. In fact, the goddess was blind. Or she wore a blindfold. In current usage, however, "fortune" has an entirely positive meaning: it refers to a kind of blessing that sometimes rains on us regardless of our merits or demerits. We can be idiots or villains and have great fortune, virtuous or intelligent and have great misfortune. (The latter term is very precise and has no connection with a god's or goddess's name.) So, whether we turn to the dictionary or to current usage, the word "fortune" bears within itself an ambiguous meaning: a disquieting and muddy implication. It fully reflects the casualness yet inexplicability of life: the mystery that in identical circumstances one wins and one loses, one gets off unhurt and one dies. And don't try to unravel it, to understand why. Just to give sense to that mystery we use the equally ambiguous expedient of the already written Destiny, or the simplistic fable of the Eternal Father who decides at his whim. The only certainty is that fortune's eyes are truly blind or blindfolded, and that this makes her unjust. It makes her illogical, absurd, the symbol itself of the chaos that set the universe in motion and still masters everything. $S = K \ln W$. Nevertheless, nothing and nobody is more loved and more desired than this goddess. Even if you have the brain of a genius and the heart of a saint you speak of her with passion or reverence, you invoke her, you confide in her your plans, your secrets, your dreams. And you forget she's a whore you shouldn't depend on, a double-dealer who suddenly turns her back on you, a traitoress to mistrust and replace with your own strengths. Which gets us to the point.

Only the whore we shouldn't depend on, the double-dealer who suddenly turns her back on us, the traitoress to mistrust etcetera, could have explained why Angelo and Sugar had reentered the headquarters unharmed. Or why Rambo and his ten marò had been spared by the rocket which had killed Leyda, her mother, her grandfather, the dog, and the goat; why Ferruccio had not been hit by the fireball which had killed Mahomet; why Luca and Nicola had not been hit by one of the hundreds of bullets that rained on their guard tower, then by the shells in the street; why Hawk had gone inside the bunker an instant before his jeep blew up; why Roberto had gotten away with a lump on his head and a little dust in his eye; why Sergeant Natale had been gravely wounded but not killed by the grenade burst on the rond-point of Shatila. In short, why the Italians had not suffered one single death throughout the five hours of hell. Thus, Eagle's cry for help was right. And not only for the Twenty-Two but for the other posts racked by the battle. That is, the Twenty-Five, the Twenty-One, the Twenty-Three, and the Twenty-Four. The Condor understood it so well that he immediately summoned the reserve company called Rapid Intervention to send five M113s to Shatila: one for each of those posts. But for almost ten minutes the M113s full of troops had been idling behind the Eagle base's rear driveway, and the order to move out had not come. In its place, a chorus of protests and a nasal voice arguing with them by radio.

"Favete linguis! Silence, gentlemen!"

"But we've got to move, sir! The hatches are closed!"

"Closed or open, you must wait! Necessitati parendum est, we have to deal with necessity, Cicero teaches us!"

"But what are we waiting for, sir?"

"Quis, quid, quod, pro quo, that doesn't concern you, gentlemen!"

And it would be superfluous to wonder whom that voice belonged to.

*　*　*

Since five-thirty in the afternoon Crazy Horse had been whinnying, kicking, scraping, snorting, and tormenting everybody with his frenzy to throw himself into the eye of the hurricane: "Come on, illustrious colleagues, let's bring those clods to their knees! Remember Cicero's maxim: bellum ita suscipiatur ut nihil aliud nisi pax quaesita videatur! Let's make war to show that we want peace! Let's imitate what Antoine-Charles-Louis Collinet, Count of Lasalle and Marshal of France, dared to do in the battle of Zhedenick! Or what Louis-Charles-Antoine

Des Aix, Chevalier of Veygoux, dared to do in the battle of the Pyramids! With three squadrons, illustrious colleagues, just three, Collinet attacked the Austrians and routed them! With only the vanguard of the Eastern Army, Des Aix defeated Bey Sediman Murad and opened the way to the conquest of Upper Egypt!" But when he had realized that the dispatch of Rapid Intervention offered him a chance to get to Shatila, his excitement had lost every restraint, and not even the unexpected outburst of Old Grouse had been able to placate him: "Enough, my friend! Stay calm, for God's sake! Control yourself!" Stay calm? Control himself? And when a gleam of light was stirring up his desires? By Jove! Did they really believe that a gentleman of his caliber, a cavalry officer who'd been blessed with the privilege of serving Her Britannic Majesty, could stand to rot in this stable like a lice-ridden nag?!? Ah, if only he could have the command of that column, lead those five M113s to Shatila, show what he was capable of! At the slightest resistance: "Bugler, sound the charge! Unsheathe your swords, my valiants!" And maybe he would even find the opportunity to declaim the exhortation that on the 13th of October 1806, in the battle of Jena, Colonel Lepic had howled at a trooper who'd ducked his head to dodge enemy fire: "Courage, my son! They're bullets, not shit!" For years he had dreamed of shouting it in the appropriate place and in its entirety, that is, outside the drawing rooms where there is always a lady who opposes the use of the virile word "shit"! And what occasion was better than this one? So, instead of ordering the five M113s to go, he'd kept them at the Eagle base's rear driveway and started pestering the Condor who moved from room to room with Pistoia and the Professor and didn't even hear him.

"General, Sir!...

"Please give me a moment, General, Sir!

"I beg your pardon, Sir!"

At last, though, the Condor heard him and stopped.

"What is it, colonel? What do you want?"

"General, Sir! I ask or rather appeal for the lofty honor of leading the column!"

"What column?"

"The Rapid Intervention column, Sir!"

"Don't talk nonsense, colonel. The Rapid Intervention left ten minutes ago."

"Nossir. I took upon myself the responsibility of detaining it at the driveway gate!"

"You... you... did what?!?"

"I detained it, Sir! So that I might ask or rather appeal for the lofty honor and assume the risks this noble enterprise involves!"

At any other time, the headquarters would have been rent by a howl comparable to the hubbub that deafened the city, and Crazy Horse would have risked ending up in the field hospital with multiple fractures and ecchymoses. But Charlie's call had deprived the Condor of the physical energy that his explosions of rage required, and overcome by discontentment he withdrew a few steps with Pistoia and the Professor.

"What do you think? Should I kill him immediately, should I kill him later, or get rid of his presence by sending him there...?"

"I wouldn't send him, general," Pistoia answered. "Just think of the ballyhoos he can cook up at the posts, if you do."

"I would, instead," the Professor answered. "In my opinion, the advantage of getting rid of him compensates for any possible damage up there."

A moment of thoughtful silence followed. Then a growl put an end to the uncertainty.

"Go ahead, colonel. But don't think you're going to Waterloo with a regiment of cavalry. And as soon as you reach the Street Without a Name, send one of the M113s to the Twenty-Four where they've been without a squad leader since Sergeant Natale was wounded. Understand? Don't try to do anything your way or I'll strangle you with my own hands."

"Yessir, General! Ipso facto, General, Sir!" And blind with joy Crazy Horse ran to his quarters to get ready.

First of all, his formal appearance. If a bullet killed him and his body were displayed for the troops to pay their respects, nobody should say valiant-but-sloppy. He thus dusted off his jacket, combed his mustache, and slapped on a few drops of 4711, the cologne preferred by Napoleon: the ceremonial he indulged in before going to the mess. Then he put on his monocle, his flak jacket, his helmet, looked at himself in the mirror, and decided that something was missing: his yellow gloves and his riding crop. He thus slipped on the yellow gloves, cradled the riding crop beneath his armpit, and looked at himself again. And now? Which piece of his outfit was missing now? The codpiece, by Jove! The genital-protecting appendix to the flak jacket! His irresponsible colleagues never used it, they said it was ridiculous and hampered their gait, but could a real man risk the very symbol of death-defying masculinity? He thus snapped on the codpiece, smiled with satisfaction, and not even noticing that he was trembling like a drenched chick quenched his excitement. So what? On the 15th of January 1675, while in Turckheim to face the enemy, didn't the great Henri de La Tour d'Auvergne, Viscount of Turenne, tremble? It was written in his memoirs: "You're trembling, you old carcass. But when you find out where I'm taking you, you'll tremble even more, I said to myself." Mumbling you're-trembling-you-old-carcass-but-when-you-find-out-where-I'm-taking-you-you'll-tremble-even-more he reached his jeep and ordered the driver to take him to the Eagle base.

"Front driveway or rear driveway, sir?" the driver asked.

"Front, young man, front! Always the front!"

"Are you certain, sir?"

"Sit tua cura sequi et me duce tutus eris! Do what I tell you and with my guidance you'll be safe, Ovid says."

"Yessir."

They reached the front driveway, and nobody was there.

"See, colonel? It's the rear driveway!"

"Quiet, young man, quiet. What are you worried about?"

"Losing time, sir. We're at least ten minutes late, sir."

"That's my problem, young man. Let's stop here and wait."

"Wait, sir?!?"

"Wait, yes, wait!"

He had no other choice. The trembling had increased so much that even the codpiece was shaking, and woe to him if the Rapid Intervention's valiant realized he had fear. Fear?!? No, no: it wasn't fear. It was the legitimate concern experienced by Henri de La Tour d'Auvergne at Turckheim, by Kellermann at Preussisch-Eylau, by Collinet at Zhedenick, by Des Aix at Marengo! It was the normal excitation which overwhelms any warrior on the verge of hurling himself into the fire. It was... By Jove, it was really fear. Thorough fear. How to control it? Maybe by reciting its definition as given by the psychology textbooks he had studied at the Military Academy: "Fear is a transitory emotional state which derives from a negative form of uncertainty, an irrational feeling that affects reason and prevents one from reacting with logic, an illness that must be conquered with the will..." He silently recited it. But the trembling increased even more, and heedless of the additional minutes he was losing he turned again to the driver.

"Young man, do you know the oration that Esprit Fléchier composed for the death of the great Turenne?"

"Esprì who? Turè who?" the driver exclaimed.

"Turenne! Henri de La Tour d'Auvergne, Viscount of Turenne and Marshal of France, Gods of Heaven! Esprit Fléchier, the French prelate

and man of letters who in 1673 was admitted to the Académie Française for his splendid funeral orations! It is his masterpiece, the one he
composed for the death of Turenne! You really don't know it?!?"

"Nossir. The only orations I know are the Pater Noster, the Ave
Maria, and the Requiem Aeternam."

"That's bad, young man. Bad. But it's never too late to learn: I'll fill
in the gap by telling you its most celebrated passage. Here it is: 'Don't
define the word "valor" as the useless, vainglorious, desperate courage
of those who seek danger for danger's sake. That is, those who risk
their lives for no reason or to receive the applause of the throng. Valor
is the pondered and calculated courage that arises at the sight of the
enemy, that considers every favorable possibility, that expresses itself
when the soldier feels ready, that faces the difficult enterprises and does
not attempt the impossible ones, that trusts nothing to chance, that
takes its time under fire, that in this way fulfills its duties...' Beautiful!"

"If you say so, colonel, sir..."

"The whole world says so, young man! Keep in mind that the concept expressed by Esprit Fléchier is substantially the one expressed by
Spinoza in his *Ethica:* Audacia est cupiditas. Audacity is greed. You do
know who Spinoza is: don't you?"

"Spinozzo, sir?"

"Not Spinozzo, by Jove, Spinoza! Baruch, which means Benedictus,
meaning Benedict, Spinoza! The great Dutch philosopher who was
born in Amsterdam in 1632 and died in The Hague in 1677! The
author of *Metaphysica, Ethica,* and *Tractatus Theologico-Politicus!* But
what do they teach you in the schools? You really don't know about
Spinoza?!?"

"Nossir. But I know that if we don't go to the rear driveway, the
Rapid Intervention column will never reach Shatila," the driver cut him
short. And without asking his permission, he drove to the rear driveway
gate where the protests were reaching a paroxysm.

"We want to move, dammit!"

"We have had enough of waiting for God knows what and whom!"

"Let's go by ourselves!"

He immediately forgot his fear. Snapping a disdainful favete-linguis
he jumped on the first M113, dismissed the gunner, took his headgear,
put it on in place of the helmet. Then emerging to his waist from the
hatch he placed himself at the Browning, cut off radio contact with the
Operations Room, and one by one the five M113s quit the base to
head for the Street Without a Name. Every turn of the tracks, a caress
that renewed his excitement. Well, he was not going to Turckheim or

to Zhedenick or to Preussisch-Eylau with the thoroughbreds of the Grande Armée. He did not see manes rippling in the wind, teeth chomping at the bit, hooves pawing the ground in eagerness to gallop against the Austrian or Russian or Prussian or English or Belgian or Dutch artillery. But the pride of leading this column and the pleasure of emerging to his waist from this hatch made him fully forget the vulgar times he had the misfortune to live in, and to hell with the concept of audacity-is-greed! To hell with Baruch-Benedictus Spinoza, Esprit Fléchier, Henri de La Tour d'Auvergne and their pondered courage! There are moments when seeking danger for danger's sake is the sacrosanct right of a man. And now that he'd cut off radio contact, now that the Condor couldn't persecute him with his bullying, he intended to enjoy that right to the last drop. Don't-think-you're-going-to-Waterloo-with-a-regiment-of-cavalry, the boor had growled. But who if not the cavalry had shown more heroism at Waterloo?!? Who if not the Dragoon Guards of Henry William Paget, Marquis of Anglesey and Count of Uxbridge, had confronted the batteries of the Grand Alliance?!? Who if not the squadrons of Édouard-Jean-Baptiste, Count of Milhaud and of Charles, Count of Lefebvre-Desnouettes, had attacked Wellington's infantry at Hougoumont and at La Haie Sainte? And weren't they armored vehicles that nowadays took the place of horses? Indeed he had a most excellent reason to feel as if he were going to Waterloo and to do things his way. In fact he wouldn't send any M113 to the Twenty-Four: he would burst into the Twenty-Three with the whole column. As for Lepic's phrase, the moment had come. Because he was arriving at the Street Without a Name where the gunbursts grazed his body emerging to the waist from the hatch, the pilot begged him to hunker down, and what opportunity could be better? What circumstance more appropriate? To completely rejoice in it, he only had to reopen radio contact with the Operations Room. He reopened it. He raised himself even higher, adjusted his monocle, caught his breath, and emitting a joyful cry he spat the phrase into the microphone.

"Courage, my valiants! They're bullets, not shit, Lepic said!"

Then, followed by the other M113s and by a chorus of go-fuck-yourself-you-and-Lepic, he turned left to reach Shatila. Thanks to the open thoroughfare he entered from the Twenty-Three and burst into the Main Street of Shatila wondering if in the Operations Room they'd heard him clearly.

*   *   *

They'd heard him clearly. After a silence of more than twenty minutes, that courage-my-valiants-they're-bullets-not-shit had struck their ears like a stone falling into the middle of a pool.

"What did he say?!?" bawled the Condor, infuriated.

"What did he say?" stammered the Professor, disconcerted.

"What did he say?" exclaimed everybody else, baffled.

"He said what you heard: some of his bullshit!" barked Pistoia, not surprised. "But now he does worse. Listen, listen!"

They listened. Now the radio was carrying the echo of an argument in English and French.

"Sir! You are not a gentleman, Sir!"

"Shut up, you bloody imbecile!"

"Sir! You are grosser than my stableboy! And I don't deal with stableboys!"

"Tais-toi, espèce d'idiot. Shut up, you idiot. Et va-t'-en. Beat it."

"Monsieur! Si vous ne moderez pas votre langage, je vous prends à coups de cravache! Sir! If you don't moderate your language, I'll swat you with my riding crop!"

"What is he doing?!?" asked the Condor, even more infuriated.

"What is he doing?" asked the Professor, even more disconcerted.

"What is he doing?" asked everybody else, even more baffled.

"He's arguing with the governmentals who won't let him pass! I told you that he would cook up some ballyhoo!" barked Pistoia, even less surprised.

The Condor looked at him in dismay.

"Go there and settle this business, Pistoria. Quick!"

"With my balls to the wind, general!"

"But no shooting this time. Is that clear?"

"Yessir. My Sardinian pattada and nothing more!" Pistoia replied.

2

There are lovers of war who going through the atrocious experience of battle change in a radical way. They realize they loved something to be hated and, unearthing their true nature, they take off their mask: gradually or all at once, they pass to the opposite side of the barricade. Sugar's case, Sandokan's case, as we know. There are others instead who having no mask to take off (because their love coincides with their true nature) don't change at all. And this was the case of Crazy Horse: always faithful to himself and to his world, always deaf to the oaths of those who didn't understand his folly. Yet it was also the case of Pistoia, and those five hours had undeniably demonstrated it. Even during the moments of greatest tension Pistoia had retained his warmonger's arrogance: the grit of the hunter and gambler who stays at war like a fish in the water, and of course he had dreamed of going to Shatila as much as Crazy Horse. Really with his balls-to-the-wind he thus ran to get the Sardinian dagger which had contributed so conclusively to the destruction of the truck at Bourji el Barajni. Then he grabbed the rest of his gear, jumped in a jeep, and happily plunging into the crackle of gunfire reached the Twenty-Three. He cheekily parked on the communal grave, the-dead-don't-write-tickets, and proceeded on foot. The Sixth Brigade's armored cars had in fact returned with a supply of ammunition and clogged the thoroughfare again, the outgoing cannonade intensified the confusion, and only two M113s had managed to take position: those for the Twenty-Three and the Twenty-One. The rest of the column was halted with the motors running, and the first M113 was blocked at the corner of the long narrow street that led to the Twenty-Five. It didn't take long to locate it. Now almost completely emerged from the hatch thus standing like the hero on an equestrian monument, his head encased in the gunner's headgear and his monocle flashing with indignation, Crazy Horse was lashing his crop against two governmentals who barred his way with a jeep. And lashing his crop he whinnied, he whinnied...

"Sirs! I already told you I don't deal with stableboys!"

"And we already told you to shut your mouth," retorted the pair.

He studied the situation. Well, it wasn't as bad as it had seemed from a distance: the two governmentals had the cross at their necks. Meaning, Gassàn's name could be dropped. Moreover, they were sloppily sitting on the back of the jeep and the front pointed to the Main Street. Meaning, the matter could be solved without the use of the Sardinian pattada. All that had to be done was to forewarn the pilot of the first M113 then grab the jeep of the two governmentals and move it.

He called Crazy Horse.

"Colonel, colonel!"

The monocle fell down to dangle inertly from its chain. The crop bent down, the whinnying became an outraged exclamation.

"Captain! Why are you here? What do you want?!?

"To give you a hand, colonel, and to be sure that you keep quiet. Keep quiet!"

He called the pilot.

"Pilot! Do you hear me, pilot?"

A joyful voice answered.

"Yessir! Loud and clear, sir!"

"Keep your motor running. And as soon as I say all-clear, move your ass. Understand?"

"Yessir!" an even more joyful voice answered.

"And call the others, tell them to do the same!"

"Yessir!"

Good, now he could get to work. And while the two governmentals stared at him in a stupor, unable to stop him, he leaped on the jeep. He moved it with a double shout.

"Haza amr men Gassàn, Gassàn's orders! All clear, pilot, go! Move! Go!"

Amidst murmurs of relief, and with Crazy Horse who didn't know whether to be grateful or angry, the M113 moved. Immediately followed by the second and by the third it turned the corner, entered the long narrow street where the Amal gunfire had strangely stopped, and he tailed them suspiciously. It had been too easy, dammit: merely the deed of a traffic cop who unplugs a jam by pulling out a car. The two morons hadn't offered any resistance, the officers on the Main Street hadn't even approached to prevent the manuever, and even now that the column proceeded they behaved as if the matter had nothing to do with them. Why? Who was in charge along this street? Who had given the order to obstruct the passage with that jeep? An overzealous jerk or really Gassàn? And supposing that it had been really Gassàn, where was he? At the curve of the ex-Twenty-Five Alpha? By Christopher Columbus, it would be unpleasant having to use his Sardinian pattada on him: it isn't nice to cut a friend's throat. On the other hand, war is war. Even during the Crusades, friends butchered friends, and for sure a guy named Pistoia could not submit to bullying because the bully was Gassàn! Not to mention that... God dammit! The column was slowing down, it was stopping, and the equestrian monument was descending from his pedestal. Again he lashed his crop, again he whinnied... In Italian, this time. Gripping the Sardinian pattada, Pistoia overtook the third M113, then the second one, then the first, and here was Gassàn with twenty men pointing their M16s.

"Colonnello, le ripeto: torni indietro. Colonel, I repeat: turn back."

"Sir! Io ho una missione da compiere, I have a mission to accomplish, Sir!"

"I couldn't care less, colonel."

"You don't know to whom you're talking, Sir!"

"I do know, colonel. I'm talking with somebody who doesn't even understand his own language."

"Sir! I should challenge you to a duel, Sir!"

"And I should answer go-fuck-yourself, colonel. But I'm tired."

*　*　*

He was tired inside, Gassàn. The dwarf-hunting had exhausted him psychologically, the final moments of the wait had knocked him out morally. And, when the brahmet-bayi had hit the easy target, instead of the vital exhilaration that in such cases invigorated him, he had felt a mysterious distress: almost a resentment for the Virgin of Junieh who had granted him the favor. Thoughts very similar to those that had urged Bilal to throw away his Kalashnikov and leave the Tower had gripped him. Why go on living in the blood, why keep killing and end up being killed? For what, for whom? For the Gemayels, the Jumblatts, the powerful gangsters who exploited the people like him to prop up their bank accounts and rackets? His father was avenged by now. Dozens and dozens of symbolic bouquets of flowers had been laid on his grave at Saint Elias's cemetery, and they hadn't brought him back to life. They hadn't mitigated the icy rage that consumed his son. On the contrary, they had soured it and fed the vicious circle which imprisoned Beirut: I kill you, so you kill me, so I kill you again, so you kill me again, ad infinitum. Enough. It was time to withdraw. It was time to move to some Switzerland with his slim and elegant wife, his gracious and polite children, it was time to give up his brahmet-bayis, his thirst for revenge. And with an expression of boredom on his handsome face, he had sat again at the wheel of the jeep with the 106mm cannon. He'd reentered Sabra. But there he had seen the wounded from his company, the dead collected in the Tower which didn't interest anybody anymore: in an overflow of rage he had taken three squads of riflemen, reached Shatila, and placed himself at the curve of the long narrow street where he'd stopped Crazy Horse. The fact is that the soul's rebellions are irreversible: the setback due to the overflow of rage hadn't restored at all his combativeness. In total indifference, he now faced Pistoia who approached him clutching his Sardinian dagger.

"What did you say to my colonel, Gassàn?"

"I said that I should answer him go-fuck-yourself," Gassàn answered in Italian.

"Apologize and let him pass, Gassàn."

"I don't think I will, Pistoia."

"No?"

"No, Pistoia."

Right under the noses of the twenty riflemen handcuffed by the same stupor that had paralyzed the two morons of the jeep, the Sardinian dagger flew upward and pressed against Gassàn's throat.

"Do as I say or I'll slit your throat, Gassàn."

There was a sardonic sneer.

"Cut it out, Pistoia. Don't make me shoot you."

"We would die together, Gassàn."

The sardonic sneer became a bitter smile.

"It would sadden me for you, Pistoia. Weren't we friends?"

"Friends or enemies, tell your janissaries to let my colonel pass. Otherwise I'll order the M113 to roll over them, I'll kill you, you'll kill me, and we'll end like Romeo and Juliet."

The bitter smile became a sincere laugh.

"All right, Pistoia. You win. I apologize."

"Not to me. To my colonel. And make it fast."

Gassàn obeyed with a shrug. Voglia-scusarmi-colonnello, please-excuse-me-colonel. The Sardinian dagger retracted making way for Crazy Horse who excitedly clicked his heels and stood at attention.

"Sir! I warmly thank you, Sir!"

"Never mind, colonel..."

"On the contrary, Sir! Because you are a real gentleman, Sir! And while thanking you, I apologize in return for the impetuousness of my subordinate. I take the freedom of reminding you that in such cases forbearance is required. Also General Jean Lannes, Duke of Montebello and Marshal of France, as you well know, behaved in such a rough fashion during the siege of Ratisbona. Just think that after leaning a ladder against the wall of the fortress, he scrambled up with his sword and..."

"Don't worry, colonel..."

"Rebus sic stantibus, Sir, it's essential that I shake your hand and quote a maxim of Licinius: discordia fit carior concordia. Discord renders concord more sweet. Am I right?"

"You are right, colonel."

"Sir!"

And the farce concluded with his defenestration. Because while watching that scene Pistoia realized that instead of scrambling up a ladder to conquer Ratisbona, he should rob the equestrian monument of his column. So he did it, and when Crazy Horse became aware of the robbery it was too late: his M113 had left with the impetuous subordinate. What's worse, the second M113 was following him.

"Captain! For heaven's sake, where are you going, Captain?!?"

"I set out, we set out, to save time! Take the third one, colonel!"

In the third M113, the crew was resolute and sharp-witted. To keep Crazy Horse away from the radio and the Browning, they raised a wall of bodies and a chorus of obsequiousness: "Come, colonel, come. Please make yourself comfortable inside and in the back." So the three M113s could safely reach the Twenty-Five. The first, to stop in the middle of the vacant lot and reestablish the abandoned post. The second, to turn right into avenue Nasser and go to the Twenty-Four. The third, to turn left and go to the Twenty-Two where Crazy Horse poured his indignation and logorrhea upon poor Eagle.

"Behavior which deserves a court-martial, illustrious colleague! You can't imagine the affronts that scoundrel committed! And to think that in spite of his usual crimes I compared him to Jean Lannes who was, as you know, one of Napoleon's most valorous generals and not by chance is buried in Paris's Pantheon! My dear friend, Horace speaks the truth when he says sperne-vulgus, disregard-common-people! Tacitus speaks the truth when he says that common people are always ready for the worst, est vulgus ad deteriora promptum! Seneca speaks the truth when..."

"No-o-o! This is too much, I can't bear it!" poor Eagle cried when the moment came to hear Seneca's opinion. And barely controlling the only homicidal impulse of his life, the one to discharge his pistol into the vocal cords of his former Academy colleague, he did what he should have done before: he jumped into the jeep and drove off.

This took place while, with his Kalashnikov and Sergeant Natale's feathered helmet, Passepartout was joining the two Amal who fired the PK46 from the roof of the gas station. And while, with a bouquet of roses, a Christmas cake, a velvet dog, the courage that doesn't see any danger and doesn't hear any reasoning, the courage that comes from love, Ninette was about to meet him.

3

The death of a love is like the death of a loved person. It leaves behind the same grief, the same emptiness, the same refusal to accept the truth. Even if you expected it and caused it, wanted it out of self-defense or sagacity, when it happens you feel mutilated. You feel as if you're left with only one eye, one ear, one arm, one leg, one lung, half a brain, and you do nothing but invoke the lost half of yourself: the person with whom you felt whole, complete. You don't even recall his or her faults, the torments he or she inflicted on your soul, the sufferings you went through on his or her account: the regret gives you the memory of a valuable, extraordinary individual, of an irreplaceable treasure, in any case of somebody whose merits largely exceeded his or her demerits. Nor is it a relief to understand that this represents an insult to logic, an affront to intelligence, a masochism. (In love, logic doesn't help. Intelligence is useless and masochism attains psychiatric heights.) Then, slowly, it passes. Maybe outside your awareness, the grief dims and dissolves: the emptiness diminishes, the refusal to accept the truth disappears. You finally realize that the object of your dead love was neither an extraordinary individual nor an irreplaceable treasure, you replace him or her with another half or supposed half of yourself, and for a certain time you recover your wholeness. Your completeness. But your soul retains a scar that makes it ugly, a dark bruise that disfigures it, and you no longer are what you were before that death. Your energy is enfeebled, your curiosity is weakened, your faith in the future is burnt out because you sense you have wasted a piece of existence that nothing and nobody can reimburse you for... That's why, even if a love languishes without remedy, you keep it and you try to heal it. That's why, even if it is in a state of coma, you try to postpone the moment when it will breathe its last breath: you detain it and you silently implore it to live one more day, one more hour, one more minute. That's why, even when it has stopped breathing, you hesitate to bury it and in certain cases you expect to resuscitate it. Rise, Lazarus, and walk. All things that Ninette knew very well, now that she was on the verge of crossing paths with Passepartout. Now that she went to keep the appointment with her destiny.

She had repented at once for her haughty, definitive letter. After handing it over to the concierge, she had been seized by the impulse to take it back and spend a last night with her pensive Italian. Yet her will had prevailed, and she had gone back to her Ashrafieh residence: the sumptuous mansion she referred to in the letter when she said that weeping on a full stomach and in a beautiful house is more bearable than weeping on an empty stomach and in a hovel. She was still crying as she entered her home, and the tears furrowed a face very different from the one that Angelo knew: less young than he would ever imagine, incised by wrinkles which were scars left by sorrows, and as dreary as sadness itself. Seeing it, in fact, her affectionate servants had grown alarmed: "Madame! Don't you feel well, madame?!" But without an answer she had locked herself in the bedroom and sobbing George-George-George she had grabbed the photo of a handsome gray-haired man whose features strikingly resembled Angelo's: the photo of her slaughtered husband, of the man she had loved so much that the moment she'd seen his limbs scattered among the wreckage of the blown-up car she had lost her mind for months. And about those months she now remembered nothing but a nurse who pushed her wheelchair, a doctor who fixed electrodes to her skull, another one who aroused the specters of her past. The exquisite villa in the quarter of Furn el Chebbak where she had been born after the death of her father slain by the French during the revolt against their mandate. The elegant boarding school in Lausanne where she had been educated unregretfully far from a mother who delegated her duties to nannies and teachers. The luxurious apartment in London where she had lived in thoughtless freedom till the day she had returned to Beirut for the garden party given in her honor by the British embassy where she'd met the handsome gray-haired man by whom she had been immediately charmed and whom she had immediately charmed. The cathedral of Notre-Dame-du-Liban where they had married, crazy with love and heedless of those who marveled at the excessive difference of age or judged their marriage a cynical contract to join two fortunes. The eternal honeymoon which had blessed them even after the loss of a child never reconceived. The start of the civil war and the beginning of the nightmare, of the threatening calls, the messages your-husband-is-in-our-sights-so-get-ready-to-become-a-widow. The terror that they would really kill him and one morning the explosion, a voice shouting "Run, madame, run. They've killed him." Then, a silence full of inertia. The gloomy inertia in which she'd fallen after concluding that her life had ended with his. Only after leaving the clinic had she realized that life doesn't die with the death of a man too much loved, and replaced him many times. This time, with the pensive Italian who physically revived him like nobody else... Those eyes that were the same eyes, that brow that was the same brow, that nose that was the same nose, those cheekbones that were the same cheekbones, that mouth that was the same mouth, and that body that was the same body. George thirty years younger. That is why she had spoken to him, that day in August, and immediately desired him, tracked him down, transformed him into the object of her maniacal need for love. But also this love was now dead, and it had to be buried by repeating that no love can resist the absence of love. It had to be forgotten by recalling that no love is irreplaceable, that sentimental relationships are mirages we invent to fill the void, chimeras we fabricate to defeat the solitude. Thus anybody can become the object of the mirage, the instrument of the chimera.

When the sobbing had ended, she had fallen into a long heavy sleep. But the sleep only served to postpone the crisis, and at her awaking the crisis had burst to reignite the obscure disease once suspected by Angelo: the never healed madness that five years before had sent her to the clinic where the nurse pushed her wheelchair, a doctor fixed the electrodes to her skull, another one aroused the specters of her past. The sense of mutilation that comes with the death of a love had doubled. Feeling doubly deprived of one eye, one ear, one arm, one leg, one lung, half a brain she'd plunged into the regret of her pensive Italian. And more than ever the regret had given the memory of a valuable, extraordinary individual, an irreplaceable treasure, somebody whose merits largely exceeded his demerits. Oh, how enchanting his youth was! How bewitching his vitality, his ingenuous dream of finding a mathematical prescription for existence, a formula of Life! What voluptuousness there was in his physical vigor and in his almost enraged transports! She had to get him back, to recover her wholeness, her completeness... Rise, Lazarus, and walk. So at seven she'd put on an incongruous white dress that emphasized her gorgeous body, a pair of high-heeled shoes that emphasized her gorgeous legs, then the chain with the cross-shaped anchor, and ignoring the pleas of the affectionate servants don't-go-out-madame-it's-too-dangerous she had gone out. She had bought an awkward bouquet of roses, an unhandy Christmas cake, a stuffed velvet dog that in her judgment epitomized her feelings, with that absurd load she'd taken a taxi to reach the Green Line, and of course she knew what she risked. The shelling resounded all over the city, people spoke of clashes that at Gobeyre and Shatila piled dead upon dead, and since five-thirty very few dared leave the Christian Zone for the Muslim one. But the courage that comes from love doesn't heed any danger, we said, and hers was heightened by the incurable madness: without blinking an eye she had left the taxi at the Tayoune crossing, passed the rotary, reached the beginning of the short boulevard that led to rue Argàn. Here, though, she had been stopped by an Eighth Brigade officer guarding the area with a company of soldiers: "This is an operation zone, madame. Either retrace your steps or wait." So she had crouched at the foot of a pine tree, for almost two hours she had quietly remained to watch the explosions, listen to the hubbub, and like an Ophelia who goes to drown herself in a pond she now waited for the right moment to slip away.

She cast a glance at the officer who seemed to have forgotten her presence and only thought of speaking over the radio or shouting orders. She looked at the soldiers who huddling around the white mare's grassy bed grumbled among themselves and didn't even seem to notice that she was still there. She decided that the right moment had come and stood up. Careful not to rouse their attention she gathered her awkward roses, her unhandy cake, her velvet dog, started walking along the boulevard, and meanwhile she reflected on which way she should choose once she got to rue Argàn. Should she take rue Farrouk, the street that crossed Gobeyre and ended on the rond-point of Shatila, or turn right and go toward avenue Nasser? The first was certainly less exposed to fire. Taking it, however, meant entering a quarter more than inhospitable for a woman dressed like her and with a cross-shaped anchor at the neck. The second was at the center of the fighting and overflowed with shells, bullets, fragments. Taking it, however, offered the advantage of the Italian posts: in case of necessity, they might offer some shelter. She thus chose avenue Nasser and once in rue Argàn she turned right, onto the sidewalk that got to the Twenty-Two. Disregarding the shots that fell everywhere she headed for the post. But after a few steps her attention was drawn by a strange character who wearing a bersagliere's feathered helmet and waving a Kalashnikov jumped down from the roof of the gas station, stumbled over a corpse, got back on his feet, sprang forward, came toward her. And she instinctively stopped. Instinctively she placed the purse and the roses and the cake on the low wall that bordered the sidewalk, she freed her right hand and grabbed the cross-shaped anchor. She slid it around to her nape, under her long hair. Then, continuing to keep the velvet dog in her left hand, she observed the strange character more carefully. Who was he? Why did he come toward her? No, he did not come toward her. He ran in her direction, and was only a boy. An innocuous boy of thirteen or fourteen who undoubtedly had been sent to fight against his will and who taken by an uncontrollable panic now fled with the helmet a bersagliere had loaned him. Poor creature... He could have been her son... The son she had lost and never reconceived... She should stop him, console him... And moved by the most dangerous love that exists, the love called pity, she waited for him to reach her. Then she gently grabbed him by one arm.

"Esh, walad! Stop, boy."

"Let me go! What do you want? Let me go!" yelped Passepartout, really taken by an uncontrollable panic. While he had been entertaining himself on the roof of the gas station, in fact, a volley from Gobeyre had killed the two Amal with the PK46, and this had driven him out of his wits.

"Calm down, habibi. Calm down, darling..."

"Let me go, let me go!"

"Why are you so afraid, darling? Stay here..."

"No! I am not, I am not! And I don't want this, I don't want it anymore!"

"What is it that you don't want anymore, darling?"

"Thi-i-is!"

He wriggled out of her gentle grasp. He put the Kalashnikov into her right hand. He crossed rue Argàn, plunged into rue Farrouk, and from that moment all started to unfold with the rhythm of a script. An inescapable script written the day an old blind man sitting on a baby chair and smoking narghile had pointed out to Angelo the jewelry shop he was looking for, so Angelo had gone inside it and bought a residue of the happy Beirut: a gold chain holding a cross in the shape of an anchor, or rather an anchor that was actually a cross because the up-right and the crossbar formed a cross bearing a tiny Christ with a minuscule ruby that gushed from his chest... Do you see them? Passe-partout who runs with his feathered helmet, and running plunges deeper and deeper into rue Farrouk. Ninette who remains on the side-walk and, the velvet dog in her left hand, the Kalashnikov in her right, asks herself: now what do I do? But soon she decides and, abandoning the purse, the roses, the cake, she too crosses rue Argàn. She too plunges into rue Farrouk and despite her high heels she dashes off in pursuit of the boy she believes to be an innocuous boy sent to fight against his will. A boy who could have been her son, the son she lost and never reconceived. And she calls him.

"Iah walad! Boy, iah walad!"

To reach him, she thinks. To give him back his rifle. To explain to him the risks he takes getting rid of it. To tell him: don't you know what can happen if they find you without it? They can shoot you, habibi! But the more she pursues him the more the feathered helmet gains distance, and in front of the jewelry shop she halts in defeat. Better to leave it, entrust it to someone. That old man, for instance. Because there is an old man, a few paces away. Seated on a baby chair, he smokes his narghile as if the battle were taking place on another planet. Yet he seems to see everything, and should the boy come back... She approached him. Not realizing he was blind, she handed him the Kalashnikov.

"Papi! Grandpa!"

With exasperated slowness, the old man withdrew the narghile's tube from his mouth and turned his milky pupils.

"What are you giving me?"

"A rifle, papi. A boy stuck it in my hand. Then he fled and I..."

"Throw it away."

"No, papi. He might change his mind. He might come back."

"If he comes back, he finds it. If he finds it, he kills. Throw it away."

"Papi, he's just a boy..."

"The boys kill, here. Kill, kill, kill: all they know, all they do, is to kill. To die and to kill. To kill and to die. It is easy to kill. It is as easy as to die. You simply have to pull a trigger. Throw it away."

"Papi..."

"Throw it away, I said. Or hide it."

"But they might punish him, papi..."

"Throw it away. Or hide it."

He sounded so imperious in his mild detachment, so categorical, so sure of himself, that she did as he ordered. She hid it behind the door next to the jewelry shop. Then she turned her steps toward rue Argàn to go recover her purse, her roses, her Christmas cake, then to reach avenue Nasser, but the already written script didn't foresee this event. At the corner with rue Argàn the air displacement of an explosion hurled her against a wall, she fainted, and when her eyes reopened she was in a truck unloading wounded people and halting in front of a building with green flags. Around the building, a crowd of desperate women who tried to break a barrier of militiamen.

"In the name of Allah, let us in!"

"Be merciful! Let us pass!"

"We want to see them!"

"Give us a list of names!"

"Mine is named Bashir!"

"Mine, Barakaat!"

"Mine, Ismahil!"

"Mine, Sharif!"

"Mine, Alì!"

Standing over her, two male nurses who ironically pointed at the velvet dog and who clearly recognizing her stressed their derisive voices upon the appellative Madame.

"Is this dog yours, Madame?"

"Yes..."

"Can you get down by yourself, Madame?"

"Yes..."

"Then get down. Quick."

"Where am I?"

"At the hospital."

"No, I don't need anything. No..."

"You do, Madame."

She touched her lips. They were swollen and aching. She touched her nose. It was skinned and it hurt as if it were cracked. Her brow also. She observed her incongruous white dress which had become a grizzled rag, her beautiful legs which appeared disfigured by wounds, she spat out a front tooth that had come loose. Then she brought a hand to her nape to make sure that the cross-shaped anchor was still hidden under her long hair and got down.

"What hospital is this?"

"The Shiite clinic, Madame."

Yes: the Shiite clinic where one afternoon in November Charlie had sent Angelo to check if the mother of the child who needed three units of B-negative was telling the truth and where Angelo had felt the unseizable yet tangible presence of a sad apathetic Ninette never seen and never suspected... The Ninette who limping and asking for a little warmth from her absurd velvet dog was now proceeding among the bodies of the Bashirs, the Barakaats, the Ismahils, the Sharifs, the Alìs. Almost all of them, minors of thirteen or fourteen. The age of the boy who'd stuck the rifle in her hand.

*   *   *

They were everywhere. Heaped up like calves at the shambles they lay in the overflowing wards, in the packed corridors, underneath the stairways, in the bathrooms, and on the floor of the emergency room they were so many that when you walked there you trampled on them... To replace the adults decimated during the assault on the Tower, in fact, Rashid had called up dozens of untrained adolescents. He had untidily positioned them on the roofs or at the windows, and the governmental artillery had made such a massacre that in most cases the surgeons didn't even waste morphine to alleviate their suffering. They abandoned them to die, and as soon as this happened the sextons dragged them to a large room that emitted a nauseating stench then shouted to the nurses who didn't know where to place the new wounded: "One spot free! Two spots free!" The scene was horrifying. The chorus of moans, deafening. Some wept over their cauterized stumps, some howled over their sawed-off legs, some sobbed over their truncated arms, some bawled over their slashed-open bellies from which the intestines protruded with flows of shit. "Yahallah! Yahallah! Yahallah!" One, struck in the head by a huge fragment, was left with half a face: deprived of his right temple, his right ear, his right cheek, and with his nose reduced to a mush of bloody cartilage, he looked like a vivisected guinea pig. Yet he still had his jawbones, his palate, his tongue, his vocal cords, and he distinctly gurgled: "Mama, ummi, mama, please kill me. I beg you." Seeing Ninette, he flinched. He opened wide his eye, an immense blue eye which expressed an immeasurable impatience to end, and exhaled his last breath with a wheeze of relief.

"Shukràn, mama, shukràn. Thank you, mother, thank you..."

She stooped over him. Swallowing her horror, she closed his eyelid. Then, still holding her absurd velvet dog, she went to sit on the bench in the entrance. All at once she felt very, very unwell. A ferocious migraine had joined the increased soreness at her brow, her nose, her legs, her lips. Along with the ferocious migraine, a profound weariness. Along with the profound weariness, a murky apathy. And she knew why: since the day the load of Tnt had dismembered the man too much loved, she had not seen death so close. She had always been able to avoid its sight, to ignore it the way she had ignored it the day of the double slaughter: life-goes-on, darling, we-must-forget. And this had been a powerful medicine for her obscure disease. It had helped her enormously in overcoming the crises which had occurred in five years. But now that Death appeared again before her, enlarged and multiplied, now that it forced her to look at its face, the crisis begun at home was bursting to get hold of her with the symptoms that the psychiatrists had foreseen and explained. "You're a very intelligent woman, madame, and you have the right to know the truth. And the truth is that you haven't recovered: don't think that you are cured. Certain illnesses cannot be cured. They go in cycles, and any physical or psychological stress can set off a new cycle... An excessive strain, for instance. A violent emotion, a sentimental failure, a shock. You'll have periods of energy during which you'll be cheerful and talkative, lucid and uninhibited, full of desires. And periods of inertia during which you'll be melancholic and taciturn, confused and inhibited, brimful with renunciation. The latter ones produce crises which often lead to suicide or to a behavior that equals suicide. You're a manic-depressive, madame, and manic-depressives are inclined to masochism: one out of five ends up directly or indirectly killing himself. Watch out for the symptoms. The most frequent symptoms are a ferocious migraine, a profound weari-

ness, and a murky apathy. If this happens, call us at once. Agree?"
"Agree, doctor, agree." She smiled bitterly. She'd answered agree-
doctor-agree, but even if calling from Gobeyre were possible, tonight
she wouldn't. To call a doctor, to fight a crisis that may lead to suicide
or to a behavior that equals it, you need the desire to live. And suddenly her desire to live had dissolved. It had been dissolved by the
Bashirs, the Barakaats, the Ismahils, the Sharifs, and the Alìs in the
emergency room, and particularly by the boy left with half a face. By his
immeasurable impatience to die, by his wheeze of relief. "Shukràn,
mama, shukràn..." Because it had been his impatience which had made
her realize how useless it is to refuse death. How useless to hate it, to
declare I'll-never-yield, I'll-never-bend, to-its-invincibility. It had been
his wheeze which had made her understand that it is not enough to
oppose it with Life, to think or to hope that Life is the measure of all.
The mainspring of all, the goal of all. It is Death, the measure of all.
The mainspring of all, the goal of all. And Life is nothing but its instrument, its nourishment, its food. $S = K \ln W$. In other words, Mister
Boltzmann had been right in surrendering himself to it before his time,
and she might well imitate him: let herself be swallowed up by nothingness.

She passed her tongue over the hole left by her spat-out tooth, just
one of the upper incisors, she lightly caressed her nose now purple and
as monstrously swollen as her lips. With another bitter smile she
thought what a pity to have abandoned the purse in rue Argàn: it
would have been interesting to examine in a mirror the disappearance
of her legendary beauty... And the impulse to let herself be swallowed
up by nothingness grew. Who knows, maybe Death wasn't an enemy.
Maybe it was, she was, a mother. A real mother whose insatiable belly
truly offers shelter and repose. The eagerness to find that shelter, that
relief, that repose, now possessed her with such force, she said. But
then something happened. It happened that, while she was lulling herself with her eagerness and the words shukràn-mama-shukràn, instead
of the immense blue eye which expressed an immeasurable impatience
to die she saw two large eyes which expressed an immeasurable impatience to live. Angelo's eyes. And she jumped to her feet. With the
sudden, ephemeral vitality of the moribund who galvanized by an extreme spurt of energy fill their lungs to take a last breath, she rushed
out of the hospital. Oblivious of the ache of her wounds and of her
ferocious migraine, rid of her profound weariness, of her murky apathy,
she dipped into the crowd of women held back by the militiamen's
barrier, asked them how to reach the Italian headquarters. Turn right,

they answered suspiciously staring at the intruder, take the Street Without a Name, turn left, skirt the south side of Gobeyre, keep going until you reach the rond-point of Shatila and rue de l'Aérodrome. She nodded. She began walking. Limping more than ever on her high heels, shivering more than ever from the night's cold, asking more than ever for a little warmth from the velvet dog, she headed toward the Street Without a Name where the inferno was now total. The M48s marshaled in Shatila had in fact doubled their barrage, the Sixth Brigade's mortars had increased their fire, and many grenades were falling on the street. But she didn't care. She only cared to arrive as soon as possible, to know as soon as possible that Angelo was well, and at every step she repeated: "I don't want to see him, I don't want to be seen by him. All I want is to know that he is alive and unhurt. I can't die in peace if I don't know that he is alive and unhurt." She skirted the south side of Gobeyre. She reached the rond-point of Shatila where at the Twenty-Four the squad leader of the M113 that had come with Rapid Intervention saw her through the loopholes and exclaimed: "For Christsake! Does that woman have balls!" She entered rue de l'Aérodrome. She covered the three hundred yards that still separated her from the headquarters. She approached the sentry box where the carabinieri on guard got alarmed and wondered who could be that toothless hag who limped and carried a strange velvet bundle. A loon, a bum, the crazy woman of Shatila?

"Alto là! Halt right there!"

"Chi sei? Who are you?"

"Che c'é in quel fagotto? What's in that bundle?"

"Una bomba? A bomb?"

"Vattene! Scram!"

She leaned against the sandbags.

"Please, I want to know if Angelo..."

"Via, ialla, via! Beat it!"

Only one intervened in her favor.

"Let her speak, dammit! Don't you see she's almost dead?!?" Then, turning to her and speaking in English: "Come on, tell me what you're looking for."

"I want to know if Angelo is alive. Unhurt and alive..."

"Angelo, the sergeant from the Arab Bureau?"

"Yes..."

"Sure he's alive! Unhurt and alive. He just came back from Shatila."

She raised herself upright with a spurt of energy like the one that had galvanized her at the hospital.

"Really?"

"Really. I swear! But who are you?"

"Ninette... I am Ninette."

"Ninette?!?"

They shined the flashlights on her. They studied her more carefully. One by one, little by little, they recognized the sleek chestnut hair which waved in glitters of gold, the disquieting violet eyes, the long legs, the perfect body of the gorgeous woman who almost every day came with her contagious gaiety to meet the sober-looking guy from the Arab Bureau, and exploded in a chorus of incredulity.

"God dammit, you're really Ninette!"

"What happened to you, Ninette?!?"

"You lost a tooth! You broke your nose!"

"How did you get here?!?"

"We'll call Angelo at once!"

She suddenly drew back.

"No! Don't!"

"Why not?"

"Because..."

She bent over the velvet dog. She slowly caressed the tiny bloodstains that had soiled its chest and its throat. She placed it on the sandbags.

"Just give him this."

"This?!? What is it? A toy?"

"No. A gift. A farewell gift," she murmured. And she left without answering their calls.

"Ninette! Where are you going, Ninette?!?"

"Ninette! Don't go away, wait!"

"Ninette! Come back, Ninette, it's dangerous there!"

"Ninette! Stay with us, stay here!"

She didn't even hear them. She didn't need to. Now that the sufferings of her soul were over, the only thing she needed was to do what had always horrified her: to imitate Mister Boltzmann, to deliver herself to the Mother whose insatiable belly offers shelter and relief and repose. And knowing it gave her a placid happiness. It soothed her with the sense of liberation which soothes every human being who realizes that his or her vital cycle is concluded and thus, devoid of any fear or regret, goes looking for a place to die. She retraced the three hundred yards of rue de l'Aérodrome. She reached the rond-point of Shatila. Here she paused and, with a serene movement, she brought her right arm behind her neck to seek the cross-shaped anchor hidden under her long hair. With the same serene movement she slid it back to its place, well visible at her throat. Then, with the slow steps of a person who has no hurry because eternity lies ahead and eternity waits, she started walking again. She arrived at the Street Without a Name, she crossed it, and when she was on the other side she seemed to head up avenue Nasser. But she didn't. As if she had sensed that her appointment with destiny was not in avenue Nasser, it was in rue Farrouk, she entered rue Farrouk. Here she walked about fifty yards, reached the old blind man on the baby chair who impassively smoked his narghile, and she was about to say papi, has-that-boy-come-back-to-take-the-rifle, when a nasty voice struck her.

"My Kalashnikov!"

It was Passepartout who a moment before had been found by Rashid without the Kalashnikov and forced to endure his fury. You-ran-away, little-coward. You-dropped-your-Kalashnikov, filthy-deserter. Go-get-it-or-you'll-curse-the-day-you-were-born, stupid-faggot. Taken by a new uncontrollable panic he had therefore returned to search for the woman he'd given it to, and here she was. Though much less white, her white dress glowed in the dark like a lamp. And though she was disfigured, dirty with blood, he could recognize her in a blink. She recognized him too, the feathered helmet was unmistakable, and she immediately went toward him.

"Iah walad, boy..."

The nasty voice grew nastier.

"You stole it, you thief! You stole it!"

"No, habibi, no! What are you saying, darling? You gave it to me: remember?"

"I didn't give you a thing, liar! You took it, you stole it to sell it! You sold it and now he will skin me!"

"No, habibi, no. I hid it..."

"Where?!? Tell me where, you toothless hag!"

"There, darling, inside that door..."

"What door?!?"

"That one next to the jeweler's shop... Don't cry, quiet down. I'll get it, wait..."

"Don't," the old man said turning his milky pupils. "Don't do it."

"But I have to, papi. If I don't, they'll kill him. Didn't you hear?" she answered.

"I said don't. If he gets it, he'll kill you."

She smiled calmly. She stepped into the entrance next to the jeweler's shop. She picked up the Kalashnikov, went back to Passepartout who grabbed it with rage and made the gesture of running away. But in the very same moment the flames of a burning house brightened the minuscule ruby that gushed from Christ's chest, thus illuminating the cross-shaped anchor, and a howl shook rue Farrouk.

"Christian! Whore! Spy!"

Ninette just had time to spot the hand ripping the cross-shaped anchor and the chain from her neck, then the expression of Passepartout who slipped it into his pocket. An expression both obtuse and perfidious, she thought in amazement, yet as innocent as it can be for a poor wretch who has been taught to kill and destroy and nothing else. Immediately after she heard the click of the trigger releasing the percussion pin, she saw a yellow glare, she felt a volley of very hot stones that pierced her throat and her chest, then pushed her backwards. And while everything became black, motionless and black, while Passepartout howled again Christian-whore-spy, while the old blind man muttered I-told-her-don't-do-it, don't-give-it-to-him, the toothless hag dropped to the ground with a large gash in her throat and a large gash in her chest and long ribbons of blood that unbound to soak the asphalt. Thus she opened wide her stupendous violet eyes, she exhaled a long breath of assuagement, and letting the nothingness swallow her up she delivered herself to the Mother whose insatiable belly offers shelter and repose and relief. Shukràn, mama, shukràn...

This happened at midnight.

4

It was precisely at midnight, while in a shelter the Head Chaplain celebrated his Mass with the usual promises of brotherhood and peace, that the hopes of obtaining a truce seemed to vanish and the battle reached its climax. Unable to invade Gobeyre with an M48 attack from avenue Nasser because the alleys were too narrow and the tanks would have been blockaded inside them, from the sides because rue Argàn offered no access and the Street Without a Name bordered Haret Hreik as well as Shyah, the governmentals of the Sixth and the Eighth Brigades turned to the heavy artillery: the 130mm and 155mm guns that Gemayel kept in the mountains. Then Rashid responded with everything that was left: Chinese rockets, PK46 machine guns, 60mm and 81mm mortars, Kalashnikovs, Rpg. The volcano's lava overflowed the limits inside which it had been contained for almost seven hours, its lapilli hailed onto the headquarters, the field hospital, the Logistics base, the Eagle base, they splashed as far as Bourji el Barajni, and the personal drama of the Condor reached the most painful peaks. What a mistake to believe that giving orders is easy, that commanding is a pleasure. What a blunder. Because commanding means deciding for the others, deciding for the others means making choices over the hides of the others, and making choices over the hides of the others means bearing a load of torments. If you have a minimum of brains and conscience, if you are not an idiot or an irresponsible or a delinquent, every option seems like an ambush: a proposal as unstable as the patterns of a kaleidoscope that at the slightest touch shifts its mirrors to dissolve their colors and shapes and rearrange them in a different way. A square where there was a triangle, a hexagon where there was a square, a rhombus where there was a trapezium, white where there was black, yellow where there was red, green where there was pink or brown or blue. And each shape or color, an alternative which is at the same time valid and disastrous. A dilemma which tears your soul to pieces. Every leader knows it. Every person who, not being an idiot or an irresponsible or a delinquent, has found himself or herself in charge of a group. But very few know it better than a general at war. That is, a man on whose decisions the life or death of hundreds or even thousands of people (including his own soldiers) depends. And, tonight, nobody knew it better than the Condor who had finally decided to answer fire with fire. Meaning, to let the ships attack.

Around ten, Charlie had called him on the walkie-talkie from Zandra Sadr's house and said: "General, the telephones are still down in Gobeyre, and the messengers sent by His Eminence haven't come back yet. His Eminence asks us to be patient, to wait. Let's be patient, general. Let's wait..." And, though unwillingly, he'd accepted. Around eleven, Charlie had called again and said: "General, it seems that the messengers were trapped on their way back, and His Eminence has sent some couriers to look for them. He's begging us to give him another thirty or forty minutes. Let's do it, general..." And, amidst a lot of shouting, he'd granted that time too. But after the forty minutes Charlie had remained silent, Gemayel's artillery had begun blasting with the 130mm and 155mm guns, the volcano's lava had started to overflow onto the headquarters and the field hospital and the Logistics and the Eagle base and Bourji el Barajni, and head down the Condor had left the Operations Room. He'd shut himself in his office, placed himself at the radio tuned to the frequency of Albatross, the cruiser carrying the ships' commodore, and within a few moments he'd reached the stage we reach when something decides for us. It doesn't happen only in war situations. It happens in daily life. For example, in the social or sentimental relationships that cost too much grief and are worn down in the grief until they hang from a thread... If you're not an incurable gambler who resolves his dilemmas with rouge-ou-noir, les-jeux-sont-faits, rien-ne-va-plus, before cutting that thread you think carefully. Maybe it's a sturdy thread, you force yourself to think. Maybe it can remake what is worn out, you say with forced hope. And even if you bleed to death, you wait. Even if the precariousness of the relationship has frozen in an eternal wait for improvement, you postpone your decision: your impulse to cut the thread. Then, suddenly, something decides for you. What? An episode that rubs out the remains of your forced optimism. An act that erases the residue of your forced hope. A word that makes you conclude: no, it is not a sturdy thread: it is an extremely slender one, it practically doesn't exist. Enough with patience, enough with waiting, enough with hoping. Then you stretch out your hand and cut it. The Condor stretched out his hand. He lifted the microphone. And while he's bringing it to his mouth to call Albatross, let's see what he sees with his eyes dimmed by the torment of the leader who must decide for the others. Who must make his choices over the hides of the others.

*   *   *

He sees the ships that two miles off the coast move slowly with their guns and their missiles already aimed. And on each ship, behind the bridge, a large spectral room barely brightened by a fluorescent purple twilight. A kind of waterless aquarium. In the middle of the spectral room, a round and horizontal screen where mysterious ectoplasms float: fluid outlines, icy flashes. Along the wall, square and vertical screens on which emerald-green smudges flicker, swept through three hundred sixty degrees by a brush of light. Nothing else seems to move in the fluorescent and purple shade, not a sound breaks the silence. Not a single voice. In fact, at first glance you think the room is empty. You must narrow your eyes to discern the calm individuals with headphones on their ears who sit at the round and horizontal screen or in front of the square and vertical screens. The first ones, to operate strange handles which move the mysterious ectoplasms; the second ones, to operate strange keyboards which are connected with the brush of light. You observe them in bafflement, you wonder who they are. Monks performing an esoteric rite? Spiritualists trying to contact the souls of the dead? Disciples of a secret sect praying for the salvation of humanity? No. They're military men. And this is the Operative Combat Station, the OCS. As for the round and horizontal screen, it displays the synthesis of the collected and elaborated data to furnish a map of the targets to bomb. The fluid geometric outlines are the interpretations of the targets. The icy flashes are arrows that shift to point them out. The square and vertical screens show radar images from the sky, the sea, the ground. The emerald-green smudges are the electronic echoes of the beaches and mountains and villages and cities upon which the guns and missiles will pour their fire... No, here you don't see houses that burn, yellow hovels that blow up, mice with two legs and two arms that flee dragging suitcases and mattresses and televisions, uniformed acrobats who gauging their courage to the grain run under a hail of bullets, kids who fly to heaven with a pot of hummus and schawarma, little girls who die beneath the rubble with their mother and their grandfather and their goat and their dog. You don't see nineteen-year-old recruits who dirty with urine sob I-am-not-an-umbrella, proud squad leaders who almost get killed to recover their feathered helmet, magnificent dwarfs who conquer useless towers and keep singing with-my-teeth-I-will-defend-this-tower-with-my-teeth, pacifists turned into pitiless warriors who cure their hate by disintegrating their enemies with brahmet-bayis. You don't see crazy colonels with monocles and riding crops who shout heroic nonsense and offer their chest to fire, or belligerent captains who put their dagger to their friends' throats, or gorgeous women gone mad with grief who let themselves be slaughtered by young criminals and die thanking Death whom they call Mother. You don't see the uncomfortable, painful, concrete, bestial yet human war which is fought at close range and soils us with blood. No: here you see the comfortable, painless, abstract, rational yet inhuman war which is fought at a distance and does not soil us at all. The modern war. The technological war. The cowardly war we delegate to the Supreme Being with whom we have replaced the Eternal Father and Jehovah and Allah or Whatever. (All of them gods capable of some mercy, at times. Therefore visceral, imperfect.) The Supreme Being who doesn't even consider the use of mercy. The perfect god who thinks for us, works for us, judges for us, kills for us. The really omnipotent, omnipresent, omniscient god Computer.

Hallelujah, hallelujah! Who's unfamiliar with the omnipotence and omnipresence and omniscience of this wizard capable of any marvel or sorcery? He unquestionably knows everything. He indisputably can do everything. And, materialized in infinite shapes or microscopic dimensions, it dwells everywhere. In your wristwatch, in your telephone, in your television set. In the greengrocer's and the butcher's scales, in the telescope of the astronomer who studies black holes, in the calculator of the imbecile who can't even add two and two by himself. In the files of the tax offices and police stations, in the merry-go-round at the Luna Park, in the controls of an airplane or a submarine. In the secret agent's shoes or fountain pen, in your heart's pacemaker, in the doll that laughs and cries and walks, in the photoelectric cell that catches your license plate when you speed, in the satellite that journeys among the planets of our solar system and beyond. But, above all, in the implements of modern war. The technological war, the cowardly war. So, aboard these ships that the Condor now sees with dimmed eyes, it dwells in the room next to the Operative Combat Station. A brightly lit room, this one, dizzy with the buzzing of the air conditioners which maintain a constant temperature of 20 degrees centigrade (68 degrees Fahrenheit) because woe to us if his sacred mechanisms suffer a little heat or cold; because woe to us if a speck of dust or a wisp of smoke ends up among his divine neurons. Always equal to himself because aboard each ship he needs an exact copy of himself, the god stands on a paneled platform beneath which his holy tentacles extend. And in this particular case his physiognomy is that of a gunmetal-gray parallelepi-ped. His features: fifty-nine inches in height, forty-three inches in depth and in width, almost three hundred pounds in weight. To breathe, he uses an electric current of five thousand watts. To function, two operators in white smocks and white shoes and white gloves. Obse-quious and untiring, the two operators check the divine neurons, over-see the sacred mechanisms, inspect the holy tentacles, and the Omnipo-tent-Omnipresent-Omniscient congratulates them by blinking a red eye and a green one. A benign entity, you would say. A god in the service of Life like a pacemaker. Instead, when he works with the repli-cas of himself, the bloody bastard deals Death at a frightening speed. The speed of light which within a second travels from earth to the moon or circles the earth seven and a half times. At one hundred eighty-six thousand miles per second, in fact, he primes a chain of electronic consents that we could never prime, sets in motion a se-quence of electrical impulses that we could never set in motion, exe-cutes a series of simultaneous operations that we could never execute. He instructs the missiles already placed on the launching pads and simultaneously loads the guns, gives them the targets, the trajectories, the firing rate. He orders thirty shots per minute if the guns are 127mm guns, fifty-eight if the guns are 76mm guns, he commands them to divide those shots into volleys of four shells: each of them leaving as soon as the breechblock closes. Load and shoot, load and shoot, load and shoot, load and shoot, pause. Load and shoot, load and shoot, load and shoot, load and shoot, pause... Kill and destroy, kill and destroy, kill and destroy, kill and destroy, rest. Kill and destroy, kill and destroy, kill and destroy, kill and destroy, rest. And don't hope to witness some failure or interruption caused by some mistake. The bloody bastard never makes mistakes. He wouldn't even if he had a soul begging him to try: his infallibility attains the absolute. But be careful: like all gods, he exists only because men exist. The men who conceived him and begot him and suckled him and programmed him. He functions only because the calm individuals with headphones on their ears move the mysterious ectoplasms and operate the strange handles and administer his omnipotence, his omnipresence, his omniscience, his infallibility. Without them he's nothing but a vulnerable clump of electrical wires, a delicate gadget that can be ruined by a hint of heat or cold, broken by a speck of dust or a wisp of smoke. And, in order to deal Death at the speed of light, he needs a man to give him the order. Here and now, the Condor.

The Condor is well aware of this. He's equally aware that by giving the order he will end up bombarding himself, that half of the thirty or fifty-eight shells per minute will fall on the Italian sector. So, despite the severed thread, he still has a moment of hesitation. And during that moment his mind too travels at the speed of light. Every mile, every yard, every foot, every inch, a missile or a grenade that explodes inside his brain. Do you know how many things a person can think while light travels from the earth to the moon or circles the earth seven and a half times? Do you know how much a person may suffer while thinking, how much he or she may flagellate himself or herself? An apocalyptic hurricane is now spinning in his head: a whirl of thoughts and feelings as rapid as the electronic consents, the electrical impulses, the simultaneous operations carried out by the god capable of any marvel or sorcery. And, in the whirl, the haunting image of the train Grandfather used to speak of. In the locomotive, driving, he: the railwayman. In the first cars, the marò and the bersaglieri who have been in Shatila for twenty-four hours. Hungry, cold, frightened. With them, the company of Rapid Intervention and the officers who share their fate. Poor Eagle whom he has always mistreated, poor Crazy Horse whom he has always humiliated, poor Hawk whom he has always criticized, poor Sandokan whom he has always insulted, poor Pistoia whom he has always exploited. In the following cars, the paratroopers on guard at Bourji el Barajni and all the other troops staying at the Eagle base or at the Logistics as well as the personnel of the field hospital and the headquarters. In the final cars, those who are quartered at Sierra Mike or the Ruby base and who seemed to be outside the range of the battle and instead are not because Gemayel's artillery has stirred up Jumblatt's artillery... Maybe I should reknot the thread, the Condor thinks, maybe I should have an extra dose of patience and wait for Charlie's call. Or maybe I should stretch out the interval between the two phases of the order... The order begins with three words, ready-for-fire, and they are not irrevocable words. Once they're pronounced, the Computer primes the chain of consents, sets in motion the sequence of impulses, performs the series of simultaneous operations, then it stops to wait for the three additional words which really are irrevocable ones: fire-at-will. If Charlie's call came between the ready-for-fire and the fire-at-will, it would still be possible to turn back by saying: order-suspended, order-annulled. Yes, maybe it's worth reknotting the thread... Maybe Zandra Sadr's messengers are right now returning from Gobeyre with a positive response... Maybe they've already re-ported it to Zandra Sadr... Maybe Zandra Sadr has already instructed Charlie to notify the general... Maybe Charlie is about to call... Then two nearby explosions shake the headquarters, a handful of plaster chips fall on his head, he realizes that the battle has reached rue de l'Aérodrome, he recalls that fortune is a whore we must not depend on, and takes the microphone. He brings it to his mouth: "Albatross, at-tention, Albatross. Condor One here."

"Go ahead, Condor One. Albatross here," the commodore an-swered.

"Ready for fire!"

"Ready for fire," the commodore repeated.

"Ready for fire," the Operative Combat Station confirmed.

"Ready for fire," said the Computer to itself and to the copies of itself.

Then it prepared for the words fire-at-will, and it was at that moment that the Condor's walkie-talkie crackled to bring Charlie's exultant voice.

"Condor One, Condor One! Charlie-Charlie here!"

"Go ahead, Charlie..."

"General! His Eminence's messengers have returned! The Amal ac-cept the truce! It will become effective as soon as we inform the governmentals!"

Ten minutes later the truce became effective, and the Condor had to apologize to the goddess with the blind or blindfolded eyes. Even when the battle had reached its climax, there had not been any casualties among the Italians.

* * *

There hadn't been any in Shatila where a rocket coming from the northwest corner of Gobeyre and aimed at the Sixth Brigade's mortars had missed the Twenty-Eight's M113 and fallen on the opposite sidewalk killing Ahmed who stood outside to enjoy the show. There hadn't been any at the headquarters where one shell had burst on the sandbags of the Operations Room and one near the basement, that is, near the Arab Bureau and the powder magazine called Sugar's Museum. There hadn't been any at the field hospital where seven 81mm grenades had fallen but none had exploded because of faulty fuses. There hadn't been any at the Logistics, where a garage had blown up with several jeeps and no man. There hadn't been any at the Eagle base where a fifth of the camp had caught fire and the bathroom next to Eagle's Louis XVI bedroom had been destroyed. There hadn't been any at Bourji el Barajni where during the final half-hour the hail of shells had not spared a single post. There hadn't been any at Sierra Mike where a 130mm bomb had seriously damaged the infirmary in which Calogero the Fisherman lay inside a straitjacket. (Informed of his escape, Sandokan had rushed off and found him on the beach at Ramlet el Baida: a vague shape zigzagging along the seaside, a faint voice begging the wind for a boat, a-boat-to-return-to-Formìca.) And finally, there hadn't been any at the Ruby base where a Katyusha launched by the Druzes had destroyed Rocco and Imaam's oasis... Of course there had been many wounded. Those who were on the guard towers, for instance, had caught plenty of fragments. The same for those who had remained on guard at the checkpoints or at the machine guns placed on the roofs. But never in vital parts of the body, and the Head Chaplain took advantage of this to support the validity of his theories. Before the ite-Missa-est, in fact, he said that tonight the Infant Jesus had been reborn in Beirut to save the soldiers of the Italian contingent. But nobody imbibed it, and later many free thinkers posed him questions as uncomfortable as they were legitimate. If the Eternal Father is the eternal father of all men and loves them all in the same manner, they asked, why had he indulged in so many favoritisms and injustices? Why had he spared the Italians (a kindness for which they fervently thanked him, of course) and mowed down so many others? And what about Allah: what was he doing in the meantime? Was he sleeping, was he dancing with the houris, was he playing cards with the devil? Besides, aren't the Eternal Father and Allah the same thing: different names for the same mercy? Or are they truly empty hopes, useless fantasies, fruits of our imagination and desperation?

The Head Chaplain replied that human reason, so imperfect because of the original sin committed by Adam and Eve with the apple, cannot penetrate the mystery of the Lord's grand design. So they better shut up. Which they did. And meanwhile, in Shatila, the gatherers of the dead came out to start their work.

5

The doors were unbolted, the rolling shutters were raised, the windows were reopened, and like mice reentering their lair the inhabitants who had survived the desperate flight returned to their houses and their hovels. Those who had chosen to remain inside them, on the contrary, came out holding ropes. And like cats emerging from a burrow when the storm is over, in the beginning they advanced with short cautious steps: hardly breathing from fear and narrowing their eyes to locate new dangers. The truce had been announced by the governmental radio with a special bulletin, the muezzins had ratified it from the minarets with prayers of thanks to Allah, the Italians had confirmed it from their posts with jubilant howls and joyous oaths, but the people holding the ropes wouldn't trust even God himself. Only after reassuring themselves that nobody was shooting anymore, that the battle had really ceased, did they begin to walk expeditiously and with the air of going to seek something. They went to seek the dead. And as soon as they found one they stopped without saying a word, they knotted an end of rope around his or her thorax or ankles, they put the other end over their own shoulders, and dragged the corpse away. As if it were rubbish. Finding the dead was easy. They were all over though most of them were piled up in the area of the Tower, to the southeast of Sabra, around the Twenty-Two, around the Twenty-Five, and in the alleys or lanes parallel to avenue Nasser. Burying them at once wasn't easy, instead: as Gobeyre's cemetery overflowed with the corpses of its quarter, Saint Elias's cemetery accepted only the corpses of the Maronite Christians, and the Old City cemeteries were too far away, the only available place was the communal grave where improvised diggers were already at work. So along the Main Street of Sabra and the long narrow street of the ex-Twenty-Five Alpha, now abandoned by Gassàn and garrisoned by the Sixth Brigade's mortarmen with twelve jeeps, an unexpected and hallucinatory spectacle was forming little by little: two columns of shadows which seemed to drag their own shadows and which headed with laborious slowness toward the intersection of the Twenty-One. Here they met at a right angle to become a single silent procession, a spectral parade of phantoms, and filing through the space left by the M113s of the Sixth and the M48 of the Eighth they reached the communal grave where they untied the corpses. They gave them to the improvised gravediggers who immediately flung them amidst the remains of the thousand Palestinians butchered a year and four months before. There was no other way. Unless you have rivers of formalin and lots of refrigerated compartments, after a battle or a bombing or a massacre the dead must be buried at once. Otherwise they rot. They infect the living with their putrefaction. They cause epidemics, they taint the air with their stench. That sweetish, nauseating, ghastly stench that in spite of washing remains on your skin and on your hair for days. In your nostrils, for weeks nay months. In your memory, forever.

Sitting in the jeep with which he'd escaped Crazy Horse's logorrhea then halted at the Twenty-Three, Eagle observed the spectral procession and obsessively mumbled: "Holy Moses! San Gennaro, San Gerardo, San Guglielmo, Abraham, Isaac, Jacob, Jesus! This time too they cannot be less than a thousand, and for a neighborhood battle a thousand dead are so many. Too many..." At a certain point in fact he had begun to count the bodies dragged along by the gatherers, and in five minutes he'd arrived at thirty-six. From this number he had figured that between Sabra and Shatila the victims could not be less than three or four hundred, in Gobeyre at least six or seven hundred, and such a calculation dismayed him even more than the comment Crazy Horse had made while looking at the carnage in the Twenty-Two's little square: "Bagatelles, my illustrious friend, bagatelles. Thirty-two thousand French and forty-thousand Austrians fell at Wagram on the 5th and 6th of July 1809. Seventy-two thousand altogether." He was also abashed by the way the governmentals watched the unexpected and hallucinatory spectacle: maybe distracted by their own losses, very limited in comparison and yet far from being negligible, neither those with the cross at their necks nor those without it showed the slightest sign of pity or interest. And, finally, he was disheartened by the stunning silence that petrified both quarters, the total absence of noise that had followed the infernal hubbub of the seven-hour combat. Then, within that silence, an almost imperceptible chirping arose. The repetition of the word that in Arabic means help, help-me. "Saedni...saedni... saedni..." He peered into the darkness. The sound came from a young woman he had already seen emerging from the pathway that connected the Twenty-Four with the center of Shatila, running to the communal grave, fluttering around it with the frenetic movements of a butterfly blinded by a sudden light, and then bending over the hollow to examine the new bodies which had been thrown inside. Now, however, she had moved away. And as slowly as if she had consumed all her energy, she was coming toward his jeep. He addressed her politely.

"What do you want, dear?"

"Muhammad...saedni..."

"Tell me, dear! Parla, parlez, speak!"

"Saedni... Muhammad..."

"Muhammad who? Qui, chi?"

"Muhammad baby...my baby..."

"Your baby? Did you lose your baby? Hai perduto il tuo bambino, avez-vous perdu votre enfant?"

"Na'am, yes..."

"Perduto o morto, lost or dead?"

Her immense black eyes widened in horror.

"Là, no! No morto, pas mort, no dead! Talieni..."

"I don't understand, dear. Non capisco, je ne comprends pas, mish fahèm!"

"Talieni...sadiqi talieni..."

"Sadiqi talieni? Amico italiano, ami italien, Italian friend?"

"Na'am, yes!"

"Where, dove, ou?"

"Hamsa ua aeshrina..."

"Mish fahèm, I don't understand!"

"Hamsa ua aeshrina..."

She was waving her hands, while she said hamsa-ua-aeshrina. With her right hand she wiggled the index finger and the thumb, indicating two. With her left all five fingers. And Eagle began to understand.

"Due, deux, two, etnén?"

"Na'am, yes, na'am!"

"Cinque, cinq, five, hamsa?"

"Na'am, yes, na'am!"

"Venticinque, vingt-cinq, twenty-five, hamsa ua aeshrina?"

"Na'am, yes! Hamsa ua aeshrina, na'am!"

"I understand. Come with me. I'll take you there."

He helped her to get in the jeep. He left the Twenty-Three, he drove to the long narrow street that led to the Twenty-Five. Proceeding at a walking pace because the Sixth Brigade's twelve jeeps were drawn up along the south wall, he reached the vacant lot of the Twenty-Five. He got her to the M113 of the Rapid Intervention.

"This woman is looking for her child. A baby, a boy, I don't know. Anyway his name is Muhammad and he has an Italian friend at the Twenty-Five. Have you seen him?"

"Nossir," the squad leader answered. "But Muhammad is the same as Mahomet, and over there they have a dead kid whose name is Mahomet."

"Over where?"

"Behind the sandbags under the fig tree, sir."

"Who put him behind the sandbags?!"

"I don't know, sir. Maybe the bersagliere usually on guard under the fig tree. He has dug himself in there and won't let anybody take the body away."

"Who is this bersagliere?"

"The one who got the medal from the French for digging the little girl out of the water-closet, sir."

"Oh, no!" exclaimed Eagle, suddenly recalling the answer Hawk had given him by radio around nine o'clock. Nothing-colonel, nothing. A-kid-got-killed-here-at-the-Twenty-Five... The-little-boy-who-always-came-to-visit-the-bersagliere-under-the-fig-tree. And-I'm-afraid-he's-taking-it-badly... And already in anguish he turned to the young woman who now looked at him hopefully.

"Aspetta qui. Wait here."

"Na'am, yes..."

While she was saying yes, however, her eyes turned to the fig tree. They stared at it in perplexity, they moved to Ferruccio who as still as a statue blocked the entrance of the enclosure, and somehow sensing that this was the fig tree Muhammad always talked about, this was the friend for whom he'd fled with the pot of hummus and schawarma, she broke away from Eagle and ran to Ferruccio.

"Monsieur! Signore, sir!"

"Christ, oh Christ..." stammered Ferruccio recognizing Mahomet's face in her face.

"Sadiqi Muhammad? You amico, friend of Muhammad?"

"Christ, oh Christ..." Ferruccio kept stammering.

"Talieni sadiqi Muhammad? Muhammad's Italian friend?"

"Christ, no..." Ferruccio sobbed stretching an arm to send her away. But she had already understood by now, she had already slipped into the enclosure, already seen, and a shriek ripped through the Twenty-Five. An almost inhuman shriek.

"Mu-u-u-ha-a-a-mma-a-ad!"

Then, all at once, the stunning silence that had petrified the quarter broke. And from every street, every alley, every lane, every house, every hovel, every shanty, door, roof, terrace, window, from every hole, a tremendous chorus arose. A lugubrious chorus of groans and howls and voices that called the dead. The Bashirs, the Ismahils, the Sharifs, the Alìs, and the Barakaats killed in Shatila. The Leydas, the Fatimas, the Jamilas, and the Aminas killed beside the Bashirs and Ismahils and Sharifs and Alìs and Barakaats. And along with that lugubrious chorus, an unusual sound. The inimitable sound that Arab women emit by drumming the tongue against the palate and gurgling a shrill gurgle, a piercing scream made up of infinite screams whose significance changes according to the circumstance, so at times it expresses protest, at times jubilation, at times grief, and in the last case it is the most unbearable sound you can hear. A sound that seems like a weeping of Cyclopes, a sobbing uttered by hordes of tortured animals...

"Ohi-ohi-ohi-ohi-ohi-ohi-ohi!"

Even if you've heard it before, even if you know it well, hearing it again makes you shiver. Eagle had never heard it, so the effect on him was deranging. Because, all at once, he forgot the Jewish rancors in which he'd been educated. He forgot his mother, his Uncle Ezechiele, his relatives in Tel Aviv and Jerusalem, the menorah, the Torah, and with a sudden, inexorable overturn of sentiments, he felt an irresistible love for his people's worst enemies: be they Palestinians or Shiites. Those unlikable, untrustworthy, deceitful Palestinians who had stolen the happy city and destroyed it with their abuses and boasts and wars but who in their turn had been robbed of their cities and their homes and now lived like animals, like animals they ate and slept and refused to pick up their garbage and hurled insults at those who did it for them, like animals sold their daughters and sisters and wives, like animals slaughtered and were slaughtered, but like animals were buried and unburied to make room for the newly killed... Those retrograde primitive savage Shiites whose sole talents were hating and killing and obeying the muezzins, the mullahs, the ayatollahs, and blaming the others for their own miseries. Those obtuse and idle and vicious illiterates who worked the land only to grow hashish, those vampires who bred terrorists the way mice breed mice, who smiled with happiness only when they went to massacre hundreds of people with their trucks full of hexogen, but who had always been exploited and humiliated and tyrannized by everybody, Westerners included, always kept in ignorance and poverty and fanaticism, always fucked by the mosques and minarets and the singsong Allah-akbar, Allah-akbar, Allah-akbar... And along with that love he felt a profound shame for having despised them so. Along with that shame, the need to do something that would go beyond the limits of courtesy or politeness. In the grip of that need he approached the devastated creature who had fallen upon her dead son, he lifted her up. He drew her away from the guard post, he helped her to get back in the jeep, dried her tears, then he told Ferruccio to wrap Mahomet in a blanket, to lay him on her lap, and accompanied her back to the communal grave. Here, pushing aside the diggers, he gently placed the small wrapped body in the spot she indicated with a trembling finger. The spot where one year and four months before they had thrown her husband and her father and her brother and her raped daughter. He buried him with his own hands. Finally, he entrusted her to a group of women and went to the Twenty-Two to get the little girl from the crèche and bury her, too.

But Rambo wouldn't let him.

"Give her to me, Rambo..."

"Nossir."

"She has to be buried, Rambo..."

"I know, sir."

"Let me do it, Rambo."

"Nossir. I must do it myself."

"All right... Put your jacket back on."

Shaking his head, Rambo took the jacket he had covered the tiny naked corpse with. He put it on. And the incredible thing which would set in motion the final drama as well as divert Angelo's thoughts from Ninette took place.

* * *

Ninette had been dead for at least twenty minutes when, finally informed by the carabinieri and yelling why-didn't-you-call-me-all-the-same-you-stupid-bastards, Angelo had run off to trace her in rue de l'Aérodrome and the Street Without a Name and the rond-point of Shatila and avenue Nasser and rue Argàn: everywhere except rue Farrouk. The truce had already started when, deaf to the amused comments you-got-a-toy, Father-Christmas-brought-you-a-toy, he'd shut himself in his dugout to intensify his pain with anguished questions. She had come, she had come, so why had she forbidden the carabinieri to call him? And why hadn't they recognized her at once? Why did they say that she was battered, dirty, lame, and even missing a tooth? Why was the chest and throat of her absurd gift soiled with bloodstains? Then Charlie had arrived, worn out from his meeting with Zandra Sadr. He had called him and said: "It seems they're opening the communal grave and tossing in it a fuckload of corpses. I should go and see, observe the reactions of the governmentals, but the Condor wants to see me. Go in my place and watch." He'd gone. Without ceasing to pose himself questions, he'd entered at the Twenty-Five. Without noticing that Ferruccio was sobbing, he'd parked the jeep next to the enclosure under the fig tree. Without lifting his eyes toward the damn Tower that nobody wanted anymore he'd taken the long narrow street where the twelve jeeps were lined up with the headlights off, he'd stopped to watch the shadows that dragged their own shadows. Yet not even this had diverted his thoughts from Ninette. But when he saw Rambo carrying the tiny naked corpse of a child, everything changed. And he heard himself muttering two words he almost never said.

"My God!"

He wasn't the only one. It took your breath away to see that blood-stained giant who advanced all alone with the rifle on his shoulder and the Khomeini badge on his chest, carrying the tiny naked corpse of a child. It struck you more than the spectral parades of phantoms, more than the lugubrious chorus that seems like a weeping of Cyclopes, more than the young mother holding the wrapped body of her son, and the Shiite soldiers in the first jeep had the identical reaction: "Yahallah!" Moaning yahallah the driver turned on the headlights and lit Rambo's path. And the driver of the second jeep did the same. And after him the driver of the third jeep, of the fourth, of the fifth, of the following seven. One by one, as if they obeyed an order and silently passed it on to each other, all the twelve Shiite soldiers at the wheels of the twelve jeeps turned them on: within a few minutes the street became a necklace of light. Grains of light splashing swords of light that Rambo plowed with Leyda then left to the shadows behind him. Then Rambo arrived at the Main Street where the Eighth Brigade M48s and the Sixth Brigade M113s still lined up in two opposed rows, and here also two headlights went on. The headlights of a Sixth Brigade M113. And after these, two more. And two more, and two more, and two more. Vehicle after vehicle, always on that side. Until the Main Street too became a necklace of light, grains of light splashing swords of light that Rambo plowed with Leyda then left to the shadows behind him: to the dozens and dozens of dead children, dead men, dead women, dead old people. Inundated with all that light the silent procession appeared in all its atrocious details, its boundless tragedy, the Shiite soldiers understood what Bilal had understood, and a threatening roar arose from the Sixth Brigade M113s. Amidst the threatening roar, the voice of an officer who thundered out a word then three words plus the voices of his soldiers who answered with similar words. And seized by a new anxiety Angelo wondered what the officer had said, what the soldiers had answered.

CHAPTER FIVE

1

HE HAD SAID ENOUGH. "Biskaffi, enough. Ma'a-baddih-iah, I won't obey anymore." They had answered yes, enough: "Uah-nahna-kamaam, we won't obey anymore either." And those words synthesized a fury that had been ripening long before the jeeps switched on the necklace of light, the swords of light, to illuminate the procession. Analyzing the 81mm grenades that had fallen on the field hospital and hadn't exploded, all of them shot by the Shiite mortarmen of the Sixth Brigade, Sugar would have ascertained that the fuses were defective because somebody had tampered with them. The same sabotage which had taken place along the Green Line when the Shiite gunners altered the trajectory ordered by the Christian officers and instead of bombing Haret Hreik they hit the Ruby base. Observing the fragments of the shells exploded in Shatila he would also have noticed that in the alleys parallel to avenue Nasser, the stretch between the Twenty-Two and the Twenty-Four, the bulk of the carnage had been committed by the Sixth Brigade with the trick of short-range fire. A good part of it, though, had landed on the right target. That is, on the other side of the avenue. And this had contributed a lot to the shambles made by the M48 cannons of the Eighth Brigade. Six hundred dead in Gobeyre, the figure hypothesized by Eagle, plus more than a thousand mutilated. And now, three weeks later (that much time has passed since we left Angelo with his question), the wrath of the Shiite officers and soldiers had assumed frightening proportions: nine out of ten felt the same way as those who had been moved at the sight of Rambo advancing with Leyda's tiny naked corpse. "Gemayel's army has betrayed us," they growled at every pretext. "It has forced us to fire alongside the Christians and for the Christians on our homes, our children, our women, our parents, our faith brothers, on ourselves. Biskaffi, enough."

Three weeks. Things had changed very much in three weeks. To begin with, no one of the Eighth Brigade entered the Western Zone:

the only governmentals who dared pass or stay there despite the cross at their necks were the Christian officers of the Sixth, not numerous and often treated as unwanted guests. The Shiite officers and soldiers of the Sixth, on the contrary, roved the quarter at their leisure. Mocking the Condor who could not oppose it they kept their M113s side by side with the Italian M113s, and here they squabbled with the Amal. They denigrated the Eighth, they fed the rumors that an unarmed Bilal had been killed in cold blood by Gassàn, they openly spoke of the reprisals to come, accounts to settle. In short, you could see it with your naked eye that the Shiite revolt was about to burst. You could feel it in your bones that Gemayel's army was on the verge of splitting in two. One side, the Eighth with its zealots devoted to Jesus and to Saint Maron and to the Virgin of Junieh; the other side, the Sixth with its fanatics devoted to Allah and to Khomeini and to Zandra Sadr. Among the Multinational Force, in fact, the wind of demobilization was blowing stronger and stronger. Almost all the Marines of the American contingent had been transferred to the aircraft carriers that controlled the coast and the few who remained never left the trenches excavated under the rubble of their headquarters; the French strayed from the Eastern Zone only to inspect the thirty legionnaires left out of pride in the Pine Wood; Her Britannic Majesty's one hundred Dragoons ventured outside the former tobacco factory only to go buy fruit at the market; the Italians had reduced their effective force by four hundred men and surprise, surprise: Shatila was now garrisoned by the paratroopers with the marò. In the villa of the Saudi prince dead from an oysters-and-truffles indigestion there was the Ruby base. Which means the Eagle base no longer existed. The bersaglieri had left.

*   *   *

The key to this departure had to be found on the stretchers of the hospital ship that along with Gino and the other incursori fallen into Passepartout's ambush had brought home those wounded during the battle. In Italy, in fact, the favoritism practiced by the Eternal Father and the timely blindness of the goddess Fortuna hadn't provoked any Te Deum of thanks, and the arrival of those stretchers had raised fury. Along with the fury, polemics about the soundness or rather the unsoundness of sacrificing so many young people in a war that didn't concern the country. And the government had decided to withdraw part of the contingent: "Let's pull out the marò or the paratroopers or the bersaglieri. Whichever battalion the Condor chooses." Rejecting a priori the idea of giving up his cherished paratroopers, the Condor would naturally have chosen the scorned marò. Nor would Sandokan have opposed such a decision: as eager as he was to transform himself into a peaceful bourgeois with a gold watch in his fob and a Rotary card in his pocket, he asked nothing more than to leave Beirut. But to the delight of Fabio who now could see Jasmine when he wanted because Ahmed rested in a graveyard of Shyah, the navy had issued a point-blank refusal. And the ax had cut down the bersaglieri. Worse: fearing that his choice would please Eagle and eager to delay that gift as much as to poison it, the inexorable Condor had summoned him at the very last moment then assaulted his pride with a list of reprimands and accusations: not budging from the Twenty-Two until Crazy Horse's arrival, not authorizing Hawk to go rescue the two nuts of the Twenty-Five Alpha then ordering him to drop the M113 in the crater and take shelter in Habbash's house, sending Rambo and the ten marò to a hovel from which they'd emerged alive only by a miracle, burying with his own hands a Palestinian boy and letting Rambo join the procession with a badge of Khomeini on his chest and a little naked body in his arms... Only at the end had he revealed to his victim the real reason why he'd been summoned.

"Colonel, I'm afraid I have to give you good news. And I'm damn sorry for it. Within forty-eight hours you and your battalion leave."

Good news?!? After the weeping of the Cyclopes and the burial of Mahomet, Eagle had gone through a metamorphosis almost more radical than Sandokan's, and you understood it at a glance. He no longer raged at the garbage the stinking bedouins piled in front of their shanties; he no longer got irritated when somebody yelled at his bersaglieri talieni-tomorrow-kaputt or when the prostitutes provoked them by displaying watermelon-sized breasts; he no longer preached boys-don't-react, don't-defy-fate, it-doesn't-matter-if-they-call-you-queers, better-queer-than-dead; he no longer worried about the Israeli pilot who might fall into Shatila to be eaten alive by the Palestinians. And when Uncle Ezechiele had called him to reprise his torment with the question dear-nephew-what-will-you-do-if-an-Israeli-pilot-etcetera, he had shouted: "Uncle Ezechiele, don't shit on my patience. If he falls and they eat him, it is his fucking problem." He also said that the worst enemies of his people were not any worse than his people and, finally, he'd fallen in love with Mahomet's mother. All he did was repeat how sweet and unlucky she was, how much she needed affection, every day he brought her food, and never grew discouraged by her woeful refusals. "Là, shukràn, monsieur. No, thank you, sir. I don't need anything..." Thus, the words within-forty-eight-hours-you-and-your-bat-talion-leave had stunned him like a punch in the face and for a couple of seconds he'd remained more silent and motionless than a boxer who lies K.O. on the carpet. But then, surprisingly, he had been able to overcome the blow. And saying to himself that he wasn't a child or an idiot, he was a grown-up and intelligent man capable of distinguishing a Marie-Thérèse chandelier from an English or a Venetian one, a Pif-fetti inlay from a Maggiolini one, he had rebelled. Flashing his mild eyes and revealing an unforeseen boldness, he had answered: "In due respect, sir, this is the most rotten abuse of power I've ever experi-enced. Even with you. You know very well that the correct solution would be to repatriate a third of the marò, a third of the bersaglieri, a third of the paratroopers, and that my boys don't deserve your insult. Because who suffered for hours at the Twenty-One, at the Twenty-Two, the Twenty-Three, the Twenty-Four, the Twenty-Five, the Twenty-Seven Owl? Who endured for hours the shelling, the hunger, the arrogance of the Amal and the governmentals? Maybe I'm not a Napoleon, which delights me a lot, however in Shatila there was Eagle. Not you. And if I didn't budge from the Twenty-Two until the arrival of your logorrheic Chief of Staff, you never budged from the headquar-ters. So our lack of heroism matches." But with an equally surprising coldness the Condor had retorted: "Colonel, shut up and get ready because I'm clearing out the convent. Within forty-eight hours I'm moving the Ruby base to the Eagle base." And poor Eagle had been forced to bow his head then return to his quarters where, packing the menorah that had outlived the Capodimonte cup, he'd ordered Hawk to inform the troops with seven words.

"Boys, we've been evicted and we're leaving."

Evicted?!? Leaving?!? Point-blank like thieves and to pass the base on to the paratroopers?!? With the exception of Ferruccio, now enclosed in a gloomy torpor and indifferent to anything unrelated to his pot still greasy with hummus and schawarma, everybody had reacted with such a tumult that Hawk had been forced to grab his pistol and shoot three times in the air: "Calm down or I'll drill a hole in your asses one by one." So Onion had started to cry see-they-even-send-us-back-with-a-hole-in-our-asses, and Nazarene had put aside his unbelligerent theo-ries. Reembracing the principle that life consists of hate rather than love, he had improvised a speech to inform his comrades that tolerance doesn't pay, that Gandhi was an idiot, that Jainism peddled a bunch of fairy tales, that they should imitate the *Potemkin* sailors who sick of eating putrid meat had mutinied and touched off the Russian Revolution. "Having our dignity insulted is worse than eating putrid meat! Let's avenge ourselves!" And Franz, the sulky Tyrolean who spoke German, had reinforced the incitement: "Genau, right! Errichten wir die Barrikaden! Let's put up the barricades! Schlagen wir die Fall-schirmjäger ins Gesicht! Let's smash those paratroopers in the face! Hauen wir alles durch! Let's smash them all!" Only String had behaved in a rational manner. "What smashing, you lumpfish! What barricades, what *Potemkin* sailors! Listen to a cook and to a communist: revenge is a dish we enjoy cold, a tidbit we prepare with the salt of tactics!" Then he had proposed leaving the usurpers a mouse-infested base, his idea had won, and the final forty-eight hours had been spent in hiding the bait of food wherever their imagination suggested: in the tents, the depots, the offices, the various lodgings. Without remorse and inso-lently shouting at Her Highness the First Widow, the two minor wid-ows, the two favorites, the two cooks, the two nurses, the two maids, the scullery girl, the eunuch who peered through the grates of the upper floor, they had left the mansion and reached the port. A picket waving the battalion flag had paraded with the bugler playing the corps anthem, and the ship had taken them away with considerable provisions of hashish. Sic transit gloria mundi, so vanish the world's glories, Crazy Horse would have sententiously said. True. At this point, even the word bersaglieri had been forgotten. It was as if an eraser had removed it from the blackboard of everybody's memory thus eliminating them from the cast of the tragicomedy. Although continuing to garrison Bourji el Barajni, now it was the paratroopers who played the role of protagonists on the stage of Shatila and held the Twenty-One, the Twenty-Two, the Twenty-Three, the Twenty-Five. (The Twenty-Seven Owl and the Twenty-Four had been assigned to the marò.) As for the Louis XVI bedroom, now it belonged to Falcon and Gigi the Candid and Armando Golden Hands. Each of them, still in shock for the grief they had imposed upon themselves and their sweethearts.

"Armandò, Armandò! Dites-moi que ce n'est pas vrai! Tell me it's not true!"

"Malheureusement c'est vrai. Unfortunately it's true, Sister Mi-lady..."

"Gigì, Gigì! Dites-moi que c'est seulement un bavardage! Tell me it's only gossip!"

"Je voudrais bien. If only it were, Sister George..."

"Nous avons reçu une bien triste nouvelle. We've received very sad news, my friends!"

"Bien triste, very sad, Sister Espérance..."

"Mais moi j'ai peur sans vous! But I'm afraid, without you! I don't want to stay without you!"

"Ne pleurez pas. Don't cry, Sister Madeleine. Or you'll make us cry, too..."

Yes, the convent had been cleared out. The only Italian post that remained in the Eastern Zone was Ost Ten, still guarded by the five mortarmen with Lieutenant Joe Balducci and his four Marines. A big problem because the Marines had to be evacuated within the month and the riddle that had always tormented Gigi the Candid was about to become a reality: how to sneak them across the Green Line and accompany them to the trenches of their headquarters without throwing them into the claws of people who rather than giving up the pleasure of killing an American would convert to Christianity? How to convince the blond and freckled Balducci to wear a paratrooper's uniform? How to camouflage the four guys blacker than pitch thus recognizable even under a chador or disguised as muezzins? Each time he thought of this, Gigi the Candid felt the old anguish multiply in swarms of toads. Yet it isn't the four Marines he thinks of while he works with Armando on a strange machine set up behind the rear gate of the new Ruby base: three big iron bars welded in a star shape and fixed upon a dolly in its turn mounted upon tracks perpendicular to the entrance. A mobile cheval-de-frise, in short, to open and close the passageway as the Leopard does at the headquarters. It isn't the Ost Ten problem he worries about while one and a half miles away a bullet is about to miss its target fly into the camp, enter inside a tent and set off a series of unforeseen events that will knot Rocco to the Condor, the Condor to the Professor, the Professor to Charlie, Charlie to Angelo, and Angelo to what he calls the last link in the chain. That is, while the Shiite revolt is about to burst and determine the fate of the one thousand two hundred Italians who remain in the cast of our story.

2

"For God's sake, Armando, hurry up! It's almost noon!"

"I'm hurrying, colonel, I'm hurrying..."

"You're not! You're wasting time!"

"No, sir, I'm trying to figure out why this dolly doesn't roll smoothly... You're really in a bad mood today, sir..."

"You bet I am!"

And who wouldn't be, in his place, he angrily said to himself. The snags always fell on him, dammit! This morning two sycophants had informed Charlie that somebody was up to something, the Condor had deduced that the third truck was about to appear, that the defenses needed to be reinforced but the rear gate of the new Ruby base didn't have enough room for a Leopard, and who could untangle the damn muddle? Gigi the Candid, of course. Call-Gigi-the-Candid. Gigi-the-Candid-always-finds-a-solution. Gigi-the-Candid-will-resolve-the-problem... Well, he had. With the girders and the rails he used to steal from the former Beirut railroad, thief-akrùt-thief, he'd built this device. And Armando's hands had been golden as usual. But the damn wheels wouldn't roll backwards or forwards, at noon the general would come for an inspection, and... He shook his head. No, the real reason wasn't this. The real reason was that he hadn't slept. You couldn't sleep in the damn room with the awful canopy bed and the awful armoire smudged with mother-of-pearl and the awful chandelier adorned with little whores: it crawled with mice. But not normal mice: monsters twelve or sixteen inches long not including the tail, dinosaurs who sprang on top of you and devoured you alive. Throughout the rest of the base, the same story. Everything was infested. The tents, the depots, the offices, even the rooms of the upper floor where Her Highness the First Widow kept shrieking "C'est la faute des Italiens, ces salauds d'Italiens! It's the fault of the Italians, those slovenly Italians!" Slovenly, yes: in their hurry to depart, the bersaglieri had left such a mess! Chunks of cheese, sausages, butter-and-marmalade sandwiches... Attracted by the smell of the food, the dinosaurs had come out of their winter lairs and goodbye sleep...

"Got it, sir!"

"Got what?!?"

"The ball bearings are rusted!"

"If they're rusted, change them!"

No, the mice and the lack of sleep weren't the reason either. He felt so cantankerous because it was Thursday, dammit. Because the thought of Sister George, of her minute figure, her witty face, her liquefied g's, was tormenting him more than ever. And along with that the nostalgia for her regular and irregular verbs, her grave and acute and circumflex accents, her affectionate scoldings, her jocose praises. Aujourd'hui-les-ânes-volent, today-the-donkeys-fly, Gigì. He hadn't seen her since the last supper, and... What a disaster, the last supper! Denying himself the chance to make up for his new and inexplicable behavior, that is, to dine once more tête-à-tête, Falcon had committed the most stupid mistake: he had invited them again to the mess. As a result, the nicest had been Sister Françoise who by now lived at the Rizk and so hadn't come. The others, in fact... Irritated with her elusive suitor and reinstated to her past haughtiness, Sister Espérance. Disappointed with the missed opportunity to dine privately, therefore restored to her past hostility, Sister Milady. Worn out by the fear of being left without protection and unusually tedious, Sister Madeleine. Shut up inside a silence as grumpy as it was stubborn, Sister George. Only to deliver a little au revoir speech had she broken that silence, and for a few moments her customary sprightliness had seemed to revive. But while she was joking about the old tensions her glance had turned to the sixteen-step stairway now devoid of any barrier, and her voice had faded into a whisper: "Je ne peux pas continuer. I cannot go on." Then Sister Milady had emitted the whine of an animal wounded to death, Sister Madeleine had exploded into sobs, and Sister Espérance had sprung up in disdain. "Mes soeurs, saluez nos amis. Sisters, say goodbye to our friends." A disaster, yes, a disaster. All the more that, the next morning, their windows had remained shut, and in vain the departing battalion had hailed: "Arrivederci, Sister Espérance! Arrivederci, Sister Madeleine! Arrivederci, Sister Milady! Arrivederci, Sister George!" Worse: in all those weeks, he had never been able to call her. The convent telephone didn't work.

"It won't help to change them, colonel."

"Change what?"

"The ball-bearings..."

"Why won't it help?"

"Because they simply need to be oiled..."

"If they need to be oiled, oil them!"

"That's what I'm doing!" Armando Golden Hands shot back with resentment. And pretending to wipe the sweat that trickled down his temples, he dried a tear.

*   *   *

Okay, he thought while drying that tear, okay: the poor man suffered. He missed Sister George, he did nothing but turn over the pages of *Mot à mot,* and since the battalion had moved to the new base his white hair had grown even whiter. But were it possible to place their respective ordeals on a scale and weigh them, he would have demonstrated that his suffering was twice as heavy. Because, when Sister Espérance had sprung up in disdain and hissed Sisters-say-goodbye-to-our-friends, Milady had whispered: "Rejoignez-moi dans la chapelle, join me in the chapel, Armandò. I must talk to you." And counting the beats of his heart that thumped like a drum, he had joined her. Trembling from head to foot for the contact of his arm against her arm, his leg against her leg, a contact that despite the clothes seemed almost epidermic, he had sat with her on the pew in front of the altar. Then she had started to speak in a very low voice, so low that at times it wasn't even a voice, it was an imperceptible murmur, the rustle of a leaf, and yes: just remembering what she'd said made him cry. "I wanted to see you alone as I wanted to thank you, Armandò," she'd said. "But not to thank you for the many little favors you have loaded the convent with: for the huge, extraordinary gift you've given to me. The gift of making me understand who I am. Or, better, what I am not and never will be: a good nun, a real nun. Never, Armandò, never. My father was right to assert that I have too many desires, too many passions I'm incapable of controlling. He was right to believe that I wouldn't withstand the test, that I would give up the novitiate. I'm giving it up, Armandò. I won't take the vows. As soon as I leave this chapel, I'll inform Sister Espérance and Sister George and Sister Madeleine. I'll tell them the truth. All of it! No, don't say anything, Armandò. Don't interrupt me, or I won't be able to go on. Besides, I know what you want to ask. You're so practical... You want to ask what I'll do with my life. Well, I'll stay here for as long as my presence will ease the problems caused by the evacuation of the base: it would be mean to leave the sisters alone immediately. But after that, who knows? The future depends on destiny and on our Lord: I could die soon. This is a city where we cannot count on being alive tomorrow. And now that your battalion moves away, now that the convent remains unguarded... If we survive, if I survive, I'll go to Paris: maybe. I'll use my French and the law degree I took to keep my family happy and work there as a lawyer. Or maybe I'll travel the world, I'll enjoy the cheerful and comfortable existence my father envisioned for me... In either case, I hope to meet a man like you, Armandò. To meet him and to marry him and to have children with him. Many children whom I would like to tell the story of a peevish novice who didn't become a nun because of an Italian with golden hands and a golden heart. A handsome Italian who despite her abuses and reproaches and persecutions replaced the windowpanes of her convent, fixed the water pipes, erected absurd barricades on the stairway, intoxicated her with his kindnesses and his fiery eyes and his orchids... Marvelous orchids sent from Italy on a military plane, so that every week the peevish novice waited for them as a woman in love waits for her lover's flowers. And when he handed them over to her, when he stammered the double-meaning words pour-vous, for-you, she pretended to believe that they were also for Sister Espérance and Sister George and Sister Madeleine and Sister Françoise. Then she ran to put them on the altar, under a terracotta statue of the Infant Jesus, and while doing so she whispered: 'They are not for all of us, you know. They're for me. Only for me. This is a loan, Infant Jesus.' In fact those fiery eyes seduced her more than his replacing the windowpanes and his fixing the water pipes and his erecting absurd barricades. They seduced her so much that every morning she awoke looking for an excuse to go see him, every evening she fell asleep happy for having seen him, but at the same time oppressed by a sense of guilt for which she punished herself. Guess how? By keeping an embarrassing down over her upper lip, practically a mustache that she desperately wanted to remove. By denying herself the right to admit what she would have liked to admit and to shout in front of everybody: I love you, Armandò!" Yes... She'd really pronounced the words I-love-you, je-vous-aime-Armandò. And at that point the chapel had begun to whirl in such a giddy manner that he'd felt as if he were inside a centrifuge spinning at twelve g's: the prisoner of a vortex that blinded him, paralyzed him, struck him dumb. In the vortex, a jumble that mixed everything: the altar, the candles, the crucifix, the tabernacle, the missal, the statue of the Infant Jesus, the thought of his wife, that is, his own sense of guilt. And his joy. His irresistible need to reply I-love-you-too-Milady. Centuries passed before the centrifuge slowed down and stopped to give him back a body with eyes and vocal cords. To let him answer: "I love you too, Milady." Then she had brought her Gothic madonna face to his face and, with a seriousness that verged on solemnity, she had rested her mouth on his mouth. She had kissed him. At length. With passion. Finally, and very very slowly, she had moved away and whispered: "Maintenant va-t'en, chéri. Va-t'en. Now go, my darling. Go."

"But what in the hell are you doing, Armando?!"

"I put them back, colonel..."

"Put back what?!"

"The hubcaps."

"What hubcaps?!?"

"The wheel's hubcaps..."

He had left groping his way like a blind man. He had reached the esplanade, stopped to breathe the cool evening air, and after a couple of minutes he'd heard a choked voice. Sister Espérance's voice. "It's not possible! I don't believe you!" Then a small, decisive voice. Hers. "But you have to, Mother Superior. I told Armandò too." "Armandò?!? What has he to do with it?!?" "Plenty, Mother Superior, plenty. I was with him, in the chapel." "Sister! Tell me it is not true, Sister!" "On the contrary, Mother Superior. I love him. I understand who I am because I love him. But don't worry: I will not flee with him. He's a husband, a father. I won't leave you immediately, either. Whatever the cost may be, I shall not abandon you and the other Sisters. So, for the time being, I'll stay here." He sighed. He stealthily dried another tear. Ah! Gigi the Candid wondered why, in the morning, the second- and third-floor windows had remained shut and nobody had answered the arrivederci-Sister-Espérance, arrivederci-Sister-Milady, ar-rivederci-Sister-George, arrivederci-Sister-Madeleine... That's why. And yet, what made him so unhappy today was not her je-vous-aime-Armandò. Nor the memory of her long and passionate kiss, nor the consequences of her courageous confession to the Mother Superior. It was what he had just learned from Ost Ten. Because this morning, without asking anybody's permission, he'd called Ost Ten. He'd asked for news, and one of the five paratroopers had told him that the situation was getting worse: bloody clashes were taking place along the three-hundred-yard stretch and, with the Amal's help, during the night a group of Sons of God had taken the church of Saint-Michel. Led by a hysterical mullah waving the Koran and a Kalashnikov they had burned the crucifixes, shattered the statue of the saint, destroyed the relics and the tabernacle, defecated on the altar then killed the priest, and now they were transforming the church into a munitions dump: all details recounted by a Sunni Muslim who'd witnessed the havoc then hidden himself in the skyscraper. And this wasn't all. It wasn't because the paratrooper had said that at the Galerie Semaan the Sixth Brigade's soldiers kept coming to blows with those of the Eighth: last night a Christian officer who tried to quell the uproar had been beaten by a Shiite corporal. So, full of dire forebodings, he'd asked the paratrooper to go see how things were going at the convent. The paratrooper had, and here was his report. The facade of the building was once more reduced to a colander and just stepping on the esplanade meant the risk of a bullet or a fragment. The four nuns were barricaded in their rooms and Sister Madeleine was so terrorized that she kept escaping to lower herself into an old well on the property where she remained for hours reciting the Requiem Aeternam. Fearing that she would lose her mind, Sister Espérance begged the paratrooper to radio the priest who'd helped them escape during the Israeli siege and ask him the favor of reaching the convent to take the pitiable woman to the port: load her on a nonstop ship to Marseilles... As for the other nuns, they were fine and behaved with great courage. The novice, however, seemed very nervous: at any pretext she said that this was a city where you couldn't count on being alive tomorrow, and what if the Sons of God invaded the convent too? Oh, Milady! Armando dried a third tear that hung from his lashes then he gave a shove to the strange device which finally rolled along the tracks and blocked the passageway.

"Now it works, colonel."

"Good," Gigi the Candid answered without interest. Suddenly calm, he was listening to an exchange of shots that burst along the Green Line.

"It rolls right along, now: look. It blocks the passageway better than a Leopard."

"Sure..."

"What's wrong, colonel?"

Gigi the Candid bent down to pick something up and paused to examine it perplexedly.

"I don't know... But in my opinion the Condor is mistaken. In my opinion, we've worked for nothing: the tip Charlie got has nothing to do with the third truck."

"No?"

"No. Look at this."

He held out the object he'd picked up: a small rifle bullet sheathed in a shiny copper-brass alloy and with the pointed tip slightly bent by the impact with the ground.

"It's a 5.56," Armando Golden Hands said, as perplexedly. "And it's still warm."

"Just so: still warm. And a 5.56 comes from an M16. And the Eighth Brigade as well as the Sixth Brigade are equipped with the M16. And for the last few minutes, the fire along the Green Line has been nothing but M16 bursts... Maybe I'm wrong, but the governmentals are shooting at each other: that's what Charlie's tip referred to. I'm afraid that today we'll see quite a few of these small shiny bullets... If we aren't careful, somebody risks getting one in his head," he grunted reopening the passageway to a jeep full of incursori among whom was Rocco.

"Hi, Rocco!"

"Good morning, sir!" Rocco answered, festively waving his helmet.

"How's it going, Rocco?"

"Great, sir! Really great!"

"Happy again, eh?"

"Yessir! Very happy, sir!"

"One more reason to wear your helmet, kid. Put it back on your head, and don't take it off, today. Not even to scratch your pate. Understand?"

The shooting had in fact intensified, and among the trees of the park filled with the paratroopers' tents many stray bullets were whistling.

3

Rocco reached one of the tents located along rue de l'Aérodrome, slipped inside on his tiptoes to avoid waking a paratrooper who slept worn out by the night shift, and a large smile softened the awkward features for which Imaam consoled him so sweetly. You're-not-ugly-my-love, you're-handsome-because-you're-handsome-inside. Very happy, yes. The happiest soldier in the battalion, nay in Beirut, nay in the world. Could it be otherwise? He had been blessed with such a miracle, the day after the battle! Crying out Rocco-we-found-her-Rocco, the kids from Bourji el Barajni had come to the headquarters and for God's sake: there she was, as round and radiant as the sun in August. "Imaam!" "Mon amour!" What's more, soon after the bersaglieri's departure, that good man called Gigi the Candid had set him up in the camp of the former Eagle base: an ideal billet because of the tent located at the edge of rue de l'Aérodrome. When she came, she didn't even need to summon him via the carabinieri: all she had to do was stand on the sidewalk and twitter Rocco-je-suis-ici, I'm-here. He immediately vaulted the sandbag fence and off they went: to eat her roast chicken, to exchange caresses, to dream about tomorrow. Where? If it wasn't raining, behind the garbage dump. If it was raining, in the waiting room of the field hospital. Agreed, neither of these two places had the charm and the privacy of the oasis on the convent's hill: neither offered lime trees that formed a ceiling of leaves and an abandoned truck in which to hide and make love and pretend that you are already husband and wife. As a matter of fact, both of them were rather melancholic spots, and a little smelly. But when you have been all alone for months, crying and wondering will-I-ever-see-her-again, when you are poor and ugly, you learn to content yourself. And besides, hadn't they a whole life to make love and sleep in each other's arms? Wouldn't they get married as soon as they were in Italy? Wasn't the future theirs? It was. A wonderful future. The kind that awaits the protagonists of a novel with a happy ending.

He looked at his watch. Five after noon: good. Today she would come at quarter after noon, so he had ten minutes to rest. And forgetting Gigi the Candid's advice, Rocco removed his helmet. Then he stretched out with his head at the foot of the cot and his feet on the pillow: a posture that permitted him to gaze at the photo attached with adhesive tape to the waxed fabric of the tent. A photo of Imaam wearing the brown lizard-skin shoes he'd bought at Diamante in Calabria. Ah! He never tired of contemplating that star-filled mouth, those firm cheeks that she found too chubby, those full hips that she found too fleshy, those solid thighs that she found swollen with cellulite: he liked her fatness so much! And yet, what seduced him most in this photo was not her fatness: it was the shoes he had bought at Diamante in Calabria. They suited her perfectly, and they made her so happy that she wore them with every outfit. Even the blue dress. No use repeating Imaam, the-brown-doesn't-go-with-blue! She shrugged and answered: "It goes, it goes, my love. You chose it, so it goes." She also wore the Gucci scarf, and the amethyst bracelet and the Chanel Number Five. Marilyn Monroe's perfume. In the most unexpected nooks and corners, the perfume: behind the ears, inside the neckline, in her armpits. And enough to make a monk lose his head. In fact, at every sniff he said: "Let's get married at once in Beirut, Imaam!" All the more that getting married at once in Beirut was so simple! All you need to do is become a Muslim and celebrate the wedding in the Islamic way. Know how? First you get hold of two male witnesses or four female witnesses who according to the Koran count for two male witnesses, then you step inside a mosque and shout: "Ash'hadu en la'ilahe illalah, ash'hadu anna Muhammadu rassullillah! In the presence of witnesses I affirm that there exists no other God but Allah, and that Muhammad is his prophet!" The mullah doesn't even lose time asking you if Mecca is in Brazil or Luxembourg: he gives you a sheet of paper stating that you're no longer an infidel dog, that from now on you mustn't drink alcohol or eat pig meat, he wishes you mubarik which means good luck, and goodbye. To celebrate the wedding in the Islamic way, almost the same: first you call a taxi and take along the two male witnesses or the four female witnesses, then you bring them to your fiancée's home and pay her father the equivalent of a month's salary, then you sign a little contract and get her to bed. Really! The trouble is that during the separation imposed by the German measles, Imaam had read the Bible, nay the Gospels, and had been deeply impressed by Jesus Christ. Particularly, by the fact that he befriended a streetwalker named Mary Magdalene and prevented the Pharisees from stoning the adulteresses "Let those without sin cast the first stone." As if this weren't enough, she'd discovered that Jesus Christ urged his followers to take only a single wife. Meaning that he respected women a lot. And at this point she had quite lost her head. "Exactly the opposite of Muhammad who preached an-eye-for-an-eye, a-tooth-for-a-tooth, who despised women, humiliated them, bartered them with goats or camels, who said that men may have four wives and an unspecified number of mistresses!" she shrieked. Furthermore, somebody had told her that Christian women get married in white dresses with tulle veils and orange blossoms which mean virginity. God knows why, she'd loved this information as much as Jesus Christ and decided to convert to Christianity. In other words, there was no way to change her mind: to convince her to let him convert to Islam. "It would break my heart, mon amour!" Dear, sweet, marvelously fat Imaam! He was so eager to see her, to touch her, to hear her talk about Jesus Christ and Mary Magdalene and the white dress and the tulle veil and the orange blossoms, that if within five seconds she didn't twitter her Rocco-je-suis-ici, he would grant himself an earnest by kissing the photo with the brown lizard-skin shoes.

Rocco looked again at his watch which now read twelve-fourteen, and counted to five. But the twitter Rocco-je-suis-ici didn't come, so he decided to grant himself the earnest. He cocked his left foot and right elbow, he raised his head and torso to bring his face up to the photo, he turned his head forty-five degrees, and in doing so he offered his nape to the trajectory of the shots coming from the Galerie Semaan. Or, more precisely, to the bullet that a Sixth Brigade soldier had just fired at an Eighth Brigade soldier one and a half miles away. An M16 bullet like the one that Gigi the Candid had picked up nine minutes earlier. A 5.56 that, having missed the Eighth Brigade soldier, now flew in the direction of the former Eagle base. It flew toward the tent at the edge of rue de l'Aérodrome to pierce it and then penetrate Rocco's nape with a long gentle whistle.

"Zzzzzzzzzzzzzin!"

*   *   *

Oh, yes: truly inscrutable are the ways of the Lord. And truly bizarre threads intertwine them to weave the mystery of our destiny. In 1952, a few years before Rocco would come into this world, something important had happened in Whittier, California: Mr. Robert Hutton, a skillful disciple of ballistic science, had designed a cartridge whose bullet measured only one inch in length and two-tenths of an inch in diameter. That is, very small and very light. Then he had sold his idea to Remington (an old firm very famous for its typewriters, its razors, and the weapons which it manufactured in Bridgeport, Connecticut, since the time of the American Civil War) and this had caused the birth of the Remington 222. A prodigy that had won lightning success among the hunters of deer, fox, prairie dogs, and especially coyotes, so much unloved in America because they attack the herds. At the same time, Mr. Eugene Stoner, an eclectic aeronautics engineer and sincere admirer of the Kalashnikov, had designed a rifle weighing only seven pounds and capable of automatic fire. Then he had sold his idea to Fairchild's Armalite, and this had caused the birth of the Ar10: a masterpiece marred by the fact that it had to be loaded with a cartridge neither small nor light. That is, with the Nato 7.62: daughter of the Garand 7.62, stepsister of the 7.62 used by the M14 which was a Garand slimmed down to fourteen pounds, and cousin to the 7.62 that the Soviets had shortened to half an inch and adapted to the Kalashnikov. (With its cartridge, in fact, the Nato 7.62 bullet weighs almost one ounce. Stick three or four hundred of them in the knapsack of an already overloaded soldier and after a quarter of a mile listen to his curses.)

Well: just when the Remington 222 was beginning to decimate the poor coyotes and the Ar10 was about to go into production, Johns Hopkins University Medical School in Baltimore had completed a study on the lethality of portable weapons and concluded that in battle the enemy's death rate is proportional to the number of bullets shot. Meaning, it is not the well-aimed fire which kills the greatest number of enemy soldiers: it is its abundance. And this hadn't pleased the Pentagon's high-ranking officers who had retorted no, it is the well-aimed fire which kills more enemies: a good soldier does not waste bullets. It had intrigued, on the contrary, the commander of the Infantry School, General Wyman, who had come up with an obvious and crystal-clear reasoning: "If the guys of the Johns Hopkins Medical School are right, in order to win a battle or any kind of combat we've got to shoot the greatest possible number of bullets. To shoot the greatest possible number of bullets, we've got to carry in our knapsacks the largest possible quantity of bullets. Ergo, we need a smaller, much lighter bullet combined with a much lighter rifle." Then he had discovered that thanks to Mr. Stoner and Mr. Hutton such a rifle and such a bullet already existed. So he had asked them to adapt the Ar10 to the Remington 222 and the Remington 222 to the Ar10, and the Ar10 rifle had become the Ar15: only seven pounds heavy. The Remington 222, the Remington 223: still one inch long in the bullet alone, but shortened to one inch and three quarters in the length of its cartridge and only 185 grains in weight. The bullet itself, 55 grains. A few months later the patent for the Ar15 had been ceded to Colt Company, the renowned mother of the Colt 44 (used by Union soldiers during the Civil War) and of the Colt 45 (used by General Custer in his raids against the Sioux). The patent for the Remington 223 had been ceded instead to Winchester: the illustrious mother of the Winchester 73 (used by the pioneers in the conquest of the Wild West). And the magical marriage had been solemnly celebrated. The husband rifle, with the name M16; the bullet wife, with the name 5.56. And here comes the really good part of the story.

Really the good part because in 1961 President John F. Kennedy had started the American intervention in Vietnam equipping the South Vietnamese army with the M14 and the Nato 7.62, and because in height and build the South Vietnamese soldiers were as small as Rocco. Being as small as Rocco, they weren't sturdy. Not being sturdy, when they carried fourteen pounds of M14 and let's say sixteen or seventeen pounds of Nato 7.62 (more or less the equivalent of three hundred cartridges) they grew exhausted. When they grew exhausted they shot worse than usual, and instead of killing the Vietcong they got killed by them. The problem had therefore ended up in the hands of Secretary of Defense Robert Strange McNamara and his advisers: a group of Harvard-educated technocrats called the "Witty Boys." Seduced by the magic marriage, the Witty Boys had urged McNamara to recommend the M16 and the 5.56 to the president and, in his turn seduced by the Witty Boys, McNamara had said to Kennedy: "Mister President, I remind you that an M16 weighs only seven pounds and that three hundred cartridges of 5.56 weigh approximately eight pounds. This means that even a smallish soldier can carry the whole load without growing exhausted, and that in Vietnam we have an excellent opportunity to try out the Johns Hopkins theory." Kennedy had agreed, Colt and Winchester had quickly supplied ten million rounds of 5.56s and a thousand M16s, and on the 9th of June 1962 the test had taken place. In some jungle or Delta rice field a patrol of South Vietnamese Rangers had clashed with a squad of Vietcong, shooting at random and wasting an incredible amount of bullets they'd killed five of them, the bodies had been brought to Saigon for an autopsy and... The heartbreaking results of the autopsy can be found in the report which was later researched and published by a most serious expert in weapons in Washington, D.C.: Edward Azell. The thoracic cavity of the Vietcong hit in the lungs had exploded. The abdominal cavity of the one hit in the belly had exploded. The heart of the one hit in the chest had exploded. The genitals of the one hit in the buttocks had exploded. And the one who had been simply hit in a foot had died in less than twenty minutes from blood loss. In other words, a triumph. A masterstroke which explains why, seventeen days before being killed himself by two bullets, Kennedy had authorized his Secretary of Defense to equip both the South Vietnamese and the American army with the M16 and the 5.56. And why, in the following years, the magic marriage had done nothing but cover itself with glory. Hundreds of thousands of corpses spread throughout Vietnam, Laos, Cambodia, Latin America, Central America, Africa, the Middle East, wherever there was a chance to defy the equally glorious binomial Kalashnikov-Soviet 7.62 and never mind if the Kalashnikov was more widely diffused because the communist countries sold it to everybody for a very low price while the M16 was very expensive and could be bought only through the black market or the Israelis. Never mind if the prestige of the Kalashnikov remained so undimmed that in a city like Beirut even babies had it: the Kalashnikov didn't shoot the 5.56. It shot the Soviet 7.62, and who would dare compare the Soviet 7.62 to the 5.56?!? The Soviets themselves were so in love with the 5.56 that at a certain point they had copied it and improved it to use in Afghanistan.

So, in the cosmos of bullets, no bullet could compete with the tiny assassin designed by Mr. Hutton for hunting coyotes and adopted by Kennedy for hunting the Vietcong then by the Soviets for hunting the Mujadeen: the wife of the M16. And the ultimate reason wasn't even to be found in her transportability: it was to be found in the exploded heart and genitals and abdominal cavity and thoracic cavity of those four bodies, in the rapid death from blood loss of the fifth. That is, in her destructive characteristics. And here they are. To begin with, the incredible velocity of just over half a mile per second (three times the speed of sound): a prodigy that is due to her smallness and lightness which, altering the relation with the propellant charge, increase the effect of the charge itself. Then, the incredible range of at least two miles which derives from the first characteristic and from the spinning that takes place during the flight. Finally, the position of the barycenter which, being located far from the tip, causes a very precarious balance. At the slightest obstacle (let's say a leaf or the petal of a flower or a minute seed) the tiny assassin in fact loses her trim, that is, the normal inclination of the tip pointing forward. And when she meets the coveted target, a human body, she doesn't limit herself to entering. With malicious wisdom she windmills within, she turns over, she rebounds in joyous capers, and instead of producing a straight hole as large as her diameter of two-tenths of an inch she rends the flesh in gashes larger than her length: she slices and rips apart an area of almost two cubic inches. (Which is why, even if no vital organ has been touched, the victim dies of blood loss in a few minutes.) After the first half-mile, however, her velocity drops to about a quarter-mile per second, after the first mile her energy flags, and inside the coveted target she doesn't windmill. She doesn't turn over and rebound in joyous capers to rend and slice and rip the flesh apart: she pauses for a thousandth of a second to catch her breath, look around, understand where she is, then proceeds in search of an agreeable place in which to explode and destroy with a delayed burst. If she doesn't find an agreeable place, she exits leaving behind a living corpse. And this is what she did that mid-January day in Beirut after having undisturbedly crossed the one and a half miles which separated the new Ruby base from the Galerie Samaan (that is, from the point where the Sixth Brigade soldier had missed the Eighth Brigade soldier) and after having topped the sandbag fence of the camp, pierced the tent at the edge of rue de l'Aérodrome, penetrated Rocco's nape with the long gentle whistle.

"Zzzzzzzzzzzin!"

She entered the right hemisphere of the cerebellum. Satisfied, she paused for a thousandth of a second, the time to catch her breath, look around, understand where she was. Then she proceeded in search of the agreeable place in which to explode, and broke into the Hippocampus which is the center of memory. Here she found a vault with the remembrance of a childhood which had left nothing to remember but the useless and thoughtless freedom of kids, then the recollection of a squalid adolescence: a taste of youth made melancholic by the awareness of being ugly and mistreated by everybody. Come-here, get-over-there, do-what-I-tell-you. She also found the dark image of a basement lit by a tiny window: the kitchen of the seaside inn where an eighteen-year-old youngster frustrated in his dream of becoming a waiter and eating the same food as the customers, delicacies like sautéed sole and shrimp timbale, worked as a dishwasher. As he washed the dishes he peered at the feet that passed in front of the tiny window to get the people to the beach, he pined away with jealousy, and as soon as the cook asked for seawater to rinse the clams he grabbed the pail: he ran to the sea and drenched his arms and legs, enjoyed some moments of sun and sky. And this displeased her a lot. So she left the vault, the Hippocampus, and went upward: slantwise. She got to the Limbic Zone which is the center of affections and passions. Here she found mountains of never used sentiments, peaks of never satisfied desires, green hills that sprouted gratitude for a parachute and a uniform which gave him the illusion of being somebody, of counting for something. She also found huge plains of tenderness always given and seldom received, cool valleys of friendship always offered and often rejected, and moors of pity for the wretched and the defeated, for whoever was more unfortunate than he was. In the midst of the cool valleys and moors, fields of red poppies burning with love for a good and plump girl who liked his tiny eyes stuck one beside the other and inset beneath his black stripe of an eyebrow. Tesiè-adorable-de-sirièn, your-adorable-Syrian-eyes. A girl who loved him very much, who every day brought him a preposterous basket of roast chicken, who ecstatically listened to anything he said, tell-me-more, tell-me-more, who always wore the brown lizard-skin shoes he'd bought her for two hundred thousand liras at Diamante in Calabria, who wanted to become a Christian and marry him in a white dress with a tulle veil and orange blossoms because Jesus Christ respected women and befriended a streetwalker named Mary Magdalene. Among the poppies of that love, a tuft of blue irises that were the oasis with the ceiling of leaves at the convent. And the tiny assassin liked this even less. So she continued to search and climbed farther, to the left and upward: she got to the Frontal Lobe which is the center of intelligence. Here she didn't find much: no lofty peaks existed in that region, no green hills. The plains were untilled, hardly redeemed by the elementary concepts learned in grammar school or by the simple things a soldier must know, and instead of cool valleys or fields of red poppies with tufts of blue irises, a desert of sand stretched. In fact she thought this was the agreeable place in which to explode and seemed to stop, to concede an instantaneous death with a delayed burst. But just as she began to ignite the powder contained in her evil leaden heart, she noticed that lovely flowers blossomed in the sand of the desert too. The flower of an instinctive wisdom that only asked life for a little happiness with the good and plump girl, the flower of a fervid imagination that helped him to dream even when there was nothing to dream and that could see an oasis where there was only a parking lot for unusable vehicles, the flower of an innate equilibrium which made him logical and understanding and mild, the flower of an optimism which came from an infinite courage. And this vexed her so much that she quenched the sparks of her ignition, leaving behind a Hiroshima of gray matter she bore through the cerebral cortex then the occipital bone and exited. Just an inch above the left eye. Outside she continued her flight, and drilling Imaam's photo she pierced the tent again. She ended up at the foot of a tree and Rocco fell supine with his eyes open wide, his forehead spurting blood from a minuscule hole, his right hand reflexively gripping the bar of the cot. Thump-thump, thump-thump. So the sleeping paratrooper worn out by the night shift woke up and irritatedly called him.

"Rocco! What the hell are you doing, Rocco?"

Then he saw the hole above the left eye, the trickle of blood dripping down his temple, the wide-open eyes, he understood, and a scream ripped through the camp.

"Help! He got it in the head! Come quick, run!"

They all ran. Gigi the Candid, Armando Golden Hands, Falcon, the stretcher bearers. Notified by radio, also the Condor came. And behind the Condor, Charlie. Behind Charlie, Pistoia. Behind Pistoia, Sugar who immediately noticed the 5.56 at the foot of the tree and picked it up and reconstructed her incredible flight of one and a half miles: the inexplicable trajectory which threading its way among thousands of obstacles and millions of possible targets had led her to Rocco's nape. And Rocco was loaded into the ambulance. Driving past a plump girl with brown lizard-skin shoes who carrying a preposterous basket of roast chicken had halted on the sidewalk and twittered Rocco-I-am-here, they brought him to the field hospital. But the tiny assassin had performed one of those exploits the Witty Boys admired so much: by now Rocco was a living corpse. He didn't even react to mechanical goads such as the needle they pricked him with in the hope he'd moan, and in vain Gigi the Candid kept asking for an optimistic diagnosis: "He could get over it, right?" The doctors remained silent or answered: "No, colonel, no. This is an irreversible coma." At a certain point, however, one of them spread his arms and said: "Colonel, when we catch a bullet in the head we usually die at once. If we don't die at once, we die immediately after from internal hemorrhage: the cerebral mass is fed by large arteries whose rupture causes an edema which compresses the brain against the walls of the skull and smothers it. But this time a very unusual phenomenon occurred. Maybe because the bullet slowed down the moment it entered his nape, maybe because of its particular trajectory, maybe because of the head's position at that moment, maybe because of all these things together, the large arteries haven't been damaged. The edema has formed from the rupture of smaller blood vessels. So, in my opinion, he might even get off. The trouble is that it would take a neurosurgeon, a really well equipped hospital. The Rizk, I mean. But who would take the responsibility for transferring a patient in this condition?" And the Condor stepped forward.

"I do," he said. "I'll take it."

"Fine, general... But who gets him to the Rizk?"

"I do," he said. "I'll get him there."

"General," Charlie cut in, "the shooting is heavy along the Green Line. It'll be hard to reach the Rizk, and almost impossible to come back. If the Shiite mutiny has begun, we'll need you as much as Rocco needs a neurosurgeon. Don't go, please!"

But the plea only had the effect of irritating him.

"Save your advice, Charlie! Shiite mutiny or not, I'll make it! I'll go and come back! Do take care of that fatty who's whining rather than giving advice! Make her shut up!"

Then he ordered the doctor to place Rocco back in the ambulance, summoned Gaspare and his two-man escort, jumped into the jeep with them. And the short convoy left, pursued by the sobbing of Imaam who had been told that Rocco was wounded in a leg.

"Rocco! Où est qu'ils t'emmènent? Where are they bringing you, Rocco?!? I want to come with you!"

"This is not possible, dear," Charlie mumbled releasing her from the basket of chicken and handing her a handkerchief to dry her tears.

"But I'm his fiancée, monsieur, and he's wounded in a leg! A leg... Right?"

"Yes, dear. A leg..."

"Oh, monsieur! How serious is the wound, monsieur?"

"Not serious, dear. Not serious..."

"Really, monsieur?"

"Really..."

"A small bullet, monsieur?"

"Very small, dear..."

"Then why do you look so distressed, monsieur?!?"

"I'm not distressed, dear."

He was. And not so much because of Rocco or of the fear that the Condor wouldn't make it back, but because of the news he'd received this morning. The news that on Christmas Eve a woman had been shot in Gobeyre with a Kalashnikov volley. A beautiful woman, dressed in a torn but elegant white outfit, almost certainly a Christian from the Eastern Zone who wandered into the battle and who had been taken for a spy, his informers had said. Soon after the truce her riddled body had been found in front of the jewelry store on rue Farrouk, the one guarded by the old blind man who sat on the baby chair and smoked narghile, and thrown God knows where. Maybe in some common grave of that quarter. He'd then asked for a more precise description, and the answer had been: "Between thirty-five and forty. Long chestnut hair with golden highlights. Immense violet eyes. Tall, gorgeous body. Marvelous legs..." Ninette's identikit. Now he had to tell Angelo, and the mere thought of it turned his stomach.

"Oh, monsieur! If you're not distressed, I envy you, monsieur."

"Don't envy me, dear."

Around the Sixth Brigade's M113 that flanked the Italian M113 near the pathway of the Twenty-Four, meanwhile, the Amal were crowding to lay a siege. And at their command was a bearded lanky thug whom the marò on duty had never seen: Rashid. At his side, the blond boy with the cigarette butt always stuck on his lips, the Kalashnikov always over his shoulder, the Rdg8 always fixed on his belt, and Sergeant Natale's feathered helmet on his head. Khalid-Passepartout, the inevitable protagonist of the final drama.

4

The final drama took place in the eighteen hours following the exchange of shots that at noon had burst along the Galerie Semaan. It started under the pretext of a slap given by an Eighth Brigade corporal to a Sixth Brigade squad leader who had spit on him, and it evolved through the event Bilal had foreseen. That is, the fracture of the governmental army which immediately split like an amoeba whose nucleus divides to generate two nuclei incapable of living within the same cell: the Eighth Brigade on one side and the Sixth Brigade on the other. But while the Eighth maintained the integrity of its own nucleus, the Sixth continued to imitate the procedure of the amoeba which after the first split divides again to become in turn two amoebas then four then eight then sixteen up to infinity: it divided once more. On one side, a group composed of Christian officers and a few Shiite soldiers who remained faithful to them; on the other, a group composed of Shiite officers with the main body of the Shiite troops. Soon after, the second group divided into two further factions: at right the faction who wanted to deal with the Eighth and avoid a bloodbath, at left the faction who didn't. So, between brawls and scuffles, both factions crumbled to produce a myriad of stragglers at anybody's mercy and from the macabre womb of plurifratricidal war a many-headed monster was born: a multiplied demon that head after head fell into the clutches of the Amal. What's worse, it gave the Amal the entire arsenal of the former Sixth Brigade.

Tons of 5.56 and quintals of M16s which went to enrich the munitions dumps already brimming with 7.62 and Kalashnikovs, M113s equipped with 12.7mm machine guns, jeeps equipped with 106mm cannons, 120mm mortars. The mortars, the cannons, the machine guns, the rifles with which they had shot upon themselves on Christmas Eve. Then, strengthened by this abundance, the Amal launched the decisive attack. The Sons of God slipped into it with the political-religious gangs presided over by Zandra Sadr's mullahs and ayatollahs, Ludwig Boltzmann's entropy attained untouched pinnacles, and the final drama of the city became the final drama of our characters. With the exception of Angelo to whom the mysterious mechanisms of destiny would entrust a very specific task, in fact, the role of the Italians became that of insignificant spectators in the midst of a tragedy which excluded them and at the same time devoured them. And the first to pay that price was the Condor who at four in the afternoon found himself neutralized like a lion in a cage. Here are the pathetic details of the episode.

With his usual impetuosity and resoluteness, the Condor had successfully passed through the Tayoune crossing and reached the Rizk. With Sister Françoise's help he'd even mobilized an able neurosurgeon and convinced him to perform the operation the field hospital's doctor suggested. That is, to lessen the edema and somehow patch up the Hiroshima of gray matter left by the tiny assassin. On his way back, however, he had made the mistake of choosing the Museum crossing: since the first afternoon, the spot from which the Sixth Brigade's Shiite officers pressed to spread the revolt to the Old City. Rockets, gunshots, grenades that radiated throughout the entire Pine Wood. Near the racetrack he had thus been forced to abandon his jeep to take shelter with Gaspare and the escort in a cabin that seemed to be an old stable of the hippodrome, only inside it had he realized that the supposed stable was the last place on earth his pride should have chosen: a poultry house full of crazed roosters and cackling hens. An instant later a mortar shell had destroyed the jeep and radio, and Charlie's fear had come true like a prophecy: no way to reach the headquarters. Not even by foot. There were at least two miles of fire from that point of the Pine Wood to rue de l'Aérodrome: just thinking of trying to return was a folly. So, needless to say, the caged lion had become insane. Shouts. Curses. Imprecations. Kicks at the poor roosters and at the innocent hens that full of terror multiplied their cackles. Then he'd started to call the Operations Room with the only instrument he now had, the walkie-talkie, and of course he could have asked a squad to come rescue him. But in order to be rescued he had to mention the poultry house, and in vain Crazy Horse implored Sir-tell-us-where-you-are-Sir. In vain Pistoia yelled let-me-come-to-pick-you-up, give-me-an-address, a-spot. In vain Gaspare and the escort repeated give-it, general, please, general, it-is-not-a-shame-to-be-here. They only obtained new shouts, new curses, new imprecations, new kicks at the roosters and the hens. "Shut up!" In return he pestered his staff with superfluous orders, spread-the-state-of-alarm, prepare-Rapid-Intervention, double-the-patrols, re-inforce-the-roofs, and it was no use urging him to speak less: to save the batteries. He never quieted down, he never parted from that walkie-talkie which fostered his last illusion of being in command of the contingent. Meanwhile time elapsed, night fell, and the batteries really ran out. Although the voices from the Operations Room still got to him rather distinctly, his words arrived to it more and more faintly: in shreds of phrases or incomprehensible static.

"Inform... grrrr... barracks... grrrr... Sixth Brigade!"

"We don't read you, general! Repeat, repeat!"

"Infor... grrrr... grrrr... Brigade!"

At nine in the evening, while an apparently providential M48 from the Eighth Brigade approached the poultry house followed by an ambulance, the voices from the Operations Room also began to crumble in shreds of phrases or incomprehensible static. And it became clear that soon not even those would arrive.

"General... grrrr... we've... grrrr... read me?"

"No!"

"Grrrr... serious... grrrr... Shatila... read...?"

"No-o-o!"

Finally, total silence. The batteries were dead. Then, blind with fury, the lion flung himself from the cage with a pistol in his fist: pursued by Gaspare, by the escort, by the crows of the roosters and the cackles of the hens which seemed to shriek bravo-go-away-bravo, he ran toward the M48 to halt it and climb aboard. But he hardly had time to see a rocket that fell on the turret and disintegrated it: the explosion hurled him against a pine where he smashed his face then fainted, and when he opened his eyes he was in an ambulance that carried him back to the Rizk with two wounded from the blasted tank. Here the same neurosurgeon who had operated on Rocco's brain sutured with nine internal stitches and twelve external ones a soldierly slash that defaced his left cheek, Sister Françoise filled him with sedatives that didn't sedate him at all, and until dawn he lay there consuming himself with the nightmare of the train he was supposed to steer but didn't steer because it flew away in the night, steered by somebody else. God knows who.

It was steered by the Professor who had assumed command long before the walkie-talkie's batteries went dead. And who soon will insert himself into the bizarre threads of destiny by ordering Charlie to leave with Angelo for the Twenty-Four where things were taking a turn for the worse.

* * *

Despite the almost constant presence of Rashid who moved away only to go check the other posts and quickly returned, at the Twenty-Four nothing had happened but the mounting petulance of the Amal who like vultures besieged the Sixth Brigade's M113 halting in front of the pathway that led to the Main Street of Shatila. In particular, the petulance of Passepartout who showing off his feathered helmet tormented the crew: seven Shiite soldiers and a Christian lieutenant. "Enough with blocking that pathway! Give us that tank, you craven sheep! And you with the cross at your neck: move your ass! Get it to some bloody church!" Nothing more, though. In fact the Christian lieutenant, a young man with the image of the Virgin carefully glued to his pistol butt, didn't lose his self-confidence and replied: "I'm not going anywhere, stupid brat. Neither are my men. So stop provoking me or I'll thrust a bullet into your tummy." As for his men, all of them young and untrained recruits from Shyah or Haret Hreik, they didn't even answer: unknowingly demonstrating the proliferation of the amoeba now at its fourth split, they quarreled among themselves or gave voice to their differences and uncertainties. The gunner at the Browning declared that he would remain loyal to his lieutenant, and woe to whoever dared touch him. The pilot said he was ready to join the Greens, meaning the Amal, not to give them the M113. The radio operator said he was ready to give them the M113, not to join them. And for the others, one wanted both to join the Greens and to give them the M113; one wanted to sell it to the Eighth for seventy thousand dollars then divide the sum, ten thousand dollars apiece; one waited for the right moment to sneak away; one didn't know which way to turn.

"What do you think? Should I go with the Greens or not?"

"Look, I'm going home and that's it."

"You morons! Don't you realize this M113 could earn us a pile of money? The crossbearers would pay any price to get this vehicle! Let's sell it!"

"You're not selling anything to anybody, you greedy cynic! I'll drive it away with my own hands and turn it over to our people: under-stand?!?"

"Do what you want. But the first one who lays a finger on the lieutenant goes to the cemetery. Because I'll shoot him."

"Oh, yeah? But what kind of Shiite are you?!?"

"A Shiite who's not a traitor! A loyal soldier!"

At quarter to nine however Rashid had detached himself from the group, and whispering some order to Passepartout had approached the Christian lieutenant. With sudden familiarity he had taken his arm, making him turn away from the Twenty-Four he had led him toward the avenue Nasser sidewalk, and: "Lieutenant, we're all sons of Allah. What's the point of bickering among ourselves? We should discuss our misunderstandings, we should calm down our boys." The lieutenant had agreed, still walking along avenue Nasser with his back to the Twenty-Four he'd talked with Rashid for ten minutes, and only on his return to the post had he realized the cheat: surprising his crew as well as the marò, fifteen or so Amal had slipped into the pathway leading to the Main Street of Shatila; another fifteen, under Passepartout's com-mand, had shinned up the M113. This had caused a turmoil during which the lieutenant had fired a few revolver shots, the loyal soldier had burst a volley with the Browning, the one who didn't want to go with the Greens had struck the attackers with the butt of his rifle, and Passe-partout had fled: pursued by Rashid who barked you-coward-this-time-I'll-kill-you-for-real. So the marò had called Sandokan. But Sandokan had come in his metamorphosed state, and: "Quiet, boys, quiet. As Bertrand Russell says, we must vanquish the old mechanism of hate with tolerance. Thus cover your butts, let them stew in their own broth, and shut yourself inside our M113." Then he'd got inside it too and without dropping his English locutions, utmost residue of the days when he dreamed of being Robert Mitchum debarking in Normandy or John Wayne bombing Iwo Jima etcetera, he'd informed the Profes-sor.

"Condor, attention, Condor. Sierra Mike One here. Over."

"Go ahead, Sierra Mike. Condor Two here. Speak Italian and tell me what's going on."

"What's going on is that at the Twenty-Four the bedouins are bust-ing balls. Over."

"What balls? What bedouins? Speak Italian, I repeat, and clearly!"

"My balls and my marò's balls. The bedouins with the green rags, the Amal. They've attacked the governmental M113 and they've en-tered Shatila through the pathway. Over."

"Through the pathway?!? And what are you doing?!? Where are you?!"

"Inside my M113. Doing nothing. Absolutely nothing. Over."

"What do you mean by nothing?!? And what about your men?"

"They're inside with me. Over."

"Sierra Mike One! They cannot stay inside! They must go out, intervene! And so must you!"

"Impossible. I'm on the side of the trout and of the edelweiss. Over."

"What trout, what edelweiss?!? Sierra Mike One, if you don't stop speaking nonsense, I'm going to get you in front of a court-martial!"

"Get me wherever you like, Condor Two. I don't give a damn. Over."

Then he'd switched off the radio, and exactly at that point the Operations Room had tried to contact the Condor with the walkie-talkie. General-we-have-a-serious-problem-in-Shatila. But the word "serious" had been an understatement: the Amal who had entered through the pathway were all over the quarter, asking the Shiite soldiers to seize their Christian officers. And the paratroopers of the Italian posts claimed their right to fire. "Give us the authorization, for God's sake! If we don't start shooting, they'll lynch them!" Exactly what the Professor thought. But just when he is about to grant the authorization, here is Charlie coming to involve him in the bizarre threads of destiny.

"A breach has opened at the Twenty-Four: right?"

"Yes, Charlie."

"And that braggart is playing the role of Pontius Pilate: right?"

"Yes, Charlie."

"And the paratroopers in Shatila foresee a lynching of the Sixth Brigade's Christian officers, so they want to shoot and you're about to authorize them: right?"

"Yes, Charlie. Do you have a better idea?"

"Yessir, I do. The same idea as usual. The one that worked on Christmas Eve."

"On Christmas Eve there was a battle, Charlie. Tonight there's a mutiny, a revolt. And revolts don't get stopped with truces. They get stopped with shooting."

"I'm not talking about a truce, Colonel. I'm talking about going to the Twenty-Four and slapping on a band-aid to prevent the Amal from making us lose face in Shatila. Because if we lose face in Shatila, we lose Shatila. If we lose Shatila, we lose Bourji el Barajni. If we lose Bourji el

Barajni, we lose the rest of the sector and our reason for being in Beirut. Let me slap that band-aid on, Colonel."

"What kind of band-aid, Charlie?"

"A kind that permits us to bargain."

"Bargain with whom? Your friend Bilal is dead."

"I know... But the animal who took his place, Rashid, is alive and... Please, let me go to the Twenty-Four."

"It might be a dangerous waste of time, Charlie."

"One hour, colonel. All I need is one hour. Tell the paratroopers and the marò to hang in there for an hour, and I promise I'll fix the mess."

"Okay, Charlie, go ahead. But bring along an escort, an aide."

"The aide wouldn't do any good, colonel... An interpreter's enough."

"Not tonight, Charlie. Tonight you need somebody who knows how to use a gun. Bring that sullen sergeant of yours. The mathematician."

"Charlie Two? I'd rather leave him here, colonel. He's more than handy with a gun, I agree, but he's going through a difficult moment and..."

"Don't argue, Charlie."

"If you order it, sir."

So it was that Charlie called Angelo. First he called Martino who showed up unarmed as usual and had to go get his M12. Then he called Angelo who showed up holding his M12 already loaded with 9mm Parabellums. With them he got into the jeep, left the headquarters, and for sure he had no intention of speaking about the beautiful woman who had been found shot in Gobeyre. Even less did he intend to pronounce the name Ninette. But what we intend or don't intend to do weighs very little on our destiny, our lives. Through God knows which mysterious alchemies of our psyche, we almost always end up doing precisely what we didn't want to do. And all at once Charlie felt an irresistible need to pronounce that name, to tell the story of the beautiful woman found shot in Gobeyre. And he did it. Worse: he, who like nobody else knew the art of measuring words, who like nobody else abhorred brutality and mercilessness, did it with the brutality and the mercilessness of an executioner who doesn't even grant his victim the time to recite a prayer or smoke a last cigarette.

"Angelo, have you seen Ninette?"

"No..." Angelo answered unsuspiciously. "Why?"

"Because I think she's dead, son."

A frozen silence followed, during which only a feeble whine was heard. Martino's whine: "Oh, no!" Then a low, hoarse, colorless voice. Angelo's voice.

"Dead how?"

"Killed, son."

"Killed how?"

"Shot, son."

"Shot by whom?"

"By some loose dog, I guess. On Christmas Eve. In Gobeyre."

"Who says so?"

"Nobody. But this morning I was told that after the truce the sextons found the corpse of a very beautiful woman riddled by a Kalashnikov volley. They found it halfway down rue Farrouk, in front of the jewelry shop where the old blind man smokes narghile: a place where those who don't belong to the quarter rarely go... So I asked for a precise description, and the features correspond. Long chestnut hair with golden highlights, immense violet eyes, tall and gorgeous body, marvelous legs... Even the outfit seems to be the same. Because the carabinieri she talked with say that Ninette had a torn white dress, and the very beautiful woman found in rue Farrouk was wearing a torn white dress."

"Oh, chief!" Martino sobbed. "Maybe it wasn't Ninette... Maybe it was a woman who looked like her!"

"I don't think so," answered Charlie with a glance at Angelo, now totally silent. And looking as relieved as a man who has lifted a great weight from his heart, he reached the Twenty-Four.

It was almost ten in the evening, the cannons of the Eighth Brigade's M48 had extended their range to avenue Nasser. Rashid and Passepartout had disappeared, and at the Twenty-Four the siege had changed.

*   *   *

It had changed and grown worse. In fact the Sixth Brigade's M113 was now encircled by a swarm of callow vultures clearly sent to hold that easy bridgehead which, thanks to Sandokan's indifference, risked being overwhelmed. "Get back, you brats, get back! I don't like to shoot on kids, but if you don't get back I will!" shouted the Christian lieutenant. And the loyal soldier backed him up: "Young or old, I'll fire! Try to move a finger and I'll kill you all!" Far from looking frightened, though, they laughed and got closer. At a very slow pace, the pace of someone who wants to appear sure of himself, Charlie left the jeep. He passed the marò's M113 which remained shut, reached the swarm, and turned to Martino who continued to sob.

"Dry those tears and ask them who's in charge."

Martino cleared his throat, asked, and a grotesque uproar rose from the swarm.

"Ana! Me!"

"Là, inta là! No, not you! Ana, me!"

"Lasa inta, lasa hawah! Ana! Neither you nor him! It's me!"

"All the better. Ask who sent them here," added Charlie exchanging a significant look with the Christian lieutenant.

Martino asked. The uproar grew.

"Rashid! Huah Rashid! Rashid sent us!"

"Fine. Ask where Rashid is."

Martino asked. The uproar diminished.

"Gobeyre, at Gobeyre! Uah haràb mah Khalid! He went there with Khalid!"

"Good. Now tell them we're going all together to Rashid."

Martino told them. The uproar mounted again.

"Là! No, là!"

"Là kal! Not all of us!"

"Rashid là iurid! Rashid doesn't want us to!"

"Repeat to them that I want to be accompanied by everybody. And say that we know Rashid very well, that I'm his foster brother and you're his godson."

Martino said it. The uproar died out, and Charlie took the Christian lieutenant aside. In French he told him that under the pretext of being accompanied to Rashid he was taking the intruders away: especially if the Eighth Brigade's barrage reached the rond-point of Shatila, they shouldn't come back. However he advised him to take shelter in his M113 and, just in case some other group showed up, he was leaving his aide. An energetic and brave incursore. Then, without deigning to glance at Sandokan who had quietly opened the rear hatch to observe the scene and now quietly closed it again, he joined Angelo: still at the wheel of the jeep. He gave him a slap on the back.

"I leave the jeep and the lieutenant in your hands, son."

"Yes," he muttered scarcely moving his lips.

"Keep an eye on him. Be sure they don't butcher him."

"Yes."

"Park the jeep so you can watch without being watched, and avoid shooting. Understand? The last thing I need is the carcass of an Amal."

"Yes."

"That's all, and... Don't be too crushed, son. I had to tell you, didn't I? I had to lift this weight off my heart."

"Yes."

"Do you feel all right? Can I go without worrying about you too?"

"Yes."

But Charlie did worry all the same, and as he left he thought: damn me, damn me, I made a mistake by telling him the truth. I'm making a mistake by leaving him all alone. That one is capable of turning his back on the post and going in search of whoever killed his woman.

5

He didn't turn his back on anything, he didn't go in search of anybody. With a stony face he waited for the Christian lieutenant to take shelter as Charlie had advised, then he parked the jeep inside an inlet of the rampart that now enclosed a good part of the Twenty-Four. Rather than an inlet, the horseshoe-shaped niche in which Sandokan had wanted to place the M113 and which the marò had never used because they preferred to keep it on the sidewalk of the Street Without a Name: far from the governmental one. He parked it with the rear wheels backed against the niche's inner wall, the front wheels a couple of steps from the opening, then he got out and went to place himself next to the right-hand door. Since he was slightly taller than the rampart, a position that permitted him to watch without being watched on an arc of 180 degrees: to the north, about twenty yards away, the Sixth Brigade's M113; to the south, about thirty yards away, the marò's. Finally he placed the flashlight on the hood, made sure that the 9mm Parabellum cartridge was well inserted in his M12, and deaf to the thuds of the grenades now raining near the Twenty-Four, he plunged into the magma of a tearless weeping.

Dead. Killed. Shot. It was as if those three words had congealed in his brain. And yet they revealed nothing that despite his mental habit of accepting only precise data, mathematical truths, he didn't already know. Nothing that after the desperate run in rue de l'Aérodrome, the Street Without a Name, the rond-point of Shatila, avenue Nasser, rue Argàn, everywhere but rue Farrouk, he hadn't already understood. Something has happened to her, he had kept repeating while he rumpled the velvet dog. Something horrible. And later too. It had taken the sight of Rambo plowing through the swords of light and carrying the tiny naked body of a child, then the sound of the mysterious words uttered by the Shiite officer and the Shiite soldiers, to make him forget that illogical certainty. But the next morning the illogical certainty had resurrected, and with such an intensity that he'd spoken to Charlie. He'd told him everything. Everything. From the purchase of the cross-shaped anchor to the letter Martino had translated. The fact is that Charlie was too shaken by news he'd just received, the news of the death of Bilal, and listened without listening. "Don't torture yourself with doubts and fantasies, Hamlet. She was alive around midnight, wasn't she? Black and blue all over, knocked out, yet alive. Don't despair. One of these days, or as soon as she's restored her beauty, your Ophelia will show up. Wait." He had waited. Oh, had he waited! To wait, not to leave the headquarters where she could call or come at any moment, he hadn't even gone back to Gino. He hadn't even tried to settle accounts with the little criminal who had cut off his hands tossing the Rdg8. He had totally disowned the poem on love and friendship which are the same thing, the two aspects of the same insatiable hunger, the same unquenchable thirst... And in a telephone call that dripped reproach, Sister Françoise had said it to him. "He left, Angelo. He embarked on the hospital ship. And until the last moment he has been repeating see, Angelo-isn't-coming, Angelo-didn't-come. Why didn't you come, Angelo? Why?" Because it isn't true that love and friendship are the same thing, Sister Françoise. Because even when it's mixed with hate or it's born from hate, love has a power that friendship doesn't have. A power that leads us to forget our friends, Sister Françoise.

Dead. Killed. Shot. In front of the same jewelry store where he'd bought the cross-shaped anchor. Shot for what reason, for what fault? True: when we lose a beloved person, we unfailingly judge him or her from the perspective of merits and virtues. As if to multiply or justify our pain, we define him or her as good even though he or she was bad, honest even though he or she was dishonest, innocent even though he or she was guilty. But if there existed a creature incapable of doing harm to anybody, this was Ninette. Who had killed her, then? Whom would he have to kill in revenge? Yes, revenge. He had never liked revenge. He had always considered it a rough, visceral act dictated by the blindness of passions. He had never liked the idea of killing, either. Despite his skill in handling weapons, in attacking imaginary fortresses, he had always regarded the act of killing as a deed alien to his way of thinking. Which was why, the terrible Sunday of the double slaughter, it had been so easy for him to answer Ferruccio I-swear-I'll-never-kill-anybody. Tonight, instead, the idea of killing fit him better than a glove fits a hand. It attracted him, it lured him like a fruit which is ripe and demands to be eaten. And the idea of avenging Ninette seemed to him a right to exercise in the name of logic: a rational gesture, an intellectually legitimate, a morally rightful deed. Yes: intellectually legitimate before being morally valid... Damn! It is not reasonable to kill someone you don't know, as soldiers do in war. Someone you shoot at for the simple reason that he wears a different uniform and stays on the other side of the barricade, someone whom in another circumstance you might invite to drink coffee and become friends. To kill someone who has harmed you, who has robbed you of a good, who has imposed upon you a pain, on the contrary, is more than reasonable. Because it reestablishes a broken equilibrium, it makes order out of disorder, and through a positive act it erases the negative act of the individual who harmed you and robbed you and made you suffer. An operation which in mathematics is called bringing-the-system-back-to-its-initial-phase and which equals the operation of annulling the result of a problem by using the inverse of the procedure you followed to get that result. Yes: should he find the delinquent who had riddled Ninette with a Kalashnikov burst, he would kill him without hesitation. Whoever he was, wherever he found him, whenever this happened. Even here, now. To hell with Charlie's orders and recommendations, avoid-shooting, understand, the-last-thing-I-need-is-the carcass-of-an-Amal.

"Ana hunna! I'm here!"

Preceded by a sharp and malignant shriek, Passepartout had emerged from the murkiness of the Street Without a Name, and all alone was heading for the Sixth Brigade's M113 to torment again the Christian lieutenant and the faithful soldier.

"Hunna, here, hunna!"

"Hal tas ma'wai, la'im? Do you hear me, you sheep?"

"Ruha wa, la'im! Come out, you sheep!"

Halfway along the stretch that led to the M113, however, he discerned the tall figure standing near the jeep now inside the niche and, surprised to see somebody in a place that was usually empty, he stopped. He narrowed his eyes, better rearranged the strap of the Kalashnikov across his shoulder, and prepared to transfer his petulance onto the stranger.

"Ciao, italiano! Buonasera, good evening!"

"What do you want?" answered Angelo pulling the handle that chambers the round and aiming at the shadow that, almost swallowed up by the dark but visibly armed, had stopped in the middle of the stretch. Then, tightly holding the M12 with his right hand and elbow, and without losing his aim, he stretched his left arm toward the flashlight he'd placed on the hood. He grabbed it, switched it on, and the greenish disk of light illuminated a small face that in the shady glow seemed to him the muzzle of a fly to squash and devour. Globose and bulging eyes, hooked nose, overdeveloped lips. And, between the lips, a cigarette butt that looked like the sucking rostrum. A cigarette butt?!? He lifted the flashlight to check if the fly had blond hair, and the greenish disk illuminated the feathered helmet that Pistoia had alluded to on Christmas Eve. Sergeant Natale's helmet.

"Easy, italiano, easy! You blind me!"

"Who are you?"

"Khalid! Me Khalid! And me speak Italian!"

"Khalid, huh?"

"Yeah. Meaning eternal, immortal!"

"Eternal and immortal, huh? And who gave you that?"

"That what?"

"The helmet."

"No give, taken! Conquered!" rejoiced Passepartout, happy to see that the stranger had noticed his precious booty and was impressed. Then, with the imprudence of a fly that alights on a spider's web, he took a few steps forward to approach him. Meanwhile the greenish disk descended to his belt in search of the Rdg8.

"Conquered where? From whom?"

"This post here! From bersagliere in M113!"

"I see."

"Yeah! During battle!"

The Rdg8 were there. Two Rdg8 identical to the one Charlie had picked up near the fig tree of the Twenty-Five and whose serial number was almost consecutive with the number of the grenade the little criminal had used to mutilate Gino. He turned off the flashlight. He put it on the hood again. And again he gripped the M12 with both hands.

"And those? Who did you take them from?"

"Those what?"

"Those two grenades."

"No take. Gift. Rashid's gift."

"Rashid, huh?"

"Yeah. Me and Rashid bread and honey. He bread, me honey."

"Bread and honey?"

"Yeah. Me live in his house, sleep in his bed. And he fucks me, only me. Calls me honey, my sweet honey, always gives me gifts. This Kalashnikov, gift from Rashid. And in November he give me one big case of Rdg8."

"I see."

"Yeah. One full big case. Rdg8 very good. Two grenades may fix five enemies. Five! Me know!" the fly specified liming itself completely in the sticky net of the spider by now ready to squash it and devour it.

"You know, huh?"

"Yeah! Me did it!"

With the flashlight off, the fly was again a shadow almost swallowed up by the dark. But its outlines were much more distinct and its thorax looked like a silhouette on a firing range. Besides, the stupid insect had placed itself so close: right at the opening of the niche. His forefinger on the trigger, Angelo thought of how easy it would be to satisfy his need to avenge Gino as he had wanted to do in December. All too easy. And without any consequences. Thanks to the rampart that concealed him up to the middle of his head, in fact, neither the governmentals inside the Sixth Brigade's M113 nor the marò inside their M113 would see a thing. Very probably, they wouldn't even hear the noise of the outgoing bullet or that of the rifle reloading. The M48 shells were falling so near: the explosions quenched every other sound. And afterwards, who would ever know? Who would ever figure out that he had shot him? In war, corpses don't stir up police investigations, ballistics tests, autopsies... But the more he thought about this, the more he withdrew his forefinger from the trigger. The more he withdrew his forefinger, the more he realized that avenging Gino didn't stir him as much as it had the day he'd left the Rizk with his poem and said to himself that Beirut was a small place. The Gobeyre-Shatila-Bourji el Barajni triangle, still smaller. The people inside that triangle, very traceable...

"Ialla! Go away!" he suddenly said, releasing the trigger.

"Why?" a stunned voice asked.

"Because I don't want you here. Beat it!"

Confused by the dilemma that such an order implied, Passepartout drew back a little. Rashid had got so mad when he had fled from this post to escape the Christian lieutenant's revolver and the faithful soldier's Browning! If he beat it, he would get a flurry of punches or worse. On the other hand, how to stay in this comfortable and safe place if that guy didn't want him? Let's see... Maybe by seducing him, by giving himself to him for free.

"You no like me?"

"Get out, I said. Scram!"

"But me like you much! You handsome! Me want you fuck me! Gratis! Free! Fuck and fuck and cuckold Rashid together!"

"Scram. Or you'll be sorry."

As flabbergasted as he was intimidated by the chilly voice of the stranger who refused to fuck him for free, Passepartout backed off another step. He stared at the Sixth Brigade's M113, wondered if he should remain near the niche to yell once more ana-hunna, I'm-here, come-out-you-sheep, decided it would be useless, pursued another pretext, and it was at that moment that the fly floundering in the sticky net of the spider ready to perform the positive act to kill signed its own death sentence. Because, instead of proposing to cuckold Rashid, this time he dug in his jeans pocket and extracted the cross-shaped anchor he'd snatched from Ninette. Then, dangling it by the chain, he reapproached the opening of the niche.

"Hey, italiano..."

"I warned you. Go away."

"Me go, yes, go. But first me sell you jewelry for very real very good price!"

"Back off! Ialla. Back off."

"Gold jewelry. Pure gold. Me ask fifty dollars. Look!"

"Ialla. Back off. Ialla."

"Only fifty dollars! Turn light, italiano! Why no look?"

"Ialla."

"Forty dollars! Only forty! Turn light, look!"

"Ialla."

"Okay. Me go down thirty dollars! Very very good price for gold, pure gold! Look, please, look!"

"Ialla."

"Chain with anchor! Anchor with Christ! Christ with ruby! Look, look, look!"

A dreadful silence fell. A silence broken only by the barrage of 105mm shells that now fell also a few meters from the rampart and sometimes seemed to pass over it. Then the chilly voice became a voice of marble.

"What did you say?"

"Chain with anchor! Anchor with Christ! Christ with ruby! Only thirty dollars!"

"Let me see."

Slowly Angelo detached his left hand from the M12. Slowly he extended it toward the flashlight he'd rested back on the hood and switched it on again. Slowly he withdrew the hand from the hood, stretched it out toward Passepartout to take the cross-shaped anchor, brought the jewel under the beam of the greenish disk where the ruby

quivered with an almost sinister gleam. Slowly he slipped it into the left
pocket of his jacket. Then he cast a look at the Kalashnikov over Passepartout's shoulder, the Kalashnikov that Ninette had been ripped with,
and again holding the M12 with both hands he again put his forefinger
on the trigger.

"Whom did you steal that from?"

"No steal..." stammered Passepartout dropping the butt that until
now had remained balanced on his lower lip.

"Whom?"

"No steal, me swear... Mine!"

"Whom?"

It's soft, the M12 trigger. Quite soft. If you have a steady wrist and a
steady forefinger, and if you are possessed by real hate, you can savor
every millimeter of its receding: you can delay for several seconds the
release of the firing pin. And Passepartout didn't know this. Even less
he knew that the stranger had put his forefinger on the trigger again:
the beam from the flashlight resting on the hood blinded him more
than it had in the beginning, and all he could see was the rifle's barrel
pointed in his direction. But like a dog that by sniffing senses what it
doesn't know, he sensed that the forefinger pressed the trigger. And
that the trigger receded, receded, receded, that its receding wouldn't
stop, couldn't stop, because he'd made a terrible mistake: he'd offered
the stranger something that belonged to him. Something which denounced what he'd done in rue Farrouk on Christmas Eve. Something
which condemned him without hope, which consigned him to a punishment a million times harsher than the punishments Rashid used to
chasten him in his whirls of rage. The same punishment he'd inflicted
on the toothless hag who called him darling-habibi-darling. And frozen
with terror, incapable of trying a useless flight, as heartbreaking as any
creature who's about to die, even a wicked creature, a poor murderous
fly, a Khalid-Passepartout, he began to plead.

"No spara, italiano, no shoot!"

"Whom did you steal it from?" the marble voice repeated. And the
trigger softly moved backwards.

"Me give to you gratis! No spara, no shoot!"

"Whom?"

And the trigger moved back farther.

"Me give to you like gift! No spara, no shoot!"

"Whom?"

And the trigger moved back farther.

"From Christian whore, from spy! No spara, no shoot!"

"And then you killed her. Right?"

"Yes, yes, yes! But in the name of Allah, no spara, no shoot!"

"Why? Why did you, why?"

"Because Christian whore, spy! But no shoot! No spara, no spara, no spara!"

"No?" the marble voice said. And the bullet that aimed at the heart left the chamber.

It left exactly as one of the M48's shells was hitting the middle of the stretch to explode in a gigantic fan. So, with his heart pierced by the 9mm Parabellum of the M12 and his body riddled with the fragments of the gigantic fan, the poor murderous fly swayed forward then backward losing its feathered helmet. Then it dropped to the ground the same way Ninette had dropped, and without exhaling any sigh of assuagement, without thanking any mother (but what mother can a poor murderous fly thank?) Passepartout freed the world of his presence. Angelo, instead, flew against the inside wall of the rampart, and there he remained until the hatches of both M113s opened. That is, until Sandokan and the Christian lieutenant ran to him.

6

"Charlie Two, Charlie Two! Are you wounded?"

"No."

"Sergent, Sergent, êtes-vous sain et sauf, are you safe and sound?"

"Oui."

"Quelle chance, mon ami! What luck, my friend!"

"Bloody dick of a dick superdick, you must have a saint on your side: that Amal seems like a soup strainer!"

"Regardez-le: atteint en plein! Look at him: blown away!"

"What do we do with him now?"

"Il faut s'en libérer, bien sûr! We must get rid of him, of course! Do you want me to call my men?"

"No, lieutenant, I'll take care of it. Quick, marò, quick! Drag this bedouin away!"

"Yessir! At once!"

"Hey, look who it is! The one who led the group!"

"He still has the Kalashnikov over his shoulder, poor wretch!"

"What do you mean poor? He was a bastard!"

"A bastard and a coward!"

"He bugged everybody!"

"Come on, lift him up. Now he won't bug anybody anymore!"

"You morons! Don't lift him! Drag him away by the feet, bloody dick of a dick superdick!"

They dragged him away by the feet. Without seeing that in his chest there was a hole almost a centimeter wide, the hole made by a 9mm Parabellum, they brought him to the intersection with avenue Nasser. And there they abandoned him with his Kalashnikov and his Rdg8. Then everybody returned to the M113s, Angelo picked up the feathered helmet, hid it beneath the seat of the jeep, and, when Sandokan called him to make sure he was well, a calm voice answered.

"Yessir, I'm fine."

He really was fine, he said to himself as he sat at the wheel. He didn't feel any uneasiness, he didn't feel any remorse, nor any form of self-satisfaction or joy. In place of all that, a strange mixture of surprise and relief. Surprise at discovering how easy it was to do for real what he had always done for fun in the firing ranges and in the assaults on the imaginary fortresses. Relief at thinking that with one single shot he had carried out his right and performed the rational gesture, the deed which is intellectually legitimate long before being morally valid, the positive act which reestablishes the broken equilibrium and makes order out of disorder, the operation which in mathematics is called bringing-the-system-back-to-its-initial-phase. Nor did he care about the 105mm grenade fallen at the very same moment spraying the gigantic fan of fragments which would have killed the fly anyway: in spite of that simultaneity he could well say I-killed-him, I-am-the-one-who-killed-him. He could because the real killing had not taken place when his forefinger had released the trigger: it had taken place during the eternal minute in which the trigger was receding and the fly was so pitifully begging no-spara, no-shoot, no-spara. He shuddered. Pitifully, yes. To be honest, he had felt some pity. Both then and when the fly had made the obscene offer of its body. Me-like-you-much, you-handsome, me-want-you-fuck-me, etcetera. Well... A sociologist specializing in pietism wouldn't have spent many words to convince a kindhearted jury that the poor juvenile wasn't a murderer, that he was a victim of society, an outcast incapable of understanding, a pariah who had never been told the difference between Good and Evil. In short, an irresponsible victim who couldn't be blamed for his faults and who at the most deserved a few years in the reformatory. But when your soul bleeds you cannot afford the luxury of espousing the easy arguments or the ambiguous mercies of sociology. And sometimes one gets tired of those who maintain that responsibility comes with intelligence, education, welfare: do the Barabbases always go to Paradise? Do they always end up sitting

next to God? Victim or not, outcast or not, pariah or not, the fly with
the sucking rostrum had murdered Ninette. It had harmed, robbed,
imposed pain. Thus he, the harmed one, the robbed one, the pained
one, had the sacrosanct right to say: "Now we're even, Khalid-Passepartout. You killed her, I killed you."

He turned the flashlight on, he arranged it on the dashboard of the
jeep. With indifference he noted that the barrage from the M48s was
stopping and that in spite of this the Amal didn't return. Then he
rummaged in his left jacket pocket, took out the chain with the cross-
shaped anchor, brought it under the beam of greenish light and
started. There was a long chestnut hair with golden highlights entangled with the anchor's fluke. One of hers. Oh, it always hurts to find an
object that belonged to the person we loved and we lost... A pen, a
book, a button, a garment that still emanates his or her scent... But to
find one of his or her hairs is deranging. Because it is like finding a part
of his or her body, a part that has remained alive and intact... He gently
caressed it with the forefinger which had pulled the trigger. He carefully coiled it around the fluke, wrapped the whole thing in a handkerchief, and a violent itch stung his throat. An irresistible need to weep.
To weep?!? He forced himself to think of something else. He grabbed
the notebook with his mathematical lucubrations, looked for the page
where he'd copied the first part of the theorem he'd begun to solve
after the rescue of Luca and Nicola. The theorem one-is-greater-than-
zero. What solution had he chosen? Yes: departing from the axiom that
one exists, zero exists, one and zero are different, he had proceeded
with a trichotomy and considered the three hypotheses offered by the
elements a and b. The hypothesis a-equal-to-b, the hypothesis a-
greater-than-b, the hypothesis a-less-than-b. Then, discarding the hypothesis a-equal-to-b as not valid because of the axiom one-and-zero-
are-different, he had proceeded by developing the theorem ab absurdo.
That is, relying on the fact that if one hypothesis is correct, its contrary
is mistaken. At that point, however, the fear that Ninette might have
come to the Western Zone had caught him again, and... He cleared his
throat to suppress the violent itch that didn't cease, reasoning out loud
he went on: "Okay, then: as the hypothesis a-less-than-b, i.e. $1 < 0$, is
incorrect, I must set up an inequality proving that the hypothesis a-
greater-than-b, i.e. $1 > 0$, is correct... Then I must add the quantity
(-1) to both terms of the inequality and obtain another inequality *one
plus minus one less than zero plus minus one*. Like this: $1 + (-1) <
0 + (-1)$. And since $1 + (-1)$ equals 0, since $0 + (-1)$ equals (-1), I get
the inequality *zero less than minus one*. Like this: $0 < (-1)$. Then I must

multiply both terms by (-1), and by doing this I get the inequality *zero by minus one less than minus one by minus one*. Like this: $0 \times (-1) < (-1) \times (-1)$." He stopped for a moment, suddenly aware of a parallel yet alien idea which was slipping into those calculations. He blinked his eyes, suddenly blurred by a curtain of mist, he continued. "Okay, let's go on... Now, given that $0 \times (-1)$ equals 0, I get the inequality *zero less than minus one by minus one*. Like this: $0 < (-1) \times (-1)$. And given that $(-1) \times (-1)$ equals 1, I get the final inequality *zero less than one:* $0 < 1$. An outcome that, instead of proving the correctness of the hypothesis on which I based the inequality $1 < 0$, contradicts it. Contradicting it, it shows its inapplicability. Showing its inapplicability, it demonstrates the accuracy of the contrary hypothesis. That is, $1 > 0$. And here I have the proof that one is greater than zero, that something is more than nothing."

No, changing his train of thought was useless. The parallel yet alien idea remained in his mind like the itch in his throat, and the irresistible need to weep. He closed the notebook, stuck it back in his pocket, climbed out of the jeep. With his eyes still blurred by the curtain of mist, he went to check if any Amal were reapproaching the Sixth Brigade M113, and in front of the crater opened by the 105mm grenade he halted. It was a round clean hole. It suggested something... What? He went back to the jeep. He sat down again at the wheel. But in doing so he nudged Sergeant Natale's helmet he had hidden under the seat, the helmet resounded like a gong, and the parallel yet alien idea outlined itself clearly. Damn, it had been a mistake to tell himself that in war corpses don't stir up police investigations, ballistics tests, autopsies. If the corpse is not an ordinary corpse, it arouses the same fuss it arouses in a place and in a time of peace. And the corpse of Khalid-Passepartout was not an ordinary corpse. It was an illustrious corpse, a corpse that belonged to Rashid: his private property. For sure Rashid would examine the remains of his honey-sweet-honey, for sure he would see the hole sunk in his heart. A round clean hole with a diameter of 9.9 millimeters. A hole that had nothing to do with the gashes produced by the shell fragments. In other words, it wouldn't take too long for Rashid to understand that his honey-sweet-honey hadn't been killed by the fragments but by a 9mm bullet. The bullet that loaded the M12, the rifle that only the Italians used in Beirut. So, crazy with anger and grief, he too would exercise the right of revenge. He too would carry out the rational gesture, the intellectually legitimate and morally valid deed, the positive act. And this meant that with his single shot he had not reestablished any broken equilibrium, he had not made any order out of the disorder, he had not denied any triumph of Chaos, he had not performed any operation capable of bringing the system back to its initial phase. On the contrary, he had broken the equilibrium completely, he had exacerbated and multiplied the disorder, given to entropy another corpse that demanded revenge... To make a long story short, he'd fallen into an error a thousand times duller and clumsier than the one committed by Khalid-Passepartout when the stupid insect had offered him the cross-shaped anchor. The error of pouring into the concreteness of Life, into the irreversible process of Life, the laws of mathematical logic. That is, a logic which elaborates abstractedness, which can turn upside down the results of a theorem by means of reversible processes. Life cannot be turned upside down like the results of a theorem. It cannot be overturned like the inequalities $1 < 0$ and $0 > 1$ and $0 < 1$ and $1 > 0$. It cannot be returned to its initial phase. It cannot be resurrected by killing those who have killed... Then, full of horror, he realized what he had done. He had added the final link to the chain of events begun with the double slaughter in October. The missing link. He had awakened the third truck, set in motion a counterrevenge which would fall upon the whole contingent. And his stony face became a flesh face again, the curtain of mist that blurred his eyes became a cascade of water, of unrestrainable tears. He was still sobbing when, back with Martino, Charlie moaned that question.

"What happened, son?!? What did you do?!"

"I killed him," he answered, immediately collecting himself.

"Killed whom?!?"

"Khalid-Passepartout."

Then he told him the rest, and for several minutes Charlie wasn't capable of pronouncing a word. Once those minutes passed, though, he refound his voice and said: "Listen to me well, son. You did not kill anybody. You never met any Khalid-Passepartout. You don't even know who Khalid-Passepartout is or was. Period." Then he turned to Martino who looked at him totally petrified with shock, and: "As to you, listen to me as well. You never heard anything. You never saw anything. You're blind, you're deaf, and if you open your mouth you're also dead because I'll strangle you with these hands." Finally, talking to himself in a murmur: "God have mercy on us. I just signed a treaty with Rashid."

*   *   *

The treaty was much more than the band-aid he'd gone in search of. It established that the Christian officers of the Sixth Brigade would return to the Eastern Zone without further harassment and regroup there with the Eighth Brigade, that the Shiite officers and soldiers would withdraw to their barracks south of the Street Without a Name, that the Italians would return to garrison Shatila by themselves, and woe to whoever opposed it. At midnight, then, the governmental M113s that flanked the Italians in the various posts left. And two short convoys formed on the rond-point of Shatila: one which headed for the Tayoune crossing with the Christian lieutenant, his loyal soldier, the other officers who wore a cross at their necks, and one which headed for the barracks south of the Street Without a Name with the Shiite soldiers. Half an hour later the Amal lifted their siege and, after heaping up the victims of the 105mm barrage (several score that included a youngster the foreigners called Passepartout) they went raiding outside the sector. So the nocturnal nefariousness concentrated in other parts of the half-city, and the contingent did not see what the monster born from the macabre womb of plurifratricidal war was capable of. Militiamen who disguised as nurses seized the ambulances and waving the Red Cross or Red Crescent flag broke into the Eighth Brigade checkpoints, pleaded we-carry-a-wounded-baby, let-us-pass-through, and after passing through butchered their benefactors with Kalashnikov volleys. Zealots who driven by anti-alcoholic fury attacked the hotel bars frequented by occasional tourists and, along with the bottles of wine or liquor, eliminated those who were drinking. Mullahs who drunk with Savonarolian fanaticism burst into the houses, arrested the women with red polished nails or lipstick, dragged them in front of a mosque, pilloried them, then they forced them to put on a chador. And no need to underline what happened to the Sixth Brigade's Christian officers who hadn't received the order to withdraw: colonels shot by their captains, captains executed by their lieutenants, lieutenants slaughtered by their soldiers. As for the Sons of God, they were everywhere. And they burned, they sacked, they profaned the same way they'd profaned the church of Saint-Michel. Or they threatened the Palestinians, soon-we'll-take-care-of-you-too, terrorized the muezzins who had sing-songed the now suppressed appeal don't-touch-the-Italians, the-Italians-are-our-blood-brothers. All this, without Zandra Sadr lifting a hand to curb his followers. Why should he? Before beginning the revolt, the Amal hadn't even sketched out a political or military structure that would replace the fragile though existent Gemayel government, and for His Most Reverend Eminence all that anarchy was a blessing: a godsend which guaranteed him a future as the local Khomeini. And amidst such circumstances, the dawn came. With the dawn, an outcry that shook the headquarters.

"The Condor is back!"

He'd returned with a jeep kindly lent him by the Eighth Brigade, and with his unshaved beard, his baggy eyes, his swollen face, his gauze bandage covering the soldierly wound on his left cheek he seemed like the survivor of a lynching. Yet he hadn't lost a grain of his supercilious determination. "The first one who speaks of roosters and hens and poultry ends up in front of a firing squad," he snarled at Gaspare and his escort as soon as he reached the entrance. Then he went to confront a chorus of questions that would forever remain unanswered. Where had he been trapped? How had he been wounded? Why hadn't he wanted them to come and rescue him? The only one who didn't ask a thing was Charlie. He waited until the evasive don't-mind-it's-just-a-scratch had silenced the useless curiosity, then he took him aside and said what he thought of the new situation.

"General," he concisely said, "we've got to go, and fast."

The reaction was just as concise.

"I know, Charlie, I know. I'll inform our government that we must evacuate as soon as possible."

Four days later, that is, the following Tuesday, a helicopter from the flagship landed at Sierra Mike with the three-star general who during the Christmas battle had remained on a stool drying the sweat of his fear. Along with him, extreme mockery of Destiny and major misfortune for Falcon, the lance corporal Salvatore Bellezza son of the late Onofrio who God knows how had succeeded in returning to cut the throat of Alì and disfigure Sanaan. With a blissful smile on his little mouth and an unexpected shrewdness in his trapped-rat eyes, Salvatore Bellezza son of the late Onofrio carried the three-star general's briefcase which contained the papers authorizing the contingent to leave whenever and in whatever manner the Condor wanted.

So the Condor called the last briefing, and Charlie's impatience became frenzied. The evening before, in fact, his usual informants had reported to him two ugly rumors which spread in Gobeyre. First, that Passepartout had been killed by the Italians with a 9mm bullet fired into his heart at point-blank range. Second, that crazy with anger and grief Rashid was seeking help from the Sons of God to avenge himself with a spectacular punishment.

CHAPTER SIX

1

NO MATTER HOW A STORY (lived or invented) concludes, and whether or not we've divined how it will conclude, there's something disquieting in the curtain that begins to lower over its epilogue. Something that recalls the precariousness of life, its unrepeatability, its inevitable and ineluctable goal. While the wires of the mechanism holding the curtain slacken and slowly bring down the folds, we seem to be looking at a candle that little by little dies out to leave us in an obscurity full of perils. The last briefing was just that: a disquieting curtain that began to lower, a candle that little by little died out to leave them in an obscurity full of perils. And in one way or another they all felt it. But nobody felt it as much as Charlie who immediately approached the Condor and whispered: "General, during the night the British have stolen away. In spite of the unpleasant side of the matter, I really believe that we should do the same. Possibly, in the next few hours: using the navy helicopters and leaving everything behind. If we start at sunset, let's say with three helicopters every twenty minutes and twelve or fifteen men on each helicopter, by tomorrow morning we're aboard the flagship and the cruisers." An immediate departure meant in fact an acknowledgment of impotence and fear, but staying a few days more would have been a folly. Definitively split in two, the city agonized under the fire the Christians showered on the Muslims and the Muslims on the Christians, the Druzes on both of them; the airport didn't function because the Shiite guerrillas who ran it were incapable of operating the control tower and the two usable strips; the port, held by the phalangists and the Kataeb, risked falling to a siege by the Amal. From second to second the confusion intensified and the Multinational Force had become the residue of a dreary failure. Now totally hunkered down in the Eastern Zone, the French had reduced the company left in the Pine Wood to a squad of ten legionnaires; now counting almost exclusively on the aircraft carriers, the Americans had halved the number of

Marines who remained in the trenches dug under the rubble of their headquarters; and, without notifying a soul, Her Britannic Majesty's one hundred Dragoons had really left as Charlie had whispered to the Condor. Nothing remained of them but the mocking message with which Sir Montague had shattered Crazy Horse's heart: "Farewell, my dear friend. And good luck." The trouble is that the misadventure in the poultry house with the crowing roosters and the cackling hens had intensified the Condor's pride, and the idea of an immediate departure horrified him to the point of making him disregard the mortal dangers that staying a few days more would impose on the contingent. His chest outthrust and his cheek already unbandaged to show a long purple scab that evoked the duels of Heidelberg, he therefore opened the briefing with a bold announcement.

"I refuse to leave by helicopter. I refuse to steal away in the night like a thief! I want to leave by ship, with my head held high in the sunlight!" And aside from Charlie who abstained from any comment, nobody disagreed.

"Me too," the Professor answered.

"Me too," Crazy Horse answered.

"Me too," Falcon answered.

"Me too," Gigi the Candid answered.

"Me too," Pistoia answered.

"Me too," Sugar answered.

"Us too," the others answered. Including Sandokan.

"Three ships," he continued. "One for Sierra Mike's four hundred marò, one for the Ruby's four hundred paratroopers and carabinieri, one for the three hundred men of the Logistics and the one hundred working at the field hospital or the headquarters. Plus, two cargo boats which will bring back to Italy what belongs to us. Month after month we've moved to this city the equivalent of another small city, and with the exception of some empty containers I want to put everything back in the suitcase. I don't want to leave a thing. Not a biscuit, a needle, a pin. So here's the outline of my plan. Four days and four nights to dismantle the bases, load the material, move it to the port with three daily convoys. One at dawn, one at noon, and one at sunset. Tomorrow, Wednesday, the first convoys carrying the clothing, the laundries, the kitchens, the ovens. Thursday, the convoys carrying the refrigerators, the cisterns, the water purifiers, the bulk of the provisions. Friday, those carrying the generators, the radio stations, the office machinery. Saturday, those carrying the tents, the cots, the heavy weapons, and the field hospital's equipment. The night between Saturday and Sunday, the shipment with the cargo. Sunday at dawn, our departure with the M113s and the various other vehicles. A single convoy that crosses Beirut, flags fluttering. By noon, our embarking. This date, of course, will be kept absolutely secret. The troops themselves will be informed only a few hours before. Any objections?"

"None," the Professor answered.

"None," Crazy Horse answered.

"None," Falcon answered.

"None," Gigi the Candid answered.

"None," Pistoia answered.

"None," Sugar answered.

"None," the others answered. Including Sandokan.

Charlie, instead, remained silent.

"I know that this plan involves considerable risks. I know that at seeing the preparations and the ships anchored in the port, everybody will realize that we are about to leave. I know that consequently we'll lack the surprise element which has favored the getaway of the English, the withdrawal of the French from the Western Zone, the transfer of the Americans to their carriers. I know that by dismantling the bases we'll grow weaker and weaker, that by Sunday morning we'll be like a tortoise without a shell, that any dog can devour a tortoise without a shell and attack our final convoy. And I obviously worry about it. But not so much as about the hours we'll spend on the dock waiting to load the M113s and the other vehicles. One thousand two hundred men piled on a dock are an extremely easy target, and the Amal as well as the governmentals have every interest in harming us to accuse each other and increase the chaos. Poor-Italians, just-when-they-were-going-home, we'll-avenge-them etcetera. Which brings me to the subject of the only thing I'm ready to leave. Here it is. We have about a hundred containers, nineteen to twenty-five feet long, eight to ten feet wide and deep, made of solid iron. Since we need about fifty of them to transport the material, we'll fill the remaining fifty with sandbags and use them on the dock to erect a series of protective shields. Vertical trenches, let's say, inside which we'll take shelter before and during the embarking. Raise your hand if you have any objections."

Charlie raised his.

"I do, general."

The Condor smiled indulgently.

"Go ahead, Charlie. Tell us why."

"Because the most dangerous phase will not be waiting on the dock and embarking, general. It will come when the ships move away from the dock to set sail."

"Are you talking about the third truck, Charlie?"

"Yessir. The third truck coming from the sea. The kamikaze motorboat you spoke about after the double slaughter..."

"I know, Charlie, I know... But I put that fear aside because the third truck or kamikaze motorboat makes sense as long as we're in Beirut. Why should they send it the moment we leave?"

"Right. Why?" the Professor echoed.

"Why?" the others echoed. Including Sandokan.

"Because..." Charlie hesitated seeking an answer which would say enough without raising suspicions or excessive curiosity. Then he assumed the gloomy expression of a person crushed by indignation and let out a deep sigh. "Because I've been informed that an ugly story is making the rounds in Gobeyre. A slander."

"A slander? What slander?!?"

"That the young Amal who tossed the two Rdg8 in Bourji el Barajni and caused the wounding of Sergeant Natale in Shatila has been killed by the Italians, general."

A tumult exploded.

"The blond who stole his feathered helmet?!?"

"Killed by us?!?"

"But that's inconceivable!"

"Scandalous!"

"Shameful!"

"Incredible!"

"A bloody crap of a crap supercrap!"

The Condor, instead, got alarmed.

"Yes, an ugly story, Charlie... Really ugly. And which one of us would have killed him? How? Where?"

"The who, the how, and the where are mysteries that lodge in the mind of Allah, general. In fact the individual died of fragment wounds, hit by a grenade," Charlie answered without batting an eyelash. "But the worst isn't this. It is that we cannot protest. We cannot demand their apologies or explanations. It would feed the slander. And slanders, you know, are like cherries. One leads to another. At the same time, however, we should pay much attention to the rumor that Rashid has asked for help from the Sons of God to stage a spectacular revenge."

"Rashid?!?"

"Rashid."

"A spectacular revenge?!?"

"A spectacular revenge."

"Let's not get carried away, Charlie! If we paid attention to all the rumors that go around this damn city..."

"It's not gossip, general. And let's not forget that we may be alive because three months ago we paid attention to one of those rumors."

A thick silence fell. The Condor got thoughtful.

"Yes, Charlie, yes... I see your point. But even if it isn't gossip, what makes you suspect that Rashid really wants to carry out his revenge, and with a kamikaze motorboat?"

"The word spectacular, general. Remember what you said three months ago? You said: 'If I were a kamikaze who wanted to stage a spectacular slaughter, I wouldn't bother flinging myself at the bases or the headquarters with a truck or plane. I'd take a motorboat and smash it into the ship that each week arrives and leaves with the troops on leave or returning from their leave. An easy, unfailing, concentrated target. Four hundred corpses guaranteed.' "

"I remember, Charlie, I remember."

"Not to mention, you added, that in the inlets next to the port there are many motorboats: how to tell which are the harmless and which the kamikazes?"

"I remember, Charlie, I remember. And a motorboat is a nimble, very fast craft... And the ships we'll be leaving on are nothing more than ocean liners with a maximum speed of fifteen knots... You're right. Whether true or false, we must take that rumor seriously... But what can we do besides keeping our eyes open and asking the fleet to redouble the surveillance?"

"We can insure ourselves a minimum of security before the departure, general. A green light to exit the port without an unreasonable risk."

"And how?!"

"By paying a symbolic toll, general."

The tumult exploded again. Led, this time, by an infuriated Condor.

"A symbolic toll?!? I say I want to leave with my head held high in the sunlight, and you suggest I pay a symbolic toll?!?"

"Inconceivable!"

"Scandalous!"

"Shameful!"

"Incredible!"

But, again, Charlie didn't bat an eyelash.

"Not a symbolic toll in cash, general. A symbolic toll in courtesy. A favor like the one we paid for the appeal don't-touch-the-Italians, the-

Italians-are-our-blood-brothers... If you ask me, we should leave behind the field hospital."

"The... field... hospita-a-al?!?"

"Yes. With the medics and a company of carabinieri to protect them. Under the command of a superior officer, of course."

The tumult became inordinate.

"I say I don't want to leave a biscuit, a needle, a pin, and you suggest I leave the field hospital with the medics and a company of carabinieri?!?"

"He's pulling our leg!"

"He's joking!"

"It would be the same as leaving a hundred hostages!"

"And in exchange for our skin!"

"I can't believe it!"

"Me either!"

The only one who remained unruffled, this time, was Crazy Horse who jumped to his feet and brought one hand up to his monocle.

"Necessitati parendum est. We must obey necessity, Cicero teaches us! And Seneca adds: necessitas plus posse quam pietas solet. Necessity may be stronger than pity. General, Sir, I am the one who'll stay with the carabinieri to protect the field hospital!"

"Fine, colonel. Stay," grumbled the Condor, clearly lost in his thoughts and totally heedless of what Crazy Horse had said.

"Really, Sir?"

"Really, really..." Then, turning to Charlie: "Moreover, and supposing I pay the ransom you define as a symbolic toll, who can guarantee that the third truck-motorboat will not come all the same?"

"Nobody," Charlie answered sharply. "It's a gamble."

"And what are the odds of winning?"

"The same as in any gamble. Red or black, et rien ne va plus."

"And who'd be running the game?"

"The croupier, of course. The guy who tosses the balls onto the wheel and gives or takes the chips."

"Zandra Sadr?"

"Zandra Sadr. There's nobody else, general."

A long silence followed, during which the only audible sound was the drumming of five fingers asking for advice from the cherry-wood table. Then the Condor's voice rose decisively.

"Okay, Charlie, we'll take the gamble. Go see the croupier and offer him the field hospital as a chip."

And while the Professor, Falcon, Gigi the Candid, Pistoia, Sugar,

Sandokan, and the others fell into dumbstruck stillness, while Crazy Horse rejoiced ecstatically over the fine-colonel-stay, Charlie rushed over to Zandra Sadr's with Martino.

2

He came back in the afternoon, gripped by a rage that surpassed all the rages he'd had in Beirut. In fact, as soon as he reached the court-yard, he didn't even leave the jeep. He snarled at Martino go-ahead, son, leave-me-alone, then he remained at the wheel and for several minutes he did nothing but grumble at himself enough-enough-enough. Enough with staying in a city where we don't grow old, we don't die of old age. Enough with enduring sacrifice and discomfort, with sleeping in a basement on an undersize cot, deprived of a pair of clean sheets, of a soft pillow, of a woman beside me. Enough with being awakened by the singsongs of the muezzins and the thuds of the bombs. Enough with using cold water to wash my face and a stinking rag to dry it. Enough with drinking my coffee from a lousy aluminum cup. Enough with wearing the uniform of the Machine that fucks men over and reduces them to cogs in a gear. Enough with belonging to an organism which is the refugium peccatorum for anybody in search of a shelter to lodge his uncertainties or failures. Enough with playing the role of the wise and sensible adviser, of the cynical intelligent adven-turer, of the spy with a golden heart, of the idealist who stays or pre-tends to stay on the side of the ox-people. Enough with trying to imitate Lawrence of Arabia, with trying to be what I am not and never will be. I want to get out of here. I want to settle down in a city where people grow old, where they die of old age, full of wrinkles and finally tired of existence. I want to live a comfortable life, sleep in a bed with clean sheets and a soft pillow and a woman beside me. I want to wake up in a room where the sky enters with the sound of bells. I want to wash myself with hot water and dry myself with freshly laundered tow-els. I want to drink my coffee from a porcelain cup and wear gray or blue double-breasted suits, good shirts, beautiful ties, and use an um-brella when it rains. I want to quit the Machine and do a dull job. A job that lets me go to the restaurants, the theater, the movies, the soccer games on Sunday. I want to become stupid, serene and stupid, happy and stupid. Normal. As a normal man, a serene and stupid man, a happy and stupid man, I want to forget the Amal and the Sons of God and Zandra Sadr and the governmentals and the war and Beirut. And I want the same for everybody who's embarking on Sunday. I want it for my Charlies, for Stefano, for Martino, for Fifi, for Bernard le Français, for Angelo who has gotten us in this mess but in his place I would have done the same. No, I would have behaved much worse. Because I would have said fuck-you-and-your-fourteen-years, Khalid-Passepartout: he-who-kills-at-fourteen-dies-at-fourteen. Besides, the responsibility of what he did is mine. All mine. If I hadn't told him that his Ophelia had been shot in Gobeyre, now we wouldn't be in this situation. So I'd better convince the Condor to drop his pants, to pay what Zandra Sadr asks... And only at this point did he leave the jeep to finally join the Condor, inform him about the results of the meeting.

"No green light, general. As a matter of fact, the light is red. Blood red."

The Condor jumped to his feet.

"What does it mean, blood-red?!?"

"It means that they really want to get us, general, and that things are worse than I thought."

"Who says so?"

"Zandra Sadr. Because when I expressed our disdain for the slander and the threat, he seemed surprised and replied that nobody was slandering us, nobody was threatening us. But when I suggested that he make inquiries, he did and... He mentioned three motorboats, general. Not one. And mind this: I hadn't even pronounced the word motorboat."

"Tell me the exact words he used."

"Zandra Sadr doesn't use exact words, as we know. He speaks through metaphors, he expresses himself with allegories... He said: 'Yes, captain, unfortunately it's true. So true that my two ears weren't enough to listen to what I was being told.' Then I asked him if three ears would have been enough, and he answered: 'Yes, captain. Three ears. One ear for each piece of bad news I heard. And, along with three ears, three eyes. Because the third ear which doesn't exist cannot listen, and the third eye which doesn't exist cannot see...'"

"This is your interpretation, Charlie."

"No. Because afterwards he said something precise. He said: 'Captain, with two eyes only, it's very difficult to see the fire that travels three times on the water.'"

"Shit! And what about the chip of the field hospital?" hissed the Condor, sitting down to catch his breath.

"It helps. But it is not sufficient."

"It is not?!?"

"No. And now hear me carefully, general: everything has a price, in this city. Everything can be traded. Everything can be negotiated. Everything can be purchased: bought and sold. Even life. And until today we haven't been purchasing our life: we've been renting it, in exchange for blood plasma. But from today on, we have to buy it. Which means, we have to pay that toll. And in money. Not in favors."

"In money?!?"

"Yes, general. It isn't enough to leave behind the field hospital with the medics and a company of carabinieri."

"What?!?"

"Yes, general. We'll have to give it to them. As a gift."

"A gift to Zandra Sadr?!?"

"No, to the half-city represented by Zandra Sadr."

"Do you mean he had the balls to ask for this?!?"

"Yes. And without metaphors or allegories or paraphrasing. When he mentioned the fire that travels three times on the water, he spoke up loud and clear. To try stopping the fire, he said, he should offer them the field hospital. Then he explained that in doing so we would make a gift to ourselves because it wouldn't be wise to leave behind the medics and someone to protect them."

"Charlie, you're out of your mind."

"General, if I'm out of my mind, then you better resign yourself to the idea of ending up as fish food."

"I don't care if I end up as fish food! I'd rather blow up than lose my dignity!"

"I'm sure you would. But if you blow up, everybody blows up. And in all due respect: the moment you croak, please do think that for your fucking dignity you've sacrificed hundreds and hundreds of young soldiers you should have got home safe and sound."

"Charlie..." mumbled a voice that resembled very little the Condor's voice.

"Yes, general..." Charlie answered in a gentle, encouraging tone.

"Are you fully aware of what you're proposing, Charlie?"

"I am, general."

"Dignity apart, do you know how much money a well-equipped field hospital is worth? Do you know what the price is for three radiology units and an operating room, to say nothing of a mobile operating room or scintigraphy apparatus or a dental lab? Do you realize what we'd be giving to the very people who want to slaughter us?"

"I do, sir. And I'm sorry to inform you that there is more."

"More?!?"

"Yes. Because His Most Reverend Eminence also suggested, nay demanded, that we give him the provisions you want to ship back to Italy on Saturday night."

"The... provisions?!?"

"Yes. And they're worth a fortune as well. I know. But to win big we have to bet big."

"Bet?!? You're still talking about gambling?"

"Yes. And about the risk of losing. Let's not delude ourselves, general. Not even the provisions and the field hospital give us any guarantee."

"They don't?!?"

"No. And our croupier admits it. Again through metaphors and allegories he said that it might be hard to persuade all three kamikazes to cancel the attack. One out of the three could refuse and hurl himself at the first or second or third ship. In other words, with the toll we could save only two-thirds of the contingent. Well... we've got to accept all the same, general. Whether it's a straight or not."

"Charlie... It's not a matter of straight or not: it's a matter of principle! To save my principles, I would bend to any sacrifice. I'd even remain with a company of carabinieri, I would collect the field hospital's garbage every day. But... See what I mean?"

"No. I don't, general. Because with principles we won't even buy the coffins for the bodies which wouldn't be eaten by the fish. With his principles, my friend Bilal didn't buy anything. But you're the general. You decide."

A long pause followed. Very, very long. Then the Condor lifted the internal phone and called Crazy Horse.

"Colonel, bring me the list of the provisions with their prices and an inventory of all the field hospital's equipment."

"Hic et nunc! Immediately, General, Sir!" Crazy Horse neighed, drunk with happiness.

3

Honest, naive, adorable Crazy Horse. The suspicion that the Condor might have answered him mechanically, thinking of something else and for the exclusive sake of shutting him up, hadn't even occurred to him. On the contrary, after the words fine-colonel-stay, he had so much believed he would remain in Beirut to protect the field hospital that as soon as he reached his office he had grabbed the God-Save-the-Queen fountain pen and written two letters. One, short but intense, for the London lady with whom he had hoped to grow old riding over the green fields of Cornwall: "Goodbye forever, Madame. Duty calls, and I take my leave of you with these lines of Shakespeare: 'Life every man holds dear, but the brave man holds honor far more precious dear than life.' " One, longer and contemptuous for his ex-friend Sir Montague: "You fled, dear Montague. You took to your heels and discredited the glorious Union Jack. I remain, instead, with a handful of valiants to redeem the honor of the West. Soon the world will know what an Italian cavalry officer, a real soldier who doesn't forget that he served in the Seventh Brigade, is capable of. Farewell, farewell... Morituri te salutant." Then he'd given the envelopes to Old Grouse with the request that he mail them from Italy, and had rushed off to make the list of the provisions with their prices plus the inventory of the field hospital's equipment. Nineteen dense pages listing every basin, every syringe, every needle that could be found in the first aid tent or in the operating rooms, and every sausage, every apple, every biscuit that could be found in the kitchens or in the warehouses. "Flumina pauca vides de magnis fontibus orta! Great rivers sprout from tiny springs, Ovid reminds us!" Thus, while entering the Condor's office, he thought he had been summoned for a transfer of powers. He certainly didn't expect the hard blow he was about to receive between his head and neck.

"Here I am, General, Sir!"

"Read it out loud, colonel."

"Yessir. I'll begin with the provisions. Ninety-five items including the emergency supplies and excluding the rations we'll consume over the next few days. I was careful to omit nothing, Sir: not even the 210 kilos of Genovese pesto at 5.400 liras per kilo, which comes to one million and 134.000 liras, the 268 kilos of capers at 3.338 liras per kilo which comes to 894.584 liras, the 1.8 kilos of saffron at 1.804 liras per gram which comes to three million and 247.200 liras, the 15 kilos of oregano at..."

"Colonel! I'm interested in the prices!"

"Yessir, General! We have 95 million and 569.050 liras of beef, 50 million and 472.530 liras of pork, thirty million and 276.000 liras of mutton and goat, 26 million and 698.750 liras of canned meat, 20 million and 115.700 liras of prosciutto and salami and mortadella and pancetta and soprassate and sausage of various kinds, 15 million and 245.630 liras of whole chickens, 12 million and 251.760 liras of chicken breasts. Furthermore, we have 19 million and 689.810 liras of fish such as sole and cod and mackerel, 17 million and 757.000 liras of tuna in oil and salted anchovies, 14 million and 703.200 liras of spaghetti and fettuccine and tagliatelle, 8 million and 162.000 liras of ravioli and tortellini, 16 million and 825.410 liras of rice, 20 million and 601.120 liras of parmesan cheese, 14 million and 326.212 liras of other cheeses, 8 million and 518.460 liras of butter, 10 million and 111.050 liras of olive oil. We also have 13 million and 500.830 liras of cookies, 7 million and 364.000 liras of crackers, 9 million and 296.080 liras of panettoni, 7 million and 100.000 liras of condensed milk, 5 million and 725.410 liras of fresh milk, 14 million and 988.980 liras of coffee, 7 million and 781.962 liras of tea, 5 million and 980.550 liras of cocoa and chocolate..."

"The total, colonel!"

"Yessir, General! With the potatoes, beans, peas, chickpeas, tomatoes, tomato sauce, white flour, cornmeal, sugar, salt, pepper, and the other provisions you won't let me list, the total is 469 million and 63.618 liras. But this sum doesn't include fruit juice and mineral water. Nor does it include the alcoholic beverages: white and red wine, spumante, beer, liqueurs in liter bottles, minibottles, plastic packets, and whose value is 247 million and 252.906 liras. Thus, the overall sum is 716 million and 315.714 liras. A number I obtained, of course, from the wholesale prices the army is charged: the real value is much higher. As for the alcoholic beverages, permit me to clarify one point: although their quantity is considerable, it is not excessive if we consider how rigorous the winter nights can be even here. It's important that I stress it, General, Sir, because if I survive the ordeal I don't want to be accused of having drunk too much. I have never bent the elbow, Sir, and I have never allowed my subordinates to do so. Never! When it comes to drinking, I'm in total agreement with Seneca who says uti-non-abuti. Use, don't abuse."

"What in the hell has your fucking Seneca to do with it, God blasted?!?" shouted the Condor without grasping the meaning of the clarification. Then he turned to Charlie who hadn't heard the squabble and was toting up the figures on his calculator.

"A fortune, Charlie."

"Not if we divide 716 million and 315.714 by one thousand two hundred men," Charlie answered. "In food and drink, calculating the wholesale prices, the life of each of us only costs 596.929 liras and 76 centesimi. That is, well under five hundred dollars. And even if we consider the four refrigerator compartments and the generators, the value stays low. Let's say the price of a relatively good jacket or a pair of custom-made shoes."

"Refrigerator compartments? Generators?"

"Well... Meat, fish, milk, and butter are perishables. To conserve them, they'll need the refrigerator compartments. And the refrigerator compartments run with generators. Meaning, we'll have to give them those too."

"That's obvious!" Crazy Horse exclaimed, still thinking that the discussion regarded his stay in Beirut. But again the Condor did not understand.

"Save your comments, colonel. And move on to the equipment at the field hospital."

"With pleasure, Sir! Look, here I have two hundred fifty-six items. Which includes even a scale for weighing newborns whose purpose eludes me. I'll read them in alphabetical order: four aerosol machines, four air agitators, four anesthesia devices, six atomizers, twenty-six basins, one hundred ten cylinders of compressed oxygen, fifty cylinders of nitrous oxide..."

"Cut to the chase, colonel! The prices!"

"Sir, I don't know the prices of the individual items. Nonetheless, in my typically scrupulous manner, I took the opportunity to make a few inquiries. And accounting for the ambulances, the tents, the beds, the adjustable wheelchairs, the Bunker chambers, the three radiology units, the electrocardiographs, the surgery rooms, the mobile operating room, the dental lab, the scintigraphy machine, I mean the most important items, I arrived at a lump sum of three billion liras at the very least. But don't worry, General. I'm an orderly person, you know. I'll take good care of everything. Just as if this stuff were my very own."

"I know, colonel, I know," snorted the Condor, still without grasping the meaning of the clarification. "In fact, I entrust you with the task of packing up the mobile operating room and the scintigraphy apparatus."

"Packing them up, General, Sir?"

"Right. They're brand new and I want to take them back to Italy."

"Back to Italy, Sir?"

"You bet. They're too expensive. Besides, they wouldn't be able to use them."

"They wouldn't be able to use them, Sir?"

"Right."

"Begging your pardon, Sir... But why shouldn't they be able to use what they've always used? They are, they'll be, the same doctors and nurses, Sir! And I will need those items too, Sir..."

"Oh God!" exclaimed Charlie, finally aware of the misunderstanding. The Condor simply stared at Crazy Horse with irritation.

"What in the hell are you saying, colonel?!? Why in the hell should you need the mobile operating room and the scintigraphy machine?!?"

"But for the simple reason that I'll remain here to protect thus direct the field hospital, Sir!"

"What?!? Who told you that?!?"

"You did, General, Sir!"

"I did?!? When?!?"

"This morning at the briefing, Sir! When I offered to stay and you answered fine-colonel-stay..."

"Oh God!" Charlie repeated.

But the Condor shrugged.

"Who knows what I was thinking, colonel. In any case, come down from the clouds and get your feet on the ground. Although the idea of abandoning you to the Sons of God is quite tantalizing, you'll embark with us on Sunday."

"I... will... embark... with you...?!?"

"No doubt."

There was a heartbreaking whinny. The whinny of a horse who breaks a leg and begs to be finished off. Then a savage howl. A howl you would never have expected from a man of his stamp.

"General, Si-i-ir! Do thank your gods that along with being a gentleman and an aristocrat worthy of such a name, I'm a real soldier! Because I should challenge you to a duel, Sir! A duel with the saber that you don't even know how to handle! A duel to the last drop of blood!"

Then he hurled himself down the corridor and across the foyer, went up the stairs, reached the roof terrace where he started invoking the snipers shoot-me-in-the-chest-you-rascals, fire-a-bullet-through-my-heart-you-boors, and it took three carabinieri to get him. But he didn't calm down, fumbling and struggling he continued to howl I-want-to-die, mors-omnia-solvit, death-solves-everything, honesta-mors-turpi-vita-potior, an-honest-death-is-preferable-to-a-disgraceful-life. So they had to take him to the field hospital and inject a powerful dose of Valium mixed with belladonna into his bottom. Something that happened while the Condor decided to pay the no longer symbolic toll.

"Continue your calculations, Charlie..."

"Here we go, general. If I add the provisions' 716 million and 315.714 liras to the value of the field hospital, plus the 283 million and 684.285 liras which is the assessed price of the refrigerators and the generators, I get a total of four billion. One lira less, to be exact: 3.999.999.999. And if I divide that three billion nine hundred ninety-nine million nine hundred ninety-nine thousand nine hundred and ninety-nine liras by one thousand two hundred men in the contingent, I get an incredible 3.333.333,33. That is to say, three million three hundred thirty-three thousand three hundred thirty-three liras and thirty-three centesimi apiece. Meaning, each life."

The Condor smiled bitterly.

"Rather cheap for a city where everything has a price, everything can be traded, everything can be negotiated, purchased, bought and sold. Even life."

"A trifle, general. For the release of a kidnapped citizen, no Italian criminal would accept such a trifle. We may as well give up the mobile operating room and the scintigraphy apparatus."

"You're right. And since principles won't even pay for coffins, now I only have to specify the four terms I set for His Most Reverend Eminence. Then you can go and conduct the negotiations."

* * *

Charlie conducted them magnificently, once more demonstrating that the best bank account of a man is his intelligence, and in shrewdness he vied with the diabolical Zandra Sadr. He never pronounced the word "toll," alternately replacing it with the ironic term "gift" and, occasionally, the disparaging term "swag" or "loot." He never alluded to the blackmail the Condor was submitting to, and rather than behaving like one who asks for favors he behaved like one who grants them. Tons of excellent food and a complete hospital aren't gifts to bestow lightheartedly, he said through a stunned Martino, and before making such a decision the general had been thinking a lot. He'd even considered the possibility of dividing the gift in two and awarding half of it to the Christian Zone, half to the Muslim Zone. So in order to hand over all the swag to His Most Reverend Eminence, the general had set his conditions. Four conditions. First: the Italian flag and the Red Cross standard should continue to fly over the field hospital. Second: the hospital should assist everybody, not only the followers of one political-religious creed. Third: the new owners should guard it to avert acts of vandalism or plunder. Fourth: the pork meat and the alcoholic beverages prohibited by the Koran had to be transferred to the poor of the Christian Zone. A no less essential condition, this last, because the warehouses and refrigerator compartments contained an enormous amount of fresh pork and top-quality sausages, bottles of wine and spumante and liqueur and beer by the thousands, and the Italians had not the time to sort it out. Was His Most Reverend Eminence ready to accept and keep this quadruple pact? If so, he could consider himself the legitimate owner of the loot from today onward: the actual delivery would take place before the contingent embarked. That is, in a month. Yes, the general wanted to leave in a month. And, having introduced this lie, he tackled the subject that interested him most: the roulette game that despite the high stakes didn't give any guarantee on saving all three ships. Of course, he said, the general placed all confidence in His Most Reverend Eminence: not for a single moment did he doubt that, even having only two eyes and only two ears, His Most Reverend Eminence would stop the ingrates who were moved by the wind of slander. However he hadn't liked the sentence about the third eye which doesn't exist and doesn't see, the third ear which doesn't exist and doesn't hear, and found it necessary to cite an ancient Italian proverb: "Nobody is more deaf than the one who doesn't want to hear, nobody is more blind than the one who doesn't want to see." He also found it necessary to pose the following question: how did His Most Reverend Eminence intend to douse the threefold blaze of the fire that travels three times on the water?

Hieratic as usual and attended as usual by his two sons, Zandra Sadr listened without discomposure and mellifluously declared that he accepted both the gift and the terms. Yes, the Italian flag and the Red Cross standard would continue to fly over the field hospital. Yes, the hospital would assist everybody, not only the followers of one political-religious creed. Yes, the new owners would guard it to avert acts of vandalism or plunder. Yes, the food and beverages prohibited by the Koran would be sorted out and distributed to the poor in the Christian Zone. You-can-rely-on-us, captain. Immediately after, though, his tone changed. And he harshly declared that the Arab countries had some ancient proverbs too. One of them said: "If you receive a gift, offer thanks with what you have and not with what you don't have." Another one said: "Sometimes two hands aren't enough to douse three fires." So, his answer to the general was the following one: as he hadn't three eyes and three ears, he hadn't three hands either; as he hadn't three hands either, he couldn't promise to douse three fires. Yet he promised to use his single nose to sniff something burning, his single mouth to resurrect and modify the appeal that the muezzins didn't pronounce anymore at the hours of prayer. Then he resurrected it, he modified it, and that very same evening a new singsong wafted down from the minarets of the half-city.

"Samma, mishan Allah, samma! Ma'a tezi talieni min tarak! Al-talieni ekhuaatùna bil dam wa itha rahalun taraku al hadeja! Hear me, in the name of the Lord, hear me! Don't touch the Italians who depart! The Italians are our blood brothers, and departing they leave gifts for us."

Mysterious as a lie that maybe is a truth, as a truth that maybe is a lie, the appeal was repeated every day of the last four days and every night of the last four nights after the invocation Allah akbar-Allah akbar-Allah akbar. And thus Wednesday came, and Thursday, and Friday, and Saturday: all stations of a Way of the Cross that spared nobody. Not even the white mare of Tayoune who no longer budged from the grassy bed in the middle of the rotary.

4

The Wednesday Station is important for the terrible intuition that Angelo had while solving the problem of the raindrop that falls on the speeding train's window. But, since this remained a secret locked within his mind, in the eyes of everybody else the day was characterized by the stormy conquest of a dock. An event which saw Pistoia as the great protagonist. Beyond the Old City, in fact, the Amal subdued the stretch of northern coast that extended from the northwest promontory to the edge of what they aimed at: the port still held by the Christians. Hammering it with the mortars now placed in Cannons Square as well as occupying the houses next to the western basin they tried to seize the target, and to repel their attack the governmentals had closed the harbor infrastructures. Deserted, the arsenals and the shipyards. Unused, the cargo trains and the tracks. Abandoned, the drydocks and the wharves. Totally empty, the beautiful breakwater pier that from the western basin dashed off into the sea at an angle of 45 degrees with respect to the coast and after nine hundred thirty yards (eight hundred fifty meters in Angelo's problem) ended in a graceful lighthouse. Only three eastern basins operated normally. But they were in the hands of the Eighth Brigade and of the phalangists who kept them to moor the freighters which unloaded their weapons. Moreover, the harbor-master's office had been assigned to Gassàn, all of a sudden appointed colonel due to merit-in-the-field. Nobody but Gassàn had the authority to grant the use of the dock, and to the Professor's request he'd flatly answered no. "Sir, my government will confirm that no exceptions are permitted. Not even for our allies." Yet a dock had to be found. If it wasn't found, the convoys couldn't start the daily trips to transport the containers. If the containers weren't transported, the bases couldn't be dismantled. If the bases weren't dismantled, the ships heading to Beirut should be sent back. And sending back the ships meant not leaving with heads held high in the sunlight: a flight like the one of the British Dragoons would become inevitable. At dawn, therefore, the dilemma reached the breaking point. And the Condor was about to yield to the helicopter solution he'd so scornfully discarded, when a cheerful Pistoia appeared with his proposal to solve the whole business. "Don't worry, general! I'll take care of it." Then, dogged by Sandokan who held the right to supervise any operation concerning a departure by sea, he rushed to the port to confront his former friend Gassàn.

"Listen to me good, you executioner. On Christmas Eve I put my Sardinian pattada at your throat: I cannot deny it. But I didn't butcher you. And this means that you're in my debt, that you owe me your life. Ergo, cough up the dock."

And Gassàn coughed it up. He was so changed, Gassàn. The weariness that on Christmas Eve had quenched his thirst for blood and ignited thoughts very similar to Bilal's last thoughts had delivered him to a torpor of disavowal. The division of the amoeba and the defeat of the Christians had deprived him of his faith in himself, and by now he resembled very little the icy executioner who had terrorized the city for years. Weakened by a hint of corpulence that marred his handsomeness, faded by a sickly pallor that marred his healthy face, he no longer moved with the sullen energy of a panther that roves in the dark. He no longer signed his grenades with the words brahmet-bayi, his bullets with the initials bb. He no longer roamed the Western Zone in search of Muslims to eliminate according to the unavoidable duty and irrefutable right. He had even ripped the Virgin of Junieh's image from his pistol butt, even quit the habit of quoting Anatole France or Corneille, and instead of speaking about the Crusades he spoke about a dwarf wrapped in a patched jacket who had left a bitter taste in his mouth. Along with the bitter taste, the doubt of having wasted his own life. "I wanted to heal people, not to kill them..." Besides, rumors said that he'd already bought a house in Switzerland and that while waiting for the emigration visa he ran the harbormaster's office to stay far from military activities.

"Okay, Pistoia," he replied with a bitter smile. "Give a look at the three operative basins and tell me which dock you want."

Still dogged by Sandokan who had witnessed the scene with his now customary indifference, Pistoia gave a look. In the eastern basin, the best and the one that the Italians had always used, there was no room: the freighters with the phalangists' weapons unloaded with exasperating slowness and would keep the docks busy until next week. In the central basin, room existed. It also offered a certain security because the docks lay five hundred fifty yards from the houses occupied by the Amal and massive silos efficaciously protected the area from the Cannons Square mortars. But the water's depth was insufficient, and the ground space was occupied by the customs warehouses and cranes: it wouldn't hold the troops and the vehicles of the final convoy. As for the western basin, it had the defect of being too near the buildings occupied by the Amal who incessantly fired to break in. Furthermore, it was defended by the Kataeb: Gemayel's private militia. But the water's depth was sufficient, the docks were available until Sunday afternoon, and an open space of two hundred twenty by one hundred yards permitted them to erect the vertical trenches which would shelter the troops and the vehicles of the final convoy. With his arms flung wide in the gesture of a person who has no alternative, Sandokan pronounced it suitable. Pistoia agreed, and told Gassàn.

"Hey, executioner! I'm really glad I didn't butcher you!"

"And I'm glad that you're glad," Gassàn answered with the same bitter smile.

So, thanks to this bizarre relationship, the plan put forth at the briefing became effective and the Condor entrusted Pistoia with the difficult task of erecting the vertical trenches under the Amal's fire. Sugar, with the no less difficult duty of guiding the daily convoys beyond the Green Line. Each convoy, fifteen trailer trucks plus an escort of six armored cars that before passing through the Tayoune crossing stopped a hundred yards away and waited for the all-clear to be radio-transmitted by two sentries: Angelo and Bernard le Français, the Charlie who did not speak Italian. The rotary was in fact the scene of two torments: the shootings from the snipers of both factions and the continuous presence of the Amal squad leader: a dimwit who called himself Rocky and who, in order to raise the boundary bar and let the twenty-one vehicles pass through, wanted to be compensated with the red scarf he'd glimpsed at Gigi the Candid's neck during the transfer of the Ruby base. In utter bad faith Gigi the Candid had told him next-time-you'll-have-it, and the unkept promise now caused as many problems as the Kalashnikovs and the M16s hidden behind the balconies of the abandoned villas. "Ana badi fulàra, ana badi fulàra, I want the scarf!" Of course Sugar would have preferred the Sodeco crossing where there were no Rocky and no snipers. But during the spot investigation he'd realized that the oversize trailers wouldn't turn at the curves, thus had been forced to choose Tayoune and post the sentries. A most unpleasant assignment that Angelo and Bernard le Français fulfilled by parking in front of the white mare's grassy bed then placating Rocky with chocolates or cigarettes or whatever they had. And by holding their breath each time they decided to give the all-clear because the snipers were taking a rest.

Angelo's terrible intuition came in an interval between that sniper fire.

* * *

"Touchant du bois, qu'est-ce qu'on décide? Knocking wood, what do we decide? Do we give them the all-clear or not?"

"Yes, we do. Ask Rocky to raise the bar."

"Mais maintenant il recommence à mendier le foulard et moi je n'ai plus rien lui donner! But now he'll start begging again for the scarf and I don't have a thing to give him! Regarde: il a tout pris, ce misérable! Même les bonbons! Look, look: he has taken everything, that tramp. Even the candies! Il me reste seulement les petites bouteilles du liqueur au café! I only have the small bottles of coffee liqueur!"

"Give him the liqueur."

"Mais c'est un bedouin, zut! But he's a bedouin, dammit! Il ne peut pas boire du liqueurs! He cannot drink liqueur!"

"Give it to him anyway."

"Merde, alors! Shit!"

More enraged than ever, Bernard le Français left the jeep. He went over to Rocky to pacify him with the coffee liqueur, have him raise the bar, and the usual quarrel exploded at once.

"Ana badi fulàra!"

"Je t'ai déjà dit que je n'ai pas de foulards, espèce d'idiot! I already told you I don't have any scarf, idiot! Take the liqueur, you idiot, so you get drunk and your God sends you to hell!"

"Ana fulàra! My scarf!"

"Tais-toi et lève la barre, troglodyte! Shut up and raise the bar, you caveman!"

"Fulàra was sigarèt. The scarf and the cigarettes."

"Quelles cigarettes, what cigarettes?! You never asked for cigarettes! What is this cigarette story?!? Je ne fume pas, I don't smoke! Je n'ai pas de cigarettes, moi! I don't have cigarettes! Raise the bar, imbecile, blockhead!"

Finally the bar got raised and Angelo could call Sugar who was waiting with the convoy in rue Argàn.

"All clear, Condor Zed. The bar is up and the shooting is over."

"Right, Charlie Two. We're moving," Sugar answered. Then the convoy reached the rotary, crossed it, entered avenue Sami Sohl, was in the Eastern Zone, and releasing his breath Bernard le Français went back to shouting his hate for Rocky. Angelo began staring at the white mare and asking himself why, all of a sudden, he felt as if he were staring at Ninette.

Because she was beautiful with a beauty that reminded him of Ninette's beauty, maybe... Solid yet delicate body, long and perfect legs, immense eyes that turned violet, a long blonde mane that fluttered in silky waves of light evoking Ninette's chestnut hair... Or maybe because she was alone with a solitude that reminded him of Ninette's solitude, courageous with a courage that reminded him of Ninette's courage? Even when the snipers unleashed a wild volley, she did not get nervous. Even when the convoy passed at high speed, she quietly remained there nibbling the weeds... This morning an armored car had accidentally driven onto the grassy bed and skimmed her soft tail. Yet she hadn't moved, she hadn't grown scared. She'd remained there like a person who refuses to oppose destiny. As God wants, as God likes, Inshallah. He turned his head, disturbed. With redoubled pain he wondered if Ninette too had refused to oppose destiny when she had met Passepartout: as God wants, as God likes, Inshallah. And the question dismayed him. He abhorred the word destiny, he abhorred the word Inshallah: one synonymous with the other and both of them symbols of an impotence, a resignation, that offended the concept of freedom and responsibility. But the more he abhorred them, the more he felt like a puppet tugged by the threads of something or somebody who moved in step with the words destiny and Inshallah. "You got us into an infernal muddle, son. Now we're hearing loud and clear about the third truck, nay three motorboats," Charlie had said explaining that Zandra Sadr had not promised to stop the fire that travels three times on the water. So, and despite the toll, the third motorboat might still show up. And, overwhelmed by his responsibility, he had nodded. "Yes, chief. I know..." But was it really his responsibility? It was and it wasn't. It was in the sense that the 9mm Parabellum had been fired by him, that Ninette's assassin had been killed by him: intentionally and in full possession of his mental faculties. It wasn't in the sense that owing to a proliferation of events which had nothing to do with his will, the event A producing B and B producing C and C producing D and D producing E and E producing F and so on, the somebody or something had acted in a way to place him in a point of time and space where there was no alternative to what he had done.

"Mais regarde-le, ce retardé mental! But look at that dimwit, look! Ecoute-le, listen to him!"

"I'm listening, Bernard, I'm looking..."

"Maintenant il ne lui suffit pas le foulard, maintenant il veut les cigarettes! Now the scarf isn't enough, he also wants the cigarettes!"

"True..."

"Dans le cul, je lui fout les cigarettes: dans le cul! In his ass I'll jam the cigarettes, in his ass!"

"Sure..."

"Et le foulard aussi! And the scarf, too!"

"Right..."

Events which had nothing to do with his will, yes. Because if A hadn't produced B, that is, if the 5.56 hadn't been a bullet capable of reaching and piercing an obstacle even after a mile-and-a-half run, Rocco wouldn't have been hit. If B hadn't produced C, that is, if Rocco hadn't been hit, the Condor wouldn't have accompanied him to the Rizk. If C hadn't produced D, that is, if the Condor hadn't accompanied him to the Rizk, the Shiite revolt wouldn't have trapped him God knows where. If D hadn't produced E, that is, if the Shiite revolt hadn't trapped him God knows where, the Professor wouldn't have assumed command. If E hadn't produced F, that is, if the Professor hadn't assumed command, Charlie wouldn't have received the order to bring that-sullen-sergeant-of-yours-the-mathematician to Shatila. If F hadn't produced G, that is, if Charlie hadn't brought him to Shatila, he wouldn't have ended up at the Twenty-Four. If G hadn't produced H, that is, if he hadn't ended up at the Twenty-Four, he wouldn't have run into Khalid-Passepartout and... And what if the third motorboat weren't actually capable of materializing as a threat? On the basis of which elements did Charlie believe Zandra Sadr, on the basis of which arguments did the Condor ratify Charlie's fears? Granted: the three ships sent to take the troops were simple ocean liners incapable of defending themselves and of traveling faster than 15 knots. Granted: even if loaded with hexogen, let's say the two thousand six hundred pounds of hexogen the Sons of God had used to massacre the Americans, a motorboat can travel at 20 or 30 or even 35 knots and thus reach a target traveling at a much slower speed. Granted: slipping out of a bay or an inlet as near as the inlets adjacent to the western basin, a Pietro Micca could easily hit a ship outside the port. But as soon as the ship was outside the port, as soon as it rounded the lighthouse, it would be protected by the fleet under the flagship's command! It was an infallible guardian, the fleet. A guarantee, a safeguard, better than a thousand tolls. In the blink of an eye its patrol boats and helicopters and radars could sight a peril, a hypothetical human torpedo! With equal rapidity they could blast it before it neared the target! So Charlie was wrong to believe Zandra Sadr! The Condor was wrong to ratify Charlie's fears! He himself was wrong to agonize over the rebuke you-got-us-into-an-infernal-muddle! He should stop torturing himself with remorse, self-accusations, examinations of conscience! The time had come to tear this story out of his head, dammit. To cleanse his brain of it.

"Take over the radio, Bernard."

"Moi? Me?!?" Bernard le Français protested, panic-stricken at the idea of having to speak Italian if Sugar or somebody else called in. "C'est ton travail, la radio, n'est-ce-pas? That's your job, the radio, isn't it?"

"Yes, but I need to cleanse my brain."

"Tu as besoin de quoi? You need what?!?"

"To solve a problem, Bernard."

"Quel problem? What problem?!?"

He sketched a faint smile. The problem of the raindrop that falls on the window of the speeding train: the problem that the 15 knots of the ships and the 20 or 30 or 35 knots of the motorboat had brought back to his mind... You are on a train traveling at 15 kilometers per hour and it rains. You are seated alongside the left-hand window, you look in the direction in which the train goes, and you watch a drop of rain fall onto the glass. From the right to the left, that is obliquely, and forming an angle of 30 degrees with respect to the vertical. Then the train accelerates, it speeds up to 20 kilometers per hour, and the angle formed by the raindrop changes: it becomes 45 degrees with respect to the vertical. In the first and in the second case, at what speed does the raindrop fall?

"A mathematics problem, Bernard."

"Mathématiques?!?"

"Yes, with a touch of geometry and trigonometry. Because the solution is essentially graphic, but it's based on the theorems of the sine and cosine."

"Les théorèmes de quoi? The theorems of what?"

"The theorem of the sine. The one that says: in a triangle, the relation between two sides is equal to the relation between the sines of the angles opposite those sides. And the theorem of the cosine. The one that says: the square of one side of a triangle is equal to the sum of the squares of the other two sides minus the product of their length multiplied by twice the cosine of the angle between them."

"Seins and coseins?!?"

"No, Bernard: sines and cosines. In mathematics, sines are circular functions of an angle or of an arc of the circumference of a unit circle that..."

"Et à quoi ça sert? And what is the use of it?"

"The use of forgetting, Bernard. Oublier."

"Oublier quoi? Forgetting what?"

"An infernal mess, a big sorrow, the word destiny... Everything, Bernard."

"Je ne comprends pas. I don't understand."

"It doesn't matter. Take the radio."

He handed him the microphone. Still smiling the faint smile, he opened his notebook. He drew a vertical segment and, starting from the base of it a horizontal segment that pointed to the left. The vertical and the horizontal components of velocity. Then, starting from the apex of the vertical segment, he drew two diagonal segments: the path the raindrop follows with a 30-degree angle when the train is moving at 15 kilometers per hour, and the path it follows with a 45-degree angle when the train is moving at 20 kilometers per hour. He thus obtained two triangles with a side in common and, applying the theorem of the sine, he got the answer to the first question: 13.66 kilometers per hour. Then, using this result and applying the theorem of the cosine, he set up the operation $13.66^2 + 5^2 - 2 \times 5 \times 13.66 \times \cos 60^2$. He put it under a square root symbol, he looked once more at the diagonal segment with the 45-degree angle, and the faint smile faded in a hollow exclamation: "Nooo...!" While drawing the segments, in fact, he'd imagined himself to be really seated next to the window of the train, to really watch the raindrop that fell diagonally from right to left, and even when he worked on the sine and cosine theorems he'd continued to see the raindrop. Round and graceful, shiny. As harmless as a raindrop can be. But now he no longer saw it. Because in its place, now, there was a human torpedo. The third motorboat, Rashid's motorboat. Bursting from the apex of the vertical segment which had suddenly turned into the exit of an inlet next to the western basin and immediately speeding up from 20 to 35 knots, it had started to run along the 45-degree segment which had as suddenly turned into the breakwater pier and keeping itself almost parallel to the breakwater pier which formed an angle of precisely 45 degrees with respect to the coast now it

ran. It ran pointing at a ship that had just left the port. A ship full of
military men. An ocean liner that, having rounded the lighthouse at a
distance of 200 meters, headed northwest with an arc of parabola of
195 meters and with its left side facing the human torpedo...

It headed northwest at a speed of only 6 knots. So slowly that in
order to reach his target, blow up with it, Rashid had only to steer and
adapt himself to the 195-meter arc of parabola: to keep less and less
parallel to the breakwater pier, then to establish a trajectory forming an
angle of 45 degrees with respect to the liner's left side, then he simply
had to lock the rudder and arm the detonator. All the more that nobody would be able to stop him. Nobody. Not even the officers and
the soldiers on the stern and the prow and the upper deck and the
bridge who were shooting at him with pistols and rifles and Brownings.
It would be totally useless, killing him. Useless. With its rudder locked
and its detonator armed, the motorboat would complete its run anyway. It would hit the ship even if Rashid were dead. It was no use to
shoot at the hexogen, either. To begin the explosive process, in fact,
hexogen requires a powerful shock wave: an impact produced by a
detonator or a bomb, a grenade. And the guns of the fleet assembled
three kilometers from the coast remained silent. Yes, silent. A battle
fleet is not designed to protect ocean liners which are attacked by a
Pietro Micca the instant they round a lighthouse: here is what he
hadn't thought of when he'd judged the fleet an infallible guardian, a
guarantee, a safeguard better than a thousand tolls. A battle fleet needs
a lot of time to react. The time to sight the object that, blending with
the waves and the reef of the breakwater pier, moves on the surface.
The time to identify it on the radar where its echo arrives muffled by
the echo of the breakwater pier which is two meters higher and consequently the screens register only an imperceptible speck, an infinitesimal disturbance. The time to examine the object, to decide if it is a
human torpedo or an innocuous fishing boat. The time to designate
fire with the gunnery chief, to acquire the target on another radar: the
parabolic radar. The time to activate the Computer. The time for the
Computer to send electronic commands to the guns. The time for the
guns to load and open fire. The time for the grenades to hit the target.
Each phase, a handful of seconds given to the motorboat which gets
closer and closer and soon will blow up with the ship. And he knew it.

He knew it because he fired from the ship with the others, leaning
out of the left-side parapet, and because from the left side he could see
the motorboat as clearly as the traveler seated beside the train's left-
hand window sees the raindrop that falls diagonally with an angle of 45

degrees... He leaned over that parapet to watch something that right now eluded him, maybe something connected with Ninette and the formula of Life, and he opened fire when the Condor's shout ripped the air: "Stop him! Shoot him! Sto-o-p hi-i-im!" Yes, there was also the Condor. And there was Charlie, there was the Professor, there was Crazy Horse, Pistoia, Sugar, Stefano, Gaspare, Ugo, Bernard le Français, the people of the headquarters except for Fifi and Martino who for some reason were not aboard the third ship. Yes, the third ship. The last ship. The first two had already left... He fired with them, and each of them knew what he knew: that the motorboat would reach the ship because their firing was useless, because the guns of the fleet remained silent, because Rashid had locked the rudder and armed the detonator. Yet they fired all the same. Desperately. Uninterruptedly. In a hellish crackling of shots, a hellish overlapping of voices now hoarse and now shrill and now stifled. "The rifle grenades! Try the rifle grenades!" bawled the Condor. "The engine! Aim at the motorboat's engine!" howled Sugar. "Goddam those buttfuckers, those shitlickers, those faggots of rassullillah!" yelled Pistoia. "Sursum corda, hearts high! Qualis miles pereo! I die as a soldier!" whinnied Crazy Horse. And Charlie sadly grunted: "I've done what I could. I could not do anything more." Bernard le Français angrily cried: "Je n'aurais jamais dû quitter Bruxelles, zut! I should never have left Brussels, dammit!" Stefano sobbed: "Mamma mia, mamma mia!" He said nothing. He fired and that's all. He thought and that's all. A chaos of thoughts that were actually images, images that were actually regrets, regrets that were actually a delirium of syllogisms: Boltzmann who became Ninette, Ninette who became Passepartout, Passepartout who became Rashid, Rashid who became Pietro Micca, Pietro Micca who became the equation $S = K \ln W$, the equation $S = K \ln W$ which became an apocalyptic crash, a huge mushroom of red dust identical with the two he'd seen the terrible Sunday three months before... And within the delirium, the awareness that these three months had only been a respite: a postponement of the slaughter announced by Mustafa Hash. Within the awareness, the revelation that the third truck hadn't arrived that Sunday in late October because it had to arrive in another space and another time: this Sunday in late January. Then the 76mm and 127mm shells began to fall. The shells from the guns of the fleet. But they didn't fall on the motorboat, they fell in its wake, with the sole effect of raising high columns of water: the Computer was unable to hit the motorboat. Even if it had, however, it wouldn't have changed a thing. Rashid was too close by now. So close that you could see his face with absolute clarity. A wicked face full of happiness. The very happiness which three months ago had lit up the face of the kamikaze who had burst into the American headquarters, and this time you could also hear a victorious bawling: "Allah akbar! Allah akbar!" In fact the motorboat was less than sixty meters from the left side of the ship, fifty-five to be precise, and now fifty-four, fifty, forty-five, forty, thirty-five, thirty, twenty, ten, nine, eight, seven, six, five, four, three, two, one! The hollow exclamation repeated, brimming with horror.

"Nooo...!"

"Qu'est-ce qu'il y a, what is it?" asked Bernard le Français.

"Nothing... I was thinking," he murmured.

"Avec le boucan de ces salauds, de ces sadiques? With these rascals, these sadists' din?!"

Several minutes ago, in fact, the snipers had resumed their shooting, and now they were setting off dozens of 7.62s and 5.56s on the white mare's grassy bed. A sadistic entertainment to which the beautiful creature reacted by flicking her long and soft tail as if the bullets were gadflies to chase away.

"I wasn't paying attention..." he answered deducing with boundless relief that the nightmare of the motorboat had been caused by an acoustic phenomenon, not by the logic of reason.

"Tu ne prêtais pas attention, you didn't pay attention!?! Il finiront pour la tuer, ces bâtards! They'll end up killing her, these bastards!"

"You're right..."

"Bon, je ne veux pas y penser. Well, I don't want to think about it... Have you solved your riddle?"

"Almost..." he said closing the notebook still open at the page with the unsolved operation beneath the square root symbol. And, misguided by his relief, he didn't ask himself whether things could actually go as in the nightmare. Later he did, however. Because when he started working on the square root symbol to find the velocity of the raindrop that falls with a 45-degree angle on the train traveling at 20 kilometers per hour, the truth blasted again in his mind: what he wanted to know wasn't in that result. It was in the easiest, simplest mathematical problem he had ever faced. The following one.

A ship leaves an 850-meter-long breakwater pier which originates in the western basin, which forms an angle of 45 degrees with respect to the coast, and which has a lighthouse at its end. To leave the port, the ship rounds the lighthouse at a distance of 200 meters and, at a speed of 6 knots, it describes an arc of parabola 195 meters long. Keeping that arc, thus exposing its left broadside to any boat coming from the west, it heads northwest. Exactly when the ship rounds the lighthouse, a motorboat waiting in an inlet adjacent to the western basin leaves its mooring which is located 100 meters behind the foot of the breakwater pier. At an average speed of 35 knots, the motorboat dashes toward the ship to collide with it the moment its arc of parabola is completed. To this purpose it begins running almost parallel to the breakwater pier, then it slightly and constantly diverges from it to establish a trajectory which has an angle of 45 degrees with respect to the ship's left broadside. While all this happens, a fleet stays 3 kilometers off the coast. The fleet has the task of defending the ship with its 76mm and 127mm cannons. Question Number One: Can the motorboat reach the ship and hit it? Question Number Two: Can the fleet intervene before it is too late?

*   *   *

He faced it as soon as he returned to the headquarters. And he solved it like this. He began by drawing a diagram analogous to the one he had drawn for the raindrop but with a single diagonal segment and in reverse. That is, as seen by somebody leaning out of the left-side parapet of the ship. Then he indicated the elements he had to consider: the coast, the mooring the motorboat leaves to exit the inlet adjacent to the western basin, the foot of the breakwater pier and the breakwater pier itself, the lighthouse, the point at which the ship rounds the lighthouse (a point he called moment zero), the ship's course, that is, the arc of parabola 195 meters long aimed northwest, and the motorboat's course forming the 45-degree angle with respect to the left broadside of the ship. The answer to Question Number One would be given by the time the motorboat needs to cover the distance between its mooring and the end of the arc of parabola, as well as the distance the ship covers in the same time. And, to obtain it, he had to start with the length of the motorboat's path: a really plain operation which consisted of adding the 100 meters from the mooring to the foot of the breakwater pier, the 850 meters of the breakwater pier, and the 200 meters from the lighthouse to the point he called moment zero. The outcome, 1150 meters. Then, given the fact that a knot equals 1852 meters per hour and that in an hour there are 3600 seconds, he had to know how many meters per second the motorboat was covering: another plain operation which consisted of multiplying the 35 knots (the motorboat's speed) by the 1852 meters per hour and dividing the whole thing by the 3600 seconds. The outcome: 18 meters per second. Having that outcome, he divided by 18 the 1150 meters (the distance between the mooring and moment zero) and he obtained the time the motorboat needed to hit the ship along the trajectory kept by the locked rudder: 63.89 seconds which could be rounded up to 64 seconds. One minute and four seconds. And the ship? To find out how much distance the ship covered in that minute and four seconds, he had to follow the same procedure. That is, to multiply the 6 knots (the ship's speed) by the 1852 meters per hour and then divide the whole thing by the 3600 seconds contained in one hour. He did it, and he got a speed of 3.06 meters per second. So he multiplied 3.06 by the 64 seconds, and shuddered: during that minute and four seconds the ship covered 195 and a half meters. Ignoring the half-meter, absolutely negligible if compared to the ship's length, just the 195 meters of the arc of parabola: the distance that in the one minute and four seconds the motorboat covered to reach the target. The only hope that this wouldn't happen rested in the guns of the fleet's cruisers, destroyers, frigates. That is, in Question Number Two.

The answer to Question Number Two came from the time it took the fleet to react in such cases. And such time was given by a most elementary, childish addition. Ten seconds for the helicopters and the patrol boats to sight the suspicious craft. Five seconds to sound the alarm and inform the Operative Combat Station, the OCS. Ten seconds for the OCS to identify on its radar the craft's echo which arrives muffled by the breakwater pier which is two meters higher: so muffled that the screens register only an imperceptible speck, an infinitesimal disturbance. Ten seconds for the captain to examine the object, to decide if it is a human torpedo or an innocuous fishing boat. Ten seconds for the gunnery chief to acquire the target on the parabolic radar. Five seconds for the parabolic radar to make the acquisition. Three seconds for the operators to activate the Computer. Three seconds for the Computer to send the command to the guns. Three seconds for the guns to load and open fire. Three seconds for the shells to reach the target. (That's how long a 76mm grenade needs at a distance of 3 kilometers. A 127mm one needs even more.) The outcome, 61 seconds: three seconds less than the 64 seconds spent by the motorboat. In the Tayoune nightmare, however, the shells had begun to fall when Rashid was less than 60 meters from his target. Fifty-five meters, to be precise, fifty-four. And at 18 meters per second, 54 meters are covered in exactly three seconds. In three seconds, no gun can hit the mark of a very small object which runs at that speed and is three kilometers away. Worse: if the small object is approaching a ship, you have to be careful not to hit the ship. To avoid hitting the ship you have to fire slightly behind the object, doing so you end up hitting only the motorboat's wake, and... No, the fleet wouldn't be able to stop Rashid.

He said this to Charlie. But, misguided by Rashid's name the same way he had been misguided by relief, Charlie did not take him seriously.

"Rashid?" he smirked. "When I think of the third motorboat's pilot, I'm not referring to Rashid. A kamikaze must have balls. And Rashid doesn't have them."

Which brings us to the Thursday station.

5

The Thursday station is important for the bizarre rescue of Lieutenant Joe Balducci and his four Marines as well as for the dramatic good-bye of Armando Golden Hands and Gigi the Candid to Sister Milady and Sister George. Two events which were totally masterminded by Gigi the Candid and which took place soon after the dialogue between the Condor and Falcon at dawn.

"Colonel, see to the evacuation of Ost Ten."

"The evacuation, sir? When?"

"Immediately. Last night the Amal and the Sons of God seized the Galerie Semaan, the Green Line has shifted to the foot of the road that leads to the convent, and the damn three hundred yards have become a dangerous no-man's-land. A battle for possession of the hill will erupt within the next twenty-four hours, I'm afraid. So I want our five paratroopers returned to the Ruby base and the five Americans escorted back to their headquarters. By noon."

"By noon, sir?!"

"By noon, by noon! Are you deaf?!?"

"No, but who gets the Americans?"

"What do you mean who-gets-the-Americans?!? You or your men get them, God blasted! Ost Ten is your responsibility, isn't it? It's up to you or your people to escort them to safety!"

"Yessir. But Joe Balducci is white, sir. He's of Italian descent, he looks Italian. But the four Marines are black. The Amal or the Sons of God will understand immediately that they're Americans, sir, and..."

"Colonel! White or black or yellow or red or rainbow I want them safe and sound in their trenches, their headquarters, by noon: understa-a-and?!?"

"Yessir, but..."

"No buts! It's your bloody problem. You fix it."

Exactly the words Falcon had feared ever since the Condor had decided not to expose Joe Balducci and the four Marines to the risks of a transfer. Exactly the order he had expected ever since the Ruby base had been moved to the former Eagle base and the five Americans had been left with the five paratroopers on the top of the bloody skyscraper. Yet, at hearing those words and that order, he staggered. And back in the Louis XVI bedroom he dumped upon Gigi the Candid a crisis comparable to those he used to have when the idea of dying in a latrine or losing a foot and the joy of playing tennis paralyzed his bowels, full of dread he told himself that such torture had the goal of preparing him for his Great Test: his Moment of Truth.

"It's-your-problem, he bawled, you-fix-it. But answer me, Gigi: what stratagem can we use to make them cross the Green Line, the checkpoints, get them alive to the American headquarters?!? The helicopter solution is impossible because there isn't a spot to land and take off: the road is too narrow, the trees are too dense, the electrical wires are too many, and the roof of the unfinished skyscraper wouldn't support the weight. Turning to Sugar, asking him to pick them up with one of his convoys, is infeasible because he can neither change the route nor face the danger of smuggling clandestine passengers. Disguising them as paratroopers or carabinieri or marò, even more infeasible for the reasons you always state: with that pitch color and those football player physiques, they lack only the inscription USA on their foreheads..."

Wringing the red scarf he'd deceitfully promised to Rocky, Gigi the Candid let him vent his frustration without saying a word. Suddenly, however, he spoke.

"In my opinion," he said, "a way out exists."

"What way?!?"

"To sneak them out like a thief."

"Like a thief?!?"

"Yeah. The way a thief does. The first thing a thief does is hide the goods, right? When I used to rip off the railroad tracks I hid them immediately."

"But you can't hide five men the way you hide railroad tracks!"

"You can hide them better. Because they're bendable, elastic, and all it takes to hide them is some junk. Sleeping bags, knapsacks, incursori butts."

"Incursori butts?!?"

"Yeah. Incursori sitting on the sleeping bags and knapsacks that hide the five men."

"You're kidding!"

"No, I'm serious. For three months I've been puzzling my brain over this riddle. I've studied all sides of it, all its possible or impossible solutions, and concluded that the only way is to sneak them out like a thief. Give me permission and you'll see."

Falcon hesitated.

"And if Joe Balducci refuses?"

"In the beginning he will, be sure. He'll get huffy, he'll come out with some crap like I'm-a-Marine, I-don't-hide-under-anybody's-ass, I'm-ready-to-fight... But then he'll give in."

"And if the other four don't?"

"The other four will do what Joe Balducci orders. He's their lieutenant, isn't he?"

"And if the Amal want to search the truck?"

"We won't let them search it. We'll shoot, we'll fight our way through, so Balducci will be happy, our incursori will be happy, and too bad if someone gets killed. But I'm sure we can make it on the sly." He fingered the red scarf. "See this? It's the luckiest good-luck charm I ever had. Everything will go smoothly with this thing around my neck."

"Smoothly!"

"Commander... We have no other choice."

They didn't. And Falcon understood. He also understood that this wasn't a question of luck but of courage, that this was his Great Test, that he should say okay, let's-go, I'm-coming-too, that saying it he would grant himself the gift of stopping at the convent, apologizing to Sister Espérance, maybe bringing her to safety with the other nuns. The two things intersected. His desire to see Sister Espérance and his need to face his Great Test, his Moment of Truth, merged into such an impasto of feelings that his urge to go was immense. But the more he wanted to go, the more he felt the fear that in the officers' latrines induced his constipation, and at last he answered: "Fine. Go ahead." So Gigi the Candid called the Operations Room and requested the trucks, the junk, the incursori, plus an escort of carabinieri, called Ost Ten, shouted be-ready-we're-about-to-arrive, called Armando Golden Hands and buzzed follow-me-I've-got-a-good-surprise. Then he ran to the inlaid mother-of-pearl armoire and grabbed Sister George's *Mot à mot*. He opened it to the flyleaf, and without any errors he wrote: "Pour une petite femme qui a le nom d'un homme mais qui est une vraie femme et une grande femme. En souvenir d'un âne qui ne volait pas mais qui l'aimait bien et l'aime bien et l'aimera bien toujours: un âne appelé Gigì." To a little woman who has a man's name but who is a real woman and a great woman. In remembrance of a donkey who didn't fly but who loved her and loves her and will always love her: a donkey named Gigì. Finally, he stuck the book under his arm and turned back to Falcon.

"I'm going, commander."

"Okay. Go ahead," Falcon repeated. "And if you have time, give my regards to the Mother Superior."

"I'll do it, commander."

Shortly after, it was seven in the morning, four vehicles left the former Eagle base: the jeep with Gigi the Candid and Armando Golden Hands, the truck with the incursori and the junk to hide the Americans, another truck to load the observatory equipment and the five paratroopers, the jeep with the carabinieri escort. At full speed they headed for Tayoune where Rocky was sleeping off the coffee liqueur, thus the boundary bar was raised without a hitch, passing by the white mare who had for the moment survived the perfidious shooting they entered the Eastern Zone, and after a long zigzag through Furn el Chebbak they got to Hazmiye: they reached the three-hundred-yard stretch the Condor had defined a no-man's-land. A no-man's-land? It swarmed with besiegers impatient to conquer the hill. Amal who wore the uniforms of the Sixth Brigade, Sixth Brigade soldiers who wore the green armbands of the Amal, boisterous individuals who wore the black ribbons of the Sons of God around their heads and the image of Khomeini on their chests... And, among these, the mullah who had led the assault on the church of Saint-Michel: a ghastly hunchback with a crimson turban, a Kalashnikov, and a Koran dangling from his bandolier. He immediately hurled himself at the convoy to search it.

"Habess, habess! Check, check!"

"Ignore him! Don't even answer with a snort!" Gigi the Candid yelled at the incursori and the carabinieri.

They obeyed, and while the mullah rabidly barked some insult or threat, they entered the road that led to Ost Ten: now full of holes opened by the nocturnal shelling and completely deserted. But the paths to the villas also were deserted. Also the graceful olive groves, the fields that had lodged the battalion's encampment, the farm next to the glade of lime trees that had been Rocco and Imaam's oasis. And everywhere a sinister quiet stagnated: the terrifying calm which announces the explosion of a battle as a livid sky foretells the arrival of a storm.

They reached the skyscraper where the five paratroopers were already waiting downstairs with their luggage, the radios, the maps, the night-scopes, the weapons, and the personal effects of the Marines who hadn't yet left the attic floor. They inquired. Yes, the squad leader answered, combat was imminent. You felt it in your bones that it was imminent. Besides, the hill wasn't as deserted as it looked. Along the paths to the empty villas, in the olive groves, in the fields of the former encampment, in the farm next to the glade of lime trees and even on several floors of the skyscraper there were soldiers of the Eighth Brigade. They had arrived at dawn, sneaking through God knows which passage connected to the Hazmiye alleys, and infuriated at the loss of the Galerie Semaan they had positioned three companies of riflemen. It didn't take much to figure out that they wouldn't easily surrender this stronghold. But the Shiites seemed equally determined to take it. You could tell from the violence of the fire they had unleashed around two o'clock in the morning.

"Boys, what a hubbub!"

"Not only grenades. Katyushas too..."

"One skimmed the observatory. A miracle it didn't hit us!"

"You know where it ended up? On the esplanade of the convent."

"On the esplanade of the convent?!?"

"Yeah. Lots of stuff must have fallen on those poor nuns. Let's hope they're not dead..."

Gigi the Candid grabbed *Mot à mot* from the seat of the jeep and gave a nod to Armando Golden Hands.

"I'll run up there to see with my aide," he sighed. "We'll be back in fifteen minutes. Meantime, tell the Americans to come down with the rest of their stuff and get in the second truck."

Then he ordered the incursori to unload the knapsacks, the sleeping bags, the junk, warned everybody that in fifteen minutes the convoy should be ready to move, and set out.

*   *   *

The side gate lay on the ground, torn off its hinges. They climbed over it, they advanced along a havoc of scorched plants, and once at the esplanade they exchanged an incredulous look. The Katyusha had opened a chasm so deep and so wide that to proceed you had to tiptoe along its edges. As for the building, it was unrecognizable. Practically demolished, the roof from which the gutters hung down in ferrous tangles. Half-shattered by gaping holes, the facade. Totally smashed, the windows that Sister Madeleine opened to trill her cheerful laughter and to warble her nasty a-little-air-a-little-sunlight-to-forget-that-the-brutes-are-here. Completely destroyed, the canteen where Gino went to get drunk and write poems about happiness which is a monastery on the peaks of the Himalayas. Collapsed, the big door of the mess before which Armando Golden Hands and Sister Milady used to squabble or flirt. And riddled, its hall. They entered treading on a carpet of debris and broken glass, they went up the stairs of the former antirape barrier, they reached the hacked-up classrooms of the former school and kindergarten, they anxiously called out.

"Sister Milady! Sister George, Sister Espérance, Sister Madeleine!"

"Sister George! Sister Milady, Sister Espérance, Sister Madeleine!"

Nobody answered, so they reached the second floor where the devastation was complete. Overturned furniture, crumbled plates, leaking pipes, water all over. And, in place of the kitchen ceiling, a gash of mocking sky. The bedrooms were untouched, however, and subverted by a disorder that hinted at headlong flight. They called out again.

"Sister George! Sister Milady, Sister Madeleine, Sister Espérance, it's us!"

"Sister Milady! Sister George, Sister Madeleine, Sister Espérance, do you hear us?"

Again nobody answered, so they went back to the ground floor and searched the other rooms then the chapel which seemed intact too. But on the altar there was only the terracotta Infant Jesus who nabbed the orchids sent from Livorno: the crucifix and the Missal had been removed, the tabernacle of the Blessed Sacrament was empty, the monstrance and the chalice with its cruets of holy water and wine had been taken away.

"God knows where they're gone..." said Gigi the Candid with relief and disappointment.

"Maybe in the basement," replied Armando Golden Hands. "They used to take shelter in the basement, during the bombings, remember?"

"Maybe. But we can't look anymore. It's late, Armando. We must go."

"One last try, colonel. Please!"

"We must go, I tell you!"

"Please, colonel, please..."

They really had to go. Fourteen minutes had passed since they had left the skyscraper saying that they would be back in fifteen, and for sure Joe Balducci had already come down with his four Marines. Yet

Armando's please-colonel-please voiced such supplication that Gigi the Candid transferred it to himself, and snatching his arm ran to the basement. Together and not even switching on the flashlight they rushed into the corridor with the storage rooms the Syrians had used as torture chambers, and here they stopped: their hearts in turmoil. From the last storeroom on the left, a glimmer of light was filtering. A faint shine that might have been the flame of a candle.

"Sister George! Sister Milady, Sister Espérance, Sister Madeleine! It's me! Gigì!"

"Sister Milady! Sister George, Sister Madeleine, Sister Espérance! C'est moi! Armandò!"

And this time the answer came. First, three stifled whispers. Ce-n'est-pas-possible, it's-not-possible. Je-ne-le-crois-pas, I-don't-believe-it. Ce-sont-eux-je-vous-assure, it's-them-I-tell-you. Then, three shadows that cautiously leaned out of the doorway. One short and minute, one rather tall and slim, one very tall and wiry. Finally, three figures that distrustfully advanced with a candle and that in the glare of the flame turned little by little into Sister George, Sister Milady, and Sister Espérance. All three, soiled and sooty as if they emerged from the ashes of a fire. And bareheaded.

"Gigì!"

"Armandò!"

"Mes amis! My friends!"

They switched on the flashlight, they observed them in disbelief. Without her veil and wimple, Sister Espérance no longer seemed Sister Espérance. She offered in fact the unexpected sight of blonde haircut, boyish style. And making her look ten years younger, this erased all her regal haughtiness. Better: it transformed the severe warrior into a charming athlete inexplicably dressed as a nun. An identical surprise, Sister George. Because in her case an abundance of red curls and an untidy fringe transformed the little bookworm into a mischievous hippy wearing a nun's frock out of fun and double-lens glasses out of coquetry. As for Sister Milady, forget the Gothic madonna! With that shimmering cascade of raven locks, she became an inexorable sorceress under whose spells you dropped before falling in love. What's more, her upper lip's down always kept in self-punishment was finally gone. She'd removed it.

"And Sister Madeleine?" asked Gigi the Candid shifting the flashlight beam to the storage room where he saw only the sacred objects removed from the chapel, the precious sapphire crucifix that once enhanced the impeccable frock, and the olive grove painting that Sister

George had liked so much in spite of the officers' latrines he'd brainlessly included.

"Partie. Rentrée in France. Left. Back to France," the charming athlete with the blonde and boyish haircut replied with an amused smile. "She was too fearful, poor thing. Always inside that well to recite the Requiem Aeternam... Each time we had to hitch her up with the well pulley, and thank God the priest from Baabda has come. He has taken her to Junieh and put her on a boat direct to Marseille."

"You too must leave, Sister Espérance."

"Jamais, never. I already made that mistake in the past. And I won't repeat it, my friend."

"The convent is practically destroyed, Sister Espérance. There isn't even a room to stay in."

"We'll stay all the same, my friend. We have all we need, here. Look," she said pointing to the big crucifix taken from the altar and to the Missal, the monstrance, the chalice with its cruets of water and wine.

"Sister Espérance, you have nothing but a few consecrated hosts, a sip of water and a sip of wine. It wouldn't be enough to secure the survival of a cicada."

"The ways of Providence are infinite. As you should know, Our Lord Jesus Christ multipled the loaves and the fishes. And he turned the water into wine."

"Mother Superior," Armando Golden Hands put in, "we have come with two trucks and two jeeps to pick up the five Americans and the five paratroopers of Ost Ten. We can take the three of you, too. We can drop you off in Hazmiye or in Furn el Chebbak and..."

"Merci, thank you, Armandò. But I shall not accept."

"The battle we expect will start very soon, Sister Espérance."

"It will not be the first battle I go through, Armandò. I'm very well used to battles."

"But the Shiites want to take the hill, Sister Espérance. And whoever takes the hill takes the convent," Gigi the Candid insisted.

"That's one more good reason to hold the territory like a good soldier."

"Sister Espérance... when it's necessary, good soldiers retreat!"

"Not the soldiers of God, my friend. I'm a soldier of God. And I do not budge."

"Me either," echoed the mischievous hippy with the abundance of red curls and the untidy fringe. "The merciful Lord has always protected us: I don't see why he shouldn't continue to do so. And if this time he doesn't, well: we will protect ourselves."

"By throwing stones!" added the inexorable sorceress with the shimmering cascade of raven locks. "I agree with Sister Espérance and Sister George. I'll stay too. I'd rather die than abandon them."

Gigi the Candid tightened his lips and looked at his watch. Almost twenty minutes had passed since he'd said to Armando we-must-go. And they still had to tell them about the contingent's departure, to say goodbye... He raised the *Mot à mot*. He held it out to Sister George.

"Nostre livre? Our book?" she exclaimed, without understanding.

"Yes... I wrote something for you on the flyleaf, Sister George..."

"Pour moi? For me?"

"Yes... In French. I hope I haven't made many mistakes."

"Ah! Vous en aurez fait, you certainly have!" she playfully hummed. Then she adjusted the double-lens glasses, went nearer the candle, read the dedication, and: "Bravò! Not a single mistake, bravò! Merci, thank you! But why have you written in-remembrance?"

"Because we're leaving Beirut, Sister George."

"What?! When?!"

"Soon. Very soon."

Her pupils dilated.

"C'est... Is this a farewell, then?"

"Yes. We must say goodbye, Sister George."

"At once?!?"

"At once. The convoy has been waiting for a half-hour, and keeping it there is dangerous."

She started to cry.

"No... Not at once..."

"We have to. Goodbye, Sister George."

"Oui, goodbye... But you know... the donkey wasn't a donkey, Gigì... He flew... he flew as high as a gull... And I... I loved him just as much... I love him just as much... I'll always love him just as much... I even saved his painting..."

"I know, I've seen it. Don't break my heart, Sister George. Don't make me cry too." Then, turning to the charming athlete who stared at him proudly restraining her surprise and her sadness: "Falcon asked me to pass along his respect, Sister Espérance. Should I give him any message? Should I tell him anything?"

The sadness became harshness.

"Oui, mon ami. Tell Falcon that he should have come with you and Armandò. Tell him that I would have loved to embrace him. No. Forget that. What I would have liked doesn't matter. Tell him that having courage is a duty. A necessity and a duty. Tell him that he must have courage, that nothing in life counts more than courage, that life without courage is not life."

"I'll tell him. Goodbye, Sister Espérance."

"Goodbye, adieu, mon ami."

"Goodbye, Sister Milady."

"I'll walk you out," the sorceress said with decision. Then she cast a firm glance at Sister Espérance who imperceptibly nodded, she waited for Armando to say his goodbyes as well, and along with them she left the basement. Near the destroyed esplanade, though, she stopped and sought Gigi the Candid's eyes.

"Please, mon colonel. Leave me alone with him."

"Of course, my child," Gigi the Candid answered hurrying away.

It was a wordless goodbye, Sister Milady and Armando Golden Hands' goodbye. There was nothing to add to what had been said a month before in the chapel whirling like a centrifuge that spins at twelve g's. And, in some cases, words are a superfluous sound. A pesky noise. In silence he took her in his arms, in silence he caressed her now unshaded lip, in silence he offered his mouth, she offered hers. And the sinister quiet which stagnated over the hill, the terrifying calm which announces the explosion of a battle as a livid sky foretells the arrival of a storm, became a heavenly peace: a serenity which compensated them for everything. The time they'd wasted in resisting their reciprocal attraction, the sacrifice they'd endured to honor their respective pledges and commitments, the battle that soon would erupt to wipe out any hope and convey her to the ferocity of the victors, the ship that would carry him away to deliver him to the despair then to the resignation then to the more and more tenuous memory of a special love, the love of and for a novice met and lost in Beirut... Their awareness that the future was condensed in a present as short as a few instants turned every abhorrence into beauty, every discord into harmony. And when inside the chasm opened by the Katyusha a wounded cat uttered a yowl of pain, they heard a meow of joy. When among the scorched plants a hornet sourly buzzed, they heard the trill of a nightingale. And a paradisiacal music, the clatter of scurrilities that echoed from the ground floor of the skyscraper where the incursori and the Marines were quarreling.

"Call your fuckin' colonel and let's get out of this fuckin' trap, you fuckin' Italians!"

"Load us on the fuckin' truck and let us leave, you fuckin' wops and motherfuckers!"

"Get your fuckin' ass in gear and let's move, you fuckin' assholes!"

"Fuckin' dagos! Fuckin' cocksuckers!"

"Ma sentile queste bestiacce ingrate! But listen to these ungrateful animals!"

"Succhiatori di cazzi e terroni e culi bucati e fottitori di madre sarete voi! The cocksuckers and assholes and motherfuckers are you!"

"Tornate in Africa e in Alabama a grattarvi le pulci, scimmioni, cornuti! Get your ass back to Africa and Alabama and scratch your fleas, you monkeys and cuckolds!"

"Andate a cacare, fascisti! Imperialisti! Reazionari! Go shit your pants, you fascists! Imperialists, reactionaries!"

"Stracciaculi! Strippauccelli! Asswipes! Dick leakers!"

"Shut up, all of you, God blasted! That's an order, shit! Shit, shit!"

* * *

Exasperated by the delay and weighed down by their weapons, the M16s on their shoulders, the Colt 45s at their belts, the cartridge belts around their chests, and at their feet an arsenal of hand grenades, grenade launchers, bazookas, machine guns, not to mention their own stock of radios and maps and nightscopes, the four Marines had begun to bicker with the incursori when Armando Golden Hands had implored please-colonel-please. But now the quarrel had become ravenous, and Joe Balducci couldn't quiet it down. Besides, he himself was so infuriated that his shit-shit-shits hailed more intensely than his men's fuckings-fuckers-fuck-yous. Almost forty minutes, shit! With a battle coming up and the skyscraper crawling with governmental troops that probably included a few traitors or Khomeinist spies! The five paratroopers from the Ruby were already set up in the truck with the carabinieri, and instead he was here on the ground floor waiting for Mister Colonel who'd gone banging some Suzie dressed in a nun's frock! Shit, shit, shit! So, as soon as Gigi the Candid returned, swollen with grief, the dispute burst between them.

"Colonel! We've been scratching our balls for forty-five minutes, shit!"

"Hold your tongue, Joe! And order your men to lie down in the back of that truck: that's an order!"

"Lie down?!?"

"Lie down, yeah, lie down! Three with their heads facing the cab, and two with their heads facing the back! Including you! Capito? Understand?"

"No, no capito! Me no capire! What's the point of lying down?!?"

"The point of lying down is that I'm going to cover you with knapsacks and sleeping bags! Chiaro, clear?!?"

"Nossir! Why with knapsacks and sleeping bags?!?"

"Because on top of the knapsacks and sleeping bags I'm slapping the incursori's asses, that's why!"

"The...incursori's...asses?!?"

"Yep! I'm making them squat down on you. Move it, I said!"

"Squat down on us?!?"

"Precisely. And you, underneath. Hidden underneath. Do you want to move or not?!?"

Joe Balducci's rosy face grew purple.

"Nossir. Mai. Never. Never, shit, never!"

"Mai, never?!?"

"Mai! never! I'm a Marine, we're Marines! Marines don't hide under the fucking incursori's asses! Marines don't hide under anybody's fucking ass!"

Gigi the Candid's voice grew mild.

"Marines or not, you must do it, Joe. And you will."

"Nossir. Not me. Not my men."

"There's no choice, Joe. The streets swarm with bedouins anxious to eat you alive. If they see you, it ends up in an ugly fight."

"I'm not afraid to fight! I'm a Marine! I fight!"

"Joe, neither your headquarters nor mine wants to make war to bring you home. They prefer to play it cool. So I'll play it cool. Order your men to get in the truck and lie down like I said."

"Nossir. I won't listen to you."

Instead, little by little, he did.

"Shit! Are you sure your plan will work?"

"Yes, Joe. I'm sure."

"Because if it doesn't work, I'll shoot. My men will shoot."

"Mine too, Joe. But you'll see: we won't have to. Here. Take my red scarf."

"Your red scarf?!?"

"Yes. It's a good-luck scarf, Joe. A first-class mascot. And soon we'll need lots of luck. Come on, wrap it around your neck. Knot it tight."

"Okay, colonel..."

He knotted it tight. With the red scarf around his neck he ordered the four Marines to load their weapons and supplies. With another round of shit-shit-shit he convinced them to lie down as Gigi the Candid wanted. Something that required as much time as it had taken to convince him. Then he lay down beside his men, grumbled "ready," the incursori covered them with the junk, sat on top of it, and another squabble burst. Another sequence of mutual insults and scurrilities.

"Get your fuckin' ass off my fuckin' stomach, you fuckin' dago, motherfucker!"

"Fottuto sarai tu, brutto stronzo! You get fucked yourself, you shit-brain! E non parlar di mia madre sennò sullo stomaco ti ci caco, intesi? And leave my mother out of this, otherwise I'll take a dump on your stomach, clear?"

"Get your fuckin' feet off my face, you fuckin' cocksucker!"

"I cazzi li succhierai tu, bestiaccia! Cocksucking is good for you, animal! E se non la pianti, ti ficco il mio in gola, capito? And if you don't shut up I'll jam my own down your throat, got it?"

"Go fuck yourself, fuckin' wop!"

"Vacci tu, stracciaculo! You go doing it, you asswipe!"

Finally, led by the jeep with Gigi the Candid and Armando Golden Hands who had reappeared pale as a dead man, the small convoy moved on. In less than a minute it left behind the skyscraper, the convent, Sister Espérance who was ready to defend her territory like a good soldier, Sister George who in spite of her tears over the *Mot à Mot* dedication was as ready, Sister Milady who preferred to die rather than abandon them, and it reached the three-hundred-yard stretch. Again plowing through the swarm of besiegers, again ignoring the habess-check-habess of the hunchbacked mullah with the crimson turban and the Kalashnikov and the Koran that dangled from his bandolier, they reentered the quarters still in the hands of the Christians. Again making a long zigzag through Hazmiye and Furn el Chebbak they got to avenue Sami Sohl, then Tayoune where for several minutes the shooting had quieted down so Angelo immediately gave the all-clear, and at this point the inevitable took place. Because at the boundary bar there was Rocky who by now had slept off his coffee liqueur drunkenness, and was demanding the scarf.

"Ana badi fulàra."

"Ana badi fulàra?!?"

With his mind still drifting to Sister George's heartbreaking good-bye, Gigi the Candid didn't understand what he meant, and looked at him with the bewilderment of a person who hears an alarm bell but doesn't know what the alarm is for. Who was this guy? Which fulàra, foulard, was he speaking about?

"Fulàra. I fulàra. My foulard."

"I fulàra, your foulard?"

"Na'am, yes. Fulàra ahmara. Foulard rouge."

"Fulàra ahmara, foulard rouge?"

"Fiche-moi le camp et lève la barre, babouin! Tête de linotte, troglodyte! Get out of the way and raise the bar, you baboon! Empty skull, troglodyte!" howled Bernard le Français while the incursori sitting on Joe Balducci and the four Marines pointed their M12s, the carabinieri of the escort jumped to the ground to take firing positions. But Rocky wasn't impressed. Whatever they called him, he had recognized his debtor. And this time he wouldn't be satisfied with the candies or the cigarettes or the bottles that make you sleep. This time he would get the coveted scarf.

"Ahmara, ahmara. Là fulàra, là iawaz."

"Là fulàra, là iawaz?!?"

"Il dit rien foulard, rien passe! He says no scarf, no go-ahead, mon colonel!" a rabid Bernard le Français translated. "Il fait toujours comme çą, he always does this! He's obsessed with I don't know which scarf and at every convoy he busts our balls, sir!"

"A scarf...?"

"Oui, foulard rouge! A red scarf!"

Oh God. It was Rocky, the guy to whom in total bad faith he'd promised his scarf. And if he didn't pay his debt, that psychopath wouldn't let them pass. Then the incursori and the carabinieri would open fire, Joe Balducci and the four Marines would leap out of the truck to join the party, the five paratroopers would do the same, and what seemed to be a nuisance would turn into a tragedy. Too many Amal, at this crossing. Twenty at least, well armed with Kalashnikovs and Rpg, and many others were scattered among the trees of the Pine Wood. Finally forgetting Sister George's tears, Gigi the Candid smothered a curse. Then, determined to avoid a tragedy, he ordered everybody to lower their rifles. He scrabbled together the few words of Arabic he knew, and with a big smile he left the jeep.

"Ah! Inta Rocky! You're Rocky! Sadiqi Rocky, my dear friend Rocky!"

"Na'am, wa ana badi i fulàra. Right, and I want my scarf," Rocky replied, even more unimpressed. "Mish takazzar i fulàra? Don't you remember my scarf?"

"Takazzar, takazzar! I remember!"

"Wa lesh mish andak? Then why don't you have it?"

"Andi, andi! I have it, I have it!"

"Fen? Where?"

"Huna, huna! Right here, right here!"

In the meantime he approached the truck with the Marines, stopped beside it, and pretending to talk with himself he launched anxious appeals to Joe Balducci.

"Joe, I need the red scarf! Joe, give it to me! Or there's going to be trouble! Quick, Joe! Don't you hear me, are you deaf? He doesn't hear me, dammit, he doesn't!"

Joe Balducci, instead, heard him clearly. And despite the heavy encumbrance that crushed his body and prevented him from moving his hands and arms, he'd already managed to unfasten the tight knot then to slip the goddam mascot off his throat: like a sprout that makes its way through the soil's darkness and slowly uplifts itself, climbs up through the obstacles to reach the surface and blossom, become a plant, the red scarf was already threading its way through the sleeping bags and knapsacks. Inch by inch, shit by shit, it crept upward, it headed for a gleam of light, attained it, peeped out, cautiously surfaced between the legs of an incursore who snatched it with a cheery shout.

"Here it is, colonel, sir!"

And Gigi the Candid seized it impetuously, then tossed it to Rocky with another shout.

"Tieni, disgraziato! Take it, dunce!"

And Rocky took it ecstatically, then ordered his men to raise the bar.

"Iawaz! Go ahead!"

They passed through with such a frenzy that for the first time the white mare got frightened: seemed to leave the grassy bed. With that frenzy they rushed down the short boulevard that led to rue Argàn, turned in avenue Nasser, crossed the rond-point of Shatila, entered rue de l'Aérodrome, reached the airport, passed it, arrived at the American headquarters or what remained of the blown-up headquarters, got inside it. Then, while the most joyous oaths and the most glorious obscenities arose from the trenches excavated under the rubble of the terrible Sunday, the incursori removed the junk. They exhumed Joe Balducci and his four Marines. So the fuckin' dagos, the fuckin' wops, the fuckin' assholes and motherfuckers etcetera, meaning the Italians, embraced the cuckolds, the ungrateful animals, the imperialists, the asswipes, the dick leakers etcetera, meaning the Americans, and Gigi the Candid was borne aloft in triumph.

"You did it, you son of a gun!"

"You've got balls, you old fart!"

"You're a devil, man!"

"Thank you, brother."

"Grazie, colonnello."

Meanwhile, the one thousand two hundred continued to dismantle the bases. Minute after minute the small city that the Condor wanted to put in the suitcase grew smaller and smaller. It faded away, it vanished like a failed dream. And meanwhile on the western basin's dock another small city emerged: an imaginary town which embodied their hopes of not returning home inside coffins. Minuscule campaniles, miniature skyscrapers, buildings to be watched with the creative binoculars of imagination, the mirthful vertical trenches that were supposed to protect the contingent during their embarking. Mirthful because the containers were of different sizes, different colors, and Pistoia arranged them in a freakishly extravagant way: a tall one next to a short one, a yellow one next to a blue one, a green one next to a scarlet one... From afar they seemed like the towers of a San Gimignano painted with the brush of a rainbow, and he praised himself in a loud voice.

"What inventiveness, what inspiration, huh? By Christopher Columbus, even a bedouin can see that I'm an artist!"

*　*　*

He said it without his usual sprightliness, though. In an almost humble tone. Ever since the third motorboat impended over the departure, he didn't look like Pistoia anymore. His jollity sounded insincere, his boldness lacked spontaneity, and the physical exuberance which had always supported his sexual marathons was now so faded that his amatory sessions ended up being monologues about his regrets or misfortunes and that's all. Ah, damn-the-day-I-came-here. Ah, damn-the-day-I-chose-the-army. Ah, damn-the-day-I-was-born-into-this-world. Not by chance Caroline, the fiancée married to the phalangist who fell asleep as soon as his head hit the pillow, now preferred her husband: "Better than nothing..." Not by chance Geraldine, the seventeen-year-old one who hadn't any experience, each time complained: "Pistoia, but when will we dance again on the mattress?" Not by chance Joséphine, the pressure cooker he called a-wolfess-who-doesn't-use-the-bed-to-preach-the-Gospels, had started the rumor that he'd become impotent. "Poor guy, he got as floppy as an aborted soufflé." But, above all, he no longer enjoyed the atrocious sport that is the hunt of hunts, the challenge of challenges, the gamble of gambles: he hated the noises and the discomforts of war, he condemned both the Guelphs and the Ghibellines, he spat on the battle of Montaperti, he cursed the

Crusades, he said that Godfrey of Bouillon was worthy of the ferocious Saladin and when in Jerusalem Tancredi of Altavilla had behaved like a thief and a pig...

And let's pass to the Friday station.

6

The Friday station is important for the price that, with the complicity of Salvatore Bellezza son of the late Onofrio, Falcon paid to undergo the Great Test he'd always eluded or postponed. It also includes an episode that better than anything else demonstrates how unrepeatable, unsurpassable, incomparable, eternal, human perfidiousness is: the martyrdom of the white horse. Thus, we begin with it. And here is the story.

There had been a night of inertia at Tayoune. God knows why, for several hours nobody had killed anybody: an exception that had extremely irritated the snipers of the opposing barricades. To compensate for the boredom, therefore, at dawn they had reinstated the shooting around the white mare: the sadistic entertainment to which the beautiful creature reacted by flicking her long and soft tail as if the bullets were gadflies to chase away. They had done it with the usual skill, always managing to graze her body without hitting it, and until seven this had worked so well that she had gotten used to the torment. At a certain moment she had even ceased flicking her tail. But at seven a poignant whinny stirred the air. A shriek as acute as the shriek of a woman who is raped or gives birth to a child. Maybe because of the morning mist, the play of grazing the mark without hitting it hadn't succeeded: a 7.62 like the 7.62 which had killed Ninette had struck her rump. Another one, her right shoulder. Immediately after, a 5.56 like the 5.56 which had pierced Rocco's brain ran into her left thigh opening a large vermilion gash, a second doubly poignant whinny stirred the air, and crazed with pain she reared. In the hope of shaking off the three wicked stones she leaped out of the grassy bed, began galloping around it, and the real martyrdom began. It was such a temptation, that moving target, see. That big and solid and yet delicate body which galloped in pain and despair, that smooth and blonde mane which fluttered in silky waves of light, that handsome muzzle which stretched out in search of safety. It was such a lure, such an invitation to unbridle their ferocity and their cowardice: could they possibly allow her to get away with three simple wounds? And for once in total agreement, for once oblivious of their reciprocal hate, both the Christians and the

Muslims gripped their telescopic rifles. They leaned against the walls behind which they were hidden, the balconies in front of shattered windows, and joined their skills in the enterprise of destroying her. Without aiming at her head or her heart, however: otherwise she would collapse at once and goodbye entertainment. Goodbye amusement, goodbye compensation for the nocturnal boredom. Tun, tun, tun! Bang, bang, bang! Ding, ding, ding! Then she stopped galloping, searching for safety. With her belly perforated, her left hock broken, her right knee lacerated, her withers mangled, her rump torn, she went back to the grassy bed. Bleeding all over, crushed by the discovery that fighting or fleeing didn't do any good because men are too evil, human perfidiousness is everywhere, unrepeatable unsurpassable incomparable eternal, and death is the only refuge, the only hope of safety, she fell down in the middle of the weeds: of her home. And here she remained to pant, to puff, to snort, to lose more and more blood: her immense violet eyes, Ninette's eyes, wide open in a look that seemed to ask why? What did I do wrong, what? And why do I still live, why does it take so long to die? She wasn't yet dead when Angelo and Bernard le Français arrived at Tayoune, and Bernard's shout ripped the rotary.

"Assassins! Vers puants, stinking worms! Bêtes hideuses, hyènes! Filthy beasts, hyenas!"

Bernard le Français became infuriated also at Rocky and his Amal. Bastards-scoundrels-cowards, what-would-it-have-taken-to-help-her? Angelo, instead, shut himself into one of his stony silences. Then he opened his lips and murmured that she had to be finished with a bullet in her head.

"Please do it, Bernard. I can't."

The trouble is that Bernard refused. I-can't-either. And the poor beautiful creature who never bothered anybody, never had bothered anybody, continued to pant and to puff and to snort and to bleed and to suffer for two more days and one night. That is, until a compassionate hyena decapitated her from afar with two Kalashnikov bursts aimed at her neck.

Really compassionate? Anyone who well knows his or her fellow men, thus doesn't hold any illusions about them, has every right to doubt that the sentiment called compassion really exists in this world. Whatever it was, let's return to Falcon who during the martyrdom of the white mare was flagellating himself with the most uncompassionate self-examination of conscience.

*   *   *

Tell-Falcon-that-having-courage-is-a-duty.   A-necessity-and-a-duty.
Tell-him-that-he-must-have-courage,   that-nothing-in-life-counts-
more-than-courage, that-life-without-courage-is-not-life. And before
that: tell-him-that-he-should-have-come-with-you-and-Armandò, that-
I-would-have-loved-to-embrace-him. That was the message she had
sent him. The reproach. And as for courage, what a superb lesson she'd
flung in his face by refusing to leave! I'm-a-soldier-of-God. And-I-do-
not-budge. Granted: all three had refused to leave, all three had flung
that lesson in his face. But the one who made the decisions was she.
The one who set the example was she. Had she chosen to flee, Sister
Milady and Sister George would have fled as well and... Of course
thinking of her and of them all alone in the demolished convent broke
his heart. Of course imagining her and them in that basement, without
food and at the mercy of the fanatics who would conquer the hill, took
his breath away. Yet what made him suffer the way he now suffered
wasn't his broken heart, his choked breath, the hairshirt of regret. It
was the shame, the grief he felt at realizing how she had recognized his
lack of courage, and the uneasiness he felt at considering Gigi the
Candid's triumph. Had he pronounced the words I'm-coming-too, the
triumph would have been his as well. They would have said to him
as well you-did-it-you-son-of-a-gun, you've-got-balls-you-old-fart,
you're-a-devil-man, thank-you-brother, grazie-colonnello. But he
hadn't pronounced them. He hadn't gone. Once again, he had chosen
the comfortable limbo of those who don't win and don't lose: who
don't lose because they don't win, who don't win because they don't
risk, who don't risk because they don't dare, who don't dare because
they're not alive. And who are not alive because they don't have courage.

He cocked his ear at the echo of a barrage coming from Hazmiye,
the sign that the battle for the hill had started, and this exacerbated his
torment. Yes, he'd chosen the limbo of those who are not alive because
they lack courage. The limbo of those who never expose themselves,
never jeopardize themselves, never take risks and thus receive neither
praise nor blame, thus go neither to Paradise nor to Hell. The limbo of
those who always remain neutral, always spectators, always safe behind
a window from which they watch the few who expose themselves and
jeopardize themselves and take risks. The limbo of those who are afraid,
and who out of fear deny themselves even the balm of a farewell. If-

you-have-time, give-my-regards-to-the-Mother-Superior. The limbo of cowards. Fear and I are old friends, he used to say in the officers' latrine. Childhood friends, loyal friends, friends who meet everywhere and in every circumstance: when and where I have to face the enraged demonstrators who attack with iron bars and heavy stones and Molotov cocktails, when and where I have to arrest a dangerous gang, when and where I have to answer the generals who deafen with reprimands, when and where I have to jump with the parachute. However I've always faced those demonstrators, I've always arrested those gangs, I've always answered those generals, and I've never missed a parachute jump. So I'm not a coward. And such self-defense had a certain logic. It's true that to be afraid doesn't mean to be a coward, it's true that very often courage blossoms from fear, that in the end it consists of overcoming fear. The point is that such reasoning was based upon old and minor tests: in the city to which he had come and returned for the main purpose of facing the Great Test, he had shunned all the opportunities to overcome his fear. All! Aside from his trips to the officers' latrine, he hadn't done a single thing to prove that often courage blossoms from fear, that to be afraid doesn't mean to be a coward. He hadn't performed a single act that would permit him to say I'm-not-a-coward. And in forty-eight hours, he would embark. If his ship didn't blow up with a kamikaze, in a week he would be back in his placid world devoid of opportunities. And his truth would remain the truth of a phony bulldog who protects his reputation with the graves of the carabinieri gloriously fallen in the first and in the Second World War, in Northern Italy, in Greece, in Albania, in North Africa, in the antifascist Resistance. The truth of a coward whose only and sincere ideal is to die at age one hundred on some tennis court while he plays the Achilles' heel, that is, the movement he executes by shifting the weight of his body to the right heel... He shuddered. God, he said, give me another chance. Give me another opportunity, a last opportunity to prove that I'm not a coward! I don't need to have witnesses, to be borne in triumph, to hear people vociferate you-did-it-you-son-of-a-gun etcetera. I don't even care whether she finds out about it, whether she continues to think of me as a man without courage. I only care to prove to myself that I'm not a coward.

"Colonel, sir!"

He raised his sharp face that the anguish had sharpened even more, he looked with indifference at the paratrooper who called him.

"What is it?"

"Sir, Rocco's out of his coma!"

"Out of his coma?!"

"Yessir! The information just came from the Rizk, by telephone!"

"And who took it?"

"Your aide, sir!"

"Tell him to come here."

Gigi the Candid came and, full of excitement, confirmed it. Yes, all of a sudden the telephone communications between the Western and the Eastern Zones had been reestablished, so Sister Françoise had called with the incredible news: during the night Rocco had opened his eyes and asked for his watch and his girl. "Imaam...watch...Imaam." Since then he continued to repeat Imaam-watch-Imaam, and Sister Françoise warned that this didn't give them any reason for illusions: the mumbling was mechanical, the cerebral lesions remained, and at any moment the poor boy could plunge back into the coma. However, a crumb of hope now existed and... With a quivering that shook his whole body, Falcon interrupted the explanation.

"Where is this Imaam?"

"Who knows? Not even Rocco had her address. She refused to give it because of her parents who wouldn't like to see her married to a Christian. All she said to him was that she lived near the Cité Sportive."

"And the watch?"

"I have it here."

Gigi the Candid opened a drawer and took out a black plastic chronometer. The one on which Rocco had checked the time and counted the seconds before raising his body and offering his nape to the trajectory of the 5.56 that flew in the direction of the new Ruby base. Falcon grabbed it and slipped it in his pocket.

"I'll bring it to him."

"You'll bring it to him?!?"

"Yes, at once."

"But why? It makes no sense! As I told you, he probably isn't even aware of what he says! Really, is it worth risking your life for such a thing?"

"I think so."

"I don't! Tayoune swarms with snipers! At the boundary bar is the idiot who made all that fuss and got my red scarf!"

"I'll cross at Sodeco."

"What?!? Sodeco is worse! This morning even the Sons of God are there! Those who seized the church of Saint-Michel! If you meet the mullah who led them yesterday, the hunchback with the Koran and the crimson turban, you might be in trouble! Think of it! And think of your escort, dammit!''

"I'm not taking any escort."

"No escort?!? I don't understand..."

"It doesn't matter, Gigi... You don't have to understand," he cut him off. And full of gratitude for God who had given him a last opportunity to demonstrate that he wasn't a coward, he rushed to his jeep where Salvatore Bellezza son of the late Onofrio was waiting with his tiny trapped-rat eyes and his firm intention of butchering Alì as well as disfiguring Sanaan.

"At your command, colonel, sir!''

"You?!?"

It sounds incongruous, but despite his uncured and incurable stupidity, Salvatore Bellezza son of the late Onofrio was no longer the defenseless oaf that Falcon had tortured with the Torquemada technique and sent back to Livorno with the promise of making him languish in jail for thirty years. Even less was he the fragile larva that, after the cruel farewell of his Saint Rita, had been picked up and carried away by the armpits and ankles. Adversities strengthen the weak, the proverb says. And, thanks to adversities, in those few months the fragile larva had turned into a caterpillar fully able to bear the inclemencies of existence; the defenseless oaf had survived blows that would have destroyed any normal person. For example, three suicide attempts. The first, swallowing seven 9mm bullets for whose removal the medical officer had prescribed seven enemas of very hot saltwater: one enema per bullet. The second, gulping down a flask of sludge that he'd collected from the barracks' sewer and that the medical officer had refused to pump. The third, hanging himself from the blessing hand of the marble-sculpted Saint Gabriel who towered in the battalion chapel as patron of the paratroopers. Snapped off by the weight, the blessing hand had fallen and bounced on his head to lacerate the left occipital region with a bad wound the medical officer had coldly enlarged. "And let's hope you die, this time." But, above all, he'd survived his hate and the hate of whoever had lived next to him in those months. To begin with, the personnel of the infirmary who had not only performed the seven enemas for the seven bullets but pumped out of his stomach the sewer sludge that the medical officer had refused to pump and sutured the bad wound the medical officer had coldly enlarged in the hope of seeing him die. Then, his bunkmates who couldn't sleep at night because of his endless whimpering I-want-to-go-back-to-Beirut. Then, his lieutenant and his captain and his major and his colonel who from dawn to dusk were pestered by his request please-send-me-back-to-Beirut-or-I'll-kill-myself. Finally, and more than anybody else, the real victim of the situation: the battalion chaplain who, besides having a Saint Gabriel maimed and unable to bless the paratroopers, after every suicide attempt had to listen to the true reason why he wanted to return to Beirut. That is, the story of a certain Alì to be butchered and of a certain Sanaan to be disfigured. Knowing the true reason, in fact, gave him a serious dilemma: to respect the secrecy of the confessional or to spill out the whole matter so that the request please-send-me-back would be ignored? Yet, one ugly morning in January, the priest had untangled the uncertainties. "May God forgive me, Salvatore Bellezza son of the late Onofrio," he'd shouted, "but if I don't succeed in sending you back, I'll break to pieces that son of a bitch Saint Gabriel who didn't support your weight and I'll convert to Buddhism." Then, saying that the poor guy only wished to help the unhappy city's inhabitants and contribute to peace in the Middle East, he'd started pestering everybody in his turn. He'd even interceded with the Vatican, the President of the Republic, the Minister of Defense, he'd won, and to be sure that his protégé really left for Beirut he'd personally accompanied him to the three-star general. He'd witnessed his departure. "Go, damn ballbuster, go! Go butcher your Alì and disfigure your Sanaan! Go and pop off, drop dead! Mors tua, vita mea." Which means, in Latin, your death is my life.

It sounds equally incongruous but when Salvatore Bellezza son of the late Onofrio had realized that the Italians were dismantling the bases and that he was back only to leave again, he hadn't yielded to discouragement. On the contrary, he'd posed himself a series of very shrewd questions. One: since the abominable couple lived in the Old City, that is, far from the base, would he be able to butcher him and disfigure her before embarking? The answer: no. He wouldn't. Two: how to solve the unexpected problem? The answer: by remaining in Beirut. Three: with what expedient could he remain in Beirut? The answer: by getting himself reassigned to the carabinieri squad on guard at the embassy. Four: who had the authority to reassign him to the carabinieri squad on guard at the embassy? The answer: the Condor. Five: who had the authority to ask the Condor? The answer: Falcon. Therefore he needed to obtain Falcon's pardon. And to obtain Falcon's pardon he needed to whip up a good spiel, a self-criticism of the kind made by the heretics during the Inquisition and by the communists during the communist heyday. Something like this: "Colonel, sir, I've come back for the purpose of expressing my regret and remorse. I'm here to recognize that by smearing the walls with amorous messages, abandoning the machine gun, waking up His Excellency the Ambassador Glass Eye and the entire quarter, by punching my squad leader and making him spit his two upper premolars as well as his two lower premolars for a total of four teeth, I deserved your severe judgment. I demonstrated that I was truly a schizophrenic lunatic, a raving paranoid, a criminal, a discredit to the Carabinieri Corps, to the Army, to the Fatherland, and the Flag. Plus, a blind dolt. Real blind and a real dolt. Because the girl I loved and called my fiancée wasn't at all a virtuous maiden, a Saint Rita of Cascia. She was exactly what you said: a little yet a big tramp, a cheap hooker, a whore who led me by the nose. So I want to rehabilitate myself, colonel, sir. I want to erase my dishonor, redeem my crimes, and be worthy once more of the Carabinieri Corps, of the Army, of the Fatherland and the Flag. That's why I'm asking to remain in Beirut, to rejoin the squad on guard at the embassy, to protect His Excellency the Ambassador Glass Eye who sacrifices himself so much and doesn't even have a golf course to play golf. To the last drop of my blood I want to defend him from the Druzes, the Sons of God, the Amal, the phalangists, the Kataeb, his friends and his enemies including the husband of the Laundress. I mean the cretin who served as ambassador to Cuba and who played with automobiles like James Dean. And if you won't forgive me, colonel, sir, if you won't ask the general to leave me in Beirut with the squad on guard at the embassy, I'll kill myself." Then he'd committed the whole tirade to memory, a three-day and three-night exertion, and posted himself near the jeep of Falcon who now stared at him with wide-open eyes.

"You?!?"

"Yessir, colonel, sir. Me! I've come back for the purpose of..."

"When did you come back, God dammit?!?"

"Tuesday morning, colonel, sir, for the purpose of..."

"And how did you do it?!? Whom did you come with?!?"

"With the three-star general from Rome, sir. By helicopter and for the purpose of expressing..."

"And who is the irresponsible animal, the scatterbrain who made you come back?!?"

"The battalion chaplain, sir. He interceded with the Vatican, the President of the Republic, the Minister of Defense, then he said: go, damn-ballbuster, go. Pop-off. Drop-dead. Mors-tua, vita-mea. But he didn't mean it, sir, and he wept with joy for my joy."

"Bellezza! Thank God I don't have time to listen to you, I have to run to the Rizk..."

"To the Rizk, sir?!?"

"To the Rizk. Get out of my way. Quick."

"Nossir, sir. Because I'm the one who will bring you to the Rizk."

"What?!?"

"Yessir. So you don't go alone, I'll protect you, and I'll recite my self-criticism on the way."

"Your self-criticism?!?"

"Yessir. A self-criticism like the heretics made during the Inquisition and the communists during the communist heyday."

"Bellezza, you want to die. Whether by my hand or somebody else's hand you want to die."

"Oh, never mind if I die, sir! I've died so many times in these months! Once more, once less..."

And moved to pity, Falcon signed his own penalty.

"Come. We'll cross at Sodeco," he said.

*   *   *

The battle for possession of the hill had just begun when, with Rocco's watch in his pocket and Salvatore Bellezza son of the late Onofrio at the wheel, Falcon left the base and headed for the Sodeco crossing. Naturally he hadn't forgotten that Sodeco swarmed with more snipers than Tayoune, that this morning even the Sons of God were there, that if he met the hunchbacked mullah with the Koran and the crimson turban who had tried to stop the Ost Ten convoy he might be in trouble. And he was very scared. But proving that to be afraid doesn't mean to be a coward, that very often courage blossoms from fear yet consists of overcoming fear, gave him a solace he had never known: a happiness he had never felt. You know, the happiness that occurs when we undertake something monstrously difficult and we carry it out without the help of others or even in spite of others. A task that everybody hampers, for example, a rebellion that everybody opposes, a challenge that everybody advises against... The silent, proud, and yet humble happiness of which we are the sole author and beneficiary. The solitary, private, secret happiness that rewards or alleviates the lack of real happiness.

He also felt very pleased for having complicated the Great Test with a ball and chain like Salvatore Bellezza son of the late Onofrio, and glad for having overcome so quickly the irritation caused by his unexpected return. Poor scapegoat, he thought, how he must have suffered at leaving Beirut. Never-mind-if-I-die, sir. I've-died-so-many-times-in-

these-months! Once-more-once-less... I was unfair to him, I was cruel.
I called him Bruttezza, wether, eunuch, I told him that he was not a
man, that between his legs he hadn't even a pinhead... Well, maybe he
isn't a man, nevertheless he has managed to return and with a three-
star general. Maybe he is a wether, nevertheless he has had the guts to
face me and follow me to the Eastern Zone. But what is he saying,
now, what does he want? A moment ago he was talking about Saint
Rita of Cascia and a little tramp who actually was a big tramp, a whore,
now he's talking about the carabinieri, the Fatherland, the Flag... No,
about a glass eye he wants to protect from the Druzes and a very
cretinous ambassador who is married to a very rich laundress and who
plays like James Dean. What in the hell has all this to do with Beirut?
Maybe he's lost his mind from dying so many times. Or maybe I'm not
listening to him. I'll listen to him later... And meantime Salvatore Bellezza son of the late Onofrio was driving, conducting him to the appointment with a destiny of which he was the indispensable though
unaware accomplice. He drove atrociously. To better recite his self-
criticism he tore his hands from the wheel, he gesticulated, he groped,
and missed obstacles by a hair. Driving in this way he had covered rue
de l'Aérodrome and avenue Nasser, crossed the rond-point of Sabra,
skirted the Pine Wood, entered rue Becharà, and now he approached
the Sodeco crossing which was usually open and consisted of a simple
wooden bar.

"Shut up and speed up," Falcon ordered impatiently.

"Yessir!" he replied lurching into the zigzag of alleys that Sugar had
rejected because the trailers wouldn't turn at the curves. And skidding,
swerving, steering, alley after alley and curve after curve, he reached the
checkpoint where he braked in confusion. Hey! It was closed with
chevaux-de-frise and coils of barbed wire: why? Behind those chevaux-
de-frise and coils of barbed wire there were tons of guys with black
ribbons around their foreheads and the image of Khomeini on their
chests: why? There was also a hunchbacked mullah with a crimson
turban and a Kalashnikov and a Koran that dangled from his bandolier:
why? And now this mullah knelt down, pointed the Kalashnikov, aimed
at the jeep to indicate that they couldn't pass. How strange!

"Turn back, turn back!" Falcon yelled.

"Back, sir?"

"Back, yes, back! Quick, dammit, quick!"

"Yessir..." he stammered. Then he pulled up to make a U-turn, hit a
cheval-de-frise, braked once more to go into reverse, and the engine
stalled.

"Don't stop here, for God's sake!"

"The engine stalled, sir..."

"Start it again, for God's sake!"

"It doesn't want to start, sir..."

"Try again, try again!"

"Yessir..."

He started it, finally. He completed the turn. But as he completed it, he tangled the rear bumper in a coil of barbed wire and, destroying half the barrier, he drove off with it. He dragged it like a tail of tin cans lashed to the car of two newlyweds. Clink-clink! Clink-clink! Clink-clink!

"What are you doing, you idiot?!?"

"It got stuck to the rear bumper, sir..."

And just as he said it-got-stuck-to-the-rear-bumper-sir, while saying it he turned to go back to rue Bechará and offered the right side of the jeep to the hunchbacked mullah, there was a shout: "Allah akbar!" Along with the shout, a crackling of gunfire then a crackling of 7.62s that hit the license plate and the taillights and the back corner. Into that crackling, the crash of a bullet that pierced the metal of the right door. The door beside which Falcon was sitting. And Falcon saw his right leg jerk up then fall back on the footboard and soak it with blood. He felt a tremendous pain in his right foot, a pain that radiated from the heel, and he realized that perforating the shoe's thick leather the bullet had penetrated his right heel. The heel of the Achilles-heel movement. So he grabbed an arm of the idiot who hadn't noticed a thing and hadn't the vaguest idea of what had happened.

"To the field hospital, quick!" he panted.

"To the field hospital, sir?"

"Yes! Hurry up, for God's sake, hurry up!"

"Oh! Aren't you well, sir? Did you get an upset stomach?"

"Hurry..."

"Then we aren't going to the Rizk anymore, sir?"

"Hurry..."

At the third hurry he finally hurried, and still dragging the coil of barbed wire like a tail of tin cans lashed to the car of two newlyweds, still skidding and swerving, he reached the field hospital. Still without having the vaguest idea of what had happened, he turned Falcon over to the doctors who transferred him to the operating table and liberated the foot and grew speechless with incredulity. After passing through the obstacles of metal and thick leather then losing its trim, in fact, the 7.62 had exploded inside the bone and accomplished a ruin very similar to the ruin that would have been accomplished by a 5.56. The heel no longer existed. The tarsus and the astragalus and the scaphoid were reduced to a handful of fragments. The cuboid and the cuneiform bones were also gone. And in place of the phalanges and the metatarsus there was a mass of bloody cartilage.

"They got me in the Achilles' heel, right?" gasped Falcon trying to overcome the unendurable pain.

"Yes, colonel."

"Tell me if I'll be able to play tennis again..."

"And you tell us what the hell you were doing at the Sodeco crossing," a dismayed surgeon replied evasively.

"I was bringing a watch..."

"A watch?!? Why, God dammit, why?!?"

"To prove to myself that I'm not a coward," he murmured faintly. Then he lost consciousness, and they amputated his foot. Or what remained of it.

Which brings us to the final station, the Saturday station.

7

My hashish does no harm.
It's good stuff, it comes from Bekaa,
from the green valleys of Baalbèk.
And it is cheap.
Buy a kilo, soldier, and smoke it.
Smoke it, smoke it!
You have nothing else to help you forget
this sad story
and this sad city.

The sun was setting and the woman's melancholic voice was singing the dope growers' dirge that on the evening of the double slaughter had risen over rue de l'Aérodrome, when without diverting their eyes from the white mare now in the extreme of her agony Bernard le Français ordered Rocky to raise the boundary bar and Sugar crossed Tayoune with the final containers. The ones in which he had loaded the weapons of his Museum, the radios, the telephones, the equipment of the Operations Room, and the furnishings of the headquarters where nothing remained but the large cherry-wood table with a pair of chairs and the oil painting of the emir. At about the same time Pistoia completed the construction of his little San Gimignano, the three ships sent

to board the one thousand two hundred men of the contingent appeared on the horizon, and the fleet led by the flagship arrayed itself
along the coast to oversee at gunpoint the last day and the last night of
the Italians in Beirut. Then the Condor called Crazy Horse and asked
him to break the silence about the departure date, let the officers tell
the troops that they would leave tomorrow morning. He called the
Professor and asked him to inform the Christians and the Druzes, to
request that they facilitate the embarking by suspending their fire at
sunrise. He called Charlie and asked him to convey the same request to
the Amal, to notify Zandra Sadr that the field hospital and the provisions would be delivered before the final convoy assembled. Then he
locked the door of his former office, crouched among the baggage, and
burst into sobs.

"God, God, God..."

You wouldn't have recognized him that Saturday afternoon, that eve
of the departure. His eyes bleary, his cheeks swollen, and his soldierly
slash marred by an ugly fistula which had formed beneath the scab, he
was by now the shadow of the handsome man to whom the soubrette
had yowled from the stage general-you are-a-stud-you-are-a-cake.
Even his extraordinary energy had vanished. With the energy, his au-
thoritarian boldness. Yes, he thought as he sobbed, yes: he would leave
in the sunlight, the colors flying, not on the sly like the British
Dragoons. Yet he left in total defeat and with a tremendous need to
apologize to himself, to the man and to the soldier whose pride he was
about to destroy. Oh! They had been all wounds to his pride, the bitter
pills he'd swallowed in Beirut. All. Beginning with the appeal Don't-
touch-the-Italians,   the-Italians-give-us-blood,   the-Italians-are-our-
blood-brothers, now modified with the indecorous Don't-touch-the-
Italians-who-depart,   the-Italians-are-our-blood-brothers-and-depart-
ing-they-leave-gifts-for-us. But the toll nay the ransom that tomorrow
morning he would pay in beefsteaks and prosciutti, ravioli and tortellini, radiology units and ambulances, electrocardiographs and wheelchairs, surpassed any other wound. It was a self-injury, a self-humilia-
tion which took away even his wish to live and to go home. Go home?
Well, thanks to his pride sold at the paltry cost of three million three
hundred thirty-three thousand three hundred thirty-three point thirty-
three liras apiece, he brought home or hoped to bring home one thousand and two hundred men: in his personal case, though, what did it
mean, to-go-home? Nothing more than to return to the daily grind of
small bloodless wars, to reinstate himself within the false or ambiguous

rules of a world in which what counts doesn't count and vice versa, to reintegrate himself into the dreariness of the so-called normal existence... Home wasn't a joy, for him. It wasn't a relief. It was a pseudo-elegant penthouse in a pseudo-elegant quarter of Rome. Eight rooms, two bathrooms, air conditioning, garage, and silverware to pull out when you invited some important person to dinner. Or some friend who wasn't a friend. It was a bed to share with a wife he hadn't missed and who surely would welcome him by singsonging the litany of supposed sacrifices borne in his absence. It was a clerk's schedule in an office surrounded by malevolent colleagues who would envy his temporary celebrity and spit on him the poison of gossip or slander. It was the squalid struggle for promotion, the wait for the pension. The pension! Life becomes a spout dripping tedium and renunciation when you retire on the pension. You fade away when you retire on the pension. You get old, you wither, you die out of inertia. Much better to die of hexogen, then. And at once, in Beirut. The problem was that, if he died of hexogen in Beirut, those one thousand and two hundred men would die with him: his pride would have been sold in vain and...

"God! God! God!"

He sobbed for this too, for the suspicion that he'd sold his pride in vain: an eventuality he associated with the fear of having badly driven his train. Maybe I am a bad general, he said, one of those who bring their soldiers back home in coffins. Maybe I've been wrong to waste so many days with the convoys, the containers, the vertical trenches, not to slip away like the English and to gamble, to delude myself with a chip which wasn't a winning chip. Maybe I've not pondered enough. I haven't given enough importance to certain warnings, for example to that ubiquitous "three" that kept resurfacing and multiplying and dividing itself... Three trucks, three motorboats. Three ships, three battalions. Three months since the double slaughter. Three million three hundred thirty-three thousand three hundred thirty-three point thirty-three liras of toll, no, of ransom, apiece. And the third truck that never turned up, the third motorboat that might turn up, the third eye that can't see, the third ear that can't hear, the third ship. Just a coincidence, a banal fluke? It is the most vulnerable, the third ship. Because by letting the first two ships depart, the hypothetical kamikaze can easily study the course to take: calculate the time he needs. Not to mention the fact that, after the departure of the first and the second ship, the third group will be seized by a kind of relaxation. A dangerous optimism. Come-on-boys, there-is-no-two-without-three, we'll-make-it-as-well... He'd carefully planned the self-defense of each ship. He'd ordered the placement of ten riflemen on the bridge, ten on the fore-castle, ten on the quarterdeck, ten on the main deck, and twenty on the lower decks. He'd personally selected those riflemen and told them to open fire at the slightest alarm, to shoot at anything moving on the water's surface, including the most innocent fishing smack. Besides, he himself would be on the third ship: if the kamikaze came, he would personally direct the counterattack. But an obscure instinct told him that not even his presence would be of any use. Nor would the fleet with its computers and its cannons, its technology. Despite the rain of fire the motorboat would hit the target, the ants would once again gobble up the elephant and... He sobbed until Crazy Horse knocked on the door to say that Falcon was being transferred to the Rizk and asked to see him.

"I'll be right there. Thank you."

Stretched out on the cot of the ambulance, his right foot amputated and his eyes shining with fever, Falcon welcomed him with a coura-geous smile. He had asked to see him, he murmured, to urge two favors. The first had to do with the tennis racket in his luggage: a painful relic he intended to give as a souvenir to Sister Espérance, the Mother Superior at the convent. She had been a famous tennis player, she surely would appreciate the gift, and maybe it could be sent to her through the governmentals who now held the Ost Ten skyscraper. The second concerned Lance Corporal Salvatore Bellezza whom he had chased in November for a minor infraction and who had returned Tuesday morning with the three-star general from Rome. Awakening from the narcosis, he had found him at his bedside and had been forced to listen to an interminable but dignified rigmarole about his wish to redeem himself by remaining in Beirut with the squad on guard at the embassy. That is, the squad he'd belonged to. Poor wretch: he didn't have an Einstein brain, and at times he tried people's patience real hard. However he was full of goodwill, as sincere as incapable of harming a fly, and it would be worth granting his request.

"Please, general."

"Okay, colonel. We'll do," he replied, touched. And without wast-ing any time in investigations, half an hour later he ordered that Salva-tore Bellezza son of the late Onofrio be reassigned to the carabinieri squad on guard at the embassy. The tennis racket remained where it was, however. Because during the night the hill had been conquered by the Amal. The convent had been taken by the Sons of God, and the news concerning Sister Espérance as well as Sister George and Sister Milady was very, very bad.

*   *   *

My hashish does no harm.
It's good stuff, it comes from Bekaa,
from the green valleys of Baalbèk.
And it is cheap.
Buy a kilo, soldier, and smoke it.
Smoke it, smoke it!
You have nothing else to help you forget
this sad story
and this sad city.

Night was falling and the woman's melancholic voice was still singing the dope growers' dirge when the officers broke the silence and told the troops that they would leave tomorrow. A task nobody executed more willingly than Sandokan, by then so impatient to quit Beirut and to follow in the footsteps of his pacifist and antimilitarist father, that he had already shaved the shaggy and sunbleached beard, the long drooping mustaches, the goatish sideburns, and now offered a face that seemed the symbol itself of mildness: as anonymous as the voice with which he whooped his concise announcement.

"Knapsacks on your shoulders, kids! We embark tomorrow."

How did they react? Most of them, the same way we react to a miraculous panacea, an elixir which restores our health or our inner truth. And the first one to benefit from it was Calogero the Fisherman who, prisoner of the straitjacket the medical officers had prescribed to prevent him from escaping and swimming to Formìca, had spent the whole month inside the Sierra Mike infirmary and done nothing but shout out his distress: "Apìti a tunnara, open the net! Nu sugno un tunnu de mattanza, I'm not a tuna to harpoon! Sugno u picciotto, I'm a boy! U cristiano, a Christian!" As soon as he heard that knapsacks-on-your-shoulders-kids-we-embark-tomorrow, he quieted down and: "Where are we going?" "Home, Calogero." "Your home or my home?" "We, to ours. And you, to yours." "Allura lassàtimi fari li buzzi che nun scappo chiù. Then let me pack my bags: I won't run away anymore." An equally speedy recovery came over Roberto the Laundryman who after repenting for insulting Jesus with the story of Saint Lazarus's catalepsy and the threat to vote communist had suffered an attack of mysticism, told everybody he had been saved by a heaven-sent angel, and decided to become a monk. "Yes, I shall enter a monastery of Capuchin brothers. And to repay that miracle, I shall put myself at the service of the unhappy people who end up forgotten like umbrellas." At Sandokan's announcement, though: "I kidded you, suckers! It wasn't an angel who descended from heaven! It was the headquarters sergeant who brought the batteries to Twenty-Seven Owl!" Then, yelling that he was sick and tired of being an irreprehensible citizen, he declared that he couldn't wait to get back to San Remo and indemnify himself with a good gamble at the Casino plus a good fuck with a whore. As for Luca and Nicola, both fainted from emotion. And when they came to their senses, they were completely changed. "Hemingway was right," Luca said, "in war a man really becomes a man. Now that I've been under fire, proven I have balls, I'm no longer a Peter Pan looking for Never-Never-Never Land in Kensington Gardens. In Venice, I will no longer waste my time dancing with Donatella or loafing around San Marco Square. I will write a novel called *For Whom the Cannon Sings* and disclose all my intrepid experiences: from the French flag to the naked woman. How about you, Nicolin?" "I'm going to become a war correspondent. War is so exciting," declared Nicola rushing off to add his jubilation to the jubilation of the healed.

"Hurrah! Evviva! Hurrah!"

Others reacted instead with the indifference or the quiet sadness which accompanies the end of a relationship you've suffered too much for, paid too much for, so that in concluding it you don't even feel a sense of riddance: you only feel indifference or quiet sadness. And this was the case with Rambo who always wearing the Khomeini badge passed half his time at the communal grave to chase away the goats that sullied the spot where he'd buried Leyda. "Oh, yeah?" he absently mumbled. "Too bad. I will no longer be able to chase them away." As for those who were leaving behind a girl, a love, the most crushed was Fabio who on Wednesday had said to Jasmine: "I won't go without you. I'll put you inside an M113, hide you in the ship's hold, and bring you to Italy. With my squad leader's aid it shouldn't be difficult. He's a friend, he'll not raise any objection." And in vain Jasmine had tried to dissuade him: "Don't ask for the impossible, Mister Coraggio. Allah has given us more than we expected: let's be content with what we had." As sure as he was that he would succeed, at the announcement he really asked for his squad leader's aid. The squad leader grabbed him by the neck yelling you-nitwit, you-moron, are-you-out-of-your-mind, if-you-try-I'll-send-you-to-jail, and the poor devil fell into a depression like the one he'd fallen into after John's decapitated head. But Matteo too underwent a serious breakdown. Because during the day a navy helicopter had unloaded the last round of mail for the marò, among that mail there was a letter from Rosaria, and this said: "Dear Matteo, out of respect for the loyalty and consistency I always insisted on, I must confess why I urged you to risk your skin in the mess of Beirut. No, not because of your thesis on the Middle East. Honestly, I couldn't care less about it. I urged you because I needed to get free of you for a while, to understand if I was or I wasn't in love with a charming old man who was courting me. Well, I was. Head over heels. And I married him. Now I am Mrs. Caruso, the consort of the Caruso family's capo. Yes, the Carusos who control the fish market: the rivals of the Badalamenti. I hope this doesn't bother you." Doesn't bother you?!? The most raging pain had blinded him, his sagacity had vanished and, instead of calling Dalilah to tell her that he would leave the next day and that his heart was broken, that night he called her to overcome the affront to his reputation as a Sicilian male. "Dalilah, Dalilah, I'm a cuckold! Dalilah, Dalilah, Rosaria packed me off here so she could marry an old mafioso, the head of the Caruso family! Please help me! Please make love with me or I'll never feel like a man again!" "Moi I'm not une infirmière nor a whore d'un bordel. Go à l'enfer and bon voyage," Dalilah replied in her bizarre mixture of English and French. Then she shut her window. And to overcome the affront, the mafia, Palermo, Beirut which was a Palermo multiplied a thousand times, women who are selfish and cruel no matter which race or religion they belong to, the thesis on the Middle East that he would never write, Matteo followed the advice of the dope growers' dirge. He bought a kilo of hashish and smoked a good part of it. He smoked so much that he soon lost his mind and ended up inside the straitjacket they'd just taken off Calogero the Fisherman, shouting his despair in the most incomprehensible Sicilian.

"Aiutuuu! Lassitimi gghiri, aiutuuu!"

He wasn't the only one to follow the advice of the dope growers' dirge, let's be clear about it. The last night many of them bought hashish. Almost all. They bought it from whoever sold it, whoever offered it. And in Beirut everybody sold it, everybody offered it. They bought it from the Syrian who owned the grocery next to the Twenty-One and who gave free rolling paper reproducing the five-dollar bill with Abraham Lincoln and the Lincoln Memorial. (Yes, the grocery where Ferruccio used to send Mahomet and where Mahomet demanded compensatory damages in pistachio nuts or pumpkin seeds.)

They bought it from the Palestinian who ran the gas station in the little square of the Twenty-Two and who kept the cylinders of compressed gas that terrified Eagle during the battle. (Yes, the gas station from whose roof Passepartout had jumped a few moments before finding Ninette in rue Argàn and giving her the Kalashnikov.) They bought it from the Bourji el Barajni butcher who had the shop opposite the statue of the Unknown Soldier. (Yes, the statue at whose foot Gino had stopped to write his poem about the October sun of his childhood and the black wings of Death that flew away promising to return.) They bought it from the workers of the firm that manufactured the dolls' heads with the inscription "Palestinian Revolution" and from kids who wanted to be paid in chocolate not in money. (Ten chocolates for ten grams of hashish, fifty chocolates for fifty grams.) They bought it from Sheila, the cute schoolteacher who gave herself to the officers free of charge, and from Fatima, the harlot in blue jeans who banged the marò in the jeep at the bottom of the former pool near the Twenty-Seven. They bought it from Farjane, the charming fox who in her best Sunday dress went from post to post asking the soldiers will-you-please-marry-me, and from Jamila, the hungry little girl who stole String's food rations. (But all she wanted in exchange, poor Jamila, was a roast chicken.) They bought it from the Gobeyre militiamen, from the Sixth Brigade deserters, from the pimps, the mullahs, the muezzins, and also from the blind old man of rue Farrouk. They bought it blond, black, red, brown. They bought it in powder, in sticks, in chunks, in loaves both round and square, rectangular and cylindrical, packed in cotton and in linen bags, with the stamp Extra Quality or without, with the Cedars of Lebanon trademark or without. And very often they smoked it immediately. All the more that last night because the medical officers wouldn't come to take their urine samples, the sector leaders wouldn't make their inspections and yell if-you-smoke-hashish-I'll-kick-your-ass, I'll-slap-you-under-arrest. Oh, did they smoke it! The Condor and his General Staff would never know how much of it they smoked. But from every base, every post, every M113, every guard tower, every sentry box, every checkpoint, the odor of hashish arose. The unpleasant odor that drug users call perfume and instead is a stench of burnt shit and rosemary, rotten musk and resin, at the same time soft and pungent, delicate and spicy, nauseating, as fetid as the greed of the vampires who produce it or deal it. The painful odor, the painful stench, which is the stench of weakness, of sluggishness, of cowardice. In fact it pleases those who lack the courage to face life, who lack the balls to keep life alive, who lack the imagination it takes to appreciate life. Those who have not the intelligence to love life in spite of its hardness and filth and horrors. Some smoked it for the first time, spurred by a curiosity for too long repressed or rejected, the naive curiosity of children who, excited by the recommendations don't-touch-it, woe-to-you-if-you-touch-it, get snoopy and touch it. The curiosity of Eve: our mother Eve who, under the illusion of discovering what Good and Evil are, yielded to the Serpent and ate the apple. Let's taste it, let's try it. Might it really be an aphrodisiac, a mystical medicine which dissolves all anxieties and sorrows and fears, a magical serum of happiness? Might it really give you the courage you lack, the balls you lack, the imagination you lack, the intelligence you lack? Or will it reduce you to a larva who dies like a larva? "Come on, let's find out," said the snoopy children. The irresponsible Eves. Hundreds of children in uniform, of Eves dressed as soldiers: the rifle in their hands and the damn apple in their mouths. And when they didn't taste it or consume it, they hid it. In their boot heels, their rifles, the wheels of the jeeps, the motors of the armored cars, the hollows and slots of the M113s and the Leopards. To bring it to Italy, to smoke it there or resell it, to spread the plague, to diffuse the most unpleasant stench of burnt shit and rosemary, rotten musk and resin, at the same time soft and pungent, delicate and spicy, nauseating, as fetid as the greed of the vampires who produce it or deal it. The painful odor, the painful stench, which is the stench of weakness, of sluggishness, of cowardice...

"How much are you packing?"

"Me, three two-hundred-gram bricks."

"And you?"

"Me, four two-hundred-fifty-gram sacks."

"You too?"

"Yeah. I got twenty sticks of sixty grams each."

The one who packed more than anybody, perhaps, was Fifi. While Stefano and Gaspare and Ugo chased away Bernard le Français who had gone to the Pink Room to borrow Lady Godiva, Fifi hurried off to buy three kilos in chunks which he stashed in his knapsack and in every possible hole. Including those of his own body. All chunks that, through a slipup or a mockery of destiny, would arrive safe and sound in Italy and get him to the Taormina cemetery six months later.

*   *   *

My hashish does no harm.

It's good stuff, it comes from Bekaa,

from the green valleys of Baalbèk.
And it is cheap.
Buy a kilo, soldier, and smoke it.
Smoke it, smoke it!
You have nothing else to help you forget
this sad story
and this sad city.

Night had fallen, and the woman's melancholic voice hadn't yet stopped singing the dirge, when Charlie returned from his final meeting with Zandra Sadr and entered the Arab Bureau where only a few objects remained: the rifles, helmets, the poster of the delectable feminine legs on which somebody had scrawled in large letters if-you-don't-have-brains-have-legs, plus an empty trunk and the filing cabinets of the secret archive. With a bored gesture he tore down the poster, threw it away, in a bored voice he called the Condor to inform him that His Eminence had guaranteed the morning truce, then he opened the locked iron drawers and started pulling out the mysterious documents he had never permitted his Charlies to look at. The names and surnames of his Shiite or Palestinian informants, the identities of the foreign spies stationed in Beirut, the biographical and professional profiles of the terrorists exported from Libya or Syria or Iran, the identikits of the most bloodthirsty Sons of God, the topography of the camps where they were trained and indoctrinated by the ayatollahs, the addresses of the hideouts where the Westerners kidnapped by the various groups probably languished, the correspondence stolen God knows how from the embassies' secret services, the lexicon of unsuspected and unsuspectable personalities involved in weapons contraband or in the drug traffic, the inventory of arms smuggled to the Arab countries by the Israelis, the Americans, the French, the Swedes, the Italians, the English, the Greeks etcetera. And also the indisputable evidence that the double slaughter in October had been accomplished with Russian hexogen provided by the Damascus government. Also the backstage intrigues behind the innumerable political murders that had taken place in the capital, including the price paid by the notables who'd commissioned them. Also a list of the persons eliminated on the sly by the Palestinians when they were masters of the city and a certain Arafat was its king. In short, the encyclopedia of all the malfeasances hidden or unmentioned out of fear or convenience. Finally, some newspaper clippings. And, among the clippings, a December 1978 copy of the magazine *L'écho du Liban* whose cover bore the photo of a famous Supreme

Court judge murdered some years before with a load of Tnt in the Ashrafieh quarter. Inside the magazine, two photos of his young and gorgeous wife.

He pulled them out of the drawers, he placed them in plastic envelopes that he numbered, one by one he lined them up inside the trunk. And meanwhile he bitterly asked himself what the sad city had given to him, he bitterly answered: nothing good. Nothing positive. It hadn't rescued him from solitude because solitude was a distinguishing feature of his nature and because living with others, inventing ties and affections, doesn't help us to feel less alone. It hadn't snatched him away from melancholy because melancholy was the fruit of his solitude. It hadn't freed him from rancor because rancor was the fruit of his melancholy. It hadn't infused him with enthusiasm because enthusiasm is a privilege of youth, and to feel enthusiastic at forty you must have sublime incentives or the talents of an artist. It hadn't materialized his dream of becoming a Lawrence of Arabia because in order to become a Lawrence of Arabia you must be a Victorian aristocrat born in a Wales manor and educated at Oxford, a refined man, an ingenious histrion. A world-class adventurer. He was a petit bourgeois, instead, a guy born in a modest little villa of Bari, a plebeian of our times. Maybe a little more intelligent than the people he dealt with every day, but essentially uncouth and devoid of brilliant qualities. This made him a mediocre adventurer, a second-rate hero condemned to sacrifice himself in trivial undertakings. In a negative sense however, the sad city had given him a lot. Practically, all. Because by forcing him into shabby intrigues and shopkeepers' compromises it had exacerbated his pessimism, intensified his skepticism. The typical skepticism of those who marvel at nothing. And those who marvel at nothing believe in nothing... Dammit, until three months ago he did believe in something. For example, in the necessity of changing a world that doesn't change and doesn't function because it's ruled by the stupidest hierarchy in existence. The hierarchy of those who have nothing and thus count for nothing, who have little and thus count for little, who have much and thus count for much, those who have too much and thus count for too much. He was staying or wanted to stay on the barricade of the poor and the ignorant: on the side of the eternal ox-people who plow other people's land for a thread of hay, sweep their streets, console themselves by begetting swarms of children, instruct themselves by reading a half-book they found in the garbage. Bilal's side. Not Gassàn's. And staying on Bilal's barricade means staying there even if the Bilals are named Rashid or Passepartout. But when he'd discovered that Angelo's innocent, harmless, defenseless Ophelia had been killed by Passepartout, when he had seen how Rashid orchestrated the victories of the ox-people, he had concluded that there is no difference between the Bilals and the Gassàns. Because the Bilals and the Gassàns, the poor and the rich, the ignorant and the learned, are two sides of the same coin: two aspects of the same mistake. A mistake called Man. Because it is Man, not the world, who doesn't change. Whether he is rich or poor. It is Man, not the world, who doesn't function. Whether he is ignorant or learned. It is Man, not the world, who keeps alive the stupidest hierarchy in existence. And to hell with the chatter of those who in good or bad faith say the contrary. To hell with the ideological impostures and the evangelical lies about poverty justifying any fault, or ignorance acquitting any crime. To hell with the forgive-them-Father-they-know-not-what-they-do. They know, they know... They know, and this was the damn reason why he didn't believe in anything anymore. The reason why, if the motorboat were to arrive tomorrow, he would die believing in nothing. And dammit, dammit, dammit, what death is more death than a death which comes when you believe in nothing?!?

He angrily grabbed the copy of *L'écho du Liban*. Angrily he threw it onto the plastic envelopes already arrayed inside the trunk and said to himself: blessed are those who believe in something. In the Eternal Father, in the Devil, in love, in hate, in justice or privilege, in money or not money, in a next life or in this one. In something! We die so much better when we believe in something. We die so much less. And if the motorboat were to arrive... Maybe it would. Maybe it had been useless to convince the Condor to swallow his pride, to pay the ransom. Maybe he'd been naive to tell himself all those I-want, I-want, I-want. He would never settle in a city where people grow old and die of old age, full of wrinkles and finally tired of existence. He would never sleep in a bed with clean sheets and soft pillows and a woman beside him. He would never awaken in a room where the sun enters with the sounds of the bells etcetera. He would never get to become stupid, serene and stupid, happy and stupid, normal. Zandra Sadr had been so strange today. He didn't seem at all like the loathsome santon who deals with people from the summit of his hieratic stateliness. He sighed, he tossed, he fretted. He behaved as though he were crushed by some guilt or some defeat, and never looked him in the eye. What's more, he didn't speak like an oracle, he didn't express himself in the usual phrases full of hidden significance. He spoke like a common mortal, and skipping the pluralis majestatis he'd said that he wouldn't attend the delivery of the provisions and of the field hospital. "No, I won't be coming, captain.

I'm old, those things tire me. I'll send my sons. And please: do avoid ceremonials. Do limit the formalities as much as possible. A handshake and a document attesting to the donation will be enough." He had also avoided confirming the acceptance of the four terms put forth by the Condor, and raising the subject had been of no use. Repeating those terms, even less. "Most Reverend Eminence, forgive me if I insist. But my general wants to be certain that the Italian flag and the Red Cross banner will continue to fly on the field hospital's flagpole, that the field hospital will continue to assist everybody and not only the followers of one political-religious creed. He also wants to be sure that the pork meat and the alcoholic beverages forbidden by the Koran will be sorted out and given to the poor of the Christian Zone, that no act of vandalism or plunder will take place..." Each time he'd answered with an evasive I-understand, I-understand. But the worst had happened when they had parted. Because at that point his bowed face had raised, his downcast eyes had lifted, and: "Captain, unfortunately in all churches there are bad faithful, individuals incapable of obeying their shepherd. So I must bid you goodbye with a proverb that suits the circumstances: man proposes and God disposes. Inshallah, captain. I'll pray for you and your people." In other words, he had passed on to the Almighty the job of saving the ransom's payers.

He shot a glance at Angelo and Martino who silently helped him pack up the archive, and a violent cramp twisted his stomach. A spasm very similar to the spasm he'd felt the day the two bastards the law defined as parents had shown up to take his daughter Gioia, and she had exploded into those cries Dada-no Dada-no. Dammit, he thought, how young they are! They're so young that they still believe in everything. Should the motorboat arrive, they would die believing in everything. Maybe there's a death much worse than the death that comes when we don't believe in anything anymore: the death that comes when we still believe in everything. And this conclusion made him so enraged that he stopped placing the documents in the plastic envelopes. He stopped numbering the envelopes, lining them up, and with quiet contempt he dumped the still-full drawers into the trunk. All together. As if they were garbage. Whoosh! Whoosh! Whoosh! Then he turned to Angelo and Martino.

"Burn them," he said.

"Burn them?!?" Martino exclaimed in disconcertment.

"Burn them?!?" Angelo buzzed in disbelief.

"I said burn them. And in a way that no trace remains."

"Yes, chief..."

They hoisted the trunk and carried it to the courtyard, at that time very dark and deserted. They poured a can of gasoline into a big trash can, they set fire to it, they started to burn the documents in a way that no trace would remain. Envelope by envelope, page by page, without haste. And without curiosity for what they contained, though the flames that flickered in vivid tongues of reddish light ripped up the darkness illuminating the terrible secrets down to the last word.

8

"Samma, mishan Allah, samma! Ma'a tezi talieni min tarek! Listen, in name of God, listen! Don't touch the Italians who depart! At talieni ekhuatouna bil dam wa itha rahalun taruku al hadeja! The Italians are our blood brothers and departing they leave gifts for us!"

The woman's melancholic voice had faded away with the dope growers' dirge and from the minaret of the mosque in rue de l'Aérodrome the muezzin was casting the futile appeal, when Angelo and Martino began to burn the newspaper clippings among which was the old copy of *L'écho du Liban*. Still without haste and without curiosity. Especially Angelo who, locked inside the theorem he had solved at Tayoune, awaited the dawn like a man condemned to death. His mind, a magma of thoughts totally alien to the terrible secrets the flames illuminated down to the last word. The thought of a past he now saw with nostalgia, as unappreciated luck and a joy to remember: the bus that carried him from Brianza to Milan and from Milan back to Brianza, the yoke of the family that nagged him with complaints and reproaches, the boredom of the provinces where nothing happens and the only relief is to flirt with the girl next door, the poster of Einstein's witty face and his divine equation, the years spent scaling impervious mountains and descending into the abysses of the sea and leaping into the sky from dizzying heights, the army that compressed the roots of his intellect and pruned the foliage of his maturity to reduce him to a dwarf tree but also to amuse him and to prolong his youth... Then, the thought of a present that didn't arouse any nostalgia and that on the contrary crushed him with the awareness of his guilt. The murderous fly who struggled in the sticky net of the spider ready to squash it and devour it. That poor murderous fly who begged no-spara, don't-shoot, no-spara. The insidious problem one-greater-than-zero which instead of making order out of disorder had introduced a new element of disorder and favored the triumph of Chaos. The raindrop that falling from the apex of the vertical segment became Rashid who pointed at the third ship and locked the rudder and armed the detonator and bawled his victorious Allah-akbar. And, above all, the thought of Ninette. A thought that renewed the questions he used to ask himself at the beginning of their relationship and that now he condensed into a brief, obsessive query. Who-were-you, who-were-you, who-were-you.

He had repeated it so many times, today. For instance, when he had caressed again the cross-shaped anchor with the golden hair rolled around the fluke. That living residue of a dead creature. Or when the compassionate hyena at Tayoune had ended the white mare's agony by shooting the two Kalashnikov bursts aimed at her neck: the second one so precise that the beautiful head had come off the beautiful body as if the bullets were the blade of a guillotine, as if severed by the blade of a guillotine it had tumbled down the grassy bed, and gushing a fountain of blood had rolled to the Pine Wood boulevard where it had remained. Her immense violet eyes, Ninette's eyes, wide open in a flash of relief and her white teeth disclosed in a smile that seemed a thanks. Who-were-you, who-were-you, who-were-you. Only one question haunted him as much: the one provoked by the riddle with which her letter concluded. "I wish you to find the formula you search for. The formula of Life. (It exists, darling, it exists. I know. I can even put you on its trail: it does not derive from a scientific calculus, it is not a mathematical term. It's a word. A simple word that here we pronounce at any pretext. It promises nothing, I warn you. Yet it explains everything, and it helps.)" A word, he kept saying, a word. How can a word explain what numbers do not explain, how can a word help where numbers do not help? And if it does, have I been wrong to believe that my search should take place by means of the sorceress capable of a thousand enchantments and a thousand wonders? Maybe yes. Maybe the answer is not in the abstraction of pure thought, in the bodilessness of numbers. Maybe it really is in the physicality of a word. After all, mathematics has already failed me once: the moment I believed that by shooting Khalid-Passepartout I would cancel the negative act with a positive act: return the system to its initial state... A word! A simple word that here is pronounced at any pretext. But if it is pronounced at any pretext, why haven't I ever heard it? Why don't I hear it now? Do the thunders of war smother its sound? Or is its sound more inaudible than the one of a feather falling on a flower, than the silence of a star exploding in the void? Is it an infrasound of not even two hertz, is it an ultrasound of thousands and thousands of hertz, that is, a sound too low or too high to be registered by human eardrums? Nevertheless a word is not only pronounced, is not only learned through its sound. A word can be written. It can be read, seen! It is also a visible image! So why haven't I ever seen it? Why don't I see it now? And in his laborious pondering he didn't realize (but he would) that we not only hear and see a word: we live it, we breathe it, we touch it. In his wearisome ratiocinating, he didn't understand (but he would) that besides being a sound and a visible image a word is a tangible object: flesh of our flesh. Because its physicality belongs to us, has belonged to us, for millions of years: since the time when we were not yet human and thus we were not capable of thinking, of explaining why one is greater than zero. The remote time, the primordial time, in which everything began and we began. The unseizable time which seems to have vanished from our memory and instead dwells inside it to provide us with the only form of knowledge that never fails: the one that comes from intuition, from instinct.

And having cleared this small problem, let's move on to Martino who unlike Angelo awaited the dawn with joyous impatience. His only worry, finding a way to share his truth with Angelo. That is, availing himself of the Word made flesh to pronounce the three little words he had never pronounced: I-am-gay.

*   *   *

Deaf to the pessimism which had taken possession of Charlie after Zandra Sadr's farewell, and trusting the only form of knowledge that never fails, Martino was absolutely certain that he would leave Beirut alive. Never mind Rashid's threats, he told himself burning the clippings among which was the old copy of *L'écho du Liban,* never mind Charlie's fears: I'm going home. I feel it, I know it. Home, home! God, what a marvel to return home, to take off the gray-green uniform that hampers you and doesn't suit your complexion, to slip back into your tight jeans and Pierrot shirt or into the shocking-pink outfits you wore to mock the perfumed diplomat who cruised you and Albert in Cairo! What a delight to no longer sleep in the Pink Room, no longer see those wardrobes destroyed by macho idiocy, those walls smeared with the bacchanalia of blondes and brunettes, with the orgy of breasts and vaginas and buns and garter-bedecked thighs! What a blessing to no longer witness the sex competitions of Gaspare and Ugo who by now have learned to make love with Lady Godiva and pass all their nights in the bathroom while poor Stefano cries they-abuse-her, they-soil-her, they-treat-her-worse-than-a-prostitute! What a consolation to no longer dwell in this den of desires and temptations where you like one guy because he's stalwart and unreachable, another because he's solid and unbreakable, another because he's grave and mysterious, another because he has Beppe's buttocks and sun-gilded body, and the rest for no reason whatsoever! What a liberation to no longer endure their vulgar jokes and no longer pretend to be like them, no longer live in the terror of betraying yourself and being stuck in the pillory like a plague victim! What a relief to stop acting always zealous and polite and obliging, yes-dear, no-dear, sure-chief, at-once-chief, so that they accept you and give up suspicions! What a pleasure to feel free again to consider your truth an uncomfortable truth but not an impure peculiarity, not a fault to be pardoned, not an illness to be cured with an antibiotic called Woman! You're a faggot and you'll remain a faggot, my dear. So forget the Lucias and the Brunellas, the Adilés and the Giovannas, look for a second Albert and have a queer's life: the future is a promise that begins tomorrow.

Yes, he was really happy, Martino. So happy that he had not bought even a gram of hashish. Do you need hashish, joints, snorts, when the future is a promise that begins tomorrow? But he refused to leave without performing a gesture that would redeem the shams he'd imposed on himself, an act of pride that might replace the kind of fear in which he'd lived in Beirut. Thus, before the departure, he wanted to share his truth with somebody: to pronounce in front of somebody the three little words. Somebody who would listen to him with respect, who would understand him, console him, maybe even express admiration. You're-a-brave-man, Martino. You're-honest, Martino. You-have-dignity. And to realize this dream he'd chosen Angelo: an ideal interlocutor, in his opinion, since he guarded the terrible secret of the Amal killed at the Twenty-Four. I'll tell him the same things I've told Lady Godiva, he thought while burning the precious documents. I'll begin with the arrogant faggots who cackle like hens when people reject them or who shield themselves behind Michelangelo's and Leonardo da Vinci's homosexuality as if being a homosexual signifies being a genius capable of carving the David or painting Mona Lisa, and I'll state at once that I judge them mostly unpleasant. Then I'll face the subject of the army that hates faggots and doesn't permit them to wear the uniform, and I'll say that I enlisted all the same because I was misled by the slogans the army uses to swindle the naive. A-man-has-to-scrve-as-a-soldier, to-become-a-man-you-need-to-become-a-soldier, etcetera. In short, I'll explain that I hoped to find in the army a much better medicine than the antibiotic called Woman, thus an instantaneous recovery, instead I found the other face of queerness: the equally squalid and grotesque phenomenon of male chauvinism, the cult of the fragile cylinder the soldiers invoke at every pretext. Then I'll say that this helped me to understand that being a faggot does not mean not being a man, it simply means not being a male, but I don't want to be a male: I want to be a man and... And at this point he decided. It was almost one in the morning, the vivid tongues of reddish light illuminated the papers more brightly than ever, and Angelo was bending over the trunk to pick up the old copy of *L'écho du Liban*.

"Angelo, I have to tell you something..."

"Yes..." Angelo replied, picking up the old copy of *L'écho du Liban*.

"Something very, very important..."

"Yes..." Angelo replied, stopping for the first time to observe what he was about to toss in the fire.

"A very, very cumbersome secret. As cumbersome as those that we're burning."

"Yes..." Angelo replied, drawing closer to the flames to better see the cover of the magazine.

"And I'll begin with the premise that I've never been able to put up with faggots..."

"Yes..." Angelo replied, still absent-minded and staring at the cover.

There was a photo on the cover. The photo of a handsome middle-aged man with gray-silver hair and features that strikingly resembled his own. Or, better, the features that would have been his own if he were what he had dreamed of being and at least thirty years older. A high and spacious forehead incised with wrinkles revealing an existence full of burdens and responsibilities, eyes grown heavy and disenchanted from seeing too much, cheeks grown dry and hollowed from resting two little, a mouth very severe nay hard. So hard that not even the lips swollen with sensual sweetness managed to soften it. And, beneath the photo, a banner headline: "Qui était l'homme qui auriat pu sauver notre pays." Who was the man who could have saved our country. Beneath the headline, in smaller letters: "Our coverage on pages 13–14–15." At the top left, the date: 15 December 1978.

"Particularly the faggots who boast about their homosexuality and display it in parades, impose it on other people, Angelo. See what I mean?"

"Yes..." Angelo replied, looking for page 13 and beginning to read the article.

It was an article about the highest magistrate of the Lebanese Supreme Court, Chief Justice George Al Sharif, assassinated a week before, at fifty-eight, as he turned on the ignition of his Rolls-Royce and set out to go to attend the opening of the university's academic year. A charge of Tnt, so massive that the car had disintegrated and nothing had remained of the body but a few shreds. It began with a political analysis of the crime, certainly committed by one of the three groups in power: the so-called Warlords, that is, the mighty and honored gangsters who controlled Beirut; the Palestinians of Habbash or of his rival Arafat who equally contended with the Warlords for dominion of the city; and the followers of a tiny Shiite sect called the Black Tulips or Sons of God which had recently joined the rainbow of violence. It continued with a biographical sketch of George Al Sharif, scion of a great Maronite family that for decades had played an essential role in the struggle for the independence of Lebanon, nephew of a famous politician who had been the principal drafter of the 1926 Constitution suspended by the French in 1939, heir to fabulous riches that included oil wells in Nigeria, financier of the railroad that in 1961 had connected the capital with Damascus and Aleppo, and a magistrate of great courage: known and admired for the firmness with which he opposed anybody who nourished the country's backwardness and contributed to the rainbow of violence. Finally, the man whom the good people wanted to see as president of the Republic and, until the age of fifty, the most inveterate and most desirable bachelor in Beirut.

"So I've always viewed my homosexuality as an impure peculiarity, Angelo. As a fault to be pardoned, an illness to be cured..."

"Yes..." Angelo replied, always without paying any attention to his words and turning to page 14.

On page 14 the article told about the woman for whom George Al Sharif had given up his celibacy: Natalia Narakat, twenty-six years younger than he, like him the offspring of a great Maronite family that had always struggled for the independence of Lebanon, heiress to fabulous riches that included gold mines in South Africa, and famous for her extraordinary beauty. But she was also known for her intelligence and her strong personality, the journalist wrote, and for a rather bizarre trait: the fact that she never spoke French, the language everyone in Lebanon spoke. She refused to out of hatred for the French who had killed her father, a well-known mathematician as well as an indomitable patriot, during the bloody repression of the 1945 uprising. And the details of the tragedy, which had happened a few months before her birth, were contained in an interview that Natalia Narakat Al Sharif had given to the London *Times* on the eve of George Al Sharif's assassination.

"That's why I didn't dodge my draft notice, Angelo. See, I really thought that the army would provide me with the cure and the recovery I hadn't been able to find in Lucia, in Brunella, Adilé, Giovanna..."

"Yes..." Angelo replied, continuing to read the article which contained an excerpt from the interview.

An excerpt from which you could derive the portrait of a proud, fearless woman. "Yes, I know that language quite well," Natalia Narakat Al Sharif had told the correspondent from the London *Times*. "As a child I spoke it better than I spoke Arabic: my nanny was Swiss, from Lausanne, and my mother sent me to the École française. But when I was informed that the French had killed my father, that in cold blood and well knowing his identity they had shot him while he was leading a nonviolent cortege, I swore that I would no longer pronounce a single syllable from their vocabulary. I also swore that I would never set foot in France. And I kept both promises. I don't have the slightest idea of what Paris or the Côte d'Azur is like. Nor do I care. And in French I don't even say thank-you or goodbye." On the other hand, the article continued, she spoke perfect English. She had learned it in London, where she'd moved at fourteen to-avoid-hearing-people-express-themselves-in-French, and where she had spent the rest of her adolescence then her early youth. In Beirut, in fact, she had returned the day of her twenty-fourth birthday to attend a garden party thrown in her honor by the British embassy. There she had met George Al Sharif, and a month later she had married him. A lightning-fast love, as inevitable and as inexorable as the love in a Greek tragedy, she had defined it to the London *Times* correspondent. "You know...given the considerable difference of age, some people think that ours was a marriage of convenience: a cynical contract to join our fortunes. Others believe that I found in George the father I never knew: a protector, a guide. Nonsense: I fell in love, I'm in love, with him. Body and soul. So much in love that, if in a street or elsewhere I see a man whose features resemble his, my heart jumps into my throat and I feel the irresistible urge to bump into him and so have the pretext to engage him in a conversation: find out who he is. No, I didn't marry George out of some cynical interest in or need for affection and protection. I didn't even marry him out of admiration, although there's plenty to admire about him and I admire him enormously. I married him for love. A lightning-fast love, as inevitable and as inexorable as the love in a Greek tragedy. Should I lose him, I would become insane. I would end in a psychiatric clinic." And the prediction had come true, the journalist told in the last lines of page 14: now Natalia Narakat Al Sharif was in a psychiatric clinic where, according to the doctors, she was cured of a serious form of manic depression. Not true. Hers wasn't simply a case of manic depression. It was a clear-cut case of unquestionable madness: even if she returned home, a full recovery had to be excluded.

"What I'm saying, Angelo, is that I've surrendered to my truth," Martino concluded with a sigh.

"Yes..." Angelo replied, flipping page 14 and going to page 15.

"And I can finally say those three little words: I am gay!"

"Yes..." Angelo replied, looking at page 15.

"Angelo!"

"Yes..."

"I said I-am-gay!"

But his time Angelo didn't even murmur an empty yes. He remained silent.

He remained silent because he was totally annihilated. And he was totally annihilated because he had seen something, on page 15. Something that, in spite of the undeniable clue offered by the fact that Natalia Narakat Al Sharif refused to speak French and knew English perfectly, in spite of the particular concerning the death of her too much loved husband, he was not ready to see: two large photos of Ninette. One where radiant with happiness and splendidly dressed in her wedding gown she was leaving the church of Notre-Dame-du-Liban on George Al Sharif's arm. One where overcome by an unbearable despair she was struggling with servants who uselessly tried to hold her and keep her from looking at the human shreds that lay among the wreckage of the disintegrated Rolls-Royce.

"Angelo! Aren't you listening to me, Angelo?!?

"Angelo! Didn't you hear what I said?!?

"Angelo! Why don't you talk to me, why?!?"

He didn't because now the annihilation was reinforced by the sight of a title between the two photos. A title that said: "La formule de la Vie." The Formula of Life. And under the title, a statement that said: "How do I resolve the problem of living with this stream of threats aimed at George, I mean in this mixture of happiness and terror? My friend, it's like asking me if the formula of Life exists. Yet I'll answer, I'll do it starting from a sentence that I happened to hear while I was watching a movie on TV: by chance and without paying real attention to it. An extraordinary sentence. So extraordinary that I still wonder whether it is a famous aphorism born from the mind of a great philosopher or the accidental stroke of genius born from the pen of a clever screenwriter... Listen: 'Life is not a problem to solve. It is a mystery to live.' It is, my friend, it is! Nobody can argue the contrary. Thus, the formula exists. It consists of one word. A simple word that here we pronounce at any pretext, that promises nothing, that explains everything, and that helps in all cases: Inshallah. As God wants, as God likes, as God will want, as God will like. Inshallah.''

* * *

Determined to repay themselves for the damages of the truce which at dawn and for several hours would deny them the pleasure of killing and being killed, the Christians and Muslims were meanwhile preparing a reciprocal assault along the Green Line. And very soon, with the contribution of the Druzes who blindly fired from the Shouf Mountains, the bacchanal broke out. Barrages of 105s, 106s, 130s, 155s, mortar shellings, Katyushas, machine guns, Rpg, M16, Kalashnikov volleys. Of course, accompanied by the chorus of the stray dogs' howls and of the crazed roosters' crows for help. "Help! Help! Cock-a-doodle-do, help!" A couple of grenades fell also on the headquarters courtyard, and a fragment wounded Martino who was dragging the empty trunk away. It hit him in the gluteus, poor Martino. And this was the beginning of the last night.

9

A very long night, the last night. At the headquarters, nobody slept. Some wandered through the empty rooms or went up and down the stairs like souls in pain. Some cursed between their teeth or belched out the wildest profanities. Some chain-smoked or stunned themselves with whiskey and coffee liqueur. Some helped themselves by pretending to help others. Pistoia, by dispensing his now false jollity: "Let's cheer up, guys, 'cause tomorrow they'll fuck us with the fireworks and we'll go straight to the bottom!" Sugar, by offering technical advice: "I said it and I repeat it: if it comes, shoot at the engine! Not at the hexogen!" Crazy Horse, by declaiming verses from the *Aeneid:* "Revocate animus maestumque timorem mittite! Forsan et haec olim meminisse juvabit. Free your souls of sadness and fear! Perhaps one day you will like to remember, Virgil says through Aeneas!" As for Charlie, he was so nervous that when the Condor had the bad idea of awarding him a promotion on the field, he snapped: "In due respect, general, if you knew in which part of the body I'd put your promotion..." Only the Professor appeared cool and relaxed. Yet anxiety devoured him, and for good reason: at a certain moment, he had gone out to the courtyard and spoken with Angelo. A conversation that, after packing the *Dialogues* of Plato, the *De Libero Arbitrio* by Erasmus of Rotterdam, Kant's *Critique of Pure Reason,* and the rest of his ponderous library, he reported in the letter to the wife who didn't exist. Twenty dense pages that at dawn he stuck in an envelope addressed to himself.

* * *

I'm writing this letter in the state of mind of a man who may be living the last night of his life, my dear, and if I survive I'll destroy it. (Letters written in the face of death keep their meaning and dignity only when the person who wrote them is dead. Otherwise they sound embarrassing, ridiculous.) Shall I die, shall we die? Shall I survive, shall we survive? Both hypotheses are valid. In fact my colleagues swing back and forth on a seesaw that fluctuates between the most complete optimism and the most complete pessimism: now they claim that nothing is threatening us, that all three ships will safely leave the waters of Beirut, and now they insist that the third truck will arrive just from those waters to hit just the ship on which the headquarters personnel will be embarking. I dread the first hypothesis, though. I expect to die. Because...God, how cruel and sadistic chance can be! An hour ago, while I was strolling along the corridors, I noticed a fire that flickered in the courtyard. I ran outside to see what was burning, and guess whom I found in front of a trash can of ignited gasoline? The interpreter of the Arab Bureau and the sergeant-mathematician who inspired the key character in my miniature Iliad. As downcast as if he had suffered a tremendous disappointment or a deep humiliation, the first one was burning some papers he picked up from a trunk. As petrified as if he had seen a ghost or had been shocked by the most undreamed-of revelation, the second one was staring at a magazine he held in his hand. And in the light of the reddish flames he seemed so aged that for a moment I wondered if it were really him. A forehead incised with wrinkles revealing an existence full of burdens and responsibilities, eyes grown heavy and disenchanted from seeing too much, cheeks grown dry and hollowed from resting too little, a mouth very severe nay hard. So hard that not even his lips swollen with sensual sweetness managed to soften it, and he looked more than fifty years old: the father of himself. I approached him. Attributing all that to an overflow of grief (the gorgeous woman he unknowingly loved was executed in Gobeyre during the Christmas battle), I patted him on the shoulder. Then I took the magazine from his hands, I tossed it into the flames, I led him to the former briefing room where I preached him a little sermon about time that heals all wounds, about the joy of living that would bloom again in Italy, and for a little while I was under the impression that he agreed. With his head bowed, he nodded. But at the word Italy he raised that face thirty years older than his, and: "Sir, we shall not go back to Italy. And I can demonstrate why." Then he did. And, though his demonstration is rather an enthymeme, I mean a reasoning that lacks the premise on which it is based, though I sense in it a gap that hides something...

His certainty derives from a trigonometry problem he enunciates with three elements which I find arbitrary because of the missing premise. One: that the kamikaze motorboat be hidden among the numerous motorboats moored in the inlet next to the western wharf we'll leave from. Two: that such motorboat move exactly when the ship exits the port and, at the speed of six knots, set an arc of parabola pointing northwest. Three: that the motorboat dash against the ship at the speed of thirty then thirty-five knots while keeping a trajectory of forty-five degrees with respect to the ship's left side. All elements according to which the ship and the motorboat cover the stretch of sea leading to the point of collision in the same time: sixty-four seconds. So, after explaining his calculations and the obtained result, he said: "Sir, it's inevitable that the motorboat hits the ship, and that the ship blows up." I rebelled. I protested that the results of a problem are valid when they are supported by the elements from which the problem departs, and his elements didn't support anything because rather than elements they were reasonable fantasies: logical conjectures deduced from the calculus of probability. Who told him that the motorboat existed and was hidden in precisely that inlet?!? Who told him that it would really move the moment the ship exits the port, that it would really accelerate from thirty to thirty-five knots, that it would really keep a trajectory of forty-five degrees with respect to the left side of the ship?!? Who told him that the ship would really exit the port at the speed of six knots and with an arc of parabola pointing northwest?!? And even if things developed in the way his reasonable fantasies and logical conjectures anticipated, who told him that the fleet's cannons wouldn't hit the motorboat before the motorboat would hit the ship?!? But he didn't stir an inch, and raising those eyes grown heavy and disenchanted from seeing too much he coolly replied: "Mathematics, sir. In mathematics, absolute certainty never exists. To reveal an unknown quantity we always start with reasonable fantasies, logical conjectures that we deduce from the calculus of probability. And if a probability borders on certainty, speaking of certainty is more than legitimate. And I promise you that the probability of being hit by the motorboat borders on certainty. As for the 'almost' which separates abso-*

lute certainty from near certainty, its name is destiny: Inshallah. As God wants, as God likes, as God will want, as God will like: Inshallah." In short, he shut me up. Later, though, he did worse. Because when I asked him if he had found the formula he was searching for, the formula of Life, he replied: "Yes, sir. I just gave it to you. It is the word Inshallah. Destiny, Inshallah. But it is a word I abhor, and in order to accept it, I must disprove the formula of Death." Well...this knocked me down. Because whether he disproves or not the formula of Death, I too abhor the word destiny, the word Inshallah. Most people see it as a hope, a good omen, and identify it with their trust in the divine mercy. I see it as a submission, instead, as a renunciation of ourselves. Heavenly-Father, Omnipotent-Lord, Jehovah, Allah, Brahma, Baal, Adonai, or whatever-they-call-you: choose-for-me, decide-for-me. No thanks. I refuse to delegate my will and my mind to God. I refuse to renounce myself, to submit myself. A submitted man is a dead man before he dies, and I don't want to be dead before I die! I don't want to be dead when I die! I want to be alive when I die!

I want to be alive when I die, and I've never felt so alive. My heart has never beat better, my lungs have never breathed better, my brain has never thought better: how many things it thinks tonight! So many that to tell them all I should live for millennia. And if the calculus of probability offers a near certainty bordering on absolute certainty, ahead of me there are no more than twelve hours of life: just the time to tell you a few of those many things. Which? Well: to begin with, that I don't believe anymore in the trade I used to believe in deeply. The soldier's trade. And how to explain to you such metamorphosis? Maybe with the story I heard last night. A loathsome, terrible story... Remember Sister Espérance, Sister George, Sister Milady, Sister Madeleine, Sister Françoise, the five nuns I wanted to include in the cast of my miniature Iliad? Well, the latter two are safe and sound: Sister Madeleine in Marseilles where she managed to escape and Sister Françoise at the Rizk as usual. But Sister Espérance and Sister George and Sister Milady who had remained inside the convent... I was informed by Gigi the Candid, in his turn informed by an Amal who'd impotently or cowardly witnessed what is now called the-martyrdom-of-the-three-nuns. Poor Gigi. He wept like a child, and as he wept he repeated: "I cannot tell Armando, I cannot tell Falcon... I cannot, I cannot..." Sister Espérance was lucky. She died fighting, repelling the Sons of God with the altar's crucifix, in the basement where they'd found them. Using it like a sword she split open the face of their leader, a hunchbacked mullah with a crimson turban and the Koran dangling from his bandolier, and a Kalashnikov volley in the chest downed her. Sister George, no: she was not lucky. Rabid over his split-open face, in fact, the hunchbacked mullah dragged her up into the chapel. And here killed her slowly: with bayonet thrusts. Meanwhile she prayed, she recited the Ave Maria. "Je vous salue, Marie, pleine de grâce, le Seigneur est avec vous, soyez vous bénie entre toutes les femmes et béni soit le fruit de vos entrailles..." As for Sister Milady, look: there were at least thirty Sons of God. And after stripping her naked and tying her up, one by one they raped her and sodomized her. Yes: just like the Palestinian women who were raped and sodomized by the phalangists during the Sabra and Shatila massacre, just like the Maronite women who were raped and sodomized by the Palestinians during the Damour massacre. Then they left her to die: they didn't even bother to finish her off with a bullet. This city of infected hyenas. This necropolis run by necrophages for whom killing or being killed is the way to live. The only way. This capital of militarism, the most abject militarism, where even the children are soldiers and the soldier's trade has replaced every other. Because those Sons of God were soldiers. That mullah was a soldier. A soldier, soldiers, of an irregular army, but soldiers. As soldiers they had conquered the hill, as soldiers they had died to conquer it, as soldiers they had burst into the convent... My dear, it's too easy to blame these turpitudes on the war. Too easy to take shelter behind the abstract entity called war, that term "war" that we keep referring to as if it were an original sin or a divine curse. The subject to face and condemn is not the war. It is the men who make war, the soldiers, it is the most ancient and unchanged and unchangeable trade which exists: the soldier's trade. The trade that I loved, I respected, I idealized, and that I now repudiate. Because I've identified its fundamental error, its congenital taint.

What error, what taint? In my first letter I wrote that the protoanthropoid guarding his cave, the hominid who used his cudgel to keep enemies and wild beasts at bay, was a soldier. Yes, he was. A soldier identical to the soldiers who stayed in the sentry boxes of our bases, at our checkpoints, on our guard towers, in our posts at Bourji el Barajni or Shatila. Exactly identical: I remember him well. Because I knew him well three million years ago, when I too was a protoanthropoid, a hominid. I called him by name. I called him Rocco, I called him Rambo, I called him Ferruccio, Fabio, Matteo, Luca, Nicola, String, Nazarene, Onion, Stefano, Martino, Fifì, Gaspare, Ugo, Bernard le Français, Salvatore Bellezza son of the late Onofrio... And never mind if he didn't wear a uniform, if he didn't have a flak jacket or a helmet, if he went naked or covered with an animal pelt. Never mind if he couldn't walk erect and didn't stand at attention. His age was identical, and so was his naiveté, his credulity, his innocence, his habit of grumbling and complaining about everything. I'm-cold, I'm-tired, I'm-scared, I-want-to-bang, I-want-to-go-home. I re-

member this, too. And then I remember that I felt such a pity for him, such a tenderness. Each time he complained, I felt like saying: all right, son, go warm yourself up. Go take a rest, go get over your fear, go bang your girl, go home. I'll guard the tribe in your place, I'll chase the mammoth away from the cave. The point is that the soldier's trade doesn't consist solely of guarding his tribe, of chasing the mammoth away from his cave. It also consists of enlarging his tribe's territory, of increasing his tribe's power and faith. A task the soldier accomplishes by recalling the first lesson he has been taught. One, those who don't surrender their territory or give up their faith are enemies. Two, enemies are to be destroyed. Three, destroying them is the right and duty of every soldier as well as a privilege granted by the impunity of the soldier's trade. So, when he's ordered to exercise that right and duty and privilege, the protoanthropoid I called and call Rambo or Ferruccio or Fabio or Matteo or Luca or Nicola or String or Nazarene or Onion or Stefano and so on, obeys. In spite of his naiveté, his credulity, his innocence, his habit of grumbling and complaining about everything, he goes off to conquer the other caves: to enlarge his tribe's territory, to increase his tribe's power and faith. No longer cold, no longer tired, no longer scared, no longer pathetic, he breaks into them. He raises his cudgel and, certain of performing an act for which he will be praised not punished, he kills whomever he finds. Men, women, young people, old people, children, nuns. In the name of God, of Allah, of Jehovah, of Brahma, of Baal or whatever, in the name of capitalism, of communism, of fascism, of socialism, of nazism, of liberalism, of democracy and naturally of the fatherland, he shatters the chest of Sister Espérance who defends herself with a crucifix that is her sword. He stabs Sister George who doesn't even defend herself and recites the Ave Maria. He undresses, ties up, rapes, sodomizes Sister Milady. He leaves her to die without even bothering to finish her off with a bullet. And when he's ordered to exercise his right and duty and privilege upon his own tribe, I mean upon the supposed enemies who live in his cave, he obeys in the same way. Once more in the name of God, of Allah, of Jehovah, of Brahma, of Baal or whatever, once more in the name of capitalism, communism, fascism, socialism, nazism, liberalism, democracy, and naturally the fatherland, kills his own brothers and sisters. He shoots them, he stabs them, rapes them, sodomizes them, then leaves them to die. Skip the hypocrisies and the illusions: not always but often, soldiers stain themselves with atrocious guilt. Not always but often, and whether they go naked or covered with an animal pelt, whether they wear the galloned uniforms of a regular army or the slapdash ones of an irregular army, they commit atrocious crimes. Felonies for which, if they were civilians, they would be arrested by *the police and tried by a jury and condemned to death or to life in prison. Or, at least, judged insane and shut up inside an asylum. When I wrote that the uniform is a monk's cowl, a Franciscan concept, an act of humility, I wasn't thinking of this. Tonight I am, instead, and I feel myself a party to those crimes. Because, although I never taught my soldiers to kill nuns, although I never ordered them to practice violence inside or outside their cave, I told them that destroying the enemy (or whomever we define as the enemy) is the soldier's right and duty and privilege. Directly or indirectly, I also told them that to kill as a civilian is a crime which sends you to jail or to the gallows or to the asylum; to kill as a soldier is a virtue which gets you gold and silver medals and laurel crowns. In short, I cheated them. I made them believe that there are two ways of judging Good and Evil. Two opposed concepts of Good and Evil.*

No concept is more aleatory and misunderstood than the concept of Good and Evil: we know it. From the day men realized they were men (a terrifying discovery that I'm very happy to have not been a witness to) we have done nothing but use that concept without giving it an objective definition. All those we've collected in about fifty centuries are transient exegeses, interpretations offered or dictated by an epoch's fashions or a society's prejudices, as well as mendacities imposed by fanaticism or by momentary interests. In any case, discouraging imbecilities: you'll admit it, and... No, my dear, I don't forget what I used to say back in the days when we discussed the problem with the sacred texts at hand: the alluring days when the sentences of Plato and Plotinus, Saint Augustine and Descartes, Spinoza and Kant, flew around us like confetti. Demanding an objective definition of Good and Evil made sense when Good and Evil were two ethical categories, a moral problem, I said. It made sense when God and the Devil were alive and God vouched for Good by promising Paradise, the Devil vouched for Evil by threatening Hell. That is, when the great religions of salvation determined our behavior. And sin was taken seriously. But now that God and the Devil are dead, killed off by our Nietzsches and Freuds and Marxes, now that the great religions of salvation have been discredited by our science and our rationalism, now that Paradise and Hell have become a pair of fables, sin is no longer taken seriously: Good and Evil no longer constitute two ethical categories, a moral problem. At the most, they represent a medical problem: a state of psychic health or non-health, a balance or imbalance due to the biochemical phenomena that influence our brain's functions. Thus, I used to say, an objective definition no longer makes sense. Tonight I don't say it. Even though I continue to reject the idea of an Almighty and of a Satan, even though I keep refusing the metaphysics of the Beyond, tonight I say that there was some truth in the arguments of those who took sin seriously. The arguments of the Messiahs who promised Paradise or threatened Hell to induce men to be a little less wicked, the arguments of the apostles who through the Messiah's deification appealed to their willpower and responsibility. And I add: it is not possible that Good and Evil are composed of hemoglobin and chlorophyll, vitamins and hormones. It is not possible that they depend on metabolism, on the biosynthesis of carbohydrates and lipids and proteins, on the percentage of nucleic acid and phosphorus the gray matter contains. It isn't possible that willpower counts for nothing, that responsibility is worthless, that even science mutters Inshallah! And if I'm wrong, if the heirs of Nietzsche and Freud and Marx are right, then I issue a challenge to them. I defy them to produce Good in the pharmaceutical laboratories: to manufacture an ointment or an unguent, a syrup, a pill, a suppository, an intravenous or intramuscular injection. A vaccine that prevents us from raping, sodomizing, killing in our own cave or in the caves of others. A medicine that can be purchased at the drugstore. Otherwise we must reinvent the moral problem. At the cost of reviving God and the Devil, Paradise and Hell, and risking new Torquemadas and having to fight them again, we must reinvent it and provide the objective definition. Objective and simple, easy, usable everywhere and forever. Something like this: "Good is what does good, meaning goodness. Evil is what does evil, meaning badness." And then we must exhume the idea of sin, the consciousness of sin. We must teach once again that those who do evil commit sin and those who commit sin must be punished. Dead or alive. Finally, we must translate all this into every language, scribble it on every wall, print it in every newspaper, broadcast it over every radio and TV: until everybody learns it by heart. Everybody, beginning with the soldiers I cheated with the two ways of judging Good and Evil, the two opposed concepts of Good and Evil. Anyway, whether I live or I die, I'm bidding the soldier's trade farewell.

Whether I live or I die, I bid farewell to the writer's trade too. No: I shall not give birth to my miniature Iliad, the novel I intended to write with a smile on the lips and a tear in the eyes. The lucid madness is dissolved, the pregnancy is aborted, and if you ask me what aborted it... Well, I could answer that the euphoria I felt playing the drum of literary voluptuousness and of creative heroism has faded away because I've realized that along with being a monstrous sacrifice, an unbearable solitude, a Tantalan torture (the masochism that Colette spoke about), writing is something worse: a perpetual discontent with ourselves and therefore a perpetual trial of ourselves, a perpetual condemnation of ourselves. (Oh, do I despise the impromptu writers, the amateur writers, the phony writers who think they can piss gold and do not know the self-discontent, the self-trial, the self-condemnation!) In other words, I could answer: "My dear, I've discovered that I don't like writing, that as a matter of fact I hate it, that without being Mozart I make mine the tragic rebuttal with which the poor wretch silenced an idiot who pestered him by repeating how beautiful music is. 'Monsieur, moi je déteste le musique!' Sir, I do detest music!" I could also answer that I've reflected upon the writer's trade in the same way I reflected upon the soldier's trade, and that also in it I've found congenital taints: organic defects which devalue the monstrous sacrifice and ridicule the perpetual self-condemnation. For example, by no means is it the most useful work which exists. The eighteenth-century philosopher Jean-Baptiste d'Alembert was right when he said that on a desert island, a poet (read writer) is not very useful. A land surveyor, yes. On a desert island, I add, any peasant or carpenter or cobbler or gravedigger or midwife or toothpuller is more useful than a writer. When it comes to the immediate necessities of existence, the writer is a superfluous trinket. An unnecessary item. In an organized community, instead, he may turn out being as useful as a peasant or a carpenter or a cobbler or a gravedigger or a midwife or a toothpuller, but he becomes a double-edged sword: a two-faced Janus who, maybe, unwillingly or unaware, can cause and does cause a lot of trouble. No, my dear, I'm not denying the metaphor of the dowser who finds water in any desert, the allegory of the eternally pregnant cow who delivers calves in the form of ideas. I'm not disavowing the gifts of Merlin the Wizard, his ability to see things the others cannot see, to hear things the others cannot hear, to imagine things the others cannot imagine, to anticipate and conveys ideas. Indeed the writer may achieve such miracles. But, here comes what in my second letter I didn't stress: an unavoidable hindrance prevents those miracles from producing the best results. What hindrance? Well... Miracles are stuff which belong to the realm of saints. And, far from being a saint, a writer is a man or a woman with all the flaws of a human being (often aggravated by his or her excess of receptivity), all the impotences of a human being (often magnified by the public exposure that the writer's trade requires). So, not always is the water he or she finds pure. Not always are the calves he or she delivers healthy. Not always are the ideas he or she anticipates and conveys splendid ideas...

Let's be frank: sometimes they're not even ideas. They're masturbations of ideas, ideologies that enslave the intelligence and prevent us from having ideas, inanities that on paper seem to be noble dreams and in daily reality show themselves to be gross blunders. Other times, instead, they're diabolical suggestions: poisonous projects that can only lead to carnages.

In the best cases, they're sacrosanct protests which in good faith intend to eradicate a cancer but end up generating another cancer. (You must admit that behind every bloodbath called revolution there is a book. Behind every constitutionalized insanity there is a book. Behind every act of collective violence there is a book. Behind every genocide, a Mein Kampf.*) And what about the writers who nourish the cancer by licking the feet of the king or the queen in charge, that is, by prostituting themselves to the power that pays in money and privilege? What about those who preach well but do the contrary of what they preach? Every mea culpa of the writer should include the interminable list of those hypocrites. Just to give you a hint: the Senecas who counsel frugality but live in luxury, who urge for rectitude but heap up fortunes by purchasing for a few sesterces the properties of the citizens Nero exiled or executed. The Montaignes who plead for solidarity but hole up in their castle when the cholera epidemic reaches Bordeaux where they serve as mayor, so that it's no use begging them   mister-mayor-please-poke-your-head-out-on-the-balcony-and-say-a-few-encouraging-words. The Rousseaus who exhort the citizens to educate the young but abandon to a squalid orphanage their five children borne by poor Marie-Thérèse Levasseur. The Alfieris who hail liberty but tyrannize their relatives and beat their insufficiently zealous valet until he spits blood, or who break the bones of the barber guilty of cutting off one of their ringlets. The Tolstoys who sing the joys of matrimony and the duties of humanitarianism but betray their wives and deflower their maids and ravish the defenseless women hoeing their land. The Marxes who condemn the infamies of capital but marry the wealthy baroness, choose their friends only among the rich, and get angry if their daughter falls in love with a penniless clerk... In short, and although I cannot argue with Seneca when he wittily says that being able to preach the right things doesn't mean being able to practice them, although I know that in the end writing is an art (a cursed art) not an apostolate to be exercised in the name of public utility, although I realize that every creative work is polluted by human inconsistencies and duplicities, I could answer that what aborted the pregnancy of my miniature Iliad was an intellectual disenchantment. But I would be telling a lie, my dear: the real reason why I shall never write my novel with a smile on the lips and a tear in the eyes is quite different. It is that, like you, I do not exist. I am nothing but a product of fantasy, a divertissement littéraire, an invention expressed through words and committed to a papery essence. In fact this novel has already been written by someone else. At this point, it only lacks an epilogue.*

Just so, my dear. Just so. Shall we finally solve the charade and reveal how things really are, always were? Not long ago a shadow with a knap-

sack on its shoulders, the shadow of the Saigon journalist, fell on this letter. And using the words I used to announce my pregnancy she said to me: "I did write that book, Professor. I did bring forth the novel in which I wanted to tell the unchanged and unchangeable story of Man who at war manifests his whole truth because nothing reveals him as much as war, nothing exacerbates with the same strength his beauty and his ugliness, his intelligence and his stupidity, his bestiality and his humanity, his courage and his cowardice: his enigma. Now I only have to give it an epilogue." Then she summarized it for me, and while I listened I felt as if I were dropping into the abyss of a mise-en-abîme. You know, the ploy of painting or photographing a mirror which reflects a second mirror which in its turn reflects the first mirror, each one reflecting the other to infinity, in a succession of images that become smaller and smaller, darker and darker, so that when you look at them you feel as if you are dropping into an abyss... Because everything she said, everything, coincided with the book I thought I was writing: with the novel I thought was my novel. The theme developed on the framework of an equation expressing the eternal struggle between Life and Death; the plot sewn with the concept of destiny that our reason rejects and that a mysterious mechanism alien to our free will confirms; the multitude of characters including the key character of the young mathematician who sees Boltzmann's $S = K \ln W$ as the formula of Death and thus combats it by searching for the formula of Life; the arc of time in which the story unfolds, that is, the three months from a Sunday in late October to a Sunday in late January; the curtain that rises on the stray dogs that eat themselves up and the double slaughter that sets off the chain of events; the haunting third truck that the Christmas battle seems to dispel and instead materializes... Finally, the dilemma (always unspoken yet always present) which in the last pages looms with the question: is it really destructive, the Chaos that according to Boltzmann's equation devours Life? Is it really Death that wins over Life? I tried to defend myself, to take advantage of the mise-en-abîme. "Then I wasn't wrong to suspect you of being my alter ego," I mumbled. But she shook her head. "On the contrary, Professor: it was you who were the alter ego. My alter ego. The time has come to admit it, Professor: you do not exist. Like the others, you are only a product of fantasy: a divertissement littéraire, an invention expressed through words and committed to a papery essence. It was I who moved the puppets on the tragicomedy's stage, Professor. It was I who laughed with them and at them, who wept with them and for them, who loved and hated and suffered with them, who died with them. It was I who feared not having enough fingers to hold the many threads I'd created. You, Angelo, Ninette or rather Natalia Narakat Al Sharif and

*George Al Sharif, Passepartout and Rashid, Bilal and Gassàn, Charlie,
the Condor, Crazy Horse, Eagle, Sandokan, Sugar, Pistoia, Falcon, Gigi
the Candid, Armando Golden Hands, the five nuns, Imaam, Sanaan,
Leyda, Mahomet, the five Americans, the white mare of Tayoune, the
extras, the crowd of the young soldiers that you knew, I knew three million
years ago when I too was a protoanthropoid and had to fight the mammoth... Each of you, an alter ego of myself. An aspect or a possible aspect of
myself, an image reflected in the mirror with which I tried to tell once
again the unchanged and unchangeable story of the two-handed mammal fitted for standing erect etcetera, much funnier than the other mammals and more touching than any other animal." I rebelled. I retorted
that no, I was not like the others. Because by means of me she had done
something deeper than telling a story: she'd explained it! And even if I
were like the others, hadn't she written that words are tangible objects?
Hadn't she defined them as flesh of the flesh, the Word made flesh? I
physically existed, by now, I was flesh of her flesh. She couldn't suppress my
physicality, then! She couldn't annul it, reduce it to a papery essence! The
fact is that all writers, all, say one thing and do another. While I was
struggling to stay alive, my puppeteer vanished with her belongings. That
is, with the book and the tomorrow which might have been ahead of me.*

*Now I only have a few pages, a few hours to go, and look: the dawn is
about to rise. The night is melting into a tender violet, the rackets of the
nocturnal combat are fading. Along the corridors, the bustle has multiplied, the voices have grown in volume. "Get ready!" they yell. "The convoy is assembling!" Soon they will call me, I'll have to say goodbye: see how
short life is? Too, too short! Whether we're made of words and paper,
whether we're made of flesh, it lasts no longer than a desert flower. One of
those flowers that blossom at daybreak and wither at sunset. I never saw
them, but somewhere I read that they're very beautiful. Maybe they're very
beautiful because they last only the space of a day. This makes them precious and... They've called me. They call me. I must go. Goodbye, my dear,
goodbye. And thank you. Because although you were just a product of
fantasy, an image reflected in the mirror, an idea, you gave me more
than a person in the flesh. Is solitude, then, the only companion we have to
feel less alone? Is fantasy the only reality? Are being born and living and
dying a dream like the dream of dreams, that God whom we implore in
despair, whom we demand to exist when we know or we think that he does
not exist, that he has been invented by us?*

EPILOGUE

THAT DAY THE SUN ROSE to bring the bluest sky ever seen in Beirut (or so it appeared to anyone who scanned the sky in the hope of finding there a sign of good luck), and as it rose the cannons fell silent. With the cannons, the mortars. With the mortars, the machine guns and the Kalashnikovs and the M16s and the Rpg. From that moment the truce became effective, and a flagship helicopter could safely land on the paved esplanade of the Logistics base to pick up Martino who whined face-down on a stretcher while Charlie consoled him. "Don't complain, fool. Thanks to a couple of holes in the butt, you're going home." Soon afterwards the helicopter took off for the Rizk where it picked up Rocco who kept mumbling Imaam-watch-Imaam and Falcon, who unaware of Sister Espérance's fate, bid his goodbye to Sister Françoise with these words: "Please, Sister, as soon as possible ask the Mother Superior to write me and tell me if she liked my tennis racket." At almost the same time, Sugar and Pistoia left the headquarters to return Salvatore Bellezza son of the late Onofrio to his old embassy squad then to reach the port and organize the arrival of the final convoy. Before leaving, however, Sugar did something for which in the past he would have arrested himself: he halted in front of the hideous painting he had always considered an imperishable work of art, the portrait of the emir in his yellow turban and blue cloak, and under Pistoia's incredulous eyes he stole it.

Two minor events which deserve some details. The reinstatement of Salvatore Bellezza son of the late Onofrio, in fact, was not appreciated. At the mere sight of his face, the squad leader who had lost the two upper and the two lower premolars started to howl I'll-kill-him, I'll-kill-him, and Glass Eye was seized by an attack of hysteria. I'll-resign-I'll resign! The theft of the emir's portrait, on the contrary, had a glorious outcome. Here it is. Before dawn, a freighter full of weapons for the phalangists had anchored at the western wharf's dock acquired by Pistoia. Exploiting the vertical trenches it now unloaded artillery pieces, and there was no way to make its captain give up the intrusion: he said that he'd been authorized by Gassàn and, unless Gassàn ordered him to go, he wouldn't go. Shrugging his shoulders Gassàn added that he couldn't give such an order because the eastern wharf was full, that the Italians had to be patient, that they could embark tomorrow, and all at once Pistoia remembered the Pistoia he had once been. He went to the jeep, grabbed the painting Sugar had hidden under his bags, crashed it so furiously over the head of Gassàn that the poor guy remained with his neck stuck through the emir's face: the emir's forked beard and emerald-ruby clasp under his throat, the half-moon eyebrows and the yellow turban with the teardrop pearl under his nape. "And if you don't order that gatecrasher to clear out on the double, you won't make it to Switzerland, Gassàn. Because this time I'll cut your throat for real: understand?" Gassàn understood, gave the order, and the freighter moved out.

After receiving word that the wharf and the dock had been freed, the Condor authorized Charlie to proceed with the payment of the toll. A bitter ceremony which took place in the former briefing room with Zandra Sadr's sons escorted by twelve heavily armed militiamen avidly staring at the large cherry-wood table, and which developed in the most disastrous way. Because, when Charlie reiterated the four conditions put forth by the Condor and solicited the assurances that in the farewell encounter His Most Reverend Eminence had avoided with an evasive I-understand, I-understand, a sepulchral silence fell. And when he suggested sealing the promise with a handshake, the tall bearded son grumbled that he didn't shake hands with anybody and the blond one extended his hand as though he expected it to be kissed. The meaningful episode was followed by the delivery of the field hospital where, seeing for the last time the costly ambulances that would have aroused the envy of a deluxe clinic, the tidy wards with their neatly made beds and their immaculate sheets, the operating rooms, the radiology units, the dental lab, the torrents of medicine and blood plasma, a medical officer fainted and had to be laid on a stretcher. Immediately after there was the delivery of the provisions, and this time it was Charlie who got sick. Of course Charlie knew very well that the 716 million and 315.714 liras calculated on the discount prices the wholesalers give to the army corresponded to mountains of food and rivers of beverages: a lavishness which could have appeased the hunger of the entire city for weeks. Not by accident, during the negotiations, he'd used the disparaging terms swag and loot. Yet, and in spite of the meticulous list provided by Crazy Horse, he hadn't realized that two-fifths of the mountains consisted of pork and sausages. Four-fifths of the rivers, of wine and beer and liqueurs. So, when the gigantic refrigerators and the immense warehouses were opened, he wobbled. In a fit of dizziness he sat on a peak of prosciutti, leaned against a wall of bottles, and mumbled: "I'm about to pass out. Uncork something and let me have a drop." At Bourji el Barajni and Shatila, meanwhile, the marò and the paratroopers vacated their posts, and a sorrowful scream was rebounding from house to house: "Al-talieni tarak, the Italians are leaving!" With the cry, the vain plea: "Min tarak! Don't leave, min tarak!" And, almost always, those who cried were the same ones who used to torment and deride them with threats and the insults: talieni-maccaroni-manjukin, Italians-macaroni-faggots, talieni-ibn-sharmuta, Italians-sons-of-bitches, talieni-tomorrow-kaputt, Italians-tomorrow-your-turn. Suddenly those alien soldiers who picked up their trash, who gave them free medical treatment, who put gladiolus on the communal grave, who defended them from the Shiites and the phalangists and whoever wanted to make them pay for their past cruelties had become indispensable and irreplaceable. Min-tarak, don't-leave, min-tarak.

Once the toll was paid and the Bourji el Barajni and Shatila posts were vacated, the final convoy assembled along rue de l'Aérodrome and the Street Without a Name: two huge columns that meeting at a right angle at the rond-point of Shatila extended all the way to the airport and to the Ramlet el Baida littoral. The M113s, the Leopards, the armored cars, the tankers, the trucks with cranes or trailers, the jeeps, the motorcycles, the transports full of troops. And, around the two huge columns, a spectacle which would have enraged Rashid more than ever. Girls in despair who searched for their paratrooper or their marò: "Franco! Dove sei, where are you, Franco?" "Mario! Rispondimi, answer me, Mario!" Paratroopers and marò who leaned out of the transports or the armored cars or the tanks, and with broken voices answered them: "Farida, sono qui! I'm here, Farida!" "Leila, vieni qui! Come here, Leila!" Children who clambered up on the M113s and the Leopards to say goodbye and to hand their friends a gift: "Edoardo! Io portare pistacchi per viaggio! Me bring you pistachios for travel!" "Antonio! Io dare te ancora hashish per Italia! Me give you more hashish for Italy!" Women who sadly waved their handkerchiefs: "Ma'a salama! Goodbye, ma'a salama!" Among the women, a tiny old one in chador who blew kisses and shrieked: "Viva Gesù! Long live Jesus!" And, behind her, Imaam who sobbing and jumping from vehicle to vehicle said to everybody: "Monsieur, je vous en prie, I beg of you, do you know if Rocco's wounded leg is healed? Monsieur, je vous en prie! If you see Rocco, tell him that I shall always wait for him!'' The convoy was supposed to be led by the Professor. But, just as he was about to take command of it, a wild shout rent the air. The shout of the Condor who at the verge of exasperation yielded to Crazy Horse's querulous request. "Okay, colonel, go! God blasted, go! Scram or I'll stuff that bloody monocle down your throat!'' Soon after, Crazy Horse jumped on the headquarters' Leopard. Red with joy and emerging from the hatch in the equestrian statue pose he'd assumed on Christmas Eve, he went to place himself at the head of the column arrayed along rue de l'Aérodrome. Then he unsheathed his riding crop, and: "Qui nihil sperare potest desperet nihil! Those who have nothing to hope don't despair for anything, Seneca says! Let's go, valorous gentlemen!''

Followed by a chorus of go-fuck-yourself-and-Seneca, touch-your-balls-for-good-luck, the Leopard crossed the rond-point of Shatila and entered avenue Nasser. It passed the corner that had been the corner of the Twenty-Four, the vacant lot that had been the vacant lot of the Twenty-Five, the little square that had been the little square of the Twenty-Two, it turned onto rue Argàn, onto the short boulevard that led to Tayoune, it reached the spot where the white mare's head had rolled gushing its fountain of blood, and right there a whinny echoed throughout the entire Pine Wood. "Halt, for heaven's sake! Halt!'' Then, while the convoy halted, Crazy Horse climbed out of the Leopard. He approached the beautiful head by now covered with flies, he looked at the immense violet eyes wide open in a flash of relief, at the white teeth disclosed in a smile that seemed to say thanks, he mounted the grassy bed where the big white body lay also covered with flies. Here he bent down to examine the wounds in the belly, in the hocks, the withers, the knee, the rump, he understood what the snipers had done, and quivering with indignation he turned to the crew in the Leopard. He said: "Get down, gentlemen, and form a picket! For we must pay our respects to this brave soldier!'' Embarrassed and over-whelmed by the paradox, five paratroopers formed the picket. At the present-arms they gripped their M12s, stood at attention, at attention they observed ten seconds of silence. Then they climbed back on board, swerving to avoid the brave soldier's head the Leopard moved again, the convoy followed, and at that time an extraordinary thing happened. One of those things that induce you to make a transient, momentary peace with the human race. Because, although nobody had given the order, every vehicle swerved in the same manner. Every one. Including those who were two miles back, thus didn't even know why the convoy had stopped. Not a single track, not a single wheel, grazed the handsome muzzle or the long silky bloodstained mane. Yet, avoiding that tiny obstacle was difficult. Very difficult. The head lay in fact in the middle of the boulevard and if you swerved too much to the right you ended up scraping the trees, if you swerved too much to the left you ended up mounting the grassy bed and squashing the body. Worse: as the flies had turned the white of the muzzle into gray, and its gray blended with the gray of the asphalt, from afar it was not visible. Only when you reached the end of the boulevard you saw it. But at this point it appeared in front of your vehicle like a cat that springs from the dark, and you had less than a second to swerve.

As soon as the two columns were out of the Italian sector, the Condor ordered that the Italian flag still flying in the headquarters courtyard be hauled down. Surprisingly choking back his tears he rolled it up, he took the wheel of his jeep, and preceded by a squad of carabinieri he left. He went to join the convoy's tail. An instant later the twelve militiamen who had accompanied Zandra Sadr's sons returned with an electric saw. They reentered the empty villa, they sawed in four sections the untransportable cherry-wood table that during the signing of the notarial acts had stirred their desires. They loaded the sections into a station wagon, and beneath the eyes of the multitude that still crowded rue de l'Aérodrome they drove off. Then, encouraged by the example, the Amal who now guarded the field hospital broke loose. And the looting began. It began and developed at a vertiginous speed: the swiftness of piranhas that attack a cow fallen in the water and strip its flesh off, reduce it to a skeleton. In the space of a few minutes the costly ambulances, the supplies of blood plasma, the avalanches of medicine, the mobile operating room, the scintigraphy machine, the radiology unit, the dental lab disappeared to be sold in the black markets of the Old City. And what remained was ransacked by the multitude that still crowded rue de l'Aérodrome, in a Boltzmannian chaos which combined the most disconcerting barbarity with the most touching innocence. Nice girls who already forgetful of their Marios and their Francos invaded the wards to gather pillows, mattresses, sheets, bibs, towels, and doing so they tore them, they rent them, they soiled them. They reduced them to rubbish. Cute children who already oblivious of their friends Edoardo and Antonio hurled themselves upon unknown and irresistible toys: laryngoscopes, ophthalmoscopes, keratinoscopes, droppers, test tubes, anesthesia masks, enemas. "Jamil! Beautiful, Jamil!" Decent women who already unmindful of their kindhearted ma'a-salama-farewells savagely scuffled for the possession of the sole newborn scale or smashed the glass cabinets to snatch objects of probable household use: surgical scissors, lancets, tweezers, hemostatic pincers, forceps, medication trays, basins, mysterious pans which were bedpans and strange flower vases which were bed urinals. (The tiny old woman in chador who'd shrieked in Italian long-live-Jesus contented herself with surgical suturing needles, poor thing. They were curved, with thread already attached, thus excellent for sewing buttons or mending dresses, and she liked them so much that she filled all her pockets with them.) Savages who plundered the electrocardiographs they mistook for photocopy machines, the electroencephalograph screens they mistook for television sets, the x-ray aprons they mistook for flak jackets. Vandals who brandishing hammers destroyed what they didn't need or didn't like. Idiots who shattered good pieces of furniture just to pick up a nail or a screw. When there was nothing left to loot and waste, they dismantled the tents. Or, rather, they demolished them. In some cases, by loosening the poles and letting them collapse; in others, by dissecting them with the lancets. They dragged them away and of the precious field hospital of which Crazy Horse had scrupulously counted every basin and syringe and needle, all that remained were two rags trod upon by innumerable feet: the Italian flag and the Red Cross banner. But it didn't end here. Because, after stripping off the flesh of the cow and devouring its skeleton, the piranhas swarmed over to the Logistics esplanade. Here they saw the bolted warehouses and the sealed refrigerators, they forced the locks and the bolts, and...

They came from every house and every hovel, every villa and every shack, this time. They came from Sabra, from Shatila, from Gobeyre, from Shyah, from Haret Hreik, from Bourji el Barajni, from Ramlet el Baida, from the outskirts of the Pine Wood, from the area near the airport. Poor and rich, semi-poor and semi-rich, very poor and very rich. The latter, represented by their servants or relatives. (Her Highness the First Widow sent them all: the two minor widows, the two favorites, the two cooks, the two nurses, the two maids, the scullery girl, and the eunuch.) They came in hordes. With suitcases, with sacks, with carts, with cars. To watch them was terrifying. They dived into the refrigerator compartments, into the warehouses, and crushing each other, battering each other, threatening each other, they grabbed whatever fell into their hands: enormous sides of beef and small cans of capers, wheels of parmesan and portions of chickens, cases of spaghetti and whole lambs, oranges and dried codfish. Scattering half the stuff and breaking whatever was breakable they stuffed the suitcases, the sacks, the carts, the cars, soaked with sweat they rushed off to deposit the loot at home, then came back and started all over again. In less than an hour the esplanade became a fetid and slimy lake of flour, olive oil, milk, pickles, sugar, coffee, tomato sauce, cocoa, squashed fish, broken eggs, melted butter, marmalade. A multicolored slough where they slipped and fell and got up to slip again, fall again, become more and more soiled, ludicrous masks of greed. Finally, and always escorted by the militiamen who had sawed the cherry-wood table, Zandra Sadr's sons reappeared with thirty robust men plus five mullahs and a sheik dressed in black. Black cape, black headgear, black scarf. Without expressing any surprise at the disappearance of the field hospital they moved to the edge of the esplanade, ordered the militiamen to fire two or three rounds into the air, the militiamen fired, and amidst cries of panic the plunderers began to flee. The swarm thinned out. It became an inert maniple of bruised old men, dented women, scratched children, poor wretches among whom the eunuch of Her Highness the First Widow wandered waving a frozen chicken and seeking the two minor widows. "Mesdames, Mesdames!" So the sheik dressed in black moved forward. Turning to the inert maniple he pronounced the sentence that Zandra Sadr's eldest son had decided after seeing that orgy of pork and sausage and alcohol.

The pig is a filthy animal, he said. The pork and the sausages are filthy food. Satan's food, impure stuff, harràm. Woe to those who touch it: harràm. Alcohol is a poison that leads men to commit illicit acts, spirits are iniquitous beverages. Satan's liquids, impure stuff, harràm. Woe to those who drink it: harràm. Well knowing this, the Italians have left scandalous amounts of these impurities, and in the name of mercy they've asked His Most Reverend Eminence to transfer them to the destitute of the Eastern Zone. Mercy?!? Would it be mercy to heed such a suggestion? On the contrary: it would be an incitement to vice, a spur to sin, an insult to Allah. Thus, let it all be destroyed. Then he winked at the thirty robust men, and the thirty robust men catapulted themselves against Satan's food. Refrigerator after refrigerator, shouting harràm-impure-harràm, they hauled out of the compartments the nefarious pig cutlets, pig sirloins, pig ribs, pig short ribs, pig legs, pig hindquarters, pig fillets, pig livers, pig feet, pig trotters. They piled them up on the fetid slimy slough. Warehouse after warehouse, again shouting harràm-impure-harràm, they hauled out the evil prosciutti of San Daniele, the wicked cotechini and zamponi of Modena, the disgraceful salami and salamini, mortadelle and pancette and soprassate, sausages, and finocchione. They piled them up in the same way, then, they moved on to Satan's liquids. The velvety red and crispy white wine, the excellent sweet and dry spumante, the opulent Marsala, the ambrosial malvasia. And the bottles of whiskey, of cognac, of grappa, of brandy, of anisette, of Carthusian liqueur. And the incomparable quinquila liqueur produced by the Italian Pharmaceutical Institute, the minibottles of coffee liqueur, the plastic sacks of cordials, the beers. All by the thousands. Always shouting harràm-impure-harràm they dumped these too in the fetid slimy slough, they smashed them with Kalashnikov volleys, and at this point the five mullahs moved forward. They lit a fire, and while the bruised old men, the dented women, the scratched children joined the shouting, while human idiocy triumphed once again, the alimentary holocaust took place. Dozens and dozens of stakes, pyres of the new Inquisition, which in an exhalation of oily smoke and a flickering of pale azure flames released an inebriating odor of alcohol mixed with a nauseating stench of burnt meat.

"Harràm, harràm!"

"Satan's food, harràm!"

"Harràm, harràm!"

"Satan's liquids, harràm!"

"Harràm, harràm!"

Meanwhile the convoy advanced into Christian Beirut. With its hundreds and hundreds of vehicles it meandered like an interminable iron snake along the three miles of its way, and Crazy Horse's Leopard drew closer and closer to the harbor: it aproached the entrance where repenting of the scarce generosity shown in the last days Joséphine and Geraldine and Caroline had come to ask for Pistoia's forgiveness, and where Pistoia chased them away. "Move it, move it, you selfish sows! I don't want your lousy goodbye kiss!" In the western wharf the ship assigned to the marò had already moored at the dock, the metallic gangways had already been hooked to the embarkation deck, and the commander (a sea captain who used to navigate on summer cruises) looked very afraid. "I don't like it, I don't like it. This is a place where you lose your skin," he sighed. Then the iron snake arrived, followed by the Condor who unaware of the looting and the razing and the Inquisition burning grumbled: "Good, good. I think the ransom has worked!" Behind the Condor, Charlie who knew nothing as well and mumbled: "Let's hope, let's hope..." Behind Charlie, Angelo who after the encounter with the Professor had somehow understood which path he should follow to disprove the formula of Death given by Boltzmann and accept the formula of Life offered by Natalia Narakat Al Sharif. He had understood it, yes. However he hadn't yet found the clue he needed to get into the path, and he sought it, he sought it... He sought it everywhere he felt he might find it. In the faces of people, in the shapes of things, in the noises, the colors, the sea that splashed against the dock, the sun that blazed, the sky now so blue that to him it also appeared as the bluest sky ever seen in Beirut.

And here are the events through which he got that clue.

* * *

In the total silence imposed by the officers who feared an inopportune uproar from joy and nervousness, the one thousand two hundred men assembled with the vehicles along the horizontal trenches of the imaginary San Gimignano. The Sierra Mike vehicles were loaded aboard the first ship, the four hundred marò embarked with Sandokan, the riflemen positioned themselves in the way the Condor had established. Ten on the roof of the bridge, ten in the forecastle, ten on the quarterdeck, ten on the main deck, twenty on the lower decks. Then (it was exactly eleven in the morning) the gangways were removed, the hatches were closed, the frightened captain ordered the anchor raised, the fleet's helicopters lowered their altitude to better spot any possible attack, the vedettes on the cruisers and the frigates and the flagship aimed their telescopes, the officers in the Operative Combat Station glued themselves to the radar screens, and the ship moved away from the dock. While everybody held his breath in spasmodic tension, it left the western wharf and covered the eight hundred fifty meters of the channel that skirted the landward side of the breakwater pier. At the speed of six knots (the six knots Angelo had hypothesized to solve his trigonometry problem) it reached the lighthouse and rounded it, with its left broadside facing the hypothetical arrival of the hypothetical motorboat it started the arc of parabola heading northwest. While everybody let out his breath in relief it completed the arc, settled on its route, so the second ship entered the western wharf. On the orders of another very frightened sea captain who used to navigate on summer cruises it dropped anchor, loaded the vehicles then four hundred paratroopers, and this time two episodes characterized the embarking: the crisis of Fifi who drunk with hashish but no fool yelled I-want-to-leave-on-this-ship until Charlie convinced the Condor to satisfy him, and the syncope of Armando Golden Hands to whom Gigi the Candid had just revealed that Sister Milady was dead. "I can't keep it any longer, Armando. Milady is dead. They've killed her with Sister George and Sister Espérance." "It's not true," Armando Golden Hands replied. Then he collapsed, struck by syncope. The second ship hoisted its anchor at one in the afternoon, and its departure was identical to the first one. Identical the tension that made everybody hold his breath when it moved away from the dock, left the western wharf, covered the eight hundred fifty meters of the channel, reached the lighthouse, rounded it, started the arc of parabola with its left broadside facing the hypothetical arrival of the hypothetical motorboat. Identical the relief that made everybody let out his breath when the arc was completed and the route was settled. Then the third ship moored, little by little the vertical trenches emptied out, the imaginary San Gimignano turned back into a series of containers around which an unbearable smell of hashish lingered, and at three in the afternoon the final four hundred men went on board. With them, Angelo who immediately placed himself on the main deck and leaned against the railing of the dock side. The right side.

* * *

He felt very, very old. The fifty-eight years that George Al Sharif's face had transferred to his face, thus canceling his twenty-six years, had become three million: the three million years he had lived since the days when he guarded the cave of his tribe and chased the mammoth. He felt so old that everything seemed to have happened in the remote, primordial, unseizable time. A mere image, by now out of focus and almost dissolved, the gorgeous woman he no longer called Ninette but Natalia Narakat Al Sharif. A vague remembrance, by now liquefied and devoid of pain, her letter and the photo where radiant with happiness she left the church of Notre-Dame-du-Liban and the other one where overcome by despair she struggled to look at the human shreds. A concluded episode, by now without any importance, the trauma of discovering her identity and realizing that he'd been loved by proxy: a banal proxy due to his resembling the man she really loved. A healed wound, by now nearly invisible, the grief over her death... The very very old people don't suffer like the young. Even their griefs are exhausted, watered down. But just because of his tremendous oldness, because of his experience begun three million years before, he was sure that soon he would find the clue. He was sure for he had finally sensed that the clue lay in the remote time, the primordial time, the unseizable time which seems vanished from our memory and instead dwells inside it to provide us with the only knowledge that never fails: the one that comes from intuition, from instinct. He narrowed his eyes grown heavy and disenchanted from seeing too much, he watched the fire that the

Inquisition stakes had scattered to the warehouses now raising additional clouds of smoke, and he shook his head. No, in that triumph of human idiocy there was nothing that could bestow what he needed. He watched the minarets of the chipped mosques, the campaniles of the pitted churches, and again he shook his head. No, in those symbols of human impotence there was nothing either. He watched the infrastructures of the harbor, the arsenal, the dockyards, the piers, the cranes, the trains, the buildings, and once more he shook his head. No, not even in those products of human diligence was there what he needed... He then brought his eyes to the ship: to the Condor who inspected the riflemen ready to shoot, to Crazy Horse who declaimed his usual maxims, to Pistoia who barked his usual curses, to Sugar who distributed his usual advice, to Charlie who kept silent, to Stefano and Gaspare and Ugo who at the top of the forecastle were scuffling with Bernard le Français, to Bernard le Français who grabbed a bundle from their hands, raised it over his head, made the gesture of flinging it down into the water. And he slowly approached them. "What are you doing?" he sternly asked. "Ils n'ont pas voulu me prêter leur poupée, hier soir, et je vais la noyer. They didn't want to lend me their doll, last night, and I'm going to drown her," he roared. Then he flung the bundle down, and after a slow torpid flight Lady Godiva splashed into the water where she remained to float: her legs spread wide and her arms open in a pathetic appeal for help. "Shitty French!" Ugo yelled. "Save her! Throw her a rubber ring, save her!" Gaspare cried. Stefano instead repressed a sob and murmured: "Save her! As if she were a woman. She is not, I tell you. She's only pajamas sewn to a wig. And to think that I loved her so much, that for her I suffered so much, I got myself into so much trouble! Well... Maybe with people it happens the same. You love a person, for that person you suffer, you get yourself into a bunch of trouble, and one day you realize that it wasn't worth the pain: the person was only pajamas sewn to a wig. Don't you think so, Angelo?" But his question remained unanswered. Because during that truthful assertion Angelo had heard a tumult coming from the dock. A beastly, chaotic tumult in which he had grasped the sound of the word Inshallah. "Inshallah! Inshallah! Inshallah!" And finally awaking the awareness that slept at the bottom of his memory, the ancestral call of the remote and primordial and unseizable time we belong to, he had returned to the main deck to see who thundered the word, the formula, he still had to accept.

It was the stray dogs who at night invaded the city. The terrible dogs who taking advantage of the people's fear poured through the deserted streets, the empty squares, the abandoned alleys, and where they came from nobody knew because during the day they never appeared. The perverse dogs who like men divided into bands consumed by hate, who like men wanted only to tear each other to pieces, who like men slaughtered each other for the mere conquest of a sidewalk made precious by food scraps and scum. The mysterious dogs he had never seen. Yes, it was they. And they were not ghosts. In the flesh they burst onto the dock, they ran toward the ship and yelping, growling, barking, bawling, thundering that sound, the sound of the word Inshallah, they leaped against the closed hatches. It was they and they were horrendous. Filthy, bloody, covered with sores, encrusted with tinea, some with only one eye, one ear, three paws... But each of them vibrated with such an imperious, impetuous, indomitable vitality, such an eagerness and determination to live, that they seemed healthy and intact and beautiful: splendid. And the clue revealed itself in all its evidence. Why, though they slaughtered each other every night, every night they died, did these dogs never die nay survived so gloriously? Wasn't it because, far from expressing resignation and impotence, the word Inshallah meant eagerness and determination to live? Wasn't it because Chaos is Life not Death, because Life not Death is the ineluctable and irreversible tendency of all things, from the atom to the molecule, from the planets to the galaxies, from the infinitely small to the infinitely large? Wasn't it because it is Life that absorbs the energy of whatever and whoever tries to oppose its essence and process, it is Life that uses it to arrive more quickly at its final goal, and rather than being the destruction yet self-destruction of the Universe that goal is the construction yet self-construction of the Universe? In such a case the formula given by Boltzmann and the formula offered by Natalia Narakat Al Sharif would have meant the same thing: $S = K \ln W = $ Inshallah. Death, just what he had wished for one Sunday in October when he was only twenty-six years old and expected to understand with his intellect not with instinct or intuition: the instrument of Life, the food of Life. Dying, only a momentary standstill. A pause to rest, a short sleep that prepares us to be reborn and live again and again and again: forever, to infinity. In such a case? Had he said *in such a case* as if it were a hypothesis? No, no. It was not a hypothesis: it was a certainty! He could not prove that it was a certainty. Nobody could prove it, nobody would ever prove it. Yet it was so: he felt it. He felt it, therefore he knew it, with every cell of his body and every pore of his skin and every fiber of his nervous system that it was so. That being alive means being immortal. And offering to the sun a face completely restored to his youth, his now immortal youth, he went to place himself on the left broadside of the ship.

*   *   *

At exactly three in the afternoon they raised anchor. The third ship moved away from the dock and, pursued by the beastly chaotic tumult, it left the western wharf. While the fleet's helicopters lowered their altitude to better spot any possible attack, while the vedettes on the cruisers and the frigates and the flagship aimed their telescopes, while officers in the Operative Combat Station glued themselves to the radar screens, while everybody held his breath in spasmodic tension, it covered the eight hundred fifty meters of the channel that skirted the landward side of the breakwater pier. At the speed of six knots it reached the lighthouse, it rounded it. Exposing its left broadside, it began the arc of parabola that pointed northwest. And it had covered about thirty meters when Rashid's motorboat burst out from the apex of the vertical segment of Angelo's trigonometry problem. That is, from the inlet adjacent to the western basin. Immediately speeding up to 35 knots, it started to run along the diagonal segment with the 45-degree angle. That is, along the reef of the breakwater pier. Slightly and constantly diverging it adapted itself to the ship's arc of parabola, it established the trajectory forming another angle of 45 degrees with respect to the ship's left broadside, then Rashid locked the rudder. He armed the detonator, and all unfolded as Angelo had demonstrated in his problem. The square root of $13.66^2 + 5^2 - 2 \times 5 \times 13.66 \times \cos 60^2$. And filthy, bloody, covered with sores, encrusted with tinea, some with only one eye, one ear, three paws, horrendous and yet splendid, dead a million times, billions of times and yet alive, alive thus immortal, that night the stray dogs again invaded the city.